BIRTHRIGHT

One of the bankers strolling just before noon along Lombard Street happened to catch a glimpse of the elegant woman inside the limousine.

'It's Deborah de Kronengold!' he exclaimed. 'Here.'

She was a redhead and very beautiful, with a high, clear forehead and a long neck. Her mouth was firm, as was her chin, which bore just the suggestion of a cleft. Her eyes, large and searingly blue, never wavered from the entrance to the granite building, sun glinting off its glass dome, that commanded the far side of the courtyard.

There was a time when waiting for the doorman to swing open the door before her and her grandfather's progress into the bank's marble rotunda had sent prickles down her back. That would not happen now, she knew. Leslie, her father, had expunged those feelings. In a very short time she would leave him with no money and less honour.

Deborah nodded to her driver's eyes in the rearview mirror, directing him to head into the courtyard. Triumph began to curl into the shape of her smile. Now, at last, she was ready to seize her birthright.

'Love, avarice and international high finance . . . a novel on a grand scale'

Publishers Weekly

Birthright

JOSEPH AMIEL

In the beginning is my end.
T.S. Eliot
'*East Coker*', *Four Quartets*

SPHERE BOOKS LIMITED

First published in Great Britain by
Hamish Hamilton Ltd 1985

Published by Sphere Books Ltd 1986
27 Wright's Lane, London W8 5SW

The epigraph is reprinted by permission of
Faber & Faber Ltd from '*East Coker*', *Four Quartets*
by T.S. Eliot

TRADE
MARK

Set in Compugraphic Plantin

Printed and bound in Great Britain by
Cox & Wyman Ltd, Reading

For my father

PROLOGUE

One of the bankers strolling just before noon along Lombard Street happened to catch a glimpse of the elegant woman inside the limousine. Stunned, he threw courtesy aside, grabbed his friend's arm and pointed.

'It's Deborah de Kronengold!' he exclaimed. 'Here.'

Both men stood transfixed for a long moment as the long black vehicle turned in front of them into Mercy Lane. Beyond, they could see the open gates of the most famous merchant bank in London, perhaps of the world, the Kronengold bank. Like everyone in the City, they were aware of the warfare between the young woman in the limousine and her father, who controlled the financial institution that had made their family a legend for the better part of two hundred years. As if fearful for their own safety, the two onlookers scurried on, whispering, wondering.

The chauffeur started to turn the car into the gap where the tall iron gates were swung back. Deborah de Kronengold tapped on the glass partition and held up her hand, halting him. She wanted to observe the Kronengold bank for a moment.

She was a redhead and very beautiful, with a high, clear forehead and a long neck. Her mouth was firm, as was her chin, which bore just the suggestion of a cleft. Her nose, thin and straight, was made distinctive by nostrils lifted into delicate, nearly translucent wings. Her eyes, large and searingly blue, never wavered from the entrance to the granite building, sun glinting off its glass dome, that commanded the far side of the courtyard.

A doorman in black top hat, knee breeches, and green velvet tail-coat stood there at attention as the redoubtable Peckerill had once stood, the silver buckles on his patent leather shoes similarly gleaming. There was a time when waiting for the doorman to swing open the door before her and her grandfather's progress into the bank's marble rotunda had sent prickles down her back. That would not happen now, she knew. Leslie, her father, had expunged those feelings. He had lied and defrauded and stolen. His viciousness had gouged out of her the affection she had once held for him and for his bank. In the seventeen years since she had last seen him, when she had angrily charged from his presence at the bank and from England, he and Kronengold bank had become synonymous; his deceit had corrupted it in her mind, and his ineptitude had undermined its reputation in the financial world. In a very short time she would leave him with no money and less honour. Her hatred would be satisfied, her vengeance achieved. Life really does make you pay for your deeds in the end, she thought.

Deborah nodded to her driver's eyes in the rearview mirror, directing him to head into the courtyard. Triumph began to curl into the shape of her smile. Now, at last, she was ready to seize her birthright.

Part One

The Family

CHAPTER ONE

It has often been written that the Kronengolds are different from other people. On a spring afternoon in 1951, when Deborah de Kronengold was nearing her sixth birthday, she learned she was different from other Kronengolds.

She had always known she was different in one way, of course: her red hair. She yearned to have brown hair like her mother, whom she adored. Her mother appeared thoughtful when Deborah deplored her own hair colour, not happy or indulgent, as she usually seemed when they were alone together. At those moments she would hug Deborah or reach forward impulsively to take her daughter's hand and tell her how fortunate she was to have such beautiful hair. But, in the very possessiveness of her grip, Deborah could sense her mother's worry.

A beautiful child with bright blue eyes from which a startling and precocious intelligence shone, Deborah was the only daughter of one of Britain's richest families. Despite such gifts, she had remained an affectionate little girl, sweet and considerate, but she possessed a prodigious store of energy.

From the very first, Nanny Duhamel, a young Frenchwoman engaged to watch over Deborah and perfect her French, had found herself unable to cope with her charge's high spirits and curiosity. 'It is the red hair . . . that red hair,' the harried nursemaid usually grumbled desperately as she raced after Deborah like a white kite the child suddenly yanked here to chase a squirrel or there onto some playground apparatus that brought her to the very rim of danger – and always when the inexperienced young woman least expected it.

Nanny Duhamel breathed a sigh of relief at the end of this particular spring afternoon, when she could finally shepherd Deborah out of Hyde Park through the Park Lane exit in the direction of home. The Frenchwoman considered the day far more successful than most. Deborah had not added a new scrape to the small scabs that covered her knees and elbows like shifting squall clouds, and her hat and dress were still reasonably clean.

The woman and her charge were only a couple of streets away from the house when, without warning, Deborah's face suddenly lit with a smile and she sprinted off. She had caught sight of her older brother, Richard, who had spent the day with his school friends, still in the middle of the Easter holidays. Following at his back like a square-sailed galleon was his elderly Nanny Stock, too old to take on an energetic new charge like Deborah, but kept on out of obligation by the family. She both protected Richard and propelled him with a subtle dominance the young Frenchwoman admired, but feared she would never master.

Richard was nine, three years older than Deborah. Like his parents, Richard had dark hair and eyes. His skin was pale and his physique very thin, conveying an impression of delicate health. As Deborah approached him, she could already sense that his attitude towards her now would be the sort of tolerant disdain he had increasingly adopted when they were in public, particularly when he was with his friends. 'You're a child,' he took pains to explain to her at such moments, 'a tedious, silly child.' The first time, she was too offended to react. The next time she had kicked him in the shins as hard as she could, and been rewarded with a punch on the arm and then a slammed door between them. The exclusion hurt far more than the blow.

Deborah fell into step beside Richard and tried to begin a conversation, but all his attention was focused on the yo-yo he snapped down and up ahead of him as he walked, and Deborah was forced to watch him in silence. He had promised to play with her the night before and refused when he became absorbed in his stamp collection. He had then told her they would play today, and Deborah was eager for his company. She glared at the yo-yo as if at a mortal enemy.

The Kronengold mansion rose like a grey fortress above one entire side of the Mayfair square. A black iron fence, like giant hair combs set on their spines, guarded the stone building's periphery. As they neared the front gate, Richard loosened the string around his middle finger, permitting Deborah her opportunity. She ripped the yo-yo out of his hand and raced ahead, the red hair whipping behind her like a cavalry guerdon. Richard gave chase, but she was too quick, bounding onto the stone pediment and statue at one side of the entrance and then scampering up the iron stanchion beside it to the top. Her hat had blown off, the white stockings had ripped, but Richard could not reach her. Balanced atop the narrow iron beam, feet planted between the pointed spikes, smiling at her advantage over him, she raised the yo-yo above her head.

'Richard, if you climb after me, I'll throw it into the traffic.'

Nanny Stock had already gripped Richard's arm, her responsibility thus seen to.

'*Viens ici! Viens ici, je t'en prie!*' Nanny Duhamel's face, white with fear, tipped up to Deborah. She wanted to run into the house to summon help from one of the menservants, but feared to leave Deborah, for an instant.

'Please . . . please . . . come down,' she begged helplessly, her arms bound to her sides, as if with ropes, by the possibility that an impulsive move on her part might cause the child to slip.

Deborah ignored her. 'Richard, if I give it back, do you promise to play with me after supper until bedtime?'

'It's no concern of mine what you do with it,' he answered. 'I have another.'

His indifference was infuriating to her after days of it. 'You're a liar, Richard Edgar Henri de Kronengold! This one is your favourite.'

She drew back her arm and studied his face. His mouth was quivering faintly.

'And we play Happy Families,' she pressed.

'Snakes and Ladders,' he countered reluctantly.

'Young lady, you are coming down!'

Her father's voice. She looked towards the sound. He and her grandfather were striding towards her; she had not noticed the arrival of the black Rolls that brought Father and Grandfather back from the bank. Grandfather's mansion spread over the next adjacent side of the square, so they occasionally rode home in one car. Her father was tall and strong, quite capable of reaching and lowering her.

'Snakes and Ladders,' Deborah swiftly agreed, and bent towards her father. Looping her arms around his neck, she dropped into his arms. 'Good afternoon, Father.'

Leslie de Kronengold displayed a cold, imperious expression that came easily to him. His face was dominated by a high brow and a large, thin nose, and he customarily spoke in quiet, confident commands, as if all the thinking had already been done and others must unquestioningly obey. Deborah had perceived that his manner was different with her mother; she seemed to soften him – he listened when she spoke. At an early age the little girl had set her mind to win him over as her mother had done, and she soon found that, if she was fearless in replying to his questions and could pierce his frequent boredom with humorous answers, he would be entertained and interested. This time he did not give her the chance.

'You could have been injured. Everyone on the street was watching.'

'Especially Richard. He was much too frightened to come after me.' She glanced slyly over her shoulder at her brother, his hand still shackled to Nanny Stock's. 'Now he has to play Snakes and Ladders with me all evening.'

'It will be quite a long while before you have permission to play games again. You are going to bed right after supper.' He put her down. 'Go to your room.'

Deborah was indignant. 'I wish I had fallen and hurt myself, then you would have been too sorry to punish me.'

'To your room!'

Reluctantly, she turned into the entrance, glancing at her grandfather's round face as she did so. His mouth was turned up into his moustache with amusement.

Deborah had spent very little time with her grandfather in her young life. He was a remote, Olympian figure who dominated the family – and much of the financial world as well, she was later to learn. She could hear the deference even in her father's voice. The smile, a clear sign of Grandfather's approbation, so raised her spirits that she almost failed to hear her father mutter to him, 'When I agreed to take her in, I didn't think we'd be getting an uncontrollable savage.'

Deborah squared her shoulders at the insult and kept walking, wondering what he meant.

The beginning of the nineteenth century was turbulent and unpredictable. Winds of democracy, unleashed by the French Revolution, were blowing across Europe, sucking war behind them like debris, until war in the person of Napoleon became the gale itself. In such times clever men could do well.

In Frankfurt there was such a man, Solomon ben Abraham, the only son of the goldsmith Abraham ben Itzakh. He had grown up with none of his father's superb skill at transforming cold, hard metal into gleaming beauty, and his father had feared for the boy's future: for generations beyond memory the family had produced renowned goldsmiths, so useful to the nobility that their house had been left relatively unscathed by the butchery that periodically assaulted the Jewish ghetto. Abraham soon realized, however, that his son had been born with a gift as rare as his own. He understood money in a way that amounted to a kind of genius. He could manipulate it with all the dazzling facility of an artist his paints or a composer his notes. By the age of ten Solomon could calculate exchange rates and all the coin values of Europe's profusion of duchies and principalities and nations at near instant speed. Before his bar mitzvah he had turned the front room of the family house into a store, from which he sold Abraham's work at prices the artisan had believed impossible and to which he soon added other goods imported from all over Europe.

As the years passed the store outgrew these quarters, and Solomon, now a young man, rented part of the house next door. He could have afforded to build his own by then, but there was no empty land left behind the heavy gates that, on Sundays and Christian holidays, locked Jews into the overcrowded Frankfurt ghetto. For the sign above his store he chose three golden crowns, the mark his father and those who came before him engraved on the bottom of their gold articles. Crowns had been chosen to denote family pride and derived in feeling from the five gold balls that were the insignia of their former patrons, the Medici. The turmoil that followed Lorenzo's death drove Solomon's ancestors from Renaissance Florence, and they settled eventually in this bustling Teutonic city on the Main River. Beneath the three crowns – the insignia was reduced from five to three as a show of respect – Solomon directed the sign painter to write, not MERCHANT, but MONEY CHANGER, and he took the gold crowns for a surname: Kronengold. In money itself, he sensed – one of the few careers permitted a Jew – was his future and the future of the sons his shrewd, virtuous wife had started to bear him.

If one were then to have picked a family that would rise to

dominate the finances of Europe, surely one would have skipped the little building with three crowns over its door in a street only twelve feet wide in a teeming ghetto of outcasts. But Solomon Kronengold understood money. And his wife bore clever sons. And that was the beginning.

Having failed to rein in Deborah's stubborn impetuosity in full view of her employer, Nanny Duhamel was grim-faced as she set out the child's supper in the day nursery. Deborah was too preoccupied with her own thoughts to notice. She had been pondering her father's remark since the moment she had heard it, but the possible meanings so threatened her that she pulled back time and again from the conclusion towards which her young, but highly logical, mind seemed to be pointing. She decided to wait for her mother. Other adults often rolled their eyes and put her off when she asked questions. Her mother always took as long as it required to answer them.

Her parents were going to a charity ball that night. Deborah never doubted that, despite the edict of punishment, her mother would come to her bedroom to kiss her good night. Deborah first floated on the expectation of how beautiful her mother would look when she appeared in the doorway, and then shrank in anticipation of the devastating information she might be concealing. Deborah felt small and frightened in the large bed at the centre of the night nursery. In the darkness the pink canopy she always thought of as protecting her now seemed capable of hurtling down upon her with crushing weight.

She tried to evade her fears by imagining the gown her mother would be wearing. Although Madeleine de Kronengold spoke perfect English, she was actually a French Kronengold who had married a distant cousin; separated by many generations, they were joined by the common history and investment-banking interests that linked all the Kronengolds. Being French and fashionable, she favoured Paris for her clothes, and among the Paris designers she favoured Dior, who had allowed women to be feminine again, in the longer skirts and rounded forms of his revolutionary New Look.

Deborah glanced up at the first sound of light footsteps approaching her room. Trailing red organdie, Madeleine de Kronengold glided through the doorway with confident grace, like a tropical bird darting between crowds of umbrella-sized leaves without leaving the barest quiver behind. Round her neck was an exquisite ruby and diamond necklace. From her ears hung the matching ruby drop earrings; on her wrist was the bracelet, and on her finger the ruby ring.

Deborah clapped her hands in admiration. Her mother would be the prettiest woman at the ball; she was *always* the prettiest woman wherever she went.

Madeleine de Kronengold was as beautiful as her daughter believed her to be. A fawn's soft eyes peered out of an oval face. Small-boned, her slim tall body was characteristic of her branch of the Kronengolds. Her mouth revealed her personality best. Serene at rest, it illuminated her face with spontaneous smiles.

But tonight Madeleine's mouth was set in anticipation of the firm verbal chastisement she would add to her husband's. 'Your father and I are very annoyed at your behaviour,' she began sternly, seating herself on the edge of Deborah's bed.

Deborah listened dutifully to the recitation of her sins, her attention gripped by the spectacle of her mother's hair. Tiny spaces between the ends of the curly dark brown hairs had been set aglow by the passage light behind her, flaring the rim into an aura around her head. Deborah forced herself to concentrate on her mother's words as the lecture drew to a close.

'Dee, will you promise me never to take such a foolish risk again?'

Deborah nodded with contrition; smiling with relief at having got through this unpleasant task, Madeleine bent to kiss her daughter good night.

Now Deborah could express her own concern. 'Mummy, I heard father say he didn't know I'd be a savage when he agreed to take me in. What did he mean?' Deborah saw her mother's body stiffen, and she held her breath.

' "Agreed to take" – oh, Dee, you must have misunderstood,' Madeleine said in an oddly strained tone.

'That's what he said.'

Madeleine's shoulders sank. Her wide brown eyes stared into Deborah's without blinking, as if hypnotized by headlights on a dark road crossing.

'I had hoped . . . when you were older,' she finally said. Her voice seemed to come from another part of the room. She glanced down and spent much too long straightening the blanket. 'I'm sorry it has come out this way. Perhaps it's for the best.'

She brushed a stray lock off Deborah's forehead and took a deep breath. 'Dee, six years ago, at the end of the war, I gave birth to a baby girl who died.'

'Like Calico's kitten?'

'Yes, just like that.'

Tears were forming in the corners of Madeleine's eyes. 'I had wanted a second baby very much. Just after the war ended, cousin Nathan telephoned my brother, Pierre, who was in Italy, and told him what had happened. They both knew how much having a little girl meant to me.' She gently touched Deborah's cheek. 'Our family – your uncle Pierre's and mine – owned factories and a bank in Italy before the war, and Pierre had spent the war there, so he had many friends. One particular friend was a nun who was in charge of an orphanage where children were protected from the war and given a . . . home.' The last word caught in her throat. She lifted her eyes to Deborah's. 'Your uncle Pierre decided to bring me the most beautiful, most wonderful little girl he could find to be my very own.'

Madeleine embraced her daughter, their cheeks close. She could feel Deborah's heart pounding.

'Dee, you were only a few weeks old,' Madeleine whispered. 'You were the most marvellous baby in the world. He chose you for us out of all the other babies. And we adopted you.'

Deborah had no idea what that meant, but it frightened her. 'What's adopted?'

'Do you remember when I told you how babies are born?'

Deborah stared at her mother, barely nodding; she had struggled to understand Madeleine's very simplified explanation.

'Well,' Madeleine continued, 'you had . . . you had a different mother you grew up inside of until you were ready to be born. Then I became your mother.'

'Where is she?'

Madeleine could hardly hear her own answer. 'She died too. You needed a new mother.' Madeleine's heart cried out for all the distress battering her daughter. 'My darling, I wanted so much to be your mother.'

Deborah lurched apart from Madeleine. 'You mean I'm . . . like the war orphans?'

'Yes,' Madeleine murmured.

'Is Richard adopted?'

'No, but that doesn't mean we love him any more than you.'

'He belongs to you, and I don't!' The inescapable knowledge raked her soul and racked her small body with sobs. Even as Madeleine seized her in a hug to smother physically the misery consuming this child she loved so deeply, a void engulfed Deborah, a black horror, isolating her from every other living being, every familiar object in the universe. Someone went shopping and brought home a child, Deborah thought. Much as one chooses a puppy, she had been chosen as a gift for this woman and her husband in London.

'Does Richard know?'

'Hardly anyone knows. I went to the hospital to have my baby and returned home with you.'

'Promise me, promise me you'll never tell anyone else.'

'If you don't want people to know, we'll never tell a soul.'

'Father won't tell either?'

She nodded. 'I'll speak to your father this very evening.'

Then Deborah began to ask questions. She wanted every scrap of information associated with her birth and adoption and her natural mother; each bit was precious. Madeleine tried to remember – but knew too few of the facts to hold back the menace. Finally Deborah asked, 'The other little girl – the one who died like the kitten – what was her name?'

'We never gave her a name. She died so quickly.'

Deborah thought a while about the little girl who had no name. 'If I had died, would I have a name?'

'You were born healthy and sound.'

Deborah pulled away. 'If *she* was born healthy and sound, would I have a mother?'

Madeleine was unable to answer.

'Would I still be your daughter?'

Desperate to offer consolation, Madeleine resorted to repeating, over and over again, how much she loved her daughter and what Deborah meant to her.

But in the little girl's eyes, like blue mirrors, Madeleine could see, reflected back, that hers had become the face of a very kind stranger.

Gradually, when the tears would come no more, Madeleine's protestations of love and a child's need to be loved shrank the void around Deborah until it was only a tiny hole of black doubt that darted inside her. They hugged and talked and even laughed, but much later, when she lay in bed alone in the large, dark room, Deborah was left with the dreadful certainty she was far too young to be able to put into words, but which was no less real to her young mind, that she would forever bear within her that vacuum of imminent terror into which everything that was important to her would always threaten to collapse.

Deborah's behaviour during the days that followed alternated between outbursts of rash recklessness and lows of lethargy and dependence. Both states were borne with equal fortitude by her mother, who spent many hours with her. Nanny Duhamel was kind, bringing chocolate at bedtime and playing with her when she might normally have left her alone, but it was Madeleine who held the small, shattered spirit together. What Deborah allowed no one, especially her brother, to see was the inner tempest driving such behaviour before it: gusts of rage directed both at the biological parents who had deserted her and at the family who had adopted her. She stared for long stretches at the betraying, tell-tale differences in her looks, loathing them.

Deborah dimly understood that she must be grateful to the father and mother who had taken her in, that her food and shelter, her survival, were dependent on their goodwill. She could not risk incurring their displeasure; they had adopted her, so they could *un*-adopt her, couldn't they? What would become of her then? Perhaps her real parents weren't dead after all. Perhaps they were searching for her at this very moment, but did not know she had been snatched from their Italian homeland. How could she let them know? How could she find them? Were these new parents keeping her from them, like a prisoner? The gap between her terrors and the contentment she would have to dissimulate served to deepen her torment.

Leslie de Kronengold rarely involved himself in his daughter's life. And during this period, for reasons of business, he was home even less than usual. Although Madeleine had alerted him that Deborah had become greatly disturbed upon learning of her adoption, he gave no indication of awareness on the few occasions his and his daughter's paths crossed. In typical British fashion, he believed that expressions of sentiment promoted weakness and lack of self-reliance in a child. Although she secretly longed for it, now that Deborah understood his remark, nothing on earth would force her to seek some sign of concern from her father. The following week, realizing that time was only increasing Deborah's agitation about her birth, Madeleine asked her cousin Nathan de Kronengold to visit them. They had been close since childhood. Nathan's father had been a top banker in Berlin before the war. Nathan had fled Germany in the late Thirties. By then his father was dead, and his mother doomed because she refused to leave ('The Jews are good Germans. The Nazis will soon realize that,' she had told him). His bank and assets confiscated as the price of freedom, Nathan had temporarily taken a job operating the Swiss bank owned by the British Kronengolds. That had led him into military intelligence work for the British under his cover of Swiss banker. A bachelor, he now lived in England and was a partner in a small merchant bank started before the war by an émigré cousin, Hans Blaustein.

Deborah always enjoyed visits from cousin Nathan. Huge in stature but very gentle and jolly, he never spoke patronizingly to her; he patiently played endless games of rummy, and never failed to arrive without sweets for her and Richard stuffing his high pockets. But, on this visit, no amount of chocolates or joking in his sweetly comic German accent could lift her spirits. At Madeleine's urging, Nathan explained to Deborah that his only role in her adoption had been to tell Pierre on the telephone how heartbroken Madeleine was and to suggest that Pierre, so influential in Italy, might be able to find a healthy baby for her and her husband – the war had orphaned so many. Perhaps Pierre could tell Deborah more about her background, he suggested.

The following day, Madeleine took Deborah on her first plane journey, to Paris, aboard the family's DC-3. They could shop and spend some time with Grand'mère. Both knew, however, that the primary purpose of their trip was to see Pierre.

At the end of the Second World War, in every country where the Kronengolds survived, at least one of them was capable of preserving or even of restoring extravagant affluence for all the rest. In France the saviour was Deborah's uncle Pierre, then still in his twenties; when he began, in part he had his wife's wealth to prop up his bank but for the rest he had only the legendary Kronengold name to borrow against, and that became his collateral. In Amsterdam it was the brothers Pieter and Carl. In Frankfurt, Vienna, and Milan, either nothing or no one was left to rebuild.

Pierre de Kronengold was Madeleine's older brother and the inheritor of the French barony upon the death of their father, Henri, during the war. The latter had taken refuge in England along with Pierre's wife and son and, of course, Henri's own wife, Deborah's Grand'mère. Pierre had come alone tonight to the *palais* the Kronengolds had inhabited since the days of Louis XVIII and in which Grand'mère still lived.

Never allowed to dine with adults at home, Deborah sat stiffly and quietly at the long table. Frequently, her eyes strayed from Grand'mère – erect as a bulrush, grey hair swept atop her head into soft clouds – to the portrait of Grandpère, hung all alone on the yellow wall behind her. Deborah tried vainly to find Grandpère's sternness in Pierre's shy, considerate face, as he sat with an arm hooked casually over the back of his chair. Like Richard, her brother, he appeared fragile. His shoulders were slightly stooped and his voice and expression were soothing. The tassel of brown hair that fell across his forehead and the eyeglasses teetering atop the bridge of his nose added the final touches to an appearance that was more a bookkeeper's or a scholar's than that of the soldier her mother claimed he had been in the war. The only quality that seemed at all soldierlike to Deborah was the dash of persistence in his questions; he was always truly interested in knowing how Deborah was and what she had been doing.

After dinner Pierre, Madeleine, and Deborah retired to one of the salons. Like the dining room, it was large and decorated in an ornate French period style similar to that of most Kronengold houses: gilt rococo moulding; a painted ceiling; fabric wall coverings obscured or punctuated by tapestry murals, fine paintings, and art objects; brocade-upholstered chairs and sofas; and cabinets inlaid with varying shades of wood. As she had at the great oak front door, Deborah carefully averted her eyes from the Kronengold coat of arms carved into the mantel with its three crowns and its motto, Unity and Fidelity, that had been carefully explained to her. It seemed to rebuke her personally now for trespassing on the purity of the family's honour. Deborah flounced down on an oversized sofa, feeling very small and nervous. To ease her discomfort, Pierre chose a place beside her on the sofa. He took her small hand in his as he began to tell Deborah how he had found her.

Near the end of the war, Pierre had learned from Nathan that his sister's baby had died at birth and that the doctors had told her she could have another child only by adopting one. Before leaving Italy for France to begin the task of rebuilding the shattered fortunes of the French Kronengolds, Pierre returned to Turin, the region where the family had purchased a factory complex half a century earlier, to pay a visit to the orphanage at the Convent of Santa Raffaella, which his family had long supported, to overcome potential anti-Jewish antagonism. Pierre's voice was soft as he spoke and his eyes appeared to focus far away, as if viewing himself in the past.

'Whenever I visited the convent, I would walk through the orphanage with Sister Teresa and discuss its problems, as my grandfather and father before me had done with the abbesses before her. I told her how much my sister wanted a daughter. On the third floor was the nursery. It was a long, white room with cribs along the walls. Two nuns were sitting by a table in the centre of the room, each feeding an infant. Sister Teresa and I walked from one crib to the next while she told me about the child in each.

'In the far corner something caught my eye. I saw a tiny hand playing with the white crib bars. I looked into the crib and was startled by the infant in it. Her colouring, for one thing: bright red hair and the largest blue eyes.'

'Like a clown!' Deborah blurted out.

'Like cabochon sapphires.' Pierre smiled. 'Do you know what they are? Round sapphires. The best of them have stars shining within them, as your eyes do. Sister Teresa explained to me that a doctor from a nearby town had brought the child there when it was born . . . just after its mother died.'

Madeleine reached protectively for Deborah's free hand. But Deborah drew both hands into her lap.

'Who was . . . my mother?'

Pierre shook his head. 'The doctor knew only that the woman had no family. The child's father had been killed in the war.'

Deborah's eyes had turned to glass. 'That's all you know about them?' she finally asked.

Pierre thought a moment. 'I remember Sister Teresa saying that the doctor told her the mother had the same colouring you do and was also very beautiful.' He smiled again at the recollection. 'I had never seen such a beautiful baby. Suddenly the child reached out –'

'But it was me. Why do you keep saying "the child"?'

He bent his head apologetically. 'You. You reached out and began playing with your toes, gurgling like babies do – you seemed so pleased with such a wonderful trick. Around your neck I noticed a gold chain with a small gold cross.'

Deborah's anguish deepened. Nanny Duhamel wore a cross and had explained what it signified.

'I'm not even Jewish.'

'The doctor thought your mother was Jewish and was wearing the cross to hide her religion from the authorities. They tried to capture Jews in those days, you know. Wearing a cross was a good way to disguise oneself. The doctor said that she herself named you before she died.'

'Is Deborah a Jewish name?'

'It comes from the Bible. In Hebrew it's Dvora. She was a wise judge who rallied the Israelites to defeat their enemies thousands of years ago.'

'But why did you keep the name Deborah?'

'We Jews had all gone through so much. The fight for Israel was about to begin. Besides, you seemed a very clever baby.'

'You don't have to be very clever to find your toes,' Deborah said grumpily.

'Not one of those other babies your age could have done it.'

She fought back the accommodation of a smile. 'I wish you had named me Mary.'

Deborah didn't speak again for a long time, allowing the whole story to replay through her mind like a film. Finally, she sought Uncle Pierre's eyes again.

'Am I really special?'

'Very special,' Madeleine replied just an instant before he did.

Deborah could feel the tears beginning to come again. 'I come from nowhere.'

Madeleine opened her purse and lifted out a tiny gold cross on a chain. The child stared at it, trying to see in the cross's shape or colour where it had come from, who had made it, and, most of all, the woman who had worn it and had named her Deborah. Madeleine lowered the cross into Deborah's open palm. The small fingers closed on it, seeming to clutch without conscious command. The sharp metal points cut into Deborah's skin, but the pain increased the reality of her scant birthright. She squeezed harder, staring at her fist until the white-hot pain drove every thought but itself from her mind and she became lost in it, coming back to awareness only when she noticed her tears had fallen on the heel of her hand. Her mother was speaking again.

'When Uncle Pierre brought you to us, it was a miracle. I can't imagine life without you. I love you more than you can ever know.'

Deborah flung herself at her. 'Oh, Mummy, I love you too.'

She snuggled her cheek into the cool blue silk dress and gazed at the familiar rope of pearls as large as ripe grapes around her mother's neck. She could feel security flowing back into her muscles and bones. Whoever her shadow parents might be, obscured in the dimness at the edge of the room, she knew that the flesh-and-blood mother she held loved her. And, although the tiny demon of doubt about who she really was still nestled inside her, she no longer doubted her mother's love.

A flash of childish fear or intuition at the moment made her whisper, 'Don't ever leave me, Mummy.'

'I would leave everything in this world before I left you, Dee.'

Content, Deborah hugged Madeleine for a long while without thinking. Then she sat up. She wanted Pierre to retell the story, not because she didn't remember every word, but because it was all she had. That, a tiny cross, and a first name. Everything else, she felt, was an act of charity.

Soon afterwards Madeleine decided to invite as many of the British Kronengold family as could come to their London house for the Passover seder, a ceremony erected on family and religion – elements now dangling dangerously from her daughter's sense of belonging.

Eating matzos rather than leavened bread during the eight days of Passover was a detail of religious observance that had long since slipped from the family's small inventory. As religion had gradually lost its appeal to upper-class Christians during the nineteenth and twentieth centuries, so had it done to the Kronengolds. But they always dutifully appeared at synagogue during the High Holy Days. Not only would the Kronengolds' absence be considered letting down the side, but it would also violate the family's superstitious, unspoken understanding of a covenant by which God had agreed to allow the family to flourish while so many other Jews suffered so dreadfully.

For generations Kronengold dinner parties had been traditional gathering places for the mighty and the gifted. Several times in Deborah's short life she had been presented to Winston Churchill. She had curtsied obediently, but nearly erupted with giggles at the sight of the long cigar protruding from the aged infant face into hers. Once Matisse, who had been commissioned to do a painting for one of the drawing rooms, had dashed off a pencil portrait when she was introduced to him. But before tonight she had always been swiftly herded out by Nanny or one of the other servants after her ritual moment of courteous prettiness, bearing with her the recollection of smart clothes and magnificent jewellery, which she would later do her best to re-create, using crayons, scissors and paste, so that she could play at dressing up.

Tonight was an awesome occasion for Deborah: she was to dine at a large gathering with adults for the first time. Menservants in black livery swung back the great doors to the dining room. Deborah gasped. The chandeliers and sconces glittered like clutches of huge diamonds against the soft glow of red velvet walls.

Grandfather sat at the head of the table. Lord Kronengold was of medium height, but to her child's eye he always appeared to be a giant – larger than her much taller father. He had a ferocious countenance: great scowling eyebrows that sat above his eyes like bushy black sentinels and, guarding his mouth in a similar manner, an old-fashioned moustache that had not changed its shape through decades of family photo albums. A waistcoat covered the dome of his large stomach.

Like the rest of his suit it was, as always, black.

As the man who owned the bulk of the British Kronengold assets and controlled I. Kronengold & Sons, the family's legendary merchant bank, he would normally have been looked up to by the others. But he had long ago proved himself to be one of those rare sons of genius the family uncannily produced just in time to lead it through critical years. His time had come just after the Second World War, when the bank's assets had been slashed by war losses and much of the ancient building in Mercy Lane that had housed generations of Kronengold bankers had been razed by bombing. Samuel de Kronengold and the bank's employees worked endless hours in the half of the bank that remained. He brilliantly leveraged investments in businesses that would thrive in the post-war boom he foresaw. In addition he was the major force resuscitating and uniting London's banking capability and, through that, much of the nation's industry.

The Kronengold interests and the rest of the City had soon risen like phoenixes from the rubble of Hitler's bombardment and, like phoenixes, the new appeared to be very much like the old. The men who then came each day to the City as their fathers and grandfathers had – in striped trousers, morning coat, and top hat; or in black suit, bowler hat, and carrying a rolled umbrella – determined that they had good reason for optimism, even for complacency. Once more it was good to be an Englishman and, as always, if the example of Lord Kronengold was any criterion, blessed to be a Kronengold.

Samuel was no observer of Jewish ritual. He considered much of it nonsense, but he had a strong sense of family and had rich recollections of Passover seders as a boy. Although still vigorous, he was now in his mid-sixties and becoming increasingly concerned about the accelerating entropy and the loss of entrepreneurial spirit among the Kronengolds. He began the evening by recalling the words of Solomon Kronengold to his sons: 'It is hard to be a Jew. But it is harder to be nothing.' Then he nodded to Nathan, the most religiously observant of those present, who explained that the Passover dinner, the seder, is a reminder of the Jews' deliverance from Egyptian slavery thousands of years ago – and that such redemption is still spiritually possible for everyone.

Raising his glass, Nathan intoned the prayer for the wine, and the age-old ritual-dinner began.

Among the many relatives along the sides of the long dining table were Deborah's parents, her father's shy brother and sister-in-law, Charles and Cora, Grandfather's gregarious nephew Malcolm and Malcolm's ex-actress wife, Lavinia. Malcolm was on the board of the family holding company, but was perfectly content to allow Samuel to run things while he tended his art collection. Other Kronengold adults and their children made up the rest of the party.

Deborah was the youngest child present. She had been carefully schooled for several years in the table manners expected of an upper-class young lady, but she was nonetheless bewildered by the number of forks, knives, spoons, and glasses set out before her. When in doubt, she had been told, use the outside utensil, but no meal could possibly have so many courses. There was so much an adult had to know, she decided. No wonder it took so long to become one.

For children the high point of a seder is the hunt for the afikomen, a piece of matzo wrapped in a napkin that is hidden when none of them is looking. Deborah was all concentration, never taking her eyes off the square of napkin-covered matzo beside her grandfather's plate. She was determined that the prize – traditionally money, she was told – would be hers.

But she had anticipated too soon. When dinner was finally brought in by a file of servants bearing gleaming silver trays, her attention was captured by the display. The butler led, his white collar high and starched, his black bow tie alert, like rabbit's ears. Behind him were the liveried footmen. The young girls who worked for the family followed, their backs straight, their cheeks slightly flushed at the notice their entrance was receiving.

'At last!' Malcolm cried out. 'Another minute, and I'd have converted out of pure hunger.'

Everyone laughed. Deborah's gaze shifted back to the napkin. It was gone! In that short moment of letting down her guard, someone had whisked it away. Halfway down the table, Malcolm was standing behind one of the relatives. Grandfather's eyes seemed to be laughing at her. All her advantage lost, Deborah folded her arms and glared at him.

When the children were finally unleashed, yapping and scuffling, she bounded to the head of the table. The others searched chuckling dinner guests or opened the doors of cabinets along the walls or peeked behind pictures, but she was convinced it had to be near Grandfather; her surveillance had been broken for only that single instant. Malcolm, empty-handed, had been too far down the table; he had been a decoy. Deborah studied Grandfather's face. He stared as intently at hers, his eyes once again seeming to laugh at her predicament.

'Deborah, you'd better hurry – someone else will find it,' Malcolm's wife, Lavinia, prodded.

The heavy older man and the little girl continued to study each other.

She could see clearly it was not in his lap or under his chair. Hands locked across his stomach, he sat unmoving in the tall chair. He seemed much stiffer than earlier in the evening. Of course! She plunged into the space separating his back from the upholstery. Having observed her sudden movement, the other children were rushing towards them. She groped around frantically. The bottom of his jacket felt hard and flat; her hands scrabbled underneath it – and the prize was hers. Triumphantly, she held up the glorious square white parcel. The adults applauded and cheered. Richard was fuming. The ignominy of being bested by someone as young, as insignificant, and as female as she was almost too crushing an embarrassment to bear. It would be days before he spoke to her again. She resolved not to care.

'My prize!' she demanded.

'What do you want?' Samuel asked.

'Money. That's the prize . . . isn't it?'

'Perhaps some sweets.' His tone was teasing.

'But it's supposed to be money!'

'Deborah, speak to your grandfather with more respect,' her mother interjected sharply.

But she was not to be diverted. She continued to stare him down.

Samuel broke into a wide smile. 'I honestly believe this monkey would go so far as to destroy my reputation in the City if I failed to pay what I owe her.'

He lifted her onto his knee. 'You sit here with me, little Deborah. Tomorrow morning I will withdraw one entire gold guinea from the bank just for you.'

She hadn't the slightest idea what the value was of the coin Grandfather had named, having never possessed, nor needed to, even so much as tuppence in her life. 'Is that a lot of money?'

'A fortune,' he assured her. 'And afterwards we shall go to a grand restaurant, you and I, to discuss important financial matters.'

Deborah had never been to a restaurant, but had often stood yearning to join her mother as she pulled on her gloves and adjusted her hat in the mirror.

'Do you promise?'

He solemnly extended his hand. 'Is my credit good until tomorrow?'

They shook hands, and she collapsed happily against his chest. Then, as he remembered his own grandfather doing every Passover, he began to tell Deborah and the other children the history of the family.

As the nineteenth century was beginning, Solomon Kronengold sent his eldest son, Isaac, to England as his agent. In 1642 Jews had been permitted by Oliver Cromwell to return to England after four centuries of exclusion. The years since then had witnessed a steady increase in their number. A short, almond-eyed young man with pronounced Semitic features, Isaac spoke only German when he arrived in the City of London.

The buying and selling, the bargaining, the lending, the very closeness of people in the City when Isaac Kronengold arrived among the tangled skein of narrow streets – today still bearing names like Threadneedle, Old Jewry, Poultry, Bishopsgate, and Cheapside – were native territory to him. He began by exporting goods to Germany, but soon surmised that the real growth industry was not textiles or ceramics, but the credit he extended on them. By the second year he had bought a building between King William and Lombard Streets, in Mercy Lane. Over the door he placed a sign displaying three crowns, as his own father had once done, and the words 'I. Kronengold & Co,' the 'Co.' later to be replaced by 'Sons'.

Solomon sent his second son to Paris before he was twenty, and others, in turn, to Amsterdam, Vienna, and Milan. The youngest remained with their father in the narrow house in the Frankfurt ghetto. All six of the Kronengold brothers, but the eldest most of all, had inherited their father's genius for finance. And in their footsteps, for generation after generation, would march half a dozen branches of the dynasty.

Inflation, scarcity, and the need to transport money beyond

guarded, war-ravaged borders brought desperation to some in Europe. To the Kronengolds they brought the opportunity to rise from squalid oppression to security, to dignity. In his own city each son built a branch bank that prospered beyond the avarice of potentates; they became the richest, most powerful bankers in the world, financing nations and early ventures of the Industrial Revolution: railways, Bessemer steel plants, steam-driven ships. Their partnership was linked by more than codes, couriers, boats, and carrier pigeons; they thought as one, united by the creed old Solomon had laid down: Unity and Fidelity.

Initially, Kronengolds tended to marry other Kronengolds, first because they genuinely liked and, more importantly, trusted each other; second, because few brides' fathers could provide the heavy dowry befitting marriage to a Kronengold except another Kronengold; and third, because the family capital was thereby kept intact. When they did marry outside the family, the alliance was always an advantageous one for the firm, originally involving other Jewish bankers – Rothschilds, Warburgs, Blausteins, and the like – and, later, the most elevated among the nobility. By tradition, only the sons could own shares in the banks; the daughters formed blood links among the influential aristocratic husbands they married outside the family.

Soon the Kronengolds were too rich and too powerful – and had too many friends in high places dependent on them – to be denied aristocratic titles of their own. At the pinnacle of society in their countries – usually grudgingly because of their Jewish roots – they became the intimates of royalty, resided in vast palaces, were waited on by regiments of servants, and amassed superb art collections and racing stables. Yet the various branches of the family still comprised a loosely bound unit. Even when the Kronengold banks in different countries under different cousins were split into separate firms, the cousins still relied on each other across borders and visited each other for holidays.

Always, they still felt themselves planets in a single solar system that revolved about the singularity of their heritage. Always, they still felt themselves held in orbit by the creed that had impelled the family's success: Unity and Fidelity.

Samuel sought every child's eye and, finally, Deborah's. 'Without the family, we are just like any other people with money who come and go. But together, as one, we are invulnerable.' Recognizing that she did not understand, he added, 'Making sure the family prospers – does well – and our name goes on, that is our purpose in life, little one. Nothing is more important.'

After the seder, Madeleine accompanied Deborah upstairs to tuck her into bed.

'Mummy, does Grandfather know I'm adopted?'

'Yes, Dee, he does.'

'I think he likes me all the same.'

Madeleine kissed her daughter's forehead tenderly. 'I think he does – very much. You like him, don't you?'

'Yes. Because he's fair. A lot of adults aren't to children, you know.'

'What was the best part of the whole evening, Dee – finding the matzo?'

Deborah thought a minute, then shook her head. 'Being allowed to stay up with the family. Mummy, is that what it was like before the war? The whole family together like that?'

'A little bit. We were younger, of course. And there were many more of us, from all over Europe.' Her eyes grew unfocused as she thought about it. 'I seem to remember us all being so foolishly full of hope.'

And then a shiver rasped along Madeleine's spine. She had remembered that day in Valtary when hope and youth had died.

CHAPTER TWO

A year later, by the summer of 1952, to all outward appearances the wound opened in Deborah as a result of her discovery of her adoption had healed over and left her once again cheerful and high-spirited. She kept her inner agitation to herself. When alone, as she often was, her shame about her origin would sometimes well up to smother her thoughts and all the joy that should have nourished her. She wondered about the dead little girl who had no name, did not, in Deborah's reverie, even have a face – only a luminous, perfect light shining from her: that other little girl never would have done the awful things for which Deborah was constantly getting into trouble. At times like those, Deborah believed that Leslie and Madeleine must wish with all their hearts that their real daughter, their own perfect real daughter, had lived and that they had never agreed to take the naughty Deborah in.

She often felt guilty when she thought back to what she knew of her beginnings, and afraid that her adoptive parents might read her thoughts and resent her ingratitude. Hadn't they saved her from oblivion, given her her very life? But the fantasies would not cease. She wondered what her life would have been like if her birth parents had lived, what *they* would have been like. Often the family she imagined in play were the phantoms from whom she had truly sprung, sometimes a king and queen, sometimes a knight and his lady; but always one was the beautiful mother with her daughter's red hair, who would announce to the assembled nobles that the only name pretty enough for her perfect daughter was Deborah.

Loved as ardently as before by Deborah, the mother with whom she actually lived seemed at those times a kind of celluloid figure glued on the earlier woman, each dissolving into and confusing the wholeness of the other. Often the two mothers bore the same face, like a paper cut-out doll with different-coloured wigs and clothes. Her fantasy father was tall and manly, like her adoptive father, but he bore vague, idealized features and always smiled and was tender.

Deborah's anxieties and her consequent fears and fantasies, although troubling to her, did not sap her vitality or her confidence. She had been nearly six when she learned of her adoption, and a sturdy self-possession had already been formed within her. Likewise, Nanny Duhamel's return to France the previous autumn could have been far more traumatic if her replacement had not been a tutor who began her schooling, throwing open to her consuming curiosity the mysteries of the adult world. In the minutes before the tutor's arrival, Deborah often grew physically excited nearly to trembling in anticipation of what the day held in store.

Deborah's studies ended in June, when the family moved for the summer months to their vast country estate, Clove Hill. Clove Hill always seemed a magical place to Deborah. As a very small child, she was often asleep in the night nursery of the London house before the family left for the weekend, the sights and sounds of Mayfair outside her window. In the morning she would awake at Clove Hill and run to her window. Outside now were meadows and trees, flowers knelt over by gardeners, fountains and birds chattering to each other. The world had transformed itself for her delight. Even after she was old enough to understand that Clove Hill was a different place to which she was driven by car, some of the magic still lingered, revealing itself in the sun's spectrum glint off dew-drops beaded on blades of grass and hedge leaves, or in the fog rolling up the lawn's long incline like the waves of a mischievously contrary sea.

The replica of a huge French château had been built at the end of the last century by her grandfather's father, one of the grandsons of Isaac, the first Kronengold to settle in England. Other Kronengolds bought or built other great houses in the area, near enough to their relatives to drive over for a family lunch or to joint the same hunt. One, for instance, had purchased a perfect small Tudor mansion, which then became the old wing of a perfect large mock-Tudor mansion.

Clove Hill, however, was the family jewel. Samuel's father, apart from being far and away the richest man in England, was a man of some culture. When he thought it time to build his monument, the only design that satisfied him was a French Renaissance-style palace, the only site a hill in

Hampshire. The top had to be sheared off, gullies filled in, woods moved, roads built, rivers diverted, pipes laid, workers transported and housed, and a railway company coerced into building a spur line. Thousands of acres, encompassing farms, woods, villages, and churches, were bought up around the site. As the building rose to its profusion of cone- and pyramid-roofed turrets and its parade of chimneys, agents in half a dozen countries purchased art and furnishings at his direction, shipping wooden crates full of treasures to Clove Hill. Entire rooms from great European houses of the past were dismantled, sent off, and reassembled within the walls of the new building. Having an interest in ornithology, Samuel's father did the traditionally Kronengold thing and sprinkled the estate with hundreds of rare, colourful birds. The very scale of the undertaking served to prove the newly-elevated Lord Kronengold a titan worthy of his exalted place atop the financial pillar that supported much of the Victorian Age's optimism, enterprise, and grandeur.

Clove Hill was passed on to Samuel, the eldest son, who added a wing to house his own art collections and converted one of the outlying farms into a thoroughbred stud. In honour of his father he increased the collection of birds. Peacocks strutted across the front lawn in stately beauty. Mynah birds welcomed visitors in several languages, and doves were dyed every colour of the rainbow to amuse the eye. When Samuel's wife died soon after the war, he insisted that his son and daughter-in-law consider the house their own. Leslie and Madeleine abandoned plans to buy a country house. His requests and suggestions had the force of family law. Much of the summer and many weekends in the spring and autumn the house was filled by their guests, by Samuel and his guests (fewer as he grew older), and, all too occasionally, by other children.

Deborah quickly grew very bored that summer of 1952. For her seventh birthday her parents had given her a pony, Gypsy, who was black as an opal, but she was not allowed to ride alone. She had no playmates, and Clove Hill was filled with adults. Richard was often able to invite a friend to join him; most times he was with Peter Rowell, whose nickname, Bash, was an excellent expression of his exuberance. Blond and blue-eyed, Bash was handsome and sure at an early age of his good looks and charm. Bash's family was also among the elite of merchant banking.

Ploverdale, the Rowells' country house, was nearby. For twelve or so decades I. Kronengold & Sons and Rowell & Co. had done business, and the two families had maintained cordial and useful, if not intimate, social relations. The closeness in the two boys' ages brought them together, although Bash's recklessness alarmed Richard as much as it attracted him. Deborah was captivated by Bash Rowell and convinced that her own fearlessness would have made her a fit companion, despite her being a girl and three years his junior; she would have given anything to join them, but Richard would not hear of it. The only time he would play with her was when no one else was available. She was very bored indeed.

Deborah's liberation arrived on an August day that proved climacteric in her life, although it began in disappointment and tedium. Her father and his guests, including Richard and Bash, had gone off shooting grouse on the private moor that was planted each year with heather and gorse and had been stocked with the birds brought down from Scotland in truckloads the night before. The head gamekeeper was required to wear a kilt. Indeed, the Kronengolds' money seemed to have brought Scotland to a more convenient doorstep, something which was both mocked and appreciated by the weekend guests, who included the Foreign Secretary Anthony Eden; Harold Macmillan; the managing directors of two other top merchant banks, one of whom was Bash Rowell's father; three industrialists; a noted Shakespearean actor; and assorted prominent people. Deborah had begged to join the group assembling in the forecourt, but her father sharply criticized her for displaying unladylike tendencies. Old Jamison, the head stable lad, was assisting the gamekeeper, and left her with only a vague hope that he might have time to take her for a short ride if the men grew bored and returned early from the shoot.

Madeleine and the women guests would be going off to a local flower show, but Deborah, having made her exclusion from the shoot a matter of principle, refused to join them.

For a few minutes after watching the men drive off in the Land Rovers, she had been angry and full of self-pity. Her self-righteousness grew when the women left, but she soon became tired of moping in her bedroom and began wandering through other rooms, seeking anything that might pass for diversion. She got under the servants' feet as they tidied the drawing room and prepared tea in the kitchen. She had moved outside and was desultorily chasing multichrome doves across the lawn when she noticed a team of matched greys pulling an open carriage up the driveway.

Ecstatic over the break in the tedium, she raced towards the low steps separating the driveway and the wide terrace in front of the château's entrance, where she knew the carriage would halt. A startled peacock flew upwards nearly knocking her over, but she paid little attention to it. The passenger in the carriage, she knew, of course, had to be Grandfather. His mind might roam expertly around in the present and future, but his body always felt more at home in the leisured pace of the Edwardian Age. He hated twentieth-century machines – barely accepting the earliest of them, the automobile. Tolerating cars for only as long as it was inconvenient not to, he invariably travelled to the village by train and around the countryside by horse-drawn carriage. For the entire summer, he had been either abroad on business or on his yacht for pleasure.

Deborah and he had spent three afternoons together in the past year. The first was after the seder, when they had gone off to lunch together at the Savoy Grill, and then to the zoo in Regent's Park. She wanted to visit the monkeys and then watch the hippos yawn, which they seemed to do nearly all the time they were awake. She explained that they had always reminded her of huge lavatory seats lifting, and Samuel had laughed so violently that his hat blew away, and they both had to scamper after it. Then they had sat on a bench and talked. She hardly knew him and had endless questions to ask, mostly about what life used to be like. She asked about Grandmother, who died when she was too young to remember, and about the 'oldentime' Kronengolds. She wanted to know what happened in that mysterious place all men went off to during the day, 'the bank'. She asked what foods and colours were his favourites, what games, and so on. He seemed to have just as many questions for her. He brought her home at dinnertime after allowing her so many sweets that Nanny wisely decided to skip the meal.

The next time he spent the day with her, he had a lunch set out on the veranda overlooking the gardens behind his London house. When they strolled about the garden, she insisted on walking beside him along the top of a low wall. She did it, she told him, so they could be the same height and talk like grown-ups.

Now, as he stepped from the open carriage, Deborah flew into his arms.

He greeted her happily. 'I was afraid you'd be off somewhere on your pony.'

'Nobody will let me do anything.' Her voice wallowed bravely in its despair.

'But you wrote to me that you had been given a pony.'

'You got my letter!'

'I could read every word,' he assured her. 'But your spelling leaves something to be desired.' He gestured into the carriage. 'Look, I have brought you a present that spells perfectly.'

A young man Deborah had not noticed slid over to the near seat and stepped out. He was the least orderly person she had ever seen. His jacket – a heavy tweed one, though this was summer – hung askew, as if an overworked salesman had hurriedly tossed it onto a hanger. The knot of his paisley tie was hidden under a flap of his shirt collar, exposing an opening in his shirt where the second button should have been. Listless locks of brownish-blond hair flopped randomly across his forehead.

'Deborah, I have brought you a tutor, Jason Latham. From America. Where much of the future for your generation will be. You can be certain that I have found his credentials faultless.'

The absurdity of such a statement failed to occur either to Samuel or to his granddaughter; it seemed perfectly natural that one Kronengold should vouch for an employee's references when recommending him to another, even to a seven-year-old.

'Have you been in America, Grandpa?'

'Certainly not!' His tone conveyed all his distaste for such a notion. 'Mr. Latham came *here*.'

'How do you do, Mr. Latham?' Deborah ventured.

He shook her hand with a shy smile and then self-consciously dropped his gaze.

The three of them began walking along a path bordered by box trees clipped into spheres. At the end was the geometric Elizabethan garden laid out beside one of the wings of the house. Jason Latham tended to fall behind by a step or two out of courtesy, or perhaps so as not to be called upon to speak.

'Mr. Latham is a scholar,' Samuel explained. 'He has been to Oxford and, before that, studied literature at Yale University, which I'm told is among America's better efforts to approach the sort of education we provide at Oxford and Cambridge.'

'But, Grandfather, I had a tutor all year, and now Mummy has entered me in a school. I start after the summer.'

He brushed the air, effectively disposing of that arrangement. 'No longer. Mr. Latham will be tutoring you instead of that woman . . . or some school.' Scorn infused his last words. 'I won't have your mind cluttered by a lot of second-rate people, your originality squashed into everyone else's tedious shape. Five mornings a week should do very nicely. And there'll be people for languages and sports. And every Tuesday and Friday you and I will have lunch and then spend the afternoon together.'

Samuel paused before an airy model of a Japanese temple in which half a dozen nightingales flew. He whistled, but received no response. In the evening they filled the air with their music; Deborah's window opened above this garden, and she was often rocked to sleep by their singing. The two men and the little girl then turned onto a path in the garden. Samuel set a determined, zigzag pace towards the fountain in the centre. His speech was similarly decisive.

'Mr. Latham is rather weak on the fine arts. That will therefore be my responsibility. And, of course, economic matters. As for your pony, it seems only sensible that, if you have one, you should be allowed to ride it. I will take up the matter with your parents.'

So many of the important things in her life seemed to have been decided upon that Deborah was too confused as yet to be grateful about the prospect of expanded mobility. 'Grandfather, is Mr. Latham to be a present for Richard as well?'

'Richard,' he repeated thoughtfully. 'Unfortunately, the school that your parents selected for him has already done its worst to what there was of him, and Richard is well on his way to becoming a gentleman, God help him.'

'But what about when you're away?'

He smiled down at her. 'This summer I finally had some time to myself. I confess that the leisure grew heavy on my hands. Unlike the time I've spent with you.'

Usually the thorniest and most peremptory of men, brilliant, impatient, easily bored, Samuel de Kronengold had found himself drawn to Deborah's bright mind and vivacious manner. She possessed a capacity for originality that had attracted his interest and, unexpectedly, had held it.

Deborah stood at the edge of the fountain, trying to sort out her thoughts, staring without awareness at the muscular marble men and women locked into contortions by marble fishes and sea serpents.

So much attention after so arid a day, and to be addressed so directly and in a tone approaching equality – uncharacteristic of Grandfather, to say the least – was pleasing to Deborah, but something was troubling her.

She finally spoke up. 'Grandfather, what am I to do for friends? At school I was hoping to meet other children.'

He appeared sincerely perplexed. 'Why on earth would you wish to spend time with children?'

Samuel had in fact done more than hire a tutor, it turned out; he had purchased a library. Around one o'clock that afternoon several vans arrived stacked high with boxes of books. Deborah came to the thoroughly logical and demoralizing conclusion that this education Grandfather had ordered for her would entail her reading through every book in the hundreds of cartons issuing from the vans. Her heart grew heavy; she would never be allowed out of the library.

Much earlier in the afternoon than Deborah had expected, the lorry piled high with dead grouse appeared at the pantry door, and the shooting party returned in the Land Rovers and trooped towards the forecourt in front of the house. Richard brought up the rear like a dragging tailpipe. His feet scuffed the grass; his eyes were downcast. Leslie turned back on the stone terrace's broad front step and awaited Richard's arrival like a vengeful archangel perched above a cathedral entrance. Deborah hurried up. When she reached them, her father was already talking heatedly to her mother, who had returned with the other women to greet the shooting party.

'Richard shot four straight birds, right off the bat, as well as any man among us. Really first rate! Then he refused to go on. Wouldn't fire another shot all day!' Leslie spun away in disgust.

Tea had been laid on the terrace. The two adults moved

towards the tables and their guests, Madeleine reluctantly. She was the parent who listened to Richard's concerns and comforted him; she would speak with him alone later. Deborah caught sight of Grandfather stopping her parents. He was talking firmly to them, she supposed about the matters he and she had discussed that morning. Concerned about her brother and uncertain about Grandfather's proposal, she remained with Richard. Richard's face was an agony of conflict. Terrified of Father, his anguish was so great he divulged it with little prompting. He had been looking forward to his first shoot. But the first sight of dead birds being dropped at his feet by the dogs and the sheer numbers piling up revolted him.

'We killed hundreds, Dee. We couldn't eat that many in a year of grouse dinners. They'll sell them to butchers' shops in London tomorrow. Dee, we were out there to slaughter birds for butchers' shops. I couldn't lift my gun back up to my shoulder. But Bash kept blasting away from behind the next butt.' He blinked back tears. 'Bash loved it. Look at him over there.'

Bash Rowell was talking to his father and another man. His young body was bent like a longbow, tautly, beautifully insolent with the day's giant step to manhood. Richard, agonizing, seemed every bit as courageous to Deborah's inexperienced eyes. But she knew he didn't feel it. All the time he spoke, he gaze was on his father, whose back was kept pointedly turned to them.

Leslie rarely rode before the fox-hunting season began in November – summer was for shooting and fishing – and he was a man of disciplined habits. But, at Samuel's urging, he immediately spoke to Old Jamison about Deborah's reliability on a horse and then rode out with her to assess this for himself.

Rain had kept Gypsy in her stall the day before, and she was jittery with energy. Both the young girl and her pony longed to stretch out full all the way to the lake. But her father had stressed tersely that he was as concerned about Deborah's sense of responsibility as about her equestrian skills. She kept Gypsy well reined in, and they trotted sedately all the way.

Leslie's jaw was set in furrows; neck and back rigid, his mind still dwelling on Richard's disgrace earlier that day. The posture bespoke a mood Deborah had been exposed to before;

she kept her silence. In the last few months, she had begun to break through his severity by appealing to his interest in archaeology. The opportunity had occurred by chance. She had asked her mother who King Tut was – it was such a funny name for a king. Her mother insisted that her father could tell more about him than almost anyone, because when Leslie was at Cambridge he had hoped to become an archaeologist and had studied ancient cultures. With some reticence, Deborah had approached her father and had been delighted when he put his arm around her and led her to the library. There, he pulled down thick volumes from the walls of books and showed her pictures of the golden treasures found in Tutankhamen's tomb, explaining how the Egyptians' life was a preparation for their afterlife. From there he launched into a lecture on the culture of the Greeks and Romans.

He spoke with animation until long past her bedtime; thoughts tumbled out. She sensed that he wanted her to understand this long-dead world that captivated him, and felt herself nearly bursting with love for him. But when she asked him why he hadn't become an archaeologist instead of a banker, his face and tone petrified. He replied only that when his older brother, Edgar, died, the duty became his.

Madeleine prided herself on openness, never blocking out the truth from her children or distorting it. When Deborah inquired of her about Edgar's death and her father's attitude, Madeleine's face grew sombre, and it required a few minutes before she was composed enough to reply. Finally, she said that Edgar was Leslie's older brother. He was a banker who had died just before the war. Leslie was left with no alternative to his family duty; his father told him he would go into the bank.

Deborah asked if there was a photo of this Uncle Edgar who had died seven years before she was born. Madeleine drew from the bottom drawer of her desk a metal box, which she unlocked. From it she took a photo and handed it to her daughter. A handsome young man in ski clothes stood on snow-covered ground. Behind him were hazily defined figures skiing. The sun was in his eyes, and he was squinting, but the good looks and the wide smile made one like him immediately. The young woman beside him was shielding her eyes from the sun with one hand. The other hand, a diamond ring glinting on it, was extended towards the camera. She was laughing, as if he had just said something funny to her.

Deborah handed back the photo to her mother, understanding from Madeleine's bereft, averted eyes – although not the reason why – that she would rather not be asked any more questions, particularly about why she looked so happy in the photo.

At the path near the lake, where the light between leaves turned the horses flickering piebald, Leslie slowed his mount to a shambling walk and glanced sideways at his daughter. A miniature person on a miniature house, she still sat with upright pride. An unaccustomed grin creased his face.

'Young lady, I thought there was no possible way for you to restrain yourself so long. If I hadn't been with you, would you have been so . . . contained?'

Deborah bit her lip, hoping he would pass on to another topic.

'Well?' he asked again.

She giggled, tension releasing at last. 'I'd have been to the windmill by now.'

'I suppose I just know too little about girls. I keep expecting you to be gentler.'

'I really do try, but after a while I get bored and restless.'

'And probably need to get out and ride to use up all that energy.' Surprise was in his voice, as if the possibility that girls had something in common with boys had never occurred to him. Deborah's hopes rose.

They pulled up where the brook tumbled into the lake. The horses lowered their heads to drink the running water.

'How do you feel about Grandfather's plans for you? Mother is concerned that you might be better off in a school.'

'Would I have to read every one of the books that arrived today?'

'Whatever made you think that? No, only schoolbooks, and those you decide to read for pleasure.'

Relieved, she answered, 'Then I think I want to do it.'

'I had a tutor as a boy.'

Deborah waited for him to add to that observation, but he didn't. Finally, she felt compelled to give a reason for her choice. 'Grandfather is very interesting to be with.'

'Yes, I thought that might be it. He can be quite overwhelming. Did he say why he chose you and not Richard?'

Deborah heard the threat of rage in her father's

voice – against her? Against Richard? She was not sure, but sensed a lie here would be safer than the truth. She had never lied to anyone before, much less to her easily vexed father, and waited for certain discovery and punishment as she answered him.

'Richard's studies are so much more important than mine. He didn't want to interrupt them.'

Leslie grew silent and recalled with chagrin how futile his own desires had always been in the face of his father's dictates. To this day, Lord Kronengold's opinion was the only one that mattered on any important business decision. The newspapers lionized Leslie as the young star of the Kronengold empire, but he was realistic about his chafing subservience. Now his father had been overcome with a sudden enthusiasm for Deborah's development. Leslie found that galling because he remembered a similar enthusiasm when he himself was a child – for his older brother, Edgar. His father had taken an inordinate interest in Edgar's tutoring, spent hours each day with him, allowed Edgar to accompany him to the bank and to meetings. Only when his father, with utmost reluctance, had sent Edgar off to Eton, did he finally focus his attention on his younger sons, Leslie and Charles, who had also been tutored.

Leslie was a solid student, not dazzling like Edgar, but conscientious and traditional-minded. Leslie could still remember his father's irritation at the slowness of his calculating and at his failure to comprehend the complex business questions his father posed, more suitable for someone with Edgar's years and training than his own. And he had an even firmer recollection of the bleakness of his soul when, during one of his turgid, rambling answers, his father had abruptly interrupted to announce that he was sending him to boarding school the following week. Leslie knew, with the clarity of perfect foresight, that he had failed his father, and that all the rest of his life he would fail himself.

Now, so many years later, his father had found a new comen to guide across the universe, to pin his hopes on: Deborah. And, again, with the same clarity of that boyhood moment in his father's study, he could see that Richard, the product of his own flesh, was simply a living extension of his own inadequacies projected forward into time.

Suddenly, Leslie resented the child beside him, the child forced on him when Madeleine learned why she had lost her own baby. And he felt the vague beginnings of antagonism towards her stirring within him – for her brilliance; for her beauty; for her vitality; for not being his; and for being an ever-present accusation of his failure. If he had fought the feeling down, cast it away, the alienation towards the child that he allowed to germinate at that moment might never have taken root, but he was so riled by self-reproach that he found the idea of attaching blame to Deborah strangely intriguing, like a scab he could not resist picking. When he eventually spoke, however, his voice did not deviate from its customary forceful, slightly bored tone.

'Want to race a bit back to the house? Really give the horses a workout?' He was riding Wave Crest, a once-good racehorse converted to hacking because of a docile disposition.

'It wouldn't be a fair race,' she observed thoughtfully. 'I'd have too much of an advantage.'

'I didn't mean we would race *against* each other.' But he was intrigued. 'Why do you think you'd win?'

'You'd have to take the roads or the meadows the whole way round. Gypsy and I are short enough to run under the branches in Blendon's Wood, nearly to the house.'

A look of bewildered repugnance at the child's tactics crossed Leslie's face.

'I thought the point was to get there first,' Deborah said weakly.

'Some things are understood.'

They galloped back at a good pace, opening up the last quarter-mile across a meadow. Leslie had to go round the apple orchard. Deborah took a path through it.

Madeleine was waiting in front of the passageway into the stableyard, watching them sweep towards her.

'She's not a bad rider, Maddy,' Leslie acknowledged after reining up. 'She should be safe on her own.'

'Not bad? She's superb,' replied Madeleine, her Gallic zestfulness uncurbed by exposure to a decade and a half of English reserve. 'She's like part of the horse.'

'Does that mean I can ride by myself?' Deborah asked as they proceeded into the stableyard.

'I suppose so,' her father finally conceded.

Deborah's 'Thank you!' was so explosive it startled the horses. She flipped off and handed her reins to a groom who had hurried up.

Madeleine had come to observe Deborah but wanted to say something to her husband. 'Leslie, please try to put Vivienne at ease this weekend.'

'Oh Lord, you didn't invite her for the entire weekend?' His tone was firmly disapproving.

'Vivienne is outrageous, I know, but I love her for it.'

'Every newspaper has had a field day with her.'

'You sound as moralistic as the Archbishop of Canterbury. She'll behave. Her daughter's with her. I thought it would be fun for Dee to have a girl her age here.'

Madeleine kissed her husband lightly on the cheek, a very un-English public display of affection that always flustered him. He had been as captivated in their youth by her disconcerting naturalness as he had been by her looks – which had infatuated him long before he had any hope of possessing her. In private moments, like this, it still could touch him in ways he had never suspected were important, and almost invariably make him feel even less worthy of her.

Still afloat on the exhilaration following her father's decision – and his lean praise – Deborah slipped impulsively in front of her mother and hugged him. He awkwardly patted her head and then, mortified by her cheek resting against his chest, pulled back.

'Just be sure you ride responsibly, young lady, or you'll find yourself confined to your room.'

As she walked off with her mother, she gave him a childishly flirtatious smile of appreciation. The grim set to his mouth deepened.

Madeleine led Deborah to the conservatory, her favourite place. The huge glass area at one end of the house had been made into a tropical wonderland. Among the exotic plants and vines, brilliantly coloured birds – parrots, cockatoos, macaws, toucans – flew freely about. Madeleine had telephoned the butler's pantry from one of the kiosks placed at strategic points around the grounds, and lemonade awaited their arrival. They picked out a bench near groups of orchids varying in colour from shades of white through violet to black. Behind them was a cluster of tall stems, each bearing a large orange flower, like jungle versions of the day lily.

'What has she done?' Deborah asked.

'Who?'

'Your friend.'

Madeleine laughed warmly. 'I'm afraid she's just gone through a rather public divorce. Vivienne couldn't exist without scandal. She's incorrigible, but she has a heart of gold. I've met her daughter. You two have a lot in common.'

'What's her name?'

'One of the early months, I think. Certainly not January or February.'

Madeleine grew quiet, her gaze fixed on the stately orange blooms. They were angled both to the sun that warmed them and to each other like the faces of elegant women.

'I wish I weren't so timid on horseback,' she finally said. 'I'll never share that time with you when you're galloping off here and there. You're growing up too fast, Dee. I'm starting to lose you already.'

Perturbed, not understanding what she had done to cause dismay, Deborah clutched her mother's arm. Madeleine placed her hand over Deborah's. 'Children grow up too fast. You're so quick and clever, it just seems to be happening even earlier than I had imagined it would.'

'But you're always busy.'

'The only time I ever feel the slightest bit useful is when I'm working at Immigrant House.' Madeleine devoted much of her spare time to a social service for refugees. 'It seems as if all the business in my life takes place around me, and my job is to show up because the table is laid. I sometimes wonder what I'm doing here.' Madeleine was speaking more for herself than for her daughter, who did not fully understand what she meant.

'You mean like how at night sometimes I still wonder who I really am?'

Madeleine spun around and hugged Deborah fiercely. 'You are my daughter, as completely as if I had given birth to you. You are Deborah *de Kronengold*.'

'Will I grow up to be like you? Or like somebody else I don't know?'

Because she had no answer, Deborah thought, her mother gathered her in more tightly. 'You'll be yourself. Dee, you will grow up to be somebody wonderful, more wonderful than you and I can possibly imagine. It's my fault you're worried. Yes, it is. We must make a special effort to set aside time to talk privately and do things together and not let anything interfere with our time alone. Let's both try.'

Deborah thought about revealing the lie she had told her father a little while before. It troubled her and was all confused with her concern for Richard, her anger at being excluded from the shoot, and the questions she had about the new direction in which Grandfather had set her life. But just then guests began wandering into the conservatory, already dressed for dinner. Deborah kept her thoughts to herself.

Lady April Thornley proved to be a revelation. Already eight, she was a fund of the most sophisticated knowledge, which frequently settled topsy-turvy in her head. Deborah came upon her engaged in an argument with Bash Rowell in the children's wing, a suite of rooms on the second floor widely separated from the slightest opportunity of disturbing an adult. The noise they were making was evidence of the architect's wisdom. Bash was maintaining, with a haughtiness representative of a family whose female line could be traced back to Agincourt, that April could not be certain the Duke of Grenford really was her father, judging by the talk about her parents' divorce he had overheard among his father's group.

'Of course he's my father,' April replied with consummate élan. 'Mother says that is the one thing a woman cannot afford to make a mistake about. She always spent April at Grenford.'

Deborah introduced herself and pulled April away.

The two of them became acquainted as Deborah washed and changed. The similarity Madeleine had observed in them must be their outspokenness, Deborah soon decided. Physically, they were not at all alike. Deborah was tall for her age and slim as a boy, with blue eyes, hair the colour of conflagration atop her head, and straight features that she considered barely tolerable. April seemed to be a bouquet of circles: dark round eyes in a round face, dark curly hair, and a short, chubby body. Her mouth, too, was round in a way; when closed it looked perpetually drawn together for kissing. Deborah was fascinated by her eyelashes, long swooping wings that made one fasten on her eyes and forget her chubbiness. She was rarely silent. Within half an hour Deborah – and the maid helping her dress – had heard the most intimate details of April's mother's love affairs. Deborah didn't understand many, and judging by the maid's wide-eyed attention, this was not the sort of thing one spoke about in front of the servants. But silencing April was impossible. Deborah was captivated.

'She drives men mad with desire,' April confided proudly to Deborah as they watched her mother from their hiding place on the minstrels' gallery above the drawing room. Most of the men, drinks in hand, were clustered around Vivienne Thornley. The recently-divorced Duchess of Grenford was too extravagant, too striking in her looks for anyone to take the time to decide whether she was truly beautiful. Her eyes and hair resembled her daughter's, but little else in her lean stance and lush features did. She seemed to be concentrating much of her madness-inducing power on the oversized target of Nathan de Kronengold, one of the few bachelors present. Lying on her stomach on the balcony, peering down between the posts supporting the railing, Deborah was beginning to suspect she did not totally grasp a great deal that was happening in that part of the room. She decided she would ask April later.

She tried to catch her grandfather's eye as he went by, but he was engrossed in a conversation with his old friend Anthony Eden about the direction of the British economy. There was someone present whose opinion he particularly valued and thought the Foreign Secretary should hear on the subject. He pulled his cousin Nathan away from the knot around Vivienne Grenford. Anxious not to be left out, Leslie joined them just as Nathan began to speak.

After a mild apology for what he was about to say, Nathan condemned as dangerous, self-eluding bravado the tiny island's attempt to swagger like such giant powers as America and the Soviet Union. Massive defence expenditures were draining the country's limited resources, and costly social programmes would drain the people's moral and economic incentive. Compared to other countries, England was investing little capital in new industrial capacity, technology, or products. Since coming to live there, Nathan had drawn the conclusion that the English were a people who would accept anything but change, and who did not value winning as much as losing gracefully. 'To put it simply,' he ended in his usual fatalistic tone, 'we are headed down the road to destitution.' He advised the others to invest outside Britain.

Leslie was appalled, claiming that Nathan's remarks were baldly unpatriotic, particularly reprehensible in an émigré.

Eden considered it impolitic to comment. Samuel was quietly thoughtful.

Madeleine had been at the front door welcoming newly-arrived guests and so had entered the drawing room a few minutes after the others. She was wearing a white accordion-pleated crêpe dress from Dior, and her entrance was noticeable. The approving murmurs and smiles that greeted her brought a flush of embarrassment to her cheeks, and she swiftly began introducing new guests to the others. Her eyes sought out Leslie, who was now engaged in a political discussion with Eden and several other men. Leslie had been toying with the idea of running for Parliament, but she doubted whether he would either relinquish his privacy or tolerate his removal to the Lords on Samuel's death. At bottom, she had learned, Leslie was a solitary man, difficult to know well and more difficult to reach.

Taking a weak whisky and soda from a footman's tray, she surveyed the room and concluded that things were going well. None of the nearby little groups of guests needed a hostess's touch. She glanced at the walls. New green silk material had been put on them, and the moulding brightened with new gilt. She was pleased at how much fresher the drawing room looked. She was about to begin a slow circumnavigation to greet those newcomers she had not yet welcomed to Clove Hill when she was startled by a voice behind her.

'I say, the Whistler bears a striking resemblance to you.'

Robin Rowell was leaning casually against a wall, one hand in his pocket, the other holding a drink. He was blond and, like his son Bash, quite handsome. His features were more finely carved than his son's, and the posture held more leisurely, but he wore the same tinge of insolence in his gaze and the same charming smile. Madeleine turned towards him.

'Oh, it's you, Rob. The woman in the portrait is an ancestor of mine, and related in some way to Leslie as well. The rumour is she had a mad affair with Whistler, but couldn't be sure whether he loved her for her wealth or herself.'

'Why quibble?' He flashed an amused smile. 'You say "rumoured"?'

'We Kronengolds bury our secrets so deep one can never be sure.'

'There used to be a saying at our bank that doing business with the Kronengolds was like putting one's head in the lion's mouth. I wonder if that holds true for a relationship with their women.'

'We try to keep our mouths firmly shut.'

'Then Leslie is a lucky man indeed.'

Robin Rowell considered Madeleine de Kronengold a beautiful woman, but his own interest in her began to awaken only when he realized that his banter was not correspondingly arousing her interest and leading to the more intimate flirtation he practised as a matter of habit.

Robin Rowell, the sixth Earl, had always got what he desired. His parents, the servants and, later, others had indulged him – as he indulged Bash – as if it were his birthright by reason of wealth, family position, and grace in appearance and manner. Women were particularly drawn to him because of those qualities – and because of his indifference. They sensed that the pleasure they gave him was transitory and, intellectually at least, passionless. He had married solely to continue the line and add a few more influential, titled family members to the Rowell genealogy. His wife had obliged him quickly by producing a son and thoughtfully departing the earth at the same time, thus allowing him to return to the bachelor life he so enjoyed. He remembered her with some fondness for both those acts. Contrary to what that might imply, he was not a ruthless man, although it might appear so to a casual observer. Rather, he was simply unsentimental about his wants and opportunistic about satisfying them.

Intrigued by Madeleine, he was about to continue their conversation when she suddenly introduced herself to a stranger standing near them.

'Max Holtz,' the man responded in a thick German accent. He had a pugnacious face, prominent cheekbones, jaw, and brow, and a brooding look to his eyes. He half-bowed courteously from the waist and shook their hands.

'You're Samuel's guest,' Madeleine remembered. She had an inkling she knew him.

'Lord Kronengold is very gracious. I'm over from South Africa. He is kind enough to employ me to oversee his interests in Johannesburg.'

'We've met before, haven't we?'

'I'm honoured.' He bowed awkwardly. 'But the circumstance was not a pleasant one. I escaped from Austria in 1938 with some members of your family.'

Recollection stabbed through her. She remembered him now. His presence at the time had been inconsequential to her, but she remembered him nonetheless, a background figure in a tableau that lingered painfully fresh in her memory: on a railway platform near her family's estate in France, harshly lit by bare light bulbs, Leslie and this other man were lifting a coffin down from the luggage van. They had travelled all day from Vienna to Valtary, where a family celebration was to take place. She and Pierre had come to greet the train, but neither could have known beforehand what it would bring.

The night before, a mob of Nazi toughs had run amok through the streets of Vienna and noticed the lights on in the Kronengold bank. Edgar was in the bank with his young brother, Leslie. They were helping the aged patriarch of the Austrian Kronengolds to transfer out of the country as much of his family's assets as possible before they all fled to safety the next day. Edgar had travelled from Switzerland the day before to slip capital back through clandestine routes to the Swiss bank he ran. Leslie, who had promised his father to give banking a three-year trial before choosing archaeology, was working in the Vienna bank as a trainee.

The mob had charged the locked doors of the bank. Edgar, trying to bar them, was killed when the mob surged through. The old man was trampled to death seconds later. Leslie was able to escape with others out the back. Early the next morning the eldest of the Kronengolds was hastily buried, and the few family members left alive in Austria – Leslie and two old women – climbed aboard the train with Edgar's coffin. This man, Holtz, the most muscular of the employees at the Viennese bank, was chosen to help carry Edgar's coffin. His chance reward after years of working for the Kronengolds – when young men at other firms with less talent were being rewarded with partnerships – turned out to be Edgar's precious train ticket out of Nazi Austria. Escape. But how could they know the searing resentment he harboured against this family that had wiped out his grandfather's little Austrian bank in the 1890s, an incidental casualty they probably did not even notice during one of their fabled financial coups? They saw only a diligent young man with a strong back.

The Kronengolds had chosen luckily. At the border his forged German papers convinced the Austrian police to let them all through. Any obligation to the Kronengolds imposed on him by the reward of the train ticket he considered cancelled.

Running happily down the railway platform to greet the travellers, Madeleine caught sight of the coffin. Leslie's eyes, encountering hers, were drowning in desolation. Then she knew. Her life suddenly began crumbling under the soles of her feet. Edgar, her fiancé, *was* her life. They were to have been married in two days at the Château. Now she was as dead as he, but she would have to go on living.

'I remember you now,' Madeleine said to Holtz.

He appeared grateful. 'I had only the clothes on my back.'

Max Holtz had never forgotten Madeleine de Kronengold. She looked so lovely that night on the platform, the grief illuminating her beauty like a mourning candle. He possessed nothing and needed their generosity. She was so far above him – a Kronengold, a rich, hated, fragilely perfect Kronengold. He could say nothing about his feelings, just as he had always concealed his burning grudge against the Kronengolds and made a show of gratefulness for each crumb that they threw him – oblivious of his hatred. This time it was the offer of a job in the French Kronengold's Paris bank. Well paid, with responsibility, but always a hireling.

The position lasted until the Germans marched into France. Their appearance and his well-forged Aryan identification papers, masking his Jewish identity, afforded him what he was sure, at last, was his big chance. Surveying the confusion and hardship imposed by Nazi occupation – Henri de Kronengold forced to flee to England, his son, Pierre, isolated in Italy with the family's Italian holdings, other Kronengolds trapped in flight around Europe – Max perceived the opportunity to turn the war to his advantage. In later years others would curse the Germans for their butchery. He would curse them for losing.

Penniless after the war, he had emigrated to South Africa and a new start; his contact with Samuel Kronengold, whom he had met that fateful day at Valtary, when Kronengolds from far and wide were gathered there for the wedding, had become the main source of business there for him. But Samuel was an absentee landlord, leaving operational authority and wide discretion to Max Holtz. Now Holtz had come to England with a proposal he intended to make to Samuel that would allow him a percentage of the profits produced by his efforts in South Africa. He was ready to marshal the most convincing arguments that he was entitled to a share, that profits always increase when a manager has a personal incentive. But, in his heart, doubts sapped his resolve; he was convinced that Samuel would turn him down, not out of lack of entitlement, but simply because 'the Kronengolds never take in partners.'

Madeleine perceived, beneath Max Holtz's excessive courtesy, cross-currents awash against each other: elemental ambitions and hungers barely restrained and resentments barely concealed. They made her uncomfortable until she realized that she was merely unused to close exposure to such a nature. The British considered it good manners to mask ambition and desire with nonchalance or even apathy. Rob, for instance, was known to be an enterprising banker, but if asked, he would probably mumble that he did 'something in the City' and change the topic. Holtz, on the other hand, was a man for whom survival and then the pursuit of prosperity had been matters of will. He was as ill at ease amid those accustomed to possessing great wealth as she was with him. She cast about for some banal bit of conversation to make him feel comfortable.

'Do you shoot?' she asked him.

'Do I shoot who?'

'Birds, old man,' Rob chipped in helpfully. 'Marvellous shooting today.'

'No. I play a little tennis occasionally.'

Madeleine could imagine him on the court – smashing formlessly at the ball but winning by sheer competitive determination.

At that moment, Max Holtz caught sight of Samuel entering the room. For a few seconds he seemed to be struggling with a strong desire to continue talking to Madeleine, but then he half-bowed again, excused himself, and walked over to his patron. The way they stood Madeleine could tell who was the supplicant – around the Kronengolds most people were – but even a child could recognize that Max Holtz was not a man who assumed such a role easily.

Madeleine gazed about the room. 'Vivienne looks marvellous tonight, the centre of attention.'

Rob smiled. 'She never changes, does she? We've known

each other since childhood, actually. She was precisely the same then.'

'My daughter is like that. You can see the woman in her waiting to grow big enough to be taken seriously.'

'Were you like that as a child?'

'I was quite scatterbrained at her age, I'm sure.'

'And probably very beautiful.'

Rob's tone startled her. All hint of flirtatiousness had been stripped away. And then she realized how hard he was staring at her. Flustered by what she perceived to be his impertinence, she rushed into a reply. 'A mess, I'm afraid. And probably as tiresome then as now. By the way, I invited a really interesting woman for you to meet. Have you spoken to Lady Bosworth? She's just returned from the Amazon.'

Madeleine scanned her guests, seeking the woman. Rob spoke up to stop her.

'I thought she had made the fact common knowledge – I'm afraid I'm the reason Carolyn Bosworth went up the Amazon.'

Madeleine laughed and shook her head helplessly at the complications that had just crept into her guest list. 'Sometimes I wish I were a bit less naive.'

'Naiveté is not a quality I come across very often in the women I meet.'

Madeleine felt so discomforted that she replied with a defensiveness which sounded foolish and embarrassed her still more. 'I'm afraid you aren't used to talking to happily married women.'

'Happily married or merely used to it?'

Rob continued to stare at Madeleine with an interest that even he, so jaded by the inevitability of seduction, could not deny was far more intense than he had felt for a woman in a long while. She was beautiful, true. But it was a beauty suffused with a vibrant freshness that he found unique – and quite incongruous in a woman married to someone as stolid and unimaginative as Leslie de Kronengold.

Madeleine took several seconds to break free of the thoughts that trapped her. Her eyes flashed. 'That was a very presumptuous remark.'

'Only if the shot was wide of the mark,' Rob replied. 'I gather it wasn't.'

Madeleine felt the blood pounding through her chest with unaccustomed force. She was breathing far too heavily, and her skin felt hot. This was all so ridiculous, she thought, these reactions from a married woman. And then she recalled with chagrin what he had asked her about the marriage. All she expected out of life anymore was a serene routine. Leslie had given it to her. Most people didn't have even that. She was very grateful to him. Why had Rob Rowell insisted on reminding her there was once a dream called happiness?

'I will try my best to forget this episode,' she offered in a voice she thought sounded quite composed.

'Please don't,' he insisted. 'I know I won't.'

In the gallery above, April nudged Deborah and pointed down towards something. Deborah shifted to view that side of the drawing room more clearly. Her mother was just spinning away from Bash Rowell's father to speak to other guests, her dress twirling wide. The movement appeared so self-conscious, so unlike her mother, that Deborah continued to watch. The only thing the least bit unusual, she thought, was that Lord Rowell kept staring at her mother for so long after she had left him. Deborah didn't know why, but it bothered her.

CHAPTER THREE

In 1953 the elder daughter of the late King George VI was crowned Queen Elizabeth II in a triumphant ceremony that promoted an outpouring of joy and optimism among her subjects. Britain was predicted to be on the verge of a Golden Age, much like that reigned over by the young queen's namesake three hundred years earlier. By 1956, the country's most prominent banker had become convinced that Britain was finally about to shake off her postwar economic timidity and become again the power she had been when her empire girdled the globe. His confidence extended even more strongly to his banking and investment interests there. A major reason for his hopefulness was his granddaughter.

The four years since he had intervened in her life had been marvellous for Deborah. She had sprung up like a bamboo shoot and was now over five feet in height, but slim and angular, with no roundness yet at the hip or breast. From a distance, one noticed that she moved like an athlete, with grace and quickness. Yet, once she drew near, one saw nothing but her face, as startling as when she was an infant: red hair against white skin, both a fit setting for the sapphire eyes. Growth had not changed the shape or proportion of her facial features, and now it was evident that the promise of beauty displayed in childhood would be fulfilled in womanhood. Her face was a delicately structured oval with high, almost Eastern cheekbones and a determined chin, softened by the hint of a cleft. Her brow was high and thoughtful, her nose thin and straight. But always one was held by the eyes, not simply by their colour, but by the unyielding gaze. People were often disconcerted by such directness, adults occasionally ascribing it to impudence. But Samuel comprehended that the intensity of her look derived from a mind that rarely rested; Deborah could never be fully understood or circumscribed, he concluded, never be reduced to the predictable; a part of her would always be reaching towards the unexplored and, thus, would always be bewitching.

Deborah had also thrived intellectually in the four years since Samuel had taken an active interest in her. She consumed effortlessly the learning offered her by Jason Latham, the tutor he had engaged, and by her language, art, and music tutors. But the high points of the week for both of them were the afternoons and occasional evenings they spent together. The original two afternoons a week were now often four or five. He took her to art galleries and auctions, to the theatre and concerts, and to companies he was considering financing. When he kept a Gainsborough in Britain with a winning bid at Sotheby's, she was beside him. When he outraged the stodgy banking community (and Leslie) by engineering a take-over of a big British company by an American giant, she was at the secret meetings in his private study. He invited her to lunches both with the most impressive intellects of the day and with his succession of young girl friends. He bombarded her with material on mathematics, economics, and banking that was advanced for her years and to which few girls of any age were exposed.

Despite his commitment to her training, particularly her business training, he was not surprised to hear that her favourite times with him were the intimate, undemanding ones. They were for him as well. She loved to accompany him to the races and watch the crowd express their affection for him as if they were his friends.

She loved also to talk to him when he was not trying so obviously to stuff education into her. Often she would charm him into breaking off for tea at the Dorchester or a walk in Hyde Park. Those were usually the times when he would recount the family history, a topic as important to a Kronengold as double-entry bookkeeping or foreign languages.

'We are inseparable from our history,' he once told her when they were sitting on a park bench near the Serpentine. 'All our blessings derive from those first Kronengolds. All our obligation must go to ensure that their legacy is passed on.'

'Were they all so very clever?'

'Many were.'

'Like my daddy?'

Samuel looked away, trying to appear intent on a passing rowing-boat. 'Times changed by the middle of the nineteenth century,' he finally went on, continuing his earlier narrative as if her question had never been raised. 'The Kronengold capital and its reputation were by then so vast that the banks more or less ran themselves. Do you remember what was written about the bankers in those days in the book I asked you to read, the one by Walter Bagehot?'

She laughed. 'You always say it to me.' He smiled and waited. ' "There has probably very rarely ever been so happy a position as that of a London private banker",' she recited, ' "and never perhaps a happier".'

'Very good.'

'Is it still so happy to be a banker?' Deborah asked.

'Not as it was then.'

She gazed at him quizzically.

'The wars,' he sighed, and began to explain how the guns of 1914 had changed forever the dependable, benign, uncomplicated world the privileged had blissfully inhabited. Half a generation of young men had been obliterated in the next four years, and the others returned home disdainful of class and age distinctions, ready to work, to build, and to purchase for a better life.

New technology forged new companies, he told her, while reducing the need for reliance on family members in other countries to make swift decisions – the telephone and telegraph could now whisk one there electronically. Governments and industry devoured capital in mammoth amounts. Even in groups, the private bankers – British 'merchant' bankers, American 'investment' bankers, and French bankers in *banques d'affaires* – could never again hope to control the financial destiny of nations. New types of banks now drew vast capital from the people themselves and their businesses and pumped it back into even vaster undertakings.

'Few merchant bankers,' Samuel declared with an eyebrow raised to indicate his own distaste, 'had the foresight or stomach for the sort of banking that placed branches on every other street corner like so many grocery shops. Banks that catered to the shopkeeper and working man, that had to open their books to the scrutiny of outsiders.'

Samuel went on to tell her about the depression of the Thirties. The merchant bankers were hurt particularly badly, because the capital they lost was not the public's for the most part, but their own.

By the end of the decade a new war shattered the world for the second time in a quarter century, on a scale so vast and with a cruelty so pervasive as to make its predecessor seem a sequence of bungled training manoeuvres. The Germans wiped out whole branches of the Kronengold family. Even those who escaped were destroyed financially, their banks and factories seized, their homes and art collections gobbled up. The wealthiest Jews in Europe, they were special targets of the Nazi terror. Even German bombers over London were told to use the great glass dome of the Kronengold bank as a prime target.

Samuel stood up. Pointing his walking stick at her, he made his final point. 'They never hit it!'

In April 1956, on the occasion of Deborah's eleventh birthday, Samuel arranged for her to pay a visit to the Kronengold bank. She had asked for this privilege on her two previous birthdays, but only now had her request been granted.

That morning she dressed in a longish dark green dress, a touch inappropriate for her age but not for her destination. She did not want the people at the bank to think her a child, in high stockings and knees exposed.

Because Leslie was far more comfortable with adults and maintained, at best, only an amiable remoteness with Deborah, Madeleine considered it important for there to be another man in Deborah's life she could look up to and to whom she could feel close. Grandfather and granddaughter adored each other, and they had been good for each other. Leslie, however, seemed to resent their relationship.

Standing at the front door, Madeleine recalled the fight she had just had with Leslie, and the bitter anger she had suppressed while seeing Deborah off boiled up inside her once again. His resentment had become unmistakable after he learned that his father was taking Deborah to the bank for her birthday. That morning he had announced to his wife that under no circumstances would he go to the bank 'if that little brat is there'. His outburst, so totally unexpected, and, even more, the impersonality of his characterization of Deborah, had shocked Madeleine deeply.

'She's our child!' Madeleine had exclaimed.

'*My* child is away at school. This one is here against my will. She has seduced you all.'

As much as the words, the ugly intonation and the snapped-off twist to his mouth conveyed his rancour.

Madeleine had argued that his bitterness was foolish, that no one was taking anything from Richard by treating Deborah with friendliness, that no one judged one child against the other or against the biological parents from whom they had sprung. Dee was just a little girl who was looking forward to seeing the place where her father worked and who would be hurt and confused if he wasn't there to greet her.

'She has her grandfather,' Leslie had thrown back at Madeleine, and then retreated to his dressing room, leaving little doubt that he would make other plans for the day.

The long black car carrying Deborah and Samuel disappeared from view into the tunnel of traffic. Madeleine could imagine her now, talking faster than most people could think, besieging her grandfather with questions or observations or childish gossip. Madeleine turned back into the house. Jason Latham stood at the end of the hall, studying a piece of paper. He looked like a lost child.

'Is something the matter, Jason?'

'Deborah says that I'm to take the train from Waterloo. She hasn't told me how to get there.'

Madeleine's eyes rolled up and then down in mock exasperation. The tutor's vagueness about his surroundings had become a good-natured family joke. 'Where are you going to?'

'Windsor Castle. I thought I'd give myself a treat today.'

'The gardens will be beautiful at this time of year.' She realized how much she wanted to get away for the day. 'Jason, how would you like some company?'

The shy eyes lit up. The few encounters he had had with the delicately lovely mother of his pupil had become treasured souvenirs, lifted gingerly for viewing from the glass shelves of memory, but he was much too inhibited to initiate a conversation with her. He found himself swallowing hard, wetting his throat enough to say, 'Very much.'

'Williston can drive us. I'll be ready in five minutes. I must tell Immigrant House I won't be going in today.'

As she dashed up the wide staircase that swept to the first floor in a grand semi-circle, Madeleine felt a schoolgirl's relief at having had classes suddenly cancelled and no responsibilities to face. But the relief was mingled with apprehension. She feared unstructured time; idle moments gave an opportunity for thoughts better pushed unexamined into the mind's dark recesses – a skill at which she had become quite expert. She paused at the top of the stairs.

'We must be sure not to miss anything,' she called down to him. 'I know you'll be enchanted by the State Apartments and St. George's Chapel. And, of course, we must see the Leonardo drawings and Queen Mary's Dolls' House.' Satisfied with her conscientious agenda, she hurried on to her sitting room.

'This is my granddaughter – Mr. Leslie's daughter.'

'Welcome to the bank, miss.' The portly doorman in knee breeches and green velvet tail-coat stood within the courtyard in front of the stone façade of the eighteenth-century building in which I. Kronengold & Sons had first begun to do business. He raised his top hat and smiled broadly as he opened the wide oak doors for Deborah and Samuel.

'The first doorman at the bank wore this uniform,' Samuel explained to Deborah, who was staring at it. 'None of the uniform designs have been changed.'

Inside, an ancient butler moved forward to take Samuel's hat. 'Peckerill, this is my granddaughter, Deborah de Kronengold – Mr. Leslie's girl,' Samuel told him. 'Peckerill was here before I was, Dee,' he added.

'His lordship was barely older than you, miss, when he first came to the bank with his father,' Peckerill intoned. 'My uncle had been here before me and put in a word with the old Lord when I was of an age to seek employment.'

Samuel chuckled. 'Peckerill and I are the historians here. He was referring to *my* grandfather, the first Lord Kronengold, who ran the bank then. Your great-great-grandfather.' Samuel turned back to the old attendant. He had an odd glint of mischief in his eye. 'What would you think about a woman in the bank some day – not as a secretary, but as a banker?'

The old man's mouth opened involuntarily. He stared in awe at the red-haired child who stood before him. 'My word!' he muttered. 'My word!'

Deborah, for her part, was speechless; there had never been a woman in the bank. Shares and positions in the bank were traditionally reserved for the men in the family. She searched her grandfather's face to discover whether he was serious, but she could not tell.

Samuel guided Deborah across the black and white marble

floor to the centre of the circular marble hall. Several stories up, a domed skylight illuminated it. Passages led into wings, and a wide marble staircase looped up to higher floors. Deborah felt as if she stood inside a great silver bell.

Her grandfather broke the spell. 'The Kronengold bank has spread through the rest of the buildings on this side of Mercy Lane – the last building houses the insurance company we own a good part of – but the heart of it is still here. Isaac Kronengold and his family lived on the upper floors of the original wing at first. They moved out when the bank grew too big and needed room.'

Samuel tried to sound casual as he spoke, but he was not. It was minor legend among the Kronengolds that a child's first excursion to the family bank could offer insight into fitness for a banking career, that a special enthusiasm and an indefinable astuteness in a child possessing a banker's instinct made themselves readily apparent. Samuel was not certain he believed that, but he did remember that, on his own initial tour of the bank, he had been seized with excitement. His father and grandfather had nodded knowingly to each other as he commented or asked questions. Samuel had recognized similar traits at a young age in his son Edgar. Now he had set his heart, which still grieved for the loss of his remarkable eldest son, on finding signs of that rare talent in his young granddaughter. To people with that talent, he knew, money was more than an agreed-upon standard of exchange, or even a tool; it was an artistic medium with which the gifted could fashion elegant forms, the beauty of each directly related to its potential for profit at minimized risk. Great musicians and artists often demonstrated their brilliance when young. Why should it be any different for those blessed with the talent to increase money?

The last few years had been among the best of Samuel's life, a gift of return that he had not dared to wish would ever come again since the night he had learned that Edgar was dead. Deborah had brought life and happiness full circle in the most unexpected way. But even as he regarded the young girl's wide, inquisitive eyes and shining face, as she stood gazing up at the frosted glass dome high above the bank's hall, he knew in his heart that, despite all his love for her and the unfairness of scrutinizing every word she uttered, he would be keenly disappointed and would have difficulty continuing to shower her with attention and, yes, respect, if he failed to sense in Deborah some hint of real genius for banking. The reason was more than a grandfather's pride; this visit was one more step along the path on which he had been leading her since she was seven. Samuel de Kronengold secretly intended that, if her aptitude, intelligence, and character continued to confirm his appraisal of her, Deborah would inherit the bulk of his vast wealth. She would head the Kronengold bank because he would bequeath to her controlling interest in British Kronengold Holdings Ltd., the family holding company that owned most of the bank's stock and the other major family assets.

Leslie would be shocked, no doubt. When one considered the traditional criteria, he deserved to be his father's successor: eldest living son, dedicated worker, cautious banker. But responsibility to the ultimate welfare of the family was the very essence of Samuel's character, of what he believed set the Kronengolds apart from other families visited by good fortune, of why the family had survived the seemingly inevitable pattern of dissolution and decline to become a dynasty. And that responsibility compelled Samuel to recognize that the rapidly accelerating uncertainties of the future demanded shrewdness, tenacity, and imagination in uncommon measure of whoever replaced him as steward of the Kronengold interests. Deborah, for all her immaturity, seemed to give promise of possessing those talents in abundance. Leslie possessed too little of them, and what he did possess was often turgid or mean-spirited, rather than constructive. Charles, his second son, was sweet-natured but shy and lacked the leadership instinct. Apart from Deborah, the next generation was either in its infancy, in the case of Charles's two children, or uninspired, in the case of Leslie's son, Richard. The right choice to lead the bank into the tangled, perilous years ahead was clearly Deborah.

There was much against that choice. It might be fought on the grounds of her having been adopted, but a well-drafted will could prevent that. Furthermore, she would have to stand up to a raging Leslie, and maybe others in the bank and the family, possibly at a relatively young age. Indeed, Samuel had cancelled this ostensibly innocuous visit on Deborah's two previous birthdays because of Leslie's objections – undermining his son's wishes would only have reduced his effectiveness as an administrator – but this year Samuel refused to be put off.

The final ground for disqualifying her was her sex. Samuel had tried to ignore that issue in his thinking because of her other qualities, but whether clients and colleagues would was unknown. The greatest unknown was whether a woman might be biologically unsuited to banking. That possibility, too, could not be ignored; it was in the forefront of the questions into which he hoped to gain an insight today. So much depended on whether Deborah possessed that elusive, ultimately unteachable talent.

Samuel began the tour at the Trade Acceptance Department, where the firm itself had begun by financing other merchants' trade. The guide was a bright young man named Davis for whom the firm had some hopes.

'We lend here,' David began. 'We finance trade during the period goods are accepted for delivery by the buyer.' He paused and looked at Deborah to make sure she was following him.

'Finance in what way?' she asked.

Encouraged, the young man grew more specific. 'When a British seller gets an order for, let's say, machine tools from a German buyer who needs them for his factory, the buyer doesn't want to pay until he has the machine tools in his hands and can check them. But the seller doesn't want to ship without being paid. We know the buyer and the seller and the goods, so we pay the seller when he ships and collect from the buyer when they arrive. We charge interest on the money we provide during that interim period.'

Samuel interrupted with a question for his granddaughter. 'How much interest would you charge?'

Deborah's brow furrowed slightly in thought. She was used to her grandfather's impromptu quizzes. 'There's some risk, but not much if you know the buyer and seller. One and a half percent for, say, a six-week transaction is a good return. Ten percent on an annual basis. Maybe one more for the paperwork you have to do.'

'Right on the nail, eh, Davis?' Samuel exclaimed.

'Yes, sir,' the young man replied, nonplussed by the exchange.

Deborah turned back to Davis. 'The bank has an insurance company it gives business to. Does it own ships too? It must have a lot of business to give them.'

'We recommended Devon Star Lines, but only because they expedite our documents and are very good at resolving disputes quickly.' He went on to explain other aspects of his job.

Just before leaving Trade Acceptances, Samuel suddenly stiffened. 'Davis, you're not wearing shoes.'

'But I am, sir.'

'Shoes have laces.'

'Yes, sir.' Davis looked down at his black slip-on shoes in consternation.

To Lord Kronengold originality of thought was one thing, of dress quite another.

They left Trade Acceptances. Just beyond the doorway, Samuel took Deborah aside. 'Davis isn't high enough up yet to be let in on it, but the reason we suggest our clients use Devon Star Lines for shipping is because we own a hefty interest in the company.' Samuel expected at least an answering smile of satisfaction, but noticed, instead, that Deborah's brow was clouded; she appeared deep in thought.

'Is there something you didn't understand back there?'

'No, I think I understood,' she replied, but her eyes were no less preoccupied.

In other departments Deborah was unfailingly polite and poised, but she had grown quiet, rarely offering an unsolicited comment. Her questions were limited to those that induced her guide to continue explaining his department's functions – whether it was Commercial Loans, where the firm acted as middleman in procuring loans for companies from commercial banks; or Foreign Exchange, where various currencies were traded for international clients and for the firm's own profit; or Corporate Finance, where mergers and acquisitions and new stock and bond issues were arranged for corporations.

Exasperated by her seeming unresponsiveness, Samuel felt impelled to devise questions to probe her comprehension of what was being explained to her. Deborah's answers were invariably astute, but she volunteered little, producing few of the dazzling exchanges he had set his hopes on. Samuel feared the cause might be lack of interest – a fatal defect – which might stem from the incompatibility of a woman's basic nature with the profession of banking.

What Samuel failed to realize was that Deborah's interest

was too great to permit the performance he sought. Ideas were whirling in her head, falling into place, building a structure she could not yet describe in words, but which promised a framework so immense and yet so simple that it could accommodate everything she had been taught about finance in the past and was learning today.

It was nearly noon when Samuel led her into the Partners' Room. Several Kronengold cousins with small interests in the bank were at their antique wooden desks. Behind them, hung from the mahogany panelling, were the portraits of respected ancestors, a few of the most dignified of whom had as their lone talent the ability to be born into the family. But merchant banking had grown more complex since the war. Fearing managerial stagnation, Samuel had recruited capable outsiders. He paid them very well and gave them a good deal of responsibility – some even ran important divisions – but as yet only a Kronengold had ever been made a partner.

Deborah went to each family member to say hello, most warmly to her uncle Charles, Samuel's younger son, of whom she was quite fond. They knew of Samuel's partiality to her and his interest in her, but few, if any, apprehended that the girl's visit could bear special significance.

'I hope this place hasn't proved too boring for you,' one partner remarked kindly.

Samuel listened closely for her answer, but it was merely a noncommittal, 'Not at all.'

Samuel then brought her to his desk, set near the hearth, the traditional place of honour before the age of central heating. Near it was another large desk, the chair conspicuously empty. Neither Deborah nor Samuel mentioned it, but each time the door opened to admit someone her eyes swung hopefully towards the newcomer.

'Deborah.' Samuel drew her attention back to the tour. 'The banking world ascribes a mystical significance to this room. So many momentous decisions have been made here. As I've told you, the Kronengolds never reveal the amount of their assets. Even if we had *none*, the outside world would never know it. All merchant bankers live by the sharpness of their wits and the worth of their word, but secrecy is as much a part of the Kronengolds' operations as our capital. It inflates our triumphs and hides our mistakes. It's the best sort of publicity.'

'But we can't do without capital.'

'Well, if you're clever and trustworthy you'll accumulate capital even if you start small. But start out with a *mountain* of money, and if you're not clever, be certain you'll lose it all.'

A yellow glint on a cabinet in the corner of the room caught Deborah's eye, and she went towards it. A small gold statue rested on a pedestal. She recognized the tableau: the biblical Isaac, aged and infirm, lay on his litter. Jacob knelt before him, draped in animal skins to fool his blind father into bestowing the family birthright on him, instead of on his older brother, Esau. Jacob's head was tilted warily, his eyes peering off in the direction from which his brother would return. His body was compressed like a spring; in a moment he would flee. The father's face was at peace, serene in the mistaken belief that the benefits of his blessing had gone to the eldest in the traditional way. The entire statue was no more than four inches across, but so cunningly crafted that the figures seemed to be of heroic proportions, and the gold from which they were fashioned to glow with their inner spirit.

Deborah lifted the piece and carefully turned it over. Three crowns were engraved on the base.

Samuel smiled, intrigued by the irony of Deborah's interest in the piece. 'It's the only work by Abraham ben Itzakh that has come down to our branch of the family. For a long time it was worth only the value of the gold, because he was a Jew. Many of his pieces were melted down. Today those that remain are considered masterpieces. Perhaps if he had used a less valuable medium, like marble. . . .'

'But look, Grandfather, look how bright and rich it is. And the detail. The tiny fingers and nails. The furs and the cloth.' Her finger brushed gently across one of Jacob's sandalled feet.

'There's something magical about gold,' he concurred. Encouraged by the child's emergence from what had appeared to him to be almost a trance, he warmed to the subject. 'And not just its appearance. It can be bent and manipulated, beaten flat to a few thousandths of an inch and not break, so flat that a quarter of a million sheets would be only an inch high. Add a bit of another metal to gold, and it hardens. Gold won't tarnish. It's the best conductor of electricity, and you can draw it into the finest of wires. Most important, Dee, gold is scarce. So it has kept its value throughout history – the best money there is.'

Deborah's face was very close to the tiny representation of

Jacob, which gleamed here and there as she turned it to catch the light. Her voice was hushed. 'Even if it weren't valuable, it would still be beautiful.'

'Ah, but it *is* valuable. Let me show you something.'

Samuel led his granddaughter out of the Partners' Room to a lift. The attendant closed the door and the gate and pushed a button. The lift descended deep into the earth and bumped gently to a stop. The older man and the young girl stepped into an antechamber before a wall of steel bars. Samuel pressed a buzzer. A moment later a face appeared in a small window in the centre of the heavy steel door behind the bars. The door swung open; the barred gate slid back. They walked into a room that contained packing materials and a scale. A second lift, a platform in the centre of the room, lowered them into an even deeper basement, dark and damp beyond the glare cast by a single exposed light bulb hanging from the ceiling. Boxes and bags were stacked along the dimly lit walls. A brawny workman leaning on an axe turned as the platform descended into the dungeon's gloom. Deborah clutched her grandfather's hand.

'Good day, m'lord,' said the workman.

'Good day, Jenkins.' Samuel's voice reverberated against the granite walls. 'Why don't you show our guest what's inside the box?' He pointed to a small wooden crate on the floor.

The workman raised the axe high over his head into the darkness and then swung it down. Deborah jumped back. The crate split neatly in half, revealing a gleaming bar of gold about a foot long. Chuckling at his granddaughter's trepidation, Samuel picked up the gold bar and handed it to her. She nearly dropped it.

'It's very heavy!'

'But very valuable. Each ounce is worthy thirty-five dollars. The American government will buy it at that price. Which would come to?'

'Twelve and a half pounds sterling,' she answered with a hint of annoyance at the renewed quizzing.

'The bar weighs how much, Jenkins?'

'Twenty-five pounds, sir.'

Deborah's eyes widened as she stared at the gold bar. 'Fourteen thousand dollars!' she said after a moment, her voice awed. Then she glanced wryly at her grandfather.

'Three thousand, one hundred and twenty-five pounds sterling.'

'Look behind you.'

A pyramid of gold bars was stacked near the wall. In the dim light they appeared orange and lustreless.

'It's all "fine gold", nearly pure. Only five parts in a thousand are alloy. In addition to all our usual banking activities, we're gold merchants. We buy it and sell it. We're also an agent for South Africa in selling its exported gold.'

'Who buys it from you?'

Samuel nodded at Jenkins, who appeared eager to contribute.

'The Frenchies buy a lot of it, miss. They love it. Bury it in their backyards, stuff it up their chimneys. It's their security.'

'A lot of people feel that way,' Samuel added. 'Sometimes people escaping from war or oppression survive because of the gold they can carry. The English haven't suffered invasion or wild currency catastrophies; they'd rather invest in something that brings a return. But the Swiss and Germans buy it. Importing gold is illegal in India, but every self-respecting bride gets her dowry in gold and wears every bit of it on her wedding day. It's her security in case of divorce, widowhood – ' He picked a handful of wafer-sized bars out of one of the crates. 'We melt it into smaller sizes and sell it to Arab traders in countries where it's legal. They're called smugglers' bars. They're slipped into pockets in special waistcoats and smuggled into India on fast boats. Incidentally, the smugglers make a good deal more on them than we do.' Samuel let the wafers slide out of his palm and back into the box. 'Those bars over there may once have made up one of Abraham ben Itzakh's pieces or an ornament in the Temple of Solomon. They're all simply gold now . . . the bars, these sovereigns, the napoleons.' He scooped gold coins out of several bags. 'These American eagles.'

'My gold guinea.' Once more Deborah was deep in thought, but now the ideas were affixing themselves like panels to the framework that had been building in the recesses of her mind, defining the form, making it visible.

'Even your guinea. And once it's melted down, all anyone cares about is its value, what it can buy.' He gestured towards the pyramid against the wall. 'Jenkins, how much do you reckon that pile of gold is worth?'

Jenkins gave it an appraising glance. 'Oh, about two million pounds or so.'

'Remember, Dee, in troubled times people will pay a lot in paper money, in land, in anything, for a little bit of gold.'

He reached up to the light bulb and aimed it towards the pyramid, which suddenly gleamed with the lustre of the sun.

Samuel's gaze swung from the bright yellow bricks to Deborah. Her eyes were glistening more brightly than the metal. Samuel's patience could endure no more. He erupted angrily. 'All morning you've been quiet as a mummy. Have you no questions, no comments? What on earth is going through that mind of yours?'

For a moment longer she remained silent, entranced by the glittering metal and how it fitted into the structure she envisaged. When she spoke, her voice was touched with awe.

'All of this – this bank, all of your wealth, the value of all this gold and even of all the money in the world – is merely an idea we have all agreed to believe in!' She thought about that for an instant, then uttered a barely audible sigh. 'What a *wonderful* idea!'

Samuel de Kronengold's tension cracked into a delighted grin. He no longer had any doubts about his granddaughter.

Madeleine had had a pleasurable day at Windsor Castle, all the more enjoyable for having been stolen out of the rigorous, if unfulfilling, schedule she normally set herself. Another reason for her elation was the surprising realization that the shy young tutor was infatuated with her.

Madeleine's relationship with Leslie had grown deadeningly routine over the past few years. Not seeing her beauty or worth reflected in another's eyes had served to numb her spirit as well. She had no idea whether men considered her attractive, nor would the question have occurred to her, if her thoughts had not occasionally returned to that conversation she had had with Rob Rowell during the summer weekend four years before. She had bolstered her mental barriers against such thoughts and had avoided social engagements where she might encounter Rowell. On the few occasions that he had turned up at a ball or Leslie had invited him to shoot or fish, she made quite certain others were with her when she greeted him. But, no matter how quickly she withdrew her gaze, she could not ignore the intensity of feeling his own gaze projected, or the spasm of faintness it triggered within her. She had hidden quite well, she thought, all outward sign of the inward exhilaration. And, until the guileless, fumbling tutor had inadvertently reminded her of it, she had remained quite oblivious to her own appeal. But Jason was so obviously harmless she was disarmed.

While strolling in the Moat Garden in the early afternoon, she noticed he was sweating profusely in his heavy woollen clothing, the same heavy woollen clothing he had worn when he arrived four years before. On a generous whim, she decided to take the young man shopping for clothes that were stylish and better suited to the warm months ahead. She instructed Williston to drive them back to London. The limousine deposited Madeleine and Jason Latham in Regent Street. She took him into shop after shop and bought suits, jackets, slacks, shirts, accessories, all in a torrent of enthusiasm.

At about five o'clock Madeleine stepped back, scrutinized the bewildered tutor's appearance in the blue blazer and grey slacks he now wore, and pronounced her mission of mercy accomplished. She told the salesman to send the rest of their purchases to her house.

This last shop was in a side-street. Madeleine and Jason began to amble back along the zigzag route they had taken since leaving Williston and the car, he still astounded by the day's events, she still invigorated by them. As they turned a corner, Madeleine caught sight of a familiar figure dashing out of a doorway and onto the pavement. The man's black homburg was pulled down over his face, but she could swear it was Leslie. Curious, she quickened her pace, but as she neared the building from which he had emerged, he was no longer in view.

The narrow, squat building seemed perfectly ordinary, if shabby; tobacconist on the ground floor, a flat or office on the second. The entire row of houses was rather seedy. If she hadn't been threading her way to one of the main streets, she would never have chosen it. What could Leslie have been doing here? She was certain now that the man was he. She left Jason on the pavement and stepped into the doorway. A tiny, drab hallway ended at a second door. A single card was affixed to the wall: MLLE. DANIELLE. STRICT OBEDIENCE TRAINING A SPECIALTY.

Just then the inner door swung open. A large young woman stepped through, tying a flowered kerchief around her chin.

'Looking for somebody?' she asked.

Madeleine inspected her. She was in her late twenties, pretty, with wariness in her eyes and hardness chiselled into lines just beginning to appear around her mouth. Her bright blonde hair was undoubtedly dyed.

'Are you Mademoiselle Danielle?'

She nodded. 'Mabel, actually. French names are good for business.' The voice was Cockney and hostile. 'What do you want?'

Madeleine improvised. 'I just saw your card. I'm looking for someone to train my dog.'

'Your dog?'

'It says on your card "strict obedience training".'

The woman's laugh was derisive. Her accent in reply mocked Madeleine's upper-class intonation with perfect fidelity. 'Akshully, my deah, I don't train dogs – hate the bloody beasts, don't ya know. I train men – it pays better.'

'I'm afraid I don't understand.'

The accent was again belligerent Cockney. 'Do you live in cloud cuckoo land? This is London, Duchess. Nineteen fifty-six. Some girls walk the streets. But I have regular clients who come here, and the police can't touch me.'

Madeleine felt as if the woman had kicked her in the stomach. She could hardly breathe in enough to speak. 'Then – "obedience training" means they pay you . . . to order them around as well.'

'Aren't you the clever one!' Dismissing Madeleine from her mind, the woman strode towards the door.

'That man who just left –'

'One of my regulars,' the woman snapped back, with a sauciness meant to shock. 'A banker. He loves the pain.'

The woman stepped out of the hallway. Madeleine, suddenly nauseated, fell back against the wall for support. Her eyes rolled up to the ceiling. She tried desperately to hang on to some semblance of self-possession. She inhaled deeply and stared straight ahead for nearly a minute, trying to suppress the horrified disgust, trying not to think. When she was fairly certain of her composure, Madeleine left the building too and rejoined her young companion on the pavement.

* * *

The limousine was just pulling up to the house when Madeleine spotted Leslie being let in at the front door. His back was to her. The clothes he wore were identical to those worn by the man she had sighted; even the homburg was still pulled uncustomarily low over his eyes.

She confronted him as soon as they were alone in the drawing room. Leslie was lighting a cigarette as she entered. His voice had a cozy, contented ring to it. 'Would you like a drink, Maddy? I thought I'd have a whisky.'

Madeleine was shaking as she spoke. 'Where were you today, Leslie?'

'Where?' He looked startled. 'At a factory in . . . Surrey.'

'Which car did you take?'

'It doesn't really matter, does it?'

Madeleine, usually so accommodating, was immovable. '*Which car*?'

'Jeffreys drove me.'

Any faint hope Madeleine might have harboured that the man she had sighted on the street a short while before had not been Leslie was destroyed. Jeffreys was off duty today. The only chauffeur was Williston, and he had driven her all day. Inside Madeleine something soft and loving towards Leslie fled forever. She spun round to leave the room, the nausea once again welling up inside her.

'Oh, by the way, Maddy,' Leslie called out, 'sorry about this morning. Didn't mean a word of it, of course. I'll make it up to Dee at dinner.'

She turned to stare at him. How very repentent and agreeable he now seems, she thought – I loathe him.

'You all right?' he asked.

She fled down the hall and up the stairs.

She went to her sitting room and lay down on the chaise-longue, not strong enough to hold her body up a moment longer. She had to be alone. She had to think.

How can this be happening to me? she cried out silently. How could I have allowed him to hurt me again? Oh, God help me!

'Ma'am, are you all right?'

Madeleine opened her eyes. Irma, her lady's maid, stood at the door.

'Ma'am, it's time to dress for dinner. You asked for it to be early tonight. Miss Deborah's back already and dressing for her birthday.'

Madeleine nodded numbly and sat up. She needed time to think, but she would not allow herself to ruin the dinner for Dee. She rose, went to her dressing room, and began to change her clothes.

Dinner started pleasantly enough, with friendly teasing about Jason's changed appearance. He and Samuel had been invited to share Deborah's birthday. Richard was away at boarding school, so only adults were present. Relieved after years of unexpressed anxiety, Samuel made no effort to restrain his pride in Deborah's performance at the bank. He recited her observations on the intrinsic nature of money and related how astute her later remarks had been in the Partners' Dining Room.

'You would have been delighted, Leslie,' Samuel concluded, and eyed his son pointedly.

'No doubt, no doubt,' Leslie responded a touch too heartily. 'A feel for numbers is always helpful, no matter what she does in later life.'

'Particularly if she chooses to become a banker.'

Leslie's shock at what the remark might portend about his father's thinking never passed across his face and could only be guessed at from the long instant in which animation of any kind deserted him. All his life his father had held absolute power over him. Since being told he must pursue a banking career, he had waited, patient, calculating, knowing some day power would be his. Some day his enforced impotence would be at an end and he, in his turn, would rule. Now his father was toying with him, threatening to deny him the reward that was his both by right and in return for the years spent at the bank against his will. How prescient he had been to fear Deborah's hold on his father's emotions! He spoke up. 'There's plenty of time before Dee has to make so momentous a decision.'

Leslie looked over at his daughter, applying a hearty smile to his face. She stared at him, the blue, inscrutable eyes disconcerting him, reproaching him, he thought.

'You weren't there today, Father.' Deborah spoke carefully, revealing no hint of the wound. Although the years had taught her neither to expect affection from her father nor to let him glimpse the hurt such disregard inflicted on her, each slight stabbed her deeply. Today's more than most – she had looked forward so long to visiting him at the bank.

Leslie tipped his head in the merest concession to the appearance of regret. 'Unavoidably, I had to be out of town today. Pity.'

Deborah made no reply, and the moment passed. But Leslie could still feel his daughter's intense, disturbing stare boring into the heart of his secret self. And Deborah could still feel his icy disregard.

All through dinner, Madeleine barely spoke, feeling she was about to explode. As soon as the cake had been nibbled at and Deborah's gifts opened, she escaped again to her sitting room. The only illumination was provided by a single lamp on the eighteenth-century writing table inlaid with Sèvres porcelain plaques that served as her desk. She was too distraught to sit, but paced back and forth across the colourful flower patterns of the Savonnerie carpet.

How could I have deluded myself into believing that ours was a contented marriage, she wondered in anguish, that he loved me and cared for Richard and had even come to care for Deborah? How could I have been such a fool after what happened to my baby?

Leslie had adored the army and the war, she remembered; he felt liberated and totally on his own for the first time in his life. His father was no longer in authority over him, or his mother coddling him. He did not have to live up to his brother's towering example – Edgar had been dead over a year when Leslie volunteered in 1939. To give him his due, he rose quickly from captain to higher rank. When the bombing started in London, he grew solicitous for Madeleine's safety and begged her to leave London for Clove Hill. Once she became pregnant with Richard, in 1941, Leslie insisted she also abandon the long stays in the city to be with him.

Madeleine's rude awakening to Leslie's infidelity had come at the death of her second baby, deformed and killed by a venereal illness she had no idea she was infected with and could have caught only from Leslie. The doctor who delivered the insensate creature twisted into her womb had then been forced to cut out organs within her that had become too diseased to form another child. She had regained consciousness to news of a dead child and a sterile abdomen. The doctor, anguished and embarrassed for her, had explained the tragedy's cause and the treatment she and Leslie would have to undergo.

She had confronted her husband in fury when he rushed to her hospital bed. Head hanging guiltily, mumbling weak denials, all so unlike him, he had seemed a monster to her, a murderer. At that moment she was certain, at the very least, of his indiscriminate promiscuity. And, when he fell silent, she knew that he was undeniably aware of her certainty.

Madeleine stayed in the hospital near Clove Hill to recuperate and banished Leslie to London. Submerged in depression, she was physically weak and emotionally desolate.

Two months later the war ended and Nathan, an operative in Switzerland, was able to telephone Leslie's military intelligence headquarters in London. Nathan said he had spoken that day to Pierre, who was in Italy. Pierre was recovering from a wound, but was safe and about to travel to Turin. Leslie did not confide that he and his wife were estranged, but did reveal to Nathan how deeply despondent she remained over their baby's death. Nathan suggested that Pierre bring to them, from the Turin orphanage supported by Pierre's family, an infant they would adopt. Leslie rushed down to the country to discuss it with Madeleine.

Just the thought of holding a baby again seemed to restore her to life. Her nostrils filled with the smell of talcum powder and baby skin. She yearned to shelter the unseen infant from the destruction into which the little girl had been born, to surround her and Richard with a home and family, and to free herself from the desperate prospects of making a new life alone. Leslie seemed truly penitent, blaming the war and the pressure it put on him for his infidelity. He told her how grief-stricken he was about their baby's death and that he wanted another child as much as she. He swore to be faithful and pleaded with her to forgive him. She agreed to take Leslie back.

The next night, when Pierre telephoned to discuss it with them, they told him they wanted to adopt the child.

Madeleine stopped pacing in front of the wedding photograph of her and Leslie on the writing table, and held it up to the lamp. She wore a simple white dress, Leslie his captain's uniform, the peak of his cap shading his dark eyes. Leslie appeared grave, dependable, the sort of man a woman could rely on unqualifiedly. Her face was – she stared at it, seeking to determine what troubled her about the photograph – her face was devoid of any emotion. She was merely there, in the place she was supposed to be, leaning against Leslie.

After Edgar's death, she had dragged herself back to Cambridge simply to take her mind off her grief. Leslie was in his last year there, and he began to drop in to dine with her and study together. Leslie had seemed so young scampering about in the background while she and Edgar were falling in love that it came as a surprise to realize he was a year older than she and quite attractive. As time passed, she knew Leslie was growing serious about her, yet she wasn't ready to think seriously herself. But then Samuel talked to her father by telephone, and when she came to Clove Hill for a Christmas visit, he took her aside. Although the French and English branches of the family were now only distantly related by blood, they continued to join together in business deals and at family functions. Her romance with Edgar had started at her parents' anniversary party. Since then she had become close to Samuel.

'Edgar is gone; I've come to accept that, and you must too,' he told her. 'Leslie will make a good husband. I couldn't want a finer wife for him. You know how fond I am of you. With so much in common, you two can have a good life. The war is in Poland now, but it's only a matter of time before Britain and France, too, have troops on the battlefields. It would be important for you and for Leslie to know that, amid all the turmoil, you have each other.'

And she *had* thought about it, and about how much affection she had for Leslie and how little she now expected out of life. He adored her, Leslie had solemnly vowed, and he would love her faithfully forever. Finally, reluctantly (she now remembered), she had allowed herself to love once more and agreed to marry him.

The wedding took place in June of 1940. Not a grand affair at her family's country estate at Valtary, as she had hoped, but a small ceremony at her father-in-law's London house, she in that white dress one might wear to a garden party, Leslie in the captain's uniform he was so proud of.

Her father-in-law had been sincere in the reasons he had put forth to convince her to marry his second son, Madeleine decided as she strained to remember words, intonations, facial expressions after sixteen years. Perhaps Samuel had pushed so hard for the match between her and Leslie because he had learned about his son's perversion and feared Madeleine was Leslie's last hope for a normal life and marriage to produce a succeeding generation – without leaving everything on the shy shoulders of his last child, Charles.

Should she herself have guessed Leslie's degeneracy from some hint in his mannerisms, some implication in the anecdotes he told about being bullied at school perhaps? Had there ever been marks on his body she failed to note? *Would* there be marks? Her lack of sophistication, which she had always taken for granted, was an irritating barrier to comprehension.

Madeleine had been a virgin when she married. Believing that they had their whole lives ahead of them, she and Edgar had chosen to wait until marriage before consummating their love. After his death she regretted bitterly not having shared with him that final expression of their commitment. Before her marriage to Leslie, the issue never arose; still in conflict over the new allegiance, she was reluctant to offer him what she had failed to bestow on Edgar. Should she have suspected that Leslie's sexual restraint before their marriage was more than high-minded morality? And, although she had no experience with which to compare his performance as a lover after their marriage, nothing in his behaviour, in his preferences, indicated that he required anything more than their quite normal marital relations. She herself never felt anything when they made love, and was too inexperienced to realize she was entitled to. But for his part Leslie had never seemed dissatisfied with their sex life.

Pure naiveté, she castigated herself, more delusion, just like the delusion that the pressure of the war had caused him to stray or that they were a content, well-matched couple or that she and her children were encircled by his love. What she could not strike from her mind now, as she looked at the wedding photograph of the responsible young people, was that Leslie had saved his own skin in the Vienna bank when Edgar was torn apart trying to hold back the crowd, and then wormed his way into his brother's place in her heart; and he had caused their baby's death, but won her back again when he proposed they adopt Deborah. Leslie had been central to the two great tragedies in her life and then, each time, preyed upon her grief to ensnare her.

All that evening she had been too shocked to feel sorry for

herself. But now, at last, she began to weep. She had been born with so much in life, and had taken her bounty for granted. As the sobs followed one another uncontrollably, she realized she was crying for the few things in life that mattered, the few things in life she had never lost.

She did not sleep that night, but pondered her future. She had no idea what she would ultimately do; she was certain at least that she would never again be weak or foolish enough to trust Leslie. She would never again forgive him or give him the opportunity to fail her. She would never again share his bed.

Initially unnerved by Madeleine's move out of the bedroom to a guest suite at the other end of the house, Leslie soon relaxed as he realized that Madeleine did not intend to reveal to his father and others what he feared she suspected about his sexual preferences. Perhaps she was simply emotionally overwrought about something else and wanted to be by herself for a while. He decided that each of them could do with a bit more living space and fewer mutual demands for a time. Leslie either ate supper late at home or dined at one of his clubs. His nights were now his own. Occasionally, he found he missed her company. When he approached her she was pleasant and exhibited no evidence of rancour, but no evidence either of a willingness to heal the breach between them.

Madeleine's life might have gone on in that course indefinitely had not three events occurred to alter it. The first was Royal Ascot. Samuel's racing successes had made him a popular figure in England, to a large extent diluting the animosity the general public might otherwise have felt towards so rich and insulated a capitalist. Samuel had a horse entered in the Gold Cup and invited Leslie and Madeleine to view the race with him from the Royal Enclosure.

Rob Rowell spotted her under her wide, flowered hat before she saw him. She did not realize he was approaching her until he was only a few feet away. Oddly, her first impulse was not to turn away, as in the past, but to speak to him. He looked quite the most dashing man there in his morning coat and grey top hat. They spoke for only a few minutes. Later, she did not remember much of what had been said, but knew that it had been inconsequential.

The following week he showed up at a charity luncheon she and the Duchess of Harswell were sponsoring. On an impulse she had changed the seating arrangements so that he was beside her. They talked ceaselessly from first course to coffee. A week later they met for tea near the National Gallery. She found it difficult to say good-bye. After that they met several times a week for lunch or tea, and occasionally in the country to stroll by a stream or to play tennis. Despite the unfamiliar excitement she felt when they were together, their meetings were wholly innocent. She was glad to have a friend to whom she could talk comfortably. Her life was still too complicated with unsorted emotions for her to let herself consider their relationship more than friendship. But she also knew that she had reached a point where giving up seeing him would be painful.

Being with him was very different from what she had imagined. He listened to her and was concerned about things if they concerned her. He was much gentler than she had thought he would be, gentler than he himself realized, and a touch diffident, which disconcerted him. He did not like to think of himself as possessing the 'softer' traits he believed were appropriate for women but emasculating for men. She sensed, however, that he would have hated to end their meetings as much as she.

The second precipitating factor in Madeleine's life, which happened the following autumn, was not one that affected Madeleine directly, but that altered her life profoundly because of Samuel's reaction and because of the way it helped to shred the Kronengold family's ancient fabric woven of unity and fidelity. It was the Suez crisis of 1956.

The third factor was Deborah's humiliation in front of the entire Kronengold family, assembled that summer at Valtary, Pierre's opulent estate in the French countryside.

CHAPTER FOUR

Egypt's seizure of the Suez Canal in July 1956 set in motion events on a scale far larger than a single person's or a single family's destiny. The resulting crisis four months later would threaten world peace; would shake the Atlantic alliance; would humiliate Britain, dishearten her, and hasten her decline, her self-absorption, and the fall of her prime minister. It would frustrate France and accelerate her loss of Algeria, the end of the Third Republic, and the return to power of Charles de Gaulle; and provoke hostility to Britain as a future Common Market partner. It would endow Israel with more secure borders for the next decade and a port on the Gulf of Aqaba, leading to the Indian Ocean; would safeguard Egypt and make a hero of Gamal Abdel Nasser, that nation's chief of state; and would sow the seeds of a pan-Islamic oil policy based on nationalistic needs and concerted action, which would someday bring to once poor countries wealth and power beyond their wildest hopes and shake the foundations of the industrialized world.

The first retaliation for Egypt's seizure of the Canal occurred on October 29, 1956, when Israel attacked Egyptian positions in the Sinai. Two days later, in accordance with a secret scheme previously agreed to with Israel, Britain and France began bombing Egyptian airfields, alleging they were acting to protect the Suez Canal, an essential international waterway. Israel had swept across the Sinai on schedule to prearranged positions near Suez while pressing southwards to free the Gulf of Aqaba to Israeli shipping.

As the days passed Anthony Eden, Britain's prime minister, hesitated to give the word that would unleash the French and British troops waiting on Cyprus and Malta and begin the full-scale attack. He faced a host of pressures: a popular outcry in his own country against the bombings, blustering condemnation from a Soviet Union allied with Egypt and trying to divert attention from its own invasions of Poland and

Hungary, and perhaps most telling, President Eisenhower's fear that his own NATO partners were bringing the world to the brink of war. With only days remaining before the U.S. presidential election, Eisenhower, in order to force Britain to back down, was exerting both diplomatic influence in the United Nations and financial muscle by weakening the British pound.

Fearing that Eden was about to get cold feet and leave his secret Jewish allies militarily and diplomatically high and dry, Israeli high officials cast about for someone who might approach the British prime minister and allay his fears about Eisenhower's ability to undermine Britain's currency and economy. When they learned that Eden and his wife, Clarissa, were dining at the home of Samuel de Kronengold on that very night of November 4, 1956, they asked Pierre, his French cousin, to telephone Samuel to discuss what he might say to Eden.

Although Samuel was a contributor to Israel, the Israelis were far closer to Pierre, who spent a good deal of time in their country and funded numerous projects there. The two cousins had been in negotiation for months about merging their banks into a larger, unified financial institution - after a century of separation - now that it appeared Britain would soon join the Common Market. Both men feared, among other things, that a failure to retake the Suez Canal and topple Nasser would result, instead, in toppling both the French and British governments. That would put an end to British acceptance into the Common Market for the time being and, thus, to the merger of the French and British Kronengold banks.

Samuel needed little convincing by Pierre, viewing as he did Britain's refusal to knuckle under to Nasser as a reassertion, at last, of British greatness. He spent the day rehearsing the arguments he would use to stiffen Eden's backbone.

Only after dinner, when Samuel led the men, formal in their dinner jackets, to the Trophy Room, was he able to talk alone with Eden. Although they sat in a corner and conversed for a very long time, all Samuel's persuasion proved fruitless; he found himself facing a very ill, very frightened man.

Madeleine had acted as hostess for her father-in-law. She drew the women after dinner to the Byzantine Drawing Room. There, amid its Levantine splendour, as the women exchanged inconsequentialities, Madeleine felt as if they were all wasting away in a harem. Madeleine had noticed the trapped feeling coming on earlier than usual this evening, but this time the constriction around her was so tight she could barely breathe. The personal cell in which she had been existing until then, bounded by the relatively flexible dimensions of her unhappy marriage, had shrunk to the limits of her own body. The wives invited seemed as robotic as she: either colourless and predictable or syrupy loyal and predictable. Behind their British redoubts of stiff upper lips and self-reliant airs, most of these women were either inane or hypocrites, Madeleine reflected in a burst of unkindness quite unlike her. Those with any courage probably led secret lives they hid from their acquaintances – just as she slept apart from Leslie.

While half-listening to the pretty Lady Hobin-Garroway chat prettily about her pretty garden, Madeleine suddenly recalled Vivienne's gossip about her and felt a wild compulsion to ask in the most matter-of-fact tone whether the rumours were true that m'lady's third child was not her husband's but that of a professional football player with West Ham. And whether the earth moved. But Madeleine did not. She spoke, instead, of roses and asters and spring bulbs, while she screamed inwardly for escape from the concrete conventions that had hardened around her.

Very early the next morning she drove herself and Deborah to Clove Hill for the day. The ostensible reason was so that Deborah could ride to hounds. But Rob would be at his own country house for the weekend, and they planned to meet. They had not seen each other in over a week, and she missed him.

The cream-coloured Rolls convertible was a personal indulgence she had purchased the previous year. She loved to put down the top and windows and drive alone very fast. The scenery rushing past, the endless sky, the swirls of air about her thrilled her. The moments behind the wheel provided the single daring element in her suffocating life. Once she had actually screamed her inner torment aloud. The loss of self-control had scared her, but then she had laughed as the wind muffled the sound into a puny peep. How badly I wanted to escape even then, she thought.

With Deborah in the car she drove carefully, defensively.

She glanced again at her daughter, tall and straight in her riding clothes, eyes fixed on the road ahead, the eleven-year-old face an enigma. The past three months had been desolate ones for Deborah, since the terrible incident at Valtary.

Pierre had invited Kronengolds from all over Europe to his huge estate in the French countryside for the family's first reunion since the start of the Second World War. While not so architecturally pleasing as Clove Hill, being blocky and ponderous where its English counterpart was elegant and lavish, the Château de Valtary was much larger, built on a scale to rival the homes of emperors. Inside, however, the French mansion was every bit its opulent equal. As a family duty Pierre had spent a fortune repairing the war damage and refurbishing. The evening meals in the Grand Salon recreated exactly for present-day Kronengolds the sumptuous dinners once served here to Napoleon III, Edward VII, Czars Alexander II and III, innumerable presidents and prime ministers. The wines were the great vintages of the Château's fabled vineyards. For recreation, every possible activity was available: horses and horse-drawn traps and carriages, tennis, swimming, rowing, shooting, golf on a nine-hole course, croquet. Inside was an endless concatenation of rooms filled with superb furniture, walls of books, and art treasures of all sorts.

One of the most beautiful of the rooms, a large yellow salon with white rococo scrollwork moulding, housed one of the world's great collections of rare musical instruments. Pierre had collected them over his life-time, perhaps as some compensation for having to enter banking and not pursue the musical career for which he was clearly so well suited. One night of the visit had been planned by Pierre as a family musicale in that Music Room. Apart from Pierre, a concert-level pianist, few of the amateur musicians exhibited more than a pleasant talent. That was why Deborah's violin solo was doubly surprising. Her interpretation of the Vivaldi sonata she had chosen had a sweetness and virtuosity far beyond her years. Madeleine had tried to tell him how talented she was, but he had ascribed the compliments to parental pride. Pierre was captivated, overcome. He drew from a showcase a Stradivarius that was the centre-piece of his collection. He found the sheet music for a Beethoven sonata she knew and they played together, their notes rising up like birds in perfectly synchronised flight. A chill rolled from Pierre's scalp down to his toes – she had indeed turned out be a very special child.

Next day the Stradivarius was found shattered in Deborah's violin case. She denied knowing how the violin was smashed or how it got into her violin case, but all the evidence pointed to Deborah's having destroyed it in a rage after an argument with her father. Indeed, Leslie had reluctantly offered the testimony which had condemned her. His testimony and the other evidence left no doubt about her guilt. Deborah was disgraced before the entire family.

Her grandfather, Samuel, in turn, felt hurt and betrayed at the lack of integrity and character revealed by his protégée's refusal to own up to her vandalism. He felt angrier at the humiliation to which his mis-judgement of her subjected him in the eyes of his relatives. He implored her to confess, if only to him, but when she remained silent, he swore never again to speak to her. In words echoing generations of aggrieved patriarchs, he had declared, 'You are dead to me!' Within days he had cut her out of his will.

After returning from Valtary, Deborah had retreated from the rest of the household. Leslie had wanted 'to stop all this coddling' and send her to a rigorous girls' school that would 'beat some respect for other people's property into her'. But Madeleine had refused to entertain any such plan. Deborah would stay. Her tutor would stay. And Deborah's life would go on as much like before as Madeleine could make it by taking the place of the adults who had abandoned the child. She and Deborah ate together. They went to films and exhibitions together. But, since that unexplainable episode at Valtary, the joy that had always before bubbled effortlessly from her daughter was gone. She rarely spoke unless in answer to a query. And no amount of coaxing could induce Deborah to pick up the violin again; her lessons ceased. Madeleine knew that Deborah, who had already thought of herself as different from the others because of her adoption, felt betrayed; there was a jagged emptiness inside her daughter where love for her family used to be, and Madeleine doubted it would ever fully return.

Despite Deborah's muteness, Madeleine understood how grateful she was for the security and support her mother continued to provide. When they hugged each other at

Deborah's bed-time, Madeleine would sometimes hurt from the clutch of the little girl's fingers, contracted by the inner frenzy of the desperate love her daughter bore her. At such moments Madeleine was beset by guilt for somehow having failed to protect her child better from the others' rejection and for the tiny seedling of her own doubt about whether Deborah had told the truth about the violin.

Madeleine felt no gayer as they drove into Clove Hill than she had during the drive. The trees' motley had faded to a brown that surrounded mother in country tweeds and daughter in hunting pink as they strolled to the stables.

Gypsy had long since been passed on to Malcolm's son, and probably would soon be outgrown by that child as well and be sent to her brother-in-law Charles's place; *his* children would soon be of an age to begin riding. Deborah now rode a long-legged chestnut hunter with a coat that matched her hair. Madeleine invariably thrilled to their grace and freedom as the two of them raced for a fence, the young's girl's red hair streaming behind her in unison with her mount's tail and mane. But this morning Deborah wore it tucked sedately up under her hard black cap. Madeleine felt a twinge of melancholy as she watched her trot down the road to where the riders and hounds were gathering. Such a short time ago Deborah's exuberance would have exploded about her as if she were more a roman candle on horseback than a young girl. Madeleine thought, I have failed utterly at the very little in life at which I wanted to succeed.

She and Rob had arranged to meet for a picnic, and Madeleine drove on to the empty cottage at the edge of his property where they had planned to rendezvous. He was only a few minutes late, but she was nearly frantic when his blue Aston-Martin finally appeared at the end of the road.

She ran after his car as he coasted by her to park behind the cottage, as she had done, out of sight of the road. He thought she was going to kiss him or bury her head on his shoulder when he got out of the car, but instead she stared at his face, searching it.

'Maddy! Is anything wrong?

'I love you,' he suddenly exclaimed. 'Is that what you've been waiting to hear? How can you doubt it?'

She did not reply.

Her eyes closed very tightly, in concentration. 'I need to be sure. I'm so tired of being strong alone.'

'I love you,' he repeated more slowly. When her eyelids

opened and he stared once more into the soft, tortured brown eyes, he realized with some surprise that he really did.

She raised her face to his until their lips brushed as lightly as an eyelash against a cobweb. He felt weakness plummet through his torso. For months she had avoided touching him, maintaining the illusion that they were simply good friends. For months he had refrained from trying to touch her, fearful that the fragile crystal trust suspended between them would shatter with one clumsy word or act. She seemed to him a near-perfect creature, as different from other women he had known as from other species of being. He felt diffident about approaching her and certain of rejection if he tried.

'Does it look like rain?' he ventured, his lips still only a millimetre from hers, his eyes never leaving hers to check the sunny day.

'We'd better eat inside,' she agreed.

They slipped their arms about each other's waists and, eyes still locked, walked towards the house. The picnic hamper remained on the seat of his car.

Madeleine had been brought up to believe that a woman demonstrated love for a man by offering the gift of her body for his satisfaction. For sixteen years she had submitted dutifully to Leslie, gratified at first by their intimacy and later only because she felt it incumbent to dispatch her wifely obligation. She had silently scoffed when a woman friend's novel suggested that sex held the promise of bliss for the woman as well as the man. She considered such talk a myth, necessary for propagation, that one generation of women passed on to the next, like the myth that childbirth would not be painful. Now she was prepared to prove her love for Rob, but something strange and discomforting was happening.

When they kissed in the little bedroom, the breath seemed to suck out of her. As she tried to unbutton her blouse, her fingers refused to work.

'I'm all thumbs,' she apologized.

He went into the bathroom so she would be able to undress and slip beneath the covers. He realized that he also was nervous. An element he could not define seemed new for him too. When he re-emerged she was lying naked on the quilt, her eyes closed, like a white marble idealization sculpted for an empress's tomb. The flowers on the wallpaper beyond her seemed to be falling onto her in sorrowful tribute. He experienced an unreasonable instant of near terror when her eyes remained closed and he failed to detect even the rise and fall of her breasts.

'You're not having second thoughts?' he asked, as much to check for life as to hear the answer.

'I think today I will be reborn,' she said after a very long silence.

He lay down beside her. She turned her head and opened her eyes, large eyes, darkly opaque with a mystery that numbed his will. She kissed him and he tumbled into that mystery. His arms encircled her. Their bodies fitted together from head to toe, as if they had once been cleaved apart from a single block of humanity. His body felt alive only where it touched hers. He had never wanted a woman for so long or with such intensity. Yet, now that he was about to gratify that longing, he realized that what he saw pulling him into the depths of her eyes was her hope. Its purity so shamed him that his mind reacted with a single aim: not to disappoint her. He, who had always taken his pleasure without thought, wanted the pleasure – no, the delirium – to be hers; he wanted the memory of every man she had ever looked at to be expunged in one white convulsion of rapture. And he wanted his own body's pollution of memory to be burned away in the same purification. When he touched her he was very gentle, as if his fingertips listened for singing in her flesh.

He softly kissed the crook of her neck, breathing and tasting her smells simultaneously. Her skin twitched beneath his tongue in a long rolling spasm all the way to her toes.

'How . . . how strange that feels!' she whispered huskily, her voice catching.

'Hasn't Leslie ever kissed you there?'

'No,' she breathed.

'Or here?'

She did not answer, her body bowing against his mouth and shivering at each small place he touched. The new, strange elation bewildered and unsettled her. She pulled away to look at him, almost fearful of these sensations just unearthed within her. She reached up to trace along his lips. First the top one, then the bottom. She had never imagined how soft a man's lips could be.

The delicacy of his strong features had not lied to her about his gentleness, hidden away beneath the cynical armour. She leaned forward, tentative, to kiss him. That mouth seemed so dear now. Unbidden, unexpected, the sensations rippled through her again, and then she realized that her body, her emotions, had been asleep all her adult life.

Later, when he was on top of her, the sensations, multiplied a thousandfold, became an insurrection she hoped and feared would never end. And then, suddenly, her mind and body yielded to undreamed-of serenity.

Only then did he allow his own body to echo hers. His back arched. And he erupted into her. His eyes stared forward insensibly.

But, in that anaesthetic moment, he *did* see: blue eyes in a girl's face staring at him through the window beside the headboard. Madeleine's daughter, wearing a riding hat. Horror contorted her features. Their eyes locked, grappling for possession of the woman beneath him. A last pulse, and his ejaculations ceased. His head sunk down. When he looked back up again, the child's face was gone, as if it had been an apparition, insubstantial and accusatory. But then he heard a horse's shambling walk crackle fallen leaves, the far yapping of dogs, and, a while later, in the distance, a castanet-gallop on hard-packed pasture.

She must have recognized her mother's car while riding in the field behind the house and stopped to investigate. He glanced at Madeleine. Her head was thrown back, mouth open, gulping air; she had noticed nothing. He would not tell her; if she knew, remorse would grip her and she would leave him.

After a while Rob put the incident out of his mind, rolled onto his side, and regarded Madeleine through the lassitude suffusing him. Her breathing had eased. A beatific smile lit her profile. She looked virginal, darkly unknowable. The perspiration on her skin appeared to him as the glaze crusting untrod snow, her nakedness the most inviting and forbidding of landscapes.

'You're smiling,' he observed.

'It happened. You made it happen.' And she smiled again at the smugness that enfolded her, at the occasional embers of passion that still glowed amazingly within her. For now, in the afterglow, it was amazement that dominated her thoughts, amazement that parts of her body should be capable of emitting incredibly delicious sensations she had never suspected lurked within them, amazement that she felt so young suddenly, as if the years behind her were a moment and those ahead stretched without end or care; amazement that she loved and was loved in return.

Rob turned her head gently towards him. He was overwhelmed by his feelings. 'Leave Leslie,' he whispered. 'I want to be with you all the time. You're the only woman I want.'

She did not reply, but turned her head away again and stared at the ceiling. She needed to think about what was happening, what it meant, the complications and burdens it would visit on her children.

Rob stroked her cheek with the back of a finger. 'You're not sorry?' he asked.

'Never!' she said. Doors had opened and doors had closed today. She was simultaneously delighted and timorous, but not remorseful. She needed time alone to evaluate what lay before her.

But time was flowing at its own speed, gathering the currents of her life for a sudden, churning rush. Even a Kronengold, with power over so much, could hope only to bob along on top and not be pulled under.

CHAPTER FIVE

Samuel de Kronengold cancelled a rendezvous he had looked forward to with a celebrated ballerina back from a European tour and, for three days, did not leave his town house. His talk with Eden had left him with a strong foreboding that the prime minister would seek a way to turn tail and flee Egypt. Samuel began to think through the ramifications such a backing-down would have on the world situation, on Britain's future, and on the future of the Kronengold interests.

He tried to reach Nathan to discuss his apprehension, but was told by the housekeeper that he was away on a religious retreat. Samuel knew that Nathan was subject to periods of self-doubt and depression – more than usual lately. Samuel left a message for Nathan to see him upon his return.

On November 6, the Soviets instigated mob demonstrations against the Moscow embassies of Great Britain, the United States, France, and Israel after threatening to launch nuclear rocket attacks against those countries in defence of Egypt. The world trembled that day. Nuclear blackmail or diplomatic bluff? No one was quite sure. Eden's speech to Parliament that Tuesday night sounded particularly courageous; but it mattered not a whit. Eden cracked under all the pressure, giving France no alternative but to go along with him in abiding by the United Nations' call for a cease-fire. The Soviet's nuclear threat had been the final straw to break the prime minister's will – even though it later turned out to have been a total bluff offered on Egypt's behalf in lieu of the true military intervention Nasser had requested.

The Suez débâcle set events in motion that changed the lives of the Kronengold family as well. With the United Kingdom revealed to be a toothless lion, Samuel became convinced that Britain's decline had now become irreversible – the national initiative required for an aggressive, booming economy had been dissipated forever. Suez had exposed Britain's dirty little secret – or would when people had time to reflect – that what had been a worldwide empire less than a decade before had become just another small country wallowing in its own wake, a nation of disunited individuals squabbling over crusts while the wheat went untended. Samuel decided to move the bulk of the family's investments out of Britain, with the exception of a few unusually well-run, well-positioned companies. And, as for liquid assets, keeping them in sterling was even riskier. The faster he made those changes, the safer the family's finances would be.

Banking itself would continue to be a profitable business in London, because the sophisticated City was a convenient, unfettered central point for international financial transactions. But Samuel was now determined that the family's investment capital would be directed only to countries that had the determination to succeed and to grow.

He had hoped that Nathan would join him in seeking new investment opportunities. Samuel remembered vividly how accurate had been Nathan's analysis of Britain's future when they talked years before at Clove Hill. But threats of nuclear attack flung about so carelessly had agitated a Nathan de Kronengold already deeply distraught by guilt at having survived the war when others – in his family and relying on him as spymaster – were killed. He considered his survival to be a result of a moral cowardice he would not disclose any further, but which had left him groping about for relief from his anguish, from the suffering in his soul.

These last months only Deborah had been able to lift his depression. Because of his responsibility for her coming into the family, he had always taken a special interest in her. But, from a very young age, she delighted him for reasons that had nothing to do with obligation. Her good humour and intelligence had always lit up for him their hours together. Now she too was beset by inner wounds that bled despair into her soul. He had gone to Valtary reluctantly, preoccupied by his inner torment, but was at the lakeside when the servant, observed by all the relatives seated at tables for lunch, brought the shattered violin to Pierre. Against all the evidence, Nathan had tried, like Madeleine, to defend the young girl, and despite himself had admired the stubbornness of her denial. Regardless of guilt or innocence, he had sensed how much she needed his friendship and had made it a point after that to call and see her several times a week. He could now talk to her like an adult, he found. It was only when he realized that the one thing in all the world he could not tell her – tell anyone – was the one thing crushing his soul that he would bid a hasty good-bye and flee from the house to his solitary agony. That agony had now driven him to a desperate decision.

Upon entering Samuel's study Nathan began to stride to and fro across the Persian carpet, spasmodically clenching his hands and then relaxing them. He began to talk as he walked, as if continuing a dialogue that had been engaging him for days.

'I have made a momentous decision about my life, Samuel, momentous. I intend to enter a monastery. All the money, everything that I own, will go to the Church.'

Samuel was stunned. 'That is absurd. Undoubtedly you've been working too hard. Why don't you –'

Nathan waved his hand in dismissal of that notion and began to pace all the more furiously. 'Nothing can dissuade me. Madeleine and my cousin Hans have already tried today. But I am determined. Why a monastery, you will ask? Doesn't that presuppose that this hulking Jew has decided to become a Catholic? The answer is yes. But that is a conclusion, not a reason. What then *is* the reason? Why can I not seek God in the religion in which I was raised? Why do I shop for a new religion as if my old one is a car that has worn out? I know the reason, I know the reason . . .' he said to himself, as he halted and fell silent to form his thoughts into words. Then he faced Samuel, gripped by an intensity that the other man had never before seen in him. 'Because Jews find God *in spite of* their suffering. Catholics find Him *through* suffering. I suffer, Samuel. My suffering obsesses me. Nights, sometimes days, I can do nothing but rack my mind with questions I fail to answer, with fears I fail to still.' He choked. 'I cannot endure it.'

'And you think that in a monastery, where everything is prescribed, every moment accounted for, you will find peace?'

Nathan's voice became subdued. 'I know the suffering will not be lifted right away, but by giving up material things, by living for God, by emulating the suffering of Jesus, maybe I too will be allowed to find the way to salvation.'

'What an extraordinary gamble! You, who have always

calculated so carefully until all the risks are eliminated . . . to give all you possess, all your security, to the Church without knowing whether you will find there what you seek . . . and to give up all the pleasure you've always loved: good food, women. Women! Can you do without women, Nathan?'

Nathan cried out in anguish. 'We are talking about my soul! We are talking about eternity! What is . . . is . . . fornication . . . compared to that?'

The old banker shrugged. 'I've always thought that one ecstasy must be a fairly accurate preview of any other, even of eternity – if eternity is anything at all. But then, I've always been unable to comprehend why philosophers and prophets think they have to reject the good things in life – the good things God has put in life, if you wish to view it from that perspective – in order to make contact with the God who put them here to enjoy those very things.' With compassion in his own, he sought the younger man's eyes. 'Nathan, why are you always so hard on yourself? I'm not a particularly religious man, but I believe in God. Isn't that enough for *you*?'

'How easily you express the belief I find myself unable to utter. And even if I were certain that I believed in God, even if I were, how could I be certain He believed in *me*?'

'For a Jew there are a hundred ways to reach God.'

'Thank you for not raising my obligation to the family heritage.'

'Others will. A Kronengold, the exemplar of the Jew in the eyes of so many – Christians and Jews. It will seem like desertion.'

'That failure pains me . . . but the Jews are not losing very much when they lose me.'

Samuel noticed tears beginning to cover over Nathan's eyes like raindrops on windowpanes. 'Are you so awful that you fear mercy even from your God?'

'So many died in the war, so many. Only cowards escaped.' Nathan's hands flew to cover his face. 'If Jesus will not have me either, then what will become of me?'

Samuel decided to take a long trip in order to implement his plan to move Kronengold assets out of Great Britain and into more promising investments on the Continent and elsewhere. A few months earlier he would have considered the trip excellent training for Deborah and taken her too. But he had renounced all ties to her for the lack of character she had shown during the violin incident by continuing to lie to the family – to him – after her guilt became obvious. He requested that Richard be brought back from boarding school. He would take Richard on the trip instead and begin imparting to him the knowledge and techniques essential to a future banker and businessman.

Leslie found Samuel's alarm about the state of the British economy exaggeratedly panicky and quite against the nation's best interests at a time when its sons should be rallying behind the flag. Moreover, whatever the aftermath of Suez, it would blow over in a few weeks and the course of events would return to normal. Yes, his father was too alarmist by half, and certainly unnecessarily audacious. But Leslie was pleased at what his father's actions signified for him personally. Not only would Samuel be far from the bank for many months, leaving Leslie relatively free to operate it, but he was effectively confirming his intent to bequeath the bulk of his estate to Leslie – as he had declared he would be doing shortly after Deborah fell into disgrace. A small share of the estate would go to Leslie's younger brother, Charles, and a bit perhaps would go in trust for Leslie's own acknowledged heir, his son, Richard. Bother the old man's buying and selling abroad, Leslie said to himself – how much harm could he do? What mattered to Leslie was how well things had fallen into place for his own future.

A car with driver were dispatched to the boarding school to return Richard and all his belongings to London.

Late that night Madeleine turned off her reading lamp and lay back in the darkened room in which she now slept. Refusing to rely on Leslie these last six months, building a separate life, had strengthened her and made her realize something about herself. She had allowed Leslie to assume responsibilities and then, later on, believed him when he suggested she herself was incapable of undertaking them. Now she found that she relished being self-sufficient and disposing of problems. Much of her thinking was saved for this hour. She was habitually unable to sleep until all her concerns had risen up and were at least studied for a moment or two, if not actually resolved. The last two nights she had been too exhilarated for concerns to prey on her mind, although she knew that sooner or later she would have to consider how the new factors in her life – Rob's love, her own sexuality – dictated a new equation for her future. Most nights that autumn she had pondered Deborah's problems. Tonight, however, it was Richard that preoccupied her.

They're only babies when we send them off to boarding school to learn to be independent, she reflected, and we lose them. She and her son used to be so close. But the long separations and adolescent taciturnity had hardened impenetrably what she used to believe was a mere membrane between mother and son: she realized that Richard was no better known to her than the children of her friends.

At first Richard had been bewildered at the sudden dislocation in his life. Madeleine had spent hours that evening patiently explaining how the trip would be an unparalleled opportunity to see fascinating places and gain invaluable business training from his grandfather. She tried to get him to talk about his surprise at being uprooted, his anxiety about leaving on a long trip with a grandfather he had never been close to. But Richard, eyes directed at his feet, had refused to open up to her, despite all her urging. She had perceived how troubled he had seemed, and not solely about leaving his school friends to make this trip, but she could not reach him. Finally, she had kissed him good night and left his room.

Madeleine's ruminations were interrupted by a click outside the bedroom. She sat up. Someone had entered her dressing room.

She slipped into her dressing-gown and quietly opened her door a crack. In the darkness she could make out a slim silhouette moving in front of her dressing-table. The head lifted for an instant to look at something, and became recognizable: Richard was rummaging through her things. She stepped into the room and snapped on the lamp.

'Richard! What on earth are you doing?'

Richard spun around. His eyes were large and ringed white with terror. 'Mother – I – I –' he stammered. His hand edged towards the pocket of his red flannel dressing-gown.

'Richard, what you have got in your hand?'

Richard seemed to be struck dumb. He started to cram his hand into his pocket, still staring at her.

'Open your hand!' she commanded.

A bank note crumpled into a ball dropped to the carpet.

'Bring it here!'

He stooped to retrieve it and, with agonizing slowness, placed it in her hand. She uncrumpled a five-pound note. Her gaze flew to her handbag. It was open, and so was the purse inside it. An instant later she focused once more on Richard. Her eyes melted him down, shrinking him in size. His mouth began to twitch as if the muscles were diminishing unevenly.

'Why did you take this money?' she demanded of him.

Richard finally found his voice. 'I need it.'

'You get pocket money, exactly the same amount the school recommends for every other boy in your form.'

'It isn't enough,' he bleated.

'Enough for what?'

'I can't tell you.'

'Richard, I caught you stealing. I want to know why.'

As if withering, Richard's arm involuntarily began to draw back again to the dressing-gown pocket. Madeleine noticed a thin rectangle outlined through the material.

'Hand me whatever is in your pocket.'

The terror that had electrified her son's face when Madeleine first came upon him appeared minor compared to what seized him now. He shook uncontrollably, and his eyes rolled, as if seeking an escape route independently of the mind no longer able to function. Madeleine finally had to thrust her hand into Richard's pocket. She extracted an envelope addressed to her nephew Gilbert – Pierre's son – in Paris. Inside it were three one-pound notes.

Richard broke down. There was no longer any way to hide his guilt; the fragile supports of his world were collapsing around him. Between blubbering sobs he told her that he had been the one who broke Pierre's violin. At Valtary his cousin Gilbert had coerced him into taking two old violins from a display cabinet in the empty Music Room in order to hit a tennis ball back and forth. When Richard's violin was smashed, Gilbert had blackmailed a terrified Richard into agreeing to send him five pounds a week to keep silent. Gilbert had then suggested they slip the shattered Stradivarius into Deborah's violin case, which had been left on a chair after she had played for the family earlier that evening. The two boys had exchanged the violins, putting Deborah's in the display cabinet and the Stradivarius in her carrying case.

Whenever Richard, in his confession, became overcome by

his hysteria or tried to stop, Madeleine demanded he go on. When it appeared he had no more to say, she asked the question that had troubled her during the whole of his confession.

'Richard, how could you let Dee take the blame?'

'Father saw Gilbert and me leaving the Music Room,' Richard disclosed in plaintive justification, 'but he never said anything. Not a word! He knew we had been in the Music Room and protected me, so I thought it was all right to let Dee take the blame. Ask Father. He'll tell you he knew.'

A kaleidoscope of emotions assaulted Madeleine: sadness at what the child she had formed and nurtured and loved had grown into, anger at the injustice he had done his sister, searing fury at Leslie, and determination to assure Deborah's vindication.

'We will not ask your father yet!' Madeleine said with finality. She did not want Richard drawing the strength from Leslie to recant his admission before the wrong done Deborah could be exposed.

She sat Richard down by the telephone and dialled Samuel's number. Collins, the butler, woke his employer to take the call. She related Richard's confession in detail, then put Richard on the telephone. His voice nearly inert, Richard repeated what he had told his mother and then handed the receiver back to her.

'I want you to come over here tomorrow morning,' Samuel instructed her grimly. 'About eleven. I should be ready by then with what has to be done. After that I want to see Deborah. The three of us can have lunch together.'

She heard the click, then she dialled the operator. A few moments later a groggy-voiced Pierre was on the line, and she related the story to him, again putting Richard on to confirm it and Gilbert's extortion.

'I would like to speak to Deborah,' Pierre said quietly when Madeleine came back on the line.

'She's still asleep. We're going into her room now. I'll get her to ring you in the morning.'

'All right. For now please tell her how much I regret the things I said . . . and . . .' His voice trailed off, as his attention turned to the distasteful side of the disclosure. Like Madeleine he had to face and deal with the duplicity of a son.

'*A demain*,' Madeleine said and hung up.

She took a deep breath, straightened her shoulders, and led

Richard out of the boudoir and down the corridor.

Deborah came awake at the sound of the outer door-knob to her suite being turned. Her eyes opened when her bedroom door-knob turned as well. A canal of light bisected the bedroom as the door swung back.

'Dee?'

'Yes?'

'Are you awake enough to speak?'

'Yes.'

'Richard has something to tell you.' She pushed him forward.

'I broke Uncle Pierre's violin, Dee. Gilbert and I put it into your violin case.'

Richard told the story now with none of the trepidation he had displayed to the adults. Madeleine was nearly as appalled by his callousness to the sister he had traduced as by the act itself. Having no concern that she could threaten his well-being as the adults could, accustomed to taking advantage of her devotion, he had no reticence about admitting that he had been the one to shatter her life.

Deborah was sitting up in bed. Madeleine had expected to see jubilation, relief, even vindictiveness in her eyes. She would have been happier with vengefulness than with what she saw – the pain of betrayal she had perceived in Deborah for months magnified many times. Clearly, Deborah was not surprised at her brother's revelation. Madeleine understood at last that Deborah had always suspected the boys were to blame.

An eager, ingratiating smile curled the corners of Richard's mouth. 'Nothing much I could do at that point. You do understand, don't you, Dee?'

'I understand,' Deborah slowly responded, with a starkness terrible to see in a child.

'I never could work out why you didn't tell the others you saw Gilbert and me near the Music Room that night when you were going up to your room.'

Deborah did not reply.

'Because you're her brother!' Madeleine shouted at him, as if the sheer volume could hammer a spike of loving kindness through the callousness.

'Well, it's not as if she's really one of us.'

'What do you mean?' Madeleine gasped.

'She's adopted. Lucky to be here, according to Father.'

Madeleine slapped her son's face with all the strength in her arm. He fell back, stunned and frightened.

'She is your sister! One of us! You are never to think anything different – or say it to another human being!'

Richard was snivelling, mumbling apologies. But Madeleine's thoughts were of Deborah: cutting into the child now was the probably unshakable belief that, when in doubt, the family always protected its own against the outsider.

Madeleine quickly spoke up. 'Dee, I've already called Uncle Pierre and Grandfather. They want you to know they apologize for suspecting you. They love you and will speak to you themselves tomorrow.'

At last Deborah tried to speak, but emotion stole her voice. She fought to hold back the sobs rising in her throat. Finally, the years of suppressed anguish clawing to be heard, she was able to cry out, 'And Father? Does *he* still love me?'

A chill rolled over Madeleine, but she would not allow her child to be betrayed again by sugar-coating the truth with a lie. 'Richard claims that your father saw him coming out of the Music Room with Gilbert that night.' Madeleine paused a moment to allow her daughter time to appreciate the implications of that statement, then went on. 'I want you to be with us when we confront him.'

Deborah wrestled enough self-control into her voice to reply with grim prescience. 'No. Father will lie again. This won't change anything.'

Madeleine nodded her head in rueful agreement. She sat down on the edge of the four-poster bed and placed her arms lovingly around her daughter. 'Dee – I'm *so* sorry – I don't know what to say. We all love you – I love you very much.'

Deborah's face turned towards Madeleine, and again it jolted her. It was the face of a judge who was merely hearing her out before sentencing. The glint in the blue eyes, as off a guillotine edge, condemned more clearly than words every last person Deborah had trusted with her love. In some way, each and every one – and Madeleine most of all – had betrayed her.

Leslie acted predictably when confronted by Richard's admission. Not only did he dispute his son's recollection of having encountered Leslie when leaving the Music Room, but even of Richard's having broken the violin. He praised

Richard's character for wanting to take the blame for his guilty sister. And, as for borrowing a few quid from his mother's purse tonight, the boy probably intended to go shopping early for things he would need on his trip with his grandfather. Madeleine must have scared the wits out of him, Leslie asserted, when she surprised him in her dressing room, and he was too confused to be coherent. Leslie's face, when he ceased speaking, bore an expression of innocent good-will.

Richard, standing straighter, was attempting the overture to a bashful smile as his father concluded his defence; one could reasonably look at it in that sort of way, Richard reasoned, surprised by and grateful for his father's favour.

Madeleine stood impassively in the centre of her husband's bedroom as she went through the formality of hearing him out.

'It's too late for that, Leslie,' Madeleine replied, uncompromisingly. 'Richard has already told his story by phone to Samuel and Pierre.'

Leslie's apprehensive gaze flashed to Richard, who dropped his eyes, and then back to his wife. 'You cruel, devious bitch!'

'Perhaps our relationship would have been better if I *had* been cruel.' With bitter satisfaction she noted Leslie's sudden guilty start. 'When Deborah came to us, we vowed never to reveal that she was adopted. Later, when you let it slip to her, you again vowed secrecy. Now you've told Richard.'

Leslie drew himself up. 'I will not have my son believing he owes Deborah an allegiance he does not.'

Madeleine's reply was an acid hiss. 'You are a repulsive, despicable creature!'

She moved to the door, where she stopped and looked at the son she loved still. But the truth was ineluctable. 'Poor, tortured Richard. You have become the son your father deserved.'

Madeleine spent the rest of the early morning hours pacing her sitting room in thought.

Just before eleven Madeleine walked to Samuel's house. Percival Grayson, the head of the firm of solicitors that represented Samuel and the bank, was just leaving as she arrived at the doorway to Samuel's study. His father had been Samuel's trusted solicitor until his death. Young Percy here had succeeded him. He appeared fatigued and out of sorts when she greeted him, having been up all night working on something Samuel insisted be done at once, he explained.

Seated at his writing table as Madeleine entered the dark-panelled study, Samuel peered out of the gloom like a male sphinx. He wasted no time in pleasantries.

'Deborah has got to be protected,' he declared firmly. 'After we spoke last night, I rang Grayson at home, and he set to work on a new will. I've just signed it, with Grayson and two of my employees acting as witnesses. Upon my death, what would have gone to Leslie – the major part of my estate – now goes to Deborah. She will inherit a majority of the stock in our family's holding company. As you know British Kronengold Holdings owns a controlling interest in the bank and the family's investments. She'll get all my personal wealth, this house and Clove Hill, all the furniture, and nearly all the pictures and *objets d'art* not donated to museums. You are to be the executor – and the trustee too, of course, if I die before she's twenty-one. I would have named Nathan, but that's no longer practical. I know you'll protect Deborah. That's the important thing.'

Madeleine sat down. Lion heads were carved into the corners of the heavy Victorian desk between them. On its writing surface lay the new will.

'Perhaps you'll want to change your mind about my acting as executor when I tell you I've decided to leave Leslie.'

'Break up the family?' Samuel was shocked. There had been few divorces in the family; men and women stayed together regardless of incompatibility. Both British upper-class tradition and that of the Kronengolds dictated that the continuity of the family was the major purpose of life. Lineage and heritage flowed from it and were preserved by it. Despite her sombre mood, Madeleine smiled wryly at her father-in-law's implication that there was a family structure left to break up.

Samuel was insistent. 'Children need a family, Dee most of all.'

'Samuel, Leslie doesn't even consider her his daughter.'

'Did he say that?' Samuel asked, an undertone of rage in his voice.

'Yes. But, even as husband and wife, there's no marriage left to save.'

'I hadn't realized your relationship had deteriorated that far.'

'Of course you had. You just didn't want to face it. Well,' she pointed out, 'it's my problem really. I've had to live with him, not you.'

'Is there another man?' he asked bluntly.

'After what I learned last night, I would have left Leslie regardless of any other consideration. I thought about leaving him before the summer. Last night was simply the final straw.'

'Those things happen, Maddy. You know –'

She interrupted him sharply. 'If you truly believed that, you would never have changed your will today.'

Instead of meeting her eyes, he looked away. 'Will Leslie contest a divorce or fight for custody?'

'I doubt he'll do either. He's concerned about appearances.'

Samuel's gaze flashed back to Madeleine for an instant, assessing the extent of her knowledge of his son's activities, and then away again. He settled back heavily. There was something he wanted to say. 'While waiting this morning for the will to arrive, I brooded a good deal, Maddy. About Deborah, of course. And what Leslie is like. That particularly. And you – what I may have done to you. I'm not a man who apologizes easily . . .' His voice rose self-righteously. '. . . or who has often had to, I dare say.' And then he paused. 'But, if my badgering was in any way responsible for your deciding to marry Leslie, I am deeply sorry.'

'I made the decision to marry him quite freely. Leslie just never came up to either of our expectations.'

Silence settled on them for a few moments as each tucked in the stray corners of the past. Samuel was the next to speak.

'Naturally, I will want Deborah to be the one to go away with me now, if you give your permission. It will be for several months.'

'I thought you might. Richard won't be disappointed; he was rather distressed at being pulled away from school. But I have no idea how Dee will feel about going.'

'Because of my attitude?' he muttered reluctantly.

'Partially that. Partially because she and I have never been separated for more than a week or two . . . when she was away visiting her friend April.' Madeleine's hands tightened on the carved scrolls at the ends of her chair's arm-rests. 'I'm the one it will be painful for, Samuel.' She looked down to her lap while she fought off the imminent rush of tears. Her eyes were wet when she looked up, but she was in control. 'But things between Leslie and me are likely to be rather disagreeable in the next few months. I want her out of it. She's been hurt so much already. I don't even want to tell her yet that Leslie and I are breaking up. Although, Lord knows, she's more aware of the antagonisms flying back and forth in that house than anyone. I'll write it all to her in a letter when you two are safely off on the high seas. It will be easier to explain that way.' Madeleine bit her lip at the sudden realization of how lonely she would be with Deborah gone. 'If she knows now, she might insist on staying for my benefit . . . and I might even weaken enough to let her. Samuel, you're right to choose her, she really *is* the hope of the Kronengold future.'

'Will she forgive me?'

'She'll probably put you through hell first,' Madeleine replied with a smile. 'By the time you all return, I'll have a house of my own with the children's rooms ready for them.'

Samuel leaned towards Madeleine. He spoke with unaccustomed gentleness. 'I truly want you to be happy, Maddy.'

'Thank you, Samuel.'

Samuel handed Madeleine the will. 'This is the original copy of the will which I've signed. Here it is. Put it in a good, strong safe, Maddy – wherever you think it will be absolutely secure. I don't want you to tell Leslie that I've made a new will. In my absence he's the only one capable of running the bank. When I die is soon enough for him to learn what I've done.'

Madeleine folded the will and placed it in the envelope the solicitor had brought for it. The document felt like fire in her hands as she put it into her handbag.

'I've already spoken to Pierre this morning,' Samuel went on. 'The merger between our banks is off, of course. For one thing our governments will probably fall now, and the French are likely to call on de Gaulle. He'll keep Britain out of the Common Market as long as he can.'

'And Pierre no longer trusts Leslie enough to work together with him,' Madeleine added.

Samuel's nod confirmed her guess. They both grew

reflective. Once, six brothers had built a dynasty in six countries often at war because they had acted with one mind and one heart, although each was loyal to his own country. Now, their descendants in only two of those countries, separated by a strait less than thirty miles wide, were admitting that their firms could not cooperate enough to do business together. It was no one's fault. That was just the way things were.

Two mornings later, Madeleine saw Deborah and Samuel and their entourage off to Southampton, where his yacht was moored. Then she ordered her belongings to be swiftly packed and put on the van she had hired to move them. Later, with the removal men waiting outside her suite of rooms, she went to the safe at the rear of her now empty boudoir. From her handbag she took her little red address book. On the inside cover she had written the combination. She opened the lock and swung back the round steel door. Inside was over two million pounds' worth of jewellery, cash, and government bearer bonds, the entirety of her dowry, which she swept into her large handbag. The only other items in the safe were two envelopes: one containing Samuel's will, the other her own. They, too, went into her handbag. Then she opened the door to the suite of rooms and allowed the men to remove the safe.

When they had left, she wrote a short letter to Leslie. Every word had been carefully chosen the night before as she reviewed each step of her departure. It simply said that she was leaving him and that her solicitors (Vivienne's actually, but Madeleine assumed they would represent her) would contact him soon to discuss a divorce. She had thought about informing Leslie in person, but decided she no longer owed him even that much. And, as for Rob, he was part of her new life and none of Leslie's business.

Madeleine set the letter on the pillow of Leslie's bed. In this room she had lived with him, slept with him, planned a future with him, and grown to despise him. She had left it months before and did not feel a sentimental tug. But she did feel an urge to take one last walk through the rest of the house.

Because she no longer thought of the immense edifice as hers, she saw it with stark clarity, as if for the first time. The children's rooms were empty, their clothing and most of the personal possessions gone, along with their vitality. She already thought of Richard as an undesirable relative one is burdened with for long visits. That was deplorable, she knew, and when he was living in the new house with her, she would try to reach him as she had obviously failed to do when Leslie's influence loomed over the household. But his departure was more a relief for her than a loss. It was at Deborah's bedroom that she felt a pang of grief as she peered in – the pink walls, the delicate white furniture, the four-poster bed draped with pink silk. She had brought a red-haired, smiling baby here to shield her from the ravages outside, and had been unable to fend off the onslaughts within.

Madeleine leaned her head against the doorway. Already she ached with the anticipated loneliness. Deborah lit up her soul, she realized, and brought joy to a joyless home. But now was the time for her to be weaned. She must learn to survive without her mother's intervention if she was to be an independent adult some day. Madeleine had occasionally worried whether there was not some truth in Leslie's accusation that she coddled Deborah, cushioned her from the adversity necessary to toughen her capacity for self-sufficiency. Being away from each other for an extended time was a good first step for them both. What she did not want now was to inflict her own raw, confused needs on her daughter – with both of them feeling guilty. Loneliness was the price she would have to pay for knowing when separation was more loving than an embrace. She closed the bedroom door and continued down the hall.

Only staff would be here after she left, waiting for a single occupant to return to the fifty-odd rooms designed for an opulence that was the vestige of a sweeter time already expiring when she was a child, although no one knew it.

This house, built to the scale of giants, had become, she realized, more a monument to their guileless hubris, a museum more than a home. Screened from view by stone walls, its present residents, like slightly deranged dwarfs, had played out delusions of grandeur. Room after oversized room was heaped with exquisite objects rarely noticed but necessary to fill the excess space and to adduce their tiny owners' right to reside. Here a collection of Fabergé eggs as fine as the czar's. There a salon full of magnificent clocks. Here perfect Persian miniatures. There a large Rodin marble. Here an exquisite Houdon bust of a king. There a Degas dancer in coloured chalk. Madeleine mused dejectedly that the mansion recreated those prehistoric caves where men and women long dead and forever unknown had painted their dreams on the walls until their titanic shadows, flung up by the firelight, had flickered out.

She perused the faces in the family portraits, prosperous, self-satisfied faces: some kind, some pious, some handsome, all gone. The assumptions that underpinned these people's lives were gone as well. Their luxury had ridden on the shoulders of dozens of obsequious servants who toiled for their 'betters' at low wages and knew their place. But salaries and taxes were now rising as fast as expectations, levelling master and servant. Soon, the house would cease to operate, slowed to a standstill by the irresistible tandem inertias of economics and politics. Then, other little people would pull it down because there were no giants to live in it.

Madeleine said good-bye to the cook and butler and maids she knew well. She was going on a trip, she told them. The truth was known only to Irma, her personal maid, who was leaving with her.

At the front door Madeleine wrapped her fur coat around her and walked the fifty feet or so along the façade to the garage. Irma was already in the white convertible. One of the chauffeurs opened the iron gate to the street. Despite the cutting cold, Madeleine lowered the top of the car. She drove to the house she had rented, with the radio at full volume and the woman beside her shivering.

Later that same day, Samuel de Kronengold, his eleven-year-old granddaughter Deborah, her personal maid, her tutor Jason Latham, a very pretty young girl friend of Samuel's, Samuel's butler, his private secretary, his valet, and a crew of thirty-four left Southampton aboard Samuel's yacht. Over three hundred feet long, restored to its former grandeur since being returned by the Royal Navy after the war, the *Venture* contained a swimming pool, a gymnasium and sauna, a cinema, old and modern masters in airtight frames, the usual assortment of speedy launches, a Rolls, and an amphibious aeroplane for ferrying people to and from the yacht (certainly not for Samuel's personal transportation).

Most of those aboard with no tasks stood by the rails to watch the English shore diminish, then drop below the horizon.

Her eyes fixed firmly ahead of her, Deborah stood at the bow, grimly pleased that every wave the hull traversed took her farther away from Leslie, the father who hated her, and from Madeleine, the mother she now hated.

CHAPTER SIX

Deborah tried not to think about her mother. Most of the day, when in port, it was easy. At each European city where the *Venture* docked or to which she and her grandfather travelled in the private railway carriage that met them at each port, people who worked for the Kronengolds or with whom Samuel did business would await their arrival with a list of people for him to see or potential investments to be examined. Samuel convened all day with bankers, industrialists, and lawyers, and Deborah was always beside him. Grandfather and granddaughter would squeeze in sightseeing between meetings. Back again on the high seas, Samuel would talk on the radio-telephone with the bank in London or dictate letters or cables to his secretary, and Deborah would catch up on missed schooling with Jason Latham. But at odd moments, when watching the grey ocean from a railing or when a book failed to hold her attention or when Grandfather was too busy to play chess, her mother would wander into her thoughts . . . spread naked, writhing and moaning helplessly as Rob Rowell pinned her to the bed like an insect spread out at a museum for display.

Sometimes Deborah would have nightmares about the sight. Never before that day at the cottage had she ever seen her mother, or any other woman, naked. Certainly no man. What little she knew about sex had been envisaged as a painless, if undignified, injection. What assaulted her eyes had been, first, a conjunction of racking convulsions, shocking Deborah to the depths of her being; and, then, Rob Rowell holding her at bay like a wild animal guarding her mother's twitching carcass under him. He had taken her mother from her and possessed her mother's devotion now. Deborah had been an intruder without rights or affinity to either of them.

In that moment the already trembling psychological terrain on which she stood tipped crazily. Her father had wounded her time and again, but he had never deserted her. The deserter turned out to be her mother, who had vowed her love, who had vowed she would never leave, but had abandoned husband, family, her – and mocked them all; the elegant manners, the gentle sincerity that had characterized her mother's behaviour before that moment appeared exposed as an elaborate lie. Of one thing Deborah was now sure: in the end everyone would desert her.

As her ego tumbled helplessly in the hours and days that followed the incident at the cottage, Deborah had grabbed frantically for handholds. The easiest was hatred. She hated her mother for turning to Rob Rowell, and herself for not being able to provide her mother with enough love to keep her from Rowell. Ultimately, Deborah heaped on her mother all the censure for her insecurity – even for having chosen to adopt her in the first place. The longer she hated, the more stability she regained. Deborah's love for her mother had always been the constant point that guided her and kept her from foundering. Now it was this hatred. Around it she placed, as if on exhibit, all her secret yearnings for the family from which she fantasized she had been snatched and which would have loved her because she belonged there. Her grandfather and Uncle Pierre had welcomed her back, but she expected that at any moment they might cast her off again. So she clutched her hatred for her mother to her like a furry animal, and rocked herself to sleep with it, often waking with her arms desperately hugging herself, overwhelmed by how desperately she missed her.

Deborah and Samuel left the yacht in Nice and travelled north to Switzerland for the Christmas holiday, planning to rejoin the yacht after New Year's Day. They were accompanied by secretary, butler, chef, valet, and maid. Most of those left behind were given time off. Samuel's latest young girl friend was bid a permanent good-bye.

Samuel's urgency to find more promising investments had driven him in the month since leaving England, easing only when he acquired several stretches of potential beach-resort land on the southern coasts of Spain and France and made offers on others. Several favourably placed manufacturing companies had also been proposed to him, and he was considering them. On their imminent stop in Athens, he would quietly feel out the market for selling his share in the Devon Star Shipping Line to Greek shipping owners, before it became evident that Britain's exports and need for shipping capacity would soon be on the wane.

And he wanted Deborah to see the Acropolis. He was delighted to be with her again, having missed her company much more in those black months than his pride would allow him to admit. He understood that he had not yet regained his granddaughter's trust. Only time could accomplish that. He was not by nature a patient man, but knew that in this matter at least he must be. He understood, too, that his own urgency to restructure investments and to impart his experience had been somewhat trying for her. They could both benefit from a rest and a lessening of tension. For Deborah especially, starting with her first visit to the bank and then the tense aftermath of Valtary, it had been a very long year. At St. Moritz, she could ski, which she loved to do, and he could see old friends, dispose quietly of the few business meetings he had planned there, and take the waters.

The carriage, a sumptuously appointed product of the Belle Epoque, was unhooked from the rest of the train in Geneva. After a meeting with André Leitner, the head of Swiss operations for the Kronengold bank, Deborah was taken on a tour of Geneva by Leitner, whom she had met previously in London and liked. He was a brilliant young man in whom Samuel placed a good deal of trust. Even if it had not been an obligation, Leitner would have been pleased to escort Deborah; he found her youthful zest and cleverness delightful. Samuel used the free hours to visit a cardiac specialist to confirm the diagnosis of his London doctor that his heart condition would not hamper him if he took care of himself.

Reassured, he rejoined Deborah at the station. The carriage was attached to another train. Next morning they awoke in St. Moritz.

For three thousand years St. Moritz had been a spa. Even in 1000 BC its naturally hot, carbonic iron waters were considered to have restorative powers. Ever since the Middle Ages, kings and queens had travelled there, and it had become the most famous winter resort in Europe. Superb hotels and elegant chalets now housed the world's elite. Visitors could ski down the white peaks above the sprawling village, swim in the hot outdoor pool, or 'take the cure' of the mineral baths.

Samuel's house had its own well to the hot spring, and his

therapist would be available to direct his regimen and massage him. He looked forward to introducing Deborah in the evenings to interesting and celebrated people at private parties – the Shah of Iran, inevitably, would give a party or two – and to quiet dinners alone together.

Deborah was filled with excitement at the prospect. Not only had her emotions put a considerable strain on her during the trip, but, as Samuel had surmised, acting as his constant companion and sounding board – always alert to absorb difficult information or be examined on it – had worn her down. She was always on guard now to keep his favour. She wanted very much to behave like the adult he expected her to be, but yearned for the lessened responsibility of a normal eleven-year-old.

The first day on the mountain her ski instructor, under strict orders from her grandfather, had limited her freedom to 'zlow elegant turnz' very close to him, which irritated and frustrated her.

The second day he followed the same routine. On the last run of the day down the *piste*, however, he stopped to help a woman who had fallen. Observing that the woman was merely tangled up in her equipment, not injured, Deborah swung the tips of her skis around. The slope urged them forward. Slowly, they began to respond. She wanted at least this final run to be daring and exciting. The mountain glowed as if with a healthy sunburn. She flung her arms wide to embrace it all: setting sun, snow, sky, speed. Moving faster now, like a gull swooping towards a white sand beach, she tucked her sticks against the sides of her blue and green ski suit, bent her knees, and pointed her skis into the heart of gravity. The wind cut a smile across her face. Cares began to drop away from her. Time now only for reflex and rhythm. Space within her now only for exhilaration – and the fear riding it piggyback that could throw her with awful suddenness. Crouching lower to cut down wind resistance and gain better balance, she shot by other skiers almost too fast for them to take in her presence, until there was only the speed, the mountain, and her. Awareness was reduced to the most instant of presents. Before and after was a blur that her bubble of timelessness dropped through.

A small child veered across her path. She could have circled to a line down the right side of the slope, but an urge rolled her knees and edges left, towards a rise and drop-off. She took it at full speed and sprang just before the top of the rise. Then she soared. As if too heavy for flight, the last of her concerns, which had clung to her like leeches for many months, seemed to fall to earth behind her. She felt utterly free and content, afloat on the air, euphoric, happy, her long, red hair streaming out behind her like a comet's tail. Above, the last rays of the sun bestowed their benediction on her. Below, the village of St. Moritz reached up to embrace her.

Deborah's skis sprayed a fan of snow across the front door as she came to a stop in front of the chalet. Collins, the butler, scurried out to take her skis and sticks from her. Inside the front door, she dropped hat and gloves on the hall table, got out of her ski boots and into waiting slippers, and went in search of her grandfather.

She found him in the large living room, just saying goodbye to a drug company executive and a German banker. Heavy, hewn wood beams traversed the room high above her head. The fire was blazing. She seated herself in one of the deep chairs set around an expansive coffee table.

'What did the drug company man want?' Deborah asked when her grandfather joined her.

'His company is doing research on an extraordinary drug. The market for it would be limitless.'

'Does it cure a disease, something like that?'

'No, not exactly.'

Avoiding her question, Samuel strode to the humidor and selected a cigar. Her interest was now heightened.

'Perhaps . . .' she mused aloud while rising from the chair, as if about to leave the room, 'perhaps I'm too young to be told about financial matters.'

Samuel grumbled and chopped off the cigar end with a snap of the silver cutter. 'They are trying to come up with a pill to prevent, eh hmmm, to prevent, you know . . . pregnancy. Do you understand things like pregnancy? I assume your mother has discussed the subject with you.' Samuel's tone conveyed his own reluctance to explain the topic if she had not.

'Yes.'

'Ah, well, then,' he declared, much relieved. 'You can see such a pill's value.'

'For Mother?' she replied acidly.

'For everyone.' He paused. 'Speaking of your mother, her letters have finally caught up with us. Three for you. Three for me.' Samuel handed Deborah three unopened envelopes. She did not look at them.

'Aren't you going to read them?'

She shook her head and turned to the fireplace.

Samuel was forced to go on. 'She has something rather important to tell you.'

Deborah continued to view the burning logs. Several minutes passed.

In a softer voice, Samuel tried again. 'It really is important.'

'If she's leaving my father, it's no surprise.'

'I see. There's a bit more.'

'She's seeing Rob Rowell? That's certainly no surprise either.'

'Dee, Leslie is my own son, but I can sympathize with your mother.'

'With all *your* girl friends, of course you'd sympathize.'

'Dee!' He was truly shocked.

'Will Mother be like you when she gets older, dropping one lover for the next as soon as she gets bored?'

Born during Victoria's reign, Samuel was accustomed to a discreet, if feigned, blindness towards such private matters. Like most in his class, he considered another's behaviours, sexual or otherwise, solely that other person's affair; one accepted his or her public face and he or she accepted one's own. The strict observation of conventions like these, Samuel believed, sustained civilized relationships. Deborah's precocity had always seemed delightful to him, but now it was offensive, and not only in its implications about Samuel's own behaviour. To talk about one's mother so baldly was not done, not done at all. 'Your mother is a fine woman,' he said stiffly. 'Your continued coldness is hurting her very much.'

Deborah believed otherwise, that her mother was a hypocrite who pretended to a loving concern for Deborah and the family, but whose disgusting lust had demonstrated where her true attachment lay. Deborah crushed her mother's letters into a ball and threw them into the fire. She ran from the room before Samuel could admonish her.

The last afternoon of the holiday, Deborah returned early from skiing because Samuel wished her to be present at a meeting. When the man was ushered into the living room, she recognized his wrestler's face, envious eyes, fawning manner. She remembered seeing him from the minstrels' gallery at Clove Hill four years earlier, the weekend she first met April Thornley.

'My name is Max Holtz,' he announced as he took her hand and bowed from the waist.

Max Holtz had been waiting nearly a week to see Lord Kronengold, the man whose interests in South Africa he represented. But Samuel had put him off, himself awaiting information from a secret investigation his lawyers were conducting. He now had it in hand and calmly laid it before the ex-Viennese bank employee.

Gold-bearing reefs in South Africa run in an arc like an underground river, twisting and dipping where unimaginable geological forces have heaved the dark rock. The British Springbok Mining Group, of which Samuel was a major stockholder and chairman, had been prospecting for new gold deposits south of Welcom. Holtz had been directing that search. The secret investigation had revealed that the testing site was actually a rich source of gold, but that Holtz had switched the core samples to make it appear the area was barren. He had then bought up for himself all available land in the path of the gold vein.

Deborah dared not blink for fear she might miss that millisecond when Holtz's face involuntarily flashed his guilt. Instead, he was indignant as he laid down the investigative report.

'I assure you, my dear Lord Kronengold, your lawyers have made a terrible mistake, one that would be comic if it were not so slanderous. I will get to the bottom of this matter as soon as I am back in South Africa.'

Samuel's voice rose slightly, the tone of easy affability dispensed with. 'I have taken another precaution, Max. You borrowed one million rand from a South African bank to buy that land. You mortgaged every asset you own. That loan was repayable on twenty-four hours' demand from the bank. I bought the notes from the bank, and my lawyers made the demand at your office in Johannesburg this morning. Just about now a cable to that effect is probably waiting for you at your hotel.'

Holtz leaped up. 'I will find another bank to lend me the money. You'll not take my land from me.'

Deborah was alarmed. Holtz with his squat, muscular body, appeared to be torn between rushing out to seek refinancing and flinging himself at her grandfather's throat. Her hand edged towards the bell that would summon assistance.

'Perhaps I could save you some unnecessary time in obtaining new funds,' Samuel offered with seeming equanimity. 'You will doubtless find it difficult to borrow in South Africa. The banks there have already been alerted to your fraud.' He paused as if scanning his memory for possible lenders. 'So have the banks here in Switzerland and the rest of Europe.' He shook his head sadly. 'You really do seem to be having a very poor streak of luck, old chap.'

'My God, what kind of man are you?' Holtz cried out with the ferocity of a cornered animal. 'You ruin me without even giving me the opportunity to prove my innocence.'

Deborah scanned her grandfather's face. He had jumped to a false conclusion in her own case over the violin. Perhaps he was wrong now as well. She saw no hint of self-doubt or even of compassion – no visible emotion at all.

'Max, I will take over all your assets, including that land, and cancel your bank debts. You will sign everything over to me.'

Holtz was lowering his large head like a rhinoceros contemplating its charge. 'What do I get in return?'

'I could probably take everything without giving anything in return. We have the evidence to put you behind bars for fraud and theft. That's how I'd like to proceed, because you abused my trust.'

'But that land is *mine*!' Holtz beat his chest with an anguished fist. 'You think because you are a Kronengold you can just seize other people's land when you decide you want it. One of your relatives wiped out my grandfather, my father, without a second thought. But you will not do it to me.' His eyes burned with self-righteousness. 'I have given sweat and blood to your interests in South Africa – and before the war to Kronengolds in Vienna and Paris. What did it get me? When I came to you at Clove Hill four years ago to buy a small share in the South Africa enterprise I oversee for you – the most reasonable of proposals – you dismissed me out of hand. Out of hand!' He sucked in a breath. 'But you cannot steal from me what is rightfully mine. There are laws, Lord Kronengold! There are laws!'

Holtz was nearly out of control. Deborah made up her mind

that, if he moved one step closer to her grandfather, she would ring for help. But Samuel's expression was unchanged.

'If you're referring to foreclosure laws, I admit they're a bit of a hindrance. Which is why I've decided it's worth a hundred thousand pounds to get rid of you now and not to press civil or criminal fraud charges. You'll have enough to start up again. Although I advise you you'll find a chilly reception on this side of the Atlantic for quite some time.'

Max Holtz was filled with fury and helplessness. For so much of his life, barely noticed, he had cowered in the shadow of the omnipotent Kronengolds' upraised boot. His father, too, had worked for the Austrian Kronengolds – his entire lifetime. A brilliant, loyal employee, with nothing to his name when he died. And so, as it had been when he escaped from Austria, and again after the war, Max's only choice was survival – and then to begin again.

'I'll take it,' he said bitterly.

Samuel handed him a one-page contract. When that was signed and returned, Samuel handed him the cheque.

'Lord Kronengold,' Holtz declared in a voice weighed down by persecution, 'you have defamed my good name, then used that as an excuse to rob me of all I built up . . . my land. A hundred thousand pounds is the tiniest fraction of what it was worth.'

He seemed to bend ominously towards Samuel for an instant and then lurched out of the living room. Deborah moved up beside her grandfather.

'How can you be so sure?' she asked. 'He sounded so sincere.'

Samuel showed her the unimpeachable evidence gathered by his lawyers. Convinced, she was chagrined by her sympathy.

'I had begun to feel sorry for him.'

'Don't! Ever! Watch out for him, Dee. You could see it in his eyes. Max Holtz hasn't given up. His envy of us won't let him.'

CHAPTER SEVEN

When grandfather and granddaughter arrived back at the quayside in Nice on the second day of 1957, Jason Latham was waiting. With him was the young woman Samuel had dismissed as his own girlfriend when he and Deborah had left the yacht for Switzerland. Dominique had been desolate, it seemed. And Jason, a virgin and very shy with women, had taken her to dinner and tried fumblingly to comfort her. She had been grateful and, in the way that came most easily to her, demonstrated her gratitude to the shocked young man. They spent the next ten days together in a cosy pension off the Promenade des Anglais. The world had opened up for Jason Latham, but it was also clear that he had to leave Lord Kronengold's employ. Samuel gave the young man a generous severance cheque, bade him good-bye, and went up the gangplank. It was now Deborah's turn to say good-bye to her tutor.

Leave-takings were very painful for her. Each separation or rejection was a wrench back into primal sorrow from which she never returned quite whole. This parting was more difficult for her than most. She had been his student, the organizer of his absentminded life, and his friend for more than four years.

'I only came back so as not to disappoint you,' Jason replied, recognizing as well how inadequate his words were to express his feelings. 'You and I are rather . . . rather used to each other.'

'What will you do now?'

'We thought we'd travel for a while.' He paused. 'I'll miss our lessons.'

Deborah could feel the tears forming. The sailors were already in the process of casting off; the yacht would be leaving in a minute or two. She turned to Dominique. 'Make sure he always has enough money with him for a car-fare.' Then she kissed them both and ran up the gangplank and onto the *Venture*. What stuck in her mind was how happy they looked.

* * *

Samuel felt a slight constriction in his chest as he started to resume his exhausting pace when the *Venture* reached Athens. He took that as a warning to slow down and sensibly ceased to arrange too many appointments. He found he enjoyed both the business and the leisure time more.

Greece was shipping and the Acropolis. Italy, the next stop, was a refinery, a factory complex, the Venetian canals, and the Roman ruins. From there the ship headed west, towards Malaga, where Samuel would close on the beach-front land he had bought in the little fishing villages along the Costa del Sol.

Although Samuel still spent a good deal of time on the ship-to-shore telephone, making deals from Johannesburg to Stockholm, the yacht meandered now to visit interesting sights far more than before. And there was more time to read and study when on board. Deborah found the new, relaxed pace salutary, relieving the disorientation she had often felt during two months of frenetic days and shipboard nights far from home.

Samuel took upon himself the task of teaching all the subjects the tutor had been responsible for. Often he found himself only a page or two ahead of Deborah in a textbook. And occasionally they were both in the dark. The experience of jointly learning, which put them on the same level, began gradually to expand their relationship. They had loved each other before, but in the way an influential manager and his talented performer love each other, with something selfish invested and something personal held back. Deborah had been Samuel's hope for posterity, in whom he desired to instill all of his knowledge, cunning, and power. Samuel had been Deborah's surrogate father, who lavished the attention on her that her own father was unwilling to give. But now they were becoming friends, and trust was growing between them again. They found themselves talking about their feelings, something that Samuel had always before considered an indulgence (or, worse, a weakness). For the first time he began to grow nostalgic about the past.

As the *Venture* approached Malaga, reminiscences were flooding through Samuel, seemingly to make up for a lifetime of never looking back. That morning he signed contracts for the land on the Costa del Sol and then drove with Deborah to Granada and the Alhambra, the magnificent Moorish palace he had not visited for fifty years.

Many memories came to him there beneath the slim columns and elegant friezes pierced by light into a semblance of lace.

'We are originally Sephardic Jews, Spanish Jews,' Samuel said to his granddaughter as they stood at the end of the reflecting pool in the Court of the Alberca. 'The Christians forced the last of the Arabs and Jews out of Spain the same year Columbus found the New World. In this very place a woman once told me that Columbus was actually a Jew seeking a homeland for his people, that the evidence is rumoured to be hidden in the Vatican. "Colon", his real name, is a Sephardic Jewish name.' He described the Spanish Inquisition, how Jews were tortured by the Christians and killed in the name of God.

'Like Columbus, our family had moved from Spain by then. We have a knack for that, thank God! They had gone to Florence, where their skill as goldsmiths could provide a living.'

Samuel fell silent then, staring into the long, shallow pool. He probably would not tell her now, Deborah knew from experience, but tonight, after he had time to consider, she would ask him. Maybe then her grandfather would be willing to reveal who the woman was he had first come here with.

Samuel and Deborah spoke very little at dinner, as Collins and the stewards hovered about, serving them. Afterwards, grandfather and granddaughter strolled on deck and watched occasional distant lights flicker from the receding Spanish shore in pale imitation of the stars that burned the night sky. Samuel, too, had been waiting to raise something with Deborah. Mail had reached the ship before it embarked from Malaga. A letter from Madeleine had reported that Leslie was being difficult about a divorce, but she was very happy and hoped that her father-in-law was happy for her, odd as that might seem. Her only grief was her estrangement from her daughter; Deborah had not replied to any of her letters and obviously condemned her mother for leaving her father. 'I haven't left *her*,' Madeleine wrote. 'My new house has the most beautiful rooms for her and Richard. I miss her desperately. You must make her understand that, Samuel.'

As he settled into a deckchair and waited for his butler to bring brandy for him and cocoa for her, Samuel pondered a means to make the young girl understand. But she spoke first.

'Grandfather . . .' Deborah paused to be sure she had his full concentration.

'Yes?'

'Who was the woman you came with to Granada?'

Startled, Samuel hesitated. It went against lifelong habit to speak openly of such things, especially to a young girl, but it was important for Deborah to know that people could be incompatible, as her mother and father had been, without its being anyone's fault. And that love, whenever it came, could be overwhelming and dazzling and enriching. If Deborah accepted those things, she could at least begin to understand the emotions that had swept her mother up. He had never told another soul about Stella, but he realized that he wanted to now, so that, when he was gone, Deborah would know and, maybe, sometimes remember; he wanted someone left who remembered.

'Her name was Stella Roth. She was a sculptor, a Communist, and a suffragette. Not very tall, but very beautiful, I thought, and with enough spirit for half a dozen women twice her size.'

'Her eyes?'

'What?'

'What colour were her eyes?'

'Hazel. Deep and clear and hazel.'

'You must have been in love. All the novels say if you're in love, you remember the colour of her eyes.'

Samuel chuckled. 'Perhaps that's true. The first thing I noticed about her *was* her eyes.'

'Where did you meet?'

'At an art exhibition for some prominent artists. She approached me for the funds for a *women's* art exhibition. I scoffed. She challenged me to name the women artists being shown here, or anywhere at that time in London. I couldn't. "The answer is easy," she said. "There are none. The discrimination is a disgrace." I responded that perhaps they had less talent than men, that their constitution did not permit them to reach the artistic heights that men could attain. I knew that would provoke her; I *wanted* to provoke her. She was captivating. And intriguing. She wore trousers. Trousers! We argued for nearly an hour. We were very well matched. I had spoken at debates in the Cambridge Union and was logical and incisive. She was emotional. She had more historical facts crammed into her brain than an encyclopaedia, but used them to arouse one emotionally, throwing logic to the winds, which made her own kind of logic. She was a firebrand, a lioness. I had no idea women like that existed.'

Deborah was hugging her knees in delight over so delicious a revelation coming from her grandfather. 'Did you love her madly right away?'

'I began to, I think. When I refused to acknowledge the justice of her point of view, she invited me to her house the next afternoon. It turned out that she had a surprise for me. Half the works of art were done by men and half by women, but the names of the artists had been covered. I had to guess which had been done by men and which by women. I was at a loss. She was delighted. I not only wrote her a cheque to mount the exhibition, I invited her out to dinner.'

'What did she say?' Deborah asked when Samuel hesitated.

Samuel's face screwed up with reluctance to discuss so intimate a subject. But he had made up his mind to tell her everything, and he pushed on. 'Stella said – in the same tone I'm speaking to you now – she said, "We're having dinner *here*. In bed. And, if that works out, breakfast." '

Deborah's eyes were wide as headlights. Her mouth was open.

'She was what we used to call a Bohemian, a free spirit,' he continued. 'I think she fell in love with me because I was strong and couldn't be pushed around.'

'And you fell in love with her?'

'Astonishing as it may seem – it did to me at the time – I respected Stella's intelligence. She was brilliant and gifted. We fell wildly in love. Although we rarely found a topic to agree on, we couldn't bear to be apart.' Having begun, Samuel decided it was important for Deborah to hear the whole story. 'After the exhibition, Stella and I travelled around Europe together, and then North Africa. It was my Grand Tour and her chance to see art in other countries.'

They took their drinks from the butler. Samuel waited for the man to retire.

'We had gone as far as Marrakesh and were about to head inland when we both realized we were fooling ourselves that we could remain together. I was embarrassed when she proclaimed to guides in the *medina* and donkey drivers in the *souk* that they were being used by the capitalists. She felt guilty and irritated at the luxury hotels we stayed at. She insisted on making her own bed and passing out revolutionary pamphlets in the dining room.'

Deborah was convulsed with laughter.

'Sooner or later the world intrudes, Dee, no matter how much you love each other. And we loved each other with a greater passion than I've ever come close to experiencing since.' He reflected for a moment, then chuckled derisively at the memory of his younger self. 'As if we always had a fever. That's it precisely. Light-headed and flushed, nearly delirious at times. Ridiculous. There was no way for us to keep going in such a frenzy, so different from each other. We saw the world differently, wanted different things from it. And we were both so strong. Our fights were monumental.'

'Didn't Stella want to marry you?'

'We were fortunate in being wise enough to recognize the irreconcilability of what faced us and be grateful for the short time we did have.'

'And you never saw her again?'

'Once or twice at exhibitions. She died young, only a few years later. I was married by then. She wasn't the sort to live a long sedate life. She never even lived to see women get the vote. A shame. That was very important to her.'

Samuel blew a smoke ring upwards. Stella's face was as sharply defined in his memory as the moon was in the night sky. 'For all our solid conservatism, Dee, we Kronengolds have always been wildly unpredictable when it comes to falling in love.' The smoke ring had surrounded the moon and was starting to fade into the blackness. 'Take your mother . . .'

'Rob Rowell!' Deborah pronounced sharply.

'Just a moment ago you were thrilled by the romantic nature of my own love affair.'

'She's married – with children.'

'Your parents weren't happy together. That can happen to people. I'm as sorry as you that things can't be mended between them. I don't condone divorce easily, Dee. How many times have I told you that one of our main strengths through the years has been our sense of continuity as a family? But I'm convinced that in your parents' case divorce is the only way.'

'What about her children . . . me?'

'Leaving your father doesn't mean your mother loves you

less. Perhaps she'll love you even more, if that's possible – or at least she will need you more.'

'She has someone,' Deborah reminded him, in a bitter tone.

'Perhaps that will last, perhaps not. But your mother has had disappointments in her life, and a good deal of sadness.'

'Uncle Edgar?'

He nodded. 'I think she's entitled to some peace now, and some happiness.'

Some of Deborah's anger was ebbing. 'What do you think of him?'

'Rowell? I have nothing against the man. Tough in business, but then all good merchant bankers are. If she's happy with him –'

'Why couldn't she be happy alone with me?' Deborah exclaimed in anguish. 'I was happy with her.'

Samuel's eyebrows lifted helplessly. 'It sounds so simple to a child. But adults – all animals, not just people – need to pair off. That urge is as basic as eating. Something within us seems incomplete when we're alone, happy when we're coupled with another. But we don't give up loving our offspring. Dee, I've spoken to your mother several times by phone since we've been away, and she misses you enormously. Your welfare throughout this trying period has always been of paramount importance to her.'

Deborah's expression was no longer stormy. She was watching him, assessing his statements one by one. Then she looked away, at the wake spreading out from the ship until it was lost in the dark sea like a rumour.

'Another letter came for you today,' Samuel finally said. 'And a telegram came as well.' He handed them to her.

She took them and let her gaze linger on the open telegram. Her mother was distressed because she hadn't had an answer from Dee to any of her letters. The girl's face grew concerned, and she stood up.

'It's getting a bit chilly, Grandfather. I think I'll go below. Perhaps write a few letters home.'

She kissed him tenderly on the cheek and then hugged him tightly.

'Give my love, won't you?' he said as she separated from him.

'It's late now, but perhaps in the morning . . . might I use the radio telephone?'

Samuel nodded, smiling, and watched his granddaughter's erect figure recede across the deck.

Samuel sat up late into the night staring at the sea from his high-backed chair.

His face bore such a serene expression that neither his valet nor the steward wanted to take the responsibility of reminding him how late the hour had grown.

Finally, his valet ventured to attract his employer's attention. Only when Samuel failed to respond to the murmured whispers did the servant realize that the pallor on the old man's face was not a reflection of the moon's pale light, but that Lord Kronengold was dead.

CHAPTER EIGHT

Madeleine came fully awake a few moments after she had stretched her arm across the bed and found the other side empty.

'Rob?' she called out, and her eyelids opened. Then she remembered that he had kissed her on the cheek during some earlier, hazy part of the morning and said he was driving into the village for a newspaper and some items on the grocery list. He'd be returning soon. She sat up and ran a hand through her tousled hair. She had slept naked beneath the sheet and the thick eiderdown, but she had installed a new oil furnace when she bought the cottage, so the room was cozily warm despite the snow on the ground outside.

Madeleine loved the cottage as if it were a person, and always experienced a surge of satisfaction when she viewed it after an absence or when, as now, she had just woken up in it. Large rooms. Other bedrooms for guests or the children. Oak floors. Solid wood tables and chests. Comfortable stuffed chairs and sofas, without a single French antique in the house.

She had picked out the cottage, bought it, and paid for it herself. Every other house she had ever lived in had been owned by others: father, husband, father-in-law. She rented the London house she now lived in, but this weekend cottage in Wiltshire was the first house that was really hers. No one knew her in this little bit of the countryside; the place had been purchased by her estate agent in another name. She and Rob could safely meet here each weekend, as they could not chance doing very often in their London houses or his own country house near Leslie.

She and Leslie had only very recently come to a tacit agreement. If he did not pry into her private life, she would not make an issue of his; the separation would be kept discreetly confidential, and they would put off for a while discussing a formal divorce. She and Rob had taken even greater pains to keep their love affair secret: every newspaper in the country would pounce on the story if word leaked out. She sensed that Leslie suspected she was having an affair, but probably didn't know with whom, as he had been perfectly civil to Rob during a bankers' luncheon. She herself had revealed it only to Samuel and, in a letter, to Deborah, and only because Samuel had informed her that her daughter's animosity towards her was due in large measure to already knowing about it. She had kept the knowledge of her love affair with Rob even from those few people who knew she was living apart from her husband: Vivienne, who was so indiscreet, and her brother, Pierre, who could become over-protectively critical, which was not what she needed at the moment.

Madeleine threw back the white satin cover and, ignoring the slippers placed by the bed, walked barefoot across the room to the lavatory. She was totally unselfconscious about her body now, and occasionally marvelled at the relaxation in herself. Before falling in love with Rob, she had never in her life gone to sleep without wearing a nightdress. Even after sex with Leslie she would conscientiously re-don the garment.

She stopped at the door to the bathroom to gaze through the wide windows on the far side of the living room. Beyond was an expanse of white with black details: black wire bushes and cast-iron trunks with ice-cream-ball tops, a marble concourse of white river beyond, black-hulled clouds bearing down upon the house like pirate ships. She smiled at the sense of emotional well-being she now felt, when the absence of it had been her greatest sadness before leaving Leslie.

How absurd to have fallen in love at my age, she thought, and she smiled again as she turned on the bath. The last months had been remarkable to Madeleine. She had not come apart without Leslie to lean on; she had managed her life quite well all round. There were long stretches of brooding loneliness, to be sure. And she was often beset by the dread that she would be forever estranged from her daughter, whom she missed very much. But Samuel had kept her advised of Deborah's activities and had held out the hope that Deborah would eventually reconcile herself to the new circumstances.

She waited a moment or two to accustom herself to the temperature and then lowered herself into the water. Her legs straightened. Her head tilted back until her neck was resting on the lip of the bath. There was a time, she remembered, when luxuriating purposelessly like this would have brought on pangs of guilt.

Like leaves breeze-wafted across the surface of a pond, thoughts of Rob eventually drifted to her. She loved him, and he had been good for her in many ways. The most obvious was that he had unlocked the cell where her sensuality and so many previously unknown feelings had been imprisoned. But just as important had been the effect on her of independence; she sensed that he was repelled by women who tried to draw their strength from him, which helped her to fight that inclination in herself.

A problem was his very British reserve about his feelings and concerns. He had seemed so open at first but, as they spent more time together, she perceived that he revealed only superficialities about himself, just as Leslie did, the polite conversation of good acquaintances; a bit more intimate perhaps, but not nearly enough to overcome her wariness and let her begin to think about marriage. And something else: she suspected that his courtesy and his genuine fondness for her – expressed in small, tender ways – hid from view, perhaps even from his own, a very selfish side. She had no proof for that suspicion and, in fact, tended to reprove herself for her distrust. She would learn the truth about him in time, she reasoned, and was in no rush; there were so many truths about herself she needed to discover first.

She was rinsing herself when the telephone rang. She jumped. The telephone had never rung before. Only Irma, her maid, had the number. And only for emergencies. She threw a towel around her as she ran to the kitchen.

The sky had been darkening all morning. The grey-black clouds were unnaturally white at the edges. So was the snow that blanketed the ground. Expecting more snow, Rob had not dallied in the village. He was turning into the driveway in the old estate car Madeleine had bought so as not to attract attention to themselves in the village when he heard the telephone ring inside the cottage. He knew what the telephone call would be about. He had seen the front-page story when buying the Sunday newspaper. He lifted the groceries and picked the newspaper up from the seat. The fourth ring was interrupted as he entered the cottage.

'Oh, God, no!' Madeleine cried out into the receiver. She sank onto the wooden chair beside the kitchen table. 'What did she say?' She listened, her free hand clapped to her cheek. Then she murmured, 'Let me get a piece of paper.'

Rob handed her a pen and the newspaper. She wrote along a border.

'I'll be there,' she said when she had finished writing. 'Tell them that if they call back. What did my daughter say? Tell me again.'

She closed her eyes, listening with greater concentration, then nodded her confirmation. 'We'll leave right away.'

She replaced the receiver and looked up.

'Samuel died last night.'

Rob nodded and opened the folded newspaper. A photograph and a story filled the left-hand side of the page with a prominent headline: LORD KRONENGOLD, 73, DIES AT SEA.

Madeleine felt numb. She tried to read the smaller print, but it oscillated wildly. 'His secretary and Dee rang my house from Madrid airport. They flew there on the yacht's plane with Samuel's body. They're about to get on a plane to London. My maid spoke to her. She said Dee's voice wasn't very steady. Dee wanted to speak to me, but it had taken them a long time to get a call through to London. They didn't have time to try me here.'

Madeleine faltered; remorse at not being by the telephone for her daughter sprang at her, as if from an ambush.

'What time are they arriving?' Rob prompted.

'I wrote down all the information. Dee wants me to meet the plane when it gets in.'

Madeleine stared at Samuel's newspaper photograph, which was several years old. The full black eyebrows were bunched like fists, emphasizing his indomitability.

'He was well. He told me on the phone that a Swiss specialist had seen him recently and said he was well.' She fell silent.

'He wasn't a young man, Maddy.'

'But he was well,' she repeated, as if that truth would resurrect him by proving his death a divine error. 'He was well. He told me.'

Her eyes began to fill with tears. 'I really loved him, Rob. Some people said he was high-handed. But there was a . . . an integrity to him. I could always count on him. He never said one thing and did another. He was my friend, not just my father-in-law. I'm his executor, you know.'

'Not Leslie?' Rob replied with surprise.

Madeleine's thoughts were already elsewhere. 'Dee must be shattered. She was close to him, so close.' Tears began to trickle down her cheeks. 'My poor baby! This too, this too.'

Rob felt at a loss to comfort her, and he wanted to very much. At moments like these he loved her so intensely – and was quite proud of being able to. He had seduced other men's wives before, occasionally considering himself a bit of a bounder for feeling only the satisfaction of a good kill and not something more, particularly in the face of the woman's often gushing sentimentality about the act. His love for Madeleine, in a sense, validated his own self-esteem.

He put his hand on her shoulder for lack of any words that might help. She buried her head in his shirt and wept. Finally he said, 'Get dressed. I'll put away the estate car and take out the Rolls and then lock up.'

She pulled away and nodded. Then she dried her face on the towel and stood up. 'We've got to hurry,' she agreed, and began walking to the bedroom. Then, halting in mid-stride, she turned back.

'It's an odd little irony. All his life he avoided modern vehicles whenever he could. Didn't feel safe in them. Now, today, is his first time in an aeroplane.' She sighed and continued to the bedroom.

They had driven into the heavily falling snow as if into a white room. Rob concentrated on the hedges at the borders of the snow-covered road, trying to centre the car, trying not to miss any of the turn-offs. He enjoyed the feeling of being temporarily protective of Madeleine. These weekends with her had been a haven from the unceasing tempest of his business problems. So much of the Rowell bank's overseas assets had been in Egypt. The Suez crisis had given Nasser the excuse to expropriate the Rowells' Egyptian bank branch and its assets, their factories, their hotel. Rob's hands tightened around the steering wheel. His merchant bank in London had borrowed up to the hilt and was still desperately short of money. He had kept his concern from Maddy, somewhat ashamed of himself for not being more prudent. After all, she was a Kronengold. But who would have thought there'd ever be problems in Egypt, of all places? The Middle East was practically Britain's backyard. The Rowell bank's involvement there went back over a century; he had as many Arab friends as

English. He had thought of seeking Lebanese or Saudi money to prop himself up for a while, but they might want a share of the bank in return. He reminded himself gloomily that he soon might have no other choice. Then an idea occurred to him.

'You said a while ago that Samuel had appointed you his executor. Isn't that a bit odd?'

'A bit, I suppose,' she replied after a pause.

Rob could sense her reluctance to explain and did not pursue the topic, merely noting to himself that she might be a new and promising source of capital. After a few minutes Madeleine spoke again.

'Can't we go any faster, Rob?'

'This bloody snow!'

She looked at her wristwatch. 'We're crawling. I've got to be waiting for her when the plane lands.'

Rob pressed harder on the accelerator.

'She asked for me, Rob. That had to mean something. How ghastly it must have been for her, alone with Samuel's coffin on that plane. She's so young.'

'The secretary is with her.'

'No, I mean someone she loves. That's why she wants me at the airport. Don't you see?'

Madeleine lapsed into a less agitated silence. Samuel's death would now aggravate her relationship with Leslie, but it would also give her the leverage to obtain an equitable parting from him – and, more important, protection for Deborah. A year ago she might have wondered whether she was strong enough to guide Samuel's affairs for the next ten years, until Deborah was of age and could take her rightful place as head of the Kronengold bank and the holding company. Now she did not.

'That's it up ahead,' she pointed out.

Rob turned onto the main road.

'It should be easier now,' he said. 'They probably plough this road.'

He leaned forward to get a better view between the windscreen wipers cleaning snow from the glass, and then he increased the car's speed.

'The visibility's bloody awful, Maddy.'

'Will the airport be open?'

'They can usually keep the runways free of snow for a few

hours.' He patted her hand on the seat beside him.

He did not see the curve in the road. Or, until it was too late, the large truck with the snowplough snout that suddenly loomed up in front of them.

He twisted the steering wheel and braked. The car careered to the right in a skidding spin. Madeleine's door smashed against the side edge of the plough. The hardened steel cut through the Rolls like a knife and crushed Madeleine's body.

The hospital was very near, but Rob, cradling her in a blanket in the truck, knew that it did not matter. Although attendants and nurses wheeled her quickly towards an operating theatre, and doctors alongside hurriedly covered her face with an oxygen mask, injected chemicals into her, inserted in her arms tubes connected to bottles of blood, pressed frantically on her dented-in chest – Rob knew he was watching a futile dumb show performed out of habit. She had left him already, amid the swirling whiteness.

His small suitcase beside him, Rob sat docilely on the bench in the emergency room, trying to come to grips with the finality of what had happened. The moments with her had always seemed luminous, because *she* was luminous – fresh and spontaneous and always so alive. He tried to summon up vivid recollections of her, so as to hold onto her and to delay his acceptance of the unalterability of her death, but all he could visualize was the angel-perfect profile resting against the black half-moon of steel that had sliced through the white Rolls.

Even in his distraught condition, he could not evade the knowledge that he had been the cause of her death, but he assured himself that no one could hold him responsible; with weather conditions so deplorable, it was true only in the technical sense that he had been at the wheel.

He sat up straight. At the wheel! If the police found out that he and Madeleine de Kronengold had been together in a car travelling back from her country house, the reporters would learn about their affair as well. Lurid stories would smear the two of them across every newspaper in England. There might even be speculation as to whether there had been some negligence involved in the accident. The publicity would be ghastly for him, for Maddy's family, and especially for the Rowell bank, which was shaky enough as it was. And it would all be quite unnecessary. She was dead, and none of this would bring her back; if it could, he told himself, he would gladly endure it all.

At that moment a nurse approached him diffidently, carrying the forms that would have to be filled out. She appeared to be young and unsure of herself. He gave her a sad but engaging smile. Yes, he was sufficiently recovered to answer some questions for the hospital's records. He took her hand so she could not write, gazed into her eyes, and began to relate a tragic story of love found and lost, a poignant affair between two members of the nobility, one a prominent banker, the other a married woman from a prominent banking family.

After a while he confided how much being able to tell her about his loss comforted him. And later he explained that it would be so much kinder to the dead woman's family to leave his name out of the reports. He had been in the back seat asleep when it happened, he told her. He supposed the force of the skid had thrown her across the front seat, to the other side of the car, where the crash killed her. Under those circumstances it wasn't absolutely necessary to write down he was also in the car, was it? For the sake of the woman's grieving husband and children, he would be eternally grateful to her if she spared them by leaving his name out of the reports. They've already suffered so much. He pointed to a newspaper front page announcing Samuel's death. Someone had left it on a chair.

She withdrew her hand from his and fumbled in her pocket for a handkerchief. She nodded. She would do it.

The answering thankfulness on his face was authentic; her report raised no questions, no one would look further into the matter. He took her telephone number; he would like to be able to thank her properly some time very soon. Dabbing her eyes, she smiled and began to write her report.

Afterwards, Rob went through Maddy's handbag, which he had been holding, to make certain it contained nothing that might link the two of them. Her small red address book was the only incriminating item. And then he remembered that, when she had wanted to remove jewellery from her wall safe one evening, she had looked in the back of the address book for the combination.

When the snow stopped falling, he paid someone to drive him into London, to Madeleine's house.

* * *

The long funeral cortège crawled into the cemetery like a black caterpillar. The first hearse bore Samuel's body, the second Madeleine's. The third car carried Leslie, Richard, and Deborah.

Leslie had been so shocked by the near-simultaneous deaths of his father and his wife that it was some time before he realized that he didn't mourn either of them. Rather, he was elated: all his irritants had been removed at once. With his father gone, he was now subordinate to no one, and controlled a vast enterprise. With Maddy gone, so was the risk of humiliation he feared. Beneath a drawn, grieving expression, he was already making plans.

Richard had always taken for granted his mother's love for him; as a child he had been dependent upon her as a refuge from his father's severity. He knew he should be unhappy at losing her, but instead he felt relieved. The events of the previous year had changed so much: his father had become the protector and his mother the scourge and, later, in his own mind, the constant rebuke for his deceit. He felt relief at his grandfather's death as well, although not nearly to the same degree; in twice rejecting him for Dee, in having so little to do with him, his grandfather had also been a reminder that he had not measured up. So he sat in the car and looked out at the bleak day and the snow covering everything and thought about other things.

Only Deborah felt sorrow, a misery almost unendurable; it seemed to fill the sky and press all that weight down on her. Her grief was worsened by the thought that her mother had died falsely believing her daughter still hated her. Since learning of her mother's death, Deborah's guilt had grown to monstrous size, proliferating within her until it was a condemning jury. At the same time she was beset by another guilt, irrational and, thus, much more dreadful. Not only had the two people she loved the most died and left her alone in the world forever, but she feared they had died *because* she loved them. To love people was to lose them, to be abandoned by them. And her loving, emanating from a black magic within her she could not control, might even be the cause; that was the irrational, the unspeakably terrifying part. But the proof was the letter in her pocket, written too recently for her to have sent: her mother had been alive until Deborah had written to declare her love, and her grandfather had been well.

She stood inside the huge stone mausoleum, rectangular compartments lining the walls from floor to ceiling, some open, some filled and walled off, and watched the two coffins being slipped into adjoining niches separated only by the gap, the bridge, of Edgar's resting place. She wept for her mother, who had loved her, for her grandfather, who had loved her, and for herself, who had doomed them when she loved them back.

A plaque high on the wall caught Deborah's eye: INFANT DAUGHTER OF LESLIE AND MADELEINE DE KRONENGOLD. It gave the date in the spring of 1945 when she was born and died. The little girl who had no name! Deborah gasped, but the sound was mistaken for a sob and no one noticed. The guilt that had been an inner jury became executioners shouting her crimes as they stoned: You stole her place and put her here! You took for yourself all the love that was rightly hers. As surely as if you had killed her! *Your very desires can kill!*

Nathan, beside her, grasped her hand in his, and his rough brown monk's robe scratched her inner wrist with the balm of welcome punishment. Although it might have seemed incongruous to the many people spilling out past the open bronze doors like a dark liquid, none in the family thought so when Nathan's strong baritone rang out mournfully among the others who chanted kaddish, the Hebrew prayer for the dead.

At the end of the burial service, Deborah withdrew her hand. And, although she sensed her uncle Pierre's eyes on her, she did not dare meet them. She feared the lethal power of her love.

Rob Rowell stood at the rear of the large crowd gathered to pay their last respects to England's most powerful banker, a popular figure, and to a woman born to extraordinary privilege of whom many were deeply fond. Rowell's son Bash, now a tall, handsome fourteen-year-old who was home from boarding school, stood beside him. The suddenness of Madeleine's death and his own despondency had left Rob with the need for this formal parting. No one could question his being here, especially with his son. Had he not loved Madeleine, they would still have attended because of a business and social relationship with the Kronengolds. But Rob was also there for reasons of self-interest.

The mourners parted to permit the family a path to their

cars. Leslie and his brother Charles, and Pierre and their families walked slowly down the grass slope, stopping to accept condolences and greet old friends. As Leslie turned away from the last handshake to walk the final yards to his car, Rob stepped away from his son to block Leslie's progress. Bash nodded an embarrassed sadness at Deborah, several steps behind. Since the previous summer he had shot up to his father's height. The resemblance at first sight was too close to bear. She turned away. Leslie extended his hand to Rob, but the other man did not take it.

'I have Samuel's and Madeleine's signed wills,' Rob said quietly. 'I'll be waiting at my house for you.' Rob spun on his heel and strode away, his son following – others were coming towards them.

Rob was far away when the implication of what he had said registered on Leslie. Rob must be the man having an affair with Maddy! All those long summer walks when she had gone off alone at Clove Hill! And now this declaration that he had possession of the wills. Rage boiled within Leslie. The man had humiliated him by sleeping with Maddy, by poaching on his own territory, and now he was trying somehow to hold him for ransom. But how could he have obtained the wills? He might have Maddy's but certainly not Samuel's.

Leslie took the precaution of finding Percy Grayson among the mourners, but the solicitor confirmed his worst fears. Samuel had executed a new will before going abroad, which he had not given Grayson to hold. In that will he had left nearly everything to Deborah.

Rob opened the front door himself; he had purposely given his butler the afternoon off, and Bash was in his rooms. The two men stared at each other for several seconds, each taking the measure of the other. Both were over six feet tall, Leslie an inch or so taller. Leslie had larger, more prominent features, dark hair, strong chin and nose. Rob's face was classically handsome, his hair fair. But they shared the self-confidence of their class, the habit of imperturbability.

Rob merely said, 'Won't you come in?' and Leslie followed him to a wood-panelled study. The curtains had been drawn to shield the room from outside view, and the lights turned on. Rob gestured to a seat on one side of a wide desk. He took the chair on the other. He opened the centre drawer and withdrew a folder. Inside were two documents, which he handed to Leslie.

'They're photostats of Samuel's will and Madeleine's will. I am in possession of both originals.'

Leslie glanced sharply at the other man, then took the documents and began to read.

Nearly ten minutes passed before he looked up from them. He was shaken.

'Where did you get these?'

'It doesn't matter. I have them.'

'You were having an affair with my wife!' Leslie exclaimed furiously.

'She's dead, Leslie. It's too late for blame to be laid.'

'Not a particularly felicitous phrase under the circumstances.' Leslie glanced down at the wills in his hand. 'What do you want for them?'

Rob shrugged thoughtfully. 'I assume you'll want to destroy them when you get your hands on them. Samuel's clearly cuts you out of all but a relatively small bequest. Nearly everything goes to your daughter, Deborah. Madeleine's will also makes Deborah a major beneficiary –'

'I understand their implications,' Leslie interrupted abruptly. How right he had been to fear Deborah's presence in his house!

Rob was in no hurry. 'Were earlier wills executed in your favour? Those wills would take effect if no one knew about these.'

'My father signed one last summer. It's in the solicitor's safe.'

'Fortunately, this one isn't.' Rob paused for a moment of thought. 'One would gather from the discrepancy that, although your father retained only John Grayson until John died, he did not completely trust his son Percy. You and Percy were at school together?'

'We're close friends, yes.'

'And the Kronengold bank probably accounts for three-quarters of the firm's business. There should be no problem about his suffering a lapse of memory over this new will.'

'What do you want?' Leslie repeated, then regretted revealing his nervousness. 'Well, blast it, man, we both know I want them.'

'As I read Madeleine's will, her property consisted of bank

accounts, her country home and furniture, her clothes . . . and the jewellery, cash, and bearer bonds that used to be in her safe. Without a will, no one would miss the jewellery, the cash, or the bonds, particularly if the courts named you as administrator of your loving wife's estate. Her London house was rented, so they need not even know you two lived apart.'

'How much would you estimate those "non-existent" items you wish to keep are worth?'

'A million and a half to two million pounds. Maybe more.'

Leslie's face reddened with indignation. But Rob spoke again before Leslie could open his mouth.

'However, that's a good deal less than I reckon Samuel's estate will be worth.' He watched until Leslie's expression displayed comprehension, then added, 'Fifty or maybe a hundred times less. To you – not your daughter.'

Leslie examined the knuckles of his hands clasped in his lap. By refusing this agreement with Rowell, he ended up with very little; nearly all went to Deborah. This other way Rowell got a bit that had been left to the children, but he himself won the jackpot that was rightfully his. Leslie raised his eyes.

'Agreed,' he said.

Rob extracted another document from the centre drawer, a general release of any claims against himself for any act done or property taken belonging to the Kronengolds in connection with both wills turned over to Leslie. He handed it to Leslie, who signed and returned it. Rob unlocked a side drawer. He put the general release into it and removed two envelopes. Inside each was an original will bound by a white backing and sealed. He re-locked the drawer and then handed both envelopes to Leslie.

'What you do with them is your own affair.'

Leslie slipped them into his inner jacket pocket, hesitated an instant, and then left the room. He had wanted to declare his anger at Rob's despicable behaviour but, now that they had become conspirators, that did not seem to have much point.

When he heard the front door close, Rob took the general release from the side drawer and went to his own wall safe, behind a portrait of his great-grandfather, the third Earl. He dialled the combination, opened the steel door, and placed the document in the safe beside Madeleine's property. As a precaution, in case some day he had to defend himself, the safe also contained a duplicate photostat of Maddy's will because it listed the property that Leslie had agreed to his taking.

Deborah sat dutifully at the end of the tapestry-covered sofa, occasionally acknowledging the sympathy of uncles, aunts, and cousins. Malcolm and Lavinia told her to be brave, that things would not look so bad tomorrow. Aunt Simone, Pierre's wife, said how sorry she was, but nothing more; Deborah sensed herself resented for having been proved innocent of smashing the Stradivarius, at the expense of Simone's son, Gilbert. Aunt Cora, Charles's wife, a sweet little partridge of a woman, held Deborah's hand and clucked her grief over Madeleine's death. She had sincerely loved her sister-in-law, her lone friend and ally in an extremely intimidating family. Deborah, she declared sincerely, was welcome to come and stay at any time; her little cousins were so fond of her; everyone was so fond of her. Cora fell to sobbing and was compelled to go off by herself to a chair in the corner to recover.

Deborah had cried endlessly in the days just past; she did not cry now. If there were any tears left, she would shed them only when she was alone; she had learned the cost of vulnerability. After a decent stay in the drawing room, she rose and went to her room. Pierre followed her out. He had been awaiting an opportunity to speak with her alone.

She was sitting sideways on the window seat, knees tucked up under her chin, eyes fixed on the floral upholstery patterns, when he poked his head into the room. She smiled briefly to let him know she was pleased to see him, and he entered and took the space at the other end of the window seat.

Pierre gazed at Deborah's bereft, luminous face. He felt as if he was viewing a motion picture in which only sections of film remained: the baby gurgling happily in her crib became a child toddling across a room became the little girl distraught at learning of her adoption became the eight-year-old picking apples with him in the English countryside became the older girl he had gone rowing with at Valtary last summer became the near adolescent now huddled across from him, forlorn on the window seat and yet still very beautiful, the reed-thinness of childhood departing. He yearned to see her as a grown young woman, whirling at a ball perhaps, full of joy once more. When he had brought her to this home where she would be loved, he believed he was offering the infant child a life of happiness. And he had, he was sure – had made her happy and his sister happy, had even made Samuel happy. But that act had also made him responsible for what had happened to her there. He wasn't God, who could guarantee eternity for her, but he ached as if the deaths had been his failure.

'Have you ever been to a funeral before?' he asked, by way of something to start with.

'Grand'mère's.'

'Yes, of course. But your mother's death is different, isn't it? At your age she was half your world. Your grandfather, too, was so close to you. You can't replace that kind of love in your life very easily. But I want you to know that I am always there for you if you need me, for whatever you want. I love you very much also. Because I brought you here' – his gaze dropped shyly as he spoke that phrase he was sure must embarrass her – 'I consider myself more than an uncle or godfather – a friend always, if you want one.'

Tears began to push into her eyes. She looked out of the window. Nathan's tall, robed figure, arms swinging, was just turning into the gate. He had gone to church to say a prayer for her mother's and grandfather's souls and was just returning. Doubtless he would also soon come upstairs to see her. She had his love, too, she knew.

But every fibre of her being, trained to near-instinct reaction by the experiences of her short life, cried out to her that she could really rely, in the end, only on herself. And that, if she let herself love and need others, she would doom them, too. Love and death, need and loss, were now so tangled in her mind that she feared the consequences of even a word of gratitude for her uncle's kindness.

After a minute or two of silence, Pierre stood up and then bent over and kissed the top of her head. Only after he left the room did she let the tears come again.

The next day Percy Grayson read Samuel's will to the adults in the family. Ordinarily, a distant cousin like Pierre would not have been invited to hear matters so private to the British family, but Pierre was Madeleine's brother and had expressed concern that Madeleine's children receive any legacies left to them. Leslie wanted Pierre to harbour no suspicions that would provoke him to investigate. Samuel's will being read was, of course, the earlier one made in favour of Leslie. The later one, in favour of Deborah, had been destroyed. Grayson kept silent about the matter; retaining the bank as a client was far more advantageous to him than mock heroics.

Grayson then announced that Madeleine had died intestate. They would keep searching for a will, but, in the probable eventuality that none was found, her estate would be distributed in accordance with law, among her husband and children. Leslie declared that he had no desire to inherit his wife's property. He would seek to be appointed administrator by the courts and would divide Madeleine's estate between her children.

Pierre spoke privately to Leslie before departing with Simone for Paris and was assured again that he need have no fear about the children's welfare. Regardless of the unpleasantness between Maddy and himself these last months, Leslie averred that she had always been an excellent mother; he knew that it would be difficult to fill both his own place and Maddy's in the children's lives, but he would try his utmost to do so. Because of Deborah's tender age and the closeness of her relationship to her mother, he would have to devote himself intensively to her welfare in the months and years ahead.

Leslie sounded so concerned and compassionate as he spoke those words that Pierre was swayed. When Leslie apologized for the mix-up over the broken violin and ascribed it to his own emotionally overwrought state at the time – caused by the worsening relationship with Madeleine – Pierre forgave him. He would always be a bit wary about Leslie, but he no longer doubted his brother-in-law's sincerity. They parted better friends after Madeleine's death than they had been before it.

Deborah spent that afternoon at Vivenne's house. She needed both Vivienne's rough good-heartedness and April's company. April had come down from school for the funeral and would be going back tomorrow. Like Vivienne, April would always be there, Deborah knew, when she needed her.

Upon returning home, Deborah sought out her father. She

wanted to discuss her future plans.

Leslie was, in fact, feeling quite benevolent towards his daughter. Now there was no longer a chance she could threaten his patrimony, he could afford the generosity of solicitude for her welfare. She was a very pretty child, he thought, as she stood before him, and really quite quick and bright. He, too, had been thinking about her future; it was time she went away to school. With Maddy no longer alive, indeed it was a necessity.

'Dee, I'm glad you're here. I've been meaning to speak to you. I consider it time we chose a boarding school for you.'

'I agree, Father.'

He had already decided to use whatever remained of Madeleine's estate to pay for the children's education. 'I thought Lakeley. It's the top girls' school, I understand. You'll have to take exams. And they may baulk at accepting you in mid-term. But, in light of your mother's death, and perhaps of a contribution to the school, they will doubtless make an exception.'

'I don't think so.'

'I'm sure they bend the rules a bit in cases like yours.'

'I mean I don't think I'll go to Lakeley.'

Deborah's quiet firmness gave him pause. 'Why not?'

'April is at Branton.'

'Out of the question.' His distaste for Vivienne had grown over the years. He saw no reason for the relationship with her and her daughter to continue, and every reason why it should not.

'Father, you want me at boarding school. I will only go to Branton.'

Her tone was neither arrogant nor demanding, Lesie noted. It conveyed, rather, something much more menacing – uncompromising determination to have her way. His first inclination was to refuse, and force her to accept his choice. But at this moment, with the critical matter of the inheritance still fresh in people's minds, he did not dare risk it.

'All right. If that's what you want,' he assented amiably.

'Thank you, Father. One more thing. I would like to be in April's form. She's a year older, but we seem to be doing the same work.'

'That, of course, is up to the school.'

'It will help if you talk to them, I'm sure,' she said, and then, 'May I be excused?'

Leslie nodded and watched her leave the room, straight-backed, sure of herself. For the first time, with nothing at stake, he was able to admit the astuteness of Samuel's evaluation of her. She had a will of steel. As she had always been before, so she would always remain: a living reproach to him – and a threat.

CHAPTER NINE

In 1957, after succeeding an ill and unpopular Anthony Eden as prime minister, Harold Macmillan told the British people, 'You've never had it so good.' The model Edwardian patrician, scholar, and politician, Macmillan came to power at a favourable time. The Western world's economies were thriving, and Britain was experiencing a consumer boom that gave people a false sense of optimism. Everyone, from the lowest-paid worker up, seemed to be better off. With a deft hand now at the wheel, Britain seemed to be sailing jauntily before a fair breeze at last. Amid the general euphoria, few stopped to notice that indolence had permitted worms to eat through her ancient hull; or that everyone aboard, while thrilled by the craft's shiny new fittings, had a different idea of where it was heading.

Leslie de Kronengold's accession to his father's title, property, and position as head of British Kronengold Holdings Ltd and its subsidiary, the illustrious merchant bank I. Kronengold & Sons, appeared to many symbolic of the bright new age now dawning. Samuel had been born in the 1880s. The son was not yet forty. One was a product of the steam age, the other of the atomic age. Leslie himself was swept up in the general exhilaration engendered by the run of prosperous years, the newspaper stories praising him, and the flattery of those around him. New thinking was needed for these times: scientific thinking, analytical principles applied to the banking process.

Leslie's initial moves were decisive and typical. Convinced both of Britain's imminent promise and of the erratic foolishness of his father's new foreign investments, burdened with crushing death duties that had to be paid, he took steps to put the Kronengold affairs in order. Rather than show cowardice by divesting himself of his British interests, Leslie thought he was doing both the patriotic and the shrewd thing by backing out of those foreign deals not yet consummated and selling his firm's interest in most of those that had already been sealed. Those investments included land on the Mediterranean that would one day sell for a square foot what Samuel had paid for an acre; a large block of stock in a drug company soon to announce a birth-control pill; majority holdings in three small companies engaged in various advanced electronics technologies that would eventually put them in the forefront of their fields; and, when many thought the civil unrest in the Congo that year might spread south, much of the stock acquired in the merger Samuel had just arranged for British Springbok Mining with several other South African gold-mining companies.

When an outspoken partner objected to the way Leslie insisted on running either the family's holding company, of which he was by far the largest shareholder, or its subsidiary merchant bank, Leslie irately refused to budge. In the first weeks of his tenure, he dismissed the bank executives most relied on by his father, those who would certainly have argued against his shortsighted moves. He wanted blind loyalty, no dissent, and no comparisons made to his predecessor. New people were taken on, but at each tremor of the economy – and they soon began to come more frequently – management grew a little more cautious and shrank the bank's perimeter just a bit more.

Gradually, the character of Kronengold assets began to resemble the personality of the man in charge of them: defensive, plodding, unrealistic, and uninspired – like many other British enterprises, running the old course in new clothes. One or two newcomers, like the Blaustein bank, and a few of the old merchant banks did a good deal better than simply survive with a bit of profit at the year's end. One of the latter was Rowell & Co. Because of his unpleasant personal history with the head of that bank, Leslie did as little business with it as possible. From a purely banking standpoint, he considered it and the others the toffs and touts of the banking world, just a bit too showy to be sound. Bright young people were rising to partnerships in the other firms, but there was much to be said, Leslie reasoned, for being able to telephone the Kronengold bank, ask for a partner, and talk to a Kronengold. Leslie considered himself, and so did most others, a highly responsible banker.

⋆ ⋆ ⋆

Deborah's first year at boarding school was the most painful. By the summer the numbness had worn off, and Deborah was overcome by feelings of loss, loneliness, and guilt. So much of her life had been spent in the company of Samuel and Madeleine, and so much of the love showered on her had come from them, that she felt adrift, abandoned. She would often dream of them at night and wake happily in the morning to discover the cruel hoax she had played on herself. With the intuitive sensitivity of a child for another's need, April tried to spend all her free time with her friend, so as to be there if Deborah wanted to talk about her despondency.

What Deborah was unable to express, and painfully endured in silence, were the spurs growing aberrantly into her psyche. She had no right to her own past – even her Kronengold identity was borrowed. The inner frustration built up and then erupted in episodes of towering, if unexplainable, rage, allowing anger, at least, to find release. Her sadness and her guilt found none; they crushed her.

Grandfather had been an old man, and perhaps, although she was not sure, she could have done nothing to prevent his death. But her telephone call when changing planes in Madrid had summoned her mother to the airport. That request had resulted in Madeleine's death, and Deborah suffered agonies of self-recrimination. If only she had not telephoned. . . . If only she had not then left a message when she could not reach her mother. . . . If only she had first asked the maid who answered what the weather was like in England. . . .

Her mother had died, Deborah assumed, without knowing that her daughter loved her – before Deborah could post her letter or had spoken to her. That unrepaired causeway lay across the treacherous narrows that separated Deborah from her future and kept her stalled in a rueful past. Over and over again Deborah recalled her antipathy to her mother's love affair and castigated herself for the pain her resentment had needlessly caused Madeleine.

She now thought of herself as a child who, once upon a time, had suddenly appeared on earth out of nowhere, trailing death behind her. Her murdering touch had wreaked retribution on two mothers foolish enough to love her, and now, perversely, on herself for daring to believe she was entitled to give and receive love.

Unnerved by the enormity of her villainy, too young to comprehend the arbitrariness of catastrophe, Deborah felt herself tumbling through a minatory chaos; the substitute parents, grandfather, grandmother, uncles, aunts, and home that capricious good fortune had provided were slippery toeholds that had suddenly, because of her wickedness, given way beneath her. Fearing she would tumble endlessly, she determined to expiate her sin and rescue herself by vigilant, diligent adherence to the mandates of school life. She would win the admiration of one and all by the intensity of her sincerity, the depth of her goodness. She would regain the love snatched from her. She would be the best. She would succeed at everything.

She had always studied hard. At boarding school she worked twice as hard, pursuing academic achievement as a means of proving to some unseen divine magistrate that she was worthy of being loved. Although she became captain of games in her final year, and was top of her class academically, she was not made head girl, losing to an excellent student whose insipidity was taken to be unplumbed English character. April angrily maintained that Deborah's Jewish family background had hurt her chances, which surprised Deborah, because she had almost ceased to think of herself as Jewish. She attended chapel, sang the hymns (which she thought of as a sort of folk song), and listened to sermons with no more, no less, attention than any of the other girls, envisaging Jesus as a kindly fairy-tale character along the lines of Father Christmas. The fact of her adoption meant that she could have been Christian – for, despite Uncle Pierre's bid to pacify the doubts raised by her mother's gold cross, it loomed as large in her private evaluation as her rearing in a Jewish home. And even if her birth mother *was* Jewish, as the doctor who delivered her suspected, her birth father could have been Christian, or anything. She decided she had failed to become head girl because hard work could not gloss over her failure to scrub out all her faults. Perhaps if she had worked even harder. . . .

The letter from Prinsworth, one of the women's colleges at Oxford, helped her thrust much of the self-doubt behind her. On the basis of competitive exams and an interview, they had offered her a place and a scholarship. Deborah had always maintained that she wanted to follow in her family's footsteps at Cambridge and had told her friends at Branton that she would be wretched if her mother's old college there, Girton, turned her down and she had to go elsewhere. But, the moment the letter came from Oxford, she accepted, explaining that her changed mind resulted from her admiration for certain professors at Oxford and the Prinsworth tradition. The real reason was that she sensed self-sufficiency would come only if she made a clean break with her ghosts.

Throughout the years at Branton, April was her only true friend, closer than a sister could be. Together they cursed the cold, unheated rooms and the starchy foods and vile desserts like 'spotted dick' and 'dead man's leg'. They adored the same matrons and joined in their hatred for the cold-hearted Stackey, who insisted on patrolling the rooms afer lights-out during their fourth-form year. Deborah devoted hours to tutoring her friend, but always felt April endured the sessions more as an act of kindness towards Deborah's idiosyncrasy than because she found any value in education. She related to people, not ideas. No amount of history or Latin could ever shake her assurance that her purpose in life was to assume her proper place in English society. After leaving Branton she would have a carefree time at dances and parties and with amusing friends until she married a wealthy young nobleman from the same enclave of birth and privilege from which she had sprung.

Deborah left Branton Abbey in the winter of 1961. April was already preparing with her mother for her coming out in the spring. Deborah, who would be just seventeen – a year younger – was allowed by her father instead to spend the spring and summer taking courses at European universities with enough time for sightseeing. She would be taking some art courses – a subject that gave her great pleasure, but which she would not have time for at Oxford – while brushing up her languages. Leslie was pleased to find her enhancing those social graces considered essential for the not-too-distant time when he could rid himself of responsibility for her by arranging a marriage advantageous to the family's interests. Leslie did not express that last thought to his daughter, but if he had, she would have made no objection; a prime duty of women of her class, and in the world of the merchant bankers in particular, was to link powerful families by marriage. Any romantic notions that might have grown within her during adolescence had withered during the instant of revulsion at the cottage window. She had indulged in girlish talk of boys at school – indeed, it was April's favourite topic – but only as a social necessity. The thought of an intimate relationship with a man frightened her. But, if that was her duty, then she would grit her teeth and get on with it. The final act to prove her goodness would be to place her body and loyalties at the family's service, even if it meant risking childbirth, which had killed her natural mother and thus, she thought, might do the same to her.

Deborah had an ulterior reason for studying and travelling in Europe, one she was ashamed to admit even to April because it would have meant revealing that she was adopted. She had chosen to study for the first months in Italy in order to find out who her natural parents were – and maybe even locate her father. Although her mother was dead, her natural father might still be alive.

The very first Saturday in Milan, she left the family friends with whom she was staying and hired a car and chauffeur to drive her on the autostrada to Turin.

The trip proved to be thoroughly disheartening. There was no record of her birth in the municipal building in Turin where birth records were stored. A new abbess was in charge of the orphanage at the Convent of Santa Raffaella, not the woman Pierre had told her about. There was no record in their files of a female infant born in the spring of 1945 who might have been she. Having built up her hopes for so long, Deborah was grief-stricken, as if she had just learned of her natural parents' death, for to all intents she had. Also dead was a now forever undiscoverable part of herself.

Before leaving, she peeped into the nursery. Her heart ached for the babies. They were her brothers and sisters, related by lack of relationship to anyone else – a form of wasting death: never knowing where they had come from, never sure who they would be or where they had the right to go.

She pushed a large contribution into the slot in the oak box at the door and rode back to Milan wrapped in questions and in mourning. Oddly, however, that visit had a healthy effect on Deborah. She resolved that even the small part of her mind still fixed on what-might-have-been could not face backwards;

that way lay emotional disintegration. Survival depended on looking forwards. She spent a most pleasant summer holiday. In the autumn she went up to Oxford.

Deborah de Kronengold walked grimly along the High Street, barely exchanging a word with the shorter young woman beside her. They shared Miss Davis's tutorial on the history of economics and had not found a single matter on which they agreed since the term had started. Deborah had grown to her full five feet seven inches in height. Her red hair had lost none of its sunrise brightness and was still worn long and straight. She had finely fashioned features, a classic beauty that would have aroused admiration in any age, but today her chin thrust forward belligerently and her blue eyes glared in anger. The young woman who strode just as angrily beside her was Gladys Wood. Brown hair cut to utilitarian shortness, small, pretty face aggressively free of make-up, brow perpetually furrowed to match the disapproving line into which her mouth was drawn, Gladys Wood was a firmly committed Marxist. Deborah, of course, by both birth and inclination, was just as firmly committed a capitalist. Today Miss Davis had surprised them both by telling them they were very much alike; she had enjoyed their wrangles, but the debate was now tending to slip from the academic to the personal. She requested that they follow the ancient tradition of no work in the afternoon and do something frivolous together for a change. 'Like join the Bell Ringers Society?' Deborah had asked with some asperity, displeased at the prospect of having to spend her spare time with the doctrinaire fanatic with whom she shared the tutorial.

Upon learning that neither of these excessively serious young women had so much as had a meal out of hall since arriving at Prinsworth, Miss Davis had ordered them to spend the next week pursuing a social life – together. As a start they were to go out to lunch at a restaurant that very day.

Looking into the window of the restaurant, which had stood there for hundred of years, they both hesitated. Nearly all the tables were taken by male students.

'Looks intimidating,' Gladys breathed quietly.

'Rather.'

The women glanced at each other for support, then grinned at their common anxiety.

'Back-to-back, my dad always says,' Gladys offered.
'What does that mean?'
'If we fight with our backs to each other, they can't get behind us.'
Deborah nodded. 'Back-to-back it is, then.'
Gladys squared her shoulders determinedly and walked into the restaurant. Deborah followed.
'Zuleika Dobson, as I live and breathe!' a boisterous voice called out above the buzz of voices.
Other people looked up at them.
'Who's Zuleika Dobson?' Deborah whispered to Gladys.
'You. I'll explain later.'
A figure leaped up and strode towards them. 'Dee?'
The face looked vaguely familiar, like an impressionistic portrait of someone she couldn't quite place.
'Why – it's Bash Rowell, isn't it?' She smiled warmly. She had not seen him in years, since before her first term at Branton. He was tall, and he carried himself with the same casual grace she remembered from his boyhood. His hair was wavy blond, and a lock of it fell Byronically across his brow. His blue eyes were disquieting. She tried not to look into them, which was difficult, because they stared deeply into hers.
'I had no idea you had come up to Oxford, Dee. Please join us. There's almost never a table to be had in this bloody awful place. The food's ghastly, the prices are outrageous. But it's the place to go.'
Without waiting for an answer, he led the way back to a table in a corner of the room. Deborah shrugged apologetically to Gladys. 'There doesn't seem anything else available.'
'Your social life doesn't seem a problem to me,' Gladys replied with admiration.
'Childhood friend. Another exploiter of the masses, I'm afraid.'
'I'll look the other way in his case. He's gorgeous.'
Yes, he is, Deborah thought. Absolutely gorgeous. And then she knew why his eyes had bothered her so: they recalled his father's exactly when she had spied Rob Rowell kneeling over her mother in the cottage. For an instant she was tempted to flee, but decided it was brutishly unfair to hang the son for the sin of the father.

The two others lunching with Bash were, like him, at Christ Church, but all three usually lunched at this restaurant rather than at the House. One was named George; Deborah never heard his last name, but he laughed a lot and had broad shoulders that were clearly bent over oars a good part of the day in hopes of winning a place in the Oxford boat. The other young man was lightly olive-skinned and darkly moustachioed. The sharp features and arrogant stare gave him the look of a part-time stage magician, part-time hotel night clerk. His father's brother, it transpired, ruled a Middle Eastern country floating on a sea of oil. His family had done business with Rowell & Co. for generations. He spoke perfect upper-class English and was allowing Oxford to rub off on him for a year or two, although no one, himself and his tutors included, expected him to study. His name was Salim. He knew Deborah's father and had lunched at the bank, it seemed. A bottle of red wine stood on the table. Two more glasses were procured and filled.

Deborah eyed Gladys apprehensively, fearing a sudden humiliating explosion. But that abrasive young woman was speaking quite charmingly to Salim and George about a famous lecturer in moral philosophy who never seemed to get to the point.

For a few minutes Deborah and Bash chatted about mutual friends. She had been in Germany at the time, but knew he had gone to April's coming out dance. April was mad about Bash. Her letters to Deborah and, later, her conversation were dominated by her crush on him. But he seemed quite casual now when discussing *her*, and Deborah feared April was in for a drastic let-down.

Bash observed several young men staring at Deborah and remarked, 'You've really quite turned all the heads in here. Zuleika Dobson in the flesh.'

'That's all I've heard since walking in here. Who, in God's name, is Zuleika Dobson?'

'I presume you're not reading English Literature.' His smile lifted the right corner of his mouth, a mannerism she remembered from ten years earlier. 'She's fictional. Max Beerbohm made her up in a novel. Turned every head at Oxford, but she'd love no man foolish enough to love her in return. Since they all naturally loved her at first sight, she'd have none of them. During Eights Week every single undergraduate leapt into the Isis in a mass suicide. Quite romantic, don't you think?'

The ridicule in Bash Rowell's tone clearly implied a much more cynical view of the relations between men and women.

'Genocide always is,' she replied equally cynically.

'What *are* you reading?'

'Modern Greats.'

'Ah, Philosophy, Politics, and Economics, good old PPE. Economics, first and foremost, naturally.' She nodded. 'You, madam, are gazing upon a young man also engaged in the study of that dismal science by reason of family occupation. Cruelly, my father has just advised me that I am expected somehow to pass my Schools in June. I who am the envy of one and all for not having attended the opening of a single book or dallied away a single hour at a lecture in all my three years.' Theatrically, he raised his wine glass. 'I have drunk the cup of Oxford and have now reached the dregs. Even a fourth would be most welcome. I can't hope for a first – the blighters will expect me to know a bit in order to reel in a first, and even God's infinite mercy won't stretch that far. So I pray valiantly for the barely acceptable fourth. People grin slyly when you mention a fourth, knowing the hours of wenching, and drinking – and pure decadence – that are required for a fourth. Not a matter of a dull mind, simply a matter of choice. A second or third is always dubious.'

Bash was giving a party at the digs he and Salim shared in a large three-storey house. It was to be the very next night, Saturday, a last fling before Bash buried himself 'in the bowels of the Radcliffe to absorb all the wisdom of the ages and, thus, ensure that dear Father will not amputate me at the wallet'. He would send invitations to Deborah and Gladys.

'What colleges are you at?'

'We're both at Prinsworth,' Deborah replied.

'Oh God, two Prigs. Certified virgins, without doubt.' Bash shook his head in mock despair. 'It's a sign from heaven that life is ending for me and study about to begin.'

Deborah felt her face reddening. 'Don't worry,' she snapped, 'it isn't catching.'

'But still quite curable.' He tipped his head towards her with what she recognized as too studied charm, but which she had to admit was charming nonetheless.

His face was uncomfortably close to hers. She turned to her

companion with what she hoped appeared to be casual élan. 'Insouciant, wouldn't you say, Gladys?'

Gladys pretended to appraise Bash. 'Diseased, to be sure, but definitely insouciant.'

The food turned out to be not ghastly at all, and the conversation was a playful badinage that neither young woman had allowed herself to experience since coming up. Afterwards, as they made their way back to Prinsworth, the mood held.

'Miss Davis,' Gladys announced to the sky, 'we get top marks. A party invitation less than two hours after being given the assignment. Natural talents.'

'I was sure you'd denounce them to the secret police or do something equally dreadful.'

'Not worth it. A waste of good bullets.' A thought came upon Gladys, and the smile faded. 'You know what Prince Salim told me?' Deborah was amused to note that Gladys, somewhat awestruck, used Salim's title, which she herself would never have done. 'When he was twelve his father gave him a bunch of slave girls for his very own.'

'For the boy who has everything.' Deborah's thoughts returned to her conversation with Bash, and she grew angry again. 'Men act as if virginity and wanting to save oneself for marriage are really a curse.'

'They have no idea we're people. To them we're tactical objectives.'

'You don't imagine they're really able to find girls, not the kind one pays, but Oxford women willing to play their game, do you?'

'I shouldn't think so,' Gladys replied firmly. 'No half-intelligent girl would risk her reputation or pregnancy just to do a boy a favour.'

'It would be different, of course, if they planned to be married and were very sincere about it.'

'Of course.'

Miss Davis's advice to take the afternoons off proved to be subversive, breeding a discontent that became stronger as the days lengthened and grew warmer, as Deborah's circle of friends widened, and as she allowed herself to be tempted by the parties, pleasures, causes, and clubs that abounded throughout the university and the city. She had been dutiful for so long, had for so many years repressed her naturally exuberant and independent spirit, that the Trinity term became a period of modest awakening and rebellion. The first time she stayed out at a party until late and consequently was able only to skim her reading for a course the following day, she was racked by remorse at her behaviour. But soon, like most of the girls, she was sneaking in well after the gates were locked by means of the postern gate leading into the Old Garden which was usually left carelessly open. Once, when that had been found to be locked, she had done as Gladys advised: tossed her dress over the wall and, hoisted up by the man she was with, gone over after it. It was all very innocent and, for Deborah, liberating. She found the eager attention of young men a rewarding surprise; her own valuation of herself – so far judged by the limited gauge of school achievements – began to form into the worthwhile shape reflected in their eyes.

Sexuality and its natural expression seemed to have been banished from Oxford. That stemmed in part from the women there being so few and too closely observed by the males to risk 'staining' their reputations. For the most part, however, these young people were the last of the generation that still believed in the romantic adhesion of sex to marriage, a belief that derived from two centuries of family values and the lack of reliable birth-control means. There were few non-believers in the spring of 1963 at Oxford, which made Deborah's much-feared introduction to men far less intimidating than it might otherwise have been.

Deborah did all the carefree things custom and her own inclination demanded. She reclined in a wide, low punt on a golden afternoon while a broad-backed young man showed off his skill at poling it between the banks of the Cherwell. She drank Pimms in the exquisite gardens of Worcester College and watched the swans. She won all her matches and played a major part in bringing the women's lawn tennis cup to Prinsworth. She listened with the crowd at Magdalen College tower on the dawn of May Day as the choir sang the Latin hymn. She cheered like mad during Eights Week for the college of whichever boy had invited her that day. And, in spite of what she considered nearly criminal negligence of her studies, she did quite well at those unofficial end-of-school-year exams, known as Collections, intended to give undergraduates and dons an idea of the former's progress.

The very lack of sexual expectation from the young men she went out with, grateful simply to be seen by their friends with so beautiful a young woman, endowed Bash Rowell, by contrast, with a dark and unconscious fascination to her. Among many uncertain youths, he was so very certain of his sexuality.

When they met, she often had the impression of a long-legged young stallion loping towards her and did her best to ignore the disconcerting prickly sensation on the backs of her legs.

He had many girl friends, with whom, she assumed, he was on terms a good deal more intimate than he was with her. At the wild parties he and Salim threw at their house, she frequently observed sophisticated women on his arm. Champagne flowed, and the smart crowd flocked there and danced to terrific records by a new group called the Beatles.

By May Bash was visiting Deborah's college unannounced more often, to see her in the afternoon, when men were permitted (on a few other occasions he left messages to say that he had called). He seemed to want to talk about something, but ended up simply passing an hour chatting about this and that. She always felt on edge when he was in the room. She ascribed it to the physical resemblance he bore to his father and to her inexperience in the presence of men. It was always difficult for her to concentrate after he had gone.

One Sunday morning at the beginning of June, Deborah found a note on her door to see the Principal. She went to her rooms and was told that there had been a telephone call from a hospital located about half an hour from Oxford. Young Rowell had been in a car accident the night before and had asked to see her. The Principal knew no more; she offered to call a taxi for Deborah. Deborah was on the pavement outside Prinsworth's main entrance several minutes before the taxi arrived.

Deborah had not been prepared for the sight of the up-ended Jaguar as her taxi rounded a turn. The wrecked sports car's front bumpers reached up and around either side of the oak tree like a diver's arms just before he leaves the board. Its rear, untouched, crouched beneath it like strong thighs. Into her consciousness, like a phantom wreck floating up from the deepest fathoms, rose the memory of her mother's accident.

As the taxi swept past, she could see the gaping oval that filled the driver's side of the windscreen. A low branch had speared it.

Bash could be dying! All else fled from her mind.

A quarter of an hour later Deborah stood at the open door of a hospital room. The curtains were drawn. A small bedside lamp gave meagre illumination. She could see a heavily bandaged figure propped against several pillows, its right arm elevated, its eyes closed. Dashes of iodine at odd angles imparted a grotesque look to the partly unbandaged face, like a primitive warrior's dance mask, practically the only thing in the room that was not white.

'Bash?'

The blue eyes opened. Deborah was accustomed to the automatic curl of a smile when he greeted her. The grimness as he recognized her sent a greater chill through her than the first sight of the bandages.

'Come in.'

'I would have brought flowers, but it's Sunday and . . .'

He nodded. She drew up the single chair in the small room to the side of the bed, but he indicated that she should move the chair farther down.

'Turning is a trifle trying on the neck.' She settled herself.

'Thank you for coming,' he said.

'I was worried. How are you?'

'Banged up a bit all over, I'm afraid. A rib or two. The arm is broken.' Only the fingertips of his right hand protruded from the cast that embraced the upper part of his torso. 'The clavicle too, I'm told.'

She smiled encouragingly. 'The bad-tempered clavicle.' He did not respond. She continued, 'It might have been far worse. I saw the wreck on the way here.'

'I've been thinking about that. I was convinced I was dying last night after the crash. My racing belt and a bloody tree branch had me trapped. I couldn't move my arm to open the door beside me. I was losing consciousness, as if I was tired and couldn't keep my eyes open. My very last thought was that one thinks Oxford's the pinnacle of life when one's here, that everything afterwards is secondary – perhaps petty is closer to it. One loses perspective here – and then it's too late.'

Deborah was about to reassure Bash that he need not be so

morbid, because he would soon be up and about. But then she realized she would have been furious herself at being patronized in that way.

'Do you feel different now?'

He reflected on the question. 'No, merely more foolish. To let it mean so much.'

'I don't understand.'

Bash's gaze shifted to the window and the view of the garden. 'Final Schools this week, you know.'

Deborah nodded. The third-year girls at Prin were nearly hysterical with tension.

'I won't be able to write. I'll have to skip Schools and settle for an aegrotat.' His eyes shifted back to her.

'You're left-handed,' she remembered.

His eyes still stared, unblinking, into hers – He did not reply.

'And I've never known you to bother with that racing-car seat belt . . . Oh, Bash!'

His eyes rolled back to the window. 'It was just too late to get started – too much to know – too long away to get the knack – too abstract to make myself care.'

There was a long silence. As the shock passed, Deborah was moved by this glimpse of his self-doubt, his vulnerability, as she never could have been by the mass of bravado surrounding it. One could never have believed he cared a whit about failing Schools, much less that he would risk his life to escape the humiliation. His mouth was compressed with emotion. The rims of his eyes were red above the iodine streaks that ran down his face like tears.

'Why did you ask for me?' she asked. 'Instead of someone else, I mean?'

He thought for a moment before replying. 'I wasn't certain myself why when I asked the nurse to telephone you. But, as the drugs they gave me wore off, seeing you became a necessity. I think it's very complicated.'

Deborah waited for him to go on with an expectancy that swung like a pendulum between elation and desolation. The window light had drawn a golden line along the edge of his profile. She did not breathe and knew that she could not until he spoke.

'Did you know about your mother?' he finally murmured.

'And your father, you mean?'

He nodded. 'When I saw you at her funeral, it was very awkward, but I wanted to be there to say good-bye to her. I was terribly depressed by her death. They visited me at boarding school a few weeks before she died. They were driving somewhere and stopped off. I had been troubled by something or other. Let it slip in a letter home. Your mother just said hello and tried to move away so that Father and I could chat, but he and I were both making an appalling mess of it . . . neither one of us very good at expressing our feelings. Your mother, in the kindest way, finally stepped in, and the three of us talked – actually, she and I did most of it.' Bash finally turned back to look at Deborah. 'You see, except for a rather formidable nanny, I had barely spoken to a woman before that. She understood me perfectly. I thought she was the most wonderful creature.'

'I'm not my mother, Bash.'

'I know that. I'm just trying to explain the associations you raised in my mind when we first ran into each other during Hilary.' He bent his good left arm under him, to pull himself more upright; he wanted to be able to face her. A flash of pain too intense for him to hide crossed his face. He managed to change position and then gazed intently at her. 'Despite what you may have thought, I was on my very best behaviour when I was with you. I wanted so to impress you.'

'For my mother's sake.'

'Partly. At first. But then because you had such an extraordinary amount of character. You exude it, like a scent.'

'What an awful thing to say! It sounds as if I'm sweating or something.'

'It's marvellous. Not a wishy-washy, unstable atom in you. You're incorruptible. No, no, I'm not talking about your sexual morality, Dee. I'm talking about the values with which you approach things.' She thought he had finished speaking, but then he added, 'And you're beautiful.'

Deborah glanced away in confusion. 'But I still don't understand why you wanted to tell me all this.'

'I decided that if you didn't approve of what I'd done, if you thought I'd been too much of a coward to tolerate, I'd inform my tutor that I'd crashed on purpose.'

She looked up in anger. 'How dare you put that responsibility on me!'

'That wasn't in my mind at all.' He groped to define his

motivation. 'It's . . . it's that I wouldn't lie to you, and if you were to think less of me for what I was about to do, I wouldn't do it for the world.'

How helpless he looks, she thought – the beauty he usually wields like a magic wand now bandaged or laid open in brown stripes like shallow mines. Her voice was softer when she spoke again.

'You don't know me at all if you think I would make judgements about another's conscience, particularly when the only one you've hurt is yourself. My own conscience is much too black and troubled.' She moved closer to him and touched his hand lightly with hers. 'But if it eases you to know . . . my only regret is that you risked your life out of fear of what people might think. Your life is precious. What people think is air.'

He smiled again, this time a little more like the carefree cavalier of old. 'Is my life precious to *you*?'

'Everyone's is,' she said, avoiding the question's intent.

'But mine, is it just a little bit more precious than most?'

'I'm fond of you, of course, Bash . . .' she said matter-of-factly.

His hand rolled over and clasped hers. As if nuclear fuel had slipped into place, heat suddenly radiated from their touch. She told herself that she wanted to let go but that he was holding her hand too tightly.

'I came here as soon as I heard,' she allowed.

'More quickly than you would have for another?' he insisted.

'Yes,' she finally admitted, as much to herself as to him.

His face brightened fully for the first time that day. 'You'll have to bend down if I'm to kiss you properly.'

She bent towards him in a daze. She had never kissed a man before. She felt as if her lips were melting straight through her body.

CHAPTER TEN

In 1963 many in Britain, whether sentient enough to realize it or not, were forced to confront their old values, and did not like what they saw. A major mirror proved to be the so-called Profumo Scandal. High Government officials and establishment figures were alleged to have been frolicking with call girls in the swimming pool and a cottage on the Cliveden estate. There were intimations of attempted Soviet spying across the pillow. The nation eagerly devoured every salacious morsel, made even more delectable through the immediacy of television.

Dr. Stephen Ward had rented the cottage in question and introduced the young women to the frolickers. After his conviction for living off prostitution earnings, he promptly – and most conveniently – committed suicide. John Profumo, Secretary of State for War and husband of a celebrated actress, whose only offence – apart from initially lying about his participation as a frolicker – appeared to have been against his wife, resigned and, penitent, took up charity work. The moralists breathed a sigh of relief.

It was puritanism's last gasp for a while. The nation's hypocrisy had become too apparent. For years the government and the pundits had been telling the populace to work harder, be more productive, save more, export more vigorously. Yet sterling was sinking, taxes were rising drastically, and industry was staggering. The privileged few running the show from the top of the pyramid, as they had done for the last few centuries, seemed to be bumblers and frauds. To the horror of many, classlessness and sex were rearing twin heads. Soon, those on the bottom of the social pyramid would no longer be satisfied to do the bidding of those on top. Workers would strike at the slightest provocation, a good part of the time simply out of pent-up frustration. The young would idolize rock musicians and fashion designers and would have money to spend. Young women would take the pill and no longer feel restrained by that last spectre guarding sexual morality, fear of pregnancy. Great Britain was not yet swinging, but deep out to sea the earth had shifted, and a tidal wave was sweeping inexorably towards the tight little island.

Besides the Profumo Scandal, at least three other British events of 1963 bore greater significance than was immediately apparent.

At the Labour Party Conference that year, Harold Wilson exhorted the party and the nation to seek economic and social salvation through the new technology. By the end of the following year, Wilson would be Prime Minister.

Arab nations had been attempting to flex their new economic muscle by forcing companies doing business with them to cease trading with Israel, or even with companies dealing with Israel. An insurance company's board yielded to Arab pressure and forced the resignation of a Jewish director without any apparent understanding that they might bring criticism on themselves or even that they were doing anything wrong. Accommodating the Arabs was simply good business.

Lastly, a gang robbed the Glasgow-to-London train of two and a half million pounds. Far from treating the thieves as villains, the public secretly hoped that the heroes of the Great Train Robbery would not be caught. *They*, at least, had beaten the system.

To be eighteen, living that summer in London, and in love, was like heaven for Deborah, and like hell. For many years she had feared to offer her love to anyone, wary of the tragedy that had always followed upon it like a judge's sentence. Now she was to learn that death was not the only loss risked by loving, bereavement not the only grief.

Deborah had fallen deeply in love with Bash Rowell, and he with her. She had no interest at all in meeting other young men, but the social events in London and the country weekends afforded her and Bash a guarded opportunity to see each other. Both agreed that absolutely no one could be allowed to know about their romance. Her father despised his father, whose affair with Madeleine had humiliated him; a lifetime would not be long enough to heal that wound or reconcile him to the idea of an attachment between the Kronengold and Rowell families. Leslie would consider a liaison with a Rowell an attempt to degrade him. The fragile accommodation with

Leslie that Deborah tried so hard to maintain, the family bonds sustaining her tenuous sense of security, would be unravelled irreparably. On the other hand, she was just as certain, now that she herself was in love, that sacrificing herself to her father's choice of her husband, in order for the family to gain some dubious business advantage, would be emotional suicide.

Bash gave little thought to the future. He was still very young and faced a stint abroad at a merchant bank before he was ready to join the Rowell bank, much less to think about a lifelong commitment.

April Thornley was yet another impediment to young love. Short, with dark hair, dark eyes, and a full mouth, she possessed none of her mother's sultriness. Her appeal lay in her bosomy roundness and effervescent personality. Many young men were attracted to her, but she barely glanced at them. Time and Bash's indifference had not lessened her ardour for him. On the contrary, now that she had spent a year circulating at high speed within the social whirl, she was more convinced than ever that Bash was the only man she would have. She could barely order a meal from a French menu but had learned to say 'I love Bash' in fourteen languages. She had embroidered his name across the inside of her brassière cups and bought a dog, to which she found herself allergic, in order to have a reason to walk past his house twice a day. The only person she trusted enough to confide her consuming passion to was her dear, most loyal friend, Deborah.

Several times Deborah started circumspectly to reveal to April her own relationship with Bash, but each time broke off as she sensed that such news would be ruinous, striking April deeply and simultaneously on many levels; April would lose the man she loved, however unreciprocated the feeling, and would disown the friend she had trusted utterly, who had stabbed her more deeply than any enemy ever could. So Deborah kept silent and concurred when April observed at least three times in ten minutes that Bash's greeting to her at the horse show the day before had been noticeably warm. And, yes, Deborah agreed over the over again, he did look quite dashing at Lord's . . . exactly like a hero back from the front, with his new, smaller cast and black sling.

Deborah lived for the times she and Bash could be alone together, away from others. During those moments she floated on top of the most exquisite emotions, more vivid than she had ever before experienced. A single flower could assault her senses like a carnival. A furtive walk along the Embankment was a treasure hunt of wonders. The first sight of him could evoke infinite joy, a farewell abject despair. Kissing – all they would allow themselves – could wipe away all reason and memory. His masculinity frightened her and, as she grew to trust him, attracted her like a serpent hawking an orchard of forbidden fruit.

Yet, after a few weeks in London, finding places where they could be alone and not be recognized became nearly impossible. Deborah's beauty and her family's wealth and prominence quickly drew the press's attention to her until it became a kind of madness. She had only to appear in public and photographers would leap out of hiding places and start snapping. No one doubted she was Deb of the Year. Rarely did a day go by when a newspaper or magazine failed to run her picture or an article about her. Paradoxically, the more she tried to avoid publicity the more persistent was the photographers' pursuit and the more in demand she became. She continued with her social schedule for one reason only: it allowed her to see Bash.

Deborah considered ridiculous the time and attention others paid to the social circus. She had demands on her time she considered far more important. For one thing she had a heavy reading list to complete before the autumn term, about which she was quite conscientious. Yet, she was beginning to admit that university, too, seemed damnably irrelevant, especially the PPE she was studying. As taught at Oxford, philosophy was semantic puzzles, not life; politics was unrelated to the problems facing the nation; and economics, the only one of the three topics in which she was deeply interested, possessed only a nodding acquaintance with business. The extreme measures Bash had taken to avoid humiliation at being examined about such irrelevancies had served to clarify her own growing disillusionment with Oxford. She felt bored with both study and the social marathon, and she felt unproductive.

The afternoon in mid-August before she had arranged to join her uncle Charles and aunt Cora in the south of France, she returned home from a cocktail party to dress for a dinner Salim was giving. Bash and April had both been invited.

Deborah passed her brother Richard in the hallway as she

was coming in and he was going out. Over the years, since Madeleine's death, they had become closer, Richard out of guilt and relief upon finding himself in the position of favourite child. Deborah remained wary, but was willing to extend herself to strengthen her bonds with her brother. Several times that summer she had tried to engage him in conversation, but the talk was always stilted and uncomfortable. This time he stopped her.

'Do you know Harriet Carr?' he asked.

'Yes, not well though.'

'I'm going to meet her. Father wants me to marry her. What's she like?'

Deborah was shocked by the calculation of the matchmaking and by Richard's passivity.

'She's all right, I suppose,' Deborah offered. She thought the girl a cow, totally undistinguished by any appealing quality. Her father was a peer with a large estate and castle in the Midlands. It was no doubt their ancient title to which Leslie gave the greatest weight.

Richard stood pulling at his lip, ruminating on Deborah's answer. 'I'm sure it will be all right.' He hesitated and then gazed at Deborah. 'I'm not very good with women, Dee. I'm far more comfortable with men . . . you know, in bed.'

He wandered out of the house. Deborah absorbed the waves of shock his admission produced and shook her head sadly. She had always suspected that his boarding school had fostered a streak of homosexuality in her brother. But the greater sadness was how obediently her brother bent to their father's will. She wondered if he would have been different if their mother had lived.

She went to her room and sat for several minutes on the edge of her bed, her eyes fixed on the photograph of her mother a friend of the family had taken in the conservatory at Clove Hill. The soft light allowed the subtle sculpturing of Madeleine's face to be visible, the large brown eyes not to dominate the delicate structure. Flowers were in the foreground, too close to be in focus. Her mother was looking directly at the camera, laughing at something. In all the pictures of her mother, she had seen that expression only twice, the other time being in the photograph with Edgar, her mother's first fiancé. Deborah had often wished she understood why her mother was laughing in the same way here, as if knowing what had made her mother laugh so wholeheartedly would bridge the guilt stretching to the memory of her mother dying within the whiteness of a snowstorm into which Deborah had lured her, would allow them to share a single mind, would convey to each that the other loved her. Her mother had been drawn to the father, Rob, as she was now drawn to the son, Bash. Surely her mother and she were separated by only a last incantation undeciphered or a final confidence unshared. Deborah felt lonelier at that moment than she had in years.

It was nearly eight when, dressed in a green silk gown with a long, tight skirt, she was driven to April's by Williston. She and April would walk the short distance to Salim's. If Williston or Jeffreys was ever asked to report on her whereabouts, nothing would point to Bash or his circle of friends.

Outside Salim's front door, Deborah could see, through a window, Bash in dinner jacket talking with other guests and gesticulating with his good hand, which held a drink. The sling appeared a necessary defect, like an amulet to guard against the gods becoming jealous of his perfection. Years later she would be able to recall every detail of his appearance with absolute fidelity: the lift of his chin, the blond locks that framed his face with conscious effect, the bearing that connoted his superiority with unconscious grace. And then Bash turned, seeming to know she was there, and gazed at her through the open window. The image, a rectangle pasted on black, hung in time like a painting. She felt her body vibrate, as if the air between the two of them was charged with electrical current. There was nothing of her that was not him, nothing of him that was not her.

At that moment, from the doorstep, April called back to Deborah to hurry – she had rung the bell. April was very excited; she was sure Bash had asked Salim to invite her.

Deborah would remember also the young people who were there, a biopsy-thin cross-section of young England's coming years that she thought at the time only a foreigner, disdaining or insensitive to class distinctions, could have assembled in one place – from a rock-group manager to a young stockbroker speaking in Old Boy clichés that could have issued out of a men's club a hundred years before; from a gimlet-eyed fashion photographer in an open shirt to the silent young mini-skirted woman his magazine covers had made famous.

Dinner was served in the mock Tudor hall. The long oak table had been moved to one side. Large candles lent a dim light to the panelled walls to which they were affixed. In the centre of the room, before the great stone hearth, arrangements of plush, stuffed pillows curled around a line of low tables. An Arab servant stood silhouetted at the side of the hearth, turning the spit. A glistening steer, legs splayed, revolved by the flaming logs.

Swarthy musicians and a singer played and sang hauntingly in the wailing, rhythmic, earthy style of Middle Eastern music. The strangeness on the ear, the faint echo off the high, dark ceiling enhanced the primal atmosphere. A dancer appeared, her midriff bare, veils hung from the spangled belt low on her hips. She began to sway and then to dance, her body moving in sinuous waves. Servants set bubbling hookahs on the low table. Some guests took a polite puff or two. Others inhaled. Soon they were light-headed. Mixed with the Turkish tobacco glowing in the bowls above the hookahs was the customary piece of hashish.

The dancer spun. The flames flickered and leaped in accompaniment and cast bright hues at the watchers through the tossing veils. Deborah felt herself whirling and lifting, as if the love expanding within her had filled her mind and body with a helium euphoria.

'I love you,' she whispered to Bash.

From her great height Deborah noticed – or thought she did, like a premonition of a dream not yet dreamt – a flash of face behind Bash. But when she looked again April was turned away, seemingly engrossed in conversation with Salim, who had been devoting a great deal of attention to her.

Later Deborah and Bash carried their sweet mint tea to the garden and seated themselves on a wrought-iron bench. The moonlight was a shower of silver coins falling through the gently shifting leaves.

'I feel as if we're figures in a Fragonard painting,' she whispered. ' "Lovers in the garden", something like that.' Deborah brought her lips very close to Bash's. 'What do *you* feel?'

'You ask the most awkward questions of any girl I've ever known.'

'That's no answer,' she persisted. 'You've already admitted that you love me.'

'If you must know,' he replied, laughing at her refusal to be put off, 'I want to touch you all the time.' His free hand encircled her waist. 'When I saw you through the window tonight –'

'It was like electricity,' she finished for him.

She leaned closer, finally allowing her lips to press against his. His arms drew her against him. She was afloat again, but this time the electricity had returned and was pulsing inside and around her. She pulled back to tell him again how much she loved him, to let her eyes caress his beautiful face. But a different face met her gaze, a rounder face, white and full of pain, like a second, anguished moon. April stood behind Bash, beside a tree trunk on the border of the footpath. Bash turned to follow Deborah's stunned stare. He was the quickest to speak.

'I'm sorry you found out this way,' he growled, 'but it's high time you knew.'

April's head began to swing back and forth, like a mechanical doll's, to deny the words, her own eyes.

'Deborah and I didn't want to go skulking around behind your back, April, but you made it bloody impossible to tell you the truth, gawking at me as you did.'

'April, what can I –' Deborah began, but the other girl broke away, back into the darkness, twigs cracking in the path of her retreat.

'Bash, you didn't have to be so harsh,' Deborah remonstrated.

'A dose of strong medicine is what she needs. You tried pretending there was nothing between you and me, and that's what led to this muddle.'

The bliss had been shattered. They rose and walked quickly back to the house.

Inside, Deborah searched for April. She heard soft crying in the cloakroom and knocked. 'April, let me in.'

She was about to repeat her request, when the lock turned and the door opened. April fell back against the painted roses that climbed the wallpaper. Deborah closed the door behind her. She cleared her throat.

'I wanted to tell you myself, but each time I started, you behaved as if your life would end if Bash didn't love you.'

'How cleverly you carried it off,' April muttered bitterly. 'I never suspected anything.'

'I didn't want to hurt you. If it's any comfort, I hated myself awfully for hiding it. Sometimes things just happen. When he was in the hospital after his accident –'

April raised her hand in defence. 'At least spare me that.' She stared at Deborah for a long moment, as if she were balancing the other girl in her open palm, gauging her weight. 'At school I didn't think twice about all your accomplishments, your competitiveness, except to be proud of you because you were my friend. But –'

'I'm still your friend, April,' Deborah interjected with a touch of desperation.

'*But*,' April repeated with deadly emphasis, 'I had no fears about your competing with *me*, because you were almost indifferent to being liked by boys.'

'I was terrified.'

April wiped her eyes fiercely. 'You care only about *winning*! In the end, you decided you had to beat me, too – and take the only thing I cared about.' A sob rose she could not stifle. 'I just wanted him to love me.'

'Oh, April,' Deborah pleaded, 'can't you believe it just happened?'

April closed her eyes and shook her head. 'Not yet . . . not yet. . . . You get everything you want without trying, but you still try for whatever little's left to the rest of us.'

Wretchedly, Deborah reached for April's hands. 'Please believe me,' she begged.

April's eyelids opened. 'If nothing else, leave me my self-pity.'

Deborah departed without another word.

'Where to? Ronnie Scott's?' Bash asked after he had lowered himself into the new white Jaguar sports car beside Deborah – his father had replaced its wrecked predecessor as soon as Bash's smaller cast permitted him to drive.

'I'm not in the mood for jazz tonight.' Deborah, brooding, stared straight ahead. Finally, she asked. 'Am I greedy, Bash?'

'In what sense?'

'Taking all the best things on the plate, leaving nothing for anyone else?'

'If that means you're a born winner, the answer is yes.'

Deborah's head fell back against the red leather. 'Too competitive? Always fighting for the upper hand?'

'You're serious about this?'

'Yes.'

Bash considered his answer. 'I can only speak for your behaviour towards me.' She nodded for him to continue. 'Sometimes I feel you're not sure whether I'm an enemy or a lover.'

'Especially where sex is concerned, you mean,' Deborah suggested with some diffidence. 'Is my chastity very difficult for you?'

He had vowed to himself not to pressure her into yielding to him, not to take advantage of her, not even to discuss the matter, but it was out in the open now. He nodded. 'Very.'

Teardrops clinging to Deborah's lashes glittered in the sudden light from a passing car. 'I love you, Bash, and want to make you happy – in any way you want. I'm just very new at expressing it.'

With utter deliberation, Deborah lifted Bash's hand and placed it on her breast.

'Dee!' he cried out, pulling back his hand.

'I would, you know,' she said, her voice choked with strain. 'I would let you have me right here and now.'

Bash was overwhelmed by her offering – the submission was so shocking, so total.

'Not like this, here.'

'You're going to Scotland in the morning. I'm off to France.'

'My father insisted, damn it. Six weeks before I see you again.'

She kissed him passionately. 'Six weeks is forever,' she breathed. 'Tonight, Bash. Before I lose my nerve.'

'My father's already in Scotland, and the servants will be asleep by now.'

'If one of them should see us. . . .'

He thought a moment. Then he smiled and turned the ignition key. The engine roared. He released the brake and headed into the main road. 'It's a warm, beautiful night. I'll stop off at home just for a minute. To get a blanket.'

April stayed on at Salim's house after the other guests had left. Much later, when she was high from smoking and grateful to Salim for the concern he was showing her, he led her to his bedroom. She invited him to kiss her, pleased that he found her attractive. She grew hazy and warm and let Salim pull her clothes off, half resisting and half submitting out of despair and the resentment she felt against Bash. But then it became desperately important to her that Salim find her desirable. More than anything she wanted him to want her.

As he drew her down to the bed, she whispered, 'Do you like me? Do you think I'm pretty?'

In his eyes she could discern his lust for her. She smiled and closed her eyes. Soon, like a knife, he lowered his lean body into hers. After he had settled into a rhythm between her splayed legs, her imaginings, like friends, crowded into the dark room around her to transform everything to beauty; she felt wanted. The need to possess her, the urgency pounding into her, could be anyone's, she told herself. The man could be Bash.

Bash and Deborah saw the lake at the same time, shimmering like a coin tossed across their path. They had been searching for secluded woods outside London and had simply stumbled upon the little inn by the lake. Wordlessly, they agreed, and Bash turned into the car park.

'They'll want to think we're married,' she reasoned.

He handed her his key ring. With the keys held in her fist, the gold circle did look very nearly like a wedding band. Startled, she glanced at him in embarrassment.

'I wish it were a real one,' he said softly.

There was a light on over the door, and a light on inside.

'I have something else,' he remembered. 'In the boot.'

He opened the car's boot and took out a tool kit that looked much like a suitcase. He put an arm about her waist and guided her towards the inn.

A middle-aged man in shirt sleeves was bent over the front desk.

'My wife and I –' Bash began in a voice that sounded unnaturally loud to her, 'we'd like a room, my wife and I.'

The man smiled wearily and revolved the register for Bash to sign. 'You're in luck. Usually, I'm in bed by now. But tonight I was doing the books. Ten quid a night with breakfast.'

The man led the way to a second-floor room. The furniture was old, comfortable, and the windows looked out on the silver disc of lake. He left them there, refusing a tip. He was the owner, he said.

'Sleep well,' he wished them and closed the door. He never once glanced at Deborah's wedding band, or even at her.

She sucked in a long, deep breath after the door had clicked shut. She felt embarrassed to look at Bash and walked to the window, opening it as if that would alleviate the trapped feeling, the awkwardness of being in this room in which the bed seemed to crowd out all the space. She focused on a trio of ducks, oval silhouettes, that were gliding out of the dark rushes at the shore towards the pure white at the lake's heart. The odour of grass and trees mingled with that of the hotel room, an aroma like the memory of all the people who had ever stayed there. The courage Deborah had always been able to summon at will during the difficult times of her life seemed to have fled irretrievably.

Bash! she thought, as if the name were a life preserver. She spun round. He was standing only inches from her. His blue eyes, intent on hers, seemed to pull her out of the whirling anxiety. His face, so very beautiful to her, now seemed to be the only object in the room, like a perfect painting in a crowded museum. His hands reached out to her shoulders and drew her to him. Tall as she was, she felt tiny looking up at him.

They kissed, and it seemed a kiss more important than any that had come before. It seemed to seal for all time their compact of love.

'I never thought I could love anyone like this . . . so much,' she whispered.

'You and I.' He nodded. 'We're forever.'

He feels it too, she realized. Now she remembered why she had come here: to give herself to him, because they were one. Shame and fear, childhood memories of distaste that lingered furtively at the fringes of her mind, seemed puny intimidators at this moment. He kissed her again, and she felt passion igniting in her. The worst terrors would slink away from the fire that was Bash.

Gently, he slipped the zip down along the back of her dress and unhooked her bra. He lifted both the dress and bra off her shoulders. They fell at her feet.

Her courage seemed to grow doubts then. Her arms began sliding self-consciously over her breasts. He gently pulled her hands away.

As if his eyes could stroke her, she felt a quickening in her body. She admonished it to straighten up, not to be ashamed in front of the man she loved. Not taking her eyes from his, she slipped off the rest of her clothes.

'You are so beautiful. So perfect and beautiful,' Bash said. At that moment she actually felt as beautiful as he believed her to be.

But, as he undressed, she felt awkward again, not knowing if she was expected to lie down on the bed now, anxious really about going to the bed. He might think it too forward of her, or suggest experience she did not really have. So she stood in the middle of the room, her hands stiffly at her sides, and watched Bash undress. He dropped his shirt on a chair beside his sling, almost unnecessary these last few days of healing, his jacket and tie. He was about to slip off his trousers when he thrust a hand into a pocket and placed something on the bedside table.

'What's that?' she asked.

'Protection.'

She was grateful for his thoughtfulness. She was so naive about such things; it had never occurred to her, in her romantic haze, to worry about birth control. Her friend Gladys would have demanded lectures and a reading list on the topic from her doctor at the mere contemplation of sex.

Bash reached out and extinguished the single light in the room, a lamp on the bedside table. The moon, like a tipped bucket, instantly poured milk-white rays into the room. She had gone swimming with Bash at weekend house parties and so was aware that he had the cleanly muscled physique of an athlete. But when he turned, seeing him suddenly naked, apprehensive all her adolescent years about seeing a man naked, she now found her senses overwhelmed. He was tall and lean, a wraith carried into this room, this age, on moonbeams. This time her kiss with him was innocent, as if he were the first man and she the first woman and life on earth only days old. Instinctively, her hands ascended his back and the feel of his skin, not marble now, but warm and yielding to the touch, sent a quiver rolling through her body.

They sank onto the thick quilted coverlet as if into a bower. He stretched out beside her, and the thrill that had always nearly filled her when they kissed seemed to spread through her entire body. His hands moved freely over her and touched her in places she had even been shy about touching herself. The rising unfamiliar excess of sensation frightened her. And then anxiety slipped into oblivion along with memory.

She held him, kissed him, in a blur of semi-awareness, doing and feeling things she would scarcely be able tomorrow to remember – it was all one endless moment of feeling. Everything.

When she could barely think and her skin threatened to burst, she felt Bash poised against her. She opened her eyelids to gaze at the face she loved, the one fact in the universe she could rely on. It was tight with desire.

'Forgive me,' he said.

'Will it hurt?'

Then his hips lunged, and she winced at the peal of pain, a hard little circle of it. She thrust her hips up into the hurt, embracing that destructive proof of her love. She gasped in astonishment as her insides were filled with him and his movement into her. The thrilling sensation was there now, spreading and deepening. She closed her eyes and tried to concentrate on it. The oddness of the activity and half a lifetime of trepidation about it alternated in disrupting her concentration. But she was content, like a baby being rocked from within. When Bash's muscles stiffened and he moaned, she hugged him very tight and felt they were as close as two people could be.

Later, when he was lying on his back beside her, Bash said, 'You didn't have an orgasm, did you?'

'I don't know. Maybe. I'm not really sure I know what one feels like.'

'If you had, you'd know.' He kissed her shoulder. 'I really wanted you to have one.'

She rolled on her side and propped herself on an elbow. 'Bash, it was wonderful. Much better than I ever imagined.'

'But it hurt.'

She giggled. 'Not for long.' Her eyes dropped. 'I was afraid I'd be so awkward and sexless that you'd give it up as a bad job.'

'Just looking at you was almost enough to set me off.'

'But was I . . . you know, when we were really doing it . . . were you disappointed?'

His face lengthened into a mock frown.

She punched him lightly. 'This is too important to joke about.'

A smile broke through Bash's pretence. 'Definite aptitude, I'd say.'

'Thank goodness!' She breathed deeply and fell back in content.

He laughed and raised himself up to look down at her. 'I love you.'

'You're really saying it now. By yourself.'

'It seems so easy now. What about you? You seem so comfortable without a stitch of clothing on. You ought to be embarrassed, young lady.'

She hugged him. 'Not a bit of it. Haven't you heard? I've got definite aptitude.'

His face grew serious. 'When we get back to London, we're not going to slink around and hide any longer. If I have to go to your father and tell him how much I love you, I'll do it. If he tries to threaten you, well, we don't need his money.'

'What about *your* father?'

'Religious differences within a family are less important these days. It's not the same world it used to be. He'll have to understand.'

'Would you give up everything for me? I would for you, you know,' she added without needing to.

'My life, if I had to,' he swore.

That each should love and be loved in turn seemed quite the most remarkable occurrence in their lives. Overhanging their happiness was the six weeks apart. She would be returning to England late on a Saturday night. They vowed that the very next day they would be together again, would make love again.

'Here?' Bash asked.

Deborah reflected. Aspects of memory, desire, and fear struggled within her for long seconds.

'In the west corner of your country estate, there's a white cottage. It's on the edge of a meadow. Near a copse of trees.'

'I had forgotten all about it. Funny your remembering.'

'No one lives there, do they?'

He shook his head. 'It's a guest house.'

'That's where I want to be with you that first day.'

He nodded. 'The little white cottage it is then. Sunday afternoon.'

Six weeks apart would be unbearable, they told each other over and over again. But, after that, they had their whole lives together.

CHAPTER ELEVEN

Despite Deborah's despair at being separated from Bash, she truly needed a quiet time away from the merry-go-round of the Season, in her case accelerated to a frenzy by the press. She was grateful to Uncle Charles and Aunt Cora for inviting her to their house on the Riviera. All she wanted to do was sunbathe, swim, play tennis perhaps, read, get lots of sleep, and muse on her perfect bliss. Bash was an invisible companion who rarely left her thoughts, and yet she appeared to go about her life as if nothing had changed.

The first day she went to a little shop to buy a new swimsuit. Deborah had not remembered how daring bikinis were until she arrived and looked around her. She hesitated over the choice: the one-piece bathing suits favoured by the English and Americans, which quickly took on the appearance to her of formidable body armour; or the bikini, which flirted with nudity, but seemed somehow to endow the lithe young women who wore it with a mandate for physical freedom. I'm a woman now, Deborah castigated herself. With impulsive daring she purchased a blue bikini, conservative by local standards but approaching lewdness by Aunt Cora's.

Country weekends had given her body a reasonable tan, but the white apron of skin around her midriff made her appear ludicrous. After a day in the sun, she slipped off her bikini top to be greeted in the mirror by an even more ludicrous sight: what looked for all the world like a pair of giant white spectacles across her chest. From then on, when she was not with the family, she went by herself to remote spots on the property or small cliff-guarded beaches nearby. She lay on a towel or swam in the Mediterranean with only the sun to gaze on her nudity, browning her evenly all over. She wanted to look perfect for Bash when she returned and told herself how adult and self-assured she had become. Yet, when she noticed a plane crossing the sky thousands of feet overhead, she instantly, automatically, rolled up in the towel and then spent the rest of the afternoon disgusted with her inhibitions. She punished herself by refusing to drift into reveries about Bash and the life they would have together.

In the late August the family went to a gala at the Sporting Club in Monte Carlo. Pierre and Simone were to join them. Deborah wore no jewellery. Aunt Cora had tried two of her necklaces on her, but Deborah's long neck and bare shoulders, her rise of tan bosom above the neckline of the pale blue Balmain gown she had first worn at her coming out, had the beauty of a freshness more breathtaking than the richest gems; Cora had tears in her eyes when she looked at her extraordinary niece and tried futilely not to say how proud her mother would be of her, which unleased the tears in abundance, so that she had to reapply her mascara.

Deborah waited expectantly for Pierre's first sight of her as he approached their table. She laughed with delight when she perceived his look of astonishment – he had never seen her so dressed up. He hugged her and spun her around, then stepped back to look at her again.

'Yes, I know,' she said. 'If only my mother could be here to see me.'

'Yes,' he said with enthusiasm, and then more softly, 'Oh, yes! If only she could. Your red hair, your eyes. If only she could.'

He insisted on having a photograph taken with this grown-up Deborah, which made her very proud.

Deborah had always considered her Aunt Simone a plain woman, her calculating nature making itself evident in pinched facial features. To her surprise, Deborah observed that Simone had become handsome in middle age, her appearance more elegant; she seemed now at ease with herself and her position in life.

Simone was very much in love with her husband. She had barely known the vague, reserved young man her father's affluence and her scheming had won her when his own father decided it was time for Pierre to marry. But the husband returned to her from the war was a very different man. He was decisive and poised; the war had forced him to discover a capacity for action inside the bookish shell. Fearing he might leave her and their young son, and being a highly practical woman, she offered her own great wealth to Pierre as the capital to rebuild his family fortune, nearly wiped out by bombs and expropriation. She instructed her lawyer to design a loan agreement that would attach to her husband the most binding of chains: if Pierre dared to leave her before the loans were repaid, the financial empire he was determined to rebuild would become hers. Now, after so many years, a good part of the enormous loan she had made him, and often extended, still remained unpaid, but she was content that her husband remained with her now, not because of the loan agreement's penalties, but because, in his own undemonstrative way, he had indeed grown to love her. She was even secure enough now to spend an occasional evening with other Kronengolds without feeling beset by jealousy for having married so far above her father's social station. Despite her now being the Baroness and being mentioned in all the fashion magazines, she assumed that her in-laws still looked down upon her, still always thought of her as Simone Waldensteiner, whose father's newly-made industrial wealth had paid her way into their midst.

Deborah knew very little of this, although her grandfather Samuel had once told her about the loan. She knew, however, that Simone could as easily be pleasant to her as she could be malicious. During the violin incident at Valtary, Simone had misrepresented some facts to support Leslie's twisted version, perhaps because she correctly guessed that her conniving son, Gilbert, was at the bottom of things.

'And how is Gilbert?' Deborah asked courteously in French.

Simone's face lit. 'Very well. He has entered the bank, you know. Pierre says he is most talented.'

Deborah had no doubt that the shifty young man was very clever indeed. She felt grateful that her uncle Pierre had never imposed on her the requirement that, in order to sustain her relationship with him, she must maintain close and cordial relations with his son. She did not like Gilbert, and trusted him less.

Many people came to their table to pay their respects to the Kronengolds during the gala evening. A good number were young men, Pierre observed to the others with a smile. When an attractive French actor friendly with Pierre and Simone asked them to allow him to take Deborah to a nightclub afterwards, the older Kronengolds conferred with the gravity accorded a diplomatic pact.

'It seemed so very funny,' Deborah wrote Bash the next morning (care of Salim, who would forward all her letters). 'You and I are lovers, my darling, and yet they debated as if poor Philippe were taking me on my first date. I cannot wait to see you and to touch you. I miss you so terribly.'

Bash had written her several brief letters, putting Gladys's name and address on the back to conceal their origin from her family. He told her that he thought of her constantly and never wanted to be apart from her like this again.

Deborah wrote short neutral notes to April on scenic postcards, which she sent to both London and Grenford, but she received no reply. She became determined to see April when she returned to England and to put an end to their estrangement. Even if she had to prostrate herself before her friend and beg, causelessly, to be forgiven, she would do so until she and April were reconciled.

Deborah was awake by six and dressed in a white silk dress by six thirty, although there was not the slightest chance that Bash would ring her before nine and name the place where they would meet. Her father and most of the servants were in the country for the weekend, so she found herself wandering impatiently through the London house, her route taking her only into rooms with clocks. By eight thirty she was back in her sitting room – what was once the day nursery. She pretended to read the *Sunday Times*, but retained so little that she soon gave it up and simply stared at the telephone, thinking of a hundred reasons why he had not yet telephoned her, the least logical of them to her being that it was not yet nine o'clock.

When the telephone rang – at precisely nine – she leaped and lifted the receiver so fast that hardly a vibration of the bell had sounded.

'Is it you?' she cried out.

'Yes! Lord, I missed you.'

'It was an eternity. I want to have breakfast with you, just as if this was the morning after we first made love, as if no time had passed at all.'

'The usual place. Fifteen minutes?'

'I'm there already.'

She flew out of the house.

* * *

They shocked passers-by by kissing and clinging to each other in a respectable Mayfair street and then breakfasted together at the Park Lane. They walked up Piccadilly seeking the few shops that were open. They spent the morning buying silly presents for each other that had no practical use, except to make them laugh.

Only when they could no longer delay or deny the impatience in their blood did they lock eyes, silently take up their purchases, and flag down a taxi that brought them back to where Bash had parked the open Jaguar. At that moment Bash started to say something, thought better of it, and helped her into the car.

'*Je vais à ma gloire*,' she said with a theatrical toss of head and hand.

The white cottage was much smaller than Deborah remembered. The instant she caught sight of it she felt a twinge of recollected terror and could not breathe, as if the nightmare were crushing her chest.

'We hardly use this cottage for guests any more,' Bash remarked as he turned off the road.

Listen to his voice, she told herself; listen to Bash's voice. Swim up towards it out of this blackness.

'I'm surprised you even knew about it,' he continued.

The car stopped moving. Head back against the seat, she opened her eyes and ventured a breath.

'Are you all right?' Bash asked with some concern.

'Panicked. It's not you or sex, darling – certainly not sex any longer. It's this place. I thought I was being very resolute to choose it. Chasing all my personal ghosts in one grand gesture.' She did not tell him what they were.

'Perhaps you'd like to go somewhere else,' he said tensely, confused.

She fought a smile. 'Tell me again you love me.'

'Yes, damn it,' he answered with a vehemence that seemed to reproach any doubts that had ever dared to assail him. And then his voice turned gentle, humbling her anguish. 'I wrote to you in my letters . . . you were always in my thoughts. The need to make love to you again became more painful, more of an obsession every day. Love you? I'll love you always.'

'That's a thousand times stronger than my childish fears,' Deborah whispered. Her glance dropped. 'First kiss me, Bash.'

They kissed. She could feel him trembling, and she loved him even more for the vestige of weakness he concealed.

They left the car and went to the house. Bash found the key above a porch beam, where the estate manager told him it would be.

How very ordinary it looks! she observed as she walked through the little hallway that led to the living room on one side and the bedroom on the other. And so small! She reached for Bash's hand as they turned towards the bedroom. She felt free at last of all the demons that had pursued her from this place.

She undressed unhesitatingly, smiling at Bash as she did and laughing when he called her 'dark as an African'. She teased him about the faint pinkness of his skin, his Anglo-Saxon whiteness permitting nothing deeper. This time it was Bash who seemed a touch reticent. Deborah went to him, her tall body stretching upwards against his, and kissed the clouds from his eyes.

Clean floral sheets were on the double bed. Smaller flowers traced patterns on the walls. The countryside was all around them, but the scent that invaded her nostrils as Bash lay down beside her and cupped her face in his hand was uniquely his. It tumbled her mind backwards to the first time they had lain together like this. It quickened her pulse and her breathing.

Closing her eyes, she pressed her mouth against his and then opened it to the sensuous exchange of their defencelessness. The tip of her tongue felt liquid against his. Her body too seemed to be turning liquid beneath his stroking fingertips, which felt rougher than she remembered. She liked the rough texture; she could imagine the long days he had spent in Scotland, exercising on the moors to strengthen his arm, and traced the ravines between the muscles.

Her legs parted and lifted to receive his hand before he touched the warm wetness between them. She heard herself purring and then moaning as if the sound swarmed protectively about her.

When he entered her, she gasped, tightly embracing the furnace at her core, moving against him to stoke it until the red heat stretched across the room. Nothing in life could be more wonderful, she thought. And then, without warning, as if everything before it had been a dress rehearsal, she felt herself suddenly fainting, stunned, disoriented, into ecstasy.

Her only hope, her only thought, was wanting it to go on forever. And then, when it seemed about to subside and she could think enough to tell herself that such bliss was a miracle that could never happen again, it suddenly did come over her once more, obliterating everything but the bliss. And then again and again, submerging her in happiness.

Much later, when they were dressed and she thought they were about to leave, Bash drew her back to sit on the edge of the bed.

'I have to talk to you,' he said gravely.

'You sound very serious. Not today, please, I'm much too happy.'

'It can't be put off any longer,' he said quietly. 'It's about April.'

'Has something happened to her?'

'After we left Salim's house that night, she says he raped her. Maybe she let herself be raped or they just slept together – it's not very clear. At any rate, she became pregnant.'

'Oh, no!' Deborah gasped.

'Her mother wanted her to have an abortion, which made a lot of sense. She knew of a top Harley Street surgeon who'd do it. But April refused.'

'April adores children and wants to have dozens. Besides, she wouldn't kill a fly, much less a baby.'

Bash nodded. 'Her father backed her up. He's afraid of her having an abortion.'

'Does Salim want to marry her?'

'That's out of the question. He's in line of succession to the throne, will probably end up as prime minister some day at least. The family has taken the trouble to give him a Western education for that purpose. But he'll marry a Muslim – and make an alliance.' Bash took a deep breath. 'April's father threatened a row over the matter. Remember, we're not talking about some shopkeeper's daughter here one can buy off. He's the Duke of Grenford. One of the oldest and most influential families in Britain.'

'Does April want to marry Salim?'

'No, but she was ready to . . . to avoid the disgrace. As I said, that was out of the question. His father is crown prince, the king's brother. You know how close my family's relations are with them, the banking we do over there. He telephoned my father and threatened all sorts of reprisals for allowing his son to meet such a conspiring girl.'

'April?'

'That put us squarely in the middle, you see. This could have become an international incident. And my family's interests there were in jeopardy.'

'But what about April?'

Bash's eyes dropped, and he took several seconds to reply. 'Everybody involved agrees that the only way out of this mess is for April to marry *me*.'

When he dared to glance up, Deborah was staring at him incredulously.

'You must understand,' he went on, 'I have no choice.'

Deborah grabbed hold of him. 'We love each other. You can't let them force you to marry her.'

'It's already decided,' he said quietly. 'The contracts are drawn.'

'What are you saying?'

'Salim's family will settle half a million pounds on his child and another half million on April and me for handling the business. The Duke, April, my father are all satisfied by the arrangement. More than satisfied, quite rapturous, actually.'

Her voice was hard, an adversary's. Her eyes were in pain. 'What do *you* want to do, Bash?'

'It's my duty. To the family. My own desires don't enter into it.' He paused to reflect. 'April's not a bad sort and should be a quite agreeable wife, actually. But I love you, Dee. You must believe that. This . . . arrangement doesn't change that. There's no reason for my marriage to April to change anything between us.'

'Will that be part of the contract? Half a million pounds in your bank account plus two nights a week with your mistress?'

He shook his head sadly. 'This isn't something I wanted. You know that. But we're faced with an insurmountable problem. Try to be understanding about it.'

The palm of Deborah's hand caught him hard in the mouth just as he was saying the last word. He didn't move.

She turned back to speak to him only when she was at the door.

'Tell April from me that if the point was to beat me, she

did. One question, Bash. Why did you wait until after we made love to tell me?'

'Because I love you.' He willed his voice to convey the immensity of the emotion he felt. 'Because I will always love you. So much that I couldn't stop myself from wanting you today. I was hoping that once we had made love . . .' His voice trailed off.

She finished his thought. 'That I'd be so enthralled, I'd want to stay with you regardless of your marrying someone else.' She felt tears burning her eyes and could barely manage to blurt out the regret that tore at her heart. 'I could have made you happy, Bash.'

Deborah glanced once more about the little bedroom that seemed to groan beneath the weight of all the emotions burying her, smothering her voice. Her gaze went to the window, half expecting her own eleven-year-old face to be there mocking her. Then she glanced again at Bash and was able now to pronounce again the condemnation that keened within her like a dirge. 'I really loved you.'

She ran from the house and across the wide meadow until she reached the road, where she stumbled to a walk. She was crying uncontrollably, her emotions vibrating like a scream. Rejected by the man she had finally summoned up the courage to love after nearly half a lifetime of fearing to love, she felt empty, used, violated. The dull ache between her legs was a reminder. She had been right all along about the demeaning nature of the sex act; the very passion that had gripped her only a short while before now disgusted her in recollection. Out of the purest emotions, she had opened her heart and body, and she had been pillaged by Bash's lust. How could she have allowed such a selfish monster to mean everything to her – her future, her hope? Always having had everything, he wanted to believe that this time as well he would get what he wanted. If he truly loved her – and she still believed he did – he would have to live forever knowing that his choice of April had betrayed whatever might have been good and honourable in his life.

A red wild flower stretched above a tuft of grass where a mower had evidently swerved to avoid it. Deborah collapsed beside it and cradled the flower in her hands. The small moment of beauty had been spared by the mercy of a stranger. She had been ravished by a man who had claimed to love her. Deborah's tears ran down her cheeks.

When she finally stood up and looked back, the little white cottage was a smudge among trees. I truly am a woman now, she thought. Not because I've been with a man, but because I've learned never again to trust one.

Deborah threaded her way through the woods beyond the road and climbed the grassy knoll towards the chimney tops in the distance. They rose above the Georgian house into which her father had moved after donating the rest of Clove Hill to the National Trust so as to avoid both death duties and the upkeep. He had already sold off his father's racing stable and stud farm (a sport far too flamboyant for his personality). All the way, Deborah felt she was drowning in the familiar desolation that had sucked her under at the worst moment of her life.

When she reached the house, she told her father and his guests that a friend with a car had dropped her nearby, and she went to her room.

Leslie de Kronengold's private life had turned instantly conventional upon the double deaths of father and wife, much to the financial disadvantage of Mme Danielle née Mabel of Soho and others who had come to rely on the generosity with which that particular gentleman bought their services and their silence. Leslie was no longer driven to experience abuse because he no longer felt self-hatred at failing to achieve the standards expected by his father and wife, which he had perceived to be those set by his older brother. He occasionally took out several most respectable women now, and although they slept with him, none deluded herself that she was destined to be the next Lady Kronengold. His greatest pleasure in life was being able to indulge his passion for archaeology, visiting and actively working for weeks at a time at those sites he was heavily subsidizing. In short, he was becoming that most familiar of creatures, the wealthy British bachelor: a fixture at his clubs, a treasure at dinner parties, a sound fellow to colleagues at the top of the Establishment.

His relationship to his daughter, however, was a pivotal point between the freedom of the new Leslie de Kronengold and the never quite dormant psychological forces that could still threaten to crack wide and smash to rubble the rock he had become. If she had been ordinary, he might have loved her for that. Yet, even as she was, if she had been his natural daughter, parental pride might have overcome the complex antagonisms that had distorted his attitude towards his children, laming his son and excluding his daughter. But she was not ordinary – this deb year madness was proving that – and she was not his real daughter. He had accepted her into his house out of guilt; she was his expiation for his own child's death. And, because he could put the true faces of the phantoms in her ancestry, they mocked his failings at her every triumph.

Late in the afternoon, Deborah sought out her father at the bank. It was the first time she had been there since Samuel's death, but she thought it important to meet him there.

The few partners who had not yet left for the day courteously did so when Deborah was announced and soon afterwards appeared in the doorway. As she greeted them, her gaze travelled about the room, lighting on familiar objects – portraits of Kronengolds past, the little gold statuette, the hearth. She had prepared herself for the sight of her father rather than her grandfather, behind the great wooden desk beside the hearth. But, even after so many years of coming to terms with Samuel's death, the sight of her father there seemed a mistake, an optical trick that a blink of the eye would replace. However, as the door closed behind her Uncle Charles, the last to leave, Leslie's stiffly correct torso and severe expression remained. She drew up a chair across from him.

Deborah's appearance in the bank, in the very room in which his father had favoured her, served to aggravate further Leslie's already irritable disposition. As the main adviser to a large electronics company, the Kronengold bank had been described by the *Financial Times* and others as staking its 'waning reputation' on being able to fight off the take-over attempt of a much smaller, upstart company. Just that afternoon, the latter's tactics had outmanoeuvred his own and won the day. The nasty little snipers in the press would be aiming their barbs at him for a good long while.

Deborah, too, had spent a difficult day. She awoke despondent, exhausted, having scarcely slept the night before. Hurt as deeply as a woman could be, she exerted all her self-discipline to fight the depression which tried to suck her tired body down into it. She thought of all the helpless, dependent women she knew who had been brought up to adorn a man's house and bear his children and never to achieve or even to have their own ambitions. How many were discarded, lacking skills or resources, when they were too old to obtain them?

At that moment Deborah had resolved to will her own future, which she could foresee with unnerving clarity, although without the slightest detail filled in: she would always be master of her own fate. As a child she had recognized that she could rely only on herself. Her grandfather's training had stressed self-reliance. Yet, where Bash was concerned, something in her psyche or her biology had weakened that fortitude and allowed her to entrust her happiness to him. She had suffered for that lapse. Brooding on the event that had demoralized her, Deborah's determination to be utterly independent of other people grew into a single-mindedness amounting almost to fatalism. She would never again weaken, never again put herself in a position where she need rely on another person for her material welfare or her happiness, certainly not a man.

Deborah had acted on her new imperative. She had dressed and called for a car and driver. The first stop was the London School of Economics. The next destination was a monastery on a hill looking east to the sea. An austere cell in one of the ancient stone buildings housed the only person left in England she could fully trust, her cousin Nathan. She came here or telephoned whenever she needed counsel. Occasionally, he even unburdened himself to her, admitting once to her something he had never allowed anyone but his confessor to know, that the shameful cowardice that had driven him into the monastery had occurred during the Second World War when someone died because he had fled from an arranged meeting.

Penniless now, having given away all his wealth, Nathan was on the phone to Zurich when she arrived, trading millions in stocks and bonds on behalf of the Church. The Holy See was delighted to have such financial acumen in its faithful employ.

Nathan and Deborah spoke for two hours as she thought out her future. Then she had herself driven to the Kronengold bank and asked to see Leslie.

'Father,' Deborah began after she had taken a seat, 'I've

spent a good deal of time recently thinking about my future: my education, my career.'

'Couldn't you have waited until I came home to discuss it?'

'No, I don't think so.'

He nodded, on guard about her motives even as he composed his expression along fatherly lines. 'Aren't you pleased with Oxford?'

'Not very.'

'Having trouble academically?'

'No. It just seems maddeningly pointless, out of touch with life. As if everyone there had agreed to play the same games, indulging themselves while the real world goes on without them. One feels more useless the longer one stays.'

'And you feel different in London?'

'A bit, although there's a dreariness here as well. For a time it was masked by all the scurrying about and the parties, but then the pointlessness of the same vapid people at every dance began to wear through.'

'You're a bit young to be bored with life.'

'That's just it.' She leaned forward. 'It's not life I'm bored with, but unproductive life. I've spoken to the London School of Economics. I can probably continue my education there in the evenings.'

'And during the day?'

'I wish to go into the bank.'

Leslie's eyes widened. His face reddened. On the very day that he was vexed by self-doubt because of a business setback, she had chosen to commence her long-awaited assault on his authority. The perception that such an assault would someday come was not concrete or conscious in Leslie's mind, but had long existed as an inchoate foreboding, a threat to his territorial supremacy sniffed on the breeze. The amiability he had allowed himself to extend towards her in the past few years was instantly eradicated. He knew her once more for the danger to him that she was.

'You wish to go into the bank?' he repeated emphatically, as if he could not believe what she had said. 'The *Kronengold* bank?'

'Yes, this bank, our family bank.'

'For what reason?'

'To become a banker, of course.'

'Except for secretaries, we've never had a woman in the bank,' he said warily. 'Surely you know that.'

'There are some women in banking. And Grandfather seemed to think I had an aptitude for it.'

A pencil he was holding broke in Leslie's hands with a crack like a rifle shot. His nostrils were stretched wide, and the skin over his jaw muscles was tight with anger. But his words were deliberate.

'I would not allow the bank – nor you – to undergo such an embarrassment. With your aggressiveness you would eventually want to become a partner. People would wonder why you hadn't become a partner.' He fixed his eyes on hers. 'In time there would be confusion because of the Kronengold name.'

She returned his stare. 'Because you don't consider me your daughter?'

'To outsiders, for legal matters and the like, you are, of course, my daughter. I still wish you well.' He smiled faintly. 'Your present popularity has certainly enhanced your stock on the marriage market – I've already had a few inquiries from rather solid sources. Have no fear, I'll arrange an advantageous marriage for you.' His face grew grim again. 'But, as the controlling shareholder and as a Kronengold, it's my duty to prevent a stranger from entering the bank and, perhaps, from using that opportunity to lay the groundwork for some spurious claim to ownership.'

Deborah had expected her father's response, had known beforehand everything he would say – and yet had wildly, unreasonably, hoped he would fling away his aversion and recognize at last how much she wanted him to accept her. But time had not modified his contempt in the slightest. Even his occasional cordiality was a charade. Now he had hurt her irrevocably, as he had intended to. Now there was no doubt how much he despised her.

'You've made yourself unmistakably clear,' she said.

'I hope so.' The ghost of a smile still played at the corners of his mouth.

All her life she had backed away from a final confrontation with him that he could use as justification for a final break with her. She had dreaded this moment. But now, as she recognized its inevitability, she felt a snapping of bonds that was nearly audible. An exhilaration close to ecstasy lifted her to her feet.

'I have tried to respect you because you're my father – I even tried to love you. I will no longer waste my emotions. The only thing that would have kept me in England was an offer to enter this bank, a family duty I believe Grandfather intended for me. Now my family obligations are at an end, and I may do whatever I wish with my life. In that sense you've freed me. You, of all people, should understand how liberating that is.'

Gratified by the hostile, uncomprehending expression on his face, she went on. 'You'll doubtless be pleased to learn that I've decided to move to the United States.' She kept her voice matter-of-fact. 'I want whatever inheritance is owed to me.'

Leslie pulled his chair towards his desk. He straightened some papers to mask the trepidation within, to gain time to muster his poise. 'There is none,' he finally replied in an even tone.

'None?' she was stunned.

'Your grandfather left everything to me. Your mother left almost nothing. There was no will, but in accordance with her wishes I have spent what little she did have on your and Richard's education and support.'

Deborah had always assumed she had been well provided for. All her plans depended on it. 'It seems very strange that Mother, who was so careful about her responsibilities, should not have provided a will.'

'It's a matter of public record that she died intestate. The authorities searched for one quite carefully.'

'She had expensive jewellery that was to go to me.'

'She was heavily in debt and had sold all the valuable pieces well before she died. There is no money left.'

'But my inheritance?' she inquired worriedly. 'My mother had money from her family. Where is that?'

'She left nothing.'

'A trust fund for me?'

'No. We never saw the need.'

From Deborah's very first days in the nursery, Leslie had been resentful of the possible claim that Deborah might make on the property to which he and his son were rightfully entitled. Now he had arranged it so that, without his largesse, she had nothing. Control the money and he would control her, Leslie believed. He would make her submit to his wishes for her. He would finally gain from her the respect due him.

Deborah could not keep the shock from showing on her face. The money she had saved from her allowance amounted to only two hundred pounds – about five hundred U.S. dollars. She turned away and walked to the window, suspicious, angry, deep in thought.

When she looked back at him again, she said, 'I trust you are prepared to substantiate this.' It seemed impossible to her that he had not somehow manipulated matters to deprive her.

'I have nothing to hide.' He was certain the books and records would withstand scrutiny. 'Do you intend to beg additional money from relatives?'

Deborah spat back her reply. 'I want nothing that isn't rightfully mine.'

'Admirable,' he remarked superfluously. He was relieved; the penury it so pleased him to impose upon her would have put him in a bad light with the family; questions might have been asked. 'If you are wise you will use your new-found freedom to marry well and obtain security for yourself.'

A peal of laughter broke from her throat.

'*Father!*' She stressed the word. 'Someday I will be successful on a scale that is vast even by Kronengold standards. And, when I am, I swear by whatever is eternal that I shall crush you beneath my heel!'

Leslie was about to leap to his feet – to throw her out or to strike her, he was not sure which. But he found himself paralysed by a gleam, a dominance, in her eye, a peregrine's fearlessness restrained until now out of deference to the honour she owed him. Deborah retraced the steps to the desk and stood directly before him.

'I had nothing except a first name when I came here. You fed and clothed me, and you gave me a second name. I haven't got much else from you to look back on over my eighteen years, but I thank you for that.'

She started for the door.

'If you dare try to capitalize on the family name,' he said, 'I will make your life miserable with lawsuits.'

She turned. She was smiling. 'Good-bye, Leslie.'

Deborah spent the next morning checking the public records to substantiate Leslie's assertions and the afternoon making preparations to leave England. She bought a plane ticket to

New York and withdrew the rest of her money – two hundred dollars in U.S. currency – from the bank. She sent a telegram to say she would not be returning to Oxford. She wrote good-bye notes to a few friends and relatives. And then, early Thursday morning, she boarded an airliner to Idlewild Airport.

In her handbag was a small gold cross on a chain, the single link she possessed to her identity. But she wanted to look ahead, not behind: towards potential without limitation, towards the dream always possible.

Yet for a long while she could look only back; faces she wanted to put behind her still obsessed her and held her in a state of rage: Bash, willing to give her his love but not his name; Leslie, who denied her his love as well as his name. She saw through the hypocrisy Bash and Leslie defended as family duty, the treachery for which they claimed exoneration in the name of names they dishonoured. She scorned their self-serving claims of family love and responsibility, in which she had once fervently believed. She sensed that the very idea of family cohesion – an idea she had been taught by her grandfather and mother to revere as an ultimate good – had already been dead when she was born.

Family itself was the hulk of an obligatory form, a deception to control women and use them: for sex, for connections or money, or, as in the case of Gladys' working-class mother, for domestic labour. Her own mother had finally been unable to bear marriage and family and had fled both as if from a totalitarian state. To marry was to relinquish freedom, to render up one's free will. Having resolved never to relinquish to another power over her own fate, Deborah saw marriage as precisely that sort of submission. To the husband's power was added society's power, its laws and customs, devised and administered by men to bind women hand and foot. Even sex, an essential instinct, she was now convinced, had been commandeered by society for the pleasure of men, and men alone.

Apart from procreation, the justification for sex was love – and love in all its forms had always brought her pain and grief. She feared to love again, but had learned that such feelings could not be simply ordered away. She was utterly certain, however, that even if some distant day she did fall in love with another man, she would never again allow herself to be hurt by trusting him, and she would never surrender herself by marrying him.

If Bash had offered to marry her a few days before, she would have accepted happily, blindly, and the possibility of ever achieving anything on her own would have evaporated. Her father despised her, yet considered her person a valuable asset; he could simultaneously enhance his contacts and dispose of all responsibility by arranging an adroit marriage for her. Although days had passed since her last encounters with her father and Bash, the passion of her hatred for both men, who had rejected in differing ways the love she had freely offered, had not diminished by the merest mote.

But she recognized that Bash, for all her pain at his perfidy, had no obligation to her as Leslie had. Leslie had agreed to be her father, to raise her as his own child, and he had reneged on that obligation by withholding the love that should have given flesh to the skeletal commitment. Bash, at least, had loved her. Leslie, who owed her love – the most basic bond between parent and child – had denied her even that. Solemnly she renewed the pledge she had made to destroy Leslie de Kronengold. She would some day see him poor and powerless, alone and shunned – the same conditions to which he thought he had relegated her forever. She was inflamed by her hate, and grateful for it. It was a lash that would drive her forward – towards success and revenge. She would become invulnerable, so rich and powerful that even her success would awe him – and terrify him.

Realizing that she could not live consumed by hate, she gradually concentrated the emotion into the purest distillation of commitment and allowed it to settle into her bones, forever now an essential, unconscious, integral part of her being. The pain love had caused had been unbearable; she wanted never to suffer it again. But the scars had made her skin tougher, her pain had made her wiser. No one would stop her. No man would ever again divert her. She was dedicated to her mission with a religious fervour.

She had only herself, but that could also be a strength. Others' needs could never deflect her single-mindedness or blunt her resolve. With no chains shackling her to the past, she could be born anew. She could be her own mother and father. She could create herself, whatever she was or wanted to be. She would step from the plane as from a womb, reincarnated whole in a land of limitless promise. After nearly five hundred years America was still the hope of those who sought only an opportunity for their hope. For Deborah, as for millions of other immigrants, America was still the New World.

Part Two

America

CHAPTER TWELVE

The overwhelming preponderance of Americans in 1963 believed devoutly in the democracy, capitalism, and technology that had brought prosperity, the good life – or, at least, a progressively better life – to all of them. They believed in change, which had become almost a constant, and the capacity of the nation's institutions to absorb the bombardment of the new and still remain solid. They believed in their global mission to contain the Communist menace and to spread selflessly their abundance and freedom. They believed in their young, vigorous president, who held these beliefs up before them as a standard they could march behind, who was strong enough to force the Soviet Union to withdraw its missiles from Cuba and still secure enough to sign a nuclear-test-ban treaty with that country. They believed, almost as devoutly as the Establishment coterie that held the foreign policy reins, that the time had come for America to take over from Britain as the moral leader and military policeman of the world. They believed in the promise of America. They believed in themselves.

On September 26, 1963, the day Deborah arrived in New York, the *New York Times* reported that two bombs had been detonated in a Negro Sunday school in Birmingham, Alabama, eleven days after four girls were killed there in a similar incident, and that twenty-eight Negroes were arrested in Selma, Alabama, for demonstrating in front of the courthouse. On the foreign front, the *Times* quoted a defence official, who was on a survey of the military situation in South Vietnam with Defence Secretary Robert McNamara and Joint Chief Head of Staffs General Maxwell Taylor, as saying that 'military events in Vietnam' were 'getting better and better, rather than worse and worse'; the point was rapidly being approached where 'the goals set will be reached relatively shortly.'

For most Americans in 1963, Vietnam was merely a minor

squabble half a world away, the purview of the military boys and diplomats, who knew far more than they. And the Negroes? Now that the problem had been pointed out, civil rights legislation would solve it. After all, this was America, the land of prosperity, of goodness, of ever-growing perfectability, one and united, now and forever, its good crowned by God with brotherhood, from sea to shining sea.

Deborah de Kronengold stood on the steps of the United States Sub-Treasury building beneath the commanding, over-sized statue of George Washington, who had taken the presidential oath of office here. Churning with people, Wall Street bisected the skyscraper canyon like a turbulent river rushing at her feet. The taxi driver had suggested a modest hotel in a respectable neighbourhood and then driven her down to the financial district. The taxi fare was a wild extravagance, given her meagre resources, but she was impatient to find a job and begin her new life.

She detected little beauty in the façades of the buildings on either side of Wall or Broad Streets. The beauty was in the buildings' massiveness, the walls thick and strong to contain all the energy crackling within them, all the ambition. Here, she sensed, was a country unembarrassed by ambition, nurturing energy. Here was a country for dreaming as high and as far as talent and determination could reach, to the stars and beyond. Here was a country endowed with the possibility of choice. And if the choice was to amass riches and one pursued that choice ferociously, single-mindedly, forsaking all others, every waking moment applied relentlessly to that end, every sleeping moment a grudging delay, here was a country where riches could still be won.

That was Deborah's goal: wealth so great that she need never rely on another human being again – for anything. When that goal was finally reached, there would be no doubt who she was.

Deborah descended into the current of people and, picking up their pace, asked directions as she strode along to the first of the investment banks on the list she had copied from the airport phone book. From the airport, she had telephoned the personnel directors of the first two and had made appointments for that afternoon. Her aim was to make her way on her own: partly out of pride – rejecting the Kronengold name that, in the person of her father, had rejected her – and partly because she feared that, if she obtained a job through family contacts or even if he learned she was working in the banking field, her powerful father would use his influence to have her fired. No one knew her in America; she could be anonymous. She intended to use a pseudonym – Deborah Crown – and create a past consistent with appearances on which to build her future.

The people and the enormous cars moved quickly, self-assuredly. Noise battered the air self-importantly. Jack-hammers chattered full voice at the pavement. Taxis, blaring, scooted past one another like over-sized minnows. Voices, loud and confident, jabbed the air in a cacophony of English and other languages. Energy, haste, purpose – everywhere. She felt exhilarated. All around her a welcoming vitality resonated at the determined, exultant frequency of her own. She was nearly giddy with the realization that she had arrived at last where she belonged.

Motivation, however, proved to have little effect. At the first two banks she was told they hired women only at the secretarial level, never as trainees for executive positions. They asked her to take not an aptitude, but a typing, test. At the third firm on her list, she could not talk her way past the receptionist.

Once more on the pavement, Deborah tried to fight off the disappointment that beset her. Her grandfather, known to be the shrewdest banker in England, had trained her in banking himself and encouraged her aspirations to be an investment banker, as merchant bankers were called here. She told herself determinedly that this was only the first day, that success rewarded not the dreamer, but the relentless. Tomorrow she would try again.

People were now streaming out of Wall Street's buildings. She decided to return to her hotel room and plan tomorrow's job search. The evening rush hour crowd carried her along, down into a steaming subway station, and through the open doors of a train, finally lodging her between, on one side, a fat man clutching his jacket to his wet shirt with an arm that also supported a *New York World-Telegram & Sun* and, on the other, the gouging elbows and handbags of two secretaries discussing variations of the bouffant hairdos planned for Saturday night. The crowding, the dirt, the smells, and the heat oppressed her. After several stops she suddenly felt a hand against her thigh and then groping at her pocket-book. She ripped the pocket-book away and clutched it tightly against her breast, although it held very little cash. She had placed nearly all her money – less than three hundred dollars – in the hotel safe before taking the too-expensive taxi to Wall Street.

At the next stop Deborah knifed between the doors as they opened, and she sprinted for the nearest stairs. Deprivation of air and sunlight had been nearly as oppressive as the groping hand. She stood on the sidewalk gulping air for several seconds. New York's similarity to London had deceived her. Every step here was treacherous. For an instant she felt desperate, at the mercy of unseen forces she could not fight, a victim walking blindly past ambushes and booby traps. She reached out to steady herself against a lamp post and wondered if that solidity too might be a rubber deception, bending away from her weight.

Then she began to walk, barely taking note of the scenery about her. She had never felt so alone in her life, so vulnerable. And something more – so young. She had thought of herself as capable and competent, of her short eighteen years as irrelevant. Now her age seemed a mark branded on her forehead to proclaim her naïveté and clumsiness to all. Her self-confidence seemed a laughable pretence, like whistling in the dark. Depression overwhelmed her; she felt incapable of going on.

She gloomily sank down onto one of the white marble steps encircling a fountain, which she had found in a pretty plaza near a corner of Central Park. Soon, shoes held together by string appeared in front of her gaze. Slowly she raised her eyes past the soiled trousers split at the knee and the ripped jacket covering dirt-smeared skin to an equally dirty face. A derelict stood before her, unshaven and bleary-eyed. His hand was out.

'You got some change for a cup of coffee, miss?'

Inculcated all her life with the family's charitable duty, she instinctively reached into her handbag for money. Her purse was gone, stolen on the train, she realized. It had contained only some coins, but this was one more indignity piled on all the rest.

'I've just had all my change stolen,' she apologized in a daze. 'Could I write you a cheque?'

The man gazed at her in bewilderment. Then he swiftly shuffled off, passing several excellent prospects in his haste to flee this woman's obvious derangement.

Only then did Deborah realize how humorous the exchange

had been. Laughter helped restore some of her self-confidence. Nothing had really changed – she had always known she would have to find a job quickly here to survive for more than a month or so.

Deborah stood up and began to walk down Fifth Avenue. With each step her determination grew. At her hotel she broke into a twenty-dollar bill for two candy bars and newspapers containing classified job ads – all she would allow herself to spend.

She went up to the dreary little room she had rented and wrote directly to top officials in the investment banks; only they, it seemed, had the power to accept a woman into a training programme that men could practically march into simply by demonstrating possession of a more or less functioning brain. She was willing to take intelligence tests, aptitude tests – any sort of test they thought might demonstrate her banking knowledge.

When the letters were written, she spread the newspapers out on the bed that filled nearly all the floor space in the little room and concentrated on finding a job in the Help Wanted sections – in any field – to tide her over until she could locate something in finance. Her priority now was to survive. Two things soon became clear: better-paying jobs were seeking male applicants, and those accessible to women invariably required prior experience in the field. She circled any job that looked promising and, consulting a street map, tried to group the prospects into neighbourhoods so as to waste neither time nor her scant savings getting from one to the next. She would take anything. Her primary aim was the money to keep going. She had no skills, no training. All she had was tenacity.

She stood up and walked to the window, unwrapping the second candy bar. As she ate it, she stared at the night, straining to see the future and to find in it the hope of some hope. Based only on the fierce nerve sometimes granted to those whose only other possessions are raw ambition and a hunger for revenge, she was determined the day would come when she would be the richest, the most powerful of the Kronengolds. Her vengeance then would lay waste her enemies. But, first, she must simply survive.

She heard a siren close by and then a fainter one many blocks away. This was a rapacious, a terrifying city, filled with people ready to trample her if she let them. She must run harder and faster than they. She must be cunning. She must never cease to believe in her ultimate success.

By the end of the fourth day, Deborah could feel the edges of desperation curling around her. Twice that afternoon, jobs she could have filled had been given to others less than an hour before she arrived – walking. And a language school admitted it had merely been compiling a list of potential teachers in case enrollments picked up. Her last stop that day was at a lingerie company. The ad purporting to be for an assistant to be trained by the marketing manager turned out to be for a showroom model who, in between underwear exhibitions, could handle other chores – like sleeping with buyers. The receptionist suggested that with her looks she should check out high-fashion photographic modelling. The idea of exhibiting herself repelled Deborah, but even if it had not, her face was too well-known by too many people in England for her to remain anonymous in that profession. More important, someone who worked as a model would lose all credibility when she sought a job in investment banking.

Walking home early that evening, tired and discouraged, Deborah wondered how long she would have the luxury of choice. Remembering a letter in her handbag to be posted, she stopped at a post office that was open late. On the way out of the building, she was halted by a curious and ominous sight, an entire wall of grim, hooded eyes that glinted with cruelty. WANTED, the posters announced, for armed robbery, for fraud, for murder.

The old black-and-white movies she had seen at Oxford's film society were no longer exaggerated melodrama to induce shivers from ticket buyers. The subway theft had been petty, surreptitious, invisible. Here she was assaulted by eyes aglare with the misguided ambition rampant in the New World, the lone-wolf opportunism that could suddenly, with no warning, lurch towards violence.

Late that night, she lay on the sagging mattress, hands behind her head, and stared up at a ceiling badly in need of paint. She had never lacked for money before in her life, had never even had to give her personal finances a moment's consideration. A Kronengold was concerned with obtaining a good return on capital, not with trying to meet the week's rent. Deborah realized that being poor frightened her as very few things in her life ever had. It made her feel powerless, unable to direct her own fate. Achieving wealth was not simply a form of retaliation against her father, but a necessity, first, for basic survival – something she had never thought about before – and, second, for the independence she craved.

Finally, she extinguished the lamp on the bedside table. The only light left in the room was dim and shifting, from the headlights moving along the street below. Inner shadows began to shift in response, as if great stones were being rolled back. Terrors, trapped no longer, slithered up out of their dark holes. With no money, no prospect yet of acquiring any, no family to lean upon, she was frightened, desperate. The forces she was up against appeared monstrous and brutal. Always so proud of her indomitability, she felt small; her ambition seemed self-deluding. She was frighteningly alone. For an instant she thought of her mother. Even after all these years, she still missed her terribly.

Homesick now for England and its safe familiarity, she considered going back. Then she grew angry at her weakness and rejected all intentions of returning: going back now, without being able to hold aloft a dazzling trophy, would be defeat. And so would reliance on relatives for help in procuring the success she craved – she was not entitled to aid, nor did she want any. Driven off the Kronengold domain, stripped of the false mantle of family member, she was Deborah Crown now.

I *am* Deborah Crown, she thought, a new person begetting myself. I'll survive from day to day and hand to mouth, if need be, but I *will* survive – and, surviving, I'll go on to triumph, to riches, From now on, she demanded of herself, there will be no wavering.

The next day, while walking from one job inquiry to the next, Deborah spotted a handwritten sign in the window of a French restaurant: HOSTESS WANTED. The restaurant had not yet opened for the day, so she planted herself on the doorstep and waited for the owner to arrive. He turned out to be a rough ex-chef from Marseilles. He was pleased at the fluency of her French, but that was not enough for him to hire her as the night hostess.

'My customers do not know the difference between *vin* and *pain*. Talk like me, maybe you get a job.'

Deborah imitated his accent, pouting out her lower lip exaggeratedly.

'Not bad,' he admitted, reverting to French. 'Maybe you know a waitress. I'm short a waitress for dinner also.'

'How much does a hostess earn?'

'Ninety dollars a week.'

'A waitress?'

'Twenty and tips.'

Deborah reasoned that she would have cash in her pocket at the end of the night if she was a waitress. By working hard, she could earn a lot more than a hostess. 'I'll take the waitress job.'

The restaurant owner looked at her dubiously.

'You could seat the customers yourself,' she argued, 'but who'll wait on them?'

He frowned and nodded simultaneously. 'Be here at six. You get supper.'

He turned his back on her and his attention to other matters.

Deborah stood there stunned for a moment and then nearly danced out of the restaurant.

Her luck had changed. Within hours she had a second job, one in which her clear, aristocratic English speech was an asset. An answering service hired her for the midnight-to-eight shift. That left part of the day for sleeping and the rest for pursuing a job in investment banking. She was jubilant as she headed back to the restaurant to start work. They even threw in supper, she remembered. The job was a bonzanza. Her elation crashed an instant after she realized that she had been served by others all of her life – had barely noticed them flitting inconspicuously about her – and had no idea what was expected of a waitress. She would have to watch the other waitresses carefully.

Later that night, having struggled through her first round of dinners, grateful for pointers from the other women while trying to hide her inexperience from her boss, she finally had time for a breather. She sipped some water beside the rack of tumblers just out of the dishwasher and thought about the tips now safely in her pocket. Thirteen dollars and seventy-five cents. This was the first time in days that anxiety was not abrading the edge of her mind. Thirteen dollars and seventy-five cents. And a full stomach. She was on her way.

How maliciously April would laugh to see her now! 'My God, actually reduced to working at a job!' she would no doubt comment. 'And such a grubby one at that!' And then Deborah remembered the example of her friend Gladys Wood, willing to undertake any work that would pay well enough for her to ease the burden that her being at Oxford put on her working-class parents.

As Deborah put down her glass and began to place Table 7's appetizers on her tray, she realized that she had never really understood money until these trying first days in New York. She had comprehended how it operated on the large scale, of course, how macro-economic forces impacted on national economies and industry and how to devise creative funding structures to meet a variety of corporate needs and how to analyse the most complex balance sheets. But actual pennies and dollars that could be the difference between eating and starving, between shelter and the street, were something very new to her and, she had been forced to admit, far more important. Her earlier knowledge would be the basis for her success or failure in business. But this new knowledge determined her survival.

The following Monday Deborah telephoned the investment bankers to whom she had written. Unlike Great Britain, America allowed investment banks to trade on the stock exchanges, so most investment banks were also stockbrokerage firms, usually very large ones. Deborah was able to get through to a few of the bankers. Of those who actually took her call, one turned her down harshly and another turned her down tactfully, but just as firmly. None was sympathetic to her arguments that she should be given a chance to join their training programmes on the strength of the battery of tests they often employed to identify worthwhile candidates or of her economics course at Oxford (although everyone to whom she spoke seemed to assume she had been awarded a degree). The others, secretaries and executives, told her that her letter had been referred to Personnel. There, her tactics of writing to men at the top seemed to have done some good. Several personnel employees made appointments to interview her in the coming weeks, although none sounded enthusiastic – until she made her last telephone call. The man at that last firm made an appointment to see her the very next day.

Deborah had been careful to arrange the appointment in the afternoon. By then she would have had a few hours of sleep after finishing work. She wore her best suit: dark blue, responsible looking.

Deborah's legs were shaking as she took the elevator up to the firm's offices, and she had to hold onto the handrail to steady herself. She was actually grateful that she had to wait a while in the reception area.

Her high hopes for the interview were quickly dashed when the interviewer asserted that he had misunderstood her credentials during their telephone conversation, believing her to have had prior work experience in the field of financial statistics. For a moment she considered fabricating statistical experience – she could try to pick up enough from library books to cover herself while learning. Then he admitted he was seeing her only because Mr. Ebring had kicked her letter downstairs to him. When Deborah pressed him, he confessed they probably would not have hired a woman for the job anyway. Women executives, especially junior ones, always leave to get married; they aren't dependable, he told her. Of course, none had ever been hired – senior or junior – so the theory had never been tested.

As Deborah pushed through the revolving doors and back onto the sidewalk, the loneliness she had been able to keep at bay for days charged at her just behind the heat. She had not made a single friend in this hostile city. One or two of the Frenchwomen at the restaurant were pleasant, but there were none she could ever get close to. She retreated to her hotel room to write letters to the few friends and relatives with whom she still felt strong ties. She spent the most time on her letters to her cousin Nathan, in the monastery, and to her Uncle Pierre. Later on, she would write to other relatives, and eventually word would reach Leslie and allay his suspicions that she might have gone into banking. But remembering how far away they all were only increased the loneliness. All she could tell them was that she was in America to study, that she missed them, and that she would write again soon with a permanent address to which they could reply. By that time she would have rented a post office box – she did not want anyone to know where she was or how to find her.

Deborah used her free hours during the day to search for an affordable apartment in a safe neighbourhood, but that soon became as hopeless a task as finding a job on Wall Street. She recognized that she would probably have to resign herself to taking a place in one of the outer boroughs, the travel to Manhattan deducting precious hours from the time available to hunt for a job. She decided to spend a few more days trying to find a Manhattan apartment before giving up.

By now, Deborah was beginning to pick up the little pieces of wisdom about the city that made it easier to make one's way. On Friday night, between her jobs at the restaurant and the answering service, she would race down to the Times Square news-stand for the Sunday *Times* Real Estate section, printed days in advance and distributed so early only to that stand. Few telephone calls came into the answering service after two o'clock in the morning, and Deborah used the early Saturday morning hours to peruse the newspaper for apartments.

It was barely 8.15 that particular Saturday morning in October when Deborah hurried up to the brownstone in the east Thirties. The street was shabby, with several run-down tenements on either side, but the narrow town house converted into apartments appeared fairly clean and well kept.

As Deborah began to climb the front steps, she noticed another young woman approaching the building from the opposite direction in an equally determined manner. They eyed each other for an instant, and both quickened their pace. Observing Deborah's advantage, the young woman gambled that the person showing the apartment lived on the bottom floor, reached by stairs that descended several steps below the sidewalk level. Both women pushed front-door bells.

About three minutes later, after one of the tenants had shown her the vacant apartment, Deborah raced downstairs to speak to the landlord, who indeed did live in the ground-floor apartment.

A balding, middle-aged man in a short-sleeved shirt stood in his doorway talking to the other young woman.

'I'll take the apartment,' Deborah called out as she bounded down the steps. 'The ad said eighty-one dollars rent per month.'

'I was here first,' the other woman argued firmly. 'I'll take it.'

'You haven't even seen it,' Deborah retorted.

'If you want it, then it must be all right. I've walked every foot of this city for a month, and it's the first decent apartment I could afford.'

Deborah ignored her, concentrating on the owner. 'I was the first one to say I'd take the apartment. Here's the first month's rent in cash.'

The owner shrugged. 'My wife's brother took it yesterday.'

'Damn!' both women muttered simultaneously.

'Believe me, I don't care for him any more than you do, but family is family. You know what I should get for an apartment like that?' he asked them defensively. He thought for a moment. 'I got an apartment coming vacant the end of the week.'

'I'll take it!' both women exclaimed.

'Two bedroom. One ninety-seven fifty a month. Believe me, it's a palace.'

Both women exhaled in a sigh.

'I can't swing it,' the blonde-haired young woman said to Deborah in a defeated tone. 'It's all yours.'

'I can't afford it either,' Deborah admitted.

The landlord crossed his arms and gazed first at one, then the other. 'Why don't you take it together?'

'We don't even know each other,' the blonde responded.

'Now you do.'

For the first time both young women turned to examine the other. Deborah saw a very pretty young woman of medium height, perhaps a few years older than she, with the pert features and ready smile that fitted the stereotype she had come to associate with American women.

'It would be convenient, of course,' Deborah said, 'but I've never lived with anyone else.'

'We just happened to arrive here at the same time,' the other added.

The owner flipped his palms outward. 'Look, it's got two bedrooms. You each have some privacy,' he argued. 'And it saves me the cost of running an ad.'

Deborah hesitated. 'That's less than a hundred dollars a month for each of us. I could manage that.'

The blonde bit her lip, eyeing Deborah. 'I apologize for asking this, but you don't have any terrible habits, do you? Like being an alcoholic? Or raising pet rats?'

Laughing, Deborah shook her head. Her first impression of the other young woman was very favourable. 'Perhaps we should look at the apartment.'

'I suppose so.'

'Now you're talking sense,' the owner informed them.

The apartment was on the fifth floor, the last landing on the stairway. It was small, running through the length of the narrow building, but it was neat. Both women's resistance melted. They could trudge months more and not find value like this. In the living room they faced each other.

'I fancied the bedroom at the rear,' Deborah asserted.

'That's fine.'

They both considered the proposition a moment more. Then Deborah spoke up.

'Let's give it a try.'

The other young woman nodded, breaking into a hospitable smile.

Deborah turned to the landlord. 'One hundred ninety-seven fifty a month is all right if the furniture comes with it.'

'I get thirty a month more for the furniture.'

'What if we bought our own?'

'I got a big basement.'

'This furniture isn't good enough to store.'

His eyes rolled up. 'We send over lend-lease. They send over killers.' Then he chuckled. 'All right, it's early dreck.' He warmed now to the negotiation. 'The furniture is free, but I get a month's security.'

Deborah always knew to the penny the exact amount in her bank account. Her share of the security deposit in addition to the rent would be far more than she had managed to save. 'You won't need security with two of us signing the lease.'

'Just off the boat and she talks like a lawyer.' He considered her argument and then nodded.

'And you'll paint it before we move in,' Deborah added. She had no way of knowing that the city would require a painting if he had not provided one for the requisite number of years. Instead, she tried to coax him. 'You have to admit that it needs painting.'

Grudgingly, he nodded once more. As Deborah seemed about to speak again, he quickly interrupted. 'That's it. I gave in too much already. Just to save on a lousy ad, it's costing me twice as much.'

Deborah smiled. 'I was just going to say we'll take it.' She turned to her new roommate and extended her hand. 'I'm Deborah Crown.'

The two young women shook hands. 'I'm Amanda Bailor. But everyone calls me Mandy.'

'And I'm Kropotkin,' the man informed them. 'And I think I just ended up on the short end.'

Deborah's instincts about people, honed by her grandfather, were usually excellent. They turned out to be quite accurate in Mandy Bailor's case. Pleasant and careful to respect Deborah's privacy, she was unfailingly cheerful, no matter the situation or the hour. She woke up smiling and sailed straight through the rest of the day that way. Deborah's tendency to British reserve gave way almost at once. Mandy Bailor embodied the most likeable American traits. An aspiring musical-comedy actress who had come to New York from Sandusky, Ohio, she worked at night as a waitress at the Improv, a nightclub that had opened on the edge of the theatre district earlier that year. Unknown comedians and singers appeared there for free to polish their craft and to be discovered. Twice each night, Mandy sang. All day she made the rounds of casting and producers' offices and, when she could afford it, took classes.

Mandy had been a cheerleader in high school and worked her way through Northwestern. The boy she met there was just finishing medical school and begged her to marry him, but she found him dull and the prospect of the suburban life he planned – opening a practice while she had babies and kept house – stifling. She had starred in a dozen college musicals and had trained for years. She wanted her own career and a try at stardom. She knew she could become a star, like her idol Doris Day, if she gave herself the chance.

In disclosing the outline of her own past to Mandy, Deborah stuck closely to a version of her life that paralleled the truth in most regards and went only a step or two further in others: she was an orphan, brought up in England, and her boyfriend had been killed in a car accident at Oxford. Talking about Bash as if he had not survived the accident brought a grimly satisfying, if temporary, soothing of the angry resentment towards him that still festered within her. Rather than unnerving Deborah, lying about her past emphasized the distance she had travelled from it and elicited an inner elation at having become the creation she was fashioning.

Friendship that was important to both of them quickly

grew between the two young women. The very alienness of each to New York provided a commonality of outlook and need that nurtured a close relationship wildly improbable under other circumstances. Deborah considered the theatre a frivolous career choice, in which luck played too great a part – too much power resided in the hands of others. Yet she rooted hard for Mandy when she went off for a casting call. On her side, Mandy could not believe that a person as knowledgeable about the arts and as warmly empathetic as Deborah could be dominated by a business ambition she herself considered unrealistic and unfeminine. Their differences made their conversation interesting, and their amicability and concern for each other served to make both look forward to their time together.

Having a roommate and friend with whom to share the difficulties and disappointments helped to maintain their optimism and made pursuit of the brass ring less lonely. Mandy's friendship was particularly welcome to Deborah because the acrimony with April still reverberated within her like a gong's resonance that refused to still. She remained very careful at all times not to offend Mandy in any way, overcareful really, subconsciously fearful of losing her newly-won friend. At the pit of her, deeper even than the incident with April, was her longing for her mother and the guilt she had never ceased to feel that she had caused her mother's death by asking her to drive to the airport. At the moments when she missed her mother most, Deborah felt the vague sense that she had lost her because she had never really been entitled to her. Yet she rarely had a conscious awareness of that self-reproach. Her subconscious translated the varieties of guilt into other terms: gratefulness for this new friendship, the hope that the success she hungered for would expiate the guilt.

One afternoon Deborah went to the Admissions Office of Columbia University's School of General Studies to inquire about continuing her education and to put up around the school handwritten ads for language tutoring she was offering on Saturdays and Sundays. While she was tacking the handbill to a bulletin board, a good-looking young man tried to strike up a conversation with her. She ended the conversation diplomatically and fled. The rigorous agenda she had set herself permitted no time for men. Like a marathon runner, she feared that even a brief diversion would lessen her concentration, the intensity of her effort. She was obsessed by a single goal and distrusted the temptation of anything not advancing her towards it.

Deborah allowed herself only two outlets. Mandy had a small black-and-white TV set. Occasionally they were able to watch the early news together. It was their window out of their narrow lives onto the broad landscape of the world. They thrilled to film of the young president, John F. Kennedy, with his easy grace and beautiful wife and children. He seemed to be someone in touch with their own generation, a young prince brandishing an irresistible sword. He made everything appear possible for them.

Her other entertainment was reading at the nearly silent switchboard during the early morning hours. She read financial material, to be sure, eager to acquaint herself with the difference between American and British financial methods, but she scoured newspapers and the books she took from the library as well, trying to decipher the strange practices of this new culture. America's mustang energy seemed to her to burst through in the language, and she devoured writers like Hemingway, who seemed to epitomize this country. She could even sense America in its spelling: 'color', not the British 'colour'. Without an extraneous, fancifying *u*, the word was brighter somehow, the hues more pungent. The language here was a key to the nation that printed it: more vivid, quicker, franker.

Although she was now making money and had somewhere to live, Deborah had progressed no farther towards her goal of obtaining a job in the financial industry. One or two people to whom she spoke advised her to wait until she had completed the schooling she would be recommencing at Columbia next semester. Perhaps, if she had a doctorate in economics, her credentials would be too impressive to resist, they suggested. Deborah refused to resign herself to waiting four or five or maybe more years for the hope of then beginning her climb.

But her prospects failed to match her determination. As November wound down she could look forward to only two job interviews – both on the same day – with little hope of others if those two failed to pan out. That morning, while she was brushing her hair and rethinking all the things she wanted to keep in mind during the interviews, Mandy surprised her with a good-luck cake she had baked late the night before, while Deborah was at the answering service. Mandy had a callback reading for a play later that day, so they toasted each other in hot coffee, and then Deborah set out for Wall Street.

The morning appointment was at Baitling Commodities, a firm that traded contracts to buy or sell copper, wheat, lumber, sugar, pork bellies, and the like on commodities exchanges. It was not an investment bank, but it was in the financial field and might provide the opportunity to move to a banking firm in the future. Commodities firms were considered far more freewheeling than the ultra-conservative investment banks and might be willing to gamble on taking a woman. Her appointment was with the managing partner of the small firm, an edgy, frenetic man in his forties named Corcoran, who kept her waiting in a chair across the desk from him while he took a succession of telephone calls and shot sidelong glances first at her face and then lower down. She was wearing the dark blue suit and white silk blouse she saved for job interviews. She adjusted the skirt self-consciously, fearing it was riding up. Finally, Corcoran broke off a telephone conversation and told his secretary to hold all calls. Then he shut the door and unleashed a humourless smile.

'So you want to get into commodities.'

'Very much.'

'Tell me about yourself, Miss Crown. And please don't keep personal details from me. The better I know you, the more likely I am to hire you. You know, there's big money here for the right person, Miss Crown. May I call you Debbie?'

She smiled and tried to reply with a light wit that would maintain the informality but establish respect for her as a potential equal. 'Mr. Corcoran, not even my dearest enemies call me Debbie. I'm called Dee.'

'Great. Jim's my name. But we're here to talk about you, right, Deb?' The smile flashed unexpectedly at her again.

Deborah used the opportunity to outline her Oxford education, her enrollment at Columbia and her knowledge of commodities – she had spent long hours since she obtained this appointment delving into everything she could find on the subject. She ended by telling him that she was seeking to become a trainee with the firm and thought she could do a good job for them.

'A lot of people want to get in on the ground floor with us,' he answered. 'But the person I pick has got to have something special.' He moved to the front of the desk, directly in front of her, sitting on its edge and leaning forward, his knees outside hers. 'That person will work closely with me. Evenings, some weekend trips.' He smiled coyly.

She noticed on the bookcase behind him a photograph of two lumpish kids glaring at the camera beside a lumpish woman and lumpish dog. Deborah found herself involuntarily sympathizing with Corcoran's need to philander. He was fairly attractive, clearly hardworking, a success. His reward for all that was to go home at night to those sullen mounds. She felt torn by her desperation for a job in finance, her hope that this interview would be a breakthrough for her. She thought about what Corcoran was offering. Maybe it wouldn't be so bad. At least she would have a friend to rely on. Perhaps these are the dues that everyone says one must pay in the climb up. She wanted this job so much. She pursued her argument.

'There could be an advantage in hiring a woman trader. Women shy away from investing in commodities. I could help convince them otherwise.'

'Oh, there are advantages, all right. You'll start at two hundred a week!'

'In what job?' she asked warily.

'My secretary. That girl out there doesn't know when she's got a good thing. Goddamn migraines.'

'I'm not interested, Mr. Corcoran,' Deborah announced firmly.

'Oh, only to begin with,' he quickly corrected himself. And then he smiled coyly again. 'It all depends on the kind of, you know, rapport we develop.' He leaned over to touch the ruffles on her blouse.

'I think I've heard enough, Mr. Corcoran. I'm leaving.'

He locked his knees hard against hers and loomed over her, making it impossible for her to stand up. 'Two hundred a week – and a lot of bonuses,' he whispered.

'I said I was leaving,' Deborah repeated firmly, with no effect. 'Let me up.'

'You file a few things. Answer some phones for me. If you

do have some talent for commodities, hell, that's great; maybe you can even learn a little something and help out.' He paused to take in some air, and he raised his eyes to her face. 'Shit, you're a beautiful –'

'Get away from me. Now!'

He thrust forward to embrace her. Deborah's knee caught him in the testicles only a fraction of a second later. He bent double, whimpering.

As she left, she caught a glimpse of the incomprehension that wrestled in his eyes with the pain.

Deborah walked the narrow streets in a blind fury, hardly realizing where she was heading. She had placed so much useless hope on that interview. The callousness of the man's lust disgusted her. The talent she might bring to his firm was irrelevant to him. Her ambition was a chip he could play. Life to him was commerce in the most basic urges, unadorned by such confusing frills as tenderness or even mutuality of interest.

Corcoran panting over her. A hand groping at her thigh in a crowded subway like a hungry crab in heat, then choosing instead to scuttle into the unexpected opportunity of her purse. Bash plunging himself into her before daring to reveal his marriage plans. Maleness seemed to her at that moment nothing more than muscularity for pinning or charm for deceiving a woman into place long enough to induce semen to spurt. Was sex really just as sordid as she had supposed it to be when she stared into the cottage window so many years ago? Was life commerce and commerce life all one knew and all one needed to know?

Deborah finally calmed down enough to stop at a luncheonette for a cup of tea and a sandwich. Above all she must not let her anger over the incident ruin the impression she made at her next, and last, appointment, at Hazelton, Lieb & Co.

Hazelton, Lieb was one of the great American investment banks. The firm had been started by a family of nineteenth-century pedlars who had shifted into banking, as had the Kronengolds and others, by extending credit on the goods they sold and then becoming lenders to other traders. It now had offices around the country that sold stocks and bonds to the public. The heart and brains of the firm continued to be its main office, a replica of an Italian Renaissance palazzo erected out of great stone blocks. Located there were the investment bank and the executive offices, where various partners presided over aspects of the bank's functions; by means of stock and bond offerings and commercial loans, they arranged the financing for industrial companies and utilities and for states and cities. Although they often made investments themselves in promising ventures, they were primarily middlemen, who found the capital for their clients' needs. Much of the financing was obtained from private placements with such financial institutions as insurance companies, large urban commercial banks, and pension and mutual funds. Most often, however, they joined with other securities dealers in a syndicate to sell shares of a public stock or bond issue, each firm committing to sell an agreed-upon amount to its clients – either individual investors or financial institutions. They also managed the investments for several of those accounts. Hazelton, Lieb was a superb investment bank for Deborah to join. It was also the last one of any repute that had not yet turned her down.

The woman who saw her was Mrs Lorenzo, the second person in authority in the Personnel Department, a middle-aged, dark-eyed, and heavy-set woman with wings of bleached blonde hair on either side of a lined brow.

'You're a bright, with-it, ambitious girl. But you don't even know typing and shorthand.'

'Do male candidates come in having to know typing and shorthand?'

'No.'

'I thought my letter made clear that I'm not seeking to be a secretary.'

The woman assessed the spirit she observed in the young woman's eyes and sighed. 'I'll level with you, honey. I spent twenty years as a secretary before I finally wheedled my way into this position. I've had it for nearly fifteen years and seen three men half as smart as I am brought in over me to run this department. I do the work. They get the credit and the salary.'

'There must be some women bankers here.'

The woman shook her head. 'And probably none in any other investment bank either. Real bankers, I mean. There are a few women partners on the brokerage side of a few firms, but they usually have doctorates and are still kept in the back as stock analysts. A woman even has trouble getting a decent lunch down here – the private clubs, where all the contacts and deals are made, exclude us and there aren't too many good restaurants.' The woman leaned closer. 'Look, that English accent is really attractive. American executives would fall over themselves to hire you. Why don't you take a quick secretarial course –'

Deborah's mouth was firm. 'There has to be another way.'

'You're really set on it.'

Deborah nodded. 'I've had a year at Oxford, as you can see from my application, and I'm enrolled at Columbia – in economics.'

The woman shrugged helplessly and began perusing Deborah's application once more.

The only emotion that could fight off Deborah's dejection at that instant was anger. Pampered by her grandfather, she had failed to understand what struck her now: that finance everywhere was a single, huge, very male fraternity. It was a worldwide locker room where deals were made by men who threw their arms around each other's shoulders and guffawed at tales of besting competitors, customers, and colleagues; bosses, birds, and broads. Every game has rules. On your back, dollie, so we can run the ball over you. Don't you know the rules? Sit on the sidelines until it's time to spread your legs so we can kick the ball through them. Those are the rules.

Achievement had seemed so easy when she stormed out of Leslie's study, threw her existence into a suitcase, and booked a transatlantic flight. Now, the walls on Wall Street seemed to ascend to infinity.

'Mrs. Lorenzo,' Deborah tried once more, gathering her will, 'I'm still at university and perhaps I was premature in expecting to enter the training programme. But I don't want to start out in a dead-end position either. Is there anything available that isn't a secretary's job, where the partners might accept a woman?'

The woman ruminated for a moment, her dubious expression deepening. Then she reached for a manila file on the side of her desk and began leafing through papers. Finally, she shook her head.

'Nothing. There's the librarian's job, of course. It's not quite secretarial or clerk.'

Deborah grew excited. 'Librarian?'

'That's always been designated as a man's job.'

'Does it have to be?' Deborah asked.

The woman skimmed the job description. 'You keep the books and the financial material companies have to file with the S. E. C. in order, send around the periodicals that come in, and then file them. When anyone wants something, you send it to them.' She looked up. 'It pays less than a secretary gets.'

'Does the librarian ever get asked to do research on her own?'

'Look, the truth is it's designated for men because you have to heave around boxes of books that come in. It's boring and leads nowhere. I'd hate for you to get your hopes up. We haven't had someone on a full-time basis in months. I told you, it doesn't really pay enough or provide the advancement to interest anyone.'

'*I'd* like the job. Very much. What *is* the salary?'

'Minimum wage, a dollar twenty-five an hour. Forty hours a week. But, as I said, we've always had a man in the job.'

Fifty dollars a week, Deborah calculated. When her night and Saturday classes started at Columbia, she could remain at the answering service – her shift was so slow no one minded her dozing off on the sofa as long as she got to the switchboard by the third ring. At weekends, she could continue her language tutoring and maybe even her work at the restaurant. Still, by substituting this weekday job for the restaurant, she would have less at the end of the week than she did now. But she might never have another chance to get inside a financial firm like Hazelton, Lieb – or maybe any other financial firm.

'Mrs. Lorenzo,' she said, trying to eliminate from her voice the neediness she felt inside, 'most librarians are women. The position requires an education. You'll have trouble finding anyone who's educated – man or women – at the salary you're offering. I can barely afford it, but I want the opportunity. I'm sure your boss or whoever has the last say would be glad to hire anyone who'll get things into order.'

Deborah pressed on, sensing that the woman was giving her a sympathetic hearing. 'After all you've gone through, you should be the person who's most willing to support my getting the job. You know better than anyone how foolish and destructive these prejudices against women are. All I want is a chance to prove myself.'

The older woman rose, Deborah's application in her hand.

'Mr. Weber, who runs this department, is a pretty spineless character, but I guess I can talk him into making this one little decision on his own.'

She left the room and did not return for nearly fifteen minutes. When she did, she had a smile on her face.

'I think you're crazy to take this job, but if it's what you want, you have it.'

Deborah exhaled a breath she seemed to have been holding since the older woman left. 'Thank you, Mrs. Lorenzo. Someday I'll repay this kindness. It's what I want all right.' Oh, is it what I want!

Deborah raced out of the subway station and down the street towards her apartment building. The streets were strangely empty of people, but she hardly noticed. She took the stairs two at a time to the top landing, where her apartment was. She could not wait to break the news to Mandy, who had rooted for her through all the disappointments and would be nearly as thrilled as she at the good news.

Odd, she thought, the door is open. She stepped into the apartment. Mandy and the landlord, Kropotkin, and several others were huddled around the little television set.

'What is it?' Deborah asked.

Mandy turned slowly, waiting to speak until she was looking at Deborah. 'It's Kennedy. He's been shot.'

'Oh, no!'

'They think he's dead.'

Deborah collapsed into a chair, overcome by a sense that the young president's death had been inevitable. Too many people loved him, and she knew better than anyone how death comes to the things in which people invest, not their money, but their hearts.

CHAPTER THIRTEEN

At the turn of the century, the American investment banker was a feared, envied, and somewhat sinister character, personified by the colossus who dominated American finance then, J. Pierpont Morgan. Markets were said to rise and fall at the twitch of his bushy eyebrow. He merged smaller companies to form such giants as General Electric, General Motors, and U.S. Steel. He dominated financing of the rail-roads, which soaked up much of the nation's investment capital in order to bind the nation with a transportation network. He and the others of the private banking elite, living opulent lives in Fifth Avenue mansions that are now either department stores, museums, or demolished, *were* the American financial structure.

The citizens of New York, the press and, thus, the politicians laid much of the blame for the Great Depression on the investment banks, which now included not only the traditional private banks but the large commercial banks as well. Both took deposits and invested their depositors' funds, which often were pooled time deposits or trust accounts, in public issues they themselves underwrote. 'Underwriting' meant that they pledged to buy the shares themselves if they could not sell them to investors. But there was little fear of that, with so much ready cash on deposit in their own banks. In many cases the securities' prices were inflated and their risks concealed, and they were subjected to little or no objective scrutiny. Many banks failed when much of that stock and bond value, held in lieu of the cash, proved worthless.

Based on investigative hearings, Congress passed the Glass-Steagall Law in 1933, which forced the separation of deposit and investment banking. Along with the legislation creating the Securities and Exchange Commission and regulating the underwriting and selling of stocks and bonds, this law forced a fundamental change in the way capital was sought and invested. Financial firms were forced to split apart into commercial banks that took deposits and investment banks that underwrote and sold stocks and bonds. The House of Morgan, for example, split into the commercial bank Morgan Guaranty Trust Company and the investment bank Morgan, Stanley & Co., with personnel choosing to join one or the other.

By the 1960s, the investment banks had once more become respectable, providing a wide range of financial advice and services to those who needed capital and those who wished to invest it. But most investment bankers continued to operate in the traditional ways, unaware that the vigorous economy was transforming the assumptions on which they operated. Barely visible forces surging deep beneath America's landscape would eventually burst forth and reshape it forever. Very few bankers had the foresight to sense the possibilities prowling unseen in the future and to create out of pure idea those new opportunities that would someday form into a pack of irresistible predators charging at the rest of their industry. But those who did and who had the guts to act on their prescience would make fortunes.

The librarian position turned out to be both hard work and as unprepossessing as Deborah had been warned it would be. She spent the first few weeks filing material that had accumulated, straightening up the stacks and card index, and trying to figure out a way to make herself noticed in the least noticeable of Hazelton, Lieb's departments. By then she had made friends with many in the sub-structure of secretaries and clerks that keep a major business organization functioning. She had carefully learned what every executive in the firm did, what his interests were, and what his strengths and weaknesses were. She skimmed every periodical as soon as it arrived and then, before she sent it on its route from executive to executive, she would photocopy articles of interest to particular partners or their staff and append a personal note: 'Dear Mr. Howell, I thought you'd be interested in this article on the tax implications of corporate liquidations that just came in. Very truly yours, Deborah Crown, librarian.' When she passed Mr. Howell in the corridor, she would introduce herself and ask if the article was helpful. She would try her best to get in a question he would remember, like did he think that the new IRS regulations would change the capital gains treatment of corporate reorganizations. When he expressed surprise at her knowledge, she would 'admit' that she had studied economics at Oxford and was now doing further studies at Columbia. Over a period of time, she became acquainted with all the executives in the firm. Occasionally, one would drop into the library or send a note to ask her help in researching into some matter or obtaining the financial statements for a company or an industry he was studying. This was a slow campaign, in which Deborah hoped, not only to become known, but to be thought of as a valuable adjunct to some department's efforts, so that she would be able to shift out of the library and into a junior position in one of the banking departments.

While she worked, she continued to learn, both by reading everything in the library that might be useful and by excelling at Columbia. She had a straight-A average and the recommendation of an important professor in one of her courses that she consider a career teaching economics and finance. It would never have occurred to him that a woman might actually want to enter the business world itself.

In the autumn of 1964 a young man in one of Deborah's classes asked her out for a date. Ordinarily, she turned down all such overtures – she did not have time for them; she was either in class or at work every night of the week. Moreover, her experience with Bash had left her scarred. She had come to believe that love was a disease – not the intoxicating fever her grandfather had claimed it to be, but a devastating scourge that left one crippled in spirit, forever in pain. She was not eager to expose herself again to that debilitation of her purpose, to that ravaging of her soul.

But she accepted for two reasons. He asked her to a Yankee baseball game on a Saturday afternoon, after one of her language students had cancelled. She had never been to a baseball game, and he assured her that one could not fully understand America if one did not understand baseball. There was another reason: she found him both amusing and intriguing.

His name was Matt Horton. He was a tall, blond young man from California. His family owned lumber, land, and shipping interests on the West Coast. For generations they had been sending their sons to Ivy League schools for East

Coast polishing before those young men joined the family firm. But Matt was far more thoughtful about his choices than the young men such families usually produced, wanting to be certain before he committed himself to a life of family duty. That past summer he had answered the call of activist civil rights groups. Along with over a thousand young people, he had gone to Mississippi to combat its oppressive legal and social system by registering disenfranchised Negro voters who then cast ballots to nominate a dissident, predominantly Negro delegation to the National Democratic convention. Matt had never before been exposed to abject poverty or brutal intolerance. Local government enforced the system. National government looked hard the other way. The disparity between America's pretension to social justice and its practice had shocked him.

Matt had found Deborah easy to talk to about economics. Now, driving her out to the ball park, he found her easy to talk to about his concerns.

'My family wants me to go back home to Northern Califonia . . . go into the family business. At least I won't have to start out as a logger.' He glanced at Deborah's incomprehension. 'That's how my father and grandfather had to learn the business. I did it one summer. They're willing to count that.'

'I know you want me to say that money is evil and you should turn your back on a system that oppresses the poor and all that, but I don't really believe it, Matt.'

'So I should just ignore the hypocrisy, the . . . the conflict between all the freedoms and privileges in the Bill of Rights and the exploitation the system inflicts on the masses every single moment of the day?'

'I don't understand why your being poor should help them to overcome that. If it's the masses you're doing it for, I'm sure some of them would volunteer to change places with you.' She shifted position to look at him. 'If you don't go into your family's business, what will you do?'

A car cut in front of them, and Matt had to concentrate for a moment. As soon as the traffic opened up a bit, he returned to their discussion.

'I can organize, that's what. I can march and spread the word.'

'That might make you feel good, stomping about waving a

sign. Although, for the life of me, I can't imagine you'd last too long at it without a job to pay for the paint and cardboard and, of course, the meals you'd want to eat after a hard day at the old activist trade.'

'You're laughing at me, and I'm very serious.' He was pouting.

'But not very realistic. If you really *are* serious about having some influence on causes you believe in, then the best way to do it is to use the opportunity your family wants to give you. And be grateful for it.'

'What do you mean?'

'Work your tail off. Get rich. A lot of talk by a few well-meaning, powerless people might not do much, but hard cash can. You really can influence things when you're rich. You want to change the system? Go into politics or back candidates who feel the same way you do. Better still build up your business and then train and hire poor people for the new jobs. Give them jobs. That's the best way to do something about poverty.'

'You really are a reactionary.'

'No, I just don't believe in mixing bad economics with real problems, and I don't believe in people deceiving themselves with fantasies.'

Deborah liked Matt Horton, thought him intelligent and well intentioned. She did not want to see him throwing away the marvellous opportunity that life had dealt him and that her father had denied to her.

His good spirits returned when they arrived at the game and he began to explain baseball to her. She found his eagerness to draw her into the action more American than the game. He was instantly deflated when she exclaimed, 'Oh, it's rounders!'

'No, it's baseball.'

'Then it once was rounders. Girls play it in England.'

'Girls! Look, Abner Doubleday invented baseball maybe eighty, ninety years ago.'

'I certainly hope no one has been paying him royalties all that time – because he plagiarized it from rounders.' Then she smiled ingenuously at him. 'But I'm sure the boys who play it over here do it very nicely.'

'Nicely? That's Mickey Mantle over there. And Yogi Berra. They're stars.'

She smiled at his dismay over her belittling of the national pastime, and he smiled in reply at her teasing.

Deborah was fascinated by the slang of the game. Here, throwing the ball and not the playing field was the 'pitch'. 'Homer' was not a man's name, but a way of scoring. She began to be absorbed in the game.

More differences emerged when Matt ordered beer, which she had not drunk since the conviviality of Oxford pubs.

'It's ice-cold,' she exclaimed.

'Really cuts the thirst.' Matt smacked his lips.

'You mean you drink it like that? One can hardly taste it.'

'You wouldn't want it warm.'

'Of course I would. Americans invented refrigeration and transformed it into a national religion.'

She could hear Matt humming 'Yankee Doodle' as she sipped her beer.

The Yankees staged a rally in the last inning, but it was too late.

'They just ran out of innings,' Matt declared disgustedly.

Lips clenched, green-brown eyes smouldering, his face reflected his disappointment fully, as if the loss had been deep and personal. Deborah decided that his commitment had been typically American: they were never defeated, occasionally they just ran out of innings.

Between courses, waiting at table at the French restaurant that night, Deborah reflected on how much less opaque Americans were than the British, less sophisticated really. In Europe one spoke only when one was absolutely certain of one's facts and intended effect. But Americans were so much less careful. They praised more – praise was as scant in England as meat had once been – and they were far less modest. They insisted on revealing themselves for better or worse, although they naturally assumed they were presenting themselves for better. They had a need to be liked. Those qualities were engaging, but made her feel much older than her years.

When the restaurant closed for the night and she stepped into the street, Deborah found Matt sitting in his silver-grey Pontiac convertible, the top down, waiting for her.

'How did you find out where I worked?'

'Your roommate, Mandy, told me when I called your

apartment. She thinks you don't get out enough. She was really happy I took you to the game today.'

'A born matchmaker!' Deborah was annoyed that Mandy had divulged her private life; the fact that she needed to work at several jobs to make ends meet was her own concern; she wanted no one to feel sorry for her.

'I promised her I'd take you to the Improv tonight to hear her sing. I'm only doing this for Mandy's sake, you understand.'

'I work at weekends. I have students tomorrow.'

'I love the way you say that – wee-k*end*. Like it's a tiny part of a large "kend".'

Matt's manner was humorous, but Deborah sensed how hurt he would be if she turned him down after he had waited for hours to surprise her. She relented. 'We wouldn't want to disappoint Mandy.'

Deborah had not had such a carefree day since her last summer in Europe. Except for the nagging guilt that criticized her whenever she was not hard at work at something productive, she enjoyed herself thoroughly. She laughed without reserve at three very funny aspiring comedians and she was overjoyed to find out that Mandy really was a very good singer. Deborah had been reluctant to hear her perform, fearing that her friend might reveal herself to be a hopelessly untalented dreamer.

Matt drove them home, and he and Deborah stayed up and talked until dawn. Matt did most of the talking, exploring the conflicts that were immobilizing him, often unaware that he was arguing both sides of every issue with equal commitment. Both were hungry and totally tired by the time the sun rose. They walked to a luncheonette for breakfast. Over coffee and doughnuts, he admitted that he liked her and wanted to know her better.

Deborah instantly became tense, defensive. She had been through this once and was grateful that scar tissue had finally formed over the wounds, that calluses protected all the soft tissue.

'You've seen for yourself, Matt. I work. I go to school. There isn't time in my life for anything else.'

'We seem to have found time tonight. Give it a chance.'

'Matt, I have other priorities.'

'You told me. You want to be a successful investment banker.'

'Every bit of my energy, every minute I have, goes into that.'

Matt shook his head. 'I refuse to accept that answer. I can't believe you don't feel a little something for me.'

She placed her hand on his. 'I think you're intelligent and great fun to be with and very nice.'

He leaned forward and kissed her very gently and very lightly. If he had tried to be passionate, she would have been repelled and drawn back. But he was sweet, and she found that she had kissed him back.

In early November of 1965 Helen Lorenzo and Kay Bellows took Deborah to lunch to celebrate her second anniversary at Hazelton, Lieb. Kay was executive secretary to F. Harley Hazelton, the firm's major partner. Despite the streaks of premature grey running through her hair, Kay was younger than Helen, but many years older than Deborah. Both of these women had developed a very protective feeling towards their young friend, wanting to help her but, nearly as important, to cushion her from the disappointment that her almost certain failure was sure to bring.

Helen had bad news for Deborah. She had cautiously sounded out two partners Deborah had thought might be amenable to taking her into their departments in very junior posts that were open, but neither had been willing to consider a woman. Deborah felt blocked and frustrated. She had worked hard with the limited means at her disposal to show these men that she was capable, but they had not even allowed her to put her foot on the first rung up the ladder.

'I'd be willing to bet on your judgement against most of the men in the firm any day,' Kay agreed. 'We have, haven't we, Helen and I? We invested a little in those stocks you suggested and they've risen wonderfully. But maybe men just really are better in business. Mr Hazelton says he can't do a thing without me, that I'm his right hand. But he'd never consider promoting me to another job.'

'I don't believe women are less capable, Kay, and neither do you. You'd be a terrific administrator in any capacity.'

'I haven't given up trying to find you something, Dee,' Helen pledged. 'You earned the raise you got, and you've made a great impression. All the executives admit that. One of these days one of them will be brave enough to risk hiring you.'

'I wish I were that hopeful,' Deborah confessed. 'But I can't rely on luck. Somehow, I have to *make* it happen.'

Later in the meal, over coffee, Kay revealed that her boss was displeased that the Corporate Finance Division had not done better. He intended to make that point to Vanderveer Landy as soon as final figures for the third quarter were in – Landy was head of Corporate Finance, which was responsible for obtaining capital for the firm's corporate clients and for advising them on mergers and acquisitions. In practice the first activity primarily meant arranging loans and managing syndicates that underwrote and sold new issues of stocks and bonds for the most substantial public corporations, which in many cases had been clients for a generation or more. The second activity meant that, occasionally, Corporate Finance would lend one of those blue-chip companies a hand structuring its purchase of a smaller company needed to fill out one of their operations.

Someone else's adversity can be your opportunity, her grandfather had taught her. But, in this case, only if Vanderveer Landy was aware that he desperately needed whatever she might come up with to offer. She would have to think very hard about solving problems he might not even yet recognize he had.

As soon as she arrived back at the library, Deborah made a phone call to Harriet Eldin in Accounting. But the young bookkeeper was difficult.

'I just want to study it,' Deborah assured her friend.

She had learned that Harriet had access to the firm's financial statement. Her boss was in charge of compiling the figures that detailed the firm's operating results. Hazelton, Lieb & Co. was a partnership, and those figures were released to the public only grudgingly and in the most general terms.

'All right,' Deborah compromised. 'Just the latest figures for the past year in Corporate Finance. I'm working on a special project, but no one is supposed to know.'

That had the ring of plausibility, and Harriet agreed to bring a photocopy to the library. These were preliminary figures. Her boss still had to go over them himself, but she was sure they were accurate.

All that afternoon and for succeeding days, Deborah studied the figures until she could have reproduced the statements from memory; then she began to cogitate on the course that would catapult Corporate Finance out of a very respectable malaise.

That Friday night Deborah arrived home to find Mandy elbow-deep in bills, cheques, unbalanced bank statements, and her chequebook. One look and Deborah understood.

'The show closed.'

Mandy nodded glumly. 'And my Macy's bill came in. And I can't make head or tail or how much is in my checking account.'

Mandy had finally landed a role in an off-Broadway review. Disregarding Deborah's warning, she had gone on a buying binge, charging wildly at Macy's and Bonwit Teller, the two department stores where she had charge cards. Most critics devoted less than two inches of newspaper space to blasting the show.

'They didn't just close the show, the entire nightclub went out of business. They're turning it into a strip joint. They asked me to work there.'

Deborah was aghast. 'You wouldn't take off your clothes!'

'As a waitress. But the outfits will probably be nearly as skimpy.'

'What about the Improv?'

'Bud and Silver were sorry, but they had to hire a replacement for me and don't need anyone right now.' She sounded exhausted. 'I hate to ask, but you know how hopeless I am about money and figures.'

'Sure.'

Deborah separated the papers into neat, chronological piles and began tabulating. Fifteen minutes later she turned to Mandy.

'You owe a total of eight hundred and twenty-three dollars and eleven cents to the department stores. When your last two cheques clear, you'll be overdrawn at the bank by one hundred and sixty-five dollars and –'

'No cents, please,' Mandy moaned. 'If I *had* any sense, I wouldn't have gone on a shopping spree before the show actually opened.' She sighed. 'What do I do, Dee?'

'Well, *I* can pay the rent this month and lend you, say, two hundred more to cover the overdraft and give you some cash until you find a job.'

'God, I hate to do this to you all the time.'

'It's only a loan. I could be in the same fix one day.'

'But you never are. You're so good about managing things. And being organized.'

'You're allowed to be a bit irresponsible,' Deborah remarked lightly, hoping to lift Mandy out of her depression a bit. 'You're an artist.'

'Not according to the *Voice*, the *Times*, and the *Post*.'

'They criticized the show, not you.'

'They didn't even notice *me*.'

'I'm taking Matt out to dinner tonight.' Deborah refused to allow Matt to pay unless she could reciprocate, albeit on a far more modest scale; she never wanted to be under an obligation to anyone. 'Why don't the three of us go out to dinner. My treat.'

'Jeff will probably drop over. Besides, Matt's dying to be alone with you.'

Deborah took so long to respond the pause became uncomfortable.

'He wants me to spend the night at his apartment,' Deborah finally admitted to her friend, but her tone betrayed her doubts.

'And you don't want to?'

'Well . . .' Deborah hesitated again. 'It isn't the easiest thing for me.'

'It's like swimming. Sooner or later you just have to jump off the deep end.'

A subtle change had taken place in the status of the speakers. When it came to relationships between people, particularly between men and women, Deborah looked to Mandy for advice. The midwesterner possessed instincts fine-tuned during hundreds of dates at drive-in hamburger hangouts and college parties and proms and during innumerable conversations in high school corridors and lunch rooms and over telephones. Deborah's sheltered youth had deprived her of a multitude of experiences with those her own age. Only at Branton Abbey had she been among other girls. Only at Oxford had she finally been exposed to the great mystery of boys.

'Matt's nice-looking,' Mandy continued. 'Sweet, considerate.'

Deborah groped for words that expressed her doubts. 'I just wish . . . I just wish he was a little less nice. That sounds horrible, doesn't it? I just mean that sometimes he seems exactly what I could want in a man and, a moment later, he's childishly dependent.' She paused to think again. 'What I wish is that he loved me a little less and himself a little more.'

'Or maybe you're just looking for an excuse to stay away from his apartment.'

During the nineteenth century two groups gravitated towards investment banking: established white Anglo-Saxon Protestants and German-Jewish immigrants. Soon, however, wealth and a mutuality of interest melded their descendants into almost indistinguishable groups. Each went to St. Paul's and Yale, or their acceptable equivalents, and were fellow members of the same secret societies and married each other's sisters. On occasion, those in the corporations happily relied on their old doubles partners over at the investment bank to sell a hundred million dollars' worth of bonds for them. The financial institution that had represented General Blue Chip for generations would always represent it. Sons of partners in turn became partners and paved the way for their own sons.

Analyzing Hazelton, Lieb, Deborah saw a prime example of that pattern: little innovation – a revulsion against it, really; little new blood among the partners; and a sleepiness where tenacity should have been. The managing and major partner, F. Harley Hazelton, had followed his father and grandfather into the firm and had been there fifty years. He was obviously troubled by the levelling off of the firm's revenues and profits, but unable to explain the reasons or to change the firm's direction. He would probably have been aghast if Deborah had outlined her views to him and might well have fired her on the spot for her effrontery. But his disquiet at the state of affairs was a lever she could use to pry open the door, even if only a crack, to the new attitudes that were necessary to revitalize the firm and which could provide her with the opportunity for advancement. Considering it a chief executive's job to hire good people and simply let them manage, Hazelton looked solely to his division heads to do what was necessary to keep the firm on track. If they failed to do so, he would try new men in the positions.

As Deborah saw it, if Vanderveer Landy was to reverse the decline of his division, he was going to have to risk becoming more aggressive and going after the forms of corporate finance business that she envisaged as being the wave of the future. Scientific advancement was creating new companies that would be the giants of the future. To develop with them the sort of long-term relationship it already had with older corporations, Hazelton, Lieb had to seek out these young companies now and help them to grow. That was necessary but would take time. A quicker route to inject a large stream of new income into the firm would be to get into the fast, hard game of aiding the men, the so-called conglomerateurs, who were building giant companies by acquiring other companies.

The anti-trust laws had long prohibited joining together companies engaged in the same line of business, but a new and hungry breed of fortune builder had seen the advantage in creating 'conglomerate' companies, buying up firms engaged in different lines of business and utilizing the additional earnings to increase the value of their publicly traded stock. The conglomerate corporations would then be able to borrow more money to buy more companies, or would pay with their own stock or with debt securities to be made good by their increased earnings. The investment bank locating companies willing to be acquired at the high price by the conglomerateurs, or even by less rapacious buyers, could earn enormous fees. Those men would flock to be represented by an élite financial institution, like Hazelton, Lieb, with its prestige and financial muscle. However, failure by the big banking firm's pristine moralists to jump into this promising arena would yield it to scrappy little firms that would then quickly rise to prominence.

Deborah perceived additionally that such acquisitions could be accomplished even if the company to be acquired was hostile to the take-over. The acquiring company would announce to the shareholders of a target company in which management controlled only a small minority interest its own willingness to purchase their publicly traded stock on attractive terms. The target's management might scream and go to court, but if the fight was shrewdly picked and waged, management would usually be unable to prevent a majority of its shareholders from accepting the offer and tendering their stock to the buyer. Such tactics would doubtless produce some vicious battles that the old-line investment banks were not used or, perhaps, psychologically suited to, but Deborah was certain that, if they did not move into such fields quickly, they would soon find themselves headed instead into a steep decline from which neither their old reputations nor their good breeding could save them.

As quickly as she could, Deborah assembled a carefully researched list of potential target companies, well-run publicly traded corporations that were underpriced in the stock market and vulnerable to an offer to their stockholders at a higher price. In some cases the buyer would have to offer cash, but Deborah tried to devise packages of stock or debt securities that would allow the raiding company to conserve cash while pyramiding its assets and income by acquisition. And then she made an appointment to see Vanderveer Landy.

Vanderveer Landy, known as Van by his colleagues, had gravitated towards banking in the traditional way. Not the academic sort who might thrive in one of the Wall Street law firms that drew its partners from the same gene pool as the banks, he had considered that his outgoing nature and good looks and the profusion of friends he had amassed during his short lifetime made investment banking a natural field for him after graduation from Princeton. He had, of course, grown up knowing several fathers of friends who were partners at Hazelton, Lieb, but that was true of any of the big financial firms. He picked the Hazelton firm on the advice of an uncle whose substantial financial affairs were managed by the firm and, thus, might provide a reason to move young Landy along faster than some of the other young men. Indeed, Landy's career had shot upwards with little deviation. He was a hearty, highly likeable man, whose contacts had been as useful as he had thought they would be. His ascension to the vice-presidency of Corporate Finance, the most important division in the firm, had made him heir apparent to the executive vice-president. Only thirty-seven, he was the golden boy of the firm.

Deborah had met Landy only a few months after she came to Hazelton, Lieb, when he thanked her for an article she had sent on to him. Having perceived he was not the kind to submerge himself in complex treatises, she had concentrated on short, brightly written pieces. When they had passed in the hall during the last few weeks, she had managed, with her newly acquired insight into American sports, to get in a word or two on how the Princeton team of that season was doing. He had seemed to be among the friendliest of the partners.

Once or twice he had even dropped into the library himself, instead of sending down his secretary or one of the executives under him, and they had chatted a bit.

Deborah had scheduled the meeting with Landy for a Friday, so that he would have all weekend to think about the proposal she had made and to study the materials she had compiled. A tall, handsome man with straight features and a thatch of chestnut brown hair, he was divorced and known as something of a hell raiser out of the office. But Deborah did not think that that would interfere with something as serious as his division's operations. She was wrong.

'That's an awfully keen-looking dress you've got on,' he began once she was seated. 'You always manage to look bright and fresh.'

He had, in fact, been very aware of Deborah from the first day she had approached him in the hall to chat about an article she had sent him. He considered her a knockout: spectacular blue eyes, gorgeous face and hair, and what a figure! But he had held off asking her out because of the complications that invariably ensued when one dated a girl who worked for the firm.

'Thank you, Mr Landy. I've asked for this meeting in order to present some ideas that I think can be useful to the firm and, at the same time, demonstrate my capability to move into a position in investment banking.'

'That's right,' he replied, 'you told me you were studying finance.'

Deborah was encouraged by his having remembered and began to outline her thinking.

'Say, I've got tickets to the football game down at Princeton tomorrow,' he interrupted. Same firm or not, you just have to bend the rules when a girl looks like this, he thought. 'How would you like to drive down there with me, maybe make a whole weekend of it?'

'Thank you, but I've got plans already,' she said politely, emphasizing by her tone that she had no intention of smudging the line drawn between a business and a social relationship. 'The matter I've come to discuss could open up a major new source of revenue for our firm. I've done extensive research and come up with a list of excellent companies that are ripe for acquisition.'

'Have the companies told you that?' he asked grumpily.

'They don't yet know that we're looking at them, nor would they until we've located the right client to acquire them. Some of the acquisitions might well have to be made against the wishes of the target company's management.'

'How's that?'

'Our client would publicly offer to buy the target company's shares directly from the stockholders.'

'That's a messy business which makes an awful lot of enemies, Miss Crown.' He grinned patronizingly. 'You haven't been involved in the financial world very long. Let me explain that that sort of thing just isn't done.'

Deborah gritted her teeth. Landy sounded exactly like so many English bankers she had heard, exactly like Leslie, despite the gap of three thousand miles and a different culture and accent: 'That's not the done thing, my dear, not done at all.'

A wide smile exposed Landy's white teeth and boyish charm. 'If you're sincerely interested in learning more about investment banking, why not come down to Princeton with me for the weekend?' he winked. 'There are some things I'd love to teach you.'

You're no different from Corcoran or any of the others, she thought with disgust. On the surface, better bred. But, underneath, no different, no different at all.

'Mr. Landy,' she concluded with a tight smile, 'I don't need personal instruction to know that the purpose of an investment bank is to make money for the clients and for the partners. This proposal does that – they'll make money, lots of it. If you should happen to change your mind about the direction in which you wish to take your division, I'd be glad to speak further to you.'

Deborah was disappointed but hardly surprised by Landy's rejection. In fact she had expected it; her plan depended at this stage on simply making him aware of her research. But, still, she brooded on it for much of Saturday, and finally determined to put it out of her mind. She was seeing Matt that night, and that created entirely different pressures.

Deborah felt a genuine affection for Matt Horton and wondered if, as Mandy had suggested, her inability to commit herself further really did result from the fears she knew she had about sex. He had been urging her for weeks to spend the night with him, and she had demurred. That seemed unfair to him and hypocritical. After all this time, if she was too fond of him to end the relationship, then she should be willing to sleep with him.

That sounds like brave talk, she thought, for someone who can feel at this very moment the anxiety crawling up out of her belly.

For much of that Saturday evening, Deborah had been undecided about going to Matt's apartment. They had attended a play staged in a loft by a college friend of Matt's who had also spent the summer in Mississippi. The characters had been so heavily stereotyped Deborah thought she was seeing a modern-dress production of *Uncle Tom's Cabin*. A weighty, fervent, approving discussion among members of the audience and cast had followed. Matt's expression had permitted her no inkling as to his opinion of the play.

'Wasn't that the most awful, pretentious piece of shit you've ever seen?' Matt had exploded as soon as they were out of earshot of the others.

Relieved, Deborah had slipped her arm through his, pulling him tightly against her. 'It was ghastly!'

Deborah felt very safe with Matt, unlike the way she had felt with Bash Rowell, whose subconscious allure was that one walked on a knife edge with him, always uncertain whether at heart he was a cad.

'Let's go back to your apartment,' she had murmured to Matt.

Matt embraced and kissed her before she could feel awkward. They stood in the bedroom, within the dim light cast by a lamp in the living room. The apartment was in a luxury building, not the sort of abode one expected of a student. The furniture was graceful Danish modern. His mother had insisted on finding him an apartment and furnishing it. She had done well, reflecting her son's personality deftly: clean-cut, forward looking, basic shapes, primary colours. Deborah and Matt had kissed before, but she had not let it go any farther, and nothing had been aroused within her that would want to make her go farther. Bash had been so self-assured the first time that her timidity had been swept away. Matt dissipated her fears by his gentleness. What she had feared most, however, would not go away: that Bash had so hardened her heart she would never feel anything for a man again.

They could hear the Brahms clarinet quintet drifting through the walls of the next door apartment.

'Even your neighbours want to add to our romance,' Deborah remarked.

'Good walls make good neighbours,' he quipped.

Deborah laughed without restraint. That seemed to make the ordeal easier for her. Matt undressed her slowly, kissing her as each piece of clothing fell away. She followed him to the low pedestal bed. The burgundy cotton bed-cover felt cool and welcoming against her skin. She stretched out her arms like a cat and drew him to her, trying not to think of all the barriers erected in her mind since she had last been naked with a man, with Bash. Matt kissed her now with deep passion, conveyed with a command she had never sensed in him before. Instead of the anxiety or the unresponsiveness she had expected to feel, a great peace came over her. She seemed to float far away from all the hurts that making love had come to mean to her.

'I like you,' Matt whispered. 'I really like you, but I'm afraid that if I say that to you, I'll frighten you off.'

'Not tonight, Matt. I need all the affection you can spare to get me through this.'

'I mean it.'

'I don't deserve it, but thank you.' She kissed him. 'Thank you for your sweetness.' She kissed him again. 'And your consideration.' Her last kiss seemed to go on for minutes. 'And thank you for not being scared away by –'

He placed a fingertip on her lips to hush her. And then his mouth dipped into the hollow at the base of her throat. Her long sweep of neck arched upwards, an offering of her vulnerability. His head lifted, she thought to rise up to her lips again, but then she felt him at her breast. The intimacy frightened her. She tried to pull away, but he refused to let her. Slowly, against her will, she began to experience swells of pleasure. Her fingers spread through his hair without thinking, and then pressed him to her as her nipple thickened and rose between his lips.

The peace that had cradled her so recently seemed a delusion now. She felt torn between the tactile pleasure and the willpower within her that cautioned her not to let down her defences, that this invader burrowing through would fling back her inner gates to pillage her emotions. How sweet Matt looked at her breast, she thought, distracting her from trying to examine the emotions within her tension. The sensation deepened, and prodded her to remember the joy that mingled body and soul, being cared for and appreciated, love-making that offered before it took.

She bent and kissed the tousled hair, laying her cheek upon it. She luxuriated in the warmth spreading through her and forced herself to admit also that she felt the stirring of pure animal gratification. Her flesh, long paralyzed, was taking the first halting steps towards rediscovering her biology and its needs.

Suddenly, she shuddered and a wave of weakness fluttered through her. He chose that moment to descend lower. She was so surprised that her body could still respond to a man's touch that she did not try to stop him. Only when he kissed the cleft between her legs and she shuddered beneath his tongue did she realize where he was.

She tried to cry out for him to stop. She was repulsed by what he was doing to her. But then he touched a hidden cache where fear, hope, and passion merged. She sighed as if he had opened a latch and treasures locked within were tumbling from her. Yet, the wonder was that his touch remained, and the treasures spilling out of her were endless. Then, suddenly, she separated into a hundred billion atoms flung into a vast void.

When they finally settled back into the shape of her body, they had been rearranged within. And she knew then that she would never again be afraid of her feelings for a man – they were natural and fulfilling. She understood that some men might be exploitive, but that they were ruled by the same yearnings and urges as she, urges she was finally willing to recognize.

She looked over at Matt, lying beside her.

'I hope it was okay,' he muttered. 'I was worried every second I was going to mess it up.'

Deborah sat up. 'I think you just have.'

'You're not serious.'

She placed her hand gently on his cheek, staring down at the murky outlines of the face she had come to know so well. For a little while he had created an impression of self-assuredness and enveloped her in it, but his brow must be knitted now, reflecting both bewilderment and the self-doubt that disturbed her about him.

'You're wonderful, Matt, but you're in a turmoil, so indecisive, you're not sure who you are or what you want. I'm very sure of myself – you've called it single-minded, once you even said I was obsessed. Things trouble you that I can respect, but I can't respect the turmoil that overcomes you. And it seems to be almost everything lately. Even now, when we made love, and it was beautiful, you tell me you were gripped by agonies of doubt.'

She kissed his lips very gently. 'I thank you for what you've given me tonight, Matt. You can't know how much. I might never meet another man as kind to me as you are.'

The last thing she felt as she drew away from him was his tear against the corner of her mouth.

All Tuesday Deborah refused to leave the library, cancelling a lunch date and calling a messenger for items she would normally have delivered by hand. Kay Bellows had alerted her to the meeting F. Harley Hazelton was having with Van Landy late that morning.

Please tell Hazelton that you're moving into take-overs! she kept whispering over and over again, visualizing Van Landy's worried face. That's your way out, your life preserver. That's why I timed my meeting with you for last Friday. Please tell him you're moving into take-overs!

Hours passed without a word. Deborah jumped at every phone call that jangled her receiver, but none was from Landy. Finally, when she had almost given up hope, the telephone rang again. It was Van Landy's new secretary, whom she barely knew.

'Miss Crown, Mr. Landy would like to see you.'

Deborah's eyes flicked from the telephone to the wall clock. Four forty-five. He had held out until he was afraid she might go home for the day. She responded to Landy's secretary.

'I'll be up in a couple of minutes.'

She slipped the file out of her centre drawer and forced herself to wait five full minutes before she walked to the elevator.

'You missed a great weekend,' Landy began when she entered.

'I had a pretty interesting weekend myself.'

'Hey, that's great.' He halted, trying to determine how to retrace the ground lost over the four days since she had offered to fill him in on potential take-over candidates. 'You know, I was pretty rushed the last time you were here and didn't get a chance to hear you out all the way. Why don't you fill me in right from the beginning on your ideas?'

He was the one in trouble, Deborah decided, and she need not equivocate in her approach. She fixed him with a hard gaze. 'This division isn't doing as well as it should because the kinds of corporations you've always dealt with don't have the same need for capital they once did. At the turn of the century, this firm sold millions of dollars' worth of railroad bonds. You still represent those railroads, but when was the last time they built a new track and asked you to sell bonds?'

'We represent a lot more than railroads,' he said indignantly. 'We represent some of the largest corporations in America.'

'True, but you don't represent any of the young companies, the ones that will be the giants of tomorrow. They're the ones that are growing fast and need the capital you can raise. And you aren't getting in on what will be the biggest investment banking action of the next few years – take-overs.'

He snapped his fingers, as if just remembering. 'Didn't you say something about some little research you did on companies that might be acquirable? I'd be glad to take a look at it and give you some professional advice.'

Deborah's hands did not move. 'Let me tell you what I want, Mr. Landy. You have an open line in your division's budget for an executive assistant. That job has always been a stepping-stone here to a slot as a full executive. I don't expect you to promote me to Corporate Finance executive without your having an opportunity to observe my ability. But I want your word that, as soon as I demonstrate that ability, I'll be moved up on the same basis as any man would.'

He tried to appear incredulous. 'Just for looking over your work and advising you on how to improve it?'

Deborah remained silent. He reached across his desk for one of the innumerable executive toys to which he was addicted, a wooden contraption one turned to create hectic, useless motion in rods and cogs.

'I haven't even seen your list, your approach,' he pressed

on worriedly. 'Do you even know the ropes in take-overs?'

'Cold.'

'You sure don't lack for confidence.'

Deborah nodded her thanks for the compliment. He was wrestling with several factors that demeaned him in his own eyes: asking an underling for help, hiring a woman, and committing himself ahead of time to giving her a full place in Corporate Finance if she proved herself. Now she had to offer him the means to retain his self-respect when he capitulated.

'Mr. Landy, I believe in being a team player. I work for you. This is your division. The credit is yours. And I'll always be grateful to you for recognizing my ability and giving me a start.'

He ran a hand through the chestnut hair and smiled. 'With all the work around here, I need an assistant to do the legwork, the research.'

Deborah smiled back at him. 'Then it's agreed?'

He eyed her. 'Let's see the list.'

'It's more than just a list.' Deborah opened her file. 'I think you ought to meet Harrison Walters of Corolan Steel. They've just built a new plant in Ohio to make specialty steel. I've identified a coal company, Bentley Coal & Coke, that mines exactly the grade of coal they need to fuel the new plant, that has its own coke-making capacity, and is less than two hundred miles away. The management of Bentley probably won't want to sell out at any price, but a fast take-over raid would topple them in no time. The coal and other assets are worth just over two hundred million dollars. The stock is selling at thirteen dollars a share. We can offer seventeen dollars a share, nearly a third more. The stockholders would be delighted, but the total price would still be only one hundred and ten million dollars. Corolan would get the coal it needs at only about half the price it would pay a supplier.'

'Does Corolan have cash?'

'No, but I don't propose that we offer cash. Bentley Coal has always paid a steady dividend. That's what its stockholders are used to and want. I think you should propose to Walters that Corolan issue preferred stock or a debenture that pays two percent more than Bentley's traditional common-stock dividend.'

Landy reflected for a moment. 'You have more like that?'

'A page full.'

His head bobbed as he pondered, like a worried rabbi at prayer. Finally, he decided.

'Agreed.'

'He was cornered, Mandy,' Deborah exulted. 'I got exactly what I wanted. I'm on my way.'

'I'm really thrilled for you, Dee. You deserve it.'

'A hundred and fifty dollars a week. That's enough to cover all my expenses. The other jobs will provide me with money for investing.'

'See what I mean?' Mandy's voice was very sad. 'If it was me, I would have quit those jobs and gone out shopping.'

'Is something wrong?'

Mandy nodded. 'I'm getting married.'

'That's marvellous. Jeff is a wonderful man.'

She began to cry. 'Not to Jeff. He'll never have a penny. I'm going back home to marry my old boyfriend, the doctor. He called last night to say he still wanted to marry me.'

She sought Deborah's gaze through her tears. 'I'm giving up. My suitcases are all packed in my bedroom. I was just waiting for you to come home, so I could say good-bye.'

Deborah seized Mandy's hand. 'Don't do it just because you're a little down just now. Things got better for me. They will for you too.'

'You make them happen somehow,' Mandy said with despair, 'you sacrifice for them. I don't have that . . . stamina.'

'You're just upset at not having a job,' Deborah pleaded. 'I can lend you more money now. You're sure to land a part soon.'

Mandy shook her head once more. 'I just need another twenty dollars to cover the rest of the train ticket home. He's meeting me at the station. Here I am running out on my half of the rent too,' she added, with self-disgust. 'You'll have to pay the full amount each month.'

Deborah waved her hand to belittle that burden. 'I just want you to be sure that this is what you want to do with your life.'

'I have to.' Mandy stood up. 'I'll send you whatever I owe over the next month or two. Is that all right?'

Deborah hugged her friend impulsively. 'Forget about the money. Or buy yourself the best wedding present with it. I just hope you'll be happy. Please be happy!'

'Ever after.'

They stood locked together, both knowing this would probably be the last time they would see each other, at least when they were still so close that their differences were causes for laughter and appreciation.

God damn it! Deborah screamed silently. She knew why this had happened. God damn it all the way to hell!

CHAPTER FOURTEEN

By 1967 America was beginning to pay the price of believing in its own mythology. That price was death abroad and social unrest at home on a scale none would have thought possible only four years earlier, when Deborah first set foot on American soil. Three seemingly disparate, but actually interrelated phenomena, all resting on tissue-thin hypocrisy, were responsible: the Vietnam war, racial injustice, and the rebellion of the young.

As America increased its involvement in Vietnam and more of its young died there, disillusionment began to ripple across the country and, following quickly in its wake, dissent. In mid-April anti-war demonstrations brought out upwards of 100,000 people in New York and 50,000 in San Francisco. Henry Cabot Lodge, United States Ambassador to South Vietnam, predicted the war would 'achieve very sensational results' that year. National Security Adviser Walt W. Rostow said, 'It looks very good. The other side is near collapse. In my opinion victory is near. . . . I'll show you the charts. The charts are very good.'

Race riots rocked 127 of the country's cities, killing at least 77 and injuring at least 4,000. The Reverend Martin Luther King, Jr., called the federal government 'the greatest purveyor of violence in the world' and proposed a merger of the civil rights movement and the anti-war movement.

Appalled by the butchery in Vietnam and the dichotomy between the nation's assertion of freedom for all and its practice of racial injustice, vast numbers of young people rebelled against traditional values. What came to be called the counterculture – conspicuous in homely work clothes, exotic costumes, or hand-crafted garments – began to attract a diverse population: some were revolutionaries, some were 'dropping out', some were returning to nature. All were wrapped in the euphoria of a new religion. All were certain they were about to ascend into the Age of Aquarius.

The last Sixties were a heady time in finance – the Go-Go Years. Financial, not ethical, values ruled there – the ultimate good was gain, the ultimate evil was loss – and the financial community rolled along barely disturbed by the turbulence. The stock market boomed. Shares of companies that appeared to have high growth potential sold at astronomical prices. New stock issues were snapped up. Mutual funds attracted vast capital. Mergers, acquisitions, and lightning take-over raids were creating giant conglomerate companies, the purchases usually accomplished with a minimum of cash and a maximum of the buyer's stock or its wildly concocted debt securities.

If not apparent on the surface, the turmoil affecting the rest of the country was nonetheless agitating the financial world below. Iconoclastic ideas were bombarding conventional wisdom at such a blinding rate, and new technology was creating and destroying whole industries and traditional investment strategies so quickly, that older minds, made helpless by the confusion, were in desperation turning to those of brash young people.

By 1967, change had already begun to accelerate in the financial industry. The old and honoured investment banking firm of Hazelton, Lieb & Co. was in the forefront of such financial innovation. To the amazement of many observers and the consternation of its hidebound colleagues among the old-line houses, Hazelton, Lieb had been among the most aggressive of the larger financial firms that had cast tradition to the winds and leaped into the revolution that was sweeping across its industry. Vanderveer Landy had become one of the wonder boys of Wall Street. He and the men on his Corporate Finance staff were responsible for doubling the firm's profits over the previous two years by their pursuit of vulnerable companies ripe for the raiding. As a result of its enhanced reputation, the firm had attracted many new clients interested in less savage services. Only Deborah and Landy and perhaps one or two of the executives involved in the mergers and acquisitions area of the firm knew that much of Landy's success at picking and pursuing likely target companies was due to Deborah's research, analysis, and tactics. She had been given two substantial rises, but the promised promotion had never come through. She was still his executive assistant.

Deborah had devoted two years since winning that job and

losing Mandy as a roommate almost solely to work. Even her college studies were directed at enhancing her credentials for her knowledge of investment banking. She had little time or inclination for a private life. She let out the extra bedroom to a succession of women with whom she was careful not to become too friendly. Apartment space had become even harder to come by in Manhattan, and she was able to earn far more from the room rental than Mandy's half of the rent. That and her increasing salary permitted her, at last, to build up a nest egg which she began to invest aggressively to increase her capital. Often, when exhausted from holding down her several jobs, she resolved to abandon one of them: the answering service, where she could rarely doze for more than half an hour without being woken by a ring, or the restaurant, which prevented her from using her weekends to catch up on sleep and where she feared that one day she would be spotted by someone from Hazelton, Lieb. But, each time, she recalled the additional money being earned and then multiplied by investment, and that dissuaded her.

She and Mandy wrote feverishly to each other in the first months after their parting, Deborah rarely allowing more than a day to intervene before her reply. But the letters, seemingly of their own accord, became shorter and the delays before answering became longer as the two young women, leading such different lives, had less and less of interest to say to each other. By the second year the correspondence had been reduced to notes and gifts at Christmas and on the occasion of the birth of Mandy's first child.

Deborah ran into Matt Horton less frequently at Columbia after he ceased to take business courses. She occasionally observed him from a distance, usually with people who looked slovenly and bohemian to her – Matt and the other men with over-long hair and both they and the women in working clothes.

She rarely went out in the evening. In fact she was quite happy that none of those few dates had stimulated in her the desire to see the young men again. There would be time enough for amusement when she was rich. Hardly a day passed that she did not silently admonish herself regarding one thing or another there would be time or resources for when she was rich.

Physically, she had changed little. She still walked quickly, erect to the full height of her five-foot seven-inch figure. As she had since childhood, she wore her hair very simply, parted in the centre and falling straight to just below her shoulders. The red hair framed skin that was cream white, almost translucent. But maturation, and often fatigue, could be seen about the eyes; the startling blueness now seemed set in a face that had endured trials of which the fresh-faced young woman lazily punting on the Cher could not have dreamed. Still, she was a very beautiful woman, and she was totally oblivious to the stares that followed her passage down the street.

In early June 1967, Pierre de Kronengold invited Deborah to join him on a yacht for a weekend off the coast of Puerto Rico, which he was visiting on business. He wanted to send her a plane ticket, but she insisted on buying her own. For days before leaving she could barely contain her excitement. It was the first time she had seen him, or any other family member, since leaving home. She had always adored her Uncle Pierre, and the letters back and forth had been no substitute for actually being with him.

Pierre had hired a large four-masted schooner and its crew of seventeen, so he and she could sail down the coast and, perhaps, to nearby islands, away from all the concerns of everyday life. But they had been away scarcely a day before the outside world intruded. Indeed, Deborah was forced to admit later, the outside world seemed to intrude right from the beginning.

They lay on chaises on the aft deck as the schooner glided out of the harbour, its sails set and billowing. This was their first chance to talk, but what was not said worried Deborah more than what was. Pierre appeared careworn, particularly when Deborah asked how his business affairs were doing.

'Things aren't good for private bankers in France now,' he admitted. 'De Gaulle favours the large commercial banks at the expense of the private ones, like ours.' He waved his hand in dismissal. 'But such matters are boring for beautiful young ladies.'

He replied with an unpremeditated ruefulness, however, when Deborah asked after the welfare of his wife, Simone. 'For my *own* private banker, things are always prosperous.'

Deborah supposed he had still not repaid all the massive

funds he had borrowed from Simone after the war to put his bank back into business and that both his home and business lives were difficult. If the last vestige of illusion she had sometimes entertained in her most frustrated moments still lingered that she might someday turn to Pierre for investment capital, the exchange eradicated it.

Deborah also had things to hide. As she had in all her letters, she continued to keep her career a secret from him and everyone else – she wanted no interference or questions from anyone, and certainly not the misguided charity of undeserved aid. When he raised the issue of her falling out with Leslie, she refused to discuss it, insisting he drop the matter. So she talked about her studies at Columbia as if that adjunct to her life were actually central. Pierre asked a lot of questions about the other students and their various social movements that seemed, from the distance of Paris, to be having such a profound effect on America.

Deborah was sympathetic to the goal of social justice, but believed that self-indulgence sparked many of the students. She contended that without America's affluence, they would not be protesting but, rather, would be devoting their energies to making a living or to learning the skills necessary to do so after college; the luxury of conspicuous protest was affordable only because so many had fat allowances and permissive parents.

Sadly, she went on, the war they rightly hated was proving far costlier to America than most people had yet understood – not merely to the nation's social cohesion, but to its economy as well. President Johnson had not asked for increased taxes to pay for the war, so she foresaw that deficit spending, inflation, and a cheapened dollar had become inevitable. Once those became apparent – in the not too distant future, she was willing to bet – tougher times would not be far behind. When that happened or when the news media decided to cut off the protesters' free publicity, sensing their viewers and readers were tired of being affronted by the radicals' assault on their morality, the movement would end, regardless of whether the war went on.

'I am sorry to hear you're so pessimistic.' Pierre's shoulders shrugged. 'You're probably right, of course, but I had hoped . . . well . . . that you were among those seeking to change things.'

Pierre's advocacy of protest hardly surprised Deborah; she recollected that he had always been a romantic, far happier at the piano or with a camera – even now he was taking photographs of her – than engaged with the business concerns that his family name had forced on him. What surprised her was the regret that had flitted across his face as he listened to her hard-bitten objectivity and how deeply, it seemed at that moment, the last three years had carved age into his features. He was in his fifties now. Grey hairs scored his temples where only brown once was, and great lines squeezed furrows across his brow and on either side of his mouth. The round steel spectacles that used to seem sweetly comical now made him look like a man preparing to grow old. She had always seen her mother's – his sister's – face in Pierre, and it had always been flawless and young, because she had died so young. Deborah realized that her mother, if she had lived, would have begun to look old now, her beauty slowly to diminish. For several minutes Deborah hardly heard Pierre over the din in her ears of the sadness for all three of them.

The ship had anchored off the coast of Vieques. In the Grand Saloon, where richly polished wood walls and floors set off the royal blue velvet of chairs and sofas, the table had been set for dinner on the side of the ship that faced west, where the two passengers could watch the sun set over the coast of Puerto Rico. Deborah and Pierre had just sat down at the table when the radioed message was delivered from the bridge to Pierre. Full-scale war had broken out between Israel and her Arab neighbours. Pierre was head of major Jewish organizations in France and had to fly back to Paris immediately.

The shortened visit had been stiff and not very satisfying, Deborah had reflected. Pierre had not had time to become used to dealing with her as the adult she had become, rather than as the eighteen-year-old he had last seen on the Riviera.

'It seems we are always being separated by something,' she quietly remarked as the ship weighed anchor to seek the nearest harbour from which they could disembark.

He had not heard her. His mind was already on the actions he must take on Israel's behalf. Soon, hers was on the matters awaiting her at the office.

* * *

Van Landy had often commended himself for his good judgment in hiring Deborah. For one thing, she had taken off his hands a lot of the administrative work he found so tedious. She had streamlined much of the division's decision-making machinery, freeing everyone to concentrate more effort on activities than actually produced revenue for the firm. And Landy had to admit that her confidence in her ability to spot opportune take-over targets had not been misplaced either. She had been uncanny – of course, with the proper supervision from him, he assured himself; after all, she was hardly more than a kid. Jesus, what a coldly calculating mind she had when it came to figuring out strategy! He'd hate to be competing for the top spot at Hazelton, Lieb with a guy who had a mind like that. One thing you had to be careful about, though, was not letting her talk you into anything too fast. Some of her schemes! That was where he considered his experience essential, why finance was man's work. Once in a while she would try to put him on the spot by bringing up some sort of half promise or other he might have made to her about promoting her to an executive's slot if she worked out, but how in God's name could he do that? Women were cut out to be helpers. They got too emotional. You couldn't trust them to handle something as complicated and, well, as responsible as finance. And who would take care of all the detail work for him if she was dealing with clients, actually arranging loans or take-overs, and so on? Jesus, he hated all the shit work she handled for him. He didn't have the time to do all that research on companies and potential take-over partners. And how would it look if he had a woman in an important slot? The clients would hate it, maybe want to switch bankers. He'd be a laughing-stock. She was only a kid, he remembered. There was no hurry.

Content that he need not consider seriously the promise he had made Deborah, Van Landy could ignore the deeper reasons for keeping her in her present slot. Right now he was earning all the praise. If she proved to be a capable executive, some people might begin to guess how important had been her role in the division's earlier turn-around. Moreover, her brilliance intimidated him; there was a searing kind of inevitability about her. He often felt like a small child she was leading by the hand.

Deborah, for her part, had come to like Van Landy – he

was a charming and likeable man – but those qualities were also bound up with his excessive caution and were at the heart of what she found most trying in dealing with him. In the guise of wanting to examine every problem carefully, he would take hours, sometimes days, before she could convince him to propose an unusual form of financing or a hostile take-over. They were likely to stir up antagonism from some quarter, and such battles went against his natural grain of trying to succeed by ingratiation. She felt more drained after the long hours of subtly coaxing him and surrounding him with counter-arguments than after any amount of research or study during sleep-denied nights.

In the autumn of 1967, Deborah confronted Landy head on about her promotion. She had cleared his calendar of all appointments for an hour, so there would be no interruptions while she tried to pin him down. Both arms on the desk, he leaned towards her with an expression of concerned sincerity and recounted the alleged difficulties he had had wheedling raises for her out of the executive committee. Imagine if he tried to push through a promotion. This time was just not right for such a revolutionary step, he told her. There was no doubt in his mind the committee would turn her down, and the chance for her to move up might be lost forever. Better to wait until the climate was more positive. No amount of argument by Deborah could convince him otherwise.

At the end of her fruitless session with Landy, after nearly two years as his assistant, Deborah was fed up. More important, she had already thought through what she was prepared to do about it.

Deborah had discovered that insurance companies were being forced by state regulations to hold far more cash in reserve than was foreseeably necessary to cover potential fire and casualty losses. She had been pondering a startling idea: that a corporation which brought an insurance company as a subsidiary company could do something the insurance company was itself forbidden to do – tap into the insurance company's excess capital reserves that were not needed to cover potential losses, but that the regulatory authorities insisted it not touch. Such a take-over would bring an enormous cash windfall to the buyer. Ordinarily, she would have explained her idea to Landy and searched for a client willing to undertake a raid on a likely insurance company. But now she was determined to pull off the coup herself.

For the next ten days, Deborah pored over library material and telephoned every contact she had made in the financial district. It was frustrating: she thought she had a way to get the initial money she would need, but she had to locate just the right combination of companies, which could be taken over in just the right sequence and with just the right timing. The process had seemed so much easier when she was doing it for others – opportunities then seemed to pop out at her like a jack-in-the-box. She kept slogging forward, convinced that her idea was workable if she could find the means to apply it. At last, late one afternoon, in two different telephone conversations, she heard the same rumour. After only an hour's research, she was almost certain she had found her opportunity. She telephoned John Smithline and made an appointment to see him the next day.

Deborah had been taught by her grandfather to believe that every day presented dozens of opportunities to get rich. Looking back, later on, one could see them so clearly: the Xeroxes, the Polaroids. The trick was to pick them out before the rest of the world became aware of them. And that had been the point of all her training. She was convinced that in Smithline Securities she had found such an opportunity.

At 11.30 she left her own office building, walked the two blocks to the lobby of a modern skyscraper, and looked up the suite number on the directory board. Fifteen minutes early, she paced the lobby until it was judicious to take the elevator up.

She halted for a moment at the heavy oak doorway, liking the look of it, substantial. Then she entered.

Deborah had researched Smithline Securities until late into the night. It was a small, respected investment-banking and securities-brokerage firm that offered Deborah exactly what she had been searching for: one, John Smithline was an elderly man with no heirs and no partners to complicate a sale; and two, the firm held a large number of warrants to purchase stock in Columbiana Fire and Casualty Insurance Corp., warrants that could be converted into enough stock to give her working control of that company. There was a third factor: as far as she knew, the firm had never done business with the English merchant bank I. Kronengold & Sons.

She approached the receptionist. 'I have an appointment to

see Mr. Smithline. My name is Deborah de Kronengold.'

It took all her will to utter her real name. The name sounded strange to her, assumed, another's. This appointment was the first time she had used it since entering the country. She had thought very hard about doing so. What did it matter that she felt more comfortable as Deborah Crown, an orphan she had invented, than as Deborah de Kronengold, a fraud with a borrowed lineage. Her name was the only asset she had taken from the family that had adopted her, a small enough birthright, to be sure. How dare Leslie, her father, try to intimidate her into eschewing the very family name he himself had bestowed on her, as if it were a privilege he could retract on a whim! How dare he refuse her love and every other normal, fatherly concern, and then begrudge her the little that was left to her! If her grandfather's only asset had been his name, she had decided, he would have wielded it like a club.

A few moments later John Smithline's secretary ushered Deborah down the corridor towards his office. She carefully noted the fairly large stock trading room on the right, with perhaps half a dozen stockbrokers at desks, staring up at the stock quotations that marched across the far wall. Several offices were on the left, containing, she supposed, the firm's investment banking operation. At the end of the corridor was John Smithline's office, furnished in dark woods, tufted red leather sofas and chairs, and an oriental rug.

Deborah de Kronengold was not at all what John Smithline had pictured – she was far too young, far too pretty. One never knew about the Kronengolds, though, he had heard. They were the securest buyer he could get. For them he might be flexible on the price.

Elderly, in dark suit and waistcoat, very proper, John Smithline was more or less what Deborah had pictured. He was also overweight and had a florid complexion. He moved slowly, she noted, which probably meant he wasn't well and, thus, was eager to sell. From reliable sources Deborah had learned that Smithline had been dropping subtle hints around the financial community for a few weeks that he might be willing to sell his firm for $1,200,000 in cash. She took a seat across the desk from him and, after a few minutes of pleasantries, she began to outline her offer.

'Assuming examination of the books warrants it, I'm willing

to pay a million dollars,' Deborah told him, 'but only on the following basis: one quarter in cash and the rest in promissory notes payable three months after I take over the firm.'

At that very moment, based on the latest stock market quotes for her investments, Deborah knew that she was worth exactly $21,236. That figure also took into account both her checking account balance of $58.97 and this week's salary cheque. She would use the time before she had to close on the purchase agreement to turn that twenty-one thousand into a quarter of a million; she was pretty sure she knew how – but she needed all the time before closing to do so, and she would need as well every bit of the three months after that to obtain the rest. She would have asked for six months or even four if she thought there was the slightest chance of obtaining it – her negotiating strategy here was to make a firm offer and stick to the terms no matter what. If he accepted them, she would have to come up with $250,000 at the closing and hoped to use the next three months to take over Columbiana and use its excess cash to pay Smithline his last $750,000. She had no leeway in the terms she had offered him. And, even with all her careful planning, she knew that things could fall apart if the timing did not drop into place exactly as she had foreseen. She was taking the biggest risk she had ever taken in her life.

Deborah de Kronengold and John Smithline bargained for nearly an hour. Deborah refused to budge an inch – indeed, she knew she could not. Although she never held herself out as speaking for anyone but herself, what finally clinched an agreement on exactly the payment terms she had insisted upon was John Smithline's belief that she was there to represent her family. The more firmly she denied it, the more strongly he believed that her family was behind the offer. He had checked with an English banker friend that morning, who confirmed that Leslie de Kronengold had a daughter living in America named Deborah, a redhead, very striking looking. It seemed inconceivable to John Smithline that this lone young woman, in her early twenties at most, intended to buy an investment bank on her own.

As the jetliner pierced the last remnants of daylight, Deborah could still make out the shivering surface of the Atlantic Ocean below. Since making her offer to John Smithline at midday, her mood had alternated between moments of utter serenity, because at last she had taken her destiny into her own hands and was no longer forced to rely on the goodwill of someone like Van Landy, and moments of sudden fear about the risk and the difficulties ahead. Each time the anxiety gripped her she carefully reviewed every step of her plan. And each time she concluded that, although the risk was undeniable, her reasoning was sound.

Many months before, as she had explained to her Uncle Pierre aboard the schooner, she had perceived that inflation and a weakening dollar had become inevitable in the United States. By carefully perusing such monthly international economic statistics as the balance of trade between major countries, their relative interest and inflation rates, and the purchases and sales of various currencies, she had become convinced that a major currency crisis was in the making that could multiply by ten or maybe twenty times the capital she had built up so painstakingly. As each month's figures were published, she searched for the signs. Even working twenty-hour days, seven days some weeks, she always carved out the time to analyze that month's figures.

Money was not simply a medium of exchange to her but an organic form of matter infinitely malleable into infinite forms. Dealing with it was almost an expression of her character, an innate urge, like a composer's to write music or a sculptor's to create shapes. She could read in its movement precursors of moods as clearly as in a lover's face.

Recently, Deborah had noticed some significant variations in the monthly statistics. Certain they were not aberrations but, rather, telltale jumps in earlier trends, she decided that she had, at best, two months to get into position to capitalize on an international currency crisis of major proportions.

Watching the night envelope the jet, Deborah thought about how great a step this trip was for her – financially and emotionally. In one sense, the ocean had been a wall, guarding her from the evil that threatened to swallow her on the other side until she could grow rich enough to fight on even terms. Now she was risking what little security she had come to rely on in America: her money, the distance, her anonymity. She was like a trapeze artist – fascinated by her skill and her fear and the safety awaiting her at the end of the danger. Every day not closer to her goal of real wealth and retaliation against Leslie was a day wasted. Already four years had passed – she must cut corners and take chances based on her most careful assessment. Every fibre in her being told her that the British pound would soon come under attack and plunge in value and that the U.S. dollar would quickly follow. She was flying now to Geneva to put into place the apparatus and, most particularly, the person who would be able to aid her in turning that crisis to her advantage.

Despite having slept only fitfully on the plane, as she stepped into the taxi for the short ride to the centre of Geneva, for the first time in a long while Deborah felt fresh and pleased with the way she looked. No amount of raising or lowering hemlines had been able to hide any longer that her wardrobe had fallen hopelessly out of fashion, and she had spent the afternoon scouring Ohrbach's for a suit she could afford. She had finally found a Chanel copy, a suit she loved, beige knit with black braid trim on the pockets and lapels, the first clothes on which she had splurged since arriving in the States.

As the taxi turned into the centre of the city, all sorts of memories flooded back upon her, and she had to fight to hold onto her positive mood. The only other time she had been here was with her grandfather Samuel. She had sat in on a business meeting and then been taken sightseeing while he visited a doctor for a check-up. Samuel had been so powerful, commanded such financial resources, that his success had always seemed inevitable, even among the innumerable banks that stood shoulder to shoulder like barrel-chested soldiers around the Quai de l'Ile and along the lake-front boulevards. Looking at them now, without him, she felt very small and alone. She tried to believe what Samuel had taught her, that brains were the important thing – the gift he told her she had – and that wealth would unquestionably follow.

She concentrated on remembering the city. A left turn on the Quai du Mont Blanc just past the park containing the pink and white gothic tower would bring her to the yellow awnings on the Rue Fabri. Those of the Beau Rivage Hotel first and then the Hotel Richemond's.

André Leitner was waiting for her in Le Gentilhomme, the restaurant on the far side of the Richemond's lobby. She had got to know André well when she sat in on some of her grandfather's meetings with him in London, and he had been her guide around Geneva. After the boat ride on Lake Geneva, he had taken her to the Gentilhomme for lunch. Nothing seemed to have changed: the red brocade curtains and walls, the sconces, the red velvet chairs. And André Leitner, except for more grey in his full head of hair and ample eyebrows, hardly at all. About her height, with observant brown eyes and rounded prosperous cheeks, he still looked every inch the distinguished banker, although he had been in government for the past decade. Before that he had headed Swiss operations for Samuel, and Deborah knew that her grandfather had relied on him without reservation. André had been the first person Leslie had dismissed when he stripped the bank of the hierarchy of executives loyal to Samuel. Many outsiders claimed that the Kronengold bank had never recovered from the wholesale loss.

From a small article she had read in a European banking magazine a few weeks earlier, Deborah had gleaned that André intended to leave his post in the Swiss Finance Ministry and was in discussion with several private banks about joining them. Deborah considered she had happened on a propitious moment to approach him.

Leitner remembered well the sharp-eyed little girl at Lord Kronengold's shoulder. Often Samuel would turn to her before giving his opinion in order to test her. Her astuteness had been startling, but it had seemed more like a vaudeville performance in one so young, like a child musician in shorts and bow tie standing on a wooden box to play.

Now she sat across the table from him, grown, elegant, and self-assured as she inquired about his wife and son. André had agreed to her lunch invitation out of respect for Samuel's memory, not really believing anything significant would come of the meeting, despite her statement on the telephone that she had important matters to discuss with him if he was indeed serious about leaving government service. She was hardly more than a child, and, if the rumours relayed by friends still at the Kronengold bank could be believed, had been left nothing by her grandfather. The Swiss were a cynical people; money talked far louder than schemes in Switzerland.

They both ordered fish, he the *sole d'Ostende* with Choron sauce and she the *escalope de turbot* with a sauce of champagne and caviar. Then André turned back to her, folded his hands across his lap, and asked her to tell him her plans. As Deborah began to speak, she sensed both his politeness and his very real scepticism, amounting almost to a challenge.

'To put it most simply, André,' she began, 'in less than two months, the pound sterling will crash and the dollar, which is now greatly over-valued as well, will follow. As usual, speculators and the frightened will rush to buy gold. Gold will leap upwards. In the few days of crisis, fortunes can be made.'

Shaken, André asked, 'And just what has led you to that conclusion?'

'Mainly the growing disparity in the balance of payments among the major nations, but there are other signs.'

She began to lay them out, quoting numbers, pointing out trends that he and all the other financial experts had failed to note. Facts and figures seemed to rearrange themselves into any army that marched irresistibly before her. André did not speak again for nearly fifteen minutes, as Deborah went on from her analysis to outline her strategy for capitalizing on the coming monetary crisis. He almost dared not breathe; her every word seemed to cut to the secret heart of a future only she had understood. André Leitner had always claimed that, of the many great bankers he had known in his life, only one had been an authentic genius, Samuel de Kronengold. Well before she had finished speaking, the realization came upon him that he was in the presence of a second.

'Like you,' she finally concluded. 'I was cut off by Leslie – by my father, if you will – with nothing. I won't lie to you about the limited extent of my resources, André – this is too important. My plane ticket here, the suit I'm wearing, and this meal are the three biggest expenses I've allowed myself since moving to America. I have worked very hard for four years to save twenty-one thousand dollars. With your help I must turn it into no less than a quarter of million dollars.'

'Why that specific amount?' André was curious to know.

Deborah explained about Smithline Securities, and the steps that would follow her purchase of it. Again he found himself awe-struck. Her plan was brilliant: first, because she had discovered the quirk in the law regarding insurance company reserves and, then, because of the means she had devised, with almost nothing in her pocket, to acquire both the investment bank and the far larger insurance company. Much could still go wrong, but how incredible was the conception.

When it all fell into place, Deborah told André, she wanted him to head the European office of her investment bank. But, for now, she wished him to borrow what he could against the collateral of her twenty-one thousand dollars, arrange the various brokerage accounts that would be required in the several countries and use the entire amount to do the trading for her from a nerve centre he would set up in Geneva. He was an expert trader, she knew. Gold, forbidden to be owned by American investors, could not even be traded in the United States. Deborah was British, and so the prohibition did not apply, but the trading had to take place abroad. If he wished to invest for himself, that was perfectly acceptable, but *her* trades had to be made first – and only after she gave the word by telephone at each stage of the operation.

'By when must we be ready? When will all this happen?' André inquired respectfully.

'Late October at the earliest, I would think. Late November at the latest.'

'I will be ready.'

André Leitner considered himself blessed. Twice in one lifetime he had been called upon to serve.

Deborah grew more and more apprehensive as October moved into November. Every last cent she possessed had been borrowed against and the total then invested on the assumption the British pound would fall. But, so far, nothing, not even a quiver in price, to indicate that her judgement had been correct. If the pound increased in value instead of decreased, she could be wiped out – bankrupted.

She had remained at Hazelton, Lieb because it still provided the salary to live on for the time being and because of her residue of fear that some terrible fluke or mistake would trample across all her reasoning and she would desperately need this job permanently. Moreover, the job gave her instant access to currency figures as they fluctuated minute by minute.

Americans were late-comers to the currency trading game and were wary of it. She had long ago decided that the investment bank she built would set itself off from the others by offering really expert service in international currency trading. Hazelton, Lieb had allocated two of its bond traders to execute currency trades for its multi-national clients, but they lacked the finesse and daring she respected and no trading was done for the firm's own account – which was probably just as well, she decided, given their incompetence. The men soon grew used to Deborah dashing into their room and requesting the latest quotes on pounds and dollars and francs and deutsch marks. They thought she was obtaining them for her boss.

Van Landy had been quite solicitous of Deborah since he rejected her promotion, thinking that his charm had obviated the problem and that, if he did not upset her, she would remain contented – at least for a while. She seemed as competent as always: she put together a list of regional retail store chains to be gobbled up by a growing national retailer, and she suggested ways in which Landy could structure the equipment financing for an electric utility. She was earning her keep, she told herself, even if her heart was no longer in it.

Deborah was using her holiday time judiciously. Several mornings away from her office to examine Smithline's books. An afternoon here and there to negotiate with him on details that had come up. After the first week she became convinced that Smithline Securities was worth every penny – and much more – that its owner was asking for it, but still she called for additional books and records to examine. She had to hold John Smithline off until she had the quarter of a million, but she sensed he was growing restless to close on the purchase, irritated that minute points seemed to have become significant stumbling blocks. He had not even seen a draft contract yet. Deborah kept telling him her lawyer was still working on it, but, in truth, she had not even initiated the necessary action.

Evan McAphee was a young lawyer she had come to respect at Blakely, Coggins, Marshall & Duane, the law firm that represented Hazelton, Lieb and many of its clients. They had become friends but, until she absolutely had to, she did not want either to run up legal charges or to ask him to risk a potential conflict of interest by asking him to draft her contract for purchase of another investment bank while she worked for Hazelton, Lieb. She had limited herself to extracting Evan's promise that if she ever needed a contract for something quickly, he would draft one for her.

On a morning in mid-November, Deborah arrived early at Smithline Securities to examine the books and records relating to the last possible point she could pretend was a reason for holding off on a closing. John Smithline came into the office well before his usual arrival time, prepared to give her an ultimatum. Either she set a firm date to sign the purchase agreement or he would call off the deal and seek a new buyer. He found her at the news teleprinter machines in the back of the stock trading room, engrossed in the bursts of figures clicking across the page. He waited patiently for her to notice his presence. When over a minute had passed, he spoke up.

'Miss de Kronengold, I consider that you have had more than enough time to determine that there are no hidden liabilities and that the revenue and profit are precisely what I claimed them to be. I want a draft contract to look at and a firm closing date. No more delays.'

Deborah's head rose slowly, almost regally, he thought with surprise. She was smiling broadly, and her right hand held the teleprinter paper aloft like a sceptre as she answered him.

'Shall we say two weeks from today?'

On November 18, a Saturday, at 9.30 a.m. Greenwich Mean Time, Great Britain announced to the world that her economy's problems had forced her to devalue the pound sterling by forty cents in terms of U.S. dollars – from $2.80 to $2.40.

Deborah had earlier gambled on the downward move. She had directed her bank to sell British pounds forward. The bank accomplished this in the interbank market by contracting with another bank to deliver British pounds to it in the future at $2.80 per pound. That gave her the right to deliver pounds at that price on that future date to those who had contracted to buy pounds. She had rightly counted on the pound dropping in value and becoming cheaper. The buyers of those contracts, on the other hand, were seeking to be protected against a possible rise in the value of the pound against other currencies. They might have been traders who had contracted to import goods into Britain and wanted to be certain they would be no most costly to buy in pounds when the time came to pay for them. Or, like Deborah, they might have been speculators gambling on a move in the opposite direction.

Because currency prices usually moved only pennies one way or another, Deborah needed to put up in actual cash only five percent of the price of every contract. The nearly $40,000 that André had invested for her – her capital and what he had been able to borrow for her in addition – commanded sterling contracts worth just under $800,000.

As Deborah had ordered him to do, immediately after Britain made the announcement and the price of the pound dropped, André liquidated her position by buying back – at the new $2.40 price – the amount of pounds sterling previously sold. The transaction cleared forty cents a pound in profit between the earlier sale cost and the present purchase cost. Deborah's profit and capital now totalled just under $100,000!

It was still hours before dawn when André telephoned Deborah at home to announce the incredible news. Following her advice, he too had made an excellent profit.

'Perhaps you want to stop here,' he offered.

Deborah had weighed the risk with infinite care and was convinced she had predicted correctly the events that would follow the British devaluation. This was a moment of unparalleled opportunity.

'Buy the gold,' was all she told him. 'Call me back when all the positions are in place.'

For years the United States had been giving away vast foreign aid and otherwise over-spending abroad in relation to her receipts. That imbalance had placed billions of U.S. dollars in foreign bank accounts, owned by holders who were ready to rush out of dollars at the first scare, a scare Deborah anticipated would be the delayed result of the sterling crisis. Her grandfather had taught her that gold was the universal refuge in uncertain times, and she was convinced that a crushing demand would now push its price above the $35 per ounce price. America stood ready, but would now find itself unable, to maintain. Sellers of dollars would rush in unprecedented numbers to put their money into the traditional sanctuary of the frightened, gold.

Employing all Deborah's capital and profit, André

immediately invested in contractual agreements to buy gold on a leveraged basis, putting down five percent and borrowing the balance of the purchase cost. Again, Deborah needed to put only a fraction of the total cost of the actual gold to be delivered. That would multiply her gain – or her loss – when she finally liquidated her position, received the proceeds of the sale returned to her – her five percent deposits and her profits – and simultaneously paid off the loan on the remaining ninety-five percent. Some far-sighted speculators had foreseen the pound's devaluation, but few, if any, had foreseen what Deborah was counting on, that it would be followed by a leap upwards in the price of gold and by a nose-dive in the value of the dollar.

Deborah dressed, went down to Hazelton, Lieb in the early morning hours, and, again, she waited.

What she waited for, what her instinct for finance and for the French mentality had induced her to hazard everything on, was being pondered at that moment in Paris, behind the walls of the Elysée Palace. De Gaulle, she believed, would try to force a crisis in the hope of returning the world's currencies to the gold standard, thus enriching France, which in accord with its national character had piled up a vast stock of gold.

Van Landy was away on a business trip, and Deborah did not move from the currency trading room, scanning every quote, watching for every iota of news. And, in between, stalking back and forth across the far end of the room.

At one point one of the traders started to advise a client to buy U.S. dollars, instead of French francs.

'No!' Deborah yelled at him.

Cowed, the trader reversed himself and took an order shorting the dollar. Once more Deborah began to stalk the end of the room and, as before, she waited.

The news broke like a thunderclap. De Gaulle had decided against allowing France to contribute additional bullion to the international gold pool that supported the Western currencies under attack. Deborah had gauged perfectly both the decision and its psychological effect on the public: the run out of sterling and into gold turned into a stampede. That led to the highly bearish reappraisal of the inflated American dollar that she had anticipated. Soon, bankers, investors, corporate treasurers, and speculators all over the world frantically began to sell vast amounts of dollars in exchange for gold. Gold rose like a rocket.

Jubilant, André Leitner telephoned her at her office. She now had over $200,000! Following her advice, he too had increased his already handsome profit. He advised her to cash in as he was doing. But she had one last twist of the rope to invest in, one last chance to make the money she needed to buy Smithline Securities. What she had earned so far was almost irrelevant to her if she did not have the full amount she needed. She would not deviate from her plan.

'Reverse all my positions now. Sell the gold and buy dollars.'

Deborah had no illusions that the $27 billion international gold pool would be exhausted during this run on dollars or that the temporary disparity between gold and U.S. currency would last more than a few days before returning to the previous $35-an-ounce relationship; the inflationary kettle would have to boil much longer for that to happen. When the dollar began to climb back again and gold to fall, Deborah calculated her gain and ordered André to liquidate all her positions.

Five minutes later he was back on the telephone after executing the transactions. He had the final figures. She was worth $283,000.

'Congratulations! My God, congratulations!' he shouted into the telephone. 'If only your grandfather were alive to see this. An incredible coup!'

He hung up to expedite settlement of all the trades and make certain the funds would be available at the earliest possible time.

Deborah continued to sit without moving, in a daze, receiver to her ear, staring at the white notepaper on which she had written down the figures, trying to comprehend the immensity of the total. While nervelessly directing the trades, she had refused to think of the money as really hers – it was her tool, her medium of art.

'Two hundred and eighty-three thousand dollars!' she marvelled. Audible, the words seemed to add validity to the thought. 'I've really done it. It's mine.'

For a long time she tried to believe it, to exult in it. She tried to think of someone she could share this news with, so as to extend and deepen the satisfaction until it became real.

Charging the call to her home account, she telephoned her cousin Nathan. In his little monk's cell on the English coast, Nathan de Kronengold had spent the last decade praying, meditating, and investing in the world's stock and bond markets a large part of the Catholic Church's capital. He had always been like a father to her, and they had written frequently and spoken on the telephone several times, but only now did she divulge her business involvement.

Nathan's congratulations were strangely reserved, tending to dampen, rather than heighten, her satisfaction. Pressed, he admitted to a regret that, like so many other Kronengolds before her, she had dedicated her life to money.

When she hung up, she wondered what she had been looking for. Praise? Validation? Perhaps such soberness was best. Her triumph was merely preliminary, the fuse for the far larger weapon she was seeking. And even when she possessed that next company, Columbiana Insurance, it would be merely the first step in arming herself for the war that must end in Leslie's obliteration.

Chastened, Deborah remembered that she must now quickly meet the lawyer, Evan McAphee, about drafting a contract for her to buy Smithline Securities. But, even before that, she had a prior duty. She wrote out by hand a resignation letter to Van Landy, giving two weeks' notice, but pointing out that she was owed many more weeks of vacation, which she was taking as of now. She brought the letter into his office and laid it on his desk.

He seemed at a loss at first and then offered her the promotion he had denied her for so long.

'You're too late,' she informed him. 'I've made other plans.'

'A better job? I'll match the salary.'

'I don't think so.'

'That good?' He was bewildered. 'Why are you in such a hurry?'

She thought seriously about the question before answering in the simplest way she could.

'Because I've got so far to go.'

CHAPTER FIFTEEN

Galen Stafford heard about the tender offer for control of the company he headed, Columbiana Fire and Casualty Corp., during a charity golf tournament near his Palm Beach, Florida, winter home. He had played well and needed only a bogey on this last hole to take the top prize. His second place finish the precious year had rankled with him ever since then. Just as he was about to tee off, a golf cart came racing back up the eighteenth fairway towards him. He recognized the man, overweight, in a business suit, who was being bounced from side to side by the cart, as his corporate treasurer. The man was down here from corporate head-quarters for a meeting with him after the tournament.

Sweating, fearful, the treasurer quickly explained that his office had just transferred to his motel a phone call from a *Wall Street Journal* reporter. From the reporter he learned that their own investment bank, Smithline Securities, had made an offer to purchase enough stock to take a controlling interest in Columbiana.

Galen Stafford was a large-limbed, bald-headed man who had been a basketball star in college and was now sixty-two, and his anger was legendary. It erupted now, both because his dominance over his company was threatened and because the threat appeared to come from a source he had always intimidated, John Smithline.

Columbiana was not one of the giant insurance companies, but it was good-sized and healthy and could have commanded the services of a far bigger investment bank; but that would have cost the company far more in fees, and Galen Stafford was a frugal man. He had risen through the ranks to head Columbiana, owned very little stock himself, and gave little thought to the price of his company's stock. The exception was when he was negotiating with John Smithline over the latter's fees for under-writing Columbiana's periodic stock and bond issues to raise capital. Knowing how badly the latter's small firm needed his business, Stafford had invariably forced him to accept an unduly large portion of those fees in the form, not of cash, but of warrants to purchase common stock in Columbiana. Warrants are options to purchase stock at a specified price. Underwriters often take warrants as part of their fee, but only at prices which they believe will someday be far less than the shares will be selling for on the stock exchange when they eventually wish to exercise the warrants. Galen Stafford took particular pleasure in coercing John Smithline into accepting exercise prices that were far higher than Columbiana's stock would ever conceivably sell for. Stafford got very low expenses on his underwritings, and John Smithline got low fees and some useless paper. Or so it had been for many years.

The company's treasurer now informed Stafford that a booming stock market had recently changed matters dramatically. The price of Columbiana stock was now several dollars higher per share than the price required to be paid under the terms of the warrants. In fact, a few minutes earlier, Smithline Securities had exercised the warrants by delivering a cheque to his office for $5,200,000. Smithline Securities now owned almost ten percent of Columbiana.

The man concluded, 'They've made a public offer to buy another forty-one percent of the stock from our shareholders – at five dollars more a share than the stock is selling for on the stock market. That will give them a majority of our stock. They can vote in their own board of directors and –'

'Something's crazy here,' Stafford barked. 'Has anybody had enough sense to get John Smithline on the telephone and find out what the hell is going on?'

'I've already called. His office says he's on vacation.'

The next foursome was waiting impatiently, as were Stafford's playing partners. One remarked that he might want to drop out of the tournament and take care of business, so the rest of them could play. Stafford's jaw thrust out.

'I'll hit when I'm good and ready,' he snapped. 'I'm not dropping out.'

He continued to interrogate his subordinate. Columbiana's executive committee had been alerted to assemble in the board room at four that afternoon. The firm's Wall Street law firm had been contacted, and the senior partner who represented their company would be there as well.

Stafford was trading irate insults with the other players when he finally stepped up to the tee and put all his rage into a swing that would flatten the little white ball. He topped the drive. The ball trickled into a creek that cut across the fairway fifty yards out. Stubbornly, he took a two-stroke penalty and played out the hole, losing the tournament by one stroke.

His anger stoked to volcano force, Galen Stafford stomped to his car still in his plus-fours, violet shirt, and canary-yellow slacks, and drove to the airport with his treasurer.

When Deborah bought Smithline Securities, she insisted that no public announcement be made and that John Smithline go off on his holiday without informing anyone but his lawyer and wife of the sale. During the imminent take-over fight for control of Columbiana Insurance she wanted nothing to appear to have changed at Smithline Securities and to stay deep in the background. Being both very young and a woman, she was an easy target for adverse publicity by the defending target company. Until she gained control of Columbiana, her entire scheme could topple like a house of cards.

Deborah had found in James Lacy, the young man John Smithline had lured from Goldman, Sachs to run his firm's day-to-day operations, an exceedingly capable executive. Short and feisty, he had worked his way up in finance after graduating from a state university his wife's job had helped put him through and then gaining an MBA at night while working during the day. Pleased with the opportunity to be part of building a really important financial firm, he understood that his role for the time being was to shield Deborah from the press and other potentially antagonistic eyes.

Lacy had been the one that morning who had announced to the press that a public offer was being made for controlling interests in Columbiana Insurance. He had spoken to all the reporters, and he had taken the shocked call from Columbiana. But, around noon, at just about the same time that Galen Stafford was rolling a Top-Flite golf ball into a fast-running creek on the eighteenth fairway, he had received a phone call that he could not fend off, from a very angry man who would not identify himself but said he had also been planning to launch a take-over of Columbiana and would steamroller them. He was on his way over to have it out with 'you pipsqueaks'. Lacy went in to Deborah's office to tell her about it.

In a black silk dress with elbow-length sleeves and a straight neckline, Deborah sat tall and erect behind what was once John Smithline's desk. She did not like the excessively masculine look of the furniture she had inherited, the tufted red leather and heavy woods, but it did not distract her enough to spend good money yet on redecoration. She had made only two large personal expenditures in the few weeks since purchasing the firm, both of which she considered necessities. She had increased her wardrobe with the sorts of clothes of a successful businesswoman, and she had moved to an apartment on Fifth Avenue. Although she had bought only the most basic furniture for the small apartment, she considered the prestigious address essential. There must never be the slightest doubt that she was a Kronengold.

Deborah joined in James Lacy's concern about the telephone call he had received. She told him to get the receptionist to find out more about the man when he arrived. If he was genuine, she would see him.

Deborah went back to analysing trades made in Columbiana's stock, so as to sense whether the stock market seemed to be backing her bid or rejecting it. At the moment it looked good, but Deborah could not ignore the disquieting feeling that Lacy's telephone caller had aroused. One thing she could not afford at this precise moment was a bidding war with a well-capitalized competitor.

Deborah was engrossed in the figures when she heard a noise in the corridor. She stood up to see what was causing the disturbance and caught sight of a man storming up to her secretary. He was about thirty, she judged, about six feet tall, wide and muscular, with black hair curled into tight shiny ringlets like the wool of a black sheep. His eyebrows formed a V that accentuated the power in his broad nose and square face. If she had stopped to wonder whether he was good-looking, she might have answered that he was handsome as a force is handsome – implacable, threatening. For a moment she thought there might be something familiar about the heavy cheekbones and brows, then decided otherwise; she was sure she had never met the man before.

'Look,' he growled at the receptionist running futilely behind him and the secretary trying to block his way. 'The hell with announcing me. The man I want to see is in there, and I'm going in *now*.'

'It's all right,' Deborah called out to her employees. 'Let him in.'

His head swung around, like a bull entering the ring, as he stepped into Deborah's office. She was walking round her desk to greet him, so he was for a moment unable to get a good look at her.

'I'm not going to waste my time with secretaries. Where's the guy who runs this place?'

Deborah extended her hand. 'I'm the guy who runs this place. I'm Deborah de Kronengold.'

As his gaze focused on her face, he suddenly stopped in mid-stride, not taking her hand, not even moving. An expression of stunned recognition slowly lit his features.

'Yes, you are,' he said in bewilderment. 'You're Deborah de Kronengold.'

'Do we know each other?' she asked.

The man's eyes glittered like black marbles as he considered her words and stared at her. 'We've never met, but I've waited a long time to meet you. Since Christmas of 1956. You were in St. Moritz.'

Deborah's brow furrowed. 'I *was* at St. Moritz then. With my grandfather.'

'You were there when he ruined my father.'

Deborah scanned his features and her memory carefully. 'Your father is Max Holtz?'

'And I'm David Holtz. Your grandfather robbed us of nearly everything.'

Deborah recalled every detail vividly. 'Your father tried to rob *us*. He switched core samples, secretly bought up land. I saw the report.'

Colour was rising in David Holtz's face. The young woman was far too self-possessed to be intimidated. The terrible wrongs Kronengolds had done to Holtzes for generations had been burned deeply into David's consciousness, just as his father had had them branded into his own from his earliest days by *his* father. St. Moritz was only the latest injustice in a string that stretched back into the nineteenth century, when the Holtz family's little Viennese bank and many others were wiped out by an Austrian Kronengold who had added to his millions with a devious, brilliant attack against the bonds of a large railway holding company in which they were all heavily invested. Yet David held his temper. Deborah was a

Kronengold too, and they were far too powerful to challenge without knowing the extent of her resources – just how strong she was. He softened his anger for another reason. He had seen a black and white photograph or two of her in British magazines a few years ago. She looked frivolous, insubstantial. Nothing had prepared him for the true physical impact she made: tall, bright red hair, intense blue eyes, and beautiful. He felt unsettled – the stirrings of ambivalence.

'It turned out well, though,' he said. He understood the intimacy that candour created. 'My father came to live in the U.S. then, the first time I had ever been with him for more than a few days. He and my mother were divorced in Paris when I was an infant. I hadn't spent a dozen days with him until then. He had to start all over again in America. I had just begun college, but I could help him after the school day and each summer. It really gave us a kind of bond. As angry as I was at your family, I was grateful to them too in a crazy way.'

Deborah kept silent, watching the young man as cautiously as she would a predator. She remembered Samuel's warning about Max Holtz and did not know how far to trust the son.

'The troubles we had with your grandfather only made us drive harder for success,' David Holtz said. 'The company we built has doubled its revenue for the last three years.'

'What company is that?'

'Aximation Industries.'

Deborah had heard of Aximation, but had had no idea that Max Holtz was involved in it. Aximation, she knew, had originally been a small tool company which had been used as the keystone for a dizzying series of acquisitions that had created a very fast-growing conglomerate. The acquisitions, she recalled, had been made sometimes with stock but more often with ingeniously designed debt instruments. She admired that kind of pluck and imagination. Aximation was now a big company and growing. That worried her.

'We'll do five hundred million dollars in sales this year,' he added, trying to judge her reaction. They were about to go into battle, and he wanted her to understand the strength he was dealing from.

'At this point I believe I'm expected to applaud,' she replied with light sarcasm.

'Something like that,' he retorted. 'I came here for a reason.'

'I gather you're the man who spoke to James Lacy a while ago, about our offer for Columbiana Insurance.'

He appeared angry now. 'Three or four weeks from now, we would have been ready to go after Columbiana ourselves.'

'Which means you aren't ready now.' Deborah tried to probe further. 'Why do you want an insurance company anyway? Stodgy business.'

'The same reason you do, I think.' His anger was subdued now, she could see, a negotiating stance he called on when needed.

She feigned ignorance. 'What's that?'

'Its cash reserves.'

They both smiled, sensing in the other a match to their skills. Each was impressed differently, however. David was thrown off guard because her beauty concealed a formidable mind; he wasn't used to that in the many women he had easily, almost thoughtlessly, conquered.

After a long time without an interest in a man, Deborah felt more surprise than elation at her very strong attraction to David Holtz. She usually rejected within a few minutes after meeting nearly all the young men with whom she came into contact. But David Holtz, with the energy and the agile mind of a self-made man, had a toughness that matched her own; she had been unable to make him yield an inch. Deborah mentally shook herself. Such thinking was crazy at a time like this – and about a man who threatened to destroy everything she was trying to build.

'You and your father seem to have come a long way,' Deborah said, assuming that he would want to tell her more.

'Not bad. Nowhere near what the Kronengolds are worth, but we're getting there.' He paused, the bantering negotiating tone dropped for the moment. 'It must be a great feeling to be born with all of this – to know it's yours and no one can take it away from you.'

'Yes, it must be.' David failed to note the irony in her words.

'Be honest with me,' he asked. 'What is a young, damned good-looking Englishwoman doing in a jungle like American investment banking? It's rough enough for men.'

'To put it in a sentence,' Deborah answered as honestly as she dared, 'America is a country where anyone, even a young woman, can prove that she has the capacity to become wealthy and successful on her own. And even if she's a Kronengold.'

The two stared at each other for several seconds, each assessing the strength and commitment of the other to a fight over Columbiana.

David was the first to speak. 'Regardless of whether the Kronengolds are up against us, I'll put everything on the line to acquire Columbiana. We're ready to make an offer to pay ten dollars a share above your offer.'

But Deborah thought she heard more in his voice than tenacity. She thought she could make out the merest hint of bluff.

'Are you sure this is the right battle to pick with the Kronengolds?' Doborah asked, her own tone a challenge.

'*Am* I picking a battle with the family or only with you?' he wondered aloud.

That was a question she could not let him ponder.

'Are you prepared to find out?' She let a smile play over her face. 'Besides, I think you're too good a businessman to raise the stakes of the game to the point where the prize is no longer worth the struggle – for the winner *or* the loser. Don't forget, I already own about ten percent of Columbiana's stock through exercising warrants. I have to buy only another forty percent. You have to convince shareholders owning *fifty* percent to sell to you. The odds favour me.'

She thought she could sense that he was struggling, hating to yield such a fat prize, yet fearing the consequences of a battle and all the while concerned that he might be cutting himself off from her. Now was the time to offer him a different prize.

'David, rather than scrapping over this company, to no one's benefit, let us find you another insurance company with excess cash in the reserves, a bigger one that's really worth your going after. We're investment bankers. It stands to reason that, if we could do it for ourselves, we can do it for our clients.'

'I've had enough of small investment banks. We have an appointment tomorrow with Landy at Hazelton, Lieb.'

'Van Landy can't tie his shoelaces without help. I'll make you an offer you can't ignore. To show you how good we are, I'll find you that big insurance company and, when I do, charge you only half the usual fee.'

He had not been diverted. 'I still want Columbiana.'
'Fight and all?'
He paused an instant. 'I ought to warn you. I usually get what I want. How about dinner tonight?'
She shook her head and stood up. 'Not while we're adversaries.'
'When?'
'That's up to you.'

Well before three o'clock that afternoon, Galen Stafford, still in his golfing clothes, joined his executive committee, several directors, and an armada of the company's lawyers in Columbiana's board room.

Galen Stafford had gone to Milton and Yale. He came from a prominent upper-class family and belonged to all the right clubs. He had a lot of powerful friends. The law firm that represented Columbiana was one of the handful of giant firms retained by the nation's blue-chip companies and major financial institutions. Present in the board room was the senior law partner of Columbiana's Wall Street law firm. He, too, had been born and bred into the same circles as Stafford.

By the next morning, the two men had learned a good deal about the new state of affairs at Smithline Securities and about their own defensive position. They knew they could not win by convincing stockholders that the price per share Smithline was offering was inadequate. Quite the contrary, the offer provided a healthy premium above the present stock exchange price – which itself had been far lower for decades. Their best defence would be to get the state insurance commission to refuse to approve the transfer of control, but that would fail because there were no grounds. And they had no basis for a court battle, either, another frequent defence tactic, because the lawyers were unable to identify a sustainable cause of action.

But Galen Stafford and his lawyer had very powerful friends, and, as that second day wore on and night fell, they decided that that would be their defence.

The next morning Deborah received a telephone call from the vice-president she dealt with at Metrobank and to whom she had been introduced by her own lawyer, Evan McAphee, after she purchased Smithline Securities. The banker had been eager to finance the take-over, satisfied with the collateral of the Smithline stock she owned and the Columbiana stock she would buy, knowing that the excess cash in the insurance company's reserves made all the stock far more valuable than her purchase price. But his attitude had changed radically.

'Those are demand loans, Miss de Kronengold. We can call them at any time. We want payment *now*, or else we foreclose on your stock in Smithline Securities.'

Deborah was stunned. 'It was always understood that you would be repaid as soon as the take-over of Columbiana was completed.'

'Things change,' he said with embarrassment. 'I don't have final say on policy.' He halted. 'All I can do for you – unofficially, you understand – is try to hold off a day or two before we take action.'

The news was devastating. The bank had been ready to lend her up to $40,000,000, both sides understanding that it was to pay for Columbiana stock. The bank had already advanced the $5,200,000, with which she had exercised the warrants to purchase the initial ten percent of the stock. She did not have the funds to continue the fight or even to repay the initial borrowing unless she sold off the Columbiana stock she had just purchased. She had to find another bank fast, before word of her financial problems leaked out and gave Columbiana's shareholders doubts about tendering their stock to her.

She quickly telephoned Evan McAphee, but he already knew. The bank had called him first and then said it was going to inform her. Although Metrobank had been unwilling to agree to more than a demand loan, he had made dozens of such arrangements for clients in the past. Metrobank's verbal agreement on the real terms had always been as solid as a rock. It seemed inconceivable that Metrobank would renege on its verbal promise to back Deborah all the way.

'What about a different bank, Evan?'

'I've been on the phone with other banks since the guy at Metrobank called. I'm waiting for one to call me back, and I have one or two others I'd like to call. We have to talk. Do you mind coming over to my office?'

'I'll be there in twenty minutes.'

Deborah was beginning to perceive how desperate her position really was.

Of medium height, thin, and a bit slope-shouldered, with sandy hair and grey eyes behind horned-rim glass, Evan McAphee considered himself so average looking that someone as beautiful as Deborah Crown was far beyond his powers to attract. He had been dating the same young woman for three years, the daughter of his law firm's managing partner. Linda was a well-bred, dependable, but unexciting young woman, who knew perfectly the role she would be expected to play as wife to the firm's youngest partner. She loved him and the marriage would consolidate his place in the prestigious firm. Clearly, she expected him to propose, but after meeting Deborah Evan had hesitated. For the first time it occurred to him that a woman might be more than a loyal helpmeet: indeed, he and Deborah had initially become good friends when McAphee realized much time and mental anguish could be saved if he explained to Deborah the Hazelton, Lieb matters on which he needed Landy's decisions or signatures, leaving the rest to her. More important, those conversations gave Evan the opportunity to spend some of that saved time with her. He discovered that Deborah was ambitious, yet charming; her mind could assimilate and juggle complex business matters as easily as his, yet she was feminine and warm-hearted; he admired her, yet felt protective towards her.

When Deborah first told him she was buying an investment bank, he had thought she was joking and, a moment after, that her apparent logicality might really be masking insanity. He had decided to humour her when she informed him she would have to use her real name.

'Don't tell me you have some awful first name you've been hiding? Like Ralph?'

She was too intent on her thoughts to acknowledge his joke. 'It's the last name actually. My name really isn't Crown. It's de Kronengold. I'm Deborah de Kronengold.'

Evan was about to telephone a psychiatrist friend and take Deborah over there, when she handed him her passport.

'Holy shit!' he had finally exhaled. 'Holy shit!'

The work he had since done for Deborah – the contract to purchase Smithline Securities, introducing her to Metrobank, the arrangements to go after Columbiana – had been a labour of love for Evan McAphee. But now, as Deborah's arrival was announced and he ended his telephone conversation with the president of the last possible bank to which he might conceivably have been able to switch Deborah's loan, he felt that he had failed her. All the doors were slammed shut.

'It's Columbiana's management,' he reported to her. 'Galen Stafford, really, and his lawyers. They have a lot of powerful friends who don't think it's right for a young woman to take over a bastion of old-line financial power like Columbiana Insurance. The head of Metrobank is one of those friends.'

'I guessed as much,' Deborah said quietly. 'I made one or two calls on my own before coming over.'

'You're offering the shareholders more for their stock than it's ever been worth,' Evan fumed.

'The boys in the upper-class locker room play dirty, Evan. They're standing up for everything I'm not: manhood, Protestantism, Americanism, and old age.'

'Look, it's none of my business, but the Kronengolds aren't exactly weaklings in the financial world. Couldn't, say, your father help out?'

Her eyes hardened. 'I have no one but myself.' She took a moment to collect herself. 'Evan, my best chance to raise the capital I need is in America because that's where Smithline Securities has built up its reputation. André Leitner, my European executive, is trying to interest foreign banks, but he thinks it will take weeks of negotiations because they have no history of dealing with me. I haven't got weeks. I might not even have days. At the slightest sign that my finances are weak, my credibility will be gone, and I'll be finished in finance before I've even got started. Credibility is all one really has in finance. But it's everything.'

He slammed his hands on the desk in frustration. 'Damn, I wish there was something I could do!'

'This law firm is as important as Columbiana's. Can't some of your senior partners pull some strings?'

Even looked away, pretending that he was cleaning his glasses.

Deborah guessed the truth. 'Stafford and his lawyers have got to your partners too. They have, haven't they?'

'Yes, but it doesn't matter.'

She reached for her briefcase, preparatory to leaving. 'I can understand your not being able to represent me.'

Evan replied with all the fervour in his being. 'I swear to you, nothing will induce me to drop you as a client.'

Deborah recognized the conflict that must be raging around him at this moment. Stafford and his lawyer had doubtless asked a favour of friends here, perhaps even induced this firm's clients to put pressure on its partners. His girlfriend's father and others had probably demanded that he cease to represent her. Yet, he was willing to leave Blakely, Coggins and all that he had built up here, rather than set her adrift.

'I'm very grateful, Evan,' she said. 'Right now friends are few and far between.'

Despair overcame her, and she had to stop speaking and walk to the window. She was about to lose everything she had worked and struggled for. And by means that were not legal or fair. She was up against a conspiracy, pure and simple, and she would never be able to prove a thing. She had been clever, but lacked the resources to back up her moves with the only force that mattered – money. That would have ended the conspiracy dead in its tracks. The Old Boy network might refrain from helping her, but they wouldn't put up good money to back Galen Stafford in a losing cause. However, she had no money, and the Old Boys had cut her off from the hope of finding it in time to save herself. She felt as she had when she was a child during desperate moments, sliding into the black nothingness without a handhold.

She sensed Evan at her shoulder, proffering his handkerchief.

'Don't worry, I won't cry,' she murmured.

The fact that Evan had not deserted her although he was powerless to help only made her feel more helpless, and responsible for his predicament as well.

'Yesterday someone told me the financial world is like a jungle,' she remembered. 'Not a very original thought, but accurate.'

All around me animals seem to be lunging at my flesh, she told herself despondently. There has to be a way out.

And then it came to her.

'The jungle, Evan!' she nearly shouted. 'Some animals hunt together.'

She ran to the telephone. 'How do I make a call out?'
'What's the number?'
'I don't know. It's Aximation Industries. His name is David Holtz. I want to invite him to lunch.'

Deborah waited for David Holtz to join her by the first sight she had ever visited in New York, the statue of George Washington on the steps of the Subtreasury Building. Because women are excluded from eating clubs, she had considered a restaurant, but the overcrowding promoted eavesdropping and ruined the atmosphere for a thoughtful dialogue. So, instead, hoping the suggestion was off-beat enough to intrigue him, she had told David Holtz the weather was so beautiful that she proposed they continue their earlier discussion while walking along lower Manhattan's waterfront and lunching on hot dogs. She had left the purpose for seeing him vague when he sounded so pleased to hear from her. So much the better if he believed the visit would be social and if the informality made him more amenable to what she wished to discuss. Her survival was paramount. She had very little time in which to prevent everything she was trying to build up from crashing down upon her. She must make all the moves just exactly right. They were the last ones she had.

The black limousine had barely come to a stop when David Holtz bounded out of it towards her, swinging his overcoat onto his shoulder as he took the Subtreasury Building's steps three at a time, his white breath trailing behind him.

Like a locomotive's smoke, she thought, distracted by the power in him. He was upon her faster than she had expected, his wide chest thrusting apart his grey jacket. For a moment she could not think.

'You drove down here quickly,' she finally said.

'I was afraid you'd change your mind.'

David was staring at her. In the bright winter sunlight, gold threads appeared to run through her long red hair as through a royal fabric.

'You'll get cold without your coat on,' Deborah reminded him.

He shook himself back to the present and put on the black overcoat.

'I always figured a first date should be elegant. Le Pavillon, maybe. This is crazy.'

'Absolutely,' she said with a wide smile. 'But it's a lovely day, and the streets are almost empty.'

She slipped her arm through his, invading his defences before he raised them. They cut diagonally down the steps, in the direction of the East River. His upper arm felt very large and rock-hard against her side.

'I really didn't think you'd call me,' he admitted. 'I was trying to figure out a way to call *you* without looking foolish.'

She liked his candour. It was disarming, Deborah noted, but he used it tactically, knowing the effect it had.

'*Would* you have called?'

'Yes. Probably to tell you we've decided to make our own offer for Columbiana.'

Deborah was rocked back, as if he had punched her.

'Are you okay?' he asked.

'My heel caught in the grating.' She smiled at him, as would a woman without a care in the world. 'You were saying something about making an offer?'

'I promised myself I wouldn't waste this time with you on business.'

'Just for a moment,' she coaxed.

He was reluctant, but shrugged acquiescence. 'We're thinking of offering a package to Columbiana's shareholders: one share of a new class of preferred stock and one convertible debenture for every hundred shares of Columbiana they tender. The package would pay annually about two percent more than Columbiana's present dividend and be worth seven dollars more a share than your bid.'

'It won't wash, David. I'll raise my cash offer. Those shareholders are finally sniffing a cash profit after years of holding depressed stock. They don't want funny paper.'

'Maybe,' he conceded.

Deborah pressed into the opportunity his concession afforded her. She had done extensive research on David Holtz and his company, Aximation Industries, since the day when he had stormed into her office. 'I told you when we first talked that a bidding war between us could make the stocks cost so high we'd both lose.' She paused in mid-step, then turned to him as if suddenly struck by an idea. 'Why don't you and I join forces? Buy Columbiana as partners?'

They proceeded down the street once more, silently now, until they came to the corner, in sight of the old brick buildings near the waterfront. A lone hot-dog vendor, rubbing his hands over the hot cooking compartment, huddled on the opposite corner.

David spoke at last. Hurt singed the edges of his words. 'Is that why you invited me here? For business?'

His face was so unexpectedly close to hers she could not evade it. She became conscious of the pounding in her chest and the weakness vacuuming up her innermost parts. Until now she had ignored any attraction she might feel for *him*. But his directness now forced on her the awareness that, from the very first, she had been suppressing emotions he aroused in her as a woman, urges she had not wished to acknowledge. Without losing sight of her objective in arranging this meeting, she tried to answer him with absolute honesty.

'I wanted to find a way to end our being adversaries,' she said, not having understood the depth of her own feeling until then.

He searched her face before he responded. 'I'd like to find a way too.'

After they had bought frankfurters and drinks and were walking underneath the elevated highway towards an old wooden pier jutting into the river, he pursued the point.

'What's your proposal?'

She took a deep breath.

He interrupted her. 'How can you eat it with ketchup? Ketchup is for hamburgers. Nobody eats ketchup on hot dogs.'

'Watch me.'

'Try it with mustard. Please. I can't stand to look at this.'

'What do you suggest? It already has ketchup.'

'We'll switch. I'll eat the one with the ketchup.'

'You don't like it that way.'

'It's better than having to watch you eat it.'

Deborah shrugged her shoulders. 'If it makes you happy.'

They switched hot dogs. He watched her bite into his. Her meagre half-smile out of politeness elated him.

'I knew it!' he enthused. He bit into the other hot dog. 'Hey, you know, it's not bad like this.'

He gestured towards her with the hand that held the soft drink bottle. 'Okay, what's the proposal?'

Deborah collected her thoughts and began again. 'A bank committed itself to financing our take-over. I think I can get the bank to step aside. I would switch that commitment to your company. Aximation would put up capital for my company to acquire a majority of Columbiana's stock, which would unlock the excess cash in Columbiana's reserves.'

'You'd drain the cash?' He gazed at her as he sipped.

'No. I would use it to heighten the value of the stock. First my company, Smithline Securities, would buy the rest of Columbiana's stock with an offer of some kind of bond or other debt instrument. Owning all Columbiana's stock and its cash reserves would make Smithline's stock much more valuable. I would then sell about sixty percent or so of the Smithline stock to the public at a much higher price than I paid for Columbiana's.'

'A publicly held investment bank and brokerage house?' he scoffed.

'Why not? Every other kind of company is selling its stock to the public at inflated prices. Why not an investment bank?'

'Clever,' he admitted. 'But it would sell for a lot more if the firm's name was Kronengold and not Smithline.'

A slow smile spread across Deborah's face. That had been part of her plan from the beginning. David smiled in recognition. He had the self-confidence to toss her an unspoken compliment while negotiating. She liked that. She explained the rest of her thinking. 'I would then be in a position to pay off a lot of the money I borrowed for the take-over, retain a lot of cash in the firm as working capital, and still keep some of the profit myself.'

'And you'd still control forty percent of the surviving company's stock. Enough to maintain control.' He and his father were firmly in control of Aximation Industries although their original holdings had been reduced to less than that percentage as a result of buying many companies with Aximation stock. 'What would my company end up with? You did intend to leave a little something for us.'

'I would then transfer half my forty percent or so to your company at my actual cost. We'd each own about twenty percent of the new public company's stock for less than half of what it's worth.'

'I'd finance you, you'd make a whopping profit, but we'd both come out ahead.' He leaned so close she could smell his cologne, and eyed her. 'My mother, may she rest in peace, always said, "If it sounds too good to be true, it is." You're still giving me a very lucrative deal. Why are you willing to make me a partner?'

Deborah tried to sound casual. 'As I told you, if we had a bidding war, the deal would cease to be lucrative. Half a loaf now will still be very nourishing.'

David had finished the soft drink and was taking aim at a rubbish bin. 'Assuming I put up the, what?'

'In the neighbourhood of forty million dollars.'

He clicked his tongue. 'You sure don't hang around any low-rent neighbourhoods. Which of us would actually run this company you're creating?'

'I would,' she replied quickly and firmly. 'I want full rights to vote all your shares as I see fit. My board of directors. My management.'

David exploded, flinging the bottle into the wire basket. 'I never gave up voting control in my life.'

'This is *my* deal,' she rejoined evenly. 'I own Smithline. I was the first to go after Columbiana, and I already own ten percent. If I can't control your shares, I'll break off discussions right now, and we'll fight it out.'

A corner of David's strong mouth bent in derision. 'My alternative is to fund you and then let you do whatever the hell you want with my twenty per cent of Columbiana.'

'All business decisions will be mine, but I agree to consult you before I undertake a major one.'

David Holtz glared at the blue eyes that stared without flinching at his. In them was the audacity of the Kronengolds. She was forcing him to hope that the business wisdom was in them too. But control? With all that money on the line? He was successful precisely because he made all decisions himself. Yet, even though she came out better than he did, the deal she was offering him was sensational. And he and his father's company, Aximation, would be an equal owner in a Kronengold financial firm! Even if her enterprise wasn't one of the great European Kronengold banks, the lure was overwhelming: the Holtzes had been beaten down and humiliated by the Kronengolds for so many generations; the dream that goaded him and his father onward was that, someday, they would be able to link up with and eventually absorb and become the successors to the legendary Kronengold interests.

Weighing just as urgently in his mind was his desire for

Deborah; it was nearly unbearable. If he turned her down, she might go out of his life forever.

'All right.' His accord burst out of him in an explosion of white smoke. 'The voting trust will last for three years. If you're a lousy manager, I want to be able to take control of Columbiana then.'

'Agreed. But I want your word that, if I've done a good job, the voting trust stays in effect, you buy no additional stock in my company, and I stay in control.'

'You have my word,' he pledged.

They walked along the waterfront and then back into the financial district, all the while negotiating the rest of the arrangement.

'There's one last matter,' Deborah said, halting their progress and facing David. 'I want it put in writing that any dealings I have are solely with you and not with your father.'

Her grandfather's warning still rang in her ears. But she had learned in the last two days that David Holtz ran Aximation himself. After marrying a wealthy woman, Max Holtz had willingly taken a backseat to his brilliant son and relegated himself to an elder statesman's role. Deborah's intuition was that she could trust David Holtz's integrity – he would be crafty for his own advantage, she was sure, and she would have to watch him there, but her best guess was that he would be honest. She had to go with that guess. Also he was down-to-earth and good-humoured. That counted for a lot with her. But right now she would take money from the devil if he offered it.

'My father rarely takes an active interest in day-to-day operations,' David answered, with a faint tone of resentment towards her for making the request.

Deborah pressed him. 'Then you should have no problem agreeing to his keeping his hands off.' He still hesitated. 'This last point, and we have a deal.'

David finally nodded. 'Agreed.'

'In writing.'

He nodded again. 'Do we have a deal?'

Solemnly, she put out her hand. As he took it, relief seemed to surge through her bones.

'Now that that's all decided,' David said, 'the Statue of Liberty is only a few blocks from here. We'll get a boat ride and have a chance to talk. I want to know all about you.'

Close to him like this, she could feel doubly his allure. There was more of him than other men, in every way: dynamism, warmth, cleverness, emotion. The attraction she felt was dangerous; it could give him an edge; it could divert her single-mindedness. She shook her head. 'Acquiring Columbiana is too important, David. I can't let myself think about anything personal yet.'

She had planned their route carefully. They were only a few yards from the entrance to the skyscraper in which her law firm was located. Evan McAphee was waiting in his office to draft the agreement which she wanted signed by David before the end of the day, before he got wind of the bank lock-out against her.

She guided David towards the glass doors. That piece of paper, with the brawn of concrete, would prevent her collapse. That piece of paper would be the foundation of everything.

Once Deborah had solid financial support, Columbiana's defence collapsed. To end the battle quickly, Deborah authorized James Lacy to offer Galen Stafford a two-year contract to stay on as head of the insurance operation, with lucrative retirement benefits after that. Stafford immediately met his board of directors and then issued a press release announcing that they were prepared to support her tender offer. The fight was over. A series of transactions were still to follow and a good deal of debt to be paid off, but every calculation confirmed to Deborah that she was now personally worth over nine million dollars.

Deborah was nearly delirious – a mixture of exultation and relief. She, McAphee, and Lacy shouted wildly and grabbed each other's hands to shake congratulations. Then they simply stared at each other with stunned disbelief. She tried to reach David by telephone to relay the good news, but he was in a plane in transit.

When the others left her office, she felt an emptiness, as she had after her triumph in the gold crisis. A wild impulse leaped upon her to lift the receiver and dial Leslie. If he had answered the telephone and unexpectedly, improbably, said he was proud of her, Deborah might have forgiven him every injustice he had visited on her.

He never would, she told herself. That was precisely why

she had grown to hate him so and why she ached to see him crushed. But even to have heard his scorn would have driven home the satisfaction for her, fleshed it out in some human form that would have fixed itself palpably in her consciousness.

As it was she had the joys of safety and wealth with which to warm herself. Hounded in America by the spectre of impotent poverty, she had sacrificed and risked everything to become rich. There were things she could now buy that she had taken for granted growing up: designer dresses with the style her mother had instilled in her; superbly crafted furniture that would make her home a splendid sanctuary; a chauffeur and servants to ease her life. She intended to live like a Kronengold, with a graciousness that others would admire and a grandeur they would envy. Their regard would provide the satisfaction for her. Their regard would begin to engrave her name.

Much later that evening, when as many loose ends had been securely knotted as could be for the time being, Evan McAphee noticed that Deborah was brooding when she should have been exuberant. A sensitive man who cared deeply for her and had lived the ordeal with her, he had sensed how many psychological, as well as financial, chips she had riding on the roulette wheel's spin.

'It's never quite as good as we want it to be,' he told her quietly. 'Nothing can be.' He cranked up his courage. 'May I take you out to dinner to celebrate?'

'Thank you, Evan,' she said, smiling at the prospect of his companionship. She did not look forward to going right home to her bare little apartment. And she was very fond of Evan.

She left a message with the late-shift switchboard operator at her firm that, if David Holtz telephoned, she was to tell him that the take-over fight had been won. If he had any questions, the operator was to give him James Lacy's telephone number.

She and Evan ran out of her offices and down the corridor as if escaping. They *had* escaped – from Galen Stafford and Metrobank and his law partners. They began to laugh like little children. Her earlier delight over what had happened to her today began to return.

Reviewing the victory with Evan at a quiet restaurant allowed Deborah at last to savour the achievement. She thanked him for the risk he had taken at his law firm. He tried to maintain that the animosity from his older partners had been invigorating – he had grown a bit bored.

'This fight, helping you,' he told her, his shyness sent reeling by the wine, 'gave me more gratification than any other thing I've ever done. I've never met a woman like you before.'

She took his hand. 'I would have been all alone without you, Evan. You stood by me. I'll always be grateful to you.'

Their taxicab turned the corner onto Fifth Avenue and stopped at the large stone building in which Deborah had recently rented an apartment. Parked beneath the street lamp was a white Cadillac Eldorado. Leaning against the front bumper, eating from a picnic basket beside him, was David Holtz. After his plane had landed in New York, he had received the message that Deborah had telephoned. He had rung back her office right away and learned from the operator the good news about the take-over and that Deborah had left for the evening. Thinking Deborah would want to celebrate, he had picked up a picnic supper at the Brasserie. She had taken so long to arrive, he had become hungry and begun without her.

'Congratulations,' he called out as she stepped out of the taxicab.

'How do you know where I live?' she shot back at him. She had been conscientious about keeping her relationship with David at arm's length and impersonal since signing their agreement. The take-over meant too much to her to jeopardize it with the complications that a love affair would have created. Since then, away from David, she had been quite firm in her own mind about the need to keep their relationship solely a business one afterwards as well. She intended to make that clear to him after she found out how he had discovered her private address when even her home telephone number was unlisted.

'As soon as we made our deal, I hired an investigator to do some checking on you,' he replied with a blithe wave of a drumstick, as if that was a perfectly normal thing to do.

'That's reprehensible!'

'You didn't find it reprehensible to keep from me the fact that none of the banks would finance you.'

She stood angrily before him, the street lamp encircling them and the Cadillac with light. 'That was just good business.'

He finished chewing. 'You know, even if I had known about the banks cutting you off, I still might have made the deal.'

She was intrigued. 'Why?'

'It's a hell of a deal. But that alone wouldn't have convinced me to go on the line for forty million if I hadn't learned something the day after we first had it out in your office.' He chuckled at the recollection of her self-confidence. 'Van Landy really *can't* tie his shoelaces without help. I did some checking there too.'

As he wiped his hands on a napkin, David seemed suddenly aware of Evan McAphee's presence. 'I hope it's business with him.'

'That's none of your concern.'

His voice lost its carefree tone. He placed his hand beneath her chin and tipped her face towards his.

'We both know it is.'

She held his eyes for a long moment, then she turned back to Evan McAphee, who stood beside the taxi's open door.

'Thank you, again, Evan, for everything. Tell Linda I think her boyfriend is a very brilliant lawyer and a very nice man.'

Resignation seemed to fell Evan. For a few minutes tonight he had dared to hope that his friendship with Deborah might be blossoming into romance, but, as he glanced from her to David and back, he knew there was no chance for him. He half nodded and half waved as he entered the taxi.

The taxi was just past the intersection when Deborah felt David's hands on her shoulders, pulling her towards him. She resisted; David should mean only business to her. She must be clever, must be self-protective with him. Anything more would give him a hold on her emotions that could undo her. Don't let me look at him again, she told herself. Say good night, walk away, and don't look at him.

Yet his hands held her like a vice. His face was only inches from hers. His black curls glistened beneath the street-light like a steel crown.

'Don't, David,' she wanted to say, but his mouth was already on hers, and all her strength had fled, chased away by a passion that betrayed her utterly. Then she was far away with him, making slow somersaults in a tropical bay, swimming upwards towards hazy rays of light.

'Oh, God, David,' she whispered when their lips finally drew apart, 'I was afraid it would be like this.'

Deborah's small apartment was scantily furnished. A couple of chairs and a coffee table in the living room, a bed and bureau in the bedroom.

She made no pretence about asking David if he wanted to drink, nor did he expect it. Making love was inevitable for them that night. He had perceived right from the start that she would resist him only as long as she felt herself meeting him on unequal terms; she needed her freedom as much as she needed to be loved.

Moonlight had sprayed Central Park silver, and some of it had drifted across the street and through the window, coating curtain edges, the coverlet, and the pillow with a lambent glimmer.

Deborah felt helpless now, immobilized by urges that leapt in her veins despite her most carefully reasoned resolve. David took her in his arms once more, as if she were a flower he had drawn to him to inhale her fragrance. She yielded to him as easily, her lips like petals brushing his.

Then David stood back. His black eyes gazed at her, held her in their thrall. He reached out to the button at her throat. Slowly, as if it were an ancient ritual, one by one, as time waited on his hand, he slipped each button through its slit, until the yellow dress was open to her waist. He lifted each side of the dress outwards and backwards off her shoulders and then, inch by inch down her back, as if the material were a captive's ropes he was releasing. When the dress was at her hips, he lowered himself to his knees and drew the yellow cloth downwards, exposing her long thighs. Her legs were slightly parted. He leaned forward and kissed the soft flesh inside her thighs. She shuddered, barely able to stand. And then he continued to lower the dress.

At her feet, he raised up first one and then the other, as he removed her shoes. He sat back on his heels and looked up at her, like a sculptor appraising a work in progress. His hand reached out and flicked the hook at the front of her bra. The undergarment snapped apart. Deborah shrugged to let it fall, and it too was at her feet. With a finger at each side, David slipped down her panties and her stockings held by the garter belt about her waist. They peeled off her like the skin of an orange. Then he once again dropped back on his heels and gazed up at her. She was a wood nymph in the moonlight, a dryad, a glory made of silver and light and air and magic. She was the most beautiful woman he had ever known. David Holtz understood suddenly, yet perfectly, that he would never love another woman in his life the way he loved Deborah. His fate was forever decided during that moment in which converged her exquisite beauty, the past weeks of sparring, her intelligence, his hatred and envy of her family, memories of a childhood in which he was hungry for food – before his father had the means in South Africa to help support his ex-wife and young son – and for the love and status that would make him mean something in a world that barely knew he existed, and the passion that undid him every time he looked at her.

'I love you,' he said simply. 'If you don't love me, I'll understand. It makes no difference to my loving you. Nothing will ever change that.'

Deborah knelt in front of him. She cupped his face in her hands. Her lips that kissed his seemed to be absorbing the essence of him into her. A very long while later, she began to undress him, feeling his muscular power each time her hand brushed against his body, strong and graceful as a stalking lion's, shivering when she did.

When they were both naked, on their knees, only inches from each other, as if their love and their passion were a prayer, Deborah finally spoke.

'I love you, David. Against all my best interests . . . knowing how much more difficult loving you would be than loving almost anyone else in the world . . . I love you.'

She lay back on the cold, polished wood floor although the bed was only a few feet away. She wanted their first time to be unpremeditated, elemental. David's gaze journeyed slowly down at her body, stopping at all the secret places, like a thirsting creature at an oasis.

Naked is how I will always love him best, Deborah thought. For his fearful beauty.

When he mounted her, his eyes glittering in the silvered light, she felt fullness pressing outwards to her bones, completeness she had not understood was lacking. He did not move for many seconds. His eyes never even blinked. But, when he drew back finally to thrust into her, every nerve in her body began the long rising scream towards ecstasy.

CHAPTER SIXTEEN

Buoyed up by self-confidence, a youthful America had swaggered into the Sixties. John F. Kennedy had fanned still brighter an optimism that even his death could not extinguish. By the decade's close, however, the nation was convulsed by self-doubt, and those things that were best about America – its capacity for hope and its inclination towards tolerance – were revealed to be the greatest of its illusions.

In the last months of 1967, the head of military operations in South Vietnam, General William Westmoreland, announced that the army of the South was 'on the road to becoming a competent force', and 'the end begins to come into view'. In early 1968 that reeling enemy suddenly launched a massive, prolonged offensive across all South Vietnam. United States confidence at home was shattered – even on the hawkish right. When the Joint Chiefs of the military requested yet more American ground troops, President Lyndon B. Johnson, who had personally picked bombing targets in his pyjamas during early morning hours, authorized instead a review of America's progress in Vietnam by the blue-ribbon panel his new Secretary of Defence had requested. Their bleak report forced the President to face the truth. Eyes blindly open, he had indeed led his nation into what a well-known anti-war advocate once termed 'a bloody quagmire.'

On the last day of March 1968, soon after nearly losing the New Hampshire primary to the peace-candidate Senator Eugene McCarthy, President Johnson stunned the nation by announcing he would not run for re-election, relinquishing the power he adored. By making an Indo-Chinese civil war his own, Johnson had decimated a people he had been intent on saving, and forced on his own people dissension and division greater than any since their own Civil War. He had learned at last that, without the consent of the people from whom that power flowed, he could not govern.

For all Johnson's defects, he was motivated by a genuine intent to make real what was good and generous and tolerant in the American dream of bottomless beneficence fuelled by endless plenty. Besides signalling his personal failure LBJ's announcement was recognition as well of the failure of the Great Society he had hoped to build but could not afford to finance. As Martin Luther King, Jr., put it, 'The Great Society was shot down on the battlefields of Vietnam.'

Only four days after Johnson's declination announcement, King himself was shot down. The champion of racial equality through non-violent means was assassinated by a white man in Memphis, Tennessee.

Blacks rioted in a hundred cities across the country. Chicago's iron-fisted boss, Mayor Richard B. Daley, ordered the police trying to control rioters to 'shoot to kill'.

Revolution sounded like a war drum, ominous in the American night. In May, Columbia University students seized several buildings and held off university officials for a week, until a savage police sweep routed them. That same month students and workers in France rioted against de Gaulle.

In early June, while campaigning to replace LBJ as the Democratic standard-bearer, Senator Robert F. Kennedy was shot dead, as had been his president brother. The assassin was a Palestinian Arab refugee antagonized by the Senator's support for Israel.

The disintegration of all Western civilization seemed frighteningly possible when what was later characterized as 'a police riot' descended with clubs on a relatively peaceful march to the site of the Chicago Democratic Convention. Blood flowed. The cops were in a frenzy. And television caught it all. Although many Americans were revolted by the abuse of authority, the preponderance, tired and demoralized, appeared pleased by this assertion of 'law and order'.

The Democrats nominated a candidate who tried to be all things to all people, LBJ's vice president, Hubert Horatio Humphrey. But people were analyzing him as a future president now, and he appeared a feeble choice. The anti-war movement had succeeded in deposing a president, only to find that they had assured the election of a successor they despised, as much for his lack of integrity as for their certainty that he would pursue the war into the future: Richard M. Nixon.

The press, suddenly fearful that it was out on a limb unsupported by the majority of Americans, pulled back. Walter Cronkite humbled himself before Mayor Daley on national TV to atone for criticizing him that bloody night. And, although the war would continue to rage in Vietnam for years, most of the country would be unaware of its extent because television news executives soon decided the story ought to be that the war was winding down. The TV news producers wanted positive news. They and the people wanted what would never fully return, the comfort of their illusions.

In June 1969 those illusions flickered into reality for a bright moment when American astronauts walked on the moon. A few dissenters might have grumbled at the billions diverted from social causes to beat the Soviets there, but the overwhelming masses were charged with pride. Their nation's technology, their nation's miracle, filled the TV screen for them and the world to see. Doubt and turmoil were stilled for a few blessed days while hearts hung on the drama of fragile human beings, who symbolized them all, stepping onto the most ancient of mysteries. But the feeling of national pride, the unity, the sense of purpose, could not endure for long. America was segmenting, fragmenting, splitting along a thousand fault lines. Its very diverse population no longer believed in the myths that had welded them into a nation.

August 1969 saw four hundred thousand young people gather, peaceable and loving, at the Woodstock concert in upstate New York. Many observers considered it the vanguard of the new age dawning. But a truer indication of what beckoned in the Seventies might have been the Rolling Stones concert in Altamont, California. Four people died, including a young black man beaten to death onstage by Hell's Angels. Instead of hiring trained security personnel, the concert's organizers had tried to save money by hiring the Hell's Angels – for five hundred dollars' worth of beer – to keep order while the cameras rolled to exploit the concert as a commercial movie. That same month Charles Manson and his followers were arrested for the massacre of the film actress Sharon Tate and her friends at her Hollywood home. Two of those followers would later attempt to assassinate a president.

The costs of fighting a war, excessive spending at home and abroad, and the resulting inflation hobbled America's greatest post-war achievement, its economic affluence. By the first year of the new decade, the shadow lengthening across the nation had fallen on Wall Street. The Dow Jones Industrial Average bottomed out that year at 631.

Many *Wunderkinder* had come and gone on the financial scene during the Go-Go Years. The few who lasted after harder times eradicated the optimism were both the true visionaries and the true builders. Deborah de Kronengold had proved to be among the best of them. Her firm, the D. de Kronengold Corporation, had grown at an unprecedented rate.

The Insurance Division had been expanded by the acquisition of a second insurance company and vigorous new marketing efforts. Securities Brokerage had likewise grown, both by acquiring several smaller firms and by offering better terms to outstanding brokers in other firms. She had built up from scratch a fine research staff, headed by a woman over-looked at an older firm, in order to attract large institutional buyers by offering excellent stock analyses. Evaluation of the firm's capacity to clear efficiently the back-office paperwork led to computerization and to the creation of a Computer Division keyed to servicing the financial industry.

The Investment Banking Division, however, was the one Deborah envisaged as creating the major opportunities for the rest of her firm, and its expansion during the period was spectacular. Knowing her firm was too small to attract the massive blue-chip corporations that had done business for generations with firms like Hazelton, Lieb, she concentrated on growing companies, growing industries, and growing areas of the country. By the start of the Seventies, the firm had been the main underwriter in selling to the public the stock of eleven young high-technology companies and twelve others, retaining a substantial stock interest in all of them and continuing to provide financial expertise, which was particularly helpful to the fledgling ventures. It specialized also in obtaining funds for corporate clients among the many European banks with whom Deborah and André Leitner had established close ties. And more than fifty companies, either directly or through other investment banking firms who utilized its services, now protected their export and import transactions through the D. de Kronengold Corporation's foreign currency dealing.

Deborah put all her capital into expanding the services

provided by her company in step with the clients they attracted. She held nothing back and borrowed whenever she needed more to fund expansion. But other young firms that grew wildly in the Sixties and then staggered were equally aggressive. The difference was Deborah's shrewdness in gauging economic trends. When the stock market retrenched, she had already stopped selling new issues and already counselled her clients to go bearish. Negative on gold for the present, she had been proved right when it dropped below $35 an ounce. In every case she had caused her firm's funds to firmly follow her thinking. By mid-1970 the Investment Banking Division alone had thirty-four people in responsible positions, fourteen of them women, and it sprawled over the entire floor where Smithline Securities had once occupied a corner.

Deborah's rapid rise in the financial world was acknowledged in late 1969. In the same month *Forbes* and *Fortune* magazines did profile articles on her. The latter photographed her in her newly redecorated office, handsomely modern and immaculately white, and then put her on the cover for a story which conjectured that the Kronengold genius had been reborn in her. The lead read, 'KRONENGOLD MONEY MAGICIAN: Beautiful, Young and Brilliant, She's Well On Her Way to an Empire.' The fact that both articles focused less on her accomplishments and more on a genetic heredity which only she and a few others knew was not hers added a sourness to a profile that would have otherwise gratified her. For Deborah the articles became merely a useful marketing tool to attract new clients.

Some sadness was instilled in her soon after establishing the D. de Kronengold Corporation, when she invited her friends Helen Lorenzo and Kay Bellows for dinner at her apartment. Both women had been awed by her being a Kronengold and frightened when Deborah offered them better positions than they held at Hazelton, Lieb. Kay said she was 'comfortable' where she was, although she had always complained about the discriminatory promotion practices. Deborah sadly realized Kay had subconsciously come to believe in the correctness of her subservience. By rising higher, Deborah had discovered, she had neither gained a trusted employee nor retained a trusted friend. Helen had been quiet, thinking about Deborah's offer that she become the head of Personnel, seeing in Kay's timidity a rebuke to her own. 'Yes,' she blurted out, pushing the word from her throat before she changed her mind. 'You're so smart, Dee. If you think I'm good enough, I guess maybe I am.'

Deborah had come to love the little apartment overlooking the eastern edge of Central Park and furnished it carefully, lovingly. Her favourite purchases were a Sheraton dining-room table and chairs, a tall, glass-doored cabinet from the same period, and a large sky-blue Chinese rug in the living room. Tutored early to recognize such pieces and know their value, she had paid far less than they were worth. The bare beginnings of a very modern art collection graced her walls. Once she found a superb writing desk, almost exactly like the one with Sèvres plaques in her mother's sitting room, but it made her so sad to look at that she could not sleep for the next two nights, conjuring up instead all the tragedies and guilt in her life she thought had been put well behind her. She sent the desk back to the dealer on the third morning.

Most Friday evenings she gave a dinner party, inviting influential people who began to form an ever widening circle of useful and entertaining acquaintances. A typical group might include a high government official, a writer or performer, a socialite, a newspaper columnist, and a financier or industrialist. Nathan had already confided to her that the first reports of her success, under the Kronengold name, had caused so titanic an out-burst in Leslie that half the partners stayed at home the next day to avoid his wrath. After one of her dinner parties, the wife of the British ambassador mentioned having spoken recently in London to Deborah's cousin Malcolm, who had remarked with some relish that an extremely irritated Leslie de Kronengold had cancelled *The Times* for several weeks after it ran a small article about her.

Deborah did not betray her glee at this new bit of news. Her father was worth many tens of millions of dollars and, despite the stodginess of his methods, was still a very powerful individual in world banking. It would be a good while before she had the means herself to consider challenging him, as she had vowed. Until then it was far safer strategy not to arouse him further by any remarks that might find their way back to him.

'I'm sure his displeasure,' Deborah contended, 'had to do with the recent change in *The Times's* format. After a hundred and seventy-eight years to put news on the front page rather than classified advertisements!' Deborah fought to appear grave. 'Shocking! Absolutely shocking!'

The ambassador's wife had not been fooled. 'Scandalous!' she agreed with a smile.

Most of all, the apartment was a sanctuary for her and David. He stayed there with her at least three or four times a week, when neither had social obligations imposed by business, such as dinners with clients or obligatory charity balls. They reserved for each other time when they could truly be together. Usually they had dinner after work, sometimes at a restaurant, sometimes prepared by Deborah's cook-housekeeper. Once in a while they would play tennis – at David's insistence, believing that someday he would become proficient enough to defeat her. During the summer they usually spent weekends together at the secluded beach house Deborah had bought in the Hamptons. After a while, they began to take pleasure in the entertainment New York City had to offer – a luxurious expenditure of time on which they would never have splurged if they had been alone: sports events that David liked and of which she soon became a fan; plays and concerts and opera and ballet that she liked and David, almost despite himself, began to enjoy. Yet, for all the people around them in the audience, they could have been alone together in her big bed.

Once, a Lincoln Center board member spotted them during the interval at a ballet and tried to interest them in taking an active role in the Center or in one of its performing arts organizations, but, non-committal, they fled rather than return to their seats. Coming here was their private pleasure, not an obligation. This was a gift they gave each other. Both of them thought their love ideal.

Deborah had been surprised at first by how deferential David appeared to be towards her. One night, when they were dining at an elegant restaurant, she noticed him staring at her hands as she reached for her fish knife and fork to eat the poached salmon. He sighed with relief and reached for the identical utensils beside his own plate. She realized then that he was insecure with the upper-class manners and customs to which she was so accustomed. David had been very poor as a boy, brought up by his mother who had supported him on a waitress's wages and the occasional insufficient cheque of her ex-husband, David's father, struggling equally hard to survive in South Africa. Not only was David at times put off when he recalled Deborah was a Kronengold, but the customs of wealth still felt very new to him. She wanted to let him know how unimportant they were to her, that he was her priority. She ran her hand, hidden by the tablecloth, up his thigh and whispered that she wanted to have him right there, underneath the table, while the waiter wondered where they had disappeared. He smiled tightly while he looked about self-consciously to determine whether anyone had overheard.

Only after months did he relax sufficiently to begin to appreciate her qualities of concern and humour. Until then the only person he had ever trusted enough to speak frankly to was his father, but primarily about business. He found there were few limits on his conversation with Deborah: she understood his business – in fact she had found him several excellent acquisitions – and she understood him.

David seemed to fit Deborah equally well. She needed a strong man whom she could not push around; for her, respect was the antechamber of love. Yet she instinctively resisted the sort of domination her father had tried to impose on her while growing up. The balance between the two states was very delicate, but for a very long time the balance held perfectly steady. Even their competitiveness, which made them so successful in business, seemed to pique their personal relationship. As with so many couples who enjoyed challenging each other at tennis or on a fast ski run or at Scrabble, the competitiveness heightened their lovemaking as well.

As time went on David allowed her to see more of the softer qualities in him, and Deborah liked those best. Once, when he had flu and was totally helpless, she stayed at his bedside to nurse him without leaving the apartment for days. The most powerful of men, he was rendered powerless by overwhelming nature. At such moments, despite her own tendency to self-protectiveness, she loved him so totally that, if she could have taken all his suffering into her own body to rid him of it, she gladly would have.

He could never love her in that way, she knew. And, if he had, she might not have been attracted to him. Her image of an appealing man had been formed early, by a father who denied his love. Having to resist David's subtle tendency to assert control subconsciously reassured her; she would have been frightened by the responsibility another's selflessness imposed. She needed the awareness of her own separate identity. At bottom her nature was such a loving one that she doubly feared the vulnerability to which commitment could expose her. She feared to love for so many reasons: the hurt that loving had always brought herself and often others, the hobbles it would put on her independence, and the diversion it could prove to be from her climb to the immense wealth and power that would first terrify Leslie and then ruin him.

Neither realized that their competitiveness was an augur of conflicting expectations until one night in the spring of 1970, the night of Deborah's twenty-fifth birthday. That was when they learned that the business arrangement that had brought them together was also the seed of their discord.

David was ebullient when he telephoned her that morning. He had just forced the take-over of a fast-growing oil-field services company on highly advantageous terms, solidifying Aximation's presence in that area of oil and gas exploration. He said he was giving Deborah's cook the night off and would, himself, make a special meal for them at her apartment that night. Everything had been planned for days, he told her. She was not to get home earlier than seven o'clock – it was a surprise. Knowing David's exorbitant enthusiasms, Deborah decided that the biggest surprise would be if her kitchen was still standing by seven o'clock.

Deborah arrived home that evening to find the chef of a highly respected Paris restaurant in her kitchen preparing dinner for her and David. His assistant was setting the table. David had had them both flown in that day. A florist had just delivered and was arranging enough floral displays to adorn an underworld funeral. David stood in the centre of Deborah's living room directing everyone, delighted by the extravagance of his surprise.

'Happy birthday, love!' he boomed. He enclosed her in a bear hug and then kissed her until she could not breathe. 'Well, what do you think?' he asked when they finally drew apart.

'I think it's wonderful, and I adore you for the romantic excess of it all.'

He beamed, but when he spoke the authority in his manner irked her. 'Dee, love, you speak French. There are a few things I want to tell that chef about how I like the food prepared.' He started to tick off orders he wanted conveyed.

She interrupted him with airy good homour. 'Why spend a fortune to fly a great chef over and then tell him how to cook?' She kissed David lightly on the mouth, turned on her heel, and began walking towards the bedroom. 'Call me when everything is ready. I'm going to take a shower.' She stopped and laughed. 'Or is there a surprise water ballet rehearsing in there?'

In the shower she considered how she would present to David the overall expansion plan she had devised for the D. de Kronengold Corporation. Lately, he had become resistant to her new ideas, suggesting that she might have grown large enough for the time being. She had also learned to be cautious about divulging some ideas to him because, without even realizing it, he appropriated them for his own use like an occupying army.

David talked excitedly through the champagne and caviar and the salmon mousse. Deborah wanted to bring up her new business plan, to gain some insight from David's analysis, but he had something on his own mind he seemed unable to come out with. Both were silenced by the perfection of the mussel soup and the half-dozen violinists who arrived on schedule and began to play romantic music. When the musicians moved to the far end of the living room, Deborah finally had a chance to explain to him her broad vision of the direction in which her investment bank must grow.

'David,' she began excitedly, 'it came to me all at once. My car was passing Bloomingdale's, and I realized that finance could be sold the same way. There needn't be a real estate broker and then a mortgage broker and a different insurance broker when you buy a house and a bank for your checking account and a stockbroker for investments. What if all of those things were in one firm?'

He shook his head. 'It isn't personal enough.'

She rushed on, ignoring his scepticism. 'And what if a multi-national company could count on having a branch of its investment bank located in every major financial capital?'

'You're so over-extended you haven't an extra penny to your name. Do you know the kind of capital it would take to build that kind of operation?'

'Of course, it would take a long time and a lot of money. I might not be able to build up to it for twenty years. But that's my ultimate goal.'

'You already have an office in Geneva. You're moving into commodity trading. Where does it end?'

'I thought I'd begin to look into buying a British merchant bank.'

His hand slammed on the tablecloth. 'You're like a damned fat lady in the circus! Nothing is ever enough. It's a good thing you have to come to me first with your plans.'

Deborah was incensed. She saw clearly the issue was her independence. 'David, your consultation has become interference!'

The chef, smiling, stepped to the table with the entrée on a large platter.

'*Mademoiselle, monsieur, le veau.*'

'*Merci,*' she replied. '*Quelle présentation!*'

Both David and Deborah kept their eyes on their veal and limited their comments to the excellence of the food. Only over coffee did David return to personal matters.

'Look, don't think I'm not proud of your success. I am. Truly proud. But I didn't figure it would be your life's work.' When he spoke again, his voice was subdued. 'I always figured you would give it up, or at least ease off, when we got married.'

Deborah was shocked. Early in their relationship she had mentioned in passing that marriage was something for other people, not for her. From then on she had assumed that he felt the same way.

'Is that what you've had on you mind all night, asking me to marry you?'

David beamed. He leaned forward, exactly as he did when negotiating. 'I love you. You know that. But the nights apart are driving me crazy. And you've got this whole life that I'm not a part of. That isn't the way love is supposed to be. I want to have children. I want you and me to be a real family.'

Deborah was rigid with tension. 'I'm perfectly happy with the way things are now.'

'You've worked damned hard these last years, harder than any woman ought to. I don't want that for you. I want my wife to be a lady of leisure. Here's what I propose. I'll buy your share of the company with Aximation stock and make it a subsidiary of Aximation. That will give you a nice-sized interest in my company. If you still want to keep a finger in business, you could have a seat on my board maybe.'

Deborah could barely restrain her fury. 'You want me to sit

at home while you go off to run *my* company! I cannot believe how little you understand me after more than two years together. My company is as inseparable from me as the nose on my face. It's as necessary to my survival as air and water. And the fact that you have no comprehension of that is deplorable. Worse, it's an indication of how ill-suited we are for one another.'

She jumped to her feet. 'I want you to take your violinists and your chef and your Rose Parade out of here this very instant. It's over between us.'

She took a step towards the musicians, who had just launched into a vigorous rendition of 'Golden Earrings'.

'Out of here. Right now. Not another note.'

They ground to an embarrassed halt, quickly gathered their things, and left. David closed the door to the kitchen, so that he and Deborah could be alone.

He was bewildered by her attitude. Men and women who loved each other got married. And, when they did, the woman made a home and raised a family, which was her purpose in life, and the man continued to work and provide for them, which was his purpose. In David's mind the three-year prohibition on involvement in her company's management was simply the duration of her single life. She was his, and he did not differentiate between his consuming passion for her and other motives for their relationship. Investing in her company would have served two purposes, eliminating the barrier preventing a personal relationship between them and, what he dared not express, forming a link to the European Kronengold banks, the ultimate prizes he and his father had set their hearts on some day seizing. He had always assumed that she would retire to raise their family and he would absorb her company and utilize it to build bridges to her relatives and their companies in England, France, and elsewhere.

'What's so wrong about loving you so much I want to marry you?'

'David, your attitude convinces me how right I was to decide never to marry. You don't want just marriage. You want to own me.'

In his voice was the fear that she truly intended to go out of his life. 'All I want is a normal kind of life with you.'

'Don't you see that this is normal? That having a business

is normal for a woman? It *has* been wonderful between us. Marriage would ruin all that.'

'You have this crazy ambition –'

She interrupted him. 'It isn't crazy for *you* to be amibitious.'

He had laughed at the militant women's libbers on the TV news shows demonstrating for their rights. Deborah had never ranted or raved like that. It dawned on him that all the privileges to which they were trying to assert a claim she had always automatically assumed were hers. She might very well be serious about breaking up.

'We're terrific together,' he argued. 'You can't throw that away.'

'We were both blind. Now, we're not. I love you, David, but I won't be owned. So, it's over.'

Distraught, he grabbed her arm. 'Dee, we were meant for each other. This is a catastrophe.'

She pulled her arm away. 'I have been weaned on catastrophes, David. And they taught me one thing – nothing is ever permanent.'

There was a moment of taut silence.

'Do you really want it to end?' he asked softly.

'No,' she confessed. 'But I won't ever marry, David. And I won't ever sell my company.'

'Does that mean we can't even talk about marriage later on?'

'Of course we can talk about it. But nothing will convince me to change my mind.'

He smiled. 'Leave that to me. I'm irresistible.'

She smiled too. 'Sometimes you really are.'

With her anger dissipated, Deborah recognized the complexity of David's urges. Like his hunger for wealth, his need to control her stemmed from the insecurity of his boyhood. Unsettled by and unused to a woman who refused to depend on him, he tried to devise ways to create that dependency and the safe feeling of having ensured her love. One was by marrying her. Another was by controlling the company that symbolized her freedom from him. But she was as strong-willed as he and had refused to capitulate.

Deborah finally decided that her firmness had been educational for him, that he simply needed time to get used to her independence. Their argument had been healthy, clearing the air of misconceptions. David would soon grow to accept her views, her needs.

After the chef and his assistant and their paraphernalia were gone, Deborah tried to lift his sulkiness by making love to him. The trepidations that sex had provoked in her since childhood had gradually retreated from around the safe fortress of her relationship with David; she was so sure of his love that seemingly limitless passions had been released within her. Sometimes when she climaxed he would be astounded that she was shuddering and laughing simultaneously – death and life intermingled. But now she wanted the pleasure to be his, to show him how deeply she cared.

She undressed him, refusing to allow him to embrace her or even initiate a kiss. Then she led him to her bed and threw back the cover. He lay down on the silk sheets, deep green in colour, *her* colour, a contrast to her red hair. She dimmed the lamp beside the bed, leaned over his furrowed forehead, and kissed arousal into lips that had pouted like a forlorn child's.

'Lie back, David,' she whispered. 'All you have to do is enjoy me.'

Then she licked the sweet hidden parts of his body until he was gasping. When she drew him into her mouth, sucking him deep into her and then sliding back up, circling with her tongue, he groaned helplessly, louder and louder.

'Don't!' he cried out, perturbed at not being in control of the situation, of himself, of her. And then he came.

After they had made love again, and had both been fulfilled, she lay on him and gazed down at his eyes, seeking to convey as their bodies had just done what was elemental in her soul to what was elemental in his.

'David,' she said gently, 'I need to depend on you for only one thing: knowing that what is loving and honest and mine alone in you is always there for me. That's all I need and want.'

She watched him think about that for a long time before he finally nodded. In his own mind, however, he was sure that with time he could change hers.

For a few weeks Deborah and David were careful about stepping on each other's sensibilities, but the differences that had flared on her birthday remained an unexpressed source of struggle between them, provoking irritations that had never been noticeable before. The freewheeling ease of former days often seemed to be missing. She was too touchy about any act of his that smacked of an attempt to dominate her, like his habit of sometimes making plans for both of them without consulting her. David insisted on making unsolicited suggestions about her business and was unusually guarded about his own. More annoying to her was that his possessiveness seemed to grow, rather than decline; he became increasingly jealous, prodding her for information about her social life away from him. If he learned she had spent an evening in the company of another man, even at a dinner party or a business meeting, David would become angry or sullen until she convinced him that his suspicions were unfounded.

On May 8, Deborah was walking to her office from a meeting when she became cut off by an anti-war rally marching in the Wall Street area to protest against the recent shootings of unarmed Kent State University students by National Guardsmen. At that moment she, the demonstrators, and other bystanders were set upon by two hundred hard-hatted construction workers swinging lead pipes and fists. She was not badly hurt, but the experience had been terrifying. She suddenly felt as vulnerable as in her very first days in New York. She fled, not to her own office, but by taxi to David's. From there she telephoned a security service, to hire guards for her office and a bodyguard to replace her chauffeur. Only then did she begin to feel safe again. After that, for a long time, the small animosities between her and David faded into insignificance.

That summer, when they were able to spend more time alone together at the beach and on board David's sleek motor yacht, the old rapport seemed to return. They began to have again the same sort of fun. Privately, each began to believe that the one was finally becoming accommodated to the other's viewpoint. David became convinced of it, in fact, when Deborah surprised him by accepting his father's dinner invitation.

She had not seen or spoken to Max Holtz since he had stalked out of her grandfather's ski chalet when she was eleven. As David had agreed, all her dealings with Aximation, her partner in the D. de Kronengold Corporation, had been carried out solely with David himself. She knew how much it hurt him to have at odds the two people he loved best in the world and was, in truth, extending an olive branch by meeting his father. David interpreted it as an indication that she was beginning to yield to his desire for marriage.

On the Saturday night of the Labor Day weekend, an Aximation plane flew David and Deborah the short distance across the open Sound from the Hamptons to Newport, where Max Holtz spent the summer.

Max Holtz had used the cheque Samuel gave him in St. Moritz to buy a small tool company, and his few connections in the United States to work his way into the highest social circles. Two years after his arrival, in 1959, he had met and married a very rich socialite. Her wealth and position permitted him, for the first time in his life, to live amid the respect and luxury he had always envied. Having early on recognized that his own tactical cunning was no equal to his son's true genius for business, he was very pleased to withdraw from the actual operations of Aximation and assume the figurehead role of chairman of the board of directors. His main functions for the company were as his son's sounding board and to plan long-term stratagems to attain ever higher objectives. The ultimate objective had never changed: to achieve vindication by ascending to sovereignty over the Kronengolds. He had made his dream his son's.

Thus, he had been overjoyed when David and Deborah fell in love. What a superb match his son had made! In every way! First and foremost, she was a Kronengold. Then, the efforts of her rapidly growing firm had been quite useful to Aximation, and the increasing value of its stock a handsome addition to Aximation's balance sheet. Both men had always assumed that her company would eventually become part of theirs and serve as the key to alliances with the major Kronengold banks abroad. Certainly of the British one. And, if he himself stayed in the background and was very cautious, maybe someday the French one as well – after all her mother was a French Kronengold. Who could have foreseen how perfectly events would conspire on that humiliating day in St. Moritz? All that was past. Time had been far kinder to him than to Samuel. Or, for that matter, to many of the still living Kronengolds as well. While still quite wealthy, they were no longer the financial power they once had been. He, on the other hand, had done magnificently.

Not only was Max Holtz wealthy in his own right as a result

of Aximation's success, but when his wife had died four years before, she had left most of her very large estate in a trust fund that would pay him a more than comfortable income for life and then go to charitable causes. He had also inherited an eighteen-room apartment in New York that he shared with David and houses in Palm Beach, Cap d'Antibes, and Newport. Few Jews had ever cracked the wall about the exclusive social circles at these resorts, but Max, a proven master at passing for gentile, had been escorted through by a socially powerful wife and kept suspicions to a minimum by conscientious attendance at the right churches.

When Max learned from his son that Deborah was leery of marriage, he decided the reason might be the breach between him and her grandfather that had earlier triggered off her refusal to deal with him. If that could be healed, he reasoned, she would become amenable to marrying David. He decided to invite them to dinner at the grandest of his homes, the mansion in Newport.

Newport had long been the playground of the very richest in America. In the nineteenth century they had built massive 'cottages' that rivalled one another for oversized splendour. They still spent their summers there, sailing their yachts and trading invitations to lavish parties.

Approaching Max Holtz's home in the limousine that had met them at the airport, Deborah was reminded of the great Kronengold country houses she had known as a child – Clove Hill in England and Valtary in France. She too was struck by the reversal in his fortunes since St. Moritz.

She was just stepping from the car when the front door swung back and a stocky figure in blue blazer and white slacks surged towards her. She remembered the heavily gnarled features that seemed more like some rocky landscape than a face. Around his neck was a white silk scarf stuffed into an open red silk shirt. Arms magnanimously open, he greeted her as if their families were the closest of friends. This was an energetic Max Holtz of infinite goodwill. How wonderful she looked! How often and how fondly he had thought of his late, beloved friend, his patron, her dear grandfather, the Baron – a great man, a generous man! And how was her dear father, Leslie, the young Baron? What a worthy successor to his father's example! Deborah responded with the expected replies, all the time marvelling at the appearance of sincerity that oozed from every word.

As they took drinks on the verandah overlooking formal gardens, Deborah tried to be as gracious as her host. What made her very glad she had accepted the invitation was how happy David seemed. Brusque and authoritative as he could be with many people, he was as respectful towards his father as any son she had ever known. More than respectful, she soon observed. Separated from him in infancy when his parents divorced and his mother returned with him from Paris to America, grateful beyond expression for their reunion, his attitude seemed to border on adulation. David's mother had died years before, and Max was David's only family. Deborah realized that the older man embodied all his childhood loyalties, exaggerated because he had gone so long with only the hope of a father. David's greatest fear, she knew, was that some unexpected disaster might separate them once again.

Most of the evening was spent in the cavernous dining room, seated round a gleaming table. They were served trout quenelles and veal with a mushroom and Madeira sauce. Dessert was an assortment of tiny pastries. The wines were a surprising white from the Loire, an excellent Burgundy, and a sweet Sauterne with the dessert. The conversation was without strain. Max was charming and his recollections of various members of her family had made her nostalgic. She suspected, from the way he spoke about her mother, that he had always had a secret attraction to her, which was another reason for him to be delighted by the liaison between his son and her daughter. All in all, by the time she and David were ready to take their leave and fly back to the Hamptons, she was glad she had come.

At the door Max bowed gallantly to kiss Deborah's hand. Something caught his eye. His jaw went slack. His face paled. He was paralysed. Hanging from a gold chain wrapped several times around her wrist, almost hidden by several gold bangle bracelets, was a tiny, roughly made gold cross. Coming to his senses, he straightened himself and spoke to his son.

'David, I almost forgot. There are some papers I have to give you.' He turned to Deborah, desperately trying to hide his terror. 'Would you mind our excusing ourselves for just a moment?'

In the study he grabbed David by the lapels. 'That gold

cross she wears, what do you know about it?'

'The one on her wrist?'

His whisper was almost a shout. 'Yes. What do you know about it?'

'She wears it once in while. I once asked her why a girl from a famous Jewish family would have a cross. She said it was a kind of a charm someone had given her when she was a baby.'

'Anything more? Maybe who gave it to her?'

'No, that was all.'

'Her passport! Have you ever seen her passport?'

'When we went to Bermuda.'

'Did you see her parents' names on it?'

'Leslie and Madeleine, you know that.'

'And she was twenty-five in April?' Max remembered with fear.

'Yes. Is something wrong?'

'Nothing. I must have been mistaken.' He smiled. 'No matter.'

They returned to the front hall. When Max kissed Deborah's hand a second time, he got a good look at the little gold cross. There had been no mistake.

He saw them off, waving all the time they were circling the driveway to the road. Then, the strength seeming to go out of him, he asked the butler to bring him a cognac, and he retired to his study to think.

Was it possible that she was the baby? Max was petrified by the thought. Her red hair – Leslie and Madeleine were both darker-haired. Her age. The gold cross – he had placed it himself around the baby's neck. It all matched too well to be coincidence. Almost as strong a proof as the cross was how much she resembled her Italian mother, now that he was aware of it: the same red hair, the burning blue eyes, the unyielding will. Her mother was a flame, a torch – the Torch, he remembered. And so was Deborah.

He had occasionally thought about the child and what might have happened to her. It came to him now that there was probably no way in which she could have learned who her real parents were, nor could Deborah know that he had been present at her birth. How could she? There was no birth certificate, no notary or seal, in the little hut where Dvora had given birth to her, not even a blanket. His German officer's coat had been wrapped around Deborah to keep her warm. In the guise of father, mother, and child, they had travelled through the German lines to safety. After he had left her in the orphanage near Turin, Pierre or Nathan could have arranged for their British relatives to adopt her. Leslie and Madeleine could then have bribed a local official to issue the child with a false birth certificate that listed themselves as her true parents. Max understood only too well that none of the Kronengolds wanted the child ever to be able to trace her real parentage.

Max suddenly felt his breath growing short and a sharp pain starting in his chest. He must not get excited, the doctor had warned. He put a little pill under his tongue and tried to free his mind of anxiety. Impossible.

For a moment Max questioned what Deborah's position in the Kronengold family was as a result of her anomalous parentage. Could he use it in some way to his advantage? And then another sharp pain forced him to face reality. He could never dare risk using this new knowledge he had stumbled upon. Pierre and Nathan were close to her – his son had told him so – and would go to any lengths to prevent the world from discovering the shocking truth. If they ever learned that he had found out Deborah's true identity, they would methodically vilify his name and destroy his treasured social prominence without a moment's hesitation. Worse, David would then discover the shameful truth about him – and might hate him forever. They had the evidence: a written confession he had made of his Nazi past.

Someday, perhaps, he would tell David who Deborah really was. After his death, when the truth could no longer hurt him, his son could take advantage of it.

Max shuddered. David! Deborah! My God, they were lovers. The thought was terrifying – he had to break their relationship in order to hide his own awful secret. But he could not act precipitously. David loved her too much to give her up if he was confronted directly. Max knew he must be subtle and patient; he would place wedges between the two of them that he could gradually force deeper. Yet, until the two were apart, Max Holtz knew he would not take an easy breath.

The weeks after the Newport dinner saw David and Deborah's relationship worsen. Incited by his father, David became more outspoken in trying to assert his mastery over

Deborah in every sphere until, finally, she would agree to marry him. Max insinuated that a woman like Deborah needed and wanted to be dominated, perceiving from his confused son's reports that such a stance could be the breaking point between them. Indeed, they came close to splitting up over Deborah's decision to expand abroad by buying a British financial group, at the centre of which was the highly respected merchant bank, Dandridge Brothers. She should take her time, he said, consolidate. David snapped that, if he were free to vote his stock for his own directors, he would instruct them to veto the deal.

Playing on his son's inclinations to jealousy, Max began to relate rumours, some true, some fabricated, of men with whom she had been seen, aggravating his son's simmering distrust. After carefully re-reading the investigator's report and after much brooding on everything he had learned about Deborah and her move to America, Max Holtz had come to an unexpected but no longer surprising conclusion, that an intense animosity existed between Leslie de Kronengold and the daughter who was his by adoption and not by blood. She had never received the slightest aid from him; starting in America with no money, she had struggled for years in near poverty and finally turned, not to Leslie, but to longtime enemies like the Holtzes for her capital. If that deduction was correct, Max reasoned, then perhaps her break-up with David could be turned to his own family's advantage, accomplishing precisely what Max had earlier hoped for from their marriage: control of Deborah's growing financial domain and establishment of the long-sought link with the Kronengolds.

In early October, without telling his son, he flew to London to rekindle his acquaintance with Leslie de Kronengold. When he returned from those very successful preliminary talks, he set the final machinations into motion with a carefully rehearsed lie. Knowing that David resented Deborah's friendship with Evan McAphee, Max asked him whether the lawyer had moved into Deborah's apartment building.

'Not that I know of. Why?'

'Oh, nothing,' Max replied much too abruptly.

David became insistent. 'Why did you ask?'

Max made a momentary pretence of reluctance and then said, 'I met him when he questioned me last year for that deposition I had to give in the Halsey litigation, remember?

So I know very well what he looks like. Well, I had an appointment for lab tests and was driving by Deborah's apartment house much earlier than usual this morning. I saw him coming out of her building, that's all. Nothing to become excited about. You trust her, don't you?'

Max knew that his son's loyalties were being strained and that a final jealousy could sever the ones stretching to Deborah. He strained them further.

'David,' he added, 'you wouldn't tell Deborah about this? She has enough resentment against me. Promise me you won't mention a word to her. After all, you could have found all this out on your own.'

David grunted his pledge and nearly pulled the handle from the door as he fled to his own office.

Next morning, David showed the doorman in Deborah's apartment building a photograph of Evan McAphee and promised him a hundred dollars as well as complete anonymity to tell what he knew about that man. This created no conflict of conscience for the doorman, who had already been paid five hundred dollars by Max Holtz to lie that several times he had seen the man come down from Miss de Kronengold's apartment in the early morning hours.

Devastated by what he was now sure was Deborah's faithlessness, David could barely control his anger. He did not confront Deborah, but instead scrutinized her every word, her every gesture when they were together. And, because he was jealous, her innocence appeared to him the most devious sort of dissembling. He sought his father's counsel now more than ever, and Max no longer sheathed his condemnation in disguised hints. Max excoriated her for having used and abused David. She was just like all the Kronengolds, back to the one in Austria who had bankrupted and beggared his grandfather. Trust them enough to turn your back on them, and they'll put a knife in it. Growing, he urged, that must be his and David's main concern. They must become huge, invulnerable, irresistible.

David made up his mind that he would be as secretive about his revenge as she was about her deception. She was a whore, a traitor, and undeserving of the promises she had tricked him into giving her. His father was right. Her lust had mocked his own loving passion and made him look like a fool. First she had used his money to build up a company. Then she had led him on with the hope of marriage, so that he would renew the voting trust that had tied him hand and foot for the last three years. But those three years were nearly at an end. Now he would make her pay for her perfidy. She would come crawling, and she would beg for his mercy and his love.

Only a few days later, when they were having dinner at her apartment, Deborah informed him that, just a few hours before, she had concluded arrangements to purchase the Dandridge family's stock in their British financial group. The group was publicly traded. She would immediately tender for the rest of its stock in exchange for stock in her own corporation. After some shifting of assets, about a third of the D. de Kronengold Corporation would now be traded on the London Stock Exchange and the rest on the New York Stock Exchange.

'How much does that reduce Aximation's share of your company to?' he groused.

'We'll each own about seventeen percent. More than enough together to ward off any take-over threats. David, I know you're against the purchase, but the British group is worth at least half again as much as we're paying.'

David grumbled. Silently, he gloated that she had fallen into the very trap she herself had built and he had warned her against.

After dessert, with a show of regret, he said that problems had cropped up in Aximation's Asian subsidiaries, and he would have to spend several weeks in the Orient straightening them out. His plane was leaving early, so he could not spend even this last night with her. All evening he had seemed so distant. Deborah had hoped that they could talk about it. But now she conjectured that the Asian problems had been on his mind. Her worry allayed, she told him only that she hoped he would be back very soon. Maybe they could even meet in Hawaii for a few days' holiday. At the door she kissed him lingeringly, knowing how much she would miss him.

As David kissed her good-bye, his heart was torn by his hatred and his longing for her.

A few hours later he and his father flew to London to begin their negotiations with Leslie de Kronengold.

CHAPTER SEVENTEEN

The messenger did not look to the receptionist like the usual sort who would flip an envelope onto her desk, shove the receipt at her to sign, and amble back down to a bicycle chained to a bus stop. For one thing, he was dressed in a suit. For another he spoke well, she thought. Really well. He had orders, he said, to hand the envelope personally to Miss de Kronengold. After the security guard had checked him and the package, he retired to one of the plush modern dark-grey seats to wait.

'Are you British?' the receptionist finally hazarded.

He nodded. 'Left London this morning. I'll be heading back on the next plane.'

She had never been farther than Atlantic City and was awed.

Deborah finished her meeting with the executives of Frankenthaler Aeronautics, who were seeking to tap the Eurobond market. She, James Lacy, and red-headed Steve Jacobs, head of Corporate Finance, led their guests on a tour of major areas of the firm's headquarters: the stock trading room, with over two hundred brokers gauging fluctuations in the stock market and advising clients on buys and sells; the bond room, where hundreds of millions of dollars changed hands each day on behalf of large financial institutions; the research library, with its suite of offices for analysts; the hectic currency and commodity trading rooms; and the deceptively quiet wing in which giant financings and mergers and take-overs were devised. Deborah and her executives were just seeing the Frankenthaler people out when she noticed the well-dressed man who stood as they entered the softly lit reception area.

'Miss de Kronengold?'

'Yes?'

The messenger handed her the manila envelope and slipped away. There was no return address on it, only her name and her firm's address. She tucked it under her arm and finished her conversation with Frankenthaler's chairman.

Returning to her office to take an important telephone call, she forgot about the envelope. As she ended the call and was about to take another, her eye fell on it. She slit open the envelope and viewed the contents.

The letter was typewritten and unsigned. It began: 'I doubt whether you are aware that David and Max Holtz are at present in London in secret negotiations with your father, Leslie de Kronengold. They are planning a joint tender offer that would give them control of your company. The offer would be made simultaneously on the New York and London stock markets.'

To prove its authenticity, the letter contained confidential facts and figures about her company that were known only to her partners, the Holtzes, which the letter writer alleged they had divulged in the talks. A Polaroid snapshot was also enclosed. It showed Max in the foreground and David only a step behind as they entered the gates in Mercy Lane that she remembered so well, the gates of the Kronengold bank. She had no doubt that the photograph was recent – David was wearing the camel-hair coat he had bought only a short while ago.

Deborah was thunderstruck. David had told her he was on his way to the Orient. Why would he have lied to her about his destination unless he was planning the sort of assault on her company described by the unknown correspondent? She and David had bickered more than ever recently, and he had seemed distant their last night together, but she had never doubted how much they meant to each other. However, her reason coldly told her the letter conveyed a dreadful truth that her emotions fought to deny: all the while, he had been scheming to strike at her. She felt deeply hurt. David, whom she loved most in the world, was conspiring with the man she hated most, her father, to steal from her everything she had struggled for and built.

Deborah wondered who had sent the letter to her. She guessed either her brother, Richard, or her uncle Charles, both insiders who held small stock interests in the Kronengold bank. She stared at the letter and tried to perceive from the words the person who had sat before a typewriter and picked them out. A few mistakes were apparent, as if the correspondent was not used to doing his own typing.

'Oh, God!' she suddenly exclaimed aloud, and her head dropped into her hands.

How could you do this to me, David? Of all the companies in the world to go after, why mine? But she knew the answers before she asked. You just couldn't believe that I loved you. So you had to own me.

What held her together at that moment was her instinct for survival. Even as she experienced the familiar onslaught of grief – that acid burning along the edges of her soul – some primitive part of her brain was subconsciously scanning the horizon to find the means for her defence.

Late in the afternoon André Leitner, who headed European Operations, and Neville Cooper, whom Deborah had placed in charge of her new British merchant-banking arm, arrived on transatlantic flights to join the top-secret meeting. Deborah had been examining the purported take-over scheme most of the day with James Lacy, Steve Jacobs, and Evan McAphee.

'Neville?' she inquired as soon as he stepped into the conference room.

The tall, slim merchant banker nodded. 'Yes. They're at the Kronengold bank, all right. All very hush-hush. However, our informants there tell us they've had an inkling or two that the topic being discussed is a take-over of this firm.'

Until then each person had retained the faint hope that the letter might have been a hoax or a misconception. The grimness intensified; it was almost visible, like fog. The bankers returned to the slow search for a battle plan.

Three years of building the D. de Kronengold Corporation had increased Deborah's resources enormously: she had her stock in the firm and over a million dollars in cash, but she had taken out no dividends in the three years, choosing instead to reinvest the firm's profits in expansion. Her resources were meagre beside those of either her father or the Holtzes. Together, they dwarfed her.

Hours of analysis emphasized the assets that she did have: she controlled the board of directors and owned seventeen percent of the stock, an equivalent amount to the Holtzes'; her bank contacts were now excellent, particularly in Europe; and she had the element of surprise.

By midnight two steps had been decided upon. First, Britain's Monopolies and Mergers Commission was about to approve Deborah's acquisition of the Dandridge financial group. Neville Cooper would find ways to delay the final approval, which would also serve to forestall any action by her adversaries in Britain to make a tender offer for the stock of Deborah's company. That would buy time. Second, during the extra time, Deborah and André would tour the European banks they had courted and done business with over the last three years – she needed a war chest with which to fight back. Those banks had a centuries-old tradition of discretion, and were permitted to loan a greater proportion of a stock's purchase price than were U.S. banks.

When the details had been worked out, Deborah went home for a few hours' sleep before catching the flight she and André were taking to meet bankers in Frankfurt, ironically the city in which had begun the Kronengolds' climb out of obscurity. As she often did, before turning off the light, she looked at the photograph on her bedside table of her mother laughing in the conservatory. She remembered that her mother had left his house soon after learning that Leslie had falsely accused Deborah of smashing the Stradivarius. Her mother must have felt as betrayed by the act as she herself did now by David's. And the two men had become allies! Her mother's silent laughter appeared to mock her now. For all her guilt over Madeleine's death, Deborah seemed somehow fulfilled by the link to a replication of her mother's pain. Lives intertwine, Deborah reflected sadly, and the sins of the fathers and mothers are visited on the daughters – who repeat them in endless variations.

Deborah slept poorly. Whenever she did fall asleep, she would soon wake on David's side of the bed, reaching futilely for him. They had been together for three years. Her home was his. Often he did not return to his own apartment for a week at a time. Several of his suits now hung in her cupboard. His shirts and other haberdashery were in the chest of drawers.

She had always been irked by his possessiveness. But to be loved so fiercely, she who had been starved for love so often in her life, was a kind of assurance. She was assaulted by loneliness now, not so much because she was alone – she was often alone – but because she would be alone for a long time to come. The other people she had been close to over the years, she no longer could be: Amanda Bailor was a suburban housewife who lived a thousand miles away; Matt Horton was a sociology professor at a midwestern university, mild and innocuous and ineffectual; Helen Lorenzo was now her employee – their relationship had necessarily shifted; Evan McAphee was married and expecting his first child – an intimate friendship would have been an unfair imposition on his emotions and his relationship with his wife.

David had been not only her lover, but her only intimate friend, her only confidant. And, in a way he could never understand, a protector. The nagging disquiet she had begun to notice after the first flush of a great success had passed or when she was by herself at night – not quite sadness and not quite dissatisfaction was as close as she could identify it – would be held at bay when she was with him, as if it were a voracious animal she could quiet only with success or love. He had turned on her, but she would not cease to miss him.

She and André were heartened as they made their rapid tour of European financial capitals during that next several days: not only had leading bankers come to have enormous respect for Deborah, but Leslie's arrogance over the years had alienated many of them and made them willing to back her to the hilt.

In early January 1971, the British Monopolies and Mergers Commission finally dismissed all objection to the acquisition of the Dandridge Brothers' merchant bank by Deborah's company, freeing the latter's stock for trading on the London Stock Exchange. Within hours, at a press conference held jointly in New York and London, Aximation Industries and I. Kronengold & Sons announced they were making a tender offer for a majority of stock in Deborah's company – on the New York and London stock exchanges respectively. Because Aximation already owned seventeen percent, together they needed only thirty-four percent more to gain the fifty-one percent needed for control.

As Deborah had foreseen, David was offering to buy eight percent or so more on the New York Exchange and Leslie to buy twenty-five percent in England, in order to give them equal amounts. She knew that Leslie would insist on that equality. Under American law, David could not act to add to his holdings for ten days after making the offer. So Deborah's plans had been devised to attack Leslie, the partner able to act in the interim and needing to purchase the largest amount of her company's stock.

Although Deborah was commanding her forces from her Geneva office, which was the central point for her network of borrowings, a statement under her name was released to the press in London and New York announcing that the D. de Kronengold Corporation was filing several lawsuits against Leslie's bank to halt the take-over and was claiming a hundred million pounds in damages. Deborah counted on Leslie's becoming excessively cautious in the face of the counter-attack and hesitating out of fear that he might be, one, liable indeed for damages and, two, spending large sums to buy stock in a company he would be legally blocked from controlling.

The newspapers and broadcasting media quickly picked up the story of the father and daughter of the legendary Kronengolds locked in battle. Yet, even as the wire services were flashing the news around the world, Deborah was already taking action.

She had recalled a similar situation in which her grandfather had been involved. While the other side waited for his response to their public offer, he simply went into the stock market on a massive scale and swiftly bought up control, a practice that was illegal in America, but perfectly legal in Britain. As Leslie hesitated, in order to assess the efficacy of his daughter's lawsuits, Deborah's stockbrokers went into the London Stock Exchange with an offer topping his. Her representatives were on the telephone with all the large insurance companies and funds holding blocks of stock. In less than an hour, they had rounded up over thirty percent of the stock in Deborah's company – nine-tenths of all its stock traded on the London exchange – giving Deborah now forty-seven percent of all the stock in her company. A friendly banker in Zurich had been buying up stock on the New York Stock Exchange. He stopped when he reached the four percent she needed for an absolute majority. Deborah was borrowed up to her nostrils, but she had won.

Her press conference at Heathrow was a triumphal affair. Dozens of reporters and cameramen were waiting when the plane landed. In her shabby little hotel during her first days in New York, she had vowed not to return to England without being able to hold aloft a dazzling prize. Now, at last, she was back – as a conqueror.

'She's a smashing bird, isn't she?' one of the photographers commented to his colleagues as she entered the room where microphones and lights had been set up.

Another who vividly recalled snapping her years earlier, added, 'I thought she'd catch a duke during the Season and spend the rest of her life redecorating.'

Deborah overheard him. 'Thanks, Eddie.' She winked at him. 'It's nice to be remembered.'

She stepped to the microphones and answered several questions directly related to the strategy of her defence. Suddenly, a different kind of question was heard from the back of the room.

'Miss de Kronengold, how does it feel like to beat your father for control of your company?'

On board the plane from Geneva, Deborah had anticipated the question. She had decided that it was more politic to make some noncommittal reply, but the joy of the moment was overwhelming.

'How does it feel like to win against my father?' A smile broke across her face like a rainbow. 'It feels bloody terrific!'

That was a note and a feeling she could not top. She walked quickly from the room towards the airport exit.

Neville Cooper had offered to come out to Heathrow to meet her, but she had recognized that his time could be better utilized attending to the many details still dangling. As Deborah searched for the car and driver he had sent, she thought of the people she wanted particularly to see in England. First was her cousin Nathan, to whom she often talked on the telephone. Next was either Richard or Charles or perhaps her cousin Malcolm. Even at her most dejected during the last weeks, late at night when she missed and hated David the most, she would think of her secret family ally in England who had warned her in the anonymous letter about the sneak attack in time for her to form a defence, and she would not feel quite so alone. Most probably it was Richard, she thought, who was now married to his father's choice and under his thumb, but who had once vaguely hinted at dissatisfaction in a note scribbled on a Christmas card. Whoever her secret friend was, she wanted to seek him out and thank him. She owed him so much.

Deborah had expected the chauffeur to be by the car looking for her, but he was behind the wheel and waved her in with a hand extended out of the far window. She was in too good a mood to castigate him for not opening her door.

The limousine moved off into the traffic, and she took no further notice of him until she heard him say, 'Hello, Dee.'

Surprised by the informality, she glanced up at the rearview mirror. Those blue eyes staring at her were unforgettable.

'Bash,' she exclaimed, too startled to do more than say his name. The man driving her was indeed Bash Rowell.

'I knew you wouldn't see me or take my telephone calls,' he explained. 'When I heard you were having a press conference, I came out here and bribed the chauffeur who was meant to pick you up.'

Years of accumulated contempt dripped from her words. 'You were right. I don't want to see or speak to you. What made you think I might want to?'

His eyes sought hers again in the rearview mirror. 'Because I sent you a letter telling you that your father and the Holtzes were planning to take over your company.'

Her emotions in chaotic conflict, Deborah sat silently for what seemed like miles of motorway. Finally, it was Bash who had to speak.

'If you want me to drop you off at your hotel or your bank and never speak to you again, I will.'

First Deborah had to know something. 'Why did you warn me about the take-over?'

'For the same reason I'm here now. I told you once that I had an obligation to my family which left me no choice. I had to marry April, but I would always love *you*. I finally had the opportunity to prove it.'

More miles passed before Deborah spoke again. 'I never thought I'd say this to you, Bash. Thank you.'

His voice was shaking as he replied. 'I never thought I'd hear it.'

'It's silly for us to try to talk like this,' she finally said. 'Is there any place near here to stop, perhaps to have a drink?'

He hesitated.

'Any place,' she added. 'It doesn't matter.'

He nodded and turned onto a side road. He parked near the entrance to a small hotel. The lake at the back seemed familiar. Then it struck her how very like this hotel was the one where they had first made love. She glanced sharply in the mirror.

'If you want to go somewhere else, just tell me,' he offered.

She shook her head; the memories at that other place had been good ones.

They walked past the front desk to the dining room overlooking the small lake. A waiter seated them apart from the few other guests and asked if they wanted drinks.

Watching Bash order, Deborah saw that the years had enhanced his good looks: they no longer seemed quite so unrealistically carefree. One glimpsed greater depth. The blond hair began a bit higher on his forehead. The blue eyes were more deeply set above the straight, carved features. Since childhood, she had always felt a clutch at the sight of him. After all these years of despising him, she felt it again and rebuked herself for it.

The first thing she wanted to know was how he had learned about the take-over scheme. Bash told her he had been interviewing a new man his firm was considering recruiting from the Kronengold bank. To impart an idea of the sorts of duties he had handled, the man mentioned he had recently done a study of the D. de Kronengold Corporation. Bash insisted on knowing what the study was for. With great reluctance the man revealed that Leslie de Kronengold was engaged in negotiations about a possible take-over of his daughter's firm. His partners would be the Holtzes. Bash extracted every bit of information the man had. The next morning another man, posing as a tourist, took a Polaroid photo of the Holtzes as they entered the gates of the Kronengold bank. The man immediately flew with the photograph and Bash's letter to New York.

'Why didn't you sign the letter?' Deborah asked.

'If I had, would you have believed what it contained?'

'Probably not,' Deborah admitted.

She stared at her drink a long while before she gathered the humility to speak again. 'Someone I thought was a friend turned out to be an enemy, and someone I thought was an enemy was a far truer friend. Thank you again.'

Bash had followed Deborah's spectacular career with both wonder and pride, but except for an occasional snippet mentioned to her in passing by Nathan or glimpsed in the

Financial Times she knew very little about what had transpired in *his* life over the years, apart from the fact that Rowell & Co. had thrived – his firm was probably Britain's pre-eminent merchant bank in the Middle East. Now he could fill her in on personal matters.

He and April had a daughter of their own and one son, Salim's. Salim had become a force in his country since his uncle's death and his father's succession to the throne. The boy thought of Salim as his godfather. When Deborah asked why he and April had not had more children, she sensed in Bash some of the cares that had not been present in the wildly dashing young man with whom she had fallen in love at Oxford.

'April wouldn't have any more.' He shrugged. 'She's afraid if it's a son, I'll pay less attention to the other boy.'

'Are you happy?'

'I'm neither happy nor unhappy. I'm a good banker. Much better at that than I ever was as a scholar.'

They both chuckled. Then Deborah asked a question to which she had not realized until then she wanted to know the answer. 'Is your marriage happy?'

'April's happy, I think.'

'And you?'

'I have a position in life. Duties.' He halted. He wanted desperately to reach her. 'I tried to make you understand that the last time I saw you . . . when I told you I had no choice about marrying April. You were too distraught to listen.'

Unable to stand the pain that gazing at her inflicted on his memory, his eyes dropped. 'One of my duties is to April. I would never renege on it by leaving her. She loves me very much, and I would never hurt her. It isn't happiness, and it isn't love. But I've never expected that would ever happen to me again.'

'That's why you were at the airport today?'

'Yes.'

Neither spoke for a while, but instead watched the waterfowl, too well fed to go south in the winter, paddling across the still pond like small, stately ocean liners. Deborah realized this was the first time she had felt at peace since learning that David had left her.

'Have you ever lied to me, Bash,' she finally asked, 'or done anything that might hurt me – the slightest thing – that I don't know about?'

'No. Nor would I.' His eyes were clear.

'If I ever learn you have,' Deborah pronounced calmly, 'I will do everything in my power to hurt *you*.'

A great weight seemed to be lifting from her chest, a hatred she had never sought. And beneath it, as if it had never left her, was a feeling she no longer had a reason to repress.

'Bash, I think I finally do understand the sort of duty that gave you no choice but to marry April. If you had told me just now that you wanted to leave April for me, I would have walked away and never looked back. I won't marry anyone – ever. And I'll never yield a single inch of my freedom.'

Her calm was cracking, and she had to look away, out over the lake where a bird was gliding low over the water's edge towards a landing.

'I've loved very few people in my life, Bash. And it has always brought me pain. Maybe for that reason love seemed more precious to me than it might to women to whom it has come more easily.' Her gaze returned to his eyes, bluer than the lake. 'The only commitments I want are honesty and love.'

She hesitated a moment more, then leaned forward and kissed him. Just as they had when she was seventeen, her lips felt as if they were melting down through her body.

At dusk, they made love in a room at the hotel while the waterfowl called out to each other. Then they watched the moon rise from the pond and the trees behind it as if resurrected, and they whispered about all the things the years apart had kept them from sharing. The night was as precious as Deborah had hoped.

The sun was bright and the morning warm for January when Deborah drove to the monastery on the barren cliff. Nathan was standing outside, waiting for her. He wore a heavy brown wool cassock belted with a rope. A massive man with a shaggy grey-white mane, he looked like an ancient mountain peak. She flew into his arms.

'My cousin the priest,' she teased him as she stepped back to look. 'Father Nathan. You've always been a far better father to me than my real father ever was.' She kissed him.

Nathan was crying. He wanted to say, 'You look so much like your mother, like Dvora, that my guilt is unbearable. No hole in hell is deep enough for God to fling me into.' Instead, he said how wonderful she looked, which was true, and that he prayed for her every day, which was also true. Years before he had admitted to her that the anguish which drove him into the monastery had resulted from his cowardice during the war: he was waiting in the woods for someone he was supposed to lead to safety through the Alps, but heard shooting and ran away instead, leaving the person behind. He did not tell Deborah then or now that he prayed for her every day because the person had been her mother.

'I'm not going to ask if you're proud of me,' she said as she took his arm and they began walking across the rocky landscape towards the sea. 'You'll lecture me about family unity.'

'No. You were protecting yourself.' He smiled. 'I *am* proud of you. Leslie was wrong not to take you into the bank from the very beginning. Now, he foolishly compounds matters by attacking you.'

Deborah had long suppressed her resentment at Samuel's failure to demonstrate his love by making some provision for her in his will, even in some small way. Now that resentment spurted out. 'Nathan, my grandfather left my brother some shares in the bank. I was left nothing. Why wasn't I even mentioned in his will?'

'During some phase or other when you were out of favour – the nearest I can place it is just after the dreadful violin incident – your grandfather made a new will.'

'And no one ever found a later will? Grandfather always led me to believe, during those last months travelling together, that he had made a new will after we were reconciled.'

Nathan shook his head sadly. 'I searched for one, Dee. I went to see Samuel's lawyer. He told me he had prepared a new will just before the trip, but Samuel never signed it. You know the fellow, Percy Grayson.'

'Perhaps the trip was to test my loyalty to the family. Or perhaps grandfather too thought of me as a *bastard*!' She spat out the word, making it impossible for Nathan, who knew her secret, to evade.

'Never! Not Samuel,' Nathan instantly replied, but Deborah was too consumed by this possible reason for her rejection to hear him. All her life before that moment she had not dared to form the word, even in her thoughts.

'That's why Leslie always hated me as well,' she added. 'I wasn't his.'

'Samuel loved you, Dee. He loved you.'

'Most of the time I believe it – I suppose because I have to believe there were a few people who loved me. But the doubts come when I think how he left me at Leslie's mercy.'

Nathan wanted to comfort her, but all he could think of to say was how much he wanted to heal the breach between Leslie and her. 'Perhaps now, when you can afford to be magnanimous, is the time for you to offer to heal your split –'

'No!' Deborah's reply sliced off her cousin's plea. 'You know better than anyone how he's treated me. And you know I've vowed to pay him back.' Mistaking Nathan's sadness for scepticism, she added with harsh emphasis. 'Don't doubt that I will!'

'I remember so well what the Kronengolds were like when I was a boy,' he said meditatively, gazing at the waves breaking on the rocks below. 'I was so proud to be one of them. They were like a strong chain. Threaten them in Vienna, they shackled you in Berlin or London or Amsterdam or Paris. Family, Dee. Like a chain.'

Soon they spoke of other things. He was in touch with many of their relatives. Her cousin Malcolm was loudly voicing his displeasure with Leslie's lacklustre management of the family's holding company investments and with the bank's lack of aggressiveness, particularly its failure to gain a large share of London's frenzied acquisition activity. He and the others were shocked when Leslie had announced that his most ambitious take-over effort would be against Deborah.

Near the end of her visit storm clouds darkened the sky. Deborah observed that, within this often turbulent landscape, performing so many pressure-laden tasks for the Church while his brother monks were engaged in more everyday pursuits like baking and farming, Nathan had managed to achieve a profound serenity.

'You seem at peace,' she told him.

He shrugged. 'Another form of penance.'

Deborah's talk with Nathan sparked an idea for how to debilitate Leslie's finances and isolate him. She spent much of her time in England visiting relatives and attempting to gain a better idea of the specific nature of the assets and of various shareholders' interests in British Kronengold Holdings, Ltd., the overall holding company for family investments, including the merchant bank. She learned that many of the

Kronengolds were dissatisfied with Leslie's management, but could do little because Leslie owned so large a portion of the holding company shares.

They had a right to be dissatisfied, she concluded. Many Kronengold enterprises, particularly the centrepiece, the merchant bank, had been losing money more or less steadily since Samuel's death in 1957. There had been good years, to be sure, but the poor years that followed swiftly wiped out previous gains and produced further losses. The family capital, accumulated over so many generations, had shrunk drastically several times in this century – during both world wars and the Great Depression. Rather than building it up during these more prosperous times, Leslie's uninspired leadership had eroded it. Kronengold net worth, while still large, was no longer so massive as legend continued to paint. In fact the bank had so little excess capital that Leslie had been planning to borrow from the holding company every bit of the funds to buy Deborah's company's stock.

Deborah finally devised a plan that was based on two factors. First, she knew now that the family's capital was primarily in the parent holding company and not in the subsidiary bank; the latter actually depended on the former for funds. Second, Leslie had enormous personal expenditures, for which he relied on his holding company dividends. Although his living expenses had been reduced after he had exchanged his London residence for a smaller house and donated Clove Hill to the National Trust, he had immediately increased his previously limited spending on archaeology. He was now Britain's foremost sponsor of archaeological projects. Every summer and much of the rest of the year, he could be found at one of his half-dozen digs, while allowing no one back in London to exercise authority in his absence. Deborah's strategy depended both on Leslie's not having bottomless personal or merchant-bank resources on which to draw whenever he or the bank needed more capital and on restricting his access to the well of funds in British Kronengold Holdings Ltd.

Deborah decided to approach her cousin Malcolm and her uncle Charles simultaneously. Unless both agreed to spearhead the secret revolt against Leslie, it could not succeed. Invited to dinner at Malcolm and Lavinia's house in Belgravia, she tactfully suggested that Charles and Cora should be invited because of the matter she wished to discuss with the two men.

After dinner the two women tactfully withdrew, and she broached her plan.

'I've heard from several quarters there's a good deal of irritation with Leslie's management of investment matters.'

'The man is unbearable!' Malcolm fumed. While she was growing up, her cousin, now heavy-set, bald, and fiftyish, had assumed a jocular manner with her, but her recent chain of successes and the gravity of the predicament in which the bulk of his assets were trapped dictated seriousness.

'Do you feel that way, Charles?' she asked.

Charles was naturally shy. Physically a slighter, less imposing version of his elder brother, Leslie, in whose shadow he had always lived, Charles found it difficult to express his discontent.

Malcolm prodded him. 'Come on, Charles. We've talked about it often enough, you and I.'

'Yes,' he confirmed to his niece. 'The bank, where I am, is run like Leslie's personal kingdom. Worst of all, it's run badly.'

Malcolm spoke up again. 'And we both know how badly he manages the holding company's properties – the insurance company, the stocks and bonds, the properties.'

Charles nodded.

'Would you both be willing to do something about it?'

'I think it would depend what,' Charles said sensibly, 'and how much of a limb we would be out on.'

Deborah explained her thinking. Leslie's problem – and the rest of the Kronengolds' lever – was that he owned a large portion of the holding company stock but not a majority. Perhaps because of his doubts about his eldest son's character and ability, Samuel had written a will at the time of his falling-out with Deborah that bequeathed a small but significant interest in the holding company to his younger son, Charles. Thus, Leslie did not possess absolute control of the holding company – a majority of the shares – as Samuel himself had, and could be thwarted by a united opposition. The holding company's prime investment had always been the substantial amount of shares it owned of the merchant bank, I. Kronengold & Sons, but it did not own them all. Leslie owned some shares outright, as did a few other individuals, such as

Malcolm, Charles, and Deborah's brother, Richard.

Deborah proposed that with her help Malcolm and Charles mount a clandestine campaign to organize every single one of the holding company's minority shareholders into a majority bloc. They would then have the votes to refuse to agree to a shifting of funds whenever the bank ran short of capital and Leslie tried to draw on the holding company for it. That would force Leslie to meet the bank's commitments from its own inadequate funds. In addition, the majority bloc would refuse to declare a holding company dividend, putting great personal pressure on Leslie, who had involved himself heavily and relied for his income on those dividends. If the majority bloc stayed united, Leslie would be forced to agree to their initial proposal, which would turn out to be the first step in a severing process that would continue for several years. Each time, Leslie would be coerced into giving up more of his holding company shares in return for cash and for gaining more of the bank shares owned by the holding company Malcolm, Charles, and others. Only then would holding company dividends be declared, which would allow Leslie to replenish his own capital or, if he wished, lend his dividends to the bank.

'But what if the rest of us need money to live on while we're withholding dividends from Leslie?' Charles asked with concern. 'Many of us live on those dividends.'

'We'll form a fund on which any minority shareholder can draw interest-free. Those who can will donate to it. I'll pledge myself now to contribute a million pounds to the fund when it's needed.'

Both Charles and Malcolm had been intrigued by her plan, but were fearful about taking actual steps to institute it. To some degree they still thought of her as a child. But one million pounds! That was very real indeed. The two men began to question her about the details of her scheme. She told them as honestly as she dared what her own motivation was.

'Eventually I'll be able to buy the holding company shares that Leslie has to relinquish. The assets could become much more profitable with better management. And I have as much against Leslie as any of you.'

What she kept to herself was that her ultimate purpose was to isolate Leslie and his bank from the support of the holding company capital. Alone, Leslie and the bank would be more vulnerable. She could strike at its base of clients, cut off other sources of its income and, over many years, devise ways to obliterate him.

She raised her glass of port. For over a century the family toast had been 'Unity and Fidelity!' But that seemed out of place under the circumstances. Instead, she said, 'To our success!'

They touched glasses and drank.

'What about Richard?' she asked. 'He has shares in the bank and could be hurt by what we're doing. I'd like to approach him about joining us.'

Charles shook his head with regret. 'He no longer has a mind of his own.'

'All the same, I'd like to try.'

The next day she telephoned her brother at his home and left a message that she hoped to see him before she left England. He never returned her call.

CHAPTER EIGHTEEN

Neither in England nor upon her return to New York did Deborah see or speak to David. Through intermediaries she inquired about his disposing of the stock his company still held in hers. He refused, although Deborah now possessed a majority of her company's shares and could not be uprooted from control. James Lacy snapped that David had some new trick up his sleeve. Deborah understood what her executive could not know, that David refused to give up his stock because it was his only remaining link to her; he still loved her.

What did concern Deborah was that the Holtzes were seeking ties with Leslie. As a child she had seen Max Holtz fawning effusively over her grandfather while secretly trying to steal his property. Time and again during his lifetime, she gathered, like an obsession, he had sought some involvement with the Kronengolds. Even before learning about the alliance between the Holtzes and Leslie to seize her company, she had begun to perceive that David, too, had an excessive love-hate fascination with her family, composed in equal parts of envy and rancour, which had been imbued in him by his father. In the weeks that followed, she came to recognize that David's desire for her and his need to possess her had been partly bound up in his compulsion to assert dominance over the family whose name she bore. The Holtzes' ultimate goal, she reasoned, might be to merge with Leslie or even, like South Seas cannibals who seek to gain their enemy's power and fame by consuming him, to take over the British Kronengold bank. Either eventuality would save Leslie from ruin and prevent her from realizing her own goal of destorying him. She was determined to find a means that would stop the Holtzes from aiding Leslie if they should ever try.

Deborah immersed herself in an intense study of their holdings and of Aximation Industries, probing for a weakness that would provide her with a safeguard. She eventually found one in the fine print hidden among the labyrinthine – and doubtless forgotten – clauses of a class of security Aximation had issued early in its frenzied expansion. By controlling a majority of those debentures, Deborah would have the power to control Aximation, the Holtzes' power base, if they ever threatened her again. Deborah saw to it that those debentures were quietly bought up by nominees and friends, mostly in Europe, and hoped they would never be needed.

By mid-1971, Deborah was prepared for the massive avalanche of over-valued dollars she had long been watching build up abroad to thunder down on the value of American currency. She had placed all her own and her clients' liquid assets in other currencies and was hedged solidly against the dollar. And she had made certain that all foreign loans were repayable in U.S. currency, so that a weakening of the dollar would not require more dollars for repayment. Once that was accomplished, she had given interviews to financial publications asserting that the dollar was insupportable at current levels and the Treasury Department would soon find itself unable to hold gold down to $35 an ounce. Many had called her an alarmist. Few had believed her warning.

As Deborah had predicted, America was soon haemorrhaging financially. In a futile attempt to staunch the flow of overvalued dollars pouring onto international currency markets, the American government began to sell gold and foreign currencies in order to buy dollars held abroad.

On August 15, President Richard M. Nixon finally applied a tourniquet. He imposed a domestic wage and price freeze, asked Congress to impose a ten percent surcharge on imports, and temporarily suspended the conversion guarantee of gold. No longer could the United States force a $35 per ounce ceiling on gold; for the first time in four decades, gold's value would be flexible, even volatile. And, for the first time since the Bretton Woods Conference of 1944, international currency exchange rates would not be set arbitrarily, but would shift as the relative values shifted. The dollar plummeted, and gold shot upwards. Through her London and Geneva offices, Deborah was able to orchestrate a coup for her clients and herself on a gargantuan scale. Even American clients, legally prohibited from buying gold, profited enormously. In the turmoil that would follow the break-up of the old monetary system, Deborah foresaw years of opportunity.

Deborah's achievement brought her worldwide acclaim in financial circles. Her personal gains were so staggering that she could pay off the entire debt obligation taken on during the fight for control of her company and add to her capital besides. Highly respected for her decisive take-over defence, this new success so soon afterwards began to bring through her doors the new breed of corporate executive at some of the Olympian blue-chip corporations, who understood that successful financial management demanded they look, not to clubby relationships, but to bottom-line results. Her friends in the Nixon administration, floundering in international economic waters, called on her for counsel and invited her to expand her very useful ties to the White House; she was leery of their freewheeling amorality, but was pleased to widen her influence. With her political fences in order, her existing business increasing rapidly, her own capital large, and her firm totally in her own hands and its balance sheet now impeccable, Deborah could at last plan the strategy she would employ to expand throughout the Seventies.

Experience in precious metals and commodities trading led her to plan ventures into gold mining and oil and gas exploration – she was convinced that those resources would grow in value over the coming decade. From them she hoped to create a chemical division. Computers were still in their infancy, and that would be another fertile field. And, always, the investment bank, with its increasingly extensive financial services, would be the engine generating the power to pull them all.

Deborah saw Bash only during the times her business took her to England or to the Continent, where he could discreetly join her, but she felt very grateful for their reconciliation. Her attraction to him went back almost as long as memory. Deborah had tagged along after him like a puppy when he had been her brother's friend and she a child, as dazzled by him then as she later was at Oxford. When reading Greek mythology as a girl, she always imagined that Apollo looked exactly like Bash, thinking how his easy smile could warm the planet. During the recent years apart, she had felt as if some valve within her was turned the wrong way, the juices flowed differently, something not quite right. Now, when they were together, it could have been Eights Week or the Season or the meadows around Clove Hill. April and the years between ceased to exist.

The carefree daring in him seemed to surface again as soon as he became certain once more of her love, the recklessness that had first drawn her to him when they were young. And that evoked in her a youthfulness she thought had been bleached out of her bones by the years of struggle. They went helicopter skiing in British Columbia, scuba diving in the Red Sea, and rafting in New Zealand. But the most daring night they spent involved no physical danger but, rather, being found out – and that added delicious excitement to the nostalgia: the warm June night they went up to Oxford for a costume ball, he dressed as the Thief of Baghdad and she as a harem girl. Only thin masks guarded their identities. They mingled with undergraduates and older guests. Bash was challenged by a brawny rower (dressed with consummate lack of imagination in rowing clothes) and outdrank him as easily as he might have when he too was up. Deborah simulated a few moments of a striptease when the band spotted her costume.

It was nearly dawn when they staggered onto the streets, arms flung about each other's shoulders. They wanted to see once more the places that were backdrops for the love that had bonded them here. They made faces back at the sculpted heads on the Sheldonian and chased the deer in Magdalen park. Although nostalgia had caused Deborah to drink too much, the impetus for discarding her inhibitions was not alcohol, but the masks that granted anonymity and, thus, made possible the thrill of outrageous abandonment. As both knew it would, the walk ended at the river. They took a punt and glided out onto the water, a Baghdad thief with a reclining harem girl.

Bash stopped poling, caught up in the thoughts provoked by the buildings they passed. 'Even when I was here, I knew that life for me would never be as good again, especially those last weeks, when you and I were in love.'

'And I couldn't bear the thought of coming back here for two more years without you.'

Later, floating down the Cher, they made love, not giving a damn if anyone saw them.

And, yet, they could be together so seldom. When they were apart, Deborah's nagging disquiet tended to return.

In early 1972 Max Holtz suffered a heart attack. A clinic was set up in the New York apartment he shared with David, and round-the-clock nurses employed to care for him. He seemed to be recovering. Without warning one morning, a crushing pain burst in his chest. He clutched at it and screamed in pain. He could hardly breathe.

The nurse hastened to his side, rang for a servant, and began to apply emergency measures. When the maid appeared a few seconds later, the nurse told her to telephone first for an ambulance and then for the doctor.

Within twenty minutes Max Holtz was in intensive care and recognized the inevitable. He was dying. He refused to be moved from his room and demanded that the doctor allow his son in as soon as he arrived.

David rushed to the hospital as soon as he heard. He found his father lying feebly on the bed, his pyjama top open, and wires running from his chest to an ECG machine. The doctor was leaning over him on one side, the nurse on the other. Max's eyes had been fixed on the door since David had been sent for.

'Get rid of these people,' he whispered hoarsely. 'I must speak to you.'

David looked fearfully at the doctor, then back at his father.

'Save your energy, Dad,' he implored.

'I'm dying, David. And I must speak to you before I do.'

David glanced once more at the doctor, who replied with a futile shrug. Fear erupted in David's throat. He began to shake. He adored his father. His greatest fear had always been of losing him. Max's hand clutched at his, focusing his attention.

'David!' Max shouted, summoning all his strength. 'There's very little time.'

'We'll be right outside,' the doctor assured David.

The nurse started to tidy up, but Max's glare sent her scurrying out as well. David appeared paralyzed, tears helplessly running down his cheeks.

'Shut the door and bring over a chair,' Max ordered.

David did not move.

'The door!' Max shouted again. 'We must speak about the Kronengolds.'

His son abruptly came awake and jumped for the door,

seeing the effort his father had to make to yell. When David was seated beside the bed, Max fixed him with his gaze.

'Deborah de Kronengold is already a powerful woman and will become more so, David, as powerful as any of the Kronengolds. I think she's behind this family feud Leslie seems to be having with his relatives. She hates him. Someday you may need her aid.'

At the mention of Deborah's name, David became more alert. 'She hates *me*.'

'Then listen!' he exclaimed, trying to drive home the importance of the secrets he harboured. 'What I'm about to say may turn out to be your weapon against her and the others. You'll need every tool, every trick you have to restore our family's honour.' Max closed his eyes, marshalling his strength. Then he settled his gaze again on his son.

'You must remember everything I'm about to say and never reveal a word unless there's no other way to gain your objective from the Kronengolds – or to save yourself.'

David nodded and concentrated his attention on what his father was about to say.

Max took a laboured breath. He spoke slowly. 'David, Deborah de Kronengold isn't Leslie's daughter. He adopted her. I know because the secret of how I know this is . . . why I feared so to tell you this earlier . . . is the most shameful secret of my life.'

Max Holtz was now beyond caring about the stain the secret spread on his own character. But he was gratified nonetheless that David did not condemn his sins, as Max had so feared he might. His father's survival through the chaos of war and then, afterwards, through a dozen plights that would have stopped lesser men, justified everything in David's eyes. Getting what he wanted justified everything in the end. Max held nothing back from David, hoping that someday the dark knowledge might be a lever to aid his son in gaining what he himself had failed to achieve: succession to the wealth and repute accumulated by the Kronengolds.

He confessed that he had used forged Aryan papers to save his skin during the war and had become a German officer and what he then had done. He revealed the story behind the little gold cross. And he told him who Deborah's father was. And her mother. And then something more about her that he had been able to discover only in the last few months. Stunned by the revelations, David still did as his father insisted, agreed to reveal none of it unless there was no other way to gain his objective from the Kronengolds – or to save himself from them. Only then, when Max was sure that David understood why he had done so and would have to forgive him, did he confess that he had lied to his son by claiming Deborah had had an affair with her lawyer.

Finally, Max began to speak of other matters, in a last effort to impart his advice. But, in the evening, when the final attack came, he cried out for David to renew his vow that he would achieve vengeance for him by conquering the Kronengold empire, so much of which should rightly have been theirs.

'Yes, yes,' David sobbed, seeing his father slipping visibly from him. 'I will never forget.'

David's pledge was the last words Max Holtz heard. He died a few hours later.

David nearly went out of his mind with grief. He sat by the corpse, still gripping his father's hand and convulsed by sobbing fits, until very late at night, agreeing to let the body be taken away only when he was allowed to ride with it to the funeral home. He held Max's cold hand all the way.

He stayed with the body in the funeral home's basement until one of the workers asked if they should call in people to dress his father in accordance with orthodox Jewish ritual – naked in a white shroud in a plain pine box. At last David dimly comprehended that, for all his sorrow, plans must still be made. He grabbed the man's arm.

'His best suit. He has to wear his best suit. And I want the most expensive casket you've got, whatever it is.'

'Would you prefer the casket be open or closed?'

'Open!' David gasped. He dreaded the finality of a closed coffin.

The other servants were asleep when David was let into his apartment by the chauffeur, who then departed. Despite his strength, when faced with an ultimate obstacle, a situation in which the manoeuvres of his brilliant tactical mind were futile, David became helpless. The realization that he was now alone, an orphan, without the safe stability his father had provided in his life, terrified him.

In all the world, only one person was left who had ever loved him as selflessly: Deborah. Within him the secret of her true parentage seemed to vibrate gently, guiltily, an additional cord formed by his father between them.

To David, dazed by the events and knowledge of the past few hours, the jealous struggle he had waged for control of her company seemed the haziest dream now, like a family squabble forgotten amid the nightmare of true tragedy. All he could think of was how much he loved her, how much he longed for the comfort of her companionship. The pain drove every other thought away. He would always love her. She would comfort him. Frantic to reach her, he was also nearly paralyzed amid the ruins of his life. He could barely manage to dial her number.

After two rings Deborah's voice answered. In a rush David told her he was calling, imploring her not to hang up on him. The voice continued unheeding. It was an answering machine. She would be out of town for two days, but if he would leave his name and telephone number and a short message, she would return the call when she returned.

'Dee, it's David. My father just died. I need you.'

For a long while afterwards, he cried into the receiver.

Deborah returned to her apartment after an overnight flight from Los Angeles, where she had opened a new branch office. As she undressed to take a shower, she flipped on her answering machine. Mitten Cornell invited her to a dinner party, where she would be seated beside the most divine senator. Her dentist's receptionist wanted to reschedule an appointment. The Contessa Lambarelli would be in New York next Tuesday before flying back to Rome, could Deborah have dinner with her? The auction house informed her the Kandinsky she had purchased at auction could be delivered at her convenience.

Deborah was jolted by the next voice. It was David's. Utter anguish wrenched his words. She listened to the sobbing all the way to the end of the tape.

David sat beside the open coffin in the anteroom next to the chapel. One of his hands rested on his father's, afraid of the moment when he would have to let go. Nearly everyone filing by offering their obligatory condolences were business acquaintances, for whom this occasion required a show of concern. He nodded, barely listening, his eyes wandering from his father's rouged face to the doorway. As Deborah entered, he leapt to his feet and rushed to her, as if he had sustained his courage only because of the hope she might be on her way. His reddened eyes filled with tears. He clutched her hand.

The desperation of David's bereavement summoned up in Deborah recollections of her own grief as a child and the love she had once, for so long, felt for him. When there was nowhere for him to turn, no way to fight back, when he was utterly helpless, that was when he had always needed her most – and she had always loved him most. Deborah tried to offer him words of comfort, however scant help she knew they were, realizing as she spoke that her love for David would always be as powerful an impulse as her rivalry with him. At this moment, when he was lost and desolate, when she could dispense with the armour she had donned to defend herself against him, the love poured out of her. His head fell to her shoulder, and he let himself cry.

That evening he appeared at her apartment door. His eyes were red and hollow, and he seemed barely strong enough to stand. His tears began again when she saw her. She put her arms around him, letting him feel the strength within her that could sustain him. He cried for a long while. Only after many minutes was he able to tell her that his father had confessed on his deathbed to having lied about her having had an affair with her lawyer. She listened to David's explanation, barely able to keep her outrage from spilling over into vilification of Max Holtz, of whom she had been wary all along. His father was jealous of their love, David told her; his son was all he had. It was cruel, but couldn't she understand his misguided motives and couldn't she understand how bereft David now felt – hadn't she once told him how desolate her mother's death had left her?

Deborah hugged his despair to her like a gift, and she forgave. Then she led him to the bedroom and, fully dressed, lay down beside him on the bed, cradling him against her. He finally fell asleep, for the first time in days, Deborah guessed. She stroked his black curls into place and watched him until she too fell asleep.

They woke before dawn, undressed, and made love, with a sense of gratitude that nature offered humans such solace. Then David fell asleep again.

She lay holding him in the dim light filtered through the gauze curtains. Deborah understood that David's attack on her had derived from misplaced passion, like that of the male shark, who courts the female with savage bites. Having bested David, she could generously forgive him. His return to her now seemed a very natural completion to the fullness she had sensed blossoming in her life when she and Bash, after their long separation, had first made love again.

Not one to moralize, Deborah was simply content that she had David back again. Her company was protected from him now, and he would never again dare risk losing her by trying to assert his dominance in other ways. His father had been a spur who had jabbed him into competing with her, and his father was now dead. Desperate to have her back, David would agree to her terms: no possessiveness, no strings, no marriage. Their lives away from each other were their own concern, and he would have to accept that if they were again to share times together. Neither he nor Bash would be told anything of her relationship with the other. Bash, who was married, could not insist on exclusivity. Having once lost her over the issue, neither could David. She felt a deep well of caring within her for both men; and, more important to Deborah, who had spent much of her youth deprived of the sense that she was loved, the feeling that, at last, she truly was.

Loving two men was a way of dispelling the fears she had of being owned by one of them and, subconsciously, by not being able to give quite everything of herself to either of them, of guarding them from the tragedy her love had inflicted on others. And loving two men made her feel safer that she would not be deprived of love. If something terrible should happen to either man – or if one should betray her – she would grieve, bereft, but she would still be loved.

She never wondered why the only two men she had ever loved and their families were both welded onto the history of her childhood. Or whether the urges to be loved by two men and to amass wealth might both be bound up in the same need for excess.

Such unsettling thoughts began to trouble her only years later, after she had secretly chosen one of the two men to be the father of her child, when she decided she had to know who she was.

CHAPTER NINETEEN

By 1973 the evidence was clear that the Age of Aquarius had come plummeting back to earth after a very short flight. That was the year America – if only to escape eventual defeat – finally, ignominiously, pulled its combat troops out of Vietnam. 'Watergate', a term that would come to characterize a cesspool of sleazy activity, began to come to light that year as well, resulting in near stagnation of the government until the resignation the following year of a by-then thoroughly discredited president, whose vice president had already resigned as a result of his own scandal. In October 1973 the Yom Kippur War broke out, initiated by Egypt and Syria's surprise attack on Israel. United by their hatred of Israel, the often squabbling Arab oil-producing states raised their crude-oil prices seventy per cent and announced both progressively deeper production cutbacks and an embargo on shipments to the United States and the Netherlands, countries supporting Israel. The industrial West, having built its prosperity on cheap energy and on consuming a vastly disproportionate share of the world's natural resources, was terrified by the prospect of freezing winters, rationed fuel, petrol queues, and a wild escalation in prices. Poorer countries, with far less to spend on fuel and petroleum-based fertilizers, stood to suffer even more. Inflation attacked the world in a feeding frenzy, as an apparently unpreventable succession of price rises dictated by the oil-exporting nations funnelled the world's wealth into their coffers and beggared the rest. A bleak awareness began to descend that the world's resources were finite, precious, and doomed.

For those newly independent nations without the serendipitous good fortune of saleable resources, freedom did not bring prosperity. Even the freedom itself was often short-lived. The Seventies saw one Third World country after another fall under Communist oppression or right-wing military dictatorship or religious fanaticism. Terrorism became a common weapon of political disruption all over the world.

As the Seventies ground down, more and more Americans became convinced that the nation's intentions, at home and abroad, had outstripped its capacity to realize them. Disgusted with the lack of probity in its leaders, the people elected an unknown as president in 1976, a man whose conception of America's role was similarly shrunken. An intelligent but naive and provincial Georgian evangelist, Jimmy Carter, replaced an experienced Gerald Ford, who had made the mistake of pardoning his predecessor, inadvertently tarring himself with Nixon's brush.

By May 1980, Carter had spent three and a half years floundering in the presidency. The nation's economy and the business activity that supported it were faltering. Inflation was climbing precipitously, due not only to OPEC oil-price rises, but to demands made on a swollen, out-of-control federal budget by a proliferation of programmes to aid the variously disadvantaged that had been growing since Lyndon Johnson's Great Society years. The government's role had changed from ensuring that the right to equal opportunity remain unabridged to active efforts to eradicate the adverse conditions rooted in sex, age, income, industry, the environment, and health that hindered those rights. Gold had rocketed from the once sacrosanct $35 an ounce to $850.

Having only the barest knowledge of foreign affairs when nominated, Carter had contended merely that his foreign policy would be 'moral'. He was fatally ingenuous about the motives and objectives of other nations, thinking they were the same as his, and seemingly unaware that America's interests could be furthered abroad only if he could find the grounds on which they coincided and if America's strength was respected. Applying American ethics abroad indiscriminately, without the common sense to perceive the willingness to defend more than the most apparent of American security interests, had proved disastrous. Carter's stand against the Soviet Union's seizure of Afghanistan had consisted mainly of prohibitions on Olympic participation and grain sales, penalizing America's own athletes and farmers – the only groups over which sadly he appeared to have any influence. His lone foreign-policy success, forging a remarkable peace treaty between Egypt and Israel, had aroused the enmity of the other Arab states. Now, in the spring of 1980, America's impotence seemed to be symbolized by its president's futile manoeuvring to obtain the release of fifty-two Americans still held hostage in Iran by Islamic zealots. The latter had overthrown the Shah's pro-American government in a revolution the U.S. had neither anticipated nor aided in forcibly defending against but, rather, had inflamed by granting the Shah sanctuary for medical reasons.

Only a few years earlier America had been the world's benevolent policeman: massive, self-assured, a free people in an expanding economy standing up to the forces of communism and poverty. Now it seemed a timid, bewildered hulk, its strength crippled, its sense of purpose exhausted.

Deborah de Kronengold entered the Eighties like Caesar entering Rome. Having anticipated many of the economic trends that had dominated the Seventies – uncontrolled inflation; steeply rising oil, gold, and other commodity prices; and consequent recession – and having backed her opinions unstintingly, she and DdK, as her D. de Kronengold Corporation came to be familiarly called, had flourished on an astonishing scale. That uncanny anticipatory sense brought her immense speculative gains in currency and commodities trading that she was willing to plough back into her business to accelerate its growth. The Financial Services Division now possessed one of Wall Street's most successful investment banking operations. It included a major securities and commodities brokerage firm built primarily by absorbing a succession of other brokerage firms, a mutual-fund and pension management group, several money-market funds, and a corporate finance wing that was considered the most aggressive on the Street. She had indeed begun to fashion her firm into a financial supermarket, providing a plethora of services to companies and individuals. Subsidiaries included a credit card firm; a commercial lending corporation that financed both consumer loans and large corporate ones for purchasing equipment, like aeroplanes and machinery; and an array of insurance companies. They were linked by a thriving Computer and Communications Division that serviced clients in the financial field and was now moving into telecommunications.

The Financial Services Division's operations had led to expansion into related fields. Trading crude-oil contracts on the futures markets had expanded into exploration for and development of oil and gas wells, much of the investment money for which came from DdK investors seeking tax shelter. Mortgage lending had grown into major subsidiaries engaged in real estate development, brokerage, construction, and engineering – mainly as a result of acquiring companies in those fields. The Engineering and Construction Division now had major companies building private and governmental factories and other edifices around the world. Precious-metals trading had resulted in the take-over of an excellent chemical company in the forefront of work with minerals. The latter's research scientists had moved DdK into a new field by developing the most advanced process for separating minerals from sea water to produce high-volume, low-cost fresh water.

During the early years Deborah could estimate her net worth fairly accurately at a moment's notice, mostly for her own reassurance. Now that was no longer possible or necessary. Through the mid-Seventies she had engaged in a programme of, one, organising DdK to buy up its own stock, so that there would be fewer shares outstanding, and two, using her personal capital and bank loans to buy additional remaining stock in DdK. In 1978 David sold her his block for a substantial profit, and she took the corporation 'private'. She was now the sole stockholder.

She had never forgotten how useful mystery was to a Kronengold. Executives in each division kept its income confidential, but earned lavish bonuses based on it. She and only two other people had access to the company's overall figures – James Lacy, her corporate second in command, and Steve Jacobs, now head of all financial operations. No one else knew exactly what she earned or was worth, but the public now generally accepted that she had become one of the world's richest women.

Her wealth could be measured by many yardsticks. She owned several residences, including a magnificent triplex penthouse in New York City, a house in the Hamptons twice the size of her original one, a house on Lake Geneva, and a private resort island off the coast of Italy. She maintained permanent hotel suites in London and Los Angeles. Much of her holiday time was spent on board her massive yacht, *Venture II*, as it cruised the Mediterranean. Her fleet of corporate jets, helicopters, and limousines sped her from place to place and continent to continent. Parcelled among her houses were paintings and furniture that could have formed the core of a fine museum collection. Her racing manager was just starting to acquire at auction high-priced yearling thoroughbred horses that would eventually form the basis of a racing stable.

She occupied a rarefied social position. A member of the British aristocracy and an internationally renowned financial figure, a woman of consummate beauty, intelligence, and taste, she was courted by the most élite circles, but was highly selective about her social obligations. Although she was generous with her charitable donations, more often than not she accepted only those invitations that furthered a business purpose.

Deborah's youth had often been disrupted by sudden episodes of tragedy. As an adult only one death had rasped her soul. Her beloved cousin Nathan died in 1977, not telling anyone of the painful cancer that had been consuming him like a reification of his guilt. One morning he had simply failed to wake up. The loss had desolated her for weeks. She intensified her efforts to use her growing wealth and power to eliminate uncertainty from her life.

Hating and fearing the unexpected, she worked ceaselessly to shield herself from it by planning every detail of her business and personal lives. To Deborah the future was an endless chessboard on which she identified forces gathering beyond the horizon and worked to bend them to her own uses so far in advance that they became reliable elements of her strategy by the time they occurred in the present. That gift of foresight, the freedom her wealth provided, and the knowledge that she was loved by the only two men she had ever loved had gradually brought serenity to Deborah's life. Hampered very little by ripples of personal upset, she was able to concentrate to a hardened point her driving compulsion to become so rich that she and her descendants would be secure forever, that her right to the Kronengold name could never be doubted, and that she could finally crush Leslie.

Deborah's personal life had long ago settled into a satisfying habitude that her diligently kept privacy protected. In America she spent time with David, abroad with Bash. Each man had been careful to respect her independence, and she had been careful to respect theirs. Although David and Bash might each have suspected he was not the only man in

Deborah's life, neither knew for certain who his rival was. And both, having lost her once before, feared to transgress into the sort of possessiveness Deborah detested. She loved them equally and in different ways because each man was different. Each relationship had its particular delights and, she believed, together provided a profusion of experiences and feelings that no single one could. She also believed that the moments together with each were sweeter for the separation between.

But Deborah also adored children and, each year, her desire to have a child grew greater as the childbearing years left to her diminished. In early 1980, with her thirty-fifth birthday approaching, Deborah could no longer deny the overwhelming yearning. A considerable fear menaced her, that she might die giving birth as had the mother who bore her. But that was far outweighed by the desire for a child of her own to love.

She thought long and hard to choose the father. Deborah encountered new men nearly every day. But Bash and David were the only men she had ever met who really meant something to her. Having made her own choice in life and found contentment within that choice, she would hardly pick someone else to be her child's father. David? Bash? Which one?

Unable to shake her distrust of marriage or now even of exclusivity, Deborah made the decision to keep to herself the identity of the man who would be the father, whichever man she settled on. The child was *hers*, she told herself. She would not permit it to be psychologically battered by the abuse a father could inflict. She herself had suffered that kind of hurt and would not allow this child she wanted and already loved so much to endure it.

Finally, without telling either Bash or David what she intended to do, she chose one of them to be her child's father, and purposely neglected to use any form of birth control during a weekend with him. She walked on clouds for days when the doctor confirmed she was pregnant.

Apart from the coming of her baby, Deborah looked forward to what this year would bring for other reasons. For one, she had long dreamed of establishing full-scale investment banks linked to her parent investment bank in all the major international financial capitals, but she had hesitated because of the enormous amount of cash required to fund such operations adequately. Having concentrated on the United States, Switzerland, and Great Britain, she had had neither the capital nor the time to establish herself elsewhere, apart from her small gold-trading office in Hong Kong. Now, however, she had been approached by her uncle Pierre to expand her investment bank into France by buying a substantial interest in the French Kronengold bank and, thus, instantly becoming part of an established, capitalized French presence at a fraction of the cost of starting from scratch. She had extreme reservations, however, about trying to work amicably with his son, her cousin Gilbert. Nearly a quarter of a century after the violin incident, she still found him devious and a bully. He and his clique of stockholders in the bank were adamantly opposed to relinquishing control to her, despite the lacklustre performance of the bank and its investments in recent years.

A second reason why the year seemed so promising was because DdK had recently begun construction of a huge desalination plant in Arabia that could become a model for similar ones in nearly all the water-scarce Arab countries. Additionally, her Chemical Division's Research & Development team was engaged in top-secret research she hoped would lead to a process to separate out and mine individual minerals like gold, platinum, and silver during the desalting operation, thus providing her with an endless source of wealth from the sea.

However, those other reasons for Deborah's excitement during this first year of the new decade paled beside the most important one: this was the year when, at last, she would be in a position to launch the final assault on Leslie and his bank.

Yet, despite the uncanny clarity with which Deborah had always envisaged the future, these were violent, wrenching times; and no amount of planning, however astute, could be capable of guarding her totally from their unpredictability, their treacherousness. Even a personal decision like having a baby might threaten the fragile balance of Deborah's personal life. Events out of a past she had so carefully laid to rest might suddenly rise up to stagger her. Inconceivably gigantic geopolitical forces might turn without warning, pull her onto the world stage, and menace her and all she had built. In short this was a year her serenity might be irretrievably shattered.

* * *

The first week in May began auspiciously for Deborah. At a luncheon at the Old Mill Inn on the New Jersey shore – one of her favourite restaurants – she announced to the press that her firm had come to an agreement to buy a worldwide insurance-brokerage firm with its head-quarters in that state which fitted a missing piece into the financial services structure she was building. Back in New York City, until late that night she conducted senior staff meetings for her various divisions, all of which disclosed excellent quarterly results. Only after midnight did her 707 begin its flight across the Atlantic.

Next morning, she was aboard her yacht anchored off the Spanish coast presiding over a demonstration of the desalination machinery's prototype model for Prince Salim and some of his fellow cabinet ministers. Contracts to construct the full-scale facility had long been signed and construction on the site commenced, but rumours had surged around the Arab world that the claims and specifications for the process were false, that this was an elaborate scheme to defraud them. If Deborah was to convince Salim and his colleagues to make the next contractual payment and also to convince other Arab countries chronically short of water to purchase similar desalination plants from DdK, she would have to stage a highly dramatic and effective demonstration.

In the years since the death of his uncle the king, and the elevation of his father to the throne, Salim had become an important figure in Middle Eastern politics. The role had somehow filled him out physically. His face was as sharply handsome, but it projected his responsibility now, rather than callow abandon. And arrogance was veiled by the courteousness of one who knew he possessed nearly limitless power and the capacity for ruthlessness, but understood that shrewdness made them far more effective.

Deborah's vice-president of R & D, John Rosenthal, had personally flown from Oregon with the prototype he and his fellow scientists had invented. A red-bearded man with a cat's blue eyes, he barely restrained his resentment at the Interior Minister's insulting tone. Like Salim and the others in robes and kaffiyeh, the heavy-set Arab scoffed at the apparatus he was sure would fail to produce fresh water. Rosenthal's retort was the flawless performance of his model. A moment after he flipped the switch, the machinery sucked sea water through the inflow pipe into its bowels. A large stream of clear water soon issued out of a second pipe and a thick slurry of salt and minerals poured out of a third.

This successful test meant that Deborah's company would receive a three-hundred-million-dollar payment to fund the next stage of construction. Both Salim and the Interior Minister had originally objected to her contractual insistence on total control over the plant and operations – complete ownership and supervision over everything inside the plant – but they now agreed, after seeing the demonstration, that one would naturally want to protect such an efficient fresh-water extraction system from being copied. It occurred to none of Deborah's guests that there might be any value in the slurry oozing over the side.

When Salim asked to be shown round her ship, she led him along the port gangway. He stopped her when they were alone. She thought he might have something personal to say – they had known each other for many years. Instead, he launched into a harangue: Western nations had exploited the Arabs and taken them for granted too long, always siding with Israel, always assuming the Arabs would be content merely to lend back their oil income passively. On the contrary, he continued, the Arab nations were intent on becoming a dominant force to be reckoned with by the great powers, not only economically; but politically as well.

'My Arab brothers are angered at being trifled with by the U.S and the Common Market. As we did with the oil embargo, we intend to make a show of our financial force. My personal feeling is that they are over-emotional, but . . .' He made a gesture to indicate his hands were tied. 'Please understand that any measures will not be directed at you personally or your interests.'

Salim spun on his heel and walked back to his compatriots. He rarely spoke idly, but Deborah had no idea what he was driving at.

Deborah flew on to a meeting in Madrid to discuss managing a proposed government borrowing, and then to England. There, at last, if only for a single evening, she could put her business concerns aside and see Bash.

She took a taxi the few hundred yards to the carpark of the Peggy Bedford, a popular pub near Heathrow Airport, where

Bash always met her. He was waiting for her near the handsome Tudor-style building in an inconspicuous hired car. They embraced eagerly.

'I'm sorry you weren't in the pub,' she said without releasing him from her hug. 'I'd have liked to knock their socks off by swaggering in and picking you up at the bar.'

'How can you be sure some other redhead wouldn't have picked me up?'

'You're getting on in years, a little battered and bent. You aren't much anymore, but you're mine.'

'Pretty sure of yourself, aren't you?'

Bash had changed hardly at all during the years since being reconciled with Deborah, as if being back with her had lifted the hand of care etching age on his finely modelled face. His fair hair was full, and the translucent blue eyes seemed to reflect a happiness that had not been there a decade before.

Deborah kissed him, holding his gaze with hers. 'I'm sure of *you*. Love me as much as the last time?' This question was a ritual with them.

'More or less,' he joked.

'More? Or less?' she challenged, her lips against his.

'When you put it that way. . . .'

A couple that had just parked were staring into the car. Bash prudently released the brake and drove off.

Several years before, Deborah had found and purchased the country cottage her mother had once owned in Wiltshire. There, she and Bash could be alone, away from inquisitive eyes; no one knew her there or even knew she *was* there. If Bash found it disquieting to be with Deborah in the same house where his father had been with her mother, he never said so. The closest he had come to raising it was when she first bought the house. He asked her if living in her mother's home might not make her sad. Indeed, she told him, it very well might, but that was a sadness she had lived with all her life and could never erase because she herself had caused it. During the months of travelling with her grandfather, she had forced her mother to suffer the anguish of not knowing whether she loved her. Her own anguish now was that Madeleine had died not knowing that she did. Bash had been at the funeral, she recalled, and for all the heartache it provoked was glad she could share that memory with him. Once after they had made love Deborah asked him if he thought it had been like this for their parents when they were together. Bash had not answered but Deborah herself enjoyed thinking that she was like her mother and Bash like Rob Rowell, although she would have hated such a thought when she was a child. However, life had taught her to look at love from a woman's point of view, from her mother's, perhaps. 'It's important to identify with someone,' she said to Bash, 'and I have no one else.'

Now, on that warm May evening on the terrace, they ate a supper of cold beef and Russian salad. Deborah planned to use this night to tell Bash that she was pregnant, but they had not seen each other for several weeks and she wanted the mood to be right before she raised the subject.

Bash asked about her day, and she mentioned the prototype's demonstration for Salim that morning. Bash revealed that Salim had telephoned him later with instructions that the Rowell merchant bank should include Deborah's firm in more Middle Eastern banking deals; the Arab finance minister wanted it made clear to her that his nation was delighted with the new desalination process and that any action taken against her father's bank had nothing to do with her.

Deborah was puzzled. 'Do you have any idea what he means?'

'I telephoned my father to see if he knew.' The senior Rowell had crowned his banking career by being appointed Governor of the Bank of England.

'And?'

'A rumour or two. The Arabs may rub a little dirt in Leslie's face – blacklist the British Kronengold bank perhaps.'

'What would be the point? They don't do business with it now.'

'My father thinks they may want to give the world a signal to take them seriously as a world political power. Put a little pressure on everyone not to do business with Jews, flex their muscles, that sort of thing. Make some of the other bankers and the foreign ministers hop about a bit.'

'Their boycotts of Jewish firms have never been particularly effective before.'

'Exactly,' Bash concurred. 'From my experience, these Arab tempests usually blow over in a short time and are quickly forgotten. The important thing is that it hasn't a thing to do with you.'

Deborah kept to herself that any additional pressure on Leslie was meaningless. She knew that he was already in desperate financial shape and, because of her, would have to collapse at the end of the month. The Arab boycott would barely have begun when Leslie was forced into bankruptcy.

For a while Bash and Deborah watched the sunset curl up and over the horizon until everything in sight was benignly aflame.

'I'm sorry we can't stay here after tomorrow,' Deborah said quietly. 'I promised my cousin Lavinia – you know her, Malcolm's wife – that I would go to her charity ball tomorrow night. Something or other for animals.'

Bash instantly sat upright. 'The Homeless Animals Fund.'

'Yes, that's the one.'

'Blast! April and I are meant to be going.'

Deborah attended very few social functions in London. As a result she had never run into Leslie – she wanted his first view of her since their estrangement to be when she made good her vow to ruin him. And she had been just as careful never to run into the highly social April Rowell, which simplified her love affair with Bash. Bash's wife barely existed for Deborah, whose resentment of her had evaporated after she learned that April's victory had never wrested from Bash more than a sense of duty. Deborah had his love, which was all that she wanted.

'I can't get out of this one, Bash. My cousin is chairman.'

'I'll just have to come up with some way to keep April away. No problem at all.'

Sunset over a lake had always been a special time for them. Deborah chose it for what she wanted to say.

'I've mentioned once or twice how much I want a child, Bash.' He nodded, remembering. 'Well, I'm going to have one. I'm pregnant.'

Bash was stunned by Deborah's news. He suddenly had the feeling – odd for one so earthbound – that he was standing outside his body regarding her like a scientific observer while some more primeval version of himself, the one with the feelings, was reacting. The observer in him noticed that she still looked very much as she had the first moment he had seen her at Oxford. The sunset seemed to caress her face: roseate skin, short hair seemingly lit crimson from within by hot embers, the gleam in her blue eyes lambent in the flaming light. He was not very good at noticing that sort of thing, but her face might have been a touch thinner now. Her manner was certainly more assured. He could not decide whether she was more beautiful when he had first run into her at Oxford, fresh with youth and brash confidence, or now, after so many years had polished to indistinguishability the edge where his love of her ended and she began.

'That's wonderful,' he blurted out. 'This changes everything. We have to make plans –'

She interrupted gently. 'What I want most of all is that this child *doesn't* change things. I don't even know who the father is,' she lied.

His mouth bent sadly at those words. He had long ago accepted that he could not make demands on her, and she might sleep with other men. Now, when it mattered most to him, she was confirming that, indeed, she did have other lovers. Other lovers who could have fathered the child.

'There are tests to find out who the father is,' he pressed her.

'Bash,' she replied softly, her gaze holding his. 'I do know who the father is, but I don't intend ever to tell anyone. He could be you. He could be someone else. You'll just have to live with that. I hope you can. And I hope you'll love the child as you love me, and that nothing changes between us.'

'Love him? You know how much I've wanted a son of my own, someone to carry on the family name.'

'It could be a girl?'

'Then I'll love her. She's our child.'

Deborah was caring, but unyielding. 'I don't want to marry, and you already have a wife. A position, as you once put it.'

'And you have other men in your life. You're right, of course.' He nodded sombrely and then, impulsively, he asked, 'Am I the father, Dee?'

Deborah kissed his sad eyes. 'No child should be torn by loyalty to someone who could never possibly acknowledge it.'

'That makes a great deal of sense, but . . . but April will never agree to have another child. Just to know that I'm the father would mean everything to me.'

All Deborah's life had confirmed to her that fathers were

claims made or reneged on, particularly if the child was a girl. Present, a father would be a competitor for the love she sought from her child; absent and rejecting, he would be a hunger her own love could never fill.

'No one will ever know who the father of my child is, Bash. Don't ever, ever expect any more.'

The following morning Deborah and Bash returned to London. Deborah spent a good part of the day in conference with her staff preparing strategies for the next day's meetings with top European government officials and bankers. She intended to put forth a plan to provide private financing for aspects of the proposed pipeline from Siberia's natural-gas fields to the heart of Europe.

Afterwards, in her private office overlooking the heart of the City of London, she and Neville Cooper reviewed where matters stood regarding the final assault on Leslie's bank.

By late 1975, in the wake of the disastrous plunge in British property values, Leslie had become so desperate for cash to keep afloat the projects in which I. Kronengold & Sons, his merchant bank, had invested that he had no choice but to sell off the last block of stock he still held in his family's holding company. He received in return both the cash he needed and the last of the holding company's interest in the merchant bank. Deborah had secretly put up most of the funds for the long campaign to sever Leslie from his source of capital and now she owned a large part of the holding company shares Leslie had been forced to sell for less than they were worth.

More important, Leslie dominated his son, Richard, and his executives, and made all significant decisions. With no continuing stream of new capital and no good advice to aid him, he was now running all alone. Deborah could at last go after him and cut him down.

In other ways she had been doing so since establishing her own merchant-banking presence in Britain. First, her aggressive banking executives excluded I. Kronengold & Sons from partaking in all the large underwritings they managed, such as Eurodollar bond issues to major American corporations, a two-hundred-million-Deutschmark equity issue for a German petrochemical plant, and much of the financing of the North Sea oil exploration and development.

She worked to put indirect pressure on Leslie as well. Her

bank already had insurance company interests, to which she added, and she was influential behind the scenes in the insurance company owned by the family holding company. These major financing sources for merchant-bank clients refused to lend to clients of I. Kronengold & Sons and subtly passed the word that they would not look kindly on financing requests from merchant banks that cooperated too closely with it. Without overtly attacking Leslie's business, Deborah's was secretly squeezing its client list, its income flow, and its access to capital.

In addition, Deborah's obvious success at outmanoeuvring him and guessing future financial trends was driving Leslie to destroy himself. He had developed a kind of reactive psychosis, trying to discern what he had come to believe was her supernatural predictive power and then to shadow her move for move. Each new success by her firm or miscalculation by his served to strengthen that belief. Deborah became aware of his attitude when two employees of Leslie's bank – one in gold trading, the other in currency transactions – separately approached their counter-parts in her merchant bank and secretly offered to buy information about DdK's current investment tactics. They confided that Leslie had become increasingly obsessed with her over the years. Publicity about her banking or currency or gold-trading coups often broke after a critical setback suffered by their own bank, depressing him further. He was beside himself when it leaked out through the family grapevine that Deborah had purchased most of his stock in the family holding company. That seemed to be the point at which he perceived that she was actively hunting him. Believing her to be some sort of witch dropped into his life to bedevil him, he decided the only way to fight her unrelenting, uncanny success was to invest exactly as she did, duplicating her moves in every way. He assigned a man to spot the trends DdK was pursuing by trying to observe its trading activity in the various markets. Leslie's behaviour seemed so bizarre that Deborah felt a twinge of sympathy and began to consider relenting in her vendetta. Leslie chose that moment to authorize his two bumblings spies to offer their contacts at Deborah's firm twenty thousand pounds each for hard evidence of any act of hers that would lead to her criminal conviction, even if they manufactured and planted false evidence to do so.

Deborah's rage had been volcanic when her people reported that to her. She began to feed just enough accurate information back to Leslie through her own two employees to tempt Leslie into plunging heavily in the wrong direction. Afterwards, she would let it be known that she had discerned a contrary trend and changed her strategy at the very last instant. Rather than put him off, his losses served to reinforce his belief that he must anticipate her sudden strategy shifts more precisely.

Leslie's spiralling decline was slowed by the business coming to him through David Holtz's Aximation Industries, now a large multi-national conglomerate engaged in a dozen different industries. David had widened his insurance division's scope to offer many more financial services and had purchased a securities-brokerage firm and several allied companies to expand his foothold in the finance field. I. Kronengold & Sons functioned as Aximation's British arm. Although the additional business from David helped a good deal, the opportunities he presented Leslie to undertake new ventures and take-overs jointly with Aximation required capital – as did Leslie's desperate attempts to recoup his losses by heavy speculation in commodity and currency trading – and the bank's assets were slowly but surely drying up.

In mid-1977 André Leitner reported that Leslie was quietly scouting in other countries for a twenty-five-million-pound, three-year loan to infuse badly needed capital into the Kronengold bank. Leslie's discretion was understandable; he could be badly hurt if word spread in the City about his weakened financial state. André located a pliable private Swiss bank willing to take a fee for pretending to make the loan. DdK would be the actual lender, although Leslie had no way of knowing that.

Deborah had been far cleverer than he in devising the terms, keying repayment of the loan to whatever was the dollar value of gold at the time of repayment. Leslie had yielded to the Swiss banker's adamant claim that using something as 'solid' as the price of gold avoided a potential shifting of exchange rates between the British pounds Leslie needed and the U.S. dollars the banker maintained he wanted to lend. The price of gold had since skyrocketed, which multiplied the original fifty million dollars Leslie owed by four times his original desperate borrowing. He now owed two hundred million dollars! And it fell due in a month!

But Neville Cooper had some disturbing information: David Holtz had been in London very recently to meet Leslie. No one knew much about Deborah's private life, but Neville was aware that she and Holtz had resumed their friendship and were often seen out together, although occasionally she was photographed with other escorts at social events.

'Our informants' best guess is that David Holtz was here to dicker with your father about his company buying a direct interest in the Kronengold bank.'

Long legs casually crossed, high forehead smoothly untroubled, Neville Cooper spoke with the offhandedness the English upper class customarily employed for matters of importance. Yet, educated through scholarships, he came from a working-class family – undoubtedly an actual cooper, a barrel maker, appeared prominently in his ancestry. At the time she had elevated him to the bank's managing directorship, Deborah had made clear that one of his prime objectives was to attack her father on all fronts. Neville had seen enough of such behaviour among the upper class he had chosen to join to pity his own descendants.

'I'll speak to David the first chance I get,' Deborah replied. Doing business with Leslie was one thing, but propping him up with cash was a far different matter. She then asked, 'Anything else you and I should discuss?'

Neville hesitated an instant. 'I'm glad you're going to that ball tonight. You ought to know there's been some talk around that you might be a bit too aloof in England – simply here for the money, that sort of thing.'

'In other words, acting Jewy.'

'There's that, too, yes,' he answered forthrightly. 'The ball is for a worthy charity. I'd like to alert our press-relations people you'll be there, so tomorrow's newspapers will splash your photo all over their pages.'

'I had hoped to go unnoticed.'

Neville found that very amusing.

Flashbulbs exploded as Deborah arrived at Grosvenor House, somewhat late due to a last-minute telephone call from Hong Kong. She had chosen to wear a floor-length white dress with a cinched bodice and one shoulder left bare, her eyes highlighted by her sapphire necklace and earrings. Lavinia greeted her tardy appearance with relief.

Deborah's decade of being in business with her male relatives had not always been pleasant. She had found that the Kronengold men all possessed a touch of the haughtiness and ingrained male chauvinism her father demonstrated in such abundance. Deborah had no such reservations about Lavinia, an ex-film star, vital and outgoing, whom she liked, perhaps in part because they were both outsiders to the Kronengolds.

'Thank God you're here, Dee! I told everyone you would be and would have looked a perfect idiot if you hadn't.'

Lavinia locked her arm in Deborah's and marched her into the ballroom. After several minutes Deborah realized that the only thing changed from her deb days was that the sons and daughters had replaced their parents and bred identical children to replace themselves.

Deborah had just disengaged herself from a dull conversation when she saw someone approaching she had never expected to see that night: Bash Rowell. He looked harried, quickly explaining that April had refused to cancel their plans to attend the ball. She had heard Deborah was expected and wanted the opportunity to see her again.

'She doesn't suspect anything between you and me, does she?' Deborah asked.

'On the contrary,' Bash answered in a perturbed voice, 'she wants to parade me in front of you, show off her triumph.'

Deborah smiled reassuringly at him. That was no indignity; Deborah knew where his affections truly lay.

Out of the corner of her eye, Deborah noticed a short figure walking rapidly towards them. She could never have mistaken April, who was still a profusion of circles, even to the curls in her dark hair. April wore a low-cut black dress to expose a bosom that bulged above its neckline. A ruby and diamond necklace lay on it like a line of red sea birds bobbing on ocean whitecaps.

'Dee, I thought it was you.' April's mouth widened into a smile, as if the string on her cupid's bow lips had suddenly been drawn back. The tongue behind them was still sharp. 'How wonderful to see you again! The colour of your hair, I'd know it anywhere. Although I do think that at thirty-five you might start to let it go a little darker.'

Deborah ignored the provocation. 'How's your mother?'

'Arthritis. Barbados. Young painters.'

'And your father?'

'He prowls about his castle half the night, complaining about taxes and the government.' April put a protective hand on Bash's arm. 'We've been so very happy. You never married, did you?'

Deborah let the merest beginning of a smile lift the corner of her mouth. 'I've never found a man I trusted enough with other women.'

Deborah's amiable expression erased any suspicion that might have implanted itself in April, who continued to describe the happiness of domesticity. Deborah's attention drifted to the jewellery April wore. It was magnificent. A ruby and diamond necklace, matching drop ruby earrings below sprays of diamonds, a ruby and diamond bracelet, and a startling ruby ring. Deborah had seen those pieces before, she was sure. She searched the far reaches of her memory – it must be a long time ago.

She nearly gasped aloud when she remembered. Her mother, Madeleine, had had a ruby and diamond set exactly like the one April was wearing. Deborah had been a child the last time she saw those pieces, but she had drawn them with crayons and played with them countless times under her mother's eye.

'Your jewellery is very beautiful.'

'They're my most cherished possession on earth. They were a wedding present from Bash.'

Bash added, 'They've been in our family for generations.'

'May I?' Deborah asked as she lifted the necklace to the light. April was genuinely flattered.

The immense central ruby caught Deborah's gaze. Could there be two in the world exactly like that? The first time she could ever remember seeing her mother wear her ruby and diamond set was a night scarred on her memory. It was in 1951. She was almost six. Her mother had sat on her bed, dressed to go out for the evening, and told Deborah that she was adopted.

'Been in our family for generations,' Bash repeated needlessly. 'They're an old family heirloom.'

Deborah glanced at him for an instant, trying to decipher the reason for his nervousness. Was it only April's presence? She wondered.

'Your jewellery is lovely, April,' Deborah said evenly.

'And so is yours,' April replied. 'It's so good to see you

again,' she bubbled, her natural vitality percolating upwards. 'How our lives have changed over the years, but I don't feel a day older, not a day.'

They chatted for a few minutes, until Deborah caught sight of a photographer.

'Tonight is so momentous,' she exclaimed. 'I want photos of us together like this.' She motioned to the photographer. 'Stand right next to me, April.'

'No photos,' Bash interjected. He tried to wave the man away.

'Oh, Bash,' April said, halting him. 'This isn't for the newspapers. It's just for Dee and us. He hates me to take pictures when I'm wearing the jewellery,' she explained. 'He's so afraid I'll be robbed.'

Deborah insisted the photographer take close-up shots of the Rowells together, then of her and April together, then of April alone.

When they were parting, April said ebulliently, 'You must come to visit Bash and me. You're the oldest friend we have in the world.'

Deborah's mind was a cloud chamber of angry suspicion, ablur with thoughts and ricocheting suppositions. Looming monstrous and dark above the three of them, like a towering wave, was the foreboding, not only that the jewellery had been stolen from her mother, but that Bash had always known that it was. She loved him so deeply she could not believe that he would ever deceive her, that he would ever violate the single commitment to which he had sworn the night they recommenced their love affair; honesty. But she had to be sure.

Deborah summoned a cordial smile for April. 'It was wonderful to see you again. I'll be in England for only a short stay this trip, but I'll get in touch very soon.'

As soon as she had broken free of the Rowells, she paid the photographer fifty pounds for his roll of exposed film; she wanted to leave Bash no opportunity to snatch the film away before she had possession of those pictures.

Deborah's chauffeur, an employee of her corporation, delivered her to Claridges, where she always stayed when in London, and then took the film to an all-night laboratory for processing.

* * *

Next morning, when the chauffeur picked her up, he already had the prints – with enlargements of the jewellery. Deborah had already arranged for her firm's security and investigations man to find out about them. She did not know him, but remembered being told when he had been taken on that he had built an excellent reputation at Scotland Yard.

As she perused the photographs in the limousine on her way to the office, she found herself at the centre of an agonizing conflict. On the investigation hinged her future with Bash Rowell and, seemingly arrayed in total opposition, the hope that her mother had expressed her love for Deborah by leaving her a gift the Rowells had stolen.

When Deborah returned to her office after her morning meetings and the luncheon for the pipeline group, a poorly groomed man of about fifty was waiting for her. Dark-haired and slight, he was Harry Flood, the ex-Scotland Yard inspector drawn to private industry by its far higher salary. His main function at DdK was supervising investigations of major insurance claims and of new people with whom the bank or its insurance affiliates did business. He had spent the morning in a library searching through old society magazines.

He placed the first of the magazines he had found in front of his employer. Open at a picture of her mother in her ruby and diamond set, it had been published two weeks before Madeleine's death. The caption announced that Madeleine de Kronengold had been among the committee members of a charity ball to aid Immigrant House. For a moment Deborah forgot her purpose for examining the picture and stared at her mother's face – as beautiful, with its doglike brown eyes under fans of lashes, as caring, as alive as Deborah remembered her. The time between now and then dropped away. You're going to be a grandmother, Deborah wanted to tell her. In my body is the same yearning to have a child that impelled you to take me in and love me. I wish with all my heart I had somehow been able, at the very moment you glanced into this camera, to tell you how much I loved you.

Sudden remorse – for the thousandth time in the intervening years – swept over Deborah: her mother had died not knowing how much her daughter loved her.

The detective forced her attention to the jewellery her mother wore. 'Here are very similar angles in the shots taken last night.'

For several minutes, stone by stone, Deborah compared the two sets of photographs. There could be no doubt: her mother's jewellery and April's were identical!

Deborah fell back in her chair, gazing at the desk top, but her eyes unfocused now, as she tried to comprehend the implications of this discovery. Could two identical sets of such spectacular pieces have been made? Even if Bash had not been telling the truth about generations of ownership, it was still possible that his family had bought an identical set from the jeweller who had created her mother's, although the firm would hardly be likely to risk the Kronengolds' anger by making a second set.

As if reading her thoughts, Flood produced a photograph published in the *Queen* at the end of 1963, a few months after Deborah's departure from England and six and a half years after her mother's death. It was a wedding photograph of April and Bash. He looked quite handsome, if nervous, in his morning coat. April's wedding dress had a full skirt and loose bodice – to hide her pregnancy, Deborah reasoned. Her face was radiant, triumphant in fact. She was wearing the jewellery.

The detective stolidly recounted the facts. He had been unable to find any record of the jewellery in either the bride's or the groom's family before the date of the photograph. The caption under their wedding photograph stated that 'the superb ruby and diamond parure was a gift to the bride from her husband'.

'What's the next step in such a situation?' Deborah wanted to know.

'I'm going to check whether there's any record of insurance of the jewellery.'

'Is that difficult?'

He chuckled. 'It helps to work for an insurance company. We all lend each other a hand. Do you know anyone who might recall what happened to that jewellery after your mother's death?'

'I've been told there was no jewellery left when she died.'

'Try and think, miss. There has to be somebody who still remembers. I'll come back later.'

Harry Flood reminded Deborah of a mongrel terrier: tenacious, single-minded. A good ratter, she thought. He would keep what he learned confidential while flushing every fact from every burrow.

After he had left, Deborah's index fingers formed a steeple, the apex touching her lips. Her focus glazed again. There was a mystery here that Deborah sensed was a key to the events surrounding her mother's death. Leslie had told her when she asked for her inheritance that nothing was left of her mother's to inherit. Yet, according to the date of the magazine, three weeks before her mother died she wore jewellery that even in those deflated times had to be worth at least several hundred thousand pounds.

What had happened between early 1957, when her mother last appeared in it, and late 1963, when April first wore it? Deborah could find few logical explanations. The least sensible was that her mother had disposed of the pieces in the few weeks preceding her death. The probability of that was so slight Deborah decided to disregard that explanation immediately and concentrate on likelier ones. There were only two: Leslie had sold the jewellery to Rob Rowell (Bash was a teenager then) or Rob Rowell had taken the jewellery. But, if he had taken the jewellery, he would have had to do so with Leslie's tacit acquiescence – Leslie had not told her that the jewellery had been stolen but, rather, that there *was* no jewellery, that her mother had disposed of it well before her death. Another possibility was that it had been stolen but Leslie had wanted to hide the fact from her because he had collected and kept the insurance money. Her mother was a cautious woman. Harry Flood was right: there would have been insurance.

She strongly doubted that Rob Rowell had *bought* the jewellery from her mother or, later, from Leslie. Among the bits of financial gossip her grandfather had conveyed during their long talks on his yacht was that the Rowell bank was shaky at that time because Egypt had nationalized the Rowells' substantial assets in that country during the turmoil leading up to the Suez crisis. Her recollection of Rob Rowell was that he was not one to lay out exorbitant sums of money, even if his rise from near insolvency had been dramatic enough to permit such a purchase only six years later. He would proably have given his son's bride something he already owned. And, after all that time, he might have thought it safe to allow the jewellery to emerge from its hiding place. One possibility she could discount: even after six years, Rob would have found it impossible simply to buy the jewellery from Leslie, the man he had cuckolded and made his enemy.

With the utmost logic Deborah advanced upon the likeliest explanation: Rob Rowell had taken those jewels – perhaps others as well – with Leslie's complicity! She brooded for a long while on the kind of unholy alliance Leslie and Rob might have forged. It was certainly one that Bash might never have known about. Conceivably, Bash might well believe that his father came by these jewels honestly, that in fact they were in the family's vaults for generations. With only two people involved in the conspiracy, Leslie and Rob, and both having every reason to keep silent, how was she to crack the shell sealed around them? Then she remembered what Flood had asked her: was there someone else who might have known about the jewellery?

The Members' Terrace at the House of Commons was crowded. It was a beautiful afternoon, and everyone wanted to take tea outdoors. Gladys Wood was already sitting waiting for her when Deborah arrived.

Since leaving Oxford, Gladys Wood had become a force in the Labour Party, a Member of Parliament and, in the Callaghan government, given a junior ministerial post that marked her as a comer. She had managed to retain her seat despite the previous year's Conservative victory under Margaret Thatcher, although Deborah knew from previous conversations that Gladys felt useless in a fracturing minority party that had worsened, not arrested, the nation's decline. Still a firebrand, she had learned over the years not to take herself quite so seriously.

'Look at them all, Dee.' Gladys gleefully indicated the most staid Conservative members at nearby tables. 'I always come here with scruffy Marxist professors and pugnacious union leaders who give them a tough time. They can't believe I'm here with Deborah de Kronengold. They're stunned!'

After a few minutes Deborah introduced the favour she had come to ask. She wanted to trace her mother's maid, and Gladys had been at the Ministry of Social Security under the previous government. Deborah was hoping old social security records might help. She had written down all the information she had: her mother's full name and date of birth, the address of the London house to which she had moved, and the name Irma. She had no idea what the maid's last name was.

'There must be thousands of Irmas in Britain,' Gladys remarked when she looked up.

'My mother must have been dealing with her benefits. If you could trace my mother's payment records, you might be able to find the woman's surname and where she is now.'

'I made some good friends in the ministry, but there's so little to go on –'

Deborah leaned forward abruptly. 'It's all I have!'

Gladys was shocked to hear the faint tone of desperation in her old friend's voice.

CHAPTER TWENTY

The following night Deborah was back in New York to be guest of honour at a dinner to raise money for several charities. She usually declined such things, preferring instead to make a contribution. But this award had been voted to her by the top executives of the nation's major investment institutions. Never before had it been awarded to one so young or to a woman. Even David, so competitive, subtly playing down her successes in a joking way, had expressed his admiration, confessing that he would give a lot to win that particular accolade from the financial community. Her companion for the evening, he was a financial power in his own right and had been asked to sit on the dais with twenty or so other important figures in finance. Deborah had joked that, if he hadn't been asked, he would have sulked straight through to next year's dinner.

When the lights dimmed, Deborah was introduced, and a single spot-light picked her out as she stepped onto the stage to take her place of honour. She could not see the people at the tables, but she could imagine them. Seventeen years ago none of them would give her a job because she was a woman. She had proved herself to them. Seventeen years ago, her father, Leslie, had denied her entry into the family bank. Very soon she would make good her threat to him.

That night David returned to her apartment with her. She slipped into a silk peignoir and joined him in the sitting room on the top floor of her triplex, part of her bedroom suite. She moved toward the taupe-coloured velvet sofa on which he sat. The lights were softly lit, allowing the windows on Central Park West, across the park, to glow in columns of nearer stars.

She had chosen this night to reveal her pregnancy to him. Now she hesitated. There was still a chance that Bash might be lost to her because of his deceit. What if she lost David too when he learned about her baby – or that she had no intention of divulging who the father was? As she settled herself on the sofa, David mentioned that he had seen her father in London. This touched on the other topic she wished to discuss with him, and Deborah did not want him to mistake her intentions about it. She came right to the point.

'David, you know my animosity toward my father. I want you to stop making any loans to him or investing in his bank. He's desperate for cash. Don't prop him up.'

David chuckled at what he perceived to be a transparent ploy to slow down his firm's growth in Britain. 'You invested in a British merchant bank in order to have your own British operation. Now you make a fuss if I consider doing the same for myself. You can't have it both ways.'

'That isn't the reason – I have no objection to our both dealing with the *French* Kronengold bank. There are a lot of other merchant banks in England you could acquire. Stay away from Leslie's.'

'Dee, my company is as big as yours – and we're growing fast in finance.' He smiled slyly. 'Maybe you're just worried about the competition. How can you possibly stop me?'

'I can, David. Trust me on the point. Please.' She did not want him hurt. 'I'm going after Leslie very soon. Please don't be in the way when I do.'

'You just might find yourself up against both of us.'

'David, let's drop the topic now. I suggest only that you take a look at your Series D debentures.'

'Which ones are they?'

'Just check them, David – *before* you jump into something that isn't your concern.'

His expression scoffed at her bluff, then it softened. 'Whatever you and your father have against each other, why not forgive and forget? It's about time that you mellowed. Look at me. I don't need to hustle anymore to prove myself.'

Deborah, smiling, reached up to stroke his hair. The black curls were a bit sparser, but one had to stare hard to be sure. Over forty now, he was still well muscled, if a little thicker at the waist. Deeper furrows lined his forehead, but the gleam of ambition burned as brightly. 'A bit mellower, perhaps, David, but you're still always hustling. Don't fool yourself. It's your secret weapon and your charm.'

She loved him; he was a barely stirred aggregate of cravings and sentiment and cunning that spilled over the top of him in the most human, the most appealing mixtures. She suddenly realized that, for all her confidence about David's reaction when she told him she was pregnant, she really had no idea what it would be. This had been a wonderful night, and she wanted it to continue. She did not want to risk ruining it. There would be time enough to tell David about the baby in the morning.

She bent over gently to kiss him. Their kiss deepened, surrounding them with an oblivion that excluded the entire world. David's free hand slipped to her waist and opened the peignoir. Her breasts were still firm and perfectly proportioned to her slimness. The sight of them was still exciting, arousing to him.

Soon they would make love, Deborah thought. Nothing else would exist for her when they did. Not Leslie. Not the tiny creature growing inside her.

She slipped off the peignoir, and a peal of laughter broke from her throat as she conjured up what was soon to come: the joy of his body in hers! The familiar, indescribable, wonderful joy!

Deborah woke to lightening greyness. Propping her elbows on the bed she looked at David. His brow was clenched by some disturbing dream. His eyelids fluttered as if he wanted desperately to wake from it. She kissed him, her hand massaging his knotted chest muscles.

'Wake up, David.'

His eyelids parted. He smiled and kissed her.

'David, we both have to get dressed for work soon, and there's something important I wanted to tell you.'

He hugged her. 'Let's make love.'

'This is too important to wait.'

'Would you waste an erection the size of the Empire State Building?'

'We'll make love afterwards . . . if you still want to,' she confessed and sat up to face him.

'I'd still want you in the middle of a nuclear attack.'

'I'm counting on that.' In spite of a dozen rehearsals in her mind, a hundred assurances to herself that she had correctly calculated how he would take it, she was suddenly unsure. 'David, I'm pregnant . . . it's by choice. But I don't know who the father is.'

He stared at her. 'You're – what?' His voice caught. 'You're pregnant?'

'Yes, David.' She stroked his hand that lay across his chest.

'And the father – you don't know who . . . Shit!'

He fought his rage at the implication that he was not the only man in her life, a possibility he had always deluded himself into rejecting. They had a pact – he was not to question her private life if it did not concern him. He dared not risk expressing his jealousy and losing her as a result. He waited until he had control of himself before continuing. Only then did he comprehend the second implication.

'You mean, I could be –?'

'It doesn't matter who the father is.'

His breath rushed from his lungs in a long sigh, like a collapsing balloon's. He had spent his childhood without his father and had missed him desperately. That thought prompted the emergence from the archives of his memory of the image of his father, dressed as a German officer, with a redheaded woman and her child – Deborah. It had been years since his thoughts had wandered back to his father's confession when he knew he was dying. It might have been just a myth, a tale spun out of imagination, if it were not for the document David remembered was secreted in his bank vault: a German army pass Max had filled in himself that permitted unrestricted travel throughout German-occupied Italy for a colonel and the woman and child pretending to be his wife and their infant daughter.

David had promised his father to keep to himself the secret of Deborah's parentage unless divulging it was absolutely essential. Deborah was about to have a baby, perhaps *his*, and she should know who her child's grand-parents were. *His* child, he mused. He would adore a child. Someone to carry on the Holtz heritage. But what if Deborah was so repelled by the knowledge he harboured that she aborted her baby? And what if, someday, he really did need to use that information for some ultimate strategy? Last night, she had threatened him over his proposed alliance with Leslie. If indeed she did have some means of her own to attack him, he might well need the weapon embodied in that secret. There was another reason to say nothing: his single goal in life was to make good the vow he had made to his father to infiltrate and then to subdue and eventually to own the Kronengolds; he could not chance alienating them by revealing the secret they had guarded all Deborah's life. And so, he kept silent.

'David, this doesn't have to change anything between us,' Deborah said softly. She put her hands on either side of his face, hoping the sincerity of her love for him would flow into him like a current.

'You can't believe not knowing who your child's father is won't change things.' His voice grew more emphatic. 'Damn it, Dee, you're too careful a woman not to know who the father is. I want a child. *Your* child. A father has rights.'

She heard the possessiveness in his words and stiffened her resolve. 'You – no one – will ever know. If you can't accept my child and love it for itself, as you love me – without making claims as if it were mining territory – then I had better know now.'

David faltered. 'I have to think about it.'

'I already have.' Deborah tried to make him understand.

'A child needs a father,' he cried out. 'I know.'

Her voice grew steel-hard. 'And I know how destructive a father can be. This child will have no father.'

'Dee, we've found her, your mother's maid. Her name is Irma Fingers.' Gladys Wood's voice was faint over the transatlantic cable, but Deborah heard her distinctly.

'Yes, that sounds familiar.'

'I've spoken to her on the phone. She'll see you.'

'How soon?'

'Can you make it tomorrow?'

'I'll be there first thing in the morning. Where is it?'

'Oh, that's what I was saving up to surprise you with. You know it very well. She's the head housekeeper at your family's old estate, Clove Hill.'

Deborah directed Penny, her executive secretary, to cancel all her appointments for the next two days, make the rest of the week tentative, and advise Harry Flood to be at Clove Hill at eleven o'clock the following morning – she would be arriving at 10.30, but wanted to speak to Irma Fingers alone first. At the end of the week she had arranged to fly to Paris for further negotiations with her uncle Pierre, but if necessary she could go straight from London. She did not have to telephone David about her change in plans – a few hours earlier his secretary had cancelled their dinner date, saying he had just been called out of town by an emergency.

Deborah had been displeased he had not telephoned himself, especially after the row they had had in the morning. He had stormed into her office unannounced after learning that she and her friends controlled his Series D debentures – they had refused to sell to him, regardless of what he offered. Being able to call upon a majority of the debentures, Deborah could vote him and his entire board of directors out of office at ten days' notice.

'You have a rope around my neck!' he had roared. She had calmed him down with the promise that they would discuss it that night. Now, on consideration, with both that issue and the baby agitating their relationship, she was glad about the cancellation. Perhaps the few days apart would serve to soothe his ruffled feathers.

Alone in the cabin of her 707, Deborah sat at her desk and worked for several hours. But, when the hostess withdrew after serving dinner, Deborah dimmed the cabin lights and moved to one of the deep grey seats. For a long while she watched the stars burn through the blackness outside and sat thinking. Once she had warned Bash of her retaliation if she learned he had ever lied to her or had failed to reveal the slightest thing he had ever done to hurt her. If he had knowingly kept jewels her mother had intended for her, then Bash had a lot to answer for.

Oh God, let it all be a terrible mistake he knew nothing about! she prayed. Let it all be like it was, full of love. That's all I wanted for me and my baby, that it just stay the way it was with Bash and with David.

Deborah reflected on their reaction to the baby. So sure that keeping to herself the name of her child's father was the right thing to do, she had failed to weigh heavily enough that they might want a child too or be jealous of a rival. She had desired a child so much, had thought so hard about the months she would be carrying it, the pain and risk of death she would have to undergo in giving birth to it, the fear that a father might try to take her child's love from her, that she had failed to understand the feelings of the men in her life. Her own fathers had been Leslie – destructive, hateful – and an anonymous hazy figure integrated into her biology. She could not conceive of any other paternal relationship. But now she wondered whether asking the men in her life to love her, despite possibly carrying another man's child, might not have been a way of testing the depth of their love. The chance she had taken worried her.

Despite all her contemplation in the limousine from the airport to Clove Hill, Deborah was not prepared for the emotions that inundated her as the car approached the property. When she had left England in 1963, she had closed off behind her an entire life. She no longer thought of herself as Deborah de Kronengold – although the name ultimately proved both unavoidable and useful – but as a different being begetting herself anew in the United States. She had set herself free of the centuries of national and family traditions dragging behind her like a chain of wheelless carts. She owed them nothing. Her subsequent relationships with uncles, aunts, and cousins had not dispelled that sense of separation.

Only twice before her rupture with Leslie had she investigated her past. As a child she had reluctantly accepted what was related to her about her adoption. When she was seventeen, on her Italian vacation, she had vainly checked birth records in Turin and at the orphanage. Now, once more, the past had caught her up in its coils, not to drag her back to her own murky beginnings, which no longer interested her, but to the event that was still an open wound in her soul: her mother's death.

Watching the Great Lawn move past the windows on one side of the limousine and the progression of ancient, gnarled oaks on the other, Deborah suddenly found herself struggling against an eerie perception that the car was stationary in front of a moving shot in an old film of Clove Hill. Nothing had changed: lines of red and yellow tulips still ran the length of the flower beds; a gardener was crouched as usual over the white lilies of the valley; and, farther up, near the turn in the driveway, small pink clouds floated about the rhododendron bushes as they did every spring. Beyond the bushes, forming the termination of one of the mansion's turreted wings, loomed the conservatory – glass supported into a dome by black iron ribs and enclosing a mass of tall foliage. Only at the entrance gates to the estate had she noticed a difference, a sign discreetly announcing that the property was owned for the nation by the National Trust.

The car drew to a halt before the wide stone terrace that lay between the driveway and the entrance to the house. The old movie contained a final touch of verisimilitude, tumbling her consciousness toward feelings she had sloughed off like an old, constricting carapace when she had first kicked away from England and all that had meant home. Nine former servants, like spectres, stood awaiting her in a line in front of the steps, a guard of honour in familiar livery presenting their homage. None was youthful. Most were grey- or white-haired, with faces she recognized and some she could put names to. Amid her turbulent emotions, she still comprehended that their welcome represented the bond of duty between them and departed Kronengolds they and their predecessors had faithfully served.

One man – he had been a footman, she remembered – stepped up to open the limousine's door before the chauffeur could come round to it.

He bowed as she emerged from the black car. 'Welcome back, miss,' he said, evidently so moved he was barely able to emit the words.

Deborah found herself beaming as she took his hand. 'Thank you so much. Claypool, isn't it?'

'Yes, miss,' he muttered. 'Thank you, miss.'

'You're looking well. What's your job now?'

'Maintenance, miss. I'm in charge of it.'

'No wonder the place looks so well.' Her voice betrayed her disorientation. 'And not a day older.'

'I've tried, miss,' he replied proudly.

Deborah spoke to each in turn. They had all been kept on by the National Trust. One was the old cook from whom she used to steal cooling biscuits ('A terrible rascal you were, miss – in and out of the kitchen too quick for me to scold you') and another was a gardener who also still cared for the wildly coloured birds strutting across the grass. Then, a startlingly youthful face.

'Old Jamison!'

'Begging your pardon, miss, but Young Jamison. My dad passed on some seven years now.'

'Of course, I should have known. I'm so sorry.' She remembered the man before her as a stable boy, being trained by his father someday to replace him. 'Is Gypsy's nameplate still over the old box stall?' she asked.

He looked at his feet and answered her haltingly. 'The

stables burned down last year. There's a concrete garage now.'

Deborah touched his arm impulsively. The two of them understood, as perhaps none other there could, that the change reflected the displacement of an entire way of life.

The last person in the line, standing beside Jamison, was a round, greying woman in her late fifties of average height, a ring of keys hanging from the waist of her black dress. Deborah remembered a thinner face with those grey eyes and darker hair.

'And you're Irma Fingers.'

The woman bobbed her head anxiously. 'Yes, miss.'

'You're the one I've come to speak to.' Deborah turned to the others. Emotion strained her voice. 'Thank you. Thank you all for being here to greet me today. It seemed quite as it used to be.'

She smiled at them, seeing younger faces, hearing in her mind's ear phantom voices of people long gone. Then she greeted the man waiting at the entrance who managed Clove Hill for the National Trust, and went inside with Irma.

Deborah had expected that the first sight of the vast entrance hall, with its remembered furniture and paintings and the great stairway advancing up to the second floor beside faded medieval tapestries, might trigger off once more the grief or even a touch of the self-hatred that had hung about her through much of her adolescence, but instead she found herself filled with hope.

The drawing room too was unchanged, even to the green silk brocade wall covering her mother had had installed from floor to gilded moulding. Still in place above that, Deborah saw, was the minstrels' gallery from which she and April had spied on the adults. Max Holtz had been there that day, and Nathan. She recalled how her mother had spun away from Rob Rowell abruptly, her white pleated skirt seeming from above to open like a blossom.

Amid all these memories might lie the liberating truth within the dark miasma of her mother's death.

Irma Fingers settled her plump figure onto a red silk sofa, taking care not to touch the upholstered armrests on the gilded wood. She straightened her dress, which seemed to billow from bosom to floor like black water arching downwards in gentle cataracts. To put her at her ease, Deborah asked her about herself.

Like most of those employed at Clove Hill, Irma had been born in the nearby village. She was sixteen when she had first come there to work as an upstairs maid. One summer Madeleine de Kronengold's personal maid had left her service to get married. By then a trusted employee, Irma assumed the job and went to London with her mistress in the autumn. She held the position for many years. After Madeleine's death, she worked for a family in Scotland, returning to the village to care for her aging father in 1968. Hearing that a job was available at Clove Hill, she took it and had worked her way up to head housekeeper.

'It must be a ghastly nuisance to keep this huge house clean with hundreds of sightseers swarming through,' Deborah offered sympathetically. Irma nodded vigorously – a responsive chord had been struck. Deborah went on. 'Irma, I want to speak to you about the day my mother died. You and I talked on the telephone that morning, remember? Right after my grandfather's death. I wanted to speak to my mother and had telephoned from Spain while I was waiting for a plane.'

Irma began fidgeting with her keys, eyes averted. 'I thought that was what you were coming here about. She was so good to me – always – to everyone.'

'You mean my mother.'

'Yes, miss. Losing her that day was as bad as losing my own mum. She only had *me* then to look after her, you see. She was alone then.'

'Was there someone she needed protection from?' Deborah prodded.

A tortured look appeared in Irma's eyes. Fear was wrestling with honesty. Finally she blurted out, 'It was my duty to look after her. I never trusted him, even with him being an earl and all.'

'Who, Irma?'

'Lord Kronengold told me it was all right about the safe being empty, that he knew all about it – and him being an honourable man, regardless of him having a falling out with my mistress. Really broken up he was by her death. A woman can tell those things. I never understood why she should leave such a fine, correct man. Lord Kronengold, I mean. He was very good to me.'

'But Lord Kronengold was dead.'

'No, it's the new lord I'm talking about, Mr. Leslie. He

said not to tell anyone about that night – it could stain her name, he said. I never did. I loved your mum too much to do that to her memory.' Irma twisted the keys in agony. 'I never told anyone. Your mum died with a good name, miss.'

'I want you to tell me about it, Irma.'

'Oh, no, miss. There are things sometimes it's better for a child not to know about her mother.'

'I already know about her love affair with Rob Rowell.'

Irma reacted with surprise, but the worry did not lift. 'There are other things. I promised your father I wouldn't tell a soul. But, pardon my saying so, miss, he was just too trusting.'

'Whatever happened, Irma, believe me, it's important that I know.'

Relief flooded the older woman's eyes. 'I've been wanting to tell someone all these years, but afraid too.'

'I'll protect you, if need be, Irma. But you must tell me.'

Haltingly, Irma began to talk about the day Madeleine died. A snow-storm had raged all day, and she had been anxiously awaiting her mistress's return to the London house from the airport with Deborah. Suddenly, she heard a noise on the floor below and went to investigate. She found Rob Rowell coming out of Madeleine's bedroom carrying a small satchel he claimed to have left there several days earlier. He told Irma that Madeleine had dropped him off at the railway station, that he had taken a train back from the country while she went on to the airport.

Irma thought his actions and story suspicious. She did not recall that satchel in the bedroom, but could find nothing missing after he rushed from the house. Irma was not worried that valuables might have been taken because they, including all Madeleine's jewellery, had been securely locked in the bedroom safe before the weekend.

A few days later Leslie came to the house with a probate official, and they opened the safe in Irma's presence. It was empty. Irma tried to speak up about the things that were missing, but Leslie hushed her and shooed her from the room.

'He was so worried about your mum's good name, you see.'

'Did my father say anything more to you?'

'He came to my room when the other man had gone. I tried to tell him about the jewels that were missing and the wills and the money and the –'

'She had a will?' Deborah's intensity startled Irma. 'Are you certain?'

'Why shouldn't I be certain?' Irma replied in a tone that suggested her honesty had been questioned. 'I was one of the witnesses, me and Sarah the cook, who's gone these ten years from leukaemia.'

'She had a will!' Deborah repeated numbly. Leslie had told her Madeleine died without a will, that Deborah had been forgotten by her mother – abandoned a second time.

Under Deborah's questioning it emerged that Leslie had procured Irma's silence about the matter by convincing her that Madeleine had been a secret gambler and owed a fortune to criminals. If those awful, ruthless men didn't get paid, Leslie explained to her, they would ruin Madeleine's and her children's names. Perhaps even kill the children. He also asserted that he had asked Rob Rowell to pay off the gamblers with the jewels and money in order to protect young Deborah and Richard and to keep scandal from Madeleine's name. He frightened Irma further by maintaining that the authorities might blame her for stealing the items in the safe if she mentioned them. He sacked all Madeleine's other servants, but continued to pay Irma for six months until he found her new employment in Scotland.

'Irma, think carefully. Do you remember my mother having a ruby and diamond set of jewellery?'

The housekeeper nodded. 'Certainly, miss. A necklace, a bracelet, a ring, and earrings with great hanging rubies. Beautiful they were, and must have cost a fortune. She loved them. Wore them to really important balls and such.'

'Please think very carefully. Were they locked in the safe when she went away that last weekend?'

'Absolutely. That's what I tried to tell Mr. Leslie. She had been out late the night before, wearing them, and locked them up good and tight in the safe when we were packing her things to go off to the country that weekend. That's how I know the wills and the bonds and everything else were locked in the safe. I saw them.'

'You keep saying "wills", as if there was more than one.'

'That's what I've been trying to tell you, miss. There was hers and Lord Kronengold's . The one he signed just before he and you went off on that trip. John Collins, the butler –

you remember John, miss – well, John swore to me he was a witness to that will.'

Deborah seized the woman's hand. 'How can you be sure my grandfather had this new will in the safe?'

'Because I knew everything that was in my mistress's safe. She trusted me, miss,' Irma said proudly. 'When I helped her put away the things in the safe the day we moved to the new house, I saw the envelope for the first time. I can tell you the exact words on it, "Samuel, Lord Kronengold's Last Will and Testament'. And it never left that safe until Mr. Leslie and that other man opened it and found everything was gone.'

'But it could have been a will he signed earlier?'

'John Collins lived not a hundred yards from me in the village. John swore till the day he died he was witness to a will for Lord Kronengold just a few days before you all went off on that boat, and your grandfather couldn't have had time to make another. We read about some will in the papers, but it couldn't have been the same one.'

Deborah had been edging further forward in her chair with each revelation. Now she fell back as if overwhelmed by the facts. Not only her mother's jewellery, money, and bonds had been taken, but the wills under which both her mother and her grandfather would have – must have – provided for her. Leslie had somehow connived with Rob Rowell to steal and destroy wills that favoured Deborah, wills executed at a later date that would rightly take precedence in court. That was why Leslie had claimed her mother died without a will and why the terms of Samuel's earlier will were acted upon. Deborah nearly cried out her jubilation. Her mother and grandfather had not abandoned her. On the contrary, Leslie had maliciously hacked apart the hawsers that had snugly secured her to them. Once more it had been Leslie at the heart of the plot to set her adrift. Rob Rowell got the jewellery and maybe cash and securities to put his tottering bank back on its feet. But Leslie had got much more: the bulk of Samuel de Kronengold's fortune – and Deborah at his mercy.

Deborah had one last question. 'Irma, did my mother say anything . . . of . . . anything personal about me when you telephoned her in the country that morning?'

'No, miss, she just asked me to repeat the message so she could write it down. She was broken up something terrible over Lord Kronengold's death.'

'But you're sure she left me no message . . . oh, of affection or anything of that kind.'

'Only that she was going off to the airport for you.'

The hollowness felt cold and infinite in Deborah's chest, like a bottomless cave into which she had dropped the little question. She would probably never know whether her mother was aware at the instant of her death that her daughter loved her. Deborah's wealth was now so vast that the value of the ruby and diamond set was equivalent to a dime-store trinket to other women. The primary attraction of the jewellery to her was that her mother had adored it and, like a talisman, Deborah believed, would have passed it on to her daughter under that missing will, to signify the love she felt for her. Possessing that jewellery, Deborah would know that she was loved. Damn Rob Rowell! She cursed him silently. He had stolen from Deborah the objects that signified her mother's love.

At that point Deborah summoned Harry Flood, who had been waiting in the carpark. Under Deborah's urging Irma agreed to write down all the facts and sign the statement. He would witness the housekeeper's signature. Deborah thanked her and left the room.

Oblivious to her surroundings, Deborah glided through carefully preserved rooms and gardens locked into a changeless past that actual residents – living people – would not have tolerated. Nothing she saw registered on her awareness. She might have been travelling through interstellar space, isolated within a cylinder chilled down to absolute loathing. She had hated Leslie before, but there had been a residue of petulance then, a thwarted child's desire to extract from her father, if not the affection she craved, at least the satisfaction of having provoked him to antagonism. Once or twice in the last few years – as her own rise permitted magnanimity and his incompetence had often caused him to stumble – she had even allowed herself to admit to flashes of pity for Leslie. Now, the revelation of the full measure of his crimes so embittered her that the last drop of pity lingering in her heart was frozen to a dagger of ice. Her hatred was distilled to its purest essence. Mercy was a barren rock she had passed a million light-years ago. She was headed unalterably now for the outermost blackness of primal revenge – the original black hole he had opened in the very centre of her being.

Harry Flood found her in a formal garden, staring at the statue she and Samuel had been viewing when he told her he wished to assume responsibility for her education. She was clenching and unclenching her fists with every surge of emotion. Finally, she noticed the ex-detective standing to the side with his notepad out. She beckoned him to a nearby bench and asked him to report on his investigations since last seeing her.

The first thing he had learned was that Madeleine had taken out her own insurance policy on her jewellery when she moved from Leslie's house. The policy was paid up at her death, but no claim was ever made and the pieces were never listed in her estate. He would investigate the story of Madeleine's frenzied gambling around the time of her death, but based on what he already knew about her, the possibility that she was a gambler was remote. Leslie had also told Deborah that her mother had died heavily in debt, but there was nothing to substantiate that.

He flipped a page of the notepad. Samuel de Kronengold's only known will was the one filed for probate, he told her, made several months before the voyage. John Collins, the man Irma had mentioned, was not one of its witnesses. No will was filed for Madeleine de Kronengold, who was officially listed as having died intestate.

'All we can be certain of so far, miss,' Flood insisted on reminding her, 'is that your mother's jewellery turned up six years later on April Rowell. We haven't proved Irma Fingers' story one way or the other.'

'But, if Irma *is* telling the truth, one element sticks out oddly. If Rob Rowell did come to the house and rifle the safe, then he had to know my mother would be unable to stop him or go to the police because she was already dead. Irma was waiting for her at home and didn't even know she was dead yet. How did he – hours before anyone else? Or what the safe's combination was?'

'You'd have made a good detective, miss. I've been meaning to check the story he gave the police that he returned to London by train, but other things took priority, like the insurance and trying to find evidence that he might have sold off some of your mother's other jewellery. No luck in that direction so far, but I have an appointment later on today with an acquaintance at British Rail with access to old records. After that I want to go out to the hospital where your mother died.' The detective's manner, usually brusque and straightforward, softened. 'Miss, don't jump to conclusions yet about anyone; your father, Lord Rowell, his son and daughter-in-law.'

'You and I both know that, if Irma Fingers is telling the truth, then everyone else is lying.'

'Or she might have made up that entire story to impress you.'

Either way there was still no proof Bash ever knew that the jewellery belonged to her mother. She wanted so to believe in him.

Deborah directed her chauffeur down a series of roads that led past the little white cottage where she had made love to Bash the day she learned he was going to marry April and where, years before that, she had come upon the sight of her mother naked beneath his father. Several children were playing now outside the house, and other houses had been built along the road. An estate could no longer afford the luxury of a guest house for dalliance, she observed – an irrelevant insight, she supposed, but the only one that came to her out of the numbness brought on by the layers of re-experienced pain.

Neville Cooper was eager to see her when she arrived at her London office. He filled her in on several matters. One was a sizeable loan made to one of the poorer Arab countries. The Rowell bank had let DdK take a large, profitable part in the syndication, but had totally excluded I. Kronengold & Sons. Neville guessed the Arabs were putting the boycott against Leslie's bank into high gear.

'A boycott might make Leslie's clients amenable to switching their merchant-banking affiliation,' Deborah pointed out pragmatically. She began to consider the ramifications. 'Salim has gone to some length to assure me – probably because of the desalination plant – that the Arab nations won't boycott DdK. What if they change their minds?'

'I thought the U.S. prohibited blacklisting after the last Arab boycott?'

'Some U.S. banks still ignore it. They're full of Arab money they have to placate. The U.S. depends heavily on Arab oil and might decide to favour Arab interests over DdK. What about the British?'

Neville shrugged his shoulders. 'The government here has

been kow-towing to the Arabs since the original boycott years ago. It even processes the compliance certificates Arab countries request from companies trading with them, to make sure the companies aren't dealing with Israel. If the Arabs go after us here, we can't expect any help from the British government or probably any other country in Europe – the French passed an anti-boycott law and then exempted the Arabs from it, the only ones boycotting. That's one of the risks we face if we link up with the French Kronengold bank.'

Neville's final item concerned Leslie. Only that morning Leslie had telephoned the Swiss banker whom he believed had made his loan. He was frantic to arrange a meeting to discuss postponing the massive repayment, now only a few weeks off.

Deborah's gaze went, as it often did in this office, through the stacked windowpanes to the frosted glass dome several blocks away, above the Kronengold bank. Her first view from below it had dazzled her, as if she was under a great silver bell. Now she pictured Leslie trapped beneath it, awaiting an answer from Switzerland, betraying his anxiety only by an eyelid's twitch he could not still. Occasionally his glance might stray to the gold statue of Jacob stealing Esau's birthright, and he would wonder if everything he had lied and cheated to amass was about to be wrenched from his sweating fingers.

Despite Harry Flood's admonition, she believed Irma Fingers, and she believed that somewhere there had to be proof.

'Tell André to get the Swiss bank to hold off from giving Leslie an answer,' Deborah finally declared, shifting back to Neville.

'Gold has been dropping since the high in January. He probably thinks if he can delay long enough, it will come back to where it was. And, with it, so will his debt.'

'I think gold *will* go lower, but nowhere near the price it was when he first borrowed.'

'He can't possibly repay the loan at the end of the month.'

'He might not have to,' Deborah replied, her expression as hard as Neville had ever seen it. 'He might be behind bars by then.'

Deborah's intercom buzzed. Her London secretary said a man was telephoning from Paris who claimed he was the lawyer for her uncle Pierre and that it was urgent he speak to Deborah. Deborah took the call.

She had met Alain Arnaud, her uncle's lawyer, several times

during the recent months' discussions about a possible union of her and her French cousins' banking interests in France. He had represented Pierre for many years and was one of the few people near her uncle she knew he trusted without reservation.

'*Allo. Deborah de Kronengold ici*,' she announced.

'You must come at once,' the lawyer told her. 'Pierre de Kronengold is asking for you. He is dying.'

CHAPTER TWENTY-ONE

As far as Alain Arnaud had been able to disentangle the events of the last days and briefly report them to Deborah, Pierre had collapsed before leaving for work several days earlier. An ambulance rushed him to a discreet private hospital nearby. The family doctor and specialists diagnosed that he had suffered a stroke. A blood vessel had ruptured in an inoperable region of his brain. After two days, he was still unconscious with no possibility of surgical therapy. Pierre's wife, Simone, ordered that he be removed to their Paris home with all the medical people and equipment to care for him – she wanted no word of his condition to leak out to a gossip-hungry press, she explained.

The next day, miraculously, he opened his eyes and spoke, very weak though he was, but with all his faculties. The doctor did not minimize the severity of his illness to Pierre, who demanded that his lawyer be summoned at once. When Arnaud arrived, Pierre explained the gravity of the situation and directed that his French relatives, nearly all of whom were smaller shareholders in the French bank, be called. He asked for his niece Deborah as well. He wanted to see them all as a group before he died.

Alone in the main saloon of her jetliner, tears rimming her eyes throughout the brief flight to Paris, Deborah was comforted by the thought that Pierre had made a special point of including her among the people to whom he wished to say good-bye. Since Nathan's death a few years before, Pierre remained the lone figure of an earlier generation for whom she felt deep affection, despite the unremitting nature of her aunt Simone's jealousy and of their son Gilbert's viciousness.

Deborah's eyelids clamped shut to hold back the tears. She was struck by the irony that her uncle's fine rational brain, and not the frail-looking body, should be the cause of his demise. So practical, so French, Pierre's mind had also contained just enough aberrant pathways of the dreamer to endow him with kindness and originality. Now it was failing him, the veins and arteries collapsing one after another until he was delicately yet firmly strangled.

She felt such love for this gracefully aging relation who had always loved her unquestioningly, who had once told her that her eyes when he first saw her looked like cabochon sapphires. His act of arbitrary generosity – picking her at random from the orphanage – had rescued her from an anonymous life she could not even begin to imagine and had placed her within the luxury of his sister's family. Her consolation now was that Pierre had lived a full life.

She wondered whether he had included her among those called to his bedside because he sought quick agreement now on the terms of a merger, thus ensuring his family's security within a larger, stronger financial institution. If that was what he wanted, she would gladly absorb his bank, and be generous in her terms because she loved him. But her reluctance to go forward with her cousin Gilbert as her most significant partner in the French operation lay on her stomach like an unpleasantly heavy meal. Perhaps Pierre thought that she could hold in check his son's high-handedness.

Although none of her other French relatives was as difficult as Gilbert, they were a diverse lot. Pierre had been able to keep them together as shareholders in a single spiral galaxy revolving about the bank. With him gone, Deborah predicted, entropy would ensue. The bickering French branch would be sundered by the same divisive forces inherent in an egomania that had caused the once-unified Kronengold clan to burst apart everywhere during this century – just as wider empires and cultures were similarly bursting apart. Treacheries and new alliances would eventually cobble together the French Kronengolds in several smaller, less effective banking and industrial entities. The relatives gathering by Pierre's bed like vultures would watch for the last quiver of life, to tear the body and each other apart.

The aeroplane was descending. All that remained of the day was a red pencil line on the western horizon. Above her was a spatter of stars and, somewhere below, the city in which Pierre was dying.

The street lamps cast deep shadows across the family crest carved into the oak door at the entrance of the Kronengold

Palais. The mansion had occupied a full street in the most desirable *arrondissement* for a century and a half. Without thinking, Deborah reached out to trace one of the three crowns she had feared as a child. Triumph of a sort awaited her within.

All eyes turned to Deborah as she was ushered into the red drawing room. Twenty or so relatives were conversing in small groups. Many held coffee cups. Some held stronger drinks. The conversation sputtered into silence, and all heads turned to the doorway. Deborah's eyes slowly swept the room, as if accepting the tribute of their attention, their obeisance to the power she now wielded.

Seated in the centre of the room, on a sofa placed to dominate it, was Simone. Her coffee cup hung from spidery fingers poised just below her mouth.

With lizard-quick movements Simone put down her cup and saucer and made her way to Deborah. She had not aged well. Face lifts had pulled the skin tight along her jaw and cheekbones, but ancient crevasses still ran from nostril to chin and furrowed her upper lip. The corners of her eyes pointed upwards, like a sly old cobra's. Her skin's tightness made her smile seem like an expression of vague alarm. She was dressed in black silk, as if her husband's death was a foregone conclusion.

Deborah sensed both hypocrisy in the warmth of her greeting and Simone's genuine fear about her husband's illness; clearly Simone still loved him very much. She explained in halting phrases that Pierre was slipping in and out of consciousness. They would all be called into his room the next time he was fully conscious.

After a few moments, the two women found themselves joined by a knot of relatives voicing concern about the recently-announced Arab boycott. They wanted to know Deborah's opinion about whether it would spread to the Kronengold banks, to them.

'Other worries come first!' Simone declared forcefully, ending the conversation. She took Deborah's arm. 'Gilbert, I am sure, is eager to see you.' Only then did Deborah realize that her aunt had been speaking to her in English, a subtle insult from one who found the language an unpleasant substitute for the purity of the French she refused to sully on Deborah.

As they made their way across the large room, Deborah spotted her cousin standing by the red damask curtains. He was speaking to two people seated in high-backed chairs that blocked their faces from her view. Gilbert was sleek and round with small eyes, like a well-fed muskrat. He had a thin moustache, dark like his hair, which was cut close to his head. Words like 'merger' and 'voting shares' drifted towards Deborah as she approached. To her he looked anything but heartbroken.

He greeted her with practised hospitality and then introduced one of the other two people: his icily beautiful wife. Deborah had never met her.

'It was a small wedding,' Gilbert apologized perfunctorily. And then he swung a hand toward the second person. 'You know David Holtz, of course.'

Deborah's expression revealed none of her surprise. She had just learned of her uncle's illness. Judging by his relaxed posture in the chair, David had obviously been here a long while.

'Please don't allow me to disturb your negotiations,' Deborah said to the three with a tinge of archness, and moved on with Simone.

During the course of the evening's wait, David tried to isolate Deborah for a *tête-à-tête*. She insisted on maintaining a long conversation with her old friend, her cousin Colette, and then with Colette's brother, Jean-Paul, whom she had long thought to be a talented banker. Finally, they moved off, and David took the seat beside her.

'I'd like to explain about coming to Paris without letting you know, Dee –'

Deborah interrupted him firmly. 'I'm interested only in information about my uncle's condition.'

'Gilbert made me swear not to tell anyone when he called me in New York yesterday.'

Deborah's reply was a hiss the others could not overhear. 'So you came here to scheme with your friend Gilbert. You know better than anyone what my feelings are for my uncle Pierre – better than anyone. David, there's a time when human feelings take precedence over your own self-interest.'

'You've got a hell of a nerve to lecture me on morality,' David rejoined angrily, 'after you secretly arranged to snatch control of my company any time you feel like it.'

'The only topic I'm willing to discuss right now is Pierre's health –' Her voice broke, and she reached for David's hand. 'You know, David, I want to see him once more and say good-bye – and yet I don't. I have this feeling that, as long as we're still waiting to see him, he'll stay alive. Once we see him, then he'll die.'

'Don't give up hope,' David urged. He knew what it was like to watch an older loved one fight death. One became superstitious, illogically anxious about any behaviour that might precipitate a decline in the patient's condition. And he knew, indeed he knew, what Pierre de Kronengold meant to Deborah. 'Never give up hope!'

Pierre awoke in the early morning hours. The doctor hurriedly summoned the relatives to his large bedroom on the second floor. Alain Arnaud, a small, middle-aged man with fierce eyes, was already in the room, as if he had been standing guard all night on his client and friend's behalf.

Pierre lay supine on the bed, blood and glucose dripping from separate bottles into a tube taped to his arm. His brown hair, streaked with grey, was matted wetly to his forehead. He was very pale. His eyes were closed, and dark hollows had been scooped away below them. Deborah thought he had lost consciousness again in the few minutes it took the doctor to descend to summon them from the drawing room. She was terrified that he might have died. The nurse moved swiftly to test for a pulse. The movement roused him; Pierre's eyelids fluttered, then parted. His gaze took a moment to focus and then slowly moved along the succession of sombre faces. It seemed to rest an instant on Deborah, she thought, before moving on.

Just keep him alive, she implored.

'You are all here as witnesses,' Pierre declared, his voice hoarsely subdued, but audible in the silence. 'After I die . . . there must be no question of my intentions.' He paused to gain strength. 'I have made . . . many sacrifices . . . many mistakes. But always for the good of the family, to . . . to hold it together . . . to restore its glory.' His mouth pinched sadly. 'And I have failed. The Kronengolds – all of us – we are a shadow of what we once were. Weak . . . easy prey. . . .'

Pierre's eyelids drifted together, and there was a long moment during which he appeared to have lost consciousness once more. Murmuring began to be heard from those in the room until the eyelids separated again. And, when they did, he was staring straight at Deborah.

'Only one person can make our name . . . our wealth . . . our honour . . . what it once was. Not only in France. Everywhere. And I have failed her too.' His body and face turned rigid, as if he had been suddenly gripped by a spasm of pain. Then his eyes opened again, with no less pain visible in them. His voice was a whisper, choking, when he forced out the words. 'Deborah, the last service I can do for the family is to tell the truth . . . and hope you can forgive me. The truth –' His voice faltered. 'Deborah, you must save this family when I am gone . . . rebuild it –' He emitted a rasping cough and fought to fill his lungs with air. 'I pass that . . . that duty on to you.'

The most terrible self-reproach shuddered in his eyes as she contemplated his next words. 'It is your duty,' he cried out, 'because you are my daughter!'

Gasps exploded from the listeners' open mouths.

'No, that cannot be! He is delirious!' Simone exclaimed. She hastened to Pierre's bedside. 'You are delirious! You don't know what you are saying!'

He strained to rise up on one elbow, his gaze never leaving Deborah's. Simone tried to hold him down. 'No, you must rest. You are too ill to speak rationally.'

'You are my daughter, Deborah!' he repeated, fighting off his wife's ministrations, trying to speak to Deborah as if only the two of them were in the room. 'You are the flesh of my flesh. I kept silent for the good of the family. But never a day of my life has gone by . . . never a day . . . when I did not ask God and you to forgive me.'

Deborah stood pinned against the wall in shock, unable even to think.

Pierre raised a feeble hand to the ceiling. 'I acknowledge before God and all these witnesses . . . that I am your father.' He began gasping for breath again, trying to marshal the last residue of his strength to render one final service to the family. 'Because I have legally acknowledged you as . . . as my daughter, you can . . . you can now . . . inherit a greater share of my stock . . . in the bank. Yours will be the decisive voice.'

Deborah was filled with horror. The love she had felt for

Pierre was founded on treachery. Wealth, the prize she had struggled and schemed for all her life, was being thrust at her now like a guilt offering – as payment for the agony his shunning of her had caused.

'Forgive me!' Pierre cried out, his arm reaching towards her, pulling taut the tubes connecting veins to hanging bottles. The nurse, too, was now trying to restrain the anguished man.

Deborah remained paralyzed, silent, like a fly caught in amber. And then imperceptibly, seemingly involuntarily, her head began to move from side to side.

'I love you,' he pleaded. 'You know how much I've always loved you.'

She moaned, unable to speak, her head jerking violently in the side-to-side motion.

Pierre fell back onto his pillow. White, sweating, drained of strength, capable only of the nod toward his lawyer, who had removed a sheet of paper from a folder.

Arnaud held it up. 'I have in my possession a written statement made in May 1945, signed by Pierre de Kronengold and witnessed by his cousin Nathan de Kronengold and by a Swiss notary. The document attests to Pierre de Kronengold's . . .' He began to read. ' ". . . paternity of the female infant whom my sister, Madeleine, and her husband, Leslie, and his father, Samuel, have been advised is my natural daughter. Madeleine and Leslie have graciously agreed to adopt her as their own, without revealing her true parentage, and to name her Deborah." ' Arnaud removed his spectacles and turned back to Pierre. 'Is Deborah de Kronengold that child? Your child?'

Pierre nodded weakly. 'Yes,' he whispered. Then, summoning more firmness, he said, 'The will, Alain.'

The lawyer drew another document from the folder and held it up. 'Pierre, Baron de Kronengold, has left to his wife, Simone, and to his son, Gilbert, the portions of his estate to which they are lawfully entitled. In addition sufficient assets will be sold to repay his wife the full outstanding balance of his debt to her. Approximately one-half of his estate, including most of his stock in the bank, has been left to his illegitimate, but lawfully acknowledged, daughter, Deborah.'

'He is crazy!' Gilbert shouted and flung himself at the lawyer, futilely grabbing for the will.

Gilbert was wrestled away by Jean-Paul and several other men.

'You cannot do this to me!' Gilbert hurled at his father.

'He is your son, Pierre,' Simone whined in disbelief. 'How could you do this to him?'

'She is my daughter,' Pierre replied, his voice very weak now. His gaze shifted once more to Deborah. 'And she is the last hope of the Kronengolds.'

Deborah came to life, yet her face appeared white as a corpse's.

'I want nothing from you!' she cried out in agony. 'And I owe nothing to the Kronengolds!'

She glanced left and right. In all the faces she read, not revulsion at Pierre's duplicity or pity at her years of anguish, but hatred of her for having upset their own expectations.

She broke towards the door. A man's hand reached out to stop her. She wrenched her arm away and flung herself into the hallway.

Rushing down the stairs, she heard Pierre crying out her name like a scourge at her back. She had reached the landing halfway down when Pierre's voice was suddenly strangled into silence. A moment later, she heard Simone's wail.

She launched herself down the last flight of steps.

Deborah raced down the street through swirls of early morning mist that tangled about her feet. Her only thought was to get as far away from Pierre's house and the Kronengolds as she could. Pierre may have died, but his dying words, like dragon tongues of flame, and his eleventh-hour confession to buy redemption with the one thing she did not need – his money – had incinerated every tender feeling she had ever had for him.

He had evidently demanded that the few who knew she was his child conspire to keep it secret. The reason was not hard to work out – to hide the evidence of his adultery, probably with some *contadina*, some Italian peasant girl who had died in childbirth, leaving their unwanted infant on his hands. Deborah could not blame Madeleine, who desperately wanted a child and opened her heart to take in her brother's infant. Leslie, Nathan, Samuel, they had all joined the conspiracy for good reasons: to give Deborah a home and to protect Pierre. But they had all denied her the most elemental certainty to which a child can be entitled: that she has been placed in her family by nature and cannot be disclaimed. The fairy tale they had concocted – that Pierre had chosen her at the orphanage – was, for all its poignancy, a brazen lie that had always made her feel she was an outsider among them, undeserving of their love.

Yet the men all knew she was biologically a Kronengold, a part of their family from the very instant of her birth. She was probably acceptable among them only because they knew her to be a Kronengold by blood, and not some homeless waif. The security, the peace of mind, that belonging among them by right should have provided her was, instead, snatched away at the moment they agreed – with typical male sniggering, no doubt – to condone Pierre's irresponsibility. Her own psychological welfare was never considered when her relatives switched her, bereft of a past, secretly, into the empty nursery of the British couple; their concern was the scandal that might have muddied the Kronengold name if a bastard had inconveniently appeared. It mattered not a whit to them that a black hole at the centre of her soul would threaten all her life to swallow her into a pinpoint of nothingness.

She leaned against a building to stop herself from falling over with dizziness and nausea. Her hand went instinctively to her stomach.

I will keep you safe from all this, she vowed to the small life within her, from all the evil and the selfishness and the pain. I will keep you safe from everyone!

David Holtz's taxi was a hundred yards away from the Meurice, Deborah's usual hotel in Paris, when he spotted her in the Rue de Rivoli. He dropped a hundred-franc note into the front of the taxi and sprang out onto the pavement.

'Are you all right?' he asked.

She nodded.

'I stayed a few minutes until things calmed down a little,' he explained.

'He's dead, isn't he?'

'Yes.'

Deborah slipped her arm through David's. They crossed to the flower-bordered paths of the spacious, formal Tuileries Gardens.

'I've known I was adopted since I was five or six,' Deborah explained in a toneless, reluctant voice as they strolled beneath the trees past the roundabout and swings where she used to play when visiting Paris as a child. 'Pierre told me I was an orphan he found at a convent. He and the few others I trusted lied to me all these years.'

'I always thought he was a fine man, an honourable man,' David observed. In two senses David had found Pierre's integrity remarkable indeed: in keeping his word when the war was over to vouch for Max Holtz, whom he no longer needed and must have despised; and in his refusal to condemn David for his father's past.

'I used to think he was the finest man I knew.' Her voice fell to a whisper. 'I would have given anything to have him for a father.'

'His secrecy about being your father is understandable,' David ventured as he glanced at her. 'He was married.'

Her nostrils flared. 'I was a helpless baby. He owed me a greater responsibility than he owed his wife – that fathers never fulfill! Out of a guilty conscience, he extended some affection, but he never took real responsibility for me.'

Turning into the central avenue, Deborah guided David to the Rond Point, where later in the day children with bamboo poles would prod their sailing-boats away from the concrete lip.

David had been deep in thought as they walked. 'That's all you know about your parentage then, what you learned just now?'

She sat on the edge of the pond and stirred the water with a finger, blurring her reflection. 'Yes. That's all.'

David knew much more. He debated inwardly whether to reveal the rest of what his father, on his own deathbed, had divulged about Deborah's birth. The knowledge was both a shield against Deborah and a calumny that would smear his father's – the Holtzes' – name. As his father had admonished him, he finally decided to keep silent until he had no choice but to bargain what he knew for what he wanted.

A terrible awareness seized David that Deborah encompassed all the things he desired, and controlled them. All his satisfaction rested in her hands, but she had rendered him powerless to attain it. Just when he thought he was close to succeeding to the Kronengold heritage by buying into both the British and French Kronengold banks, he discovered first that she controlled those Series D debentures to back her warning that he should not support Leslie's bank, and then, just a few minutes ago, that she had inherited a substantial share of stock in Pierre's bank. Yet those prizes were worthless in comparison to the treasure growing within her body, something he was just as powerless to possess: a child who could carry on after him and give meaning and continuity to all that he had accomplished, as he had done for his own father. Lastly – as firstly – there was Deborah herself: the most beautiful, most desirable woman he had ever known.

The thought was unbearable to him that he would never be able to claim her as his wife and have her totally devoted to him. Or that she might have other lovers – even one. He had driven that possibility from his mind years before, after their reconciliation, believing what he wanted to believe, despite their agreement not to meddle in each other's lives with other people. Knowing that his possessiveness irritated her and threatened her independence, he had decided her recent claim that another man might have fathered her child was simply a pretence to keep him from trying to swamp every area of her personal life. Of course, the child could only be his. *It had to be his!* It must bear his name and recognize his paternity; there must be a dynasty. Not just this child, but many more. Sons with his name. Like those the first Kronengold had sired.

'Dee, I've loved you for as long as I've known you. I want to marry you.'

The raw pain she heard in his voice pierced her and spoke to her own pain. She looked up at him and laid her cheek gently on his knee. 'Dear, dear David. We're trapped, you and I, by who we are and what we want. Marriage would destroy whatever we have. We'd fight constantly. We'd compete about everything. We would hurt each other and end up hurting the child.'

He was charged now by both enthusiasm and desperation. 'That's just it, Dee. That's just it. Being married means the rivalry is over. We'd be one. We could merge our companies into one massive corporation. We'd be working for the same goals then. We could take over your family's French and British banks. I'm almost set to buy into both of them right away – just like that.' He snapped his fingers. 'And your baby would have a father who loves it, and you'd have a husband who adores you.'

David waited in a limbo of agony for Deborah's answer.

When she spoke, her voice was wary. 'I choose to believe that you're concerned about me and my child. I know you love me. But we're such natural rivals, David, that the tiny suspicion always remains that the other is pursuing some ulterior self-interest. We're like wrestlers who can't break for fear the other will seize the moment to get a death grip.'

'It will be different when we're married. There'll be no reason to distrust each other.'

Deborah's laugh was liquid, a brook skipping over all the ironic pebbles in their relationship. 'How funny we are, the two of us. Afraid of you, I arranged to control those bizarre debentures. But, afraid of me, you want to merge and eliminate the threat. I want a child to love – with no father in a position to abandon it, as Pierre did me. But you want me and my child – both of us illegitimate – to carry on your name and legitimize it.' She shook her head at the irreconcilability of what they craved.

'How can you love me and not want to marry me?'

She reached upwards and took his face tenderly between her hands. 'I love you, David. But don't you think I always knew why you and your father were so drawn to the Kronengolds?' She kissed him very gently. 'I cannot give you what you want, David . . . I cannot marry you.'

He clutched her shoulders. 'Please don't refuse. Think about it, Dee,' he pleaded. 'This was a stupid time for me to bring it up.'

'All right, David. We'll talk about it some other time.'

As they walked slowly across the Tuileries, along the quais, and then over the Pont du Carrousel, Deborah talked of her childhood and, for the first time, her feelings then about being adopted. David listened and agonized over whether to reveal the last secret to her. Finally, as they neared the Café de Flore, David decided against it. He could not bring himself to relinquish his final, his only, defence.

Unable to forgive Pierre's cowardice or opportunism or selfishness – whatever it was that had motivated his deceit – Deborah did not attend the private family funeral. She returned alone to New York City on her 707.

Picking up a newspaper on the plane, her eye fell on the headline trumpeting Pierre's deathbed revelation. Suddenly, she was reliving those harrowing moments, seeing again the paper-pale arm stretched towards her, hung from intravenous tubing like a marionette's; the eyes, more white showing than brown, black crescents foretelling death imprinted beneath them; the mouth cursing her with words that begged for absolution. She dropped the newspaper and, for days, refused to read another.

Although separated by three thousand miles of ocean from the other Kronengolds, Deborah still found herself filled with an all-pervasive rage at how she had been used as a child by the relatives who had mattered to her. Normally, business problems could consume her attention totally, but now she found her mind wandering. She had a need to lash out and focus her anger on some object, but found none, and so the anger simply sizzled and bubbled, eating away at her.

On the third morning she arrived at her office to discuss a major financing with the chairman of Exxon and was greeted by a telephone call from Harry Flood. Hope and excitement mounted within her as she took the call.

'I have nearly all the facts now about what happened the day your mother died – and a good bit of what followed,' Flood told her.

'Proof?'

'Yes. Some missing pieces, but I know where to look for them.'

'Get on the next plane to New York. A car will meet you at the airport.'

Flood seemed positively jaunty as he was ushered into Deborah's presence late that afternoon. His dark hair was slicked down, and his shoes had a high polish. His suit was pressed, perhaps even new. He looked several pounds heavier and far healthier than he had only a few days earlier. The money might be better in private industry, but he had been wasting away for the kind of investigation he could sink his teeth into.

He had never been to New York before, and the view from Deborah's cloud-high windows seized his attention.

'Can you see the Statue of Liberty from here, miss? I always wanted to visit it.'

She pointed it out.

'That little lady out there?' He shook his head and turned

to recognize other sights below him. Deborah had been impatiently awaiting his arrival all day.

'You said you've learned something.'

Reluctantly, he pulled his notepad from his jacket pocket and tore his gaze from the window. Consulting the pad, he took his time walking to one of the wide white chairs. He had done a good job and was enjoying the moment.

Finally, he looked up. 'You'll remember, no doubt, that Lord Rowell claimed to have come back from the country by train the day your mother died.'

She nodded.

Flood flipped the notepad shut. 'There were no trains from Wiltshire that day, nor from just about anywhere else. The storm hit fast and early. Then the trains were cancelled.'

'You mean he wasn't with her that weekened,' she said in confusion.

'He was with her,' the detective replied quietly, 'till the very moment she died.'

'Did my mother die in a car accident?' she asked in a voice as dark and lethal as a gun barrel.

'Yes, miss, but not the way you were told.'

Flood knew what had happened that day. Everything missing from the cursory police report and hospital record had come out during his dogged inquiries. The breakthrough had come when he tracked down the snowplough driver, who recalled that a tall, slim gentlemanly type was driving the Rolls that skidded into him. He drove both the man and the injured woman to the hospital. Shown a photo of Rob Rowell taken at about that time, he swore it was the man in the accident. He signed an affidavit for Flood stating that Lord Rowell had been at the wheel of the Rolls.

'He killed her!' Deborah cried out.

'Not intentionally. The road was icy. The visibility was very poor. He skidded, and the snow-plough was there.'

Deborah was incensed. Rob Rowell was now Governor of the Bank of England, very much alive, active, admired. His driving – an instant of carelessness perhaps – had ended her mother's life twenty-four years ago. Years he had been granted and she had had ripped from her. Years in which he had garnered so much respect that he was now the linchpin of the British financial system. How cunningly he had turned murder, theft, and fraud into prosperity, influence, and honour.

'Has anyone corroborated the snow-plough driver's story?' she demanded in rage.

Flood reported that the nurse on duty at the hospital, now a supervisor, had confessed to him that she had omitted Rowell's presence that day from the hospital records and failed to mention him to the police. She too gave Flood an affidavit that Rowell had been in the car with Madeleine de Kronengold.

Flood observed that something odd was missing from the list of her belongings in the police report: her handbag. Women nearly always carried handbags in the mid-Fifties but, strangely, no handbag was listed.

'Her little address book!' Deborah suddenly cried out. 'She kept the combination to her safe in her address book. It would have been in her handbag.'

'Rowell must have kept the handbag then. That's how he found the combination to her safe.'

Flood had also learned that, because of the snowstorm, all the trains were cancelled that day. Rowell returned to London by paying a young man who had just left medical school to drive him. The driver, now a London doctor, remembered the general area in which he had dropped Rowell – very near the address of Madeleine's house and very far from Rowell's own house. With the general chaos caused by one of the worst snowstorms of the century Rowell had no worry about anyone having been notified of Madeleine's death.

Rowell's lie about having returned to London by train that fateful day created a heavier burden for Deborah than simply his own guilt. On it also hung the integrity of his son, whom she loved.

Deborah had once brought up that time with Bash. She had asked whether his father had ever mentioned anything, anything at all, about the day of her mother's death. Bash had replied that his father shied away from intimate disclosures. But, being one of the few who knew about the love affair, Bash had ventured to ask after Mrs. de Kronengold's health when he and their chauffeur met his father's train that day. His father, Bash had replied, told him that she was well and sent him her regards.

'Bash Rowell couldn't have met his father at the London station that day!' Deborah's voice was hobbled with pain.

'Young Rowell was away at school. The school records

show that the family chauffeur picked him up the next morning to bring him to London.'

'So he could give a fake report to the police corroborating his father's lie!' Deborah seethed.

Lies! *All* lies! Deborah screamed in silent agony. You were aware how much knowing about every moment of that day meant to me, and yet you embellished the lie, falsified the falsehood to mislead me years after you misled the police, tried to convince me you had been so concerned about my mother as to ask after her health and that she had sent you her regards. I've lived my life in a limbo of uncertainty about whether at the end she knew how much I loved her – seeking out even the smallest mote of knowledge about her thoughts that day. And yet, like a thief willing to steal a victim's last slice of bread, you claimed for yourself even her sole expression of regard.

Deborah leaped to her feet and rushed to the window facing south, away from Flood, not wishing to expose the anguish on her face.

You lied to me, Bash Rowell. Right from the beginning you lied to me so I would love you. Well, I did love you – much too much. And, in return, you've hurt me. You knew the truth about that day and, thus, you had to know about her jewels. I've caught you in one lie and most probably two, and I will hurt you back with all the force at my command.

Without turning round, Deborah finally spoke. 'You were going to try to track down the list of jewellery my mother insured.'

'I did, miss,' Flood replied sombrely. 'The ruby and diamond set was at the top of the list. Every single piece.'

Deborah spun round, her expression clear, no hint on her face of the pain wrenching her from the wounds she had just suffered. There would be time enough for grief and self-pity and anger when she was alone.

She resumed her seat, directing Flood to brief her on the rest of what he had uncovered. Methodically, he moved through the notes he had made. He had spoken to the widow of John Collins, Samuel's butler. The woman confirmed Irma Fingers' assertion that he had always insisted he had witnessed a will just before the yacht sailed. He had told her the second witness was the lawyer Percy Grayson. The third had been Jason Latham, Deborah's tutor. Grayson was long dead and probably part of the later cover-up, but Flood had tracked down Latham. The latter remembered Deborah fondly and acknowledged he had been a witness to such a will just days before the sailing. Deborah had occasionally wondered what had happened to the shy American after she bade good-bye to him on the dockside at Nice.

'What does he do now? Where does he live?'

Flood consulted the notebook once more. 'It seems he lives in India, miss, has for many years. Some kind of swami there, I understand, very popular, with loads of followers.' Flood coughed self-consciously, then mumbled the rest. 'Practising what he calls "orthodox promiscuity". Something about people should have as much sex as they can because orgasms are an early taste of heaven.'

'Good for him,' Deborah exclaimed vehemently, surprising Harry Flood. 'What about that missing will?'

'If we could find it, you could reopen the proceedings in probate, miss. But no luck. It probably doesn't even exist anymore. The lawyer Percy Grayson died seven years ago of cancer. I asked a friend at Scotland Yard whose girl friend works at the firm of solicitors to nose around a bit. There's nothing in their files.'

'Then, with all we've learned, we're no better off than we were. All we can prove is that Rob Rowell and his son tried to avoid scandal by claiming my mother had been alone in her car when she died.' Flood saw storm clouds looming behind his employer's narrowed eyes.

He pulled a sale catalogue from his briefcase and handed it to Deborah. It was for an auction held by one of the world's leading houses in Geneva a few months after her mother's death. Deborah flipped through the pages. He also handed her a copy of the jewellery list attached to her mother's insurance policy. Flood had checked off on both the items that corresponded identically. All but the ruby and diamond set had been consigned to the sale – anonymously.

'That really stops us dead, miss. Those auction houses don't reveal the names of buyers and sellers who want them kept secret.'

'They will this time,' Deborah said determinedly and buzzed her secretary, directing her to telephone the head of the auction house, a man with whom she had done business many times.

When the call came through, Deborah went straight to the point. Unless he turned over the records of those Geneva sales to André Leitner, the head of her Swiss operation, she would buy control of the auction house and get the records anyway – after firing him. She heard real concern in his voice as he asked whether the seller might have been prominent.

'Extremely!' she replied. 'But he's also a thief!'

After a long pause the auction-house head told her he suspected there would be a break-in at his firm's Swiss offices that night. Those records she wanted would doubtless be taken and end up at her own Geneva offices by morning.

'See that they do,' Deborah demanded. By way of thanks she told him she was looking for several Picassos and some contemporary works – a Johns, a Rothko, and perhaps a Hockney. If he would be so kind as to locate works for her to examine, and arrange a private sale, she would pay a generous fee.

Replacing the receiver, Deborah turned back to her investigator. 'You'll have the records in the morning. Please be at our offices in Geneva when they open. Ask for André Leitner. Telephone me immediately – no matter what time it is here. I'll leave word with the operator to put you through to my home.'

He nodded, then stood up, slipping the notepad into his pocket. 'Didn't get much of a chance to see New York.' He stepped towards the window once more, seeking out the lilliputian Statue of Liberty in the toy harbour below. 'You never realize how tiny the rest of the world looks from up here.'

Knowing she would be unable to sleep that night, Deborah did not try. She wandered about her large apartment, her mind consumed by the day's revelations. Rob had killed her mother and stolen from her. Leslie had conspired with him in the larceny and denied her her inheritance. By robbing her also of that expression of her love her mother had left behind for her, each had also robbed her soul. Bash, whom she had dared to trust, had perhaps hurt her worst of all; he had violated a second time the tattered remnants of belief still left to her that she might be worthy of love. She would repay them all.

The bedroom telephone rang at 3.14 a.m. Deborah picked

up the receiver before the first ring had ended.

'I'm here, André,' she answered his greeting.

'Harry Flood is here with me. The envelope was just slipped under the door.'

He described the contents. The first item was a document signed by Rob Rowell that anonymously consigned many items of jewellery to the 1957 auction – the list corresponded exactly to the list of her mother's insured jewellery, with the exception of the ruby and diamond set. The second item was a photocopy of the cheque Rowell had received in payment for the auctioned jewellery, the back of the cheque verifying that Rowell had deposited it in his own Swiss bank: £1,020,074. Nearly two and a half million dollars at the then prevailing exchange rates.

The numbers sounded to Deborah like combination-lock tumblers falling into place, opening the outer door of the terrible mystery that had cut her off from the love and security that her mother had meant to be hers. She directed André to get Harry Flood to photocopy the documents and take them to London immediately. He was to place them in her office vault.

André had one more piece of information for her: Leslie was pleading with the Swiss bank he thought was his lender to meet him. He wanted to revise the payment terms, so as to allow for more time to pay. He had even sent his son Richard there, to camp on their doorstep like a supplicating hostage no one wanted to ransom.

Events for which Deborah had planned all her adult life were moving now out of the wings and onto the stage. She must direct the timing of their appearance precisely.

'Have the Swiss banker tell Leslie that the person in charge of the loan is flying to London and will most certainly meet him. In fact, it shouldn't be very much longer.'

Deborah made one more call during those early morning hours – to the private telephone on Bash Rowell's desk. Only she and he knew the number. Only he answered calls on it.

'Dee,' he answered, overjoyed to hear from her at last. 'I was worried sick about you when I read about Pierre's death and the rest of it.'

Then he heard the uncompromising coldness in her voice.

'April was kind enough to invite me to your home. I will be there at nine o'clock tonight. Your father will also be there.'

Bash tried to put her off. 'We're committed for this evening. I'm sure my father has plans as well.'

'Tell him I wish to discuss some jewellery sold at auction in Geneva in 1957. It seems last night the documents were stolen from the auction house – by vandals, no doubt – and came into my possession.'

After a long silence, Bash muttered, 'Nine o'clock.'

CHAPTER TWENTY-TWO

The Rowells had lived in the imposing stone building near Berkeley Square since the turn of the century. Bash lived here now with his family, and his father still lived here as well, although he often came and went to his own wing through a private entrance.

Deborah indicated to the butler who answered the door that she would keep her leather portfolio and did not wait to be escorted to the drawing room. She knew her way through the house.

The first face she came upon gave her a start: a youth's face, slim and swarthy. It was simultaneously fierce, regal, and delicately beautiful – with a hunter's black eyes, a thin, faintly aquiline nose, and a soft mouth. The boy's mouth was the only feature that resembled April. Otherwise, he could have been Prince Salim, his father, at sixteen. Deborah stepped towards him.

'You must be Adam.'

His serious mien did not change. 'You're Deborah de Kronengold.'

'Your godfather tells me you'll be spending the summer with him.'

Sullenness flushed his face. 'I'm told I have no choice.'

'You would rather not, I gather.'

'I'm English,' he shot back.

Just then Bash appeared in a doorway beyond the diamond chessboard of marble. His face darkened, and Adam's sullenness instantly deepened.

'You're keeping our guest, Adam,' Bash declared tightly.

'Very good to meet you, Adam,' Deborah said, and then turned to walk to the drawing room where Bash and the others waited.

Adam nodded politely, but his gaze was on the man and could have burned holes through him.

As she entered the drawing room, Deborah's eyes fell first

on Rob Rowell, whom she had not seen since her youth. As tall as his son but thinner, his once fair hair now white and sparse, Robin, Earl of Rowell and Governor of the Bank of England, was still a very handsome man. He approached her with seeming warmth, as if impervious to the firepower she wielded. She tried to recall his face as seen through the cottage window, a rutting animal's, the eyes glazed, menacing. She realized that she had long ago outgrown the sexual terror, but not his pillaging of what seemed then – and for so long – to be every tender feeling her mother had once had for her.

April was oblivious to the tension in the drawing room. Gushing with a victor's pride to show off her house to Deborah, she did not notice the strain the men were under or that Deborah barely contained a rage like a war about to erupt. She insisted on chattering away about how wonderful her marriage was, how suited she and Bash were for each other, and how sad she had often felt for Deborah.

After a few minutes of conversation, Rob turned to his daughter-in-law and asked if she would permit him to steal Deborah away for a few minutes – he had some private memories he wanted to share with her. Bash watched nervously as they departed for his father's study.

The study's walls, ceilings, and floors were a rich wood darkened by many decades of smoke from the deep hearth and men's tobacco. On the mantel was a row of brier and meerschaum pipes. Humidors sat on the table and the desk. Hunting scenes, like windows that denied the city's tumult, hung from the walls. The stately homes of England had many such studies. Her grandfather had had one. So had Leslie. Such a masculine room conferred on its owner an authority that could exonerate his conscience for acts undertaken to uphold the great house erected around it.

Rob and Deborah took chairs across the heavy desk from each other. She waited for him to begin, but he simply stared at her for a long while.

'There's something of Madeleine about you,' he finally said. 'I gather from the newspapers her brother was your father.'

'So he said.'

Rob stared at her for several more seconds, still seeking a trace of Madeleine in what was now the perfectly carved steel of her features. Then his manner became businesslike.

'Now, what's all this nonsense about a jewellery auction?'

Without a word Deborah slid back the zip on her portfolio and handed a photocopy of the auction document to Rowell. His signature was on it. The cheque revealed without doubt where the money had gone. The originals of every document in the portfolio now resided safely in her bank's vault.

Rowell scanned the papers briefly, then assumed an expression of faint distaste. 'Leslie asked me to pay off your mother's gambling debts for him.'

'How did you get the jewellery?'

'Why, he gave it to me, of course. And a full general release at the time. I don't really think I have to answer any more –'

'Where were you the day my mother died?' Deborah demanded sharply.

Rob seemed to weigh for an instant whether to proceed on a tack of outraged refusal to answer. He decided on exasperation. 'You've forced me to reveal something I thought it better to keep from a daughter, that your mother and I spent that weekend together. As I recall, she dropped me off at the station to London.'

'That was in the police report.'

'Well, there you are. The police learned in the village where your mother kept a country house that I had been there with her. They asked me about it. I told them that I had, but came home alone by train.' He rose as if the interview was concluding.

Composed, still seated, Deborah remarked, 'Too bad the police didn't go further than simply checking the train schedules. The train you would have taken was cancelled because of the blizzard. But then, that really didn't matter, did it? You were at the hospital at the time.'

A hesitation betrayed Rob's shock. He dropped back into his chair. 'What hospital?'

'The one where you and the snow-plough driver took my mother after the crash.'

Too wily to betray himself with an incautious word, he spoke soothingly, as if to a deluded child. 'How can you possibly expect to support such a charge?'

'I'm glad you asked.' She handed him a photocopy of a document. 'The sworn statement of the nurse on duty. She admits she failed to tell the police you brought my mother to the hospital. A young doctor later drove you to London. I have his statement too.'

Deborah observed Rob trying to swallow several times. She took her time before speaking again, making Rob dangle over the edge of her next words.

'The snow-plough driver says you were driving the Rolls when it crashed into him!'

Rob's mouth parted in shock. His head fell back against the chair. Now she dropped the second affidavit before him.

'You're one step away from arrest on a capital charge,' she added grimly.

Rob had to muster all his self-discipline to reply. 'Even if it could be proved I was at the wheel of Maddy's car, there was no motive for murder. It was an accident.'

'Motive?' Deborah's eyes impaled Rob like pikes. 'Her maid has sworn she witnessed the signing of my mother's will. She has sworn it was in the safe with her jewellery, bonds, and cash when you and my mother went away that weekend – before you came back to rifle the safe's contents.' Deborah pushed Irma Fingers' affidavit towards him. 'I also have an affidavit from one of the other servants who saw you leave my mother's house only hours after her death.'

Rowell read the copy of Irma Fingers' affidavit very slowly, as if seeking to escape through a crack between the words. Gloomily, he dropped it on the pile of papers growing before him.

Deborah continued with cool detachment, the more threatening for its impersonality. 'A jury might well conclude that your attempt to hide your involvement in my mother's death and your subsequent emptying of her safe establishes ample motive for murder.'

Rob shrugged, attempting to exhibit no anxiety she could exploit. 'Surely you don't believe I intended to take that road to the airport knowing a snow-plough would be at that particular place. And that I could skid the car precisely into it, killing Maddy, but leaving me unscathed.' A thought struck him. 'And, just as surely, you don't need the property missing from her safe.' He gestured at the documents. 'You've gone to a lot of trouble here. What is it you want?'

Deborah's eyebrows converged in anger, her chin lifted – every inch the prosecutor who has just slammed closed the door on a defendant's hopes. 'Full restitution in cash for what was sold at auction – one million and twenty thousand pounds. Plus one million pounds more for the bonds and money you stole.' That guess was based on family members' estimates of Madeleine's worth. 'Naturally, I will want back the ruby and diamond jewellery that April wears –'

Rob interrupted anxiously. 'A bit sticky that – the girl thinks the jewellery's hers. Marriage contract, that sort of thing. She's rather attached to it.'

'Those were my mother's jewels,' Deborah rejoined fiercely. 'They were to go to me. I have little enough of what was hers to remember her by. You know the law, stolen goods are returned to the victim. Unless I get that jewellery at once, I'll go straight to the authorities with my evidence.'

Rob fell silent, weighing the perilousness of his position against the cost of her offer. Finally he admitted, 'The amount is about right for what I earned, but I'm entitled to keep the half that was to go to your brother, Richard. Leslie obtained his release for me when the lad turned twenty-one.'

This was the moment for her bluff. 'Her maid claims that everything was left to me and nothing to Richard.'

'That's a damned lie!' You were to get the jewellery, that's true, but the rest was to be split equally between you both.'

Rob jumped up, removed a painting from the wall behind him, and opened the wall safe. He withdrew a manila envelope from the safe. Inside the envelope were several sheets of yellowed photocopy stapled together. He handed them to Deborah.

'Your mother's will. See for yourself.'

Stunned, Deborah stared at her mother's signature. She had reasoned that someone as opportunistic as Rob might have made a copy for himself, but never dared hope that he would actually place it in her hands. With this will and if she could get her hands on the release Leslie had signed attesting to the will's receipt, she could prove Leslie's criminal guilt. He had concealed the will and permitted his wife's assets to be fraudulently disposed of.

Rob Rowell was rubbing a knuckle across his mouth. On the strength of having already produced so many incriminating documents, Deborah had tricked him into revealing he had kept a copy of her mother's will. She did not want to give him time to think. She wanted to try one more bluff.

'I'll take my grandfather's will as well.'

Rob appeared to be honestly surprised. 'I didn't keep a copy of Samuel's will. There was no reason to.'

'You must have,' she rejoined commandingly.

He shook his head. 'The only assets I was involved with and concerned about were Maddy's. I wanted releases from everyone involved with *her* will, so I kept a copy. I could never get your release, of course, but here are the others.' He handed them to her and showed her the now empty manila envelope.

'But you *saw* my grandfather's will.'

Rob nodded unwillingly; he was in so deep another concealment was meaningless, but cooperation might prove mitigating. 'I gave it to Leslie.'

'Who were the beneficiaries?' she asked.

'Except for cash bequests to Samuel's sons and Richard, everything went to you.'

Oh, God! she thought, Leslie stole everything from me! He made me feel that I should be grateful for the crumbs of financial support he threw my way. All the while he was living like a parasite on my property. Every hateful thought I've ever had about him could be multiplied a thousand times and not equal the smallest part of the vengeance he deserves.

Rob spoke up with a show of strength. He was angling to salvage his reputation at least. 'I'll agree to all your terms on one condition, that my name be kept out of everything.'

Deborah's eyes blazed. '*I* dictate the terms! Here is what you will take! You will resign from the Bank of England first thing in the morning – no man so dishonest should be in a position of such responsibility. If you do, I won't reveal you were driving the car when my mother was killed. You won't have to defend yourself against a murder charge.'

'They'll still find out eventually that I emptied her safe.' He sounded exhausted now, unable to fend her off.

'You won't be implicated if I don't press charges,' Deborah pointed out. 'But the disgrace will never go away.'

She felt a rush of satisfaction. The damning publicity surrounding Leslie's arrest would expose the corruption festering beneath the Rowell family's protestations of honour – that self-serving code that Bash had hid behind when he chose April instead of her.

She clarified the terms for Rowell. First, she would accept an immediate draft on the Rowell bank for the money owed her on account of her mother's estate, plus interest at six percent for twenty-four years. Her brother, Richard, had already agreed in his release of Rob Rowell to give up his half of their mother's property. A spasm of new anger rippled through Deborah as she realized that Richard had known for many years about the theft – and had condoned it by releasing Rob Rowell and, implicitly, by absolving Leslie. In effect her brother had become an accessory after the fact.

Deborah's second demand would trap the culprit she had been tracking most of her life. 'I want your signed statement *under oath* detailing your dealings with Leslie. A commissioner of oaths is waiting outside in my car to witness your signature.'

He nodded, hoping that this was the end.

'And lastly,' she concluded, her voice barely rising with the triumph she felt, 'I want my mother's ruby and diamond jewellery.'

Deborah had not expected or wanted April to bring the jewellery herself. But after many minutes, minutes that must have been filled with the men pleading that she had to relinquish the jewellery, April appeared in the doorway.

On one side of her was Rob, her father-in-law. His eyes were downcast, trying to avoid this playing out of his shame. Bash, white and shaking, walked slowly forward just behind on her other side, his gaze on her seeming to pull him forward as if he were on a leash. And in an open velvet box before her was the ruby and diamond jewellery. The inevitable scandal would humiliate the Rowells and cause them to be ostracised for many years to come: Rob Rowell would resign the Governorship under a cloud; vicious insults regarding the foundation of the family's present success would follow Bash for decades; and the trust other bankers had automatically accorded the firm would now be guarded, reluctant. April's own father carried one of the most respected titles in the realm, but her love for Bash had trapped her among the now disgraced Rowells.

There was no gloating in Deborah's manner as she accepted the open box, only the recognition of simple, unsparing justice. April raised her eyes for the first time. Her voice, when she spoke, still conveyed her pride.

'How delighted you must be to pay me back for stealing Bash from you! My consolation is that I still have him, and you have a loveless life.'

'This is far harder for me than you can imagine,' Deborah replied quietly. 'I'm carrying Bash's child.'

As the limousine tunnelled through the flickering gloom cast by London street lamps, Deborah opened the velvet box on her lap and held it up to catch the light sliding past the windows. Dark blood pulsed deep within the massive rubies. They seemed to be alive, to speak to her out of the past. Not of the numbers other people assigned to them as value, but of value beyond price. They told her that, although her mother and grandfather had concealed her true parentage from her, they had never discarded her; they had, indeed, loved her. Bash, however, had not only denied her their love, by hiding it, he had denied his own for her as well.

Until the moment the words came out, Deborah had been fully committed to never revealing the identity of her child's father. Why, then, had she done it? Out of spite – the ultimate triumph over April? That seemed the easy, logical answer, but she knew that was not why. She had already triumphed – over April, over Bash, over Rob, who had been the actual thief, and over Leslie, who was all but crushed and did not yet know it.

Deborah discerned that her confession resulted from her distress at not having known the identity of her own father. She wanted nothing from Bash. Indeed, her retaliation had made future contact between them nearly impossible. Moreover, bringing Leslie to trial for his crimes committed with Rob Rowell would smear the Rowell name irrevocably, and she refused to whitewash it for the sake of her child. She would not allow her child any false illusions about Bash's character. The part of her that had suffered pain over and over again – from the father who had been there and the father who had been absent – was trying to ensure that her own child would never be vulnerable to such treachery. At that moment in Rowell's study, she had understood at last that her child could never grow up whole if there was a void in its identity where a name should have been. Someday it might hate her for other things, but never for withholding the knowledge of who it was.

David had been drinking for hours in the bar of Claridges, waiting for Deborah to return. He had slipped an urgent message under her door that he had to see her. David was not drunk; rather, the alcohol had whetted his purpose to a fatalistic edge.

Time was running out on the loan Leslie had taken from the Swiss group. The British merchant banker, so long aloof, had become frantic, willing for the first time in Kronengold history to permit an outsider to become a partner in the bank. This was David's opportunity, after a lifetime of waiting. Two lifetimes, really – his father's as well. But Deborah's opposition had made him desperate. She had warned him not to involve himself with Leslie's bank, and she controlled those damned Series D debentures, a noose around his neck. Twice in the last few days he had woken in a sweat. The dream had been the same both times: he had been dangling from a paper noose, hands tied behind his back, twisting and turning, strangling.

Deborah had been emotionally wrung out when she returned to her suite. Her mind had finally shifted from what had just transpired to what lay ahead. She had decided that everything was now in place for her to launch at last the final assault against Leslie. Tomorrow would be the day. In the beginning she had resented his indifference and then had come to hate him for his acts of animosity perpetrated against her. Now she had hard evidence of outright crimes he had committed. He had tried to take everything from her and leave her nothing. Now he would be repaid in kind, left as destitute and despised as he had tried to leave her. And more: deprived of his freedom!

She needed to be fresh tomorrow. She needed sleep. She had had almost no sleep for the last forty-eight hours. Yet, when she came upon David's urgent note as she entered her suite, she telephoned downstairs. She explained how exhausted she was, but said he could come up for a brief conversation.

A few minutes later he was at her door. As he kissed her and followed her into the room, he noticed that she did indeed appear tired, but also preoccupied. He must get her to focus on his concerns.

'I tried to reach you in New York today. Penny said you were on your way to London. So I waited to speak to you here. It simplifies things.'

'David, does it have to be tonight? I have a lot on my mind.'

'I'm afraid it does.'

Deborah nodded and seated herself on the sofa. The colours of the room were subdued – smoky pastel fabrics and gleaming woods, from which were formed airily executed Art Deco furnishings. David chose a chair across from her. She was distracted, he could see, and tired too, but he had to push forward now. Leslie had insisted that it had to be now or never. He cleared his throat.

'Leslie needs an infusion of capital badly. The reason why isn't important, but because of that, for the first time, Leslie has agreed to sell an interest in the Kronengold bank to an outsider. I've agreed to have my company put up what he needs in return for a half interest in the Kronengold bank. Now, I –'

'No.'

'Just no? You have to have a good reason.'

Her eyes seared the air between them like blue oxyacetelyne flames. 'Tomorrow I intend to crush Leslie de Kronengold, as I vowed to when I left his house seventeen years ago.'

David had seen that wilful rigidity grip Deborah at other times when, rightly or wrongly, she felt her security threatened or some key objective blocked. He had to make her see reason.

'Look, you have to know how much it means to me to buy into I. Kronengold & Sons.' He ran distraught fingers through his black curls. 'Jesus, Dee, you say you love me. How can you go against me like this?'

'You say you love *me*, David.'

'More than anything.'

'Then how can you try to help the man I loathe? If I back off now my life has no meaning!'

David had wanted to say something similar, but it sounded childish now. 'Then marry me,' he said instead. 'Combined, our empire would be limitless. This antagonism wouldn't divide us then. We could swallow Leslie's bank and spit him out like a peach stone, if that's what you want. The greatest Kronengolds in his history would seem like pygmies beside us. You know how much I love you. Please—my God, please—marry me.'

Deborah felt David was crowding her into a corner, trying to extract concessions she had already declared herself unwilling to give. 'We've been over this, David,' she replied. 'I know I promised to think about it some more, but my mind is unchanged. I don't want the impositions marriage demands.'

When she thwarted him, blocked him, he wanted her so badly. Marrying her would come in time, he was sure. He had to be careful not to confuse issues now. He had something she needed, and if he bargained skilfully he was sure he would be able to trade it for Aximation's debentures and thus, for the freedom to buy his way into the British Kronengold bank. He hesitated. He had guarded the secret for years.

'Just before my father died, he told me something about you I couldn't reveal while Pierre was alive.' David was stretching the truth only a bit. He could have revealed the secret while Pierre was alive, but the powerful Frenchman would have used what he knew to blacken Max's memory. 'They met before the war and knew each other quite well during it. In fact, my father was there when you were born.'

Deborah was caught off guard. Shock flashed across her features. 'He . . . was there?'

'Yes. He guided you and your mother through the lines to that orphanage. In my safe deposit box in New York I have the pass he used.'

'Oh, David!' Deborah was on her feet, her hand involuntarily reaching forward.

'But I know more,' David spoke slowly. He could sense her eagerness. These next moments were critical. 'I know that your mother didn't die as you were told, although even Pierre might have believed that.'

'She's alive?' Deboarh gasped.

'Yes. My father had people track her down. It took months and a lot of luck.'

Deborah was bewildered. She tried to speak, but words failed her. This was the moment David dreaded, when she learned he had known about her mother all these years and had kept it from her, when he would have to play his last – his only – card. His gaze steady, his expression composed, he betrayed no hint of the desperation he felt.

'I know your mother's name,' he said, 'and where she lives. I'll trade that information for the right to buy back the debentures and be free of your threats.'

'You will *what*?' she cried out. 'Trade my mother's name for some financial paper?'

'Yes,' he responded, not flinching in the face of her scorn. 'We each get what we want. You'll be able to find your real mother. I'll get full control of my company again. A straight one-for-one business transaction.'

'What kind of creature are you? You knew who my natural mother was all these years. While you slept with me and claimed you loved me, you kept it from me. Even after I poured out my heart to you in Paris, every pain of my childhood, you still wouldn't tell me.'

David struggled to explain. 'Dee, don't you – can't you – understand my duty to restore our family's name?' The emotions battering David threatened to overwhelm him. He took a deep breath and raised his gaze to Deborah. 'I'm offering you a chance to know who your real mother is, to find her and speak to her. You yourself told me how you dreamed about that as a child.'

Deborah collapsed into the chair. The revelations of these last hours had set her own emotions vibrating at an impossible pitch. This new one was more than she could take. Now David wanted to trap her and force open the grip she had on him, her only defence.

'Do you really think I'll give you back control of your company so that you can pump money into Leslie's bank and save him from me?' she fumed. 'Yet even if he were the richest man in the world, he's now beyond saving. He's doomed!'

Misunderstanding, David plunged on. His next words, he believed, would sweep away all her arguments and force her to agree to his deal. 'Is destroying Leslie more important to you than finding your mother?'

'My mother?' she retorted sharply. 'The mother who left me worried sick that I might die in childbirth as she did?' Deborah smiled bitterly at him. '*You* tell me why I would want to see her.'

Deborah rose from the chair, walking past David to the door. He jumped to his feet and grabbed her arm.

'Mothers don't just abandon their children for no reason. I'm probably the last person left alive who knows where she is. All you've got to do is sell me the debentures.'

Deborah yanked her arm away. 'Never! I remember the last time I let myself be defenceless against you and Leslie!'

Nearly out of his mind at being thwarted in business and thwarted in love, David lunged at her and began shaking her. 'Dee, don't be foolish! You're destroying me and I love you. You have to marry me! You have to! You're carrying my child!'

David expected Deborah to try to fight him off. He was surprised when she went slack instead, and the antagonism slid from her eyes.

'David, there's something you should know. I realize now it would be wrong not to tell you. I only hope you'll understand.'

'About what?'

'The child, David.' She tried to soften her voice, even as she knew that it would not soften the blow. 'You're not the father.'

David stared at her incredulously for several seconds. Then, slowly, as if the energy source within him had been disconnected, his arms floated to his sides. Failing to gain a foothold among the Kronengolds, he had failed completely in every other way that mattered. The goal he had sought all his life – conquest of the Kronengolds – had been blocked by the only Kronengold he cared about. He loved this woman who had scorned him by having another man's child.

'Why did you do this to me?' he whispered. 'I wanted a child more than anything, someone to carry on my name, someone to whom I could leave everything I've built. You knew that!'

Again Deborah could not save him from the pain of her answer. 'Listen to yourself, David. Your reasons . . . they're wrapped up in glorifying yourself. I didn't trust you to love my child without wanting to control it, and I was right. Soon, you would have fought me for custody. Someday, you would have wanted to be the only one it loved.'

'And this lover of yours,' he snapped back at her, 'he wouldn't do that.'

'He can't.'

He shook his head sadly. 'You just picked someone who was safe! Someone who couldn't scare the hell out of you because he loved you so much. You're afraid of being hurt if you love all out – and afraid of losing whoever is able to break through and love you in spite of it.' A regretful grin climbed up one side of his mouth. 'You made sure your child could only love *you*. That's a shame. I really would have loved that kid. I really loved you. You were just afraid to let me show you how much.'

He turned to go. He had lost the three things he had always wanted most: to assume the mantle of the Kronengolds, to possess Deborah, and to pass everything on to their children.

Deborah stepped towards him. 'It doesn't have to end, David. I never wanted that. I still love you.'

'If I loved you again, your child still wouldn't be mine. I couldn't live with knowing it wasn't.'

Deborah did not answer. This time there could be no reprieve for their relationship – it was over between them. Each had been forced to pursue inner imperatives, until they finally crashed head on.

'Good-bye, David. I'm sorry it couldn't have been some other way for us. . . .'

'That red hair!' he sighed.

Then he walked towards the door, but stopped halfway. For an instant Deborah thought he might have changed his mind. But he was reaching into his jacket. His hand emerged with a white envelope, and he placed it on the table.

'What's that?' Deborah asked him.

'Your mother's name and address. It's my good-bye gift – in case you ever want to know who you are.'

'I won't look at it, you know.'

'Not you.'

He left without glancing back.

Deborah could barely sleep that night despite her fatigue. She kept replaying every moment of her night: first the triumph against the Rowells and then the irreparable break with David. Every time she felt overwhelmed by the pain of remembering that she had driven off the only two men she had ever loved, she remembered too that failure to act as she had would have been more distressing. Bash would have kept hidden from her forever the evidence of Madeleine and Samuel's love for her. By demanding all its love, David would have torn apart any child he and she had had together.

The past still imposed one obligation more upon her that had to be paid, then she would be free of it and could look to the future: the revenge she would wreak on Leslie. Once she did that, the books on the past would be closed forever. With the coming of her child, she would be able to start as fresh as the life she was bringing into the world. For seventeen years repaying Leslie had been uppermost in her mind, taking precedence over every other goal, motivating her to greater and greater success. Now the time was here.

Early in the morning she telephoned the head of the small Swiss bank that purported to be Leslie's lender. She told him to telephone Leslie immediately with the following message: at precisely noon today the Swiss bank's representative would arrive at I. Kronengold & Sons with full authority to resolve all aspects of the loan. The Swiss banker was to say no more.

Impatient for the coming confrontation with Leslie, she began to pace her hotel room as if caged. But her thoughts kept straying to last night's rupture with David. His remarks when he had left troubled her and, as they had most of the night, they continued to play over and over in her mind. Her eye fell on the letter he had left. She thrust it out of her sight, into a desk drawer. The rooms seemed too small. She called for her car and began to dress.

She stood for several minutes under the shower, trying to let the remorseless bolt of water wash away her preoccupation with David. Nothing must interfere with the perfect concentration she sought to achieve, the intensity of awareness that would make the smallest observation burn forever into her memory.

She blew her long hair dry as she sat at the dressing table and stared at her image in the mirror. You have sacrificed and gambled and prayed for this day, she told the face with the blue eyes burning back at her. Nothing you ever accomplish in the future will return to you one-thousandth part of your gratification when you see the look of utter defeat in his eyes.

She had always worn little make-up. Today was no exception, but the lipstick colour was blood red. The coat of varnish on her nails was the same predatory shade. Then she went to the cupboard to choose her garments. She did so as carefully as if for a coronation. The suit was silk and black. It must be black, she thought, because I am the messenger of his destruction.

The jewellery? Again, as always, simple. She reached into the flat case and withdrew the ruby ring. Perhaps Leslie would recognize it, perhaps not. But she would know.

Deborah tossed a sable coat over her shoulders and stopped for a last glance in a mirror. Despite her fatigue, her eyes were bright and piercing. She was older than the last time he had seen her, more confident naturally, but the hatred in her eyes had not dampened in the slightest. He would see it and remember that he had only himself to blame for instilling it there.

A fine mist was rising, she saw as she left the hotel, and the clouds had so blackened the sun that the morning looked like the hour before dawn. A few people were hurrying by, umbrellas drawn down around them like mushroom caps. The doorman opened the car door, holding high a wide black umbrella to form a mourner's canopy above her passage. She settled into the rear seat and told the driver to meander through some of London's older streets. Several hours remained before she was expected at her destination. She wanted time to think.

At ten o'clock a radio news programme informed her and other listeners that the Earl of Rowell had just made the surprise announcement that he was resigning as Governor of the Bank of England, this to take immediate effect. He blamed ill health.

That was one score settled. Her thoughts finally turned fully towards Leslie.

On impulse, she stopped at the Tower of London and walked to Tower Green where so many had been executed.

Just before noon, her car turned into Mercy Lane and approached the Kronengold bank. Deborah had planned every moment of this confrontation hundreds of times in her head since she stormed out of the bank at the age of eighteen, leaving Leslie and England behind. With the same thoroughness that had gone into forcing him backwards, step by step, to the brink of financial disaster, she had thought out every word she would say, every stance, every gesture. In her imagination she had viewed over and over again the shocked, desperate expression on his face when he realized that she had arrived at last to make good her vow to crush him – and that he had no escape.

Deborah glanced at the clock on the rear dashboard. It was exactly noon. She nodded to her driver to proceed into the courtyard towards the doorman dressed in the bank's traditional uniform of top hat, green velvet coat, and knee breeches.

At that moment a tall figure in a dark double-breasted suit emerged from the building to take up position under the canopy beside the doorman, both only a step from the misty drizzle. He was obviously uncomfortable with his act of cordiality to his Swiss lender. Although older, Leslie still radiated arrogance. Observing that imperious glare, how glad she was that in all the seventeen years since she had last seen him, she had never ceased to stalk him.

Entering through the great iron gates, the limousine halted at the entrance. The doorman sprang to the car door handle. This was the moment Deborah had dreamed about and struggled for. The door swung back. Leslie moved forward. Her gaze fixed on Leslie's face like a heat-seeking sensor on its target, Deborah stepped from the darkened rear compartment.

Leslie extended his right hand to greet his creditor but, at the sudden recognition of the person stepping out of the car, it froze.

'Deborah!' he gasped.

Standing before him was his worst nightmare come to life. He understood in that instant that she was the true lender, from whom he could expect no mercy, and that she had indeed been the dark force behind much of the bank's adversity over the years, blocking him wherever she could and climaxing her campaign by tricking him into this deceitful abomination of a loan.

Deborah smiled – his recognition of her conquest, the utter hopelessness written on his face, was every bit as satisfying to her as she had hoped for so long it would be.

'The Partners' Room!' she ordered.

Deborah swept past Leslie and pushed through the double doors into the bank, not waiting for the doorman. She paused for an instant in the vast rotunda to peer upwards into the silver luminescence that seemed to shower her like confetti. Then she ascended the staircase that ringed the circular wall, her hand caressing the ornate balustrade. An employee scuttling down, arms laden with files, halted in dumb surprise. Leslie brushed the man out of the way as he leapt up the stairs behind her.

Awaiting the appearance of the Swiss banker who held their fate, the bank's directors in the Partners' Room glanced nervously into the corridor. A flame of red hair crowning her height above a black suit, Deborah was a startling figure as she filled the doorway. Her ice-blue eyes surveyed the anxious faces in the mahogany room. One or two she recalled as younger men in the bank's departments. The others were strangers.

The last one she noticed, leaning against the mantel, was

her brother, Richard. She had been prepared to find him, according to all reports, effete and effeminate. Instead, he seemed somehow 'unrealized', a smaller, smudgy copy of his father. Once, at Deborah's insistence, her uncle Charles had approached Richard about joining the holding company group, but had been rebuffed. Richard approved of his father's business judgment and had no inclination to relinquish the role of heir apparent. Watching dismay now spread slowly across his face like a rash, she noted ironically how worthless was the title he had chosen to inherit.

The air was fibrous with ironies. A few men had jumped up to greet her, but Deborah walked deliberately to the cabinet in the corner of the room on which, doubtless ignored, sat the small gold statue fashioned presciently by her ancestor. Isaac, blind and deceived, reached out to bestow the family's birthright on the head of a usurper.

I have come back with all the fury of my righteous vengeance to destroy the bank that should have been mine, Deborah declared to herself. I have come back to claim my birthright – even if I do so by razing it.

She turned to the frightened faces with the agonizing slowness of irresistible fate. 'I will speak to Leslie de Kronengold alone,' she announced.

A few seconds later they were gone, the door closed behind them. Ignoring the fact that it was Leslie's now, Deborah walked with measured steps to her grandfather's desk near the cold hearth and seated herself. Leslie stood silently. Finally, his feet shuffling like those of a man condemned, he moved to the chair across the desk from her. Only when his anxiety seemed about to petrify him into stone did she finally speak.

'You now understand that I hold the two-hundred-million-dollar debt you owe. There is no possibility that you will have sufficient funds to repay it when it comes due at the end of business on Thursday. My lawyers have prepared the legal papers that will give me control of the bank's assets. I intend to liquidate I. Kronengold & Sons immediately and put it out of business.'

Leslie's wits had begun to return. 'I've just completed arrangements to repay everything.'

Her reply was disdainful. 'David Holtz won't come to your rescue. I've already warned him of the consequences, and he won't chance them.'

Leslie's composure fled once more. Deborah had hounded him for a dozen years, crowded him, obsessed him, as she went from one success to another. David Holtz had been his last hope. The fact that Deborah knew about the arrangement and had still come here meant she was telling the truth about having forced Holtz to withdraw.

Leslie shook himself. He must think. He must survive. But this angel of his calamity had not finished: she reached into her portfolio for papers and laid them before her. Leslie concentrated on disciplining his features to conceal the wretchedness he felt. And, as she spoke again, on trying to think.

'As soon as I leave here, I will deliver the originals of these documents to the Director of Public Prosecutions and to the Home Office.'

'What do you mean?' He was confused. 'I've done nothing illegal.'

He leaned forward to look at the documents Deborah had placed between them. She held up the top one.

'Here is a photocopy of my mother's will, which you concealed from the court.'

She held up a second document.

'I also have Rob Rowell's affidavit swearing that he gave you both that will and Samuel's will.' She displayed one more document. 'This next document is the general release you gave Rowell in exchange for the wills.'

With a gesture that swept the room, she pronounced, 'This was all mine, and you stole if from me! Samuel intended me to own and control this bank. You took everything and left me nothing! You stole my birthright! But I've beaten you.'

Surprisingly, instead of cowering Leslie rose up self-righteously. 'You aren't Samuel's rightful heir, I am – no matter how you connived to get him to sign. You were *Pierre's* child, of *his* genetic line and *his* dynasty, not mine. My child was Richard. I was entitled to pass on to him – to my own descendants – the full inheritance that was ours by right. By God, that was my duty! But it became evident soon after you came to live with us that Samuel and Maddy felt quite differently and that you were over-shadowing our real child. I know what it's like to be overshadowed by a glib, clever sibling.' His jaw set. 'My responsibility was to my own progeny, and I fulfilled it with consistent loyalty. Regardless of what Samuel's last will said, that was *my* birthright *you* were stealing.'

Her rejoinder was sharply to the point. 'You committed larceny and fraud against me – felonies that will put you behind bars for years. But your worst crime was stealing my heritage. You hated me and made me feel like an alien. I was born a Kronengold, and you all conspired to make me believe my place among you was granted on sufferance, like a temporary permit. I was your daughter – you took me in – but you never let me doubt that you despised me.'

Leslie's head tilted up with his rediscovered arrogance. 'You can blame Pierre for that. If you were denied your heritage, it was his doing, not mine. He foisted you on his sister and me and swore us to secrecy. He was a spineless coward without the strength of character to tell his wife the truth and face up to his responsibilities.' Leslie sneered. 'He was a user. He used Maddy and me to hide his adultery. He used Simone for her money. And he used you.'

Although caught off guard by Leslie's unexpected justification for robbing and abusing her, Deborah was not about to be diverted from the revenge she had pursued so long.

'You're *both* corrupt hypocrites! In the years to come, you'll often wish you were as dead as Pierre.'

She began gathering the papers, preparing to leave. Leslie searched frantically for an argument to halt her.

'I'm willing to admit privately every charge implied by those papers. But a good deal more is at stake here than my disgrace.' Deborah paused to listen. He raced on, fearing to lose her attention. 'I. Kronengold & Sons isn't just another merchant bank. When the Kronengold brothers left the ghetto to become perhaps the richest family in the world, every Jew stood taller. We were a symbol to them, an example. They too could succeed. They too could have some small power over their own lives. And we meant something to the Gentiles. They might hate us. They might murder us. But they could no longer avoid respecting us. That's what we represent – respect.'

Leslie looked away – her stare was too intimidating. 'If you crush this bank and bring charges against me, you're destroying tradition and history. We built the railways and steel mills of the Industrial Revolution. We financed the China trade in the clipper ships. Our funds built the Empire.' Observing her expression of derision at that last example, he quickly chose a different one. 'Before the Second World War, when the country desperately needed funds to start aeroplane factories for defence, the government came to *us* for the five million pounds they needed until the funds could be squeezed out of a pacifist Parliament. We gave it gladly. With no interest charged.' His voice was ringing. 'If you blacken the honour of this bank and this family by crushing me, what a tragic victory that will be!'

'I already own a far more prosperous merchant bank, only a few streets from here, one that need not be revived with millions in new capital to cover operating losses.'

'You have an obligation to this family,' he pleaded.

'Obligation?' Her laugh ricocheted round the room. 'Now, when it suits your argument, I'm part of your family.'

She began stuffing the papers into her portfolio. Leslie was desperate, but he still saw some hope in this line of argument.

'All the Kronengolds will soon be under siege. Don't delude yourself that you're any better off. No matter how friendly the Arabs seem to act towards you, someday they'll threaten you as surely as the rest of us. By destroying me, making their first attack successful, you're encouraging them to do exactly that.' His voice lowered. 'My sources – people sent to bargain with the Arabs to lift the ban – are convinced they'll go after us all. The Arabs intend to crush this bank first and then every Kronengold bank and business.'

'What reason would they have?' she countered. 'They'll have made their political point.'

'They want to leave no mistake in anyone's mind. They want to wipe us out because we're Jews and have survived two centuries of other tyrants. Our indomitability angers them. If they can smash us, they'll threaten the integrity of the entire international banking system. All the bankers and their governments are already terrified of the Arabs' immense wealth and an oil embargo; they'll cave in to the Arabs' demands about Israel, anything.'

Deborah's glare withered Leslie. 'How very foolish you are to believe I'll be dissuaded from ruining you simply because the Arabs find you as loathsome as I do!'

Leslie sensed that he might find greater success appealing to Deborah's ego. 'You're the only one among us that's powerful enough to stand up to them. You started with nothing – my God, who knows that better than I. I admit it, I've behaved appallingly to you. But you overcame everything to become a giant in world finance. You can save I. Kronengold & Sons. You can stop the Arabs. You must, before it's too late!'

He stood up to pace the narrow path behind his chair. 'I have a proposal. This bank is worth a good deal more than the sum we originally borrowed from you, although perhaps not the ludicrous figure we ended up owing. Take over the bank. Richard has only a small share. Let him keep that. I have a bit of money put by, a few assets I can sell if you'll let me. I won't starve. I'll go to Greece and concentrate on my excavations. You need never be bothered by me again.' He ceased pacing and straightened to his full height. 'But I beg you, don't let all of the tradition and honour of this bank, that generations of Kronengolds have built, become the laughing stock of envious little people – or the first victory that encourages the Arabs to wipe out all the rest of the Kronengolds.'

The zip slashing closed across the top of Deborah's portfolio sounded like a knife gutting flesh. 'The time for forging an appeal to my family loyalty was when I needed *you*, Leslie, not now, when you need *me*; and the only thing this family still stands for is its own selfishness.' Deborah tucked the portfolio under her arm. 'I do not have a single drop of pity for you. All I feel is joy at your disgrace.'

Hysterical, he cried out, '*Why?* Have you ever stopped to ask yourself *why* you've gone to such extraordinary lengths, not to regain your rights or your money, but to destroy me?'

David too had asked her why. Leslie's question was far simpler for her to answer – and much more satisfying. 'Because you tried to take everything from me, even my identity.'

But you've built a fortune several times greater than that,' he hurried on to say, 'and you'll get back almost all I have when you take over this bank, not to mention what Pierre left you when he finally faced up to his duty.' Words tumbled out in fear. 'And, as for your identity, the outside world and nearly all your relatives never had the slightest reason to doubt you were our daughter. Those few who knew Pierre was your real father knew you were as much a Kronengold as any of us. Your financial genius – even I will admit that – proves it. Isn't that enough for you? Why do you insist on disgracing the very family you wanted so to be yours?'

Deborah felt herself rooted to the floor. Lurching around

for some way to reach her as he sought to extricate himself from his predicament, he had accidentally stumbled upon a word that opened her doubts like a key: *why*. At another time Deborah would have ignored the implications of Leslie's desperate remarks and completed the kill, but David's denunciation of her the night before, coupled with his departure, had shaken her. She had always been so sure of the justness of her vendetta, but had never asked herself why revenge drove her so. She tried now to view herself from afar and saw a righteous woman wielding a sword who had no idea of her reason for wielding it. At this moment of her greatest victory, she was aware only that her deepest satisfaction derived from abandoning to the oblivion of prison and of society's revulsion the man who had abandoned her. She felt compelled to prove to herself that he, like she, belonged nowhere.

As if lightning had suddenly split the room, Deborah understood that abandonment formed the fearful black hole inside her that had threatened all her life to suck her into it. Fearing it in every relationship, to avoid the grief it could cause, she hedged her commitments and placed obstacles between herself and those she loved. David had been right about that, but had failed to appreciate that the self-defence was necessary because the men she was driven to fall in love with, like a headily addictive narcotic, were so dangerous. She was playing out compulsions instilled at the instant in childhood when she had learned of her adoption and when blackness and emptiness had become her inner step-parents.

In this new instant of doubt, Deborah realized that, unless she found her natural mother and learned the circumstances of her birth, *abandonment* – with its crippling fear of love and its insatiability for the security of wealth – would always be her birthright. And she would pass it on to her own baby.

She had given up searching for her natural parents at the age of seventeen, discerning that her emotional survival depended on submission to conditions as they had been constructed for her. The alternative was disintegration. When she came to America she had proclaimed herself born anew, her own parent begetting herself. But that bravado was a survival technique too, she comprehended. Only by unmasking the secret ghosts controlling her past could she now retrieve her necessary parts and be a whole person able to give love fully, whether to a man or to a friend or to her baby.

She had thought that destroying Leslie would end the past's hold on her but, instead, it was leading her farther back, on the very beginning.

Without another word to give Leslie either hope or despair, Deborah strode from the Partners' Room. The men waiting in the hall fell away from her advance towards the stairway as if she were the incarnation of death. The dome above seemed silently to toll their knell. All the way down the stairs, across the marble hall, and out of the front entrance, Leslie hovered at her back like a beggar hoping for a reprieve dropped by chance.

Deborah stepped out of the Kronengold bank building. The doorman held open the door of her limousine. Instead of getting into the car, Deborah turned back to Leslie. Her tone implied that what she was about to ask was of no consequence and the answering of it would offer no reward.

'Did you ever know my natural mother?'

'Not personally, although I was in touch from London with her unit and the rest of the partisans.'

'What do you know about her?'

'A heroine. Big following among the local people. Died at the end of the war giving birth to you. Or so we were told.'

'But you couldn't be sure.'

'A few years back I heard a rumour that she'd turned up in Israeli intelligence. But you always hear things like that. There's rarely any truth to them.'

'Do you remember her name?'

'Dvora, the Hebrew version of your name. Dvora Levi. She was known as the Torch.'

CHAPTER TWENTY-THREE

Except in the oil-exporting countries, the recession appeared nearly world-wide by mid-1980. Many nations were running up huge deficits as a result of the escalation in oil prices. The collapse in the price of silver shook international finance; the multi-billionaire Hunt family of Texas was forced to mortgage its oil and mineral wealth to survive. The earlier failures of the Herstatt Bank in Germany and the Franklin National in the United States were still painful memories of how the ripple effect of a large financial institution's demise could swamp a hundred others. In the United States a federal loan guarantee of $1.5 billion was rushed through Congress to stave off Chrysler's bankruptcy. General Motors and Ford reported record losses. With unemployment at its highest point in three years, the U.S. recession was declared official.

Appearing certain to head the national Democratic and Republican tickets respectively were President Jimmy Carter, who defended détente with Moscow and his lacklustre populism, and the ex-California governor Ronald Reagan, who called for a stronger military posture, reduced federal activity, and 'supply-side' economic tax cuts. Only the really committed conservatives were sure that Reagan's approach was better. The vast majority of Americans knew only that Carter's had failed.

The year-old Thatcher government in Britain had imposed austerity measures to slap the welfare-state economy out of a long slumber, but employment and the economic indicators were plummeting. A bit more slowly, but nonetheless surely, the recession was also beginning to hobble the other European nations.

Little wonder that disheartened confusion reigned everywhere: if bankruptcy failed to do one in, a terrorist or mugger might. The world was topsy-turvy, a dangerous place.

It was a time of despair. It was a time of opportunity. And it was a time when one could not be sure which was which.

The kibbutz sat on a hill top along the northern frontier of Israel. As they approached it the taxi driver Deborah had hired, a reserve officer who had fought in several wars, pointed to the low curtain of Lebanese mountains a few thousand yards beyond. The mountains hid P.L.O. mortars and raiders, he said. During the ride from Lod airport, she had also learned some other things from him. One was that although only three percent of the population lived on these kibbutz settlements, in which all property was owned and all decisions democratically made by the group, to many Israelis they embodied the utopian dream of what this nation should strive for. Another was that Dvora Levi was considered a soldier-heroine of Israel's struggle for independence and, later, a master spy, but, until her retirement from the uppermost ranks of Israel intelligence several years back, even her name had been kept secret.

The soldier in the elevated guardhouse was on the telephone a long time before waving the taxi onto the road between the pair of chain-link fences topped by barbed wire that encircled the settlement. At the shoulders of the sandwiched road was white powder that would track footprints of infiltrating terrorists across the asphalt. At night an armoured car patrolled the road.

'Everyone keeps a gun under his bed, just in case,' the driver told her.

During her El Al flight to Israel and the car trip north, Deborah had been beset by conflicting emotions: guilt that seeking her natural mother was a betrayal of the love she had just been reassured Madeleine had had for her; apprehension and curiosity and, eventually, angry resentment regarding that natural mother who perhaps had been forced to give away her child, but had later never tried to find her. Deborah soon realized that her feelings were even more complex than that, and inconsistent as well. While she still believed that no reason excused a mother for abandoning a child, she wanted desperately to find her mother and to be liked by her. She concentrated for a long time to define the nature of the yearning inside her.

An image of herself finally came into focus: she was a piece of partially woven cloth on a loom that had long ago stopped weaving because too many of the long warp threads were torn loose. Unconnected, that's how I feel, she decided, and the fabric won't ever be completed with all the right patterns woven into me until the threads are repaired.

That was why she had come there to find her mother, but she was terrified by all the unknowns to which such a choice exposed her. Fearing the unexpected, she had always manoeuvred to eliminate circumstances in which might lurk the potential to harm or grieve her. Although she was now a mature woman of power and wealth, she still harboured a child's fear she could not fend off that her mother would not want to see her and would reject her again. Deborah apprehended that Dvora Levi still had the power to maim her.

Now, approaching this armed encampment, Deborah added a new anxiety to the other. What did she have in common with this warrior, this amazon who had made a life out of war, skullduggery, and killing? If Deborah's need had not been so great, at that moment she might have turned back.

The car passed through the inner gate and parked near a stone guest house. Deborah was astonished by what she saw. She had expected to find a fortress compound – rugged, bare buildings huddled together. Instead she was within a spacious community: small but handsome houses, trees and flowers everywhere. It could have been an American suburb. *Our Town*.

A balding man in his fifties, in shorts and the ever-present short-sleeved white cotton shirt, emerged from a building that Deborah guessed was an administrative office. He strode up to her, obviously scrutinizing her face as he did so. He spoke brusquely to her driver in Hebrew.

'He wants to see your passport,' she was informed.

The kibbutz official checked it carefully and then spoke again in the raspy Semitic tongue. The driver translated a second time.

'They read here about the death of Pierre de Kronengold. He wants to know how you are related.'

'If he read the newspapers, then he knows that I'm Pierre's daughter.'

The official examined her face as if it was a museum exhibit. Then he nodded and spoke again, using his hands to indicate directions.

'He says you can go,' the driver related, and gave the directions.

Uncertain of her reception, Deborah told him to wait for her, and set off on a paved path that took her up a low rise among pine trees and then down the other side among several groupings of connected houses. It was late afternoon, and people were lounging or chatting outside their homes. Most stopped to watch as she passed. Usually capable of impeccable self-control, Deborah was very nervous, and thought the onlookers could observe her shaking.

The path bent round the last building and ended at a small house well separated from the others. A grey-haired woman, barefoot, in shorts and a short-sleeved print blouse, was bent over a row of flowers near the door, her back towards the path.

Hearing Deborah's approach, she straightened up and turned. She was tall and slim like Deborah, with the same large, intensely blue eyes set in an older face. Deborah shivered.

The woman stared unwaveringly as Deborah neared. Her expression was contained, unreadable, the only indication of her surprise the gardening shears in her dirt-stained hand that gaped open, like jaws. She seemed unable to form words for a long while.

Finally, Deborah said, 'I'm Deborah de Kronengold.'

'I know who you are,' the woman replied in a clear English accent. 'Not a day of the last thirty-five years has passed that I did not think of you. I was so sure you hated me. I was sure you would never want to find me.'

Dvora Levi stepped towards her daughter. They embraced awkwardly. Only the hungry grip of the woman's hands on her back conveyed to Deborah her pent-up longing. Deborah felt weak with relief. They parted to stare at each other again, searching for traces of themselves in the other's features.

'You . . . are . . . so beautiful.' Dvora's throat tightened at each word.

'So are you,' Deborah replied honestly. Dvora Levi's skin was tanned from working in the sun and lined by her sixty or so years, but the thin straight nose and mouth and the strong bones forming the structure of her face were those of a beautiful woman. Her hair had been red once, Deborah observed with surprise; that is how my hair will look when I'm older. She noticed the pink line rimming her mother's eyes, just as tears burned against her own.

'How did you find me? How could you know?' Dvora asked.

'I didn't even know Pierre was my father until recently, when he was dying. I gather you heard he had died.'

Dvora nodded silently.

Deborah explained. 'A friend, David Holtz, gave me your name and address.'

'The son of Max Holtz?'

'Yes. Max is dead now, but he went to a lot of trouble and expense to get hold of the information, so he and his son could someday use it as a lever against me.'

'That sounds like Max.' Dvora paused, reflecting on that distant time, then she took her daughter's hands in hers. 'Thank you for coming. I thought my life was over.'

'There is so much I want to know,' Deborah confessed. 'No one told me anything.'

'I will tell you everything. Can you stay with me a while?'

Deborah had hoped that love would well up at first sight of her mother, that years of resentment would be whisked away. But there had been no spontaneous, joyous conjunction. She still felt tentative and wary.

'Please,' the older woman urged. Deborah perceived how painful it was for this strong woman to ask – as painful as it would have been for her.

'Yes, of course, I'll stay. I brought a suitcase with me.'

Dvora sent a neighbour to retrieve the suitcase and dismiss the car and driver. Then she took her daughter's arm, as much to touch her again as to lead her into the house.

She is as anxious as I am, Deborah thought. That helped to lower the barrier a little in her own mind.

Inside the thick walls of the small living room, while Dvora fetched refreshments, Deborah seated herself on the little salmon-coloured sofa and tried to come to grips with her feelings at this extraordinary moment, but all she could sense was her inner turmoil and trepidation. Her only thought was how austere this room was, how ascetic her mother's life seemed to be.

Dvora returned from the tiny kitchen down the hall carrying a tray that supported a jug of orange juice and glasses. Deborah watched carefully as the older woman sat down on the only chair in the room, facing her, and reached for a glass to pass to her. It nearly slipped from her hand. She glanced at her daughter with a tense smile as she extended the glass. Then she leaned back, crossed her long legs, and clasped her hands over the upper knee – in a way that startled Deborah because it was so reminiscent of her own habit. She seemed about to speak, then hesitated.

'I've thought about this moment so many times, but it's difficult to start.' Dvora's throat was dry with nervousness. She paused to sip her orange juice before continuing. Finally, she said, 'It all started when we struck in the Kronengolds' steel plant in Turin, where I lived. . . .'

The first time Dvora saw Pierre de Kronengold she was standing at the head of a mass of striking workers outside the gates of his family's steel-making mill in Turin. The year was 1942. She was twenty-two years old and had been a surreptitious union organizer and a member of the secret Resistance for six years.

Her mother, Rachela, had died when Dvora was eight, from a beating meted out to her on Mussolini's express orders. Her father, Luigi Cavallo, had received the same treatment, but had recovered and courageously continued to operate their socialist, anti-government newspaper as uncompromisingly as before. He took the precaution, however, of placing his daughter in a succession of Catholic boarding schools in foreign countries, where she would be safe, would receive the religious instruction he had always wanted for her (but could not insist upon while her Jewish mother was alive), and would become fluent in a number of languages.

At the age of sixteen she had rebelled by running away from an English school – her fourth, after attending ones in Germany, France, and Spain – to be with her father and fling herself into the political and social turbulence engulfing Italy in the late Thirties. Dvora Cavallo adopted her father's extreme radicalism, involving herself in his underground newspaper, and in street demonstrations and strikes. Turin was the capital of Piedmont, where the drive to unify Italy had begun in the nineteenth century. She was a true daughter of the region: vigorous, beautiful, clever, and strong-willed. Despite her youth, Dvora soon joined her father among the tight knot comprising the leadership of Turin's underground.

It was from her Jewish grandmother that Dvora was finally able to learn about her own mother, Rachela, and about her mother's passionate Zionist beliefs that were as strong as her socialism.

By 1942 Pierre had been several years in Italy, since before the Germans had marched into Paris, when his family there had hidden what art treasures and valuables they could and, taking only their jewellery, had escaped to England. At the time Pierre was at his family's Milan bank, inherited many years earlier from a childless Kronengold branch. Despite Mussolini's new anti-Semitic decrees, Pierre had stayed in Italy to hold together what was left of the family's assets – the bank and the vast steel plant in Turin – believing himself somewhat protected because he was part of the powerful upper class.

In 1940 Britain's War Office had formed the Special Operations Executive, the SOE, a military intelligence unit, to operate behind Axis lines. Leslie de Kronengold, Pierre's British relative, had joined it in an influential position and soon recruited their cousin Nathan, who was then, after fleeing Berlin, heading Samuel's banking organization in Switzerland. Nathan, in turn, had got word to Pierre in Milan that British intelligence wanted him to gather information on Italian war production and to do his best to slow down his own plant's output, thus hindering the Axis war effort. Pierre had agreed, knowing both that he was putting at risk his family's last major assets and that he would be operating virtually alone.

Security was necessarily so tight among members of the Italian Resistance, and communications so difficult under the dictatorship in war-torn Italy, that the SOE had not yet made contact with the Italian Resistance on that day in 1942 when Pierre stepped out of the car before the gates of his Turin plant to confront Dvora Cavallo, who stood at the head of a phalanx of angry strikers. The six years since her return to Italy had forged out of the rebellious schoolgirl a hardened, dedicated patriot. She was in the forefront of this factory Resistance effort that had been disguised as a labour dispute.

Dvora had been expecting that the capitalist Kronengold would be an old man, fat with self-indulgence and indolence. She was startled by the sight of this young man in scholar's spectacles whose managers crowded around him. She decided he looked like a typical half-witted rich man's son, living proof of the rot at the core of hereditary capitalism. He ran his plant incompetently too, she had observed; anyone with an ounce of sense could have raised production by fifty percent or more.

'We demand you negotiate with us!' she yelled at him, never thinking he would agree, having behind him the government's soldiers to back up his recalcitrance.

Instead of declining, to everyone's astonishment, he nodded somewhat shyly, separated himself from his executives, and walked through the strikers and the gates, followed by the employees' strike committee. For almost an hour Dvora harangued him about his labour practices and the government's oppressive policies. When she threatened even more disruptive tactics, he stood up with an odd little smile, and said only, 'I imagine you will do whatever you have to.' And he left.

'Clearly a half-wit!' Dvora announced to the others on the strike committee when Pierre had left the room. 'And a French half-wit at that!'

She did not see him again for well over a year, until the latter part of 1943. Much had happened to both of them and to the world by then. Dvora's father had been arrested and tried before Mussolini's infamous Special Tribunal, where conviction was guaranteed. Sent to the Isle of Ponza, he contracted pneumonia and died. Twenty-three-year-old Dvora had then run the newspaper with her staff for several months but, upon receiving word of her own imminent arrest, was forced to close down the newspaper and flee into the mountains.

Dvora became an armed partisan. Having already risen to the top ranks of the underground – the *macchia* – in Piedmont, she became a key guerrilla leader, attracting many dissidents, particularly disaffected deserters from the Italian army.

Dvora was superb at languages and mimicry. She could instantly change her voice, her walk, her appearance to slip among Germans and Italians alike to gain information or perform acts of sabotage. The tenacity and daring of her band's exploits gave hope to many among the shackled Italian people. That and her red hair earned her the sobriquet 'the Torch'.

In the late autumn of 1943, a few months after British intelligence had finally established a liaison with the *macchia*, a request reached Dvora from the SOE that filled her with disgust. They wanted her group to rescue someone they claimed was a 'valuable' Allied operative being held prisoner by the Germans in Turin, Pierre de Kronengold. 'Now we're wasting our time on half-wits!' she fumed to her officers. Only because Britain had begun to supply the Resistance forces with arms they might otherwise have cut off did Dvora agree to comply.

For a long time the Germans had treated their Italian ally as a sovereign partner, but the latter's military defeats and internal dissension had prompted the Germans to send in troops and take over control of Italy, keeping Mussolini in power as their puppet. The Germans had immediately accelerated implementation of their anti-Semitic policy and begun to round up Jews. About a week before Dvora was contacted by the SOE, the Germans seized the Kronengold bank and steel plant and, as he arrived in his car at the latter, arrested Pierre de Kronengold.

Rather than being shipped off to a prison camp at once, he was incarcerated in the Germans' Turin military headquarters building. Pierre learned from his guard that there were standing orders that any Kronengold was to be held for interrogation by a specially designated SS officer. This SS man was on his way to Turin, but would have only a few days to extract his information because Pierre was scheduled to be put on board a night train and sent to a prison camp at the end of the week.

Pierre spent the next days preparing himself to resist the torture he was sure would be inflicted on him. He was determined not to divulge any information about his SOE contacts. Two days before he was to be transported out of Italy to the prison camp, he heard voices in the outer corridor, and he realized his interrogator had arrived. A moment later the lock was turned and the door opened. An SS captain stepped into the little cell. It was Max Holtz.

Germany's invasion of Paris had proved to be an opportunity for Holtz. With his falsified Aryan genealogy, he had obtained a unique position for himself with the Nazis. Reasoning that the Kronengolds and other rich Jewish families in every occupied country had tried to hide their vast capital and treasuries before they were killed or escaped, Holtz realized that his long association with the Kronengolds gave him a special knowledge of the places in which and the means by which he could track down and uncover much of that wealth. He arranged with several prominent generals that he would turn over whatever he found to them, keeping ten percent for himself. That percentage could end up totalling a vast fortune. By the time Germany had conquered all Europe and the war was won, he would be a spectacularly rich man. This was, at last, his big chance. The Kronengolds, who had destroyed his family's Austrian bank, would now have their rightful due extracted from them when he discovered their underground art vaults and secret bank accounts. The generals granted him a military commission as well, which allowed him to commandeer the resources he needed for his work.

Holtz had recently been ordered to Italy. France had been well picked over by then, and Holtz was to begin his scavenging in Piedmont, beginning with the information he could force from the prisoner Pierre de Kronengold. The prospect terrified him. They had met at Valtary when he and Leslie had escaped by train from Vienna with Edgar's body. The Frenchman knew he was a Jew and what his real name was and could unmask him to the Nazis.

As Max Holtz entered his cell and shut the door behind him, a smile broke across Pierre's tense features.

'I'd like you to make a telephone call for me, Max,' he said.

That night, having concluded that refusal would be more dangerous than compliance, Max Holtz went to a public telephone, dialled the number Pierre had given him, and said the code word to Pierre's spy network contact at the other end of the line. When the answering code was given, Holtz told the listener Pierre was scheduled to be put on board a train heading for a prison camp in Germany that left at ten o'clock on Friday night. A voice at the other end of the line then gave a series of code words to repeat to Pierre, which would confirm the message had been correctly passed.

He spent the next day, Friday, in Pierre's cell, pretending to interrogate the prisoner forcibly, all the while fearful that he himself would be arrested. He was very relieved when, at nine o'clock that night, German guards marched Pierre out to a waiting Mercedes.

'Don't worry,' their lieutenant jeered. 'Your steel factory will be following you soon. Tomorrow we start dismantling it to send it to Germany. The Italians don't fight, so Italy doesn't need its factories.'

Six streets away from the station two cars blocked an intersection, the drivers apparently engaged in furious recriminations over who had caused the minor accident. Smiling at the childishness of the Italians, the German driver got out of the Mercedes to order them to move. Suddenly, a barrage of bullets flattened the Mercedes' tyres and twenty armed partisan fighters raised their heads from behind parked cars. In less than a minute they stripped the Germans of their guns and ammunition, transferred Pierre to one of the parked cars, and left the scene without a trace.

As the getaway car sped through side streets to discourage pursuit, Pierre asked, 'Where are we going?'

A figure in the front seat turned round to him. 'Don't worry, little rich boy, we'll find a nice safe place for you.'

The voice was a woman's, and Pierre recognized it. 'Don't I know you?'

Laughing, Dvora pulled off the knitted face mask that had covered her entire head. Her red hair, darkly glinting in the dimness, fell to her shoulders.

'The strike leader!' Pierre exclaimed. Then, realizing from the colour of her hair that she must be the famous Torch, he added, 'It's an honour. But I still want to know where we're going.'

'That's none of your business,' she snapped.

'We must go to the steel plant.'

Dvora ignored the urgency in his voice. 'Did you forget your money bags?'

'We must blow it up!'

Dvora's expression became serious. 'Why?'

'Tomorrow will be too late. The Germans will begin dismantling it in the morning to ship it to Germany.'

'You'd blow up your own factory?'

'The Germans could produce two to three times the steel goods coming out of there now. It's too valuable to them.'

'You mean you know how incompetently the plant is run?'

'That was the point. Do you take me for a half-wit?'

Dvora's laughter filled the car.

They made new plans. Just before dawn, a series of explosions rocked the outskirts of Turin. The sky was illuminated by flames leaping up from a gigantic pyre that, moments before, had been the sprawling Kronengold steelworks.

Pierre was now a partisan.

Within the first month Dvora was forced to recognize Pierre's innate military talents, albeit grudgingly. When the guerrilla band began to grow short of ammunition at their mountain hide-out, Pierre gave her the name of one of his own contacts, who could place more modern weapons and ammunition in their hands. Still not fully trusting Pierre, Dvora left him at the camp with several other men while she and a larger group went for the weapons. Upon their return they had trouble locating the camp and were halted by an unseen voice demanding the password. It turned out that Pierre had organized the other men into protecting their position more effectively while hiding their other supplies and, indeed, any evidence of the camp. What had occasionally been in her absence a rather haphazard security had been prodded into alertness. He suggested, furthermore, that their supplies should not be kept in one place, but be divided into several batches and hidden in widely separated caches so as to prevent devastation to their cause if a site should be discovered. Despite her approval of the measures, she could not keep from her tone her irritation that he had made leadership decisions, in fact had taken command of the others, without her direction to do so.

Over the next few days, the band's number was augmented by several soldiers who had deserted from the Italian army. A good part of her group had originally come from the army's ranks, men who were disgusted by Fascism and were being forced to attempt to conquer other nations and repress their fellow citizens at home. Usually Dvora welcomed such trained recruits who brought their own weapons, although she had to reorientate their thinking to the guerrilla mentality of hit-and-run and survive. This time she was even more wary than usual: one of the deserters appeared too eager to express his partisan patriotism. She kept her doubts to herself, but watched him very carefully. Late one night, when all were bedded down except for those assigned to guard duty on the camp's perimeter, she saw the man rise to his knees, look stealthily around, and creep into the trees at the edge of the clearing. She stood up, her pistol drawn, and began to follow him. Another man had stood up at the other side of the clearing. It was Pierre. He nodded to her and headed into the woods on the flank.

The woods were very dark, and the false deserter moved

quickly ahead of Dvora. Often she lost sight of him. She hoped to close ground once the trees thinned out. The man was only a mile and a half from an Italian army outpost when he sensed someone behind him. He dropped to his stomach, rifle cocked. Dvora dared not move from behind the tree that hid her. Suddenly, she heard a brief scuffle and then Pierre's voice telling her she could come out. The man was dead. She found Pierre staring down at the army spy in disbelief at what he had just done: jumped on the man from behind and sliced his throat halfway through. Tiny droplets of blood spattered Pierre's spectacles.

'Why didn't you shoot him?' she asked. 'Too close to the army camp?'

'I don't know how to use a gun,' he replied, still unable to stop from staring at the dead man.

She threw an arm around him. 'It's time you learned.'

Dvora undertook personally his military training and began to listen more seriously to his suggestions. The group began to store caches of supplies at widely separated places. They changed camp sites more frequently. She had ignored his presence among her followers until then, but now began to converse with him, piqued both by his organizational skills that none of the others under her possessed and by the quiet daring that contrasted with the Italian bravado many of the others presented. She began to find that he had the ability, like her, to plan the next day's tactics without losing sight of the group's long-range strategy. Also like her, Pierre had an intellectual bent and a cultural background that gave them some common attitudes, although their differences made for lively, even sarcastic dialogue. She carefully noted, however, that he never stepped over the line into the sort of disrespect that might belittle or contest her leadership.

In private she began to call him 'your lordship', because of his father's title. Knowing she disliked being called the Torch because it emphasized her, one person, at the expense of their cause, he naturally took to calling her 'your torchship'.

Gradually, Dvora was being forced to admit that this wealthy privileged young man, in many ways so dissimilar from her, upset all her glib preconceptions about capitalists and class warfare. He was as much of a patriot as she, as capable of enduring hardships, as willing to place his life on the line, as thoughtful about the human condition. They were opposites who sensed the lacks in themselves that were strengths in the other, jigsaw-puzzle pieces that fitted – the fiery Italian socialist young woman and the analytical French capitalist young man.

For the most part the partisans had to live off the land. That meant developing a far-ranging network of secret supporters among the villagers in their territory. Those people would help the partisans' cause with recruits, with food, and by being their eyes and ears to report enemy troop movements in the area. Most of the organizing work before this had fallen on Dvora's shoulders. She soon recognized Pierre's gift of persuasion, and asked him to accompany her on the clandestine organizing journeys.

One night a violent rainstorm suddenly hit, and they were lodged together in a concealed attic of a farmhouse. Drenched, they removed their clothes in the darkness and slipped into bed.

The attraction between them had been growing in intensity in the last weeks, although neither would have admitted it, in fact denied it, emphasizing in their own minds instead the vast differences in their upbringing, their ideologies, the sparring when they chatted. Now there was silence, except for the rain drumming insistently against the single window. Neither could sleep. Neither dared move in the narrow single bed. Each listened to the other's breathing and wondered what it meant. Finally, Pierre shifted a cramped arm, which brushed against Dvora. She turned towards him and, simultaneously, they reached for each other. Their kiss was hungry and lonely and desperate.

For a short night they were sheltered from the war, from rich and poor, from reactionary and radical, from all the creeds and all the causes and all the death, trying to stretch the illusion of immortality to fit the fantasy of eternity. They clung to each other that night and made no pretence of bravery. They made love and found they loved. They fell asleep trying to shield each other from the dawn.

United in their hatred of a common enemy, they had been drawn together by a wildly passionate attraction that their differences exacerbated. The war had proven to be a common denominator, levelling them into equality, allowing them to fall in love. With death so close, only the here and now mattered. When the killing ended, Dvora and Pierre would return to their utterly opposite lives – she to socialist politics in the new Italy, he to his wife and business somewhere on the other side of the war – but the future seemed as distant and insubstantial as a dream, a desperate hope the flesh could not wait for. For Dvora and Pierre love was a far more real sanctuary.

To disguise his Judaism Pierre had melted down the gold wedding band he wore and, in a mould he whittled out of wood, recast it into a small cross, which he wore on a string about his neck. To seal their love, Dvora now gave him the thin gold chain she wore on which to hang the cross. She refused to take a gift from him in return. That was all right, she told him, because she was the poor one.

An event occurred in July of 1944 that had a profound effect on them both. Rumours had reached the partisans that Jews were being rounded up and deported in large numbers, not only in Italy, but throughout Europe. The common assumption was that detention areas had been set aside for them somewhere, villages perhaps, to isolate them from the rest of the population.

That day in July, as they had done before, Dvora's guerrillas group blew up a passing freight train in a wooded mountain area. It was carrying what they thought were military or industrial resources bound for Germany. The engine was derailed and several trucks broke open, releasing the cargo: human beings who tried to flee their captors. The German soldiers guarding the train shot back at the attacking partisans. A German major, the commanding officer, seeing the prisoners making their getaway, ordered a machine-gun unit to shift its fire so as to gun down the fleeing prisoners in their tracks – men, women, and children.

'I want him alive!' Dvora screamed at her troops.

In a few minutes most of the German soldiers were dead, and the rest had surrendered. The prisoners they had been transporting were Italian Jews. Twenty-seven had been murdered by machine-gun bullets, eight more were close to death, and eleven others were wounded. While the guerrillas released the captives in the rest of the trucks and tried to treat the wounded, Dvora went to interrogate the enemy major.

As soon as he heard her impeccable Prussian accent, the major proudly admitted, without the slightest coercion, something so shocking that, at first, Dvora and Pierre refused to believe him. He asserted that the Jews in the train – *all* the Jews deported throughout Europe – were being sent to giant extermination camps. When the railway truck had broken open, he considered it his prime duty to stop the Jews from escaping, even at the risk of his own capture.

'Jews are filthy vermin,' he explained in earnest justification for his act. 'It is in everyone's interest – not just Germany's – to wipe them out. We Aryans are curing the world of a cancer by killing them off. We have already liquidated millions, but there is still much work to be done before the Jewish problem is totally solved. We shall –'

Dvora shot him through the mouth as he spoke and, as he crumpled to the ground, through both eyes. Then she had all the remaining German soldiers lined up and executed. The partisans led the Jews they freed – the wounded and the unharmed – to members of the Resistance who could hide them. Several of the men joined Dvora's band.

Dvora and Pierre were silent for hours after their safe return to their mountain hide-out. Still stunned, they lay on the forest floor staring upwards into the night, struggling with agonizing thoughts. He held her as she wept.

'There is no God!' Dvora bitterly whispered to the stars she had once thought were God's handiwork. 'But, if there is, He is an abomination to allow millions of innocent people to be murdered because they worship Him in a different way from their killers.'

She sat up and stared down at Pierre's dimly outlined features. 'If this war ever ends, and I'm still alive, I'm going to spend the rest of my life carrying on the work my mother believed in – building a homeland in Palestine for the Jewish people.'

'When you rescued me,' he reminded her, 'the Germans were just about to put me on a train like that one, probably bound for just such a death camp. I'd be dead now. How can this be happening? Germany! The land of Goethe and Beethoven. I always thought we were living in enlightened times.' He reached up and touched her face, which was wet from weeping. 'You're right. Until we Jews have our own country we'll never be safe anywhere.'

She bent close to him. 'I want to do something irrevocable to remind me always of what I've vowed.' She thought a while, then she kissed him impulsively, seized with an idea.

'I'm going to take my mother's last name, her maiden name, Levi, so I'll never forget.'

He tried out the sound. 'Dvora Levi.'

'Jew. Zionist. Those things are in her name, and they're now in me. I'll never forget.'

'Never!' he vowed himself and hugged her against him.

Dvora began to unbutton Pierre's shirt, kissing his skin as she exposed it.

'We have a cause waiting for us at the end of the war,' she whispered. 'We *have* to survive!'

That night, in a fusion of many passions, Deborah de Kronengold was conceived.

By early 1945, Dvora's small band had grown into a brigade of three battalions, each one hundred and fifty partisans strong. Allied forces were preparing for a final, all-out offensive into Italy's industrial north. General Alexander's Allied command ordered Dvora's guerrilla force to move farther north, into the Alps – well behind German lines – to undertake the dangerous job of harrying the German army and diverting its attention from the frontal assaults soon to come.

In April, her due date near and her mobility restricted, Dvora finally agreed to Pierre's entreaties. By radio he gave the prearranged signal to Nathan, who was to meet them at an agreed-upon place in the woods south of the Swiss border, a place they had picked out on a map a few weeks before, when Nathan had ventured into Italy for a series of meetings with *macchia* leaders. Nathan would lead Dvora to a hospital in Switzerland through forest paths that snaked towards the border crossing he had bribed the Swiss to leave unobserved.

Only a short distance from the rendezvous point, a German patrol cut Dvora and Pierre off. Shots were exchanged. The two had to flee towards the south-east without ever having made contact with Nathan. Hearing the shots, Nathan fled too.

The next day, exhausted, Dvora began to experience birth pains, and she and Pierre were unable to run any more. They took refuge in a small hut on the edge of mountainous farm fields well north of Milan. The German unit searching for them surrounded the hut. Although he was ecstatic to have captured the Torch and Kronengold, the German commander was a stickler for military obedience. Instead of executing them immediately, he remembered the standing orders and sent word back to headquarters.

An hour later, through the cabin window, Pierre observed a plume of dust rising above the woods and fields and moving up the mountain towards them like an invisible locomotive. A black Mercedes convertible came into view and halted at the bottom of the hillside ploughed below. The car's lone occupant stepped from it, a stocky figure in the field-grey greatcoat and peaked cap of the Waffen-SS. The man strode quickly up the dirt path to the hut. To wear such a coat the man had to be at least a colonel, Pierre knew. Indeed that was the rank now held by the officer who entered the cabin.

Max Holtz had spent the many months since he last saw Pierre trying to track down hidden wealth, mostly Jewish, in the tangible form of art treasures. His own share of this booty had now aggregated in a bank vault into a substantial pile, which he would be able to keep for his own benefit if the Germans won the war. To his great dismay, however, just the opposite appeared to be happening. He would be a pauper again but, worse, might well be jailed for his criminal theft by the victors, his true identity and his treachery revealed. Certain the Third Reich was near defeat, Max saw the capture of Pierre de Kronengold as an eleventh-hour intercession of opportunity, as his deliverance.

'Out!' he ordered the soldiers, his Luger pointing at Pierre. 'I need only one man posted outside the door. I will get the information the Führer seeks from this Jew pig.'

'But, colonel, they are very dangerous,' the captain argued.

'Out, captain, or it will be you who is under arrest!'

The squad withdrew, leaving a young recruit outside.

Once they were alone, Max wasted no time in making Pierre and Dvora an offer. Under the alias he had assumed with the Germans, he had papers that would allow him through the German lines. He would add all their names – the baby's too when it was born – if Pierre would swear to the Allies that Max had been covertly working for the Resistance and against the Nazis all the time. No one but Pierre and Dvora would ever be allowed to know the truth. The prisoners had no choice but to strike a deal, despite their disgust with Max's amorality. But, as insurance against a likely double cross, Pierre insisted on exacting a letter which Max wrote out then and there. In it he confessed he was a German officer plundering property from the Italian government, the Church, and wealthy Jews, particularly the

Kronengolds, and that he had never been in the Resistance.

Dvora was a long time giving birth. After hours of pain, on Max's SS greatcoat spread over the dirt floor, Dvora gave birth, with Pierre's help, to a blue-eyed girl with a fringe of red hair.

'We have a daughter,' Dvora said aloud in a tone already filled with the sadness of the inevitable separation soon to come. She hugged the child desperately to her breast.

Pierre dropped to his knees beside her. 'Are you all right?'

She nodded wearily. He kissed her gently on the mouth and looked down at their daughter. The tiny face appeared to be sleeping.

'She picked herself a savage time to be born,' he observed with sorrow.

'She had no choice, poor thing. No choice at all. We've made them all.'

At that moment the infant's eyelids opened, and she appeared to stare directly at Pierre.

'Her eyes,' he said quietly. 'They're like yours . . . like cabochon sapphires. She's a very special baby.'

'Yes,' Dvora said sadly.

Max noticed the bubble of dust rising above the mountain roadway below. The Germans, alarmed at the length of time the interrogation was taking, had sent two trucks full of soldiers; they did not want partisan leaders as dangerous as these two to escape.

Max walked outside to speak to the guard. After a few words he pointed towards the village higher up the mountain. When the young man turned in the direction his superior pointed, Max shot him in the back of the head. He and Pierre then hid the body in the woods and stripped it of the rifle, a Beretta pistol the German had picked up somewhere, and ammunition.

Supported by Max and Pierre, Dvora walked down the path carrying her baby. The Germans were now too close. Pierre would have to divert them and allow the others time to make their escape. Max would escort Dvora and the baby to the Convent of Santa Raffaella. Pierre would meet them there.

He quickly unfastened the thin gold chain from around his neck. Dangling from it was the gold cross he had recast from his wedding ring. He placed it round his daughter's neck.

'In case we all get separated,' he said off-handedly, but his fear for their safety and his sadness came through. Then Pierre took his rifle and glared at Max. 'If I make it and find that either Dvora or my daughter was hurt or betrayed, I will kill you, Holtz.'

The odds made Holtz uneasy. 'But, if the Germans get you, they'll find my confession letter and know I switched sides.'

'Then pray I make it.'

Pierre kissed his infant daughter and then embraced Dvora. When Dvora turned towards Max, she was holding Pierre's pistol. She took Max's Luger from him and motioned him into the car.

'I will get them through,' Max promised Pierre gravely.

Dvora got into the car with her baby and gestured towards a dirt road scarred by twin ruts from horse- and ox-cart wheel. She knew it must lead through the woods to another road.

Pierre ran in the other direction to play hare and hounds. He found a tree on a slight elevation on the other side of the field. Wooded terrain too steep to farm was at his back. He took aim just as the first two troop trucks rounded a turn and emerged from the woods.

As he pulled the trigger, Pierre saw the windshield shatter and the driver snap back. The truck careered to the right and then spun left, smashing into a tree trunk, blocking the second truck behind it. Pierre picked off soldiers tumbling from the trucks as he moved farther back into the woods and up the mountainside.

When he was sure the Mercedes had had time to get safely away, he turned to run for an escape and felt pain explode in his shoulder. He staggered forward without breaking his stride.

Dvora's tone, sombre throughout the telling, became more so as the story neared its end. War was raging everywhere. It took nearly a week for her and her baby and Max to work their way through the warring lines to the Convent of Santa Raffaella. Pierre had not arrived, nor had he been heard from. Dvora could not wait – her troops needed her leadership. As soon as she was strong enough, she left Deborah with the nuns in the orphanage. If neither she nor Pierre made it back, the Mother Superior, Sister Teresa, was to contact Nathan in Switzerland.

The war ended in early May. Dvora rushed back to the convent while her troops occupied the Alpine area in which they had been fighting. Pierre had not been heard from, and she feared for his welfare. Her consolation was that her baby was well, and she could spend nearly every waking moment with her.

'Even when you were asleep, I sat by your crib and watched you, trying to memorize every line of your face, every fold in your plump arms, imagining what you would look like when you were grown up. At the same time my fears about Pierre were always on my mind.' Her voice dropped. 'And I knew, once he returned . . . I would never see you again.'

Dvora reached forward for a mouthful of orange juice. Recovered, she sat back. 'On the third day I was playing with you in the nursery, on the top floor, near a window that overlooked the road. A small red Fiat that had somehow held together through the war pulled up at the entrance below. Pierre got out of it. I picked you up and ran down the stairs. We were at the front door before he was. We all hugged each other . . . for what seemed like hours.'

Dvora was silent a long while, remembering, her face unfocused. 'Pierre's arm was in a sling. He had been wounded leading the Germans away from us. The bullet had fractured his collarbone, but he had been able to make it out of the woods. *Macchia* contacts in Milan had taken him to a doctor. Fighting had broken out all across northern Italy by the time he was strong enough to return to our brigade, so he fought where he was and headed towards the convent when the war ended. The nuns re-dressed his wound, and the three of us went out to the courtyard. He and I lay on the grass playing with you. All afternoon we avoided talking about the future . . .' Her gaze swung back to Deborah. 'The decision had been made by both of us just after we knew you had been conceived. Finally, we could no longer avoid it.'

Unconsciously, Deborah leaned forward, her mouth grimly drawn. Her mother's voice was firm, the anguish betraying itself only by the slowness with which she spoke.

'The course of both our lives was fixed by our commitment to a future homeland for the Jewish people. Pierre was France's most prominent Jew. It was essential that he return to his life there and rebuild his bank. Money had to be raised – lots of it – and weapons secretly purchased and smuggled into Palestine, and a secret accommodation arrived at with the French government to ease the way for all of that. His commitment to help build an Israel went hand in hand with his duty to restore the Kronengolds' wealth and influence.' She shrugged stoically. 'That meant he would have to go back to his wife. I knew that. He had nothing then but his name. His bank had been looted. He himself had destroyed a steel factory that employed thousands. Simone had the wealth to lend him so that he could rebuild.'

'So he used her,' Deborah remarked with asperity, echoing Leslie's remark.

'Pierre wasn't a user,' Dvora rejoined fiercely, 'a parasite who would just take from her and not keep his end of the bargain. If he went back to her, she would never have cause to doubt he was a true husband to her and father to his son. That was his sacrifice. But, to do that, he had to give you up.'

'What about you?' Deborah asked sharply. 'Why did *you* have to give me up?'

The older woman took a deep breath. She had always feared that someday she might have to answer that question. 'You have to know what it was like in Europe after the war. Italy was ravaged. All over Central Europe concentration camps were being liberated and piles of dead Jews were found where the Germans had no time to get them into incinerators. No one yet knew how many had been murdered. They found living skeletons too. The lucky ones! Some who had managed to make it through the war were refugees now, just coming out of hiding, wandering.'

Her voice rose. 'I had work to do. A representative of the secret Jewish government in Palestine had contacted me months before about organizing a network to collect weapons when the war ended – partisan, German, Italian, Allied. Whatever weapons we could get our hands on would be smuggled into Palestine to resist the British. Then I would lead a volunteer group behind Russian lines in Austria and Eastern Europe. Because of my languages and underground contacts, the people I could draw on to follow me, I was the logical choice. Our job was to organize secret Jewish emigration to a refugee camp in Italy. Those people would then be sneaked into Palestine – particularly Jewish soldiers and partisans, people who could fight. There was no way I could take a baby into that kind of danger. In Eastern Europe I was sure it would be only a matter of time before the Russians found out about me and my network and killed me.'

'Anybody could have worked for Israel,' Deborah countered with resentment. 'Only one woman was my mother. You owed me that by giving birth to me.'

'Would you have wanted me to have an abortion?' Dvora asked quietly.

'Is that how you saw your choice?'

The older woman hunched forward. 'I was a fighter. All my life. When I was only sixteen, I fought for the workers and against the Fascists. Then I fought the Germans. My men and I killed hundreds, maybe thousands. Do you understand? I wasn't an ordinary woman. I had skills, contacts everywhere to draw on.' There was no apology in her voice. 'I had a cause I believed in and a job I vowed to do.'

'And me?'

'Pierre and I had always assumed he would take care of your welfare in some way. When we saw Nathan some time before you were born, we learned that his sister in London had just lost her baby in childbirth and was very depressed. We had been thinking since then about asking her to take in the baby we would soon have, to raise you as her own daughter. Pierre assured me she would love you' – Dvora faltered briefly – 'as if you were her own. The first night after he arrived at the convent, through his SOE connections, he was able to telephone England and speak to his sister and her husband. She was in a hospital, sunk in depression, as I remember. An earlier call from Nathan had prepared them; they knew Pierre was the father and I was the mother. Pierre explained to them, just as he had told Nathan, that I had not been able to make it to the Swiss hopital where it would have been safe, and had died giving birth in a field. He could not keep you, he said to them, because his wife would not be understanding – about you or me. Afterwards, he assured me that they wanted you very much.'

Dvora pushed herself up to a standing position and went to the window. Bright searchlights were lit above the fence enclosing the kibbutz, etching her profile sharply against the night.

'I wrapped you up warmly and, with the nuns' help, arranged your food for the trip. I carried you out to the Fiat. Pierre was in the car with the engine running, about to leave.

First, as he had promised, he was going to Allied headquarters to vouch for Max Holtz's anti-Nazi activity. Then he would continue on to Switzerland. Nathan would put him and you on a plane to London.' She swallowed, unable to continue speaking for a moment. 'It took all my strength not to get into the car. Instead, I kissed Pierre good-bye. And then I kissed you one last time and hoped you would forgive what I had to do. I set you into a basket on the seat beside Pierre. I couldn't bear to look, so I turned round and waited a long time before turning back. When I did the car was out of sight.'

Deborah interrupted the silence. 'But why did Pierre tell everyone you had died in childbirth?'

'*I* wanted that. It wouldn't have been fair to you or the people who would make you their daughter if they thought I might suddenly appear and reclaim you. Madeleine had every right to be considered your mother. I didn't want you to be troubled by conflicting loyalties.'

'I grew up thinking you had died in childbirth,' Deborah replied intransigently. 'I was always afraid I might die the same way.'

'I'm sorry. To be truthful, I never thought you would be told you were adopted. I was sure you'd grow up thinking they were your real parents.'

'But, later on,' Deborah pressed her, 'after Madeleine died, then you could have said something. Or after I had grown up.'

Dvora slowly turned back to the room, engaging her daughter's hostile stare. 'You had every reason to hate me – a mother who gave you up. At least if I were dead, you couldn't hate me.' The muscles that kept her posture straight appeared to tighten even further with the discipline she exerted. 'I made my choice. I had to live with it.' She walked up to her daughter and gazed down at her. 'I don't ask you to approve what was forced on you without your knowledge or consent. But understand, these were sacrifices we believed we had to make for the very highest motives. For the survival of the Jewish people.'

Deborah's voice was hard and unsparing. 'I'm carrying a child now. There is no cause, no motive, noble enough to sacrifice that child for. Your recollections of tenderness to me as an infant are very poignant – and quite contrived thirty-five years after the fact. You said earlier you had nothing to live for until I showed up today. Your spying and fighting days are over. You have no husband or children. You're bored, and I brought some excitement back into your life.' Deborah cocked her head, reasserting the pride she had reined in to undertake this search. 'I think the truth is that you refused to give up a life you loved when I was born: war and danger and spying. I was an inconvenience to you. I think you abandoned me without a second thought – and wasted barely a thought on me after that.' Deborah stood up. 'I came here simply to satisfy my curiosity, and now I've done that. I'll be glad to pay someone to drive me to Tel Aviv.'

Her mother's mouth set with similar pride. 'I'll ask one of my friends to do it for nothing, as a favour to me.'

Deborah went to the bathroom. She avoided looking at herself in the mirror as she washed. At this moment she would not be able to bear the sight of a face so like that of the deceitful woman in the other room. She wanted only to run as swiftly and as far away as she could from a mother who was hers by biological accident alone and not by reason of caring.

When she left the bathroom, her mother did not appear to be in the house. Deborah assumed she had gone out to arrange for the car and driver.

Hearing a muffled sound as she walked down the hall, Deborah paused to listen. She heard it again, coming from behind a closed door. Curious, she opened the door.

Dvora sat on the edge of a bed, a framed photograph on her lap. She was sobbing and for several seconds did not notice Deborah's presence. When she did, she quickly pushed the photograph beneath a pillow and wiped at her tears with her hand.

'I will get you your car,' she whispered and started to rise.

Deborah reached past the other woman, under the pillow, and withdrew the frame. She held it up to the light, stunned by the colour photograph it contained. The shot was of her and Pierre, taken at the Monte Carlo gala, when she was eighteen. He was in a dinner jacket and she in her blue gown. They both looked very happy.

As Deborah lifted her glance, other photos in the room caught her eye. They were everywhere, on the bureau, the bedside tables, on every wall – of Deborah from infancy to the present day, and of Dvora and Pierre together on the kibbutz. Deborah moved from one to the next in a state of shock. The photographs Pierre had always insisted on taking of Deborah had been intended for Dvora.

'It never ended between you and Pierre!' Deborah exclaimed in astonishment.

Mouth open, shoulders heaving, the older woman's speech seemed stolen from her.

'He found me,' she finally whispered. 'Whenever he could come to Israel to see me, we lived together here . . .' Her voice choked. '. . . like a family – the three of us.'

Tears filled Deborah's eyes. The photographs blurred. That was what she wanted to hear. That was why she had come to Israel. She groped for the other woman's hand and dropped to a sitting position on the bed beside her.

'Always,' Deborah whispered in reply. 'Always I remained your daughter.'

'As if you were away for a day or two and would soon be back with us – here, in our home.'

Heavy with tears and elation, Deborah's head lowered onto her mother's shoulder, and her arms reached round her. Deborah hugged her tightly, allowing tears held back for a lifetime to flow between them. Slowly, she lifted her mother's hand and placed it over her stomach. There, like bubbles sliding across her belly, Dvora's grandchild was moving.

CHAPTER TWENTY-FOUR

Not once during the week that followed did Deborah think about her business. She had never before been so inactive, yet so fulfilled, despite swinging between extremes of elation and depression. She had discovered that her origin was romantic in the widest of senses and founded on an unending love. Pierre and Dvora's relinquishing of their daughter was grounded in an idealism and sacrifice that Deborah had never contemplated. Her loss had been wrenching for her natural parents. They had never forgotten her or ceased to love her. Every letter exchanged between Deborah and Pierre had been kept by Dvora, their every telephone call was recorded in correspondence.

The belief that she *had* been loved – and deserved love from others – did not instantly replace in Deborah the sense of rejection that had festered for years; at times she felt adrift between the two states. She brooded for hours, assimilating the new awareness into her bones. But there were also hours when she was grateful not to think, not to feel the depressing dislocation.

The first days spent with Dvora had been, after the euphoria, a kind of testing for them both, each groping for an appropriate position in their relationship. Although Deborah was much more open about herself than was her wont, the intimacy her mother sought often became oppressive to her, and she abruptly withdrew. Moreover, she still felt jabs of guilt that it might be a betrayal of Madeleine. The times when Deborah, in a mood of bewilderment, wanted to go off by herself to think were aggravating to the older woman, who had hungered to be with her for thirty-five years.

There were disappointments for Deborah too. The fairytale-queen image she had created, as a child, of her natural mother – or even the stereotype kindly simple peasant-woman – were nothing like Dvora Levi, who was a flinty, ascetic force, invariably hiding her own true feelings as if they were foot soldiers marching behind an armoured column. But even such negative observations were helpful to Deborah because they coerced her into focusing, one at a time, on the qualities she perceived in her newly-discovered mother. Their similarities to her own traits and the connections she had come here to seek began to emerge: independence, of course; self-discipline that subverted all attitudes which were not useful to gaining an objective; touchiness and quickness to anger; and a swift, strategic mind. Minor similarities began to emerge, too: their laughter was alike, and they found humour in the same things; other people commented that they looked alike and moved and gestured in the same way.

It was when she discussed Dvora and Pierre with other people at the kibbutz that a sense of pride about them began to grow in her. The kibbutz, which Dvora had helped to found, had always been her home when she was not in Tel Aviv or abroad for Mossad, Israel's intelligence agency. Many of her neighbours there had fought for Israel and done so bravely, but Dvora's place among them seemed surrounded by a very special garland of honour that was kept fresh by the respect they had for her. Dvora had indeed been one of the heroines of independence: never a politician, nonetheless, as a top-level official in Israel's spy network, she had known and worked with and was herself on the fringe of the revered circle that included Chaim Weizmann and David Ben-Gurion and Golda Meir.

Her neighbours' respect extended to Pierre. They knew of his wealth and his ancestory and that he was married to another woman in France, but they also knew what he had done for Israel. They considered him one of them and the secret of his life here with Dvora their own to keep as well. Deborah, who had suffered prominence in one way or another most of her life, found it fascinating to be accepted at first into their community because she was Pierre's and Dvora's daughter.

The bonds among all these people seemed to form them into a strong net knotted at each individual yet attached to the others. She pondered the paradox that the kibbutzniks had little personal wealth and lived on the edge of invasion – targets for Syrian and P.L.O. rockets, rifles always ready beneath their beds – but were so very secure in their insulated, provincial, fortress life. In contrast she had erected a very different kind of security around herself, but she too had ultimately locked herself inside it. The sense of community here made it very much a self-contained world of neighbours, and Deborah grew to appreciate how two such sophisticated people as Pierre and Dvora had been so happy here.

Nearly a week passed before Deborah was able to view both her mothers objectively. One morning, she wandered into the nursery and began to play with the babies, all the time thinking of the one growing inside her. She lifted one and nuzzled its neck, intoning a rhyme. 'Mummy will keep you safe and warm. You will never come to harm.' Those were Madeleine's words she was reciting, and that was the way Madeleine used to kiss Deborah until she was nearly of school age. At that moment Deborah sensed how much of Madeleine was in her. So much of her own desire for children derived from being showered with affection by Madeleine; the love she had received from her adoptive mother had made her capable of loving her own child. That was a psychological continuity more durable than time or even death, and it was fixed forever in her psyche. The true link to her adoptive mother, Madeleine, was psychological and unbreakable, even if not any longer exclusive. The true link to her natural mother, Dvora, was biological and unbreakable, even if no longer idealized.

As those thoughts crystallized, Deborah saw her identity as if a lifting fog had revealed the men and women out of her past converging on her, bearing their bequests of her heritage. Madeleine and Dvora. Pierre and Samuel. Even Nathan, Deborah was now grieved to realize. He had spent his later life expiating his guilt for fleeing the Alpine woods at the sound of gunfire and, he mistakenly thought, for having caused Dvora's death. He had kept the reason for his guilt from everyone. Pierre had never known that, by acceding to Dvora's request that he tell his relatives she had died, he had inadvertently crippled Nathan's life. The harm produced by the secrecy wound around Deborah was appalling to her – and all for the best of intentions, she understood at last.

Accepting that she had a rightful place in the progression of human beings who had produced her meant risking the hurts of loving and the unpredictabilities of living that no amount of farsightedness could totally eliminate. And, once she delivered Leslie up to the British authorities, it meant facing the fearsome unknown that would replace revenge in the cavity that abandonment had dug out of her.

And yet, like texture between her fingers, she could perceive a richness, a luxuriousness of potential, suffusing her life, changing it in ways she no longer automatically deflected. She could perceive threads in her character struggling to be woven into their continuations.

As Deborah left the nursery to meet Dvora for lunch, the earth felt solid beneath sure steps. A week after the original awareness had first flashed on her consciousness, Deborah believed at last that she had always been loved, had always been wanted.

Following Pierre's instructions, his lawyer, Alain Arnaud, had secretly arranged for an empty coffin to be interred at the funeral in Paris and for Pierre's body to be flown to the kibbutz for burial in the little cemetery, where Dvora would someday rest beside him. Deborah had avoided the area since her arrival, just as she had refused to attend Pierre's funeral in Paris. When she suggested that she and Dvora should take their lunch by the grove of trees on the hillside overlooking the cemetery and the valley beyond, her mother recognized it as a reconciliation on Deborah's part.

Both wore shorts, short-sleeved shirts, and white sunhats – standard kibbutz garb. As they sat cross-legged beneath a tree, Deborah remarked, 'Dressed like this, we look very much alike.'

'I've been thinking more about our differences. For instance, what motivates us,' the older woman said.

'Our ideologies, for one. My capitalism. Your socialism.'

'I think it goes deeper. Despite your success, you came here very troubled.'

'I had just learned my mother was alive. That's unnerving.'

'Perhaps,' Dvora offered, then thought a bit before adding gravely, 'Sometimes you sound so rigid. I get the feeling you'll never truly forgive me.'

'Do I sound self-righteous?'

'No, unbending, unforgiving.'

Deborah's eyes dropped to the peach she held in her hand, but the constriction in her voice revealed her anguish. 'I want to love people. I'm not just very good at it. Lately I've been finding out that I'm not very good at anything else except making money.' Her voice became intense. 'I know I love my child. I'm afraid I won't know *how* to love it.' She stared up, unseeing, in anguish, at the light skittering unpredictably through leaves moved by a breeze. 'People I loved died when I was young, and I was powerless to prevent it. Love has always brought me grief. Everything I thought was stable in my life always turned out to be an illusion that collapsed into sadness – who my parents were, family unity, the security of loved ones who would never leave me. You buried yourself in causes greater than yourself. But everything outside myself either crumbled or threatened me. Nothing lasts. Nothing can be trusted. First it was the Kronengold family in which I grew up that was fragmenting. Now, it's everything else in the world.'

Dvora took her daughter's hands. Her voice was stirred by the strength of her convictions and her compassion for Deborah. 'I believed in an Israel before there was one. I believed in Pierre's love and in our family – which you were part of – even when years went by without either of you. I believed in those things because they were important to me, not because they were possible. You must build on *something* in life. Perhaps what others feel or think or say *is* an illusion you can't be sure of – but not the way you feel about them and about what's worthwhile. Your own feelings, dreams, and hopes are the only real things in life – they give meaning to everything else.'

Deborah began to weep. 'You don't know how daring that is – to believe in all the things that always hurt you.'

Dvora put her arms round Deborah and drew her to her. Deborah wept, washing away remorse and fear and reservation.

Dvora was crying too, a flood of tears and words. 'I can't replace Madeleine – and I wouldn't want to. I'm grateful to her. She made you into a wonderful woman. But you need me in a different way. And your child will need me in yet another way.'

'Oh, yes, yes!' Deborah raised her head and searched for her mother's eyes.

'I –' Dvora began to sob uncontrollably, unable to finish. Her daughter held her, prepared to wait for hours to hear her mother's words. When Dvora finally spoke, her voice was small and forlorn. 'I . . . I need *you*.'

Their bodies together seemed to form a primitive shelter.

Later, the two women, still holding each other, walked down the hill to the mound of dirt beneath which Pierre was buried. There at last, under a searing sun, Deborah told her father that she loved him.

Walls Deborah had erected around herself brick by brick were levelled that afternoon. She felt as if she were stepping out across the rubble: naked . . . very pale in the sun . . . light-headed at the absence of the sucking black fear of abandonment at the centre of her soul . . . more deeply happy than she could ever remember being. This was not the momentary exultation she had felt on crushing Leslie and the Rowells. The happiness seemed to strum a thousand feelings inside her, a thousand strings stretching from her alone back into her past and forward into her future. Every memory and desire seemed to resonate in sympathy. Acceptance of her father, Pierre, had completed her inner foundation bridged so long with flimsy, treacherous planks. Secure now, knowing who she was, she could risk the responsibility of caring and the vulnerability of hoping.

Two days later the telephone call arrived from her executive vice-president, James Lacy. She had left orders that she was to be disturbed only in a true emergency. This was. Only hints could be conveyed over the telephone, but Deborah learned that final tests had been held by her researchers on the process to extract gold and other precious metals from the slurry of minerals being separated from sea water in the desalination process. Lacy did not dare risk letting her know whether the extraction process worked or not, but his voice sounded grave. The gravity deepened when he used code words to inform her that the Arab boycott had taken a decidedly critical turn. Lacy would say no more, but suggested they meet immediately with André Leitner and Neville Cooper.

'Tomorrow afternoon in London,' she told him. 'Have my plane at Lod airport first thing tomorrow morning.'

Deborah walked slowly from the administrative office, where the kibbutz's telephone was located, to the communal dining room, where the entire settlement took their meals cafeteria-style and where her mother awaited her. Her stay here – stolen out of time, it seemed – was about to end. She had to return to the arena of events and decisions and crises. Here, all of those had been internal. She felt as if she was returning a very different woman from the one she had been when she had arrived. She had sought answers and, miraculously, found love. Although this was her last day with her mother, there would be many more. She looked about her, at the land that her heritage had sprung from and now had reclaimed, rolling outwards from her, green and peaceful.

If you're listening, God, she thought, thank you.

The next afternoon, in her London office, Deborah saw first, alone, James Lacy, while the other men waited outside. Only he and she knew about the research effort, code-named Rumpelstiltskin, to extract precious metals from sea water. She nodded for him to take a seat. 'From your expression it looks like bad news.'

Lacy removed a top-secret report from his briefcase and handed it to her. 'Our desalination process is fantastic at purifying water – a high volume of fresh water at low cost. It just can't separate the gold and other minerals from the salt.'

Deborah was dejected by the news. She read through the confidential report detailing the results of the test just completed. As she and her scientists had always known, the water purification process was exceptional, but now they knew the process could not be refined to separate each precious element from the general mineral content of the sea water. The Rumpelstiltskin Project was a failure. She reflected sadly, 'I suppose Nature just considers fresh water a great deal more important than yellow metal.'

Deborah pressed her intercom button and summoned Leitner and Cooper into the room. She turned the meeting over to Lacy.

His tone was gloomy. 'The Arab League nations and Arab-backed banks have expanded their boycott. Originally it was only against the British Kronengold bank. Now it includes virtaully every Kronengold bank in Europe.'

'And the Kronengolds' other business firms too,' André interjected. 'Several people swore to me in confidence that the Arabs have people in each country hard at work forcing customers and suppliers to stop doing business with the local Kronengolds.'

'It's still too early to be sure,' Lacy added, 'but there isn't any doubt how drastic the situation is.' He turned to the man on his right. 'Neville?'

Our merchant-banking firm and its subsidiaries here in London haven't been bothered,' the Englishman stated. 'But Deborah is a stockholder, with a good many of her relatives, in British Kronengold Holdings. That company owns a large insurance company and several other companies.' He spoke directly to Deborah. 'During the last few weeks corporate clients have been cancelling their insurance policies. Our other business has also been falling off.'

Deborah directed her attention back to her executive vice-president. 'Jim, has Salim been advised that I have an interest in the holding company? He was clear about not including us in any boycott.'

Lacy nodded grimly. 'He telephoned me yesterday morning . . . just before I called you. The Arab finance ministers have great hopes for our desalination process and don't want to disturb relations with any company you're personally involved with. But he says a principle is at stake. The Arab nations intend to demonstrate their power by wiping out every Kronengold entity.'

'Including mine?'

'No. He was very clear they'll go out of their way to exclude you from the boycott. As part of that they want to buy your share of British Kronengold Holdings –'

'Before they destroy it?'

'Or force out your relatives and take it over.' Neville gestured around him to indicate the D. de Kronengold Corporation. 'As for this company, because you own it, we're absolutely safe. All they want you to do – and these are his words now – is to take "Kronengold" out of the name.'

None of the men dared utter another sound. Deborah's eyes had snapped wide. Her skin had turned parchment-white except for two flame-red circles on her cheeks. Ironically, the Arabs had demanded that she erase her Kronengold name just as she had discovered her right to it.

Carefully planned and vigorously executed, the Arab boycott was an all-out assault on the family that still symbolized for many the financial initiative of the Jewish people. Fearing an oil cut-off or the sudden withdrawal of Arab billions held on deposit that could shatter their economies, many nations were eager to capitulate to the Arabs. The Kronengold banks and other interests, small and separated, had little chance to survive the Arab League's embargo. They needed to join in a co-ordinated defence and to be backed by a substantial amount of additional capital. With a start, Deborah realized that they needed *her*, as Pierre with his dying words had tried to make her understand. Their only hope was if she rallied them and absorbed them into one mighty company, a world-wide investment bank that dwarfed competitors locked into a single country. That had been her private vision for many years, but the capital required to start up so many strong banking subsidiaries had always dissuaded her. Combining now with other Kronengold banks and companies could obtain this goal for her. But, by joining the others, she too might be battered into the ground. On the sidelines she would be safe. And all she needed was to change her firm's name.

She rose from her chair and walked to the window. Before her was the City, that agglomeration of financial tradition and ambition. The glass dome of I. Kronengold & Sons caught her attention first, as it always did. Her inner eye seemed to see something more: the image she had imagined as a child of her grandfather, Samuel de Kronengold, gargantuan in size, astride the City. He had always stressed that the Kronengolds were strong because they were a family, a chain that might strain at any one of them but never break, a single unit bound by values that superseded individual pique or greed or vanity.

As she thought about that chain of family she had come to acknowledge was hers by genealogy from one branch and by upbringing from another, she finally understood that she was responsible for it. She was answerable to Abraham ben Itzhak and his son Solomon and his grandson Isaac, to all their clever, dutiful sons and to all their denied daughters, as surely as to Samuel and Madeleine and Pierre. To her had come fortunes, not as a gift of leisure, but as an obligation to be met by a lifetime's duty. Her true inheritance from all who had gone before was the obligation entrusted to her to preserve the future for the next generation of Kronengolds, for the baby she carried in her womb. *That* was her true birthright: the continuity, the aspiration, the responsibility to what had come before and would follow – the sacrifice, if need be.

She even felt grateful now to know that she was Jewish – despite having always felt ambiguous about her religion. Judaism underlay the identity into which she had been born and which was now undeniably hers. It had values to which she was entitled and which bound her to her family.

Taking my place in the forefront of the Kronengolds, she told herself, binding us back together, making us a force once more – that's my purpose in life, the cause awaiting me in time from the moment I was born. Even if I fail against all that Arab power, even if I lose everything, I'll be able to hold my head high when I pass on the Kronengold birthright to my own child.

Deborah spun round, tearing her gaze from the glass dome.

'I will not change my company's name!' she declared. The room seemed to be crowded with all the invisible figures in her heritage. 'We will fight the Arabs!'

For a long time she said nothing more, trying to work out a way to battle so overwhelmingly powerful a coalition of enemies. Suddenly, she strode to her desk and quickly skimmed the final pages of the secret report on the Rumpelstiltskin Project. Then she put it down and stared at it, the whole strategy falling into place in her mind.

'We will fight the Arabs,' she finally repeated, 'but after we've levelled the odds. In order to do that, we first have to unite the Kronengolds into a single attacking army. And then we have to spin gold out of sea water.'

Until the helicopter began to descend, the estate's buildings and lands appeared to be a brightly coloured postage stamp issued by an operetta kingdom. Then the lands grew until they stretched to the horizon in every direction and the huge stone château towered above the settling aircraft.

Valtary!

Not since Deborah was eleven had the entire family gathered en masse in one place, ironically *this* place, the opulent palace in the French countryside that Deborah had inherited from Pierre. Deborah had left here in shame the last time, when the blame had wrongly fallen on her for smashing Pierre's violin. Now the lands, the building, the superb furnishing were hers.

She stepped from the helicopter, the servants were standing at attention to welcome her. She stopped an instant to take it in. The great granite façade of the château. Never beautiful, the château's square, crenellated bulk, its very survival into the age of efficiency, endowed it with a pugnacious authority. I like it, Deborah thought. It makes no apologies for its existence and dares one not to be overwhelmed. You really are pure Kronengold. Rich as hell and not apologizing for it. If I make it through all this, you old pile, I'm going to primp you up and show you off and not give a damn who sniffs at my ostentation.

Deborah strolled through salons and galleries still familiar to her, into the little bedroom where she had stayed, and into Pierre's unassuming study – so like him. She stayed there for long minutes, perusing the files stuffed with photographs he had taken, reading titles of books he had loved enough to keep by him, and fondling objects that had been his.

Finally she was ready for the Music Room. The double doors were open to receive the guests. Chairs were set out on the highly polished hardwood floor exactly as they had been when she came here to play her violin for the family. On each chair, as she had directed, was a sealed manila envelope. Inside was the memorandum of agreement drawn up overnight by Evan McAphee and his associates in New York, in telephonic consultation with Alain Arnaud in Paris, her London solicitors, and her Swiss lawyers.

Deborah stepped into the ornately pretty yellow and white room taken from a pre-revolutionary *palais*, and allowed memory to wash over her. Was she ever that child, explosive with hope and love, who had stood at the other end and played sweetly for indulgent relatives? Pierre, the origin of her musical talent, had proudly accompanied her in a sonata as if he and she were a single person, she remembered.

She walked down the aisle on the other side of the room from the windows, past the display cabinets containing Pierre's collection of rare instruments. First percussion, then brass, then woodwind, finally stringed instruments. At the front of the room were the violins, glowing with fragile elegance. She recognized the shattered and restored Stradivarius at once. Small tags identified the others: the Mandotti Stradivarius and the Koenig, the Prince William Guarnerius, and French violins by Lupot, Aldric, and Chanot the elder. There were famous bows in the case as well. It occurred to her that Pierre must have quailed at the prospect of these instruments going to Gilbert, who might have used them as mallets.

Deborah recalled the feel of a bow between her fingertips and of a violin tucked beneath her chin, the surprising beauty as bow drew sound from string for the first time. When all this was over, she would like to play again, she thought.

Deborah heard a hum in the distance growing louder, like bees swarming. She went to the window. A formation of helicopters was heading towards the château. Limousines were advancing up the drive. She glanced at her watch. Two minutes to eleven. Precisely on time. The shareholders of every existing Kronengold bank, financial institution, and major industrial entity were coming here, hoping she was their saviour.

Her executives had spoken to them on the telephone the night before, briefly outlining the purpose of the meeting and requesting their presence. None declined. During the conversations, many revealed that the boycott against them was far more comprehensive than the recent newspaper stories indicated. André Leitner's information had been accurate: Arab League bankers, government officials, and the firms with which they did extensive business (which wanted to stay in the Arabs' good graces) were putting intense pressure on every Kronengold company. Depositors were being intimidated into pulling their money out of Kronengold banks in massive amounts, new business had dried up, nervous corporate clients had begun to desert, and commercial banks had slammed shut the borrowing door on the Kronengolds and the Kronengold clients. Customers and suppliers had suddenly broken off long-standing relationships with Kronengold factories. Transporters were unwilling to ship ore from Kronengold mines. Brokers were reluctant to place policies with Kronengold insurance companies. The Kronengolds' pleas to their own governments to take action against the boycott had been met by embarrassed rebuffs; every European government feared offending the Arabs. Each day people with whom the Kronengolds dealt became more worried, and few were willing to chance Arab displeasure.

Deborah watched from the window as her relatives emptied from their vehicles and moved towards the château. All the French relatives had come by car. Simone still wore mourning. She walked up the steps with Gilbert. They halted at the top, staring straight ahead at the château's open doors. From their rigid stances, Deborah could tell they were bitter at being forced by their fear of the Arab embargo and of Deborah's economic power into meeting at the château she had 'stolen' from them.

Deborah recognized most of the other shareholders in the French bank and other French enterprises. She had last seen many of them the night Pierre died. The tallest was Jean-Paul, walking with his sister Colette. Although his influence was among the least, owing to his having inherited so small an interest in the bank, she respected him highly as a banker.

She recognized others in the French contingent: Armand, paunchy and dyspeptic, whose mistress was rumoured to have collected, through his largesse, a collection of jewellery worthy of a musuem; Michael, Gilbert's closest ally, who had always resented Pierre's hegemony as a rebuke to his own branch; weak-willed Alex, who would blow towards the stronger side – he had married a Catholic and, consequently, now felt out of place both in church and in synagogue.

The Dutch group emerged from the cars Deborah had dispatched to the private airport nearby. They were all tall and hardy, like a forest of redwoods, solid, reliable. They did not stand around at the entrance, murmuring together as the French, but, businesslike, strode quickly through the doors.

Descendants of national branches whose banks had been lost in the war were scattered among the others. Deborah admired many of them. Perhaps with some capital, perhaps with none, they had begun after the war and, to a lesser or greater degree, become wealthy again. The Belgian Leopold, named after the king his father had been favoured by, had reclaimed some of the family's African properties and managed to retain many of those despite independence and coups while rebuilding his European interests. He was an outspoken, sarcastic man. A short older woman in black walked beside a younger man no taller than she. Deborah supposed she was Olga, the widow of one of the Berlin bankers, and he was Stefan, her son. They had survived a concentration camp, moved to Luxembourg, and sold the Rembrandt returned to them against the capital to begin a private bank that had prospered.

Bent over his stick, nearly blind, Hyman was probably the oldest of the Kronengolds. Out of the country when the Viennese bank fell, he had returned to his country estate after the war, cut down all the trees, and entered the timber business. Deborah had met him several times. He and his late wife's nephew owned a chemical company with which her own did substantial business. Despite his age he would be among the most reasonable.

The German-born Lauritz lumbered out of a limousine and immediately looked about him with the caution that had protected him through the years. Nearly half a minute passed before he dismissed his driver. Among his holdings was a chain of first-class hotels built to take advantage of the increase in travel he had anticipated early on in the post-war recovery.

They were diverse, independent. In some faces still resided the impression of what had once been a strong family resemblance, but in most the likeness went deeper. If it's there at all, Deborah commented sceptically to herself.

Deborah turned away from the window and went to the little ante-chamber concealed at the front of the Music Room, originally intended for musicians awaiting their turn to play. A spyhole in the closed door, for the players to watch for their summons, allowed Deborah to observe her visitors' entrance.

The first to enter, led to his place by one of the footmen, was Pieter Kronengold, tall and broad, only faintly overweight despite his seventy or so years. He headed the Dutch branch of the family. Blunt, no-nonsense manner, likeable. The least complicated in the family. His two tall sons were with him, capable and trustworthy like their father. Deborah's Kronengold group did business with the Dutch bank.

Then came the French, more than twenty in all, in small, separated knots that reflected their dissension. Scattered among them and those who followed were the expatriates, many of whom were very rich, the heirs of those who had once been the banking kings of Berlin, Frankfurt, and Vienna.

Some of Deborah's British relatives entered next. Her uncle Charles came in with her cousin Malcolm, accompanied by eight smaller shareholders in British Kronengold Holdings. Each expression seemed hung on a wall of worry.

The last to enter the room were Leslie and Richard. Richard was fretful, nervous. Leslie stooped now, his arrogant expression merely a habit. He had waited a couple of weeks for Deborah's twin axes to fall: the arrest on criminal charges and the papers that would commence his bank's liquidation. Waiting impotently, day after day, for his execution had withered his vitality, that and the knowledge that he had failed precisely as his father had always foreseen he would. He appeared to be empty, weightless, devoid of life, propelled forward as if by a wind, his fate now an afterthought, even to him.

Just as the footmen closed the doors behind them and the murmuring fell to silence with expectancy, Deborah stepped into the Music Room and faced her relatives, nearly fifty of them, the most powerful descendants of Solomon Kronengold and his six sons. Her expression as grim as their predicament, she scanned the faces and savoured the irony of the moment. In a quarter of a century she had progressed from the skinny child hoping they would listen while she played the violin in this room to the richest of them all – and the one whom they needed most. If she could unite the isolated groups of her family into a force capable of repelling this all-out Arab assault, if she could level the walls and barriers and restore the family to one borderless nation bound by indivisible loyalty, then she would have fulfilled her duty and her destiny.

'I have asked you here today,' she began forcefully, 'because each of you is faced with a massive threat to your survival. It is only a matter of time before you are crushed. You have only two choices: to give in or to fight. I have a plan to link all our banks and interests into a single company. If you join me, you may survive. Alone, you'll certainly be destroyed.'

Deborah did not have to explain the threat they faced; they had come here seeking some means of escape. She began to present her plan. She was well on her way to creating a financial services giant, she reminded them. Her investment bank was already one of the most powerful in America, with strong operations in Britain and Switzerland, and an office in Hong Kong. She had inherited Pierre's large block of stock in the French bank. And she owned a substantial interest in the holding company which joined her and her British cousins.

Her eyes fell on Leslie. Her adoptive father's inert features confirmed her earlier observation that he was now a spiritless hulk. But her insights in Israel had allowed her to surmount her compulsion for revenge, and she had come to agree with him that his humiliation would cheapen *all* the Kronengolds in the world's eyes and would give the Arabs reason to gloat. Now she wanted only to be finished with him, to let him go, to cease punishing him, and to get on with her life – as much for her own sake as for his. Her gaze never leaving him, like twin hooks to hold him erect in his seat, Deborah announced the commutation of his sentence.

'Leslie has expressed a wish to retire from business and devote his full time to archaeology. We've decided that I will replace him as controlling shareholder in the British Kronengold bank.' She shifted her attention to the others. 'I'll be in a position to merge the major French and British family assets into my company. DdK is already extensive enough to form the basis for a worldwide Kronengold investment-banking operation that can encompass us all.'

She began to lay out the details of the banking structure she proposed. On an equitable basis, everyone would exchange his or her property for shares in Deborah's company, which would be renamed the Kronengold Financial Corporation. She estimated that her net worth was well above the richest of the others and that she would end up the major stock-holder. But they would all own proportionate amounts of shares and, in addition to earnings based on their stock ownership, each would continue to operate the bank subsidiary or other industry located in his area and to participate in its profits as an incentive. The vast capital of the reconstituted DdK would permit those local banks and industries access to far greater funds than they at present had. New subsidiary banks would be started up as well: she proposed that Jean-Paul should be installed in Milan and one of Pieter's sons in Germany. Eventually, the Kronengolds would encircle the globe, established in all the major financial centres.

Near Deborah was an easel. She lifted off a large blank card to reveal another covered with numbers. 'The figures are startling. Within a year the Kronengold Financial Corporation could control some five per cent of the free world's international investment banking. Putting new banks in Asian capitals would soon raise that percentage, while providing an opportunity for future banking growth and investment in the fastest-growing part of the world.' She pointed to her estimate of the proposed firm's capital. 'We could corner a commodity or even a small nation's currency and, most important, we'd have the resources and breadth to attract large multi-national clients, which are at present served by a patch-work of investment banks in all the countries in which they now operate. We'd control or have major positions in seven per cent of the world's property and casualty insurance companies. We would own a giant commodity and currency trading organization – the second largest in the world. And that's only the base from which we could grow.'

Deborah carefully went over the stock-ownership arrangements for the proposed company, the corporate structure, and the method for evaluating how much stock each person would be entitled to. Then she crossed her arms, an indication that what she was about to say did not derive from weakness, but from strength.

'In that regard there are a few personal matters to be cleared up before I proceed with any further explanation of my plan.' Her eyes flicked left.

'Gilbert!' He sat up, alert, full of suspicion. Simone, at his side, was coiled to spring at Deborah to defend him. 'Gilbert, I consider you a hardworking and capable banker, but one who often puts his own self-interest above the bank's. There's no longer any way in which you can seize control of the Banque Kronengold. I suggest that your future welfare can be better served by joining the rest of us. To that end I am willing to turn over to you some of my own shares in the French bank – or, rather, their equivalent in Kronengold Financial Corporation stock. One-tenth each year until, at the end of ten years, our inheritance in the French bank's share of the new company has been equalized. If at any time I judge you're acting with less than full commitment to our larger banking interests, the transfer of shares ceases.' Deborah paused, trying to communicate from some deep part of herself to its mirror-image, which she hoped resided within him, the higher significance of her act. 'This room raises unpleasant memories in both of us. We're brother and sister. I suggest that the animosity that began between us here be ended here. I think it's what our father wanted.'

Gilbert, profoundly surprised by her magnanimity, spoke. 'Your gesture is very generous.'

Deborah had no idea whether he might be able or willing to change his behaviour, but within the new business structure he could be controlled.

She now regarded Richard. Without Leslie as a model and tyrant, perhaps some natural capability would emerge. But, again, what she was about to do was an obligation paid to a higher purpose, and Richard, even if talentless, could be controlled as well.

'Richard, although I'll be taking possession of Leslie's bank stock in return for certain outstanding debts, he and I both agree that your share in I. Kronengold & Sons should remain with you. Additional shares will go to you each year on the same one-tenth-a-year basis as Gilbert will have, until you end up with shares equal to what I received on account of my ownership of I. Kronengold & Sons.'

Richard, who knew of his imminent ruin at whatever instant Deborah chose to demand repayment of her loan, was dumbfounded. He forced a smile and bobbed his head in appreciation. 'Thank you,' he finally managed.

Deborah regarded the row of chairs behind him, where Charles and Malcolm sat. 'I intend to merge my British interests, including my merchant bank and its insurance and other companies, into I. Kronengold & Sons. The whole would be far stronger if British Kronengold Holdings' assets were combined as well. Malcolm, you and I have discussed this in the past. You're far too attached to your racehorses and your life of country leisure. If your son, Howard, ever wants to apply his talent for scientific research to business, he'd be welcome.'

Her gaze swung over one seat. 'Charles, you've told me you regretted having to leave the bank, and I, for one, would be quite grateful if you rejoined it. I always felt your leaving it was a severe blow.'

'I'm . . . honoured,' Charles declared. 'I don't know how Malcolm feels, but my share of the holding company will vote to agree with the plan. There's one condition though – that my sons are given influential posts in the new company.'

'Sad to say, Charles, your sons have never exhibited the slightest interest in any activity that started before noon. But if they wish to begin at the bottom and work their way up, they're welcome.'

She widened her attention to take in the rest of the assemblage. 'That holds good for any of our sons *or our daughters*. Only the best can be allowed responsibility for matters that affect us all and future generations.'

Then Deborah's chin lifted, and her voice rang out with a fervour that she hoped would speak personally to everyone seated before her.

'We are Kronengolds. We have survived times of evil and

chaos that wiped lesser families off the face of the earth. We stand for an indomitability that cannot be allowed to die or to cower in fear.'

Her gaze seemed to be locked on every eye before her. 'Unity and Fidelity! We've forgotten what those words really mean, and how they made our forefathers strong. Unity and Fidelity! Only by pledging ourselves to those principles can we bind together into a single irresistible force and truly become a family once more. Without them our heritage is meaningless. But with them we have a heritage of greatness to pass on to the generation that will follow.'

Her last words echoed in a silence none in the room was willing to disturb. Finally, Deborah asked them all to open their manilla envelopes and carefully read the agreement that would merge them all into one company.

It was blunt Pieter who called out first a few minutes later.

'The formula to calculate a price for exchanging my stock is very fair. But, once we merge into your company, what do we do about the Arab boycott?'

All heads lifted.

'To begin with, we'll be able to put up a united defence,' Deborah replied. 'I think we've devised a counter-attack that strikes at the heart of the Arabs' power – their wealth. If the plan works, it will end Arab persecution of our family, and it will double our combined wealth.'

'Ridiculous!' the private banker Stefan muttered, making audible the incredulity on the sea of faces before her.

After swearing her relatives to secrecy, Deborah began to outline her battle plan. Gradually, the faces became more approving and, as they started to comprehend the strategy, began to nod at each other.

'This has to be done very quickly,' Gilbert remarked. 'Before word leaks out.'

Trust his scheming mind to understand instantly, Deborah thought. We may be different, but we both are our father's children.

'Exactly,' she answered him. 'Three days of gold trading from start to finish, beginning the day after tomorrow. Each move must be perfectly timed and coordinated with the next. The plan depends on our determination to attack gold with every last penny and sou and guilder we jointly possess, as if we truly believed that gold was no longer rare enough to have much value, so that the price of gold will plummet. At the same time the Arabs will be blocked by the very immensity of their gold holdings, their inability to sell a significant portion of their gold quickly because the price would then plunge nearly to zero. In other words we're using their wealth as our weapon.'

'It's brilliant!' murmured Alex.

'At least it will give us a chance,' responded the more pessimistic Leopold, who had seen borrowing sources for his consumer financing company dry up so quickly that he was faced with ruin.

Deborah's eyes swung forward again. 'The plan is very risky. One slight miscalculation, one blunder, and we'll be crushed. But the alternative is our *certain* destruction.' She did not raise her voice to exhort them now – the choice each pondered was too important to be made on the basis of heated emotion. She simply asked, 'Who will join me?'

Indecision gripped the room for a moment as each person grappled with fear or pride or insecurity. Suddenly, a chair scraped and a woman in black stood up.

'I will,' Simone said. An instant later, Gilbert was on his feet beside her.

Pieter and his sons rose at the same time as Charles and Richard. And then several more British shareholders. The hotel magnate, Lauritz, was next. The old man, Hyman, followed, helped to his feet by another Austrian, who joined him. Then they were all on their feet.

The last up was Leslie, as if lifted by the stimulus of the others.

By late afternoon, after telephone conversations with lawyers and only a few modifications to accommodate particular individual problems, the memoranda of agreement were signed, with full-scale contracts to be worked out in future weeks.

Deborah immediately went to a telephone and dialled a number that rang in Israeli intelligence in Tel Aviv. She said one word. Her mother answered with one word, and the operation was on.

CHAPTER TWENTY-FIVE

That afternoon in Athens, because it was a Sunday, a shipping broker telephoned his banker at home to say that an urgent matter had just arisen and to invite him to a restaurant to discuss a large loan. At dinner the round-faced, jolly man could barely contain his high spirits. He was negotiating a large contract to supply freighters to the American Kronengold company, he said, and wanted to be certain his banker would extend the credit he would need to charter the ships. He became anxious and tight-lipped when the banker inquired about the sort of goods to be transported.

'If I get the contract, I will need special ships.' He patted his briefcase protectively. 'That is all I'm at liberty to say.'

Invited to a taverna for drinks by the banker, the round-faced man appeared to hesitate, reminding his friend how badly he held his liquor.

'Just one,' the banker said, 'to celebrate your good fortune.'

At ten o'clock that night, the shipping broker was weaving in his chair with a silly smile on his face, keeping time to the bouzouki music with an up-raised glass of brandy. It took less than five minutes for another man, sitting at the adjoining table, to remove the briefcase to the men's lavatory, photograph its documents, and slip it back under the broker's seat. He had taken a picture of a cable from DdK requesting the shipping broker to bid on a long-term contract to supply ships with both armoured compartments for carrying precious metal and accommodation for guards. The ships were to travel from the Arabian peninsula to London.

A few minutes later the banker told his client it was getting late. He stuffed the nearly insensible shipping broker into a taxicab that rumbled off into the night.

The taxi had travelled only a short way when the portly passenger dismissed it and, suddenly quite sober, headed for a telephone.

'The goods have been removed for inspection,' he said to

the voice that answered. Then he hung up and walked off into the neon night, confident that his message would be relayed within minutes to his Tel Aviv headquarters.

On the other side of the world, an Israeli irrigation engineer at an agricultural conference in Tokyo was bragging to a group of assorted colleagues that he had just come from Oregon, where he was allowed to observe the latest innovation in DdK's top-secret desalination process.

'Salt,' he confided, 'is the least of the minerals it extracts.'

A wire-tap on the Tunisian delegate's telephone proved rewarding a few hours later. The entire episode was reported to an Arab-nation military attaché based in Japan. The latter was still in the process of sending the message on to his superior when the news that he was doing so reached Tel Aviv.

The next morning, a Monday, while Deborah's relatives returned home to convert quickly as much of their assets as they could into cash and to borrow more to the full extent of their capability, Deborah flew to Milan with Jean-Paul. On and off, Mauro Benedetto, an executive with DdK's European operation, had been exploring the purchase of a private Italian bank but, when Deborah decided that a merger of the Kronengolds was urgent, she dispatched him to Milan to press for a fast conclusion. She chose this particular bank for three reasons: the price was reasonable; prior to Pierre's arrest by the Nazis, the bank had been the property of his family, but had been seized by the Italian Fascist government and never regained; and, lastly, the bank's president was a well-connected gossip, known for his advocacy of the gold standard.

Benedetto had worked out final terms by the time Deborah arrived to sign the memorandum of agreement. She asked the departing president to stay on for a few days to help Jean-Paul become acclimatized and to represent the bank at a conference soon to take place in Rome.

As the Italian left the room, she said to Jean-Paul loudly enough for the Italian to overhear, 'You may call on the parent company for up to a billion dollars.' That titbit would fly round the international financial conference like the wind.

* * *

André Leitner had been engaged since leaving London in securing a very large loan through a hurriedly assembled consortium of Central European banks, half a billion dollars in various Arab currencies. The negotiation had become bogged down on a single point: Deborah's company was heavily borrowed with many of those banks; they now sought additional collateral. Deborah arrived in Geneva just as the luncheon meeting André had arranged was getting underway. These were worried men, she observed; a large Swiss bank had recently suffered a massive default on a loan, and the usual risks no longer seemed safe, particularly on such short notice as Deborah was asking and particularly to a member of a family targeted for destruction by the Arab states. Deborah was unwilling to include additional corporate assets as collateral – James Lacy was employed at that very moment in borrowing against those from a group of American banks, and Neville Cooper from a group of British banks.

Unable to charm the bankers into forgoing their demands, Deborah had to give them her personal guarantee. If DdK was unable to pay the loan, up to five hundred million dollars would have to be paid out of her personal fortune. They nervously agreed to make the loan on the strength of that undertaking – even though nearly all her personal fortune was comprised of DdK stock.

Because of her reputation as a shrewd investor, one of the bankers then asked her what investments looked good at that moment.

'Sell gold,' she warned. 'Believe me, gold will fall like a stone in the next few days.'

Every little bit helps, she thought as she departed for New York. From there she would conduct the complex family orchestra she had formed. The players were scattered around the entire globe, and they were about to play on instruments of pure gold.

The last instruction she gave that day was from a telephone in her New York office to Paul Ng, the director of her Hong Kong office. The Hong Kong market is the first to signal the day's gold price. From the historic January high of $850 an ounce, gold had dipped to below $600, but had recently been climbing back up. As soon as the market opened, Ng was to sell gold steadily, up to three hundred million U.S. dollars' worth, if necessary, in order to push gold down thirty dollars an ounce by the end of the day.

Deborah was back at her desk at four a.m. New York time on Tuesday. A new telephone console was in place, connected by her telecommunications and security people to all the Kronengold offices. A computer encoded the signals, making them virtually incomprehensible if the extensive precautions failed to prevent tapping. Deborah hit the red button at the top. As each receiver was lifted at the other end, a white light lit up on Deborah's console and the person receiving the call uttered the appropriate code word.

When the last light had lit up and the last code word was spoken, Deborah announced, 'Hong Kong gold closed down thirty-two dollars. Next is Zurich, then London, then New York. The plan is on.'

The Kronengold group concentrated its efforts on contracts to sell gold for future delivery because the seller needed to put up as a deposit only a very small percentage of the full price of the gold to be delivered. Their capital could command gold contracts worth twenty times those deposits. By putting enormous downward pressure on gold, the Kronengolds were forcing down the price. Their aim was certainly to make an eventual profit by later acquiring future delivery contracts to buy gold at a lower price, but they had a far more important goal – to shake the foundations of the Arab oil countries' wealth.

One of the primary causes for gold's spectacular rise over the previous year had been that the Arabs considered its purchase a safe way for them to invest the billions flowing back to them in return for their high-priced oil. If gold now dropped, the Arabs would suffer a disproportionate injury because they had bought up so much free-market gold.

Deborah's plan was carefully timed to last three days, with each successive day a stage that deepened the Arabs' awareness and anxiety. On the first day they would see the price of gold beginning to fall steeply. But that occasionally happened and would give them little pause; some government financial officials might even remain unaware of the first day's gold-trading activity – although Deborah was certain the most influential financial minister in the Arab world would ponder its implications deeply. That man was Prince Salim.

On the second day the Arabs would learn that it was the Kronengolds, now merged into one unified company, who were forcing down the price of gold. The Arab officials would begin to wonder in earnest what the gold selling meant: clearly it was a defensive tactic against their boycott, but how could a single family hope to depress gold's prices indefinitely? By the end of the second day, all the pieces of the false jigsaw puzzle would have fallen into their hands. If everything went according to plan, Arab officials would spend that night and much of the next day in worried telephone conversations.

The Kronengolds hoped the Arabs, basing their thinking on what they could deduce from the false jigsaw puzzle, would very logically conclude that the Kronengolds were selling gold because Deborah's researchers had perfected a method to extract gold endlessly from sea water during the desalination process. Such a process would overwhelmingly increase the existing supply of available gold and depress the price.

On the third day, after deciding that chemical extraction of ocean gold was certain to collapse the metal's price to that of any other plentiful commodity, such as timber or copper, the Arab governments would want to sell their gold. An ordinary gold trader armed with such knowledge might follow the Kronengolds' lead and make a fortune, but the Arabs would quickly conclude that, for them, selling was an impossibility: they possessed too much gold! Selling even a small portion of the total would, like a piston, drive the price down hundreds of dollars an ounce. Moreover, the Kronengolds had managed to collect a large amount of particular Arab-nation currencies, which they were selling for dollars and pounds; this was forcing down the value of Middle Eastern money while gold – which backed the currencies – was also falling. With their money worth less, the Arabs would have trouble paying for the billions of dollars' worth of goods and services – such as DdK's desalination plant – that they had purchased from the industrialized nations. They would have to pump more oil to pay their bills, forcing down the price of oil as well as the price of gold. Faced with such a prospect, they should be impelled by logic to conclude that their only recourse would be to come to an accommodation with the owner of the Rumpelstiltskin process, the Kronengolds, and to do it quickly, before gold's value – and their own wealth – shrank any further.

The Kronengolds had to force them to that decision no later

than the third day for several reasons. One, with more time for the Arabs to probe, Deborah's deception about the Rumpelstiltskin Project might well be discovered. Two, the growing panic would work in her favour; fear of economic ruin would stampede the Arabs towards her. Three, Deborah had calculated that the family's resources to depress gold would be exhausted by then and, with no functional cause for the decline, gold would leap back upwards.

Just as his Frankfurt bank was opening for business that Tuesday morning, Lauritz de Kronengold strode in, although he rarely travelled to Germany from his Brussels headquarters. He personally drew down the last fifty million dollars' worth of a Eurodollar loan originally made to renovate some of his older hotels, and he directed the bank to use it as his deposit to sell short gold bullion for delivery in mid-December. This would be effected by borrowing the gold from his bank and agreeing to replace it by mid-December.

'But that's over four hundred million dollars' worth of gold!' the shocked bank president replied. 'If gold rises, instead of falling, you'll be wiped out.'

The white-haired hotel magnate laughed. 'There's little chance of that.'

The story was repeated endlessly on the telephone and at the banker's club that day.

Traders who had not covered their gold position at the end of the previous day were shocked by the price when trading commenced on the Zurich exchange on Tuesday morning. Those who had gambled that gold would fall a bit overnight suddenly found they had made fortunes. Those who had gambled on a rise were desperate. Several were wiped out. Deborah felt sorry for them, but that was the gambler's chance they took. A few tried to recoup by betting on a quick rebound in the price, inasmuch as there appeared to be no good reason for the unexpected plunge. Many men have grown rich by doing nothing but watching for such dips so as to gamble then on a normal bounce back. But this was not a normal day.

At the opening of Zurich trading, gold was hit by a hundred million dollars' worth of sell orders. Whenever gold threatened to rise in price, a flood of new sell orders descended. The traders became frantic, like maniacs locked in a mirrored room. The same was true in London, when that market opened. Someone or some group with seemingly bottomless resources was driving gold into the ground.

The French are among the world's greatest gold hoarders. A gesture by the Kronengolds in France would produce far greater publicity and repercussions than anywhere else.

Gilbert called a press conference at the Banque Kronengold to announce that a medal would be struck the following year in memory of his father and to commemorate the one hundred and seventy-fifth anniversary of the French Kronengold bank. The medal would be given to valued bank customers and government officials. Most of the financial reporters regretted having bothered to come for such a dull news conference until Gilbert appeared to make a slip.

'The medal will probably be in gold, rather than silver, because of the cost.'

'Are you saying gold will fall below the price of silver?' an alert reporter asked.

Gilbert appeared to be flustered by his faux-pas, as if he had said too much. Finally, as if his honesty was forcing him to it, he predicted, 'The day may soon come when gold will be as common as sea salt.' Although I doubt it, he commented to himself.

He would say no more to the reporters, but that was enough to get sizeable press coverage for the story.

Neville Cooper had spent the previous day at I. Kronengold & Sons, examining with Richard and the other directors every aspect of the merchant bank's financial position. One of the handful of firms that confer as a group to set the London gold price twice a day, I. Kronengold & Sons had been gold merchants for more than a century, and Neville had determined that its most significant remaining asset was its gold bullion supply. But there was no need for the oversized gold inventory at present in its vaults. Deborah ordered nearly all the gold to be crated up and sold off that very day. The next morning she intended to deliver to the other gold merchants every bar of gold – and to do it in a way that would get the most attention.

* * *

The heavy selling that had followed gold around the world that day continued when New York's Commodity Exchange, Comex, opened on Tuesday with gold already down over sixty dollars an ounce overnight. Floor traders for DdK put relentless pressure on gold, selling it in every form now, not only in future contracts. In some cases orders were also being placed though unaffiliated traders from anonymous Kronengold sources in Europe.

At noon Deborah authorized DdK's public relations officer to announce to the financial press that her company intended to sell off its gold-mining operation. The move had been decided upon months earlier, but this seemed an advantageous time to make the announcement.

By afternoon the tide of desperation among gold dealers, traders, and speculators that had welled up twelve hours before in Hong Kong was rolling over America. As in Asia and Europe, speculators had bet on a rebound of the plunging price and had lost incredible sums. Worst of all, no reason for the drop had become evident, so they had no wind to blow them, no landfall to row to; one could as reasonably flip a coin when deciding on which side to be with gold.

Some observers wondered if the Russians might be doing the selling, trying to store up hard currency for grain purchases. But why would they sell in a way that would hurt the price they hoped to get for their gold? Others claimed it was the Saudis or Kuwaitis. Or maybe all the Arabs in concert; they had accumulated the most free-market gold. But their usual brokers and traders were as mystified as everyone else, and were being burned as badly. Those who employed traditional thinking and dared to go against the tide were being swept away. Fortunes were gambled and lost in minutes. And still the price of gold, heedless of the destruction it was wreaking, continued to drop – first in New York, then in Chicago, and finally in Winnipeg.

When Deborah tore herself away from her office late in the evening of that first day, gold was down a stunning $112 an ounce. Several times from her apartment, she telephoned her all-night trading desk to check on Asian markets. Sleep was minimal and fitful.

The second day, Wednesday, saw no let-up. Kronengold money refused to allow gold to rebound in Hong Kong or

Zurich. Just before nine o'clock in the morning in London, trucks stacked high with wooden crates of 400-ounce gold bars pulled up in front of the major gold-trading houses in the City. One was situated in a large avenue near an underground station, from which people on their way to work were pouring into the City. In full view of thousands, a guard on the Kronengold truck let slip a crate of gold that smashed open on the pavement, spilling out dozens of gold bars. Other guards immediately formed a protective barrier until the gold was carried inside the merchant bank taking delivery. No one could mistake the labels on the uniforms and crates that read I. Kronengold & Sons. Sophisticated onlookers, of whom there were many walking down or emerging onto that street, understood something else: the Kronengold bank was not merely engaged in the usual practice of buying and selling gold for a commission in approximately offsetting transactions, it was actively selling off what appeared to be its entire inventory of gold.

At about the same time, a jet transport was landing on the Arabian peninsula, at the seaside airstrip laid out near the site of the desalination plant DdK was constructing. Instead of taxiing to the usual unloading point, the plane stopped at the end of the runway and waited for trucks to race up to the open cargo hatch.

Huge wooden boxes were gingerly placed in the trucks as security personnel, guns drawn, guarded the shipments. The entire procedure was supervised by a red-bearded young man of about thirty.

When the last crate was safely aboard the last truck and the truck door padlocked, the red-haired man climbed into the first cab, beside the driver, and the convoy drove to the buildings at the construction site.

All this had been carefully photographed from a Bedouin tent well away from the runway. The intelligence operative was not due to submit his report and film for another two days, but this all looked so unusual and so suspicious that, leaving his assistant behind, he drove into town and put the film aboard a military helicopter.

At the capital city the film was rushed to intelligence headquarters and developed. Several shots were blown up so as to enlarge certain objects. Each observer up the hierarchical ladder saw nothing alarming in the photographs but, fearing to be mistaken, sent the pictures on to his superior.

The sixth person to see the photographs was the deputy minister of intelligence. He knew enough about the Kronengold company's activities to become excited by what he saw and to ask for an immediate meeting with his superior, the minister. Unfortunately, the latter was enjoying a very late lunch at the opulent country club that had recently been constructed. The photos sat on the minister's desk, awaiting his return.

At exactly eleven o'clock New York time, Deborah stepped to the stage of the auditorium in the Kronengold Tower on Wall Street. On the wall behind her was her company's symbol, three crowns. Beneath it were the words 'Unity and Fidelity'. Deborah rarely made herself available to journalists; the reporters knew the announcement would be important.

'I'm glad to welcome you here, ladies and gentlemen of the press. Right now, in London, Paris, Milan, Amsterdam, and Berlin, other members of the Kronengold family are also holding press conferences to make this same news public.' Her smile flashed as happily as she felt about her news. 'All of the Kronengold family's branches are merging their banks and companies into a single company, to be called the Kronengold Financial Corporation. Our purpose is to create the largest investment-banking chain in the world, with substantial holdings in other industries.'

In general terms Deborah went on to outline the merger and then accepted questions from her listeners. Near the end of the press conference, Deborah called on an accommodating reporter who had agreed to ask Deborah her opinion of the startling drop gold had taken in the last two days. As did her relatives at each of the other press conferences, Deborah explained that the Kronengolds had been heavy sellers of gold.

'I see gold going way down over the long term,' Deborah maintained honestly, and then added what seemed to be a non sequitur. 'It's a matter, as always, of supply and demand.'

Deborah returned to her office to monitor the progress of the gold sales. A lot of buying money had begun to show up on the Chicago exchange – the price was up seven dollars in the last hours. Deborah quickly reached her Chicago trader directly and ordered him to accelerate the selling.

At that moment news tickers and radio news programmes were informing gold traders around the world that the apparent cause of the plunge in gold prices over the past two days was the Kronengolds. Not for more than half a century had they possessed either the resources or the nerve to pull off so daring an operation. Those familiar with the international financial scene now understood that the Kronengolds had chosen to slug it out toe to toe with the Arab countries – David against Goliath. The mystery the Jewish banking family had always cultivated around their wealth served them well now: no one knew whether the weapon they carried into battle against the gigantic Philistine enemy was a slingshot or an ICBM.

But, for her part, win or lose, survive or perish, as she watched the prices flash on the computer screen on her desk, Deborah was comfortable with the battlefield she had chosen. Since the day Deborah had visited her grandfather's bank and seen Abraham ben Itzhak's gold statue of 'The Birthright' and the glittering pyramid of yellow metal in the basement vault – perhaps even earlier, when she had been dazzled by her grandfather's gift of a gold guinea for finding the hidden matzo – she had sensed that she and gold had almost a supernatural affinity and communication. Throughout her life gold had always proved to be her trusty benefactor. Now, aware of her Kronengold lineage, she felt as if her deftness with gold was bred into her – her genes elevating art into finance and finance into art, with both finding their natural expression in this brilliant, glistening element of nature.

In Europe, the first indication of renewed confidence in the Kronengolds came via the telephone, as many who had joined the Arab boycott against various Kronengold companies called to register their good wishes on the merger. Clearly, now that Deborah de Kronengold was siding with her relatives, this family to whom even kings once paid careful homage had again become a force to be reckoned with. In only two days, they had pushed gold down by over two hundred dollars an ounce.

At the cocktail party to welcome bankers to the Rome conference, the garrulous Italian who had just been replaced as head of the Kronengolds' new Milan bank kept telling and retelling each acquaintance he encountered how the Kronengolds had immediately begun to sell gold.

'Sell, sell, sell. And I know for a fact this Frenchman had ten billion dollars in capital at his disposal.'

Each time he told the story, the Italian banker tossed up his hands incredulously. 'When I tried to reason with him about holding onto gold, he told me, "Wouldn't *you* sell something at this price that soon will have no value?" Can you believe that? Gold – no value!'

Several listeners took special note of the words.

In the Arab country where Deborah's employees were constructing the desalination plant, the head of intelligence had spent the afternoon and early evening with friends at the country club. All the talk had been of the phenomenal, fearful drop in gold. It had grown so late that he very nearly decided against returning to his office. At the last minute he decided to go there to learn whether anything had come through his covert networks with respect to this disturbing decline in gold.

Cunning, if lazy, behind his heavy-lidded eyes and thick jowls, Prince Akim had been keeping close surveillance on the Kronengolds for several months. It was thus very natural that much of the information his diligent deputy had left for him related to that family. Prince Akim had been one of the architects of the Arab League boycott against them as the opening salvo in a revived economic war against Israel and the Jews. His cousin Prince Salim had insisted on excluding Deborah de Kronengold from the blacklist because her desalination process was essential to the nation's development plans. The most wary of all about this woman financier, Akim had accompanied Salim aboard Deborah's yacht several months ago to inspect the desalination system, but had been forced to agree that the equipment reliably produced an abundance of fresh water.

Now, as he went through the reports on his deck, so many were about the Kronengolds that his suspicion began to take root in different ground: not that the process did not work, but that it worked too well. First, a Greek shipping broker was asked to provide ships capable of carrying gold and other precious metals for the desalting plant. Then an Israeli engineer divulged in Tokyo that the Kronengold scientists could extract much more than the undifferentiated mineral content of the water. Now, there were these new reports in front of him that the Kronengolds had united – including the woman. She was disposing of her gold reserves, and they all appeared to be selling huge amounts of gold. Other reports too – from London, Paris, and now Rome – all pointing to the fact that the Kronengolds considered gold highly overvalued. What had Deborah de Kronengold said at the news conference? He went back to that report: she had said it was 'a matter of supply and demand.' In Paris one of them claimed gold might 'soon be as common as sea salt.'

Akim turned to the last item on the bottom of the pile: the photographs his deputy wanted him to look at. Two things immediately caught the intelligence head's eye: the labels on the crates being lowered from the cargo plane to the trucks, which read, 'Rumpelstiltskin Project – Do Not Open Without Top-Level Security Clearance'; and the young man with the red beard – John Rosenthal, his name was – whom he had last seen on the deck of Deborah de Kronengold's yacht. Rosenthal was her head research scientist. Akim had attempted for a year to plant a spy inside their Oregon research laboratory, but the security had been too tight. The boxes being unloaded from the plane might simply contain desalination equipment to be installed in the new plant. Or they might contain apparatus for something else, something called the Rumpelstiltskin Project.

Akim interrogated his deputy over the intercom.

'What does Rumpelstiltskin mean?'

'It is evidently a name, your highness.'

'A very odd name. What does it mean?'

'What does any name mean?'

'Find out!' Akim ordered and hung up.

An ominous feeling began to grow within him as he reviewed the material before him, but it seemed too fantastic to be credible. Some minutes later his deputy hurried back, grinning deferentially.

'Your highness, a professor of European literature at the university informs me that Rumpelstiltskin is a character in a children's story.'

'What does a children's story have to do with selling gold or desalination equipment?'

The deputy's face clouded in confusion. 'One thing, but it seems very far-fetched – this Rumpelstiltskin could make gold from straw.'

So, Akim thought as he dismissed the man, they have a project named after a character who could make gold out of something with no value – something, in other words, as cheap as sea water. The possibility that there actually was such a process shook the usually hard and ruthless minister. It all sounded preposterous, but who knew for sure with all the crazy things that were invented every day in America? He was well aware that a limitless supply produced by a cheap extraction process could undercut gold's value and destroy a massive part of the nation's wealth, and of his own as well. His personal fortune had shrunk by some fifty million dollars in the last two days.

Akim immediately ordered the telephone operator to contact the country's embassy in Washington, D.C., and locate Salim, who was there to confer with the Secretaries of State and the Treasury.

At about the same time, Deborah was telephoning in the other direction, from America to the Middle East, to her mother at Mossad headquarters in Tel Aviv. She gave the recognition password and heard, even in her mother's code response, her excitement at being back at the intelligence work she loved. Dvora began the conversation with a personal exchange.

'Are you all right?' she asked her daughter. 'The baby?'

'Yes, I'm starting to show a bit. I've taken to wearing full dresses without a waist.'

'Have you decided what you'll tell people? You'll have to say something.'

'I don't intend to say a word. This is none of anyone's business but mine.'

'At least after this is over, promise me you'll take it easy.'

Deborah laughed. 'You, of all people, concerned about what people will think and asking me to take it easy because I'm pregnant.'

Dvora broke off that line of discussion. 'You didn't call just to chat.'

'Nebuchadnezzar,' Deborah pronounced distinctly. That was the signal for the Mossad to send out the message to be intercepted by the Arabs that would reveal the purpose and confirm the effectiveness of the Rumpelstiltskin Project. But Deborah wanted an addition to it. 'Add that Rumpelstiltskin has just been tested on a barge with excellent results.'

Dvora gave her daughter the countersignal to assure her that she had received the message and would proceed to execute the plan. They hung up.

Until now the boycott against the Kronengolds had been laughably easy for the Arabs. But, suddenly, the once easy victims were attacking their oppressors in as financially threatening a manner as they had been attacked. Deborah assumed that worried Arab officials were already beginning to gather in meeting rooms or to chatter across long-distance wires from one brethren nation to another. Some would counsel using their wealth to swamp the gold markets with buy orders in a show of brutal monetary power. But others, the cleverer ones, would advise caution, wondering what the Kronengolds knew about gold that appeared to make them confident that no amount of Arab money could support the price for long. The information coming in to their various intelligence agencies would be pooled and exchanged, and the Arab leaders would ask each other if, just possibly, what all the facts seemed to imply could really be true: that Deborah de Kronengold's researchers had invented a process to mine gold endlessly from the sea. Then, hours from now, when indecision and argument were at their greatest, when hard-line boycotters were insisting on a massive purchase of gold to crush the Kronengolds and the accommodators were cautioning that such a course could be suicidal if the Kronengolds really did have a source of infinite gold supply, at that point Deborah wanted the 'convincing proof' – her false message – to reach the Arab leaders.

A few days earlier Deborah had been sure that the message would tip the scales and induce the Arabs to negotiate a truce. Now she feared her subterfuge was transparent, that they would instantly see through the whole scheme and, rather than sue for peace, would take steps to wipe out the financially spent Kronengolds. It was too late to do anything but charge forward blindly and trust, just as blindly, in providence. There remained at her disposal only fifty-three million dollars with which to hold down gold's price. When that was gone, gold would shoot upwards as if from a launching pad. Scarred gold investors, brokers, bankers, and speculators were desperate for a chance to ride the rebound upwards. She would be forced to liquidate her group's now huge holdings, simply to survive, which would accelerate gold's flight upwards as if she had attached to it a booster rocket. But it would happen so quickly that liquidating her gold position would be impossible – *everyone* would be buying. Price levels it had taken hours to pierce downwards would now be hurtled upwards in seconds. The group's losses would be catastrophic – lethal, even without the boycott.

But it was urgent that gold's price be held down for a second reason: any show of weakness now would convince the Arabs that the Kronengolds could be obliterated well before gold could flow into their coffers from a completed desalination plant. Salim might even insist that work cease on the first plant being built in his country, on the assumption that many more months would be required to build another gold-producing plant. At that point she wanted him to ponder the meaning of the additional 'fact' inserted into the false message: that tests had proved the process would work aboard a barge.

The Kronengold enterprises were so heavily overborrowed that the slightest appearance of weakness could topple them. The family had dug every last pfennig out of bank accounts and vaults, tapped every possible source of funds, mortgaged twice and three times over every piece of property they owned. They had used up nearly all of it. Only fifty-three million dollars remained with which to dupe their enemies into calling a truce. Tomorrow, the third day, the Kronengolds would fight the critical battle. By the end of it, they would either be safe and prosperous once more or destitute.

In her office, Deborah stared at the monitor screen. She hated to take her eyes off the little digits for a second. But there was an important ball that night in Washington being given by the Moroccan government. Many Arab diplomats would attend. Salim was in Washington, so he was likely to be at the ball. For psychological reasons, it was essential she be there, displaying as blithe a manner as if this were any other day.

She did not feel blithe. She felt nervous, worried. Several times in her life, she had wagered all she owned on her astuteness, but now the survival of her entire family depended on her. She tried to tell herself that the responsibility for so many others would not interfere with her judgement when the showdown came, but she could not know for certain until that moment. And that increased her nervousness.

With a final glance at the Winnipeg quotes, Deborah left her office. Her helicopter would take her to the airport and her plane, where she would dress.

Deborah had arranged for the former U.S. president Gerald Ford and his wife, Betty, to escort her to the ball; she needed to display some clout. She wore a sweeping blouson-style black gown to hide her thickening waist and, for luck, her Madeleine's ruby and diamond jewellery. She picked up the Fords at their Washington hotel in the limousine that had met her plane, and they proceeded to the ball.

Deborah was used to being the focus of photographers at public events because of the allure of her rapid rise to success, her family name, and her inaccessibility to gossip columnists eager to penetrate the well-guarded mystery of her private life. The recent revelations that had attended Pierre's death had both humanized her and piqued additional interest in her. The news and rumours of the last few days had whipped that interest into a frenzy. As she and her famous escorts emerged from the limousine to walk the few feet to the building's entrance, the press swarmed around them, pushing and jostling each other for shots of her. Reporters shouted questions. It took several minutes for the police to shoulder a path through the mob and lead the threesome to safety. Although the ex-president joked about financiers having become the rock stars of the Eighties, the three were unnerved and required several minutes to recover their composure.

Once inside the ballroom, Deborah renewed her acquaintance with several highly placed figures. She accepted congratulations gracefully on the merger of the Kronengolds, but declined to comment on the family's current 'play' in gold. Her manner was cordial to the Arab officials present, but antennae tuned to pick up any willingness to discuss conciliation, but they all carefully avoided the topic. If it was to come up, only one man had the influence to raise it: Salim.

At about eleven o'clock he arrived. Even after knowing him so many years, Deborah's instant impression was still that he was as slimly handsome as a rapier.

She waited nearly half an hour for Salim to make his way to her, if only out of courtesy. But he seemed to remain on the other side of the ballroom purposely, as if he had not decided on a final position in the Gold War, as a few were starting to call it, or worse, as if he had decided to fight it out with no cease-fire.

As a result Deborah was far more worried when she and the former president and first lady left the ball than when they had arrived. Her entire life at that moment was skidding along the thin edge of a cliff-top turn. One pebble slithering the wrong way beneath her would flip her and everything important to her over that edge.

Back in her New York apartment undressing for bed, she felt an intense desire to telephone a friend, just to talk about nothing. And then, maybe, if the conversation drifted round to it, about the fear that sometimes clawed at her when she realized the stakes for herself, for her unborn baby, and for the family depending on her. A few months ago, she would have called up David or Bash. Events had moved so swiftly these last weeks that only now was the realization sinking in that her two closest friends were gone forever: Bash, who would have bucked her up with a word or two, and David, who would have talked through the strategy with her until her doubts were stilled. She felt extremely lonely, yet simultaneously, paradoxically, extremely liberated by the knowledge that she would never again be drawn to a man by her subconscious childhood deprivations or because, like Leslie, he was a man she could not trust.

Her only intimate friend now was her mother. She looked longingly at the telephone, but did not reach for it. If her mother was out or at a meeting, she might be switched to another intelligence supervisor, and what would she say, that she was lonely and scared and needed a loving voice?

Deborah noticed that her hands were clasped across her belly. She had been doing that a lot lately – embracing her baby. She would be alone there, too. Her inner awakening during the days on the kibbutz had made her conscious of how much her child would need its father, and how much she would too – someone with whom to share the pride of their baby's first word or the burdens of its adolescence. She would never have that.

Observing Samuel and Madeleine as a child, Deborah had

never realized how heavy lay the responsibility on someone alone for matters as monumental as the welfare either of the Kronengolds or of a baby.

Deborah was woken by the ringing telephone. It took a moment to clear her head. She looked at the clock. She had fallen asleep only a couple of hours earlier.

'Hello.'

'Miss de Kronengold, this is Paul Ng in Hong Kong. I thought this was important enough to wake you for.' He and a few other key executives had her private number for such emergencies.

'Yes, go ahead, Paul.'

'I've run out of money, and gold's price is starting to slip back up. You've made an incredible profit. You might want to consider liquidating your position. I want your permission to start buying gold to cover all the sales we've made.'

'No!'

'But gold is down to –'

'Now isn't the time to question my orders.'

Rebuffed, he paused a moment. 'I have no more cash available and, as I said, gold is starting to climb back up. The other traders are testing us now, to see whether we're going to stick to our guns.'

'Spend whatever you have to to hold the price where it is. Call me as soon as trading there is over for the day, and I'll wire you the funds. I'll be in my office.'

'Yes, Miss de Kronengold.'

Deborah dressed, called for her car, and returned to her office.

That Thursday, the third day of the Gold War, was one that gold traders will never forget. They knew a fortune could be theirs if the Kronengolds suddenly changed strategy or lacked the resources to continue. After all, it had been only months since the Texas Hunt brothers and their partners had cornered silver and drawn up its price from six dollars to fifty – only to see it plummet when they could not sustain their position. But who knew how rich the Kronengolds were? After so many generations of accumulation, there might be billions more to back their gold play. A lot of wealthy men had gone broke in the last two days gambling against them. Those still left in the game wondered if they would suffer the same fate.

'Six hundred million dollars in new contracts to sell gold!' Paul Ng reported when he called her office at the end of Hong Kong trading. 'We're in the red thirty-six million dollars for deposits on our contracts.'

'I'll wire you the funds,' Deborah told him.

Seventeen million left.

Deborah hoped for quiet trading in Zurich and London, a fearful gold market worried about a confrontation with the Kronengolds. For several hours that was what she got – while having to spend very little to hold down the price. But then both exchanges were hit by a deluge of buy orders. Their floors turned into a tumult as other traders jumped on the express train.

'It's the Arabs!' André Leitner reported. 'They're trying to break us.'

'Keep selling!' Deborah demanded. 'Match them order for order!'

The other Kronengolds had nothing left, he knew. Deborah could sense him silently asking how long *she* could afford to go up against the Arabs before *her* funds ran out, but it wasn't his job to question her authority.

'Order for order,' he repeated and hung up.

Deborah's secretary, Penny, arrived early for work and found her employer pouring herself a fresh cup of coffee. The pot was nearly empty – Deborah had been there many hours.

'Let me get you some breakfast,' the young woman suggested.

'I couldn't keep it down,' Deborah admitted, permitting her secretary a fleeting glimpse of unaccustomed weakness. With her next words Deborah was herself again. 'Oh, yes, wire Hong Kong thirty-six million.'

Deborah's mouth tightened. In the first few hours today, André's bank had committed forty-one and a half million and Neville Cooper's thirty-nine million. The Comex was due to open in a few minutes, and she would have to be just as resolute there in matching the Arabs and the speculators order for order – and then in Chicago and then in Winnipeg. No, she would have to be *more* resolute. She would have to push gold even lower to intimidate the Arabs with her confidence, like a wrist wrestler forcing an opponent's hand downwards inch by inch. Only if they feared the consquences of resisting her would they be willing to sit down with her to bargain for peace.

The Comex opened in a near riot, with a heavy excess of buy orders overhanging the market. Deborah's floor traders shouted out their matching sell orders in a rapid-fire exchange with the Arabs' representatives. Many lesser players held back, fearing to wind up incidental casualties of the crossfire. But others rushed in, made heady by the intense, screaming action and the hope of riches.

Jim Lacy burst into Deborah's office with a report that their group was committed for sixty-seven million dollars' worth of deposits on Comex gold contracts, and the day had hardly begun. He had been unable to borrow a single dollar more anywhere to back their trading.

'What do we do?' he blurted out, overcome by helplessness.

Deborah shrugged – the situation seemed hopeless.

'But we can't just keep selling gold contracts like this,' he added anxiously, 'without any money to pay for it.'

'What else can we do?'

Deborah's security telephone console rang. Tel Aviv was calling.

The code words were spoken. Dvora related the facts tersely to her daughter. 'The Arabs intercepted your message several hours ago on a radio frequency they think we use to contact an operative in Syria. The truth is we use it when we want to send them on a false trail. Our best report is they believe you have a sea-water gold process, but the hard-liners have convinced the others that giving up the boycott would humiliate them. They want to see if they can overwhelm you first with their financial force.'

'For how long?'

'I don't know,' Dvora replied solemnly.

'How much are they willing to spend?'

'I don't know that either.'

The two women concluded the conversation and hung up. Deborah avoided her long-time colleague's gaze and walked to the window, her habit when wrestling with a problem. New York harbour was grey under a threatening sky. Engine smoke obscured the stern docks and wakes of ships inching in and out of the city's waterways.

At this rate of gold trading, she could not last very much

longer before the entire sandcastle washed away. She had miscalculated in two ways. First, the operation had required more capital than she had originally thought would be necessary to drive down the price. Second, she had hoped to force Arab capitulation without a fight between them on the floors of the gold exchanges – exactly the opposite of what was happening. Somehow she needed to get hold of a new source of funds, an investor perhaps willing to put up a couple of hundred million dollars for the privilege of being blasted away on all sides by the Arabs' limitless wealth. Her intuition – or her desperation – begged her to hang on just a little longer.

Jim Lacy answered the ring and flashing light on her console – the line was a direct one from the Comex floor. A moment later he reported to her, 'I've told them to keep selling into the buy orders. We're now short about a hundred million and dropping fast. By noon they figure we'll owe twice that. London is probably down the same amount, may be more. Deborah, we can't go on without cash. We'll have to default, and every bit of credibility you and your family have built up over the centuries goes down the tube. We might also all end up in jail.'

She finally murmured. 'Either way we lose everything.'

'Can I tell them at least to slow down the selling? The price will start to rise against us, but at least we may be able to handle the shortfall to some degree. I don't know.'

She nodded, at a loss. When he left the room, she watched an excursion boat round the tip of Manhattan until it was well into the East River. Then she returned to her desk and the monitor. Her fingertips in a steeple against her mouth, she watched the numbers slowly crawl back up, unconsciously calculating at each upward tick the money her group was losing.

Her secretary buzzed her. 'David Holtz is calling.'

He must be telephoning to gloat over her destruction. She snatched up the receiver.

'If you called to rub it, David –'

'I called because my traders tell me you look tapped out.'

Deborah refused to satisfy him with a reply. She was about to hang up when he said, 'You can draw on my company for up to seven hundred million dollars.'

For a instant, his words failed to register. When they did,

she was so overwhelmed by them, she did not know how to answer.

'What do you want in return? You can't have Leslie's bank. It's already a part of the family group, but if you want one of the industrial companies –'

'Nothing, damn it! Just try to sound a little grateful and let me feel a little good about it.'

Deborah had difficulty in finding her voice. 'Thank you, David. You know, I sold your bond trader my Series D debentures a day or so ago. I told my friends to do the same.'

'I'm not lending you this money because of that.'

'I know. You're a better friend than I deserve, David.'

At that instant the figures changed drastically on the monitor. David spoke up quickly. 'You'd better tell your gold traders to get on the stick.'

'Thank you, David. Thank you. But nothing I can ever say will be thanks enough.'

The Kronengold group had expended over three hundred and ninety million dollars by midday to hold the cap on the price of gold in New York and London. Each attempt by Arab buyers to push it up was met by Kronengold sell orders to force it back down. Around noon buyers seemed to hesitate, wondering whether they were throwing good money after bad. Sensing that indecision, Deborah ordered her traders to increase the rate of sales. Gold's price began to slide back downwards. With that, panic selling set in; those who had gambled on a rise suddenly became frightened that the same fate that had struck down colleagues who bet against the Kronengolds would strike them down.

A different set of figures now caught Deborah's attention: the normally rock-solid currencies of several Arab oil nations had begun to slide downwards as well – first imperceptibly and then with gathering force. Kronengolds had originally bought gold with Arab money. Now the Arabs were doing the same. The world's bankers and others were obviously making some sharp calculations about the heavy sales of those currencies and, perhaps, the monetary weakness of those nations that might be anticipating large oil revenue but had placed so much of their surplus wealth in gold. As a result bankers, speculators, corporate treasures, and finance ministers were protecting themselves by selling against those currencies. The Arabs, only a short time ago the attackers, now found themselves beset on both the gold and the currency flanks. The threatened Arab countries would have little choice but to sell gold in order to buy their own currency to prop it up. That would push gold down further. Here was the critical turning point Deborah had been trying to force for three solid days.

She sat back with relief. Now the Arabs would *have* to explore a cease-fire with the Kronengolds.

A few minutes later an aide to Prince Salim telephoned.

'His highness is most unhappy he missed seeing you last night. He is en route to New York and was hoping he might have the pleasure today.'

'It's always a pleasure for me as well.'

'Shall we say 1.30 at our consulate?'

'I'm rather busy today. Let's say 1.30 in my office.'

'A moment please.' He put Deborah on hold. She waited nearly three minutes before he was back on the line. 'Your office will be acceptable.'

Deborah rushed downstairs to the Engineering Department and described the sketches she wanted drawn up in the next hour. They were to be in her office no later than 1.15.

At precisely 1.30 that afternoon, Penny announced that Prince Salim had arrived. Deborah stood up as the door swung open, and he stepped into the room. He was dressed in a three-piece, dark blue pinstripe suit – in the Western world he rarely wore Middle Eastern garb. His moustache was thin. His black beard was clipped to a point. Burning black eyes added to the impression of savage, almost satanic good looks. Deborah could see, behind him, Penny and her two other secretaries open-mouthed.

'Salim, you're punctual! This is probably the first time. I don't know whether to feel honoured or call a doctor.'

He flicked the air in annoyed dismissal. 'It was on my way.'

As Salim walked past her into the room, Deborah gestured towards the arrangement of white sofa and white chairs around a malachite coffee table. She spent a moment conversing with Penny in low tones, her back to Salim. She wanted to give him a moment alone to note what she had just placed in open view.

Several simple blueprints and drawings were laid out as if

someone had been looking at them only a minute or two earlier. They showed an ocean-going barge with equipment on deck resembling the desalination equipment Salim had been shown on the deck of the *Venture II*. A colour rendering, of the sort customarily prepared when one is about to announce a project publicly, displayed a large pile of glittering yellow metal on the barge, just in front of the equipment. The point to be conveyed to Salim was that her firm was planning to put the equipment on barges and, in only a few weeks, could begin to pump gold from the sea.

Salim and Deborah had chosen facing chairs. She directed a cold, knowing look at him as she gathered the drawings together, rolled them up, and inserted them into their cardboard tube. Their meaning had not escaped him. If on his side he had an ocean of oil underground, they implied that she had a much larger ocean full of gold above it.

'My aide says you have been busy,' Salim began conversationally.

'I've been away, and there's a lot to catch up on,' she answered pleasantly, but noncommittally.

He nodded, not really hearing, intent on moving towards his own agenda. Suddenly, he directed his own piercing gaze at her. 'Someone mentioned to me that gold has been very active.'

'Down quite a bit the last few days, I understand.'

'They tell me it's half of what it was three days ago,' he said coolly, but Deborah thought she detected a hint of anxiety in his tone.

'I hope you haven't been buying,' Deborah replied with feigned solicitude. 'Perhaps you should sell, as we've been doing.'

'It seems we have too much gold to consider selling.' Salim stroked his beard, as if this were an academic discussion. 'That is the curse of being a world power. If we put even a small part of our holdings on the market, the price would drop another hundred or two hundred dollars an ounce.'

Deborah appeared to be mulling over his problem. 'That really does make it difficult for you. We've been telling our clients for weeks that gold is no longer a good investment.'

His hatred suddenly unsheathed, he shot at her, 'Only to someone who knows she will soon have an endless supply! Do you think we are such children we did not know why you insisted on owning everything inside your desalination plant?' He gestured towards the tube of drawings now leaning against the malachite table. 'Or that you have made tests on a barge? We have eyes everywhere.'

'How much do you know?' she asked in a pretence of guardedness.

'Everything! You have a method for taking gold from sea water while you're desalting it.'

'Oh!' Deborah seemed to resign herself to candour. 'We intended to make an announcement soon.'

Salim regarded her shrewdly. 'So the price of gold would immediately drop even further – until you can pay almost nothing to *buy* the contracts for gold to offset those you have been selling.' Something like grudging admiration entered his voice. 'You would earn billions more than you stand to earn already.'

Deborah flashed a modest little smile. 'My partners and I will do very nicely. Perhaps you've heard, all the Kronengolds have merged into my company.'

'I've heard,' he responded with a hard-eyed glare.

The toughness in Deborah's next words matched his. 'And I want you to be the first to know that "Kronengold" will remain part of the company's name.'

The two stared across the table at each other for a very long while. Deborah and her relatives had risked everything on this one, desperate, colossal bluff. The next few minutes would decide if they were fated to survive – or to expire like innumerable other families. Without shifting her stare a millimetre, Deborah said quietly, 'I take it gold is what you came to discuss with me.'

A skilled negotiator, Salim's tone when he spoke next was disinterested, advisory. 'I once heard an astounding fact, Deborah. If all the gold ever mined were placed in a single cube, it would measure only sixty-five feet long on each side.'

Deborah tried to appear surprised. 'That little!'

'Gold is valuable only if it is rare. That is why your process to mine gold from the sea is no good to you: if gold is no longer scarce, then you can earn almost nothing for it.'

'Well, yes, that makes sense.'

'Industrial uses for the metal are minor compared to its uses as jewellery *or* for investment. It will be worth very little.'

Deborah allowed herself the hint of a sly smile. 'Which is why we've been selling it.'

Salim was not used to being on the offering end of a negotiation. His manner grew stiff and formal. 'I am authorized by my government and the governments of the other Arab League nations to make you a very generous offer. If you agree never to use the process, we will call off the boycott.'

Deborah's eyes flashed. 'What? Only that?' Until now Deborah had been feigning ingenuousness, feeling him out. Now she was openly contemptuous. 'You are in no position to dictate terms! Salim, you and your fellow Arabs are in a very tight box at this precise moment. A large part of your wealth is in the form of millions of pounds of a shiny metal that will soon be cheaper than copper or zinc. Your currencies' values are slipping. Soon it will plummet. So will the price of your oil, because you're going to have to pump out a lot more of it to pay your bills. And, just like your gold, there'll be too much of it available to keep the price up.'

'We have adequate time to dispose of our gold before your process can affect the world's supply,' he remarked with no indication of the concern that had brought him to Deborah.

'You yourself said we could push the price of gold down much further and increase our profit enormously merely by announcing our Rumpelstiltskin process immediately. And if we did, because you hold enormous amounts of gold, you would lose astronomical sums.'

'But don't you yet understand that cheap gold is of little value to you? Why do you persist in going forward?'

Deborah's smugness was palpable as she explained the 'economics' of her process. 'Because gold is a lot more expensive to mine underground than it is by our process. All the producing nations – South Africa, the Soviets – will have to close their mines. We'll then have the *only* source of new supply. While formulating your offer, calculate in the value of that.'

Salim's hands were clenching and unclenching round the arms of his chair, as if he wished they were Deborah's neck. 'A few of my colleagues are doubtful that there even is such a Rumpelstiltskin process. They say we are acting like the fools in the Middle Ages who believed alchemists could turn lead into gold.'

A spasm of fear rippled through Deborah, but her expression

and her voice never changed. 'I'll be glad to convince them by releasing our story about the process to the press. We had intended to do so round about now.'

Salim again stared deeply into Deborah's eyes, seeking to be convinced. Very calmly, Deborah lifted the receiver from the telephone on the end table.

'Penny, get me the publisher of *The New York Times*. Then I'll want the *Wall Street Journal*, then AP, UPI, Reuters, and of course the network news desks.'

Deborah replaced the receiver, staring directly at Salim until the telephone intercom rang. Deborah answered it.

'Yes, Penny?' Deborah glanced at Salim. 'The *Times*'s publisher is on the phone. Do you want to speak to him or shall I?' She extended the telephone towards Salim.

His gaze flicked nervously from her face to the receiver and back again, but he did not move. After a couple of seconds, Deborah shrugged and turned her attention back to the receiver.

'Penny, *I'll* speak to him. Put him on.'

'Stop!' Salim cried out.

'Just a moment, Penny.' Deborah placed her hand over the receiver. 'I hope,' she said to Salim, 'that you have written authorization from the other governments to increase the offer on their behalf.'

'I can have it here within the hour,' he muttered. 'What will you take to kill the process?'

'Penny, apologize to him and tell him I'll have to call back later.' Deborah replaced the receiver. Her voice became conciliatory. 'Please believe me, Salim, my family and I have no desire to injure your country or any other Arab nation. We simply want to be left alone, and if we do drop the process, we want to make out as well as if we had put it into production.'

'I gather you have some terms in mind.'

Deborah laid them out. The Arabs would drop the boycott. The five nations currently considering purchase of desalination plants from DdK would commit to do so, guaranteeing the Kronengold group both a fifteen per cent profit on the two-billion-dollar construction cost of each plant and the same operating contract DdK currently had with Salim's nation. In addition, the Arab oil-producing nations would grant the Kronengolds a long-term contract – through an intermediary if they wished to save face – to purchase a million barrels of oil a day at two dollars a barrel below the actual world price. That would ensure the Kronengolds a stupendous profit, which Deborah maintained was in the range of profit they would earn by means of the sea-water gold process.

'And of course we'll require a down payment on signing. Say, a billion dollars.'

His eyes and nostrils wide with anger, Salim rejoined with quiet control, 'And just where am I to find one billion dollars in the next hour? Perhaps you'd like it in dollar bills.'

'You have more than that in gold bullion on deposit in London and Switzerland. Your banks need only shift it over to our account – at the current price at this moment on each exchange. That will save a good deal of bother and minimize gold's disruption as well.'

That part of the deal was critical. If the Kronengolds had to go out into the market and buy back either physically or in the form of gold contracts all the gold they had sold, the price of gold would shoot upwards in broad leaps, costing them phenomenal amounts. Now, however, they would be getting gold bullion to cover much of their position at the current low price, locking in an immense profit.

'Is that all?' Salim asked in a fury-strangled voice he seemed barely able to control.

Deborah nodded amiably.

Radiating passionate indignation, Salim sprang to his feet, as if about to storm out of the room. 'Instead of asking for fair terms, you try to rob us first of our gold, and now of our oil! I cannot allow my country's honour be demeaned so!'

'Nine hundred million dollars in gold bullion,' Deborah offered in reduction.

'And the oil?'

'Three-quarters of a million barrels a day for ten years,' she countered. 'No less.'

'Agreed,' Salim instantly declared, all trace of anger erased from his face.

For the next half hour they haggled over the details. Then Deborah called in Penny and dictated the terms to be typed. It would be an irrevocable offer from the Arab nations. Deborah claimed that she needed a day to consult her relatives; the Kronengold group would have until the close of business tomorrow to accept the Arabs' offer, but their banks would hold the agreed-upon amount of Arab bullion in escrow until then.

While the offer was being typed, the two read the authorizations from the Arab embassies as messengers arrived with them. In between Deborah sat motionless in her chair, afraid that the slightest move would alert him to the deception. It seemed an eternity until Penny brought in two copies of the document. Salim looked up thoughtfully after he had finished reading.

'The terms are what we agreed,' Deborah said and handed him a gold pen to sign the document with.

He gazed at the gold pen and then at Deborah, once more searching her face for the truth. Deborah willed her face expressionless, her eyelids wide open. He studied her for long seconds. Finally, Salim bent over the document and signed his name on behalf of his government and the other Arab nations.

As she took the signed offer from him, Deborah felt giddy with relief and exultation. The crisis was over. The boycott would be terminated. A profitable arrangement had been negotiated. The Kronengolds were safe.

We go on, Deborah thought. I've done my duty. I've upheld my heritage. We go on.

'A good bargain,' Salim said conspiratorially.

'A good bargain,' Deborah agreed.

'Now that it's over, tell me the truth. I couldn't take the chance when you picked up the phone – there was too much at stake – so I settled with you. But I was one of those who did not believe there was a Rumpelstiltskin process, not one that actually worked. Do you have such a process?'

Deborah smiled. 'Salim, mystery is the first law of the Kronengolds and of women. I would be breaking two laws if I did not keep you guessing.'

'You will not tell me?'

'Keep the pen as my gift, Salim. Whenever you use it, you'll wonder.'

He slipped the pen into his breast pocket and, mouth drawn in thought, he walked to the door. Suddenly, he nodded strongly. 'You have it,' he said with conviction. 'You were too confident not to have it. I was wise to settle.'

'Use the pen in good health, Salim.'

Deborah closed the door and rushed to the security telephone console on her desk. She pressed the red button and waited as white lights lit and recognition codes were uttered from London, Paris, Amsterdam, Geneva, Milan, and Berlin. She pressed the Tel Aviv button as well.

Deborah briefly summarized Salim's offer to her intent listeners. 'Any objections?'

'My God, how could there be?' one voice exclaimed.

She could hear sighs of relief.

'All right then,' she concluded. 'We start buying back gold.'

During the remainder of that day and the morning of the next, the Kronengolds quietly covered the rest of their exposed position by buying gold and gold contracts, so as to match at far lower prices what they had earlier sold. They used different traders, and more of them, to disguise their about-face and slow the climb. Just before noon on the next day, however, the rebound became unmistakable, and buying on the exchanges became frenzied. Counting the nine hundred million dollars in Arab bullion the banks held in escrow, the Kronengolds had liquidated the bulk of their gold position by then, and soon would unload the rest – at an incredible profit, doubling the newly combined group's capital, as Deborah had promised her relatives. At that point, Deborah wired the Arab countries an acceptance of the offer.

The flight from gold was over quickly. Outsiders could never be sure that there had really been a Gold War, although most floor traders were positive they knew the identities of the antagonists during that confused and savage three-day period. Most business reporters and TV commentators chalked up the sharp dip to investors' fears of instability in the part of the world that was experiencing unrest that week. One particularly astute financial reporter later asked Prince Salim if there was a link between the intense, erratic gold activity during the week and the announcement at the end of it that the Kronengolds had signed contracts to construct desalination plants in five Arab countries.

'Simply another invention of the gossip-hungry international press,' Prince Salim replied.

A few minutes after noon, Deborah drove up to town in her limousine to the Aximation Building. In the elevator she stared so hard at the last number above her head that she was slow to react when it lit and the doors opened on the ebony and chrome reception area. The receptionist was occupied with a group of visitors. Deborah walked past her and along the corridor towards David Holtz's suite. His secretary was not at her desk, but the door was open to his office. She entered.

David was going through his correspondence and dictating to his secretary. As soon as she saw Deborah, the young woman discreetly left the room and closed the door behind her.

Deborah stood in the centre of the room. Humility was very new to her, and she had rarely before ever owed anyone anything.

'Thank you again, David,' she said softly. 'For the money when I needed it. No strings attached. And for leaving me that envelope with my mother's name and address. No strings attached.'

'You saw her?'

Deborah nodded.

'Was it okay?'

'It was wonderful. You were right.'

David paused. 'I hope you aren't here to start up again what . . . what it was we had. I've thought a lot about it: I don't know if I could handle loving you with another man's child.'

Deborah took a deep breath. 'That's in the future, David. For now, I'm just grateful that you're my friend. That's when we've always been the kindest to each other.'

'Nobody's ever been a better friend to me when jealousy or our ambition didn't get in the way.'

Deborah reflected for a moment. 'We've been through a lot together.'

'Remember our first date? We walked all round the bottom of Manhattan and ate hot dogs, and you conned me into backing you.'

She chuckled. 'You're still coming up with money for me when I'm in trouble.'

Her gaze shifted to seek a tiny, distant figure through the window behind David. 'One of my employees was in New York for a few hours, and the place he wanted most to visit was the Statue of Liberty. You and I never did get a chance to visit it that day.'

David stood up. 'You free for lunch?'

'It just so happens that I am.' Smiling, Deborah slipped her arm through his. 'How about a couple of hot dogs and a boat ride?'

He drew her arm close to his side. 'Who's paying?'

'My treat,' she said. 'Mustard or ketchup, you have your choice.'

She turned to look at him. 'I've missed you, David. I've missed just being able to talk to you.' They began moving in step towards the door.

'I want to tell you about my mother.'

You'll never feel closer to your dreams

a ravishing new novel by

Caroline Gray

Orphaned, penniless, destitute, Wilhelmina Doberley arrives in New York armed only with an aching ambition to make her dreams come true.

Dreams that seem a million miles away when she starts work as a lowly chambermaid in the spell-bindingly glamorous Hotel Superb. There she discovers a world of champagne and oysters, ease and elegance – a far cry from her own life of drudge and poverty.

But Wilhelmina is determined to succeed. And when the outrageously attractive heir to the Superb begins to fall for her beauty, she knows where her destiny lies . . .

GENERAL FICTION 0 7221 41041 £2.95

Also by Caroline Gray in Sphere Books: FIRST CLASS

FROM A FORGOTTEN AGE OF ELEGANCE – A STORY OF GLAMOUR, PASSION AND WILD EXCITEMENT

ORIENTAL HOTEL

Janet Tanner

Just the mention of his name . . . and for Elise Sanderson the years simply rolled away, taking her back on a sea of bittersweet memories to those heady, dangerous days before the flames of war had ravaged the East.

Then, in the golden days of her youth, she had swept through the doors of the Orient's great hotels, into a world where bell-boys ran to answer every whim, where the champagne was permanently on ice, where elegant men in tails and women in exclusive *haute couture* danced to the endless music of orchestras.

It was then, she recalled, that she had first seen him, lounging languidly in a rattan chair, already in uniform, cigarette smoke curling lazily around half-closed hazel eyes. It was a dangerous face, she had thought in that first startled moment. A face to be reckoned with . . .

GENERAL FICTION 0 7221 83372 £2.50